T

"Cease the battle!" Urza cried imperiously. His figure blazed with light aback Gherridarigaaz. Dragon and rider descended in a column of mana energy before the storm of angels and falcons. "Cease this battle or be destroyed! I am Urza Planeswalker!"

"Tremble before him!" came a voice in mocking answer from among the angel horde.

Radiant emerged. Her figure was lit with an incandescent heat equal to Urza's. A group of archangels accompanied her, four before, four behind, and four more around the ruler of the realm. Her appearance brought a sudden hush to the battle lines. She was strange-eyed, beautiful, and terrifying.

"Tremble before this petulant god-child, this despoiler of worlds, destroyer of planes. Urza has come, my children, and when Urza comes, death always follows.

ignite your spark.

discover the planeswalkers in their adventures throughout the multiverse.

agents of artifice
by Ari Marmell

alara unbroken
by Doug Beyer

the purifying fire
by Laura Resnick

artifacts cycle i

the thran
by J. Robert King

the brothers' war
by Jeff Grubb

artifacts cycle ii

planeswalker
by Lynn Abbey

time streams
by J. Robert King

bloodlines
by Loren L. Coleman

MAGIC The Gathering
ARTIFACTS
CYCLE
II
PLANESWALKER LYNN ABBEY
TIME STREAMS J. ROBERT KING
BLOODLINES LOREN L. COLEMAN
Wizards OF THE COAST

Artifacts Cycle, Volume II

Published by Wizards of the Coast LLC

Printed in the U.S.A.

Cover art by Android Jones

First Printing: September 2009

9 8 7 6 5 4 3 2 1

ISBN: 978-0-7869-5306-6
620-25070000-001-EN

U.S., CANADA,
ASIA, PACIFIC, & LATIN AMERICA
Wizards of the Coast LLC
P.O. Box 707
Renton, WA 98057-0707
+1-800-324-6496

EUROPEAN HEADQUARTERS
Hasbro UK Ltd
Caswell Way
Newport, Gwent NP9 0YH
GREAT BRITAIN
Save this address for your records.

Visit our web site at www.wizards.com

PLANESWALKER
LYNN ABBEY

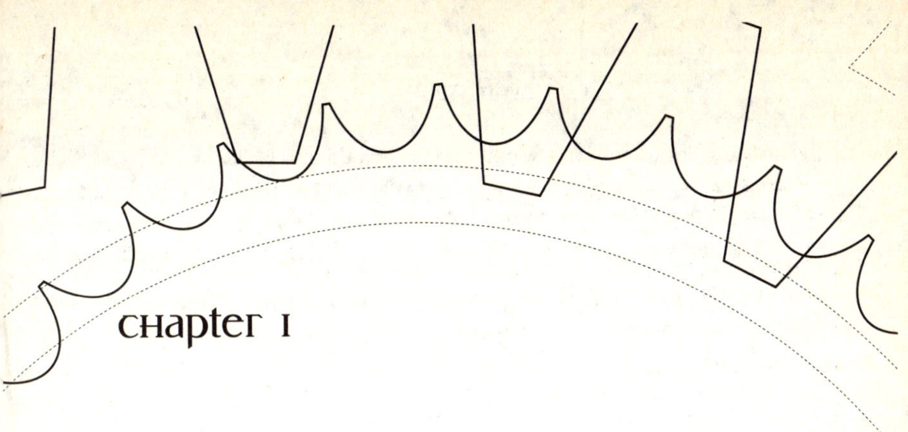

chapter 1

A man descended.

His journey had begun in the clouds, riding the winds in search of a place remembered but no longer known. He'd found the place, as he'd found it before, by following the ancient glyphs an ancient folk had carved into the land, glyphs that had endured millennia of neglect and the cataclysmic finale of the Brothers' War five years ago.

Much of Terisiare had vanished in the cataclysm, reduced to dust by fratricidal hatred. That dust still swirled overhead. Everyone coughed and harvests were sparse, but the sunsets and sunrises were magnificent luminous streaks of amber reaching across the sky, seeking escape from a ruined world.

The brothers in whose names the war had been fought had been reduced to curses: *By Urza's whim and Mishra's might, may you rot forever beneath the forests of sunken Argoth.*

Rumors said that Urza had caused the cataclysm when he used Lat Nam sorcery to fuel his final, most destructive, artifact. Others said that the cataclysm was Mishra's curse as he died with Urza's hands clasped around his throat. A few insisted that Urza had survived his crimes. Within a year of the cataclysm, all the rumors had merged in an increasingly common curse: *If I met Urza on the road, I'd cripple him with my own two hands, as he and his brother crippled us, then I'd leave him for the rats and vultures as he left Mishra.*

Urza had survived. He'd heard the curse in its infinite variations. After nearly five years in self-chosen exile, the erstwhile Lord Protector of the

Realm had spent another year walking amongst the folk of blasted Terisiare: the dregs of Yotia, the survivors of Argive, the tattered, the famished, the lame, the disheartened. No one had recognized him. Few had known him, even in the glory days. Urza had never been one to harangue his troops with rhetoric. He'd been an inventor, a scholar, an artificer such as the world had not seen since the Thran, and all he'd ever wanted was to study in peace. He'd had that peace once, near the beginning, and lost it, as he'd lost everything, to the man—the abomination—his brother had become.

A handful of Urza's students had survived the cataclysm. They'd denounced their master, and Urza hadn't troubled them with a visit. Urza's wife Kayla Bin-Kroog had survived, too. She now dwelt in austere solitude with her grandson, writing an epic she called *The Antiquity Wars.* Urza hadn't visited her either. Kayla alone might have recognized him, and he had no words for her. As for her grandson, Jarsyl, black-haired and stocky, charming, amiable and quick-witted . . . Urza had glimpsed the young man just once, and that had been one time too many.

His descent continued.

Urza had not wanted to return to this place where the war had, in a very real sense, begun nearly fifty years earlier. He wasn't ashamed of what he'd done to end the war. Filling the bowl-shaped sylex with his memories had been an act of desperation; the sylex itself had been a sudden, suspect gift, and until that day he'd neither studied nor practiced sorcery. He hadn't known what using the sylex would do, but the war had had to be stopped. The thing his brother had become had to be stopped, else Terisiare's fate would have been worse.

Much worse.

No, Urza would not apologize, but he was not pleased by his own survival.

Urza should have died when the sylex emptied. He suspected that he had died, but the powerstones over which he and his brother had contended had preserved him. When Urza had awakened, the two Thran jewels had become his eyes. All Thran devices had been powered by such faceted stones, but his Mightstone and Mishra's Weakstone had been as different from ordinary powerstones as a candle to the sun.

Once rejoined within Urza's skull, the Thran jewels had restored him to his prime. He had no need for food or rest, though he continued to sleep because a man needed dreams even when he no longer needed rest. And his new eyes gave him vision that reached around dark comers into countless other worlds.

Urza believed that in time the battered realms of Terisiare would recover, even thrive, but he had not wished to watch that excruciatingly slow process, and so he'd walked away. For five years after the sylex-engendered cataclysm, Urza had explored the 'round-the-corner worlds his faceted eyes revealed.

In one such world he'd met another traveler, a woman named Meshuvel who'd confirmed what he'd already guessed: He'd lost his mortality the day he destroyed Mishra. The blast had slain him, and the Thran powerstones had brought him back to life because he was—had always been—a planeswalker, like Meshuvel herself.

Meshuvel explained to Urza that the worlds he'd visited were merely a handful of the infinite planes of the Multiverse, any of which could be explored and exploited by an immortal planeswalker. She taught Urza to change his shape at will and to comprehend thought without the inconvenience of language or translation. But even among planeswalkers Urza was unique. For all her knowledge, Meshuvel couldn't see the Multiverse as Urza saw it. Her eyes were an ordinary brown, and she'd never heard of the Thran. Meshuvel could tell Urza nothing about his eyes, except that she feared them; and feared them so much that she tried to snare him in a time pit. When that failed, she fled the plane where they'd been living.

Urza had thought about pursuing Meshuvel, more from curiosity than vengeance, but the plane she'd called Dominaria—the plane where he'd been born, the plane he'd nearly destroyed—kept its claws in his mind. Five years after the cataclysm, Dominaria had pulled him home.

Urza's descent ended on a wind-eroded plateau.

Clouds thickened, turned gray. Cold wind, sharp with ice and dust, plastered long strands of ash-blond hair across Urza's eyes. Winter had come earlier than Urza had expected, another unwelcome gift from the sylex. A few more days and the glyphs would have been buried until spring.

Four millennia ago, the Thran had transformed the plateau into a fortress, an isolated stronghold wherein they'd made their final stand. Presumably, it once had a name; perhaps the glyphs proclaimed it still, but no one had cracked that enigmatic code, and no one cracked it that afternoon. Urza's jeweled eyes gave him no insight into their makers' language. Fifty years ago, in his natural youth, Urza and his brother had named the great cavern within the plateau Koilos, and Koilos it remained.

Koilos had been ruins then. Now the ruins were themselves ruined, but not merely by the sylex. The brothers and their war had wrought this damage, plundering the hollow plateau for Thran secrets, Thran powerstones.

In truth, Urza had expected worse. Mishra had held this part of Terisiare for most of the war, and it pleased Urza to believe that his brother's allies had been more destructive than his own allies had been. In a dusty corner of his heart, Urza knew that had he been able to ravage Koilos, even the shadows would have been stripped from the stones, but Mishra's minions had piled their rubble neatly, almost reverently. Their shredded tents still flapped in the rising wind. Looking closer, Urza realized they'd left suddenly and without their belongings, summoned, perhaps, to Argoth, as Urza had summoned his followers for that final battle five years earlier.

Urza paused on the carefully excavated path. He closed his eyes and shuddered as memories flooded his mind.

He and Mishra had fought from the beginning in a sunlit Argive nursery. How could they not, when he was the eldest by less than a year and Mishra was the brother everyone liked better? Yet they'd been inseparable, so keenly aware of their differences that they'd come to rely on the other's strengths. Urza never learned the arts of friendship or affection because he'd had Mishra between him and the rest of the world.

And Mishra? What had he given Mishra? What had Mishra ever truly needed from him?

"How long?" Urza asked the wind in a whisper that was both rage and pain. "When did you first turn away from me?"

Urza reopened his eyes and resumed his trek. He left no footprints in the dust and snow. Nothing distracted him. The desiccated corpse propped against one tent pole wasn't worth a second glance, despite the metal plates rusting on its brow or the brass pincers replacing its left arm. Urza had seen what his brother had become; it wasn't surprising to him that Mishra's disciples were similarly grotesque.

His faceted eyes peered into darkness, seeing nothing.

Now, that was a surprise, and a disappointment. Urza had expected insight the way a child expects a present on New Year's morning. Disappoint Mishra and you'd have gotten a summer tantrum, loud, violent and quickly passed. Disappoint Urza and Urza got cold and quiet, like ice, until he'd thawed through the problem.

After four thousand years had they plundered the last Thran powerstone? Exposed the last artifact? Was there nothing left for his eyes to see?

A dull blue glint caught Urza's attention. He wrenched a palm-sized chunk of metal free from the rocks and rubble. Immediately it moved in his hand, curving back on itself. It was Thran, of course. An artificer of Urza's skill didn't need jeweled eyes to recognize that ancient craftsmanship. Only the Thran had known how to forge a sort of sentience between motes of metal.

But Urza saw the blue-gray metal more clearly than ever before. With time, the right tools, the right reagents, and a bit of luck, he might be able to decipher its secrets. Then, acting without deliberate thought, as he very rarely did, Urza drove his right thumbnail into the harder-than-steel surface. He thought of a groove, a very specific groove that matched his nail. When he lifted his thumb, the groove was in the metal and remained as he slowly counted to ten.

"I see it. Yes, I see it. So simple, once it can be seen."

Urza thought of Mishra, spoke to Mishra. No one else, not even his master-student, Tawnos, could have grasped the shifting symmetries his thoughts had imposed on the ancient metal.

"As if it had been your thumb," Urza conceded to the wind. Impulse, like friendship, had been Mishra's gift.

Urza could almost see him standing there, brash and brilliant and not a day over eighteen. An ice crystal died in Urza's lashes. He blinked and saw Mishra's face, slashed and tattered, hanging by flesh threads in the cogs of a glistening engine.

"Phyrexia!" he swore and hurled the shard into the storm.

It bounced twice, ringing like a bell, then vanished.

"Phyrexia!"

He'd learned that word five years ago, the very day of the cataclysm, when Tawnos had brought him the sylex. Tawnos had gotten the bowl from Ashnod and, for that reason alone, Urza would have cast it aside. But he'd fought Mishra once already that fateful day. For the first time, Urza had poured himself into his stone, the Mightstone, and if his brother had been a man, his brother would have died. But Mishra had no longer been a man; he hadn't died, and Urza needed whatever help fate offered.

In those chaotic moments, as their massed war engines turned on one another, there'd been no time to ask questions or consider implications. Urza believed Mishra had transformed himself into a living artifact, and that abominable act had justified the sylex. It was after, when there was no one left to ask, that the questions had surfaced.

Tawnos had mentioned a demon—a creature from Phyrexia—that had ambushed him and Ashnod. Never mind the circumstances that had brought Urza's only friend and his brother's treacherous lieutenant together on the Argoth battlefield. Tawnos and Ashnod had been lovers once, and love, other than an abstract devotion to inquiry or knowledge, meant very little to Urza. Ask instead, what was a Phyrexian doing in Argoth? Why had it usurped all the artifacts, his and Mishra's? Then, ask a final question, what had he or Mishra to do with Phyrexia that its demon had become their common enemy?

Some exotic force—some Phyrexian force—had conspired against them. Wandering, utterly alone across the ruins of Terisiare, there had seemed no other explanation.

In the end, in the forests of Argoth, only the sylex had prevented a Phyrexian victory.

Within a year of the cataclysm, Urza had tracked the sylex back through Ashnod's hands to a woman named Loran, whom he'd met in his youth. Though Loran had studied the Thran with him and Mishra under the tutelage of the archeologist Tocasia, she'd turned away from artifice and become a scholar in the ivory towers of Terisia City, a witness of the land-based power the sylex had unleashed.

The residents of Terisia City had sacrificed half their number to keep the bowl out of his or Mishra's hands. Half hadn't been enough. Loran had lost the sylex and the use of her right arm to Ashnod's infamous inquiries, but the rest of her had survived. Urza had approached Loran warily, disguised as a woman who'd lost her husband and both her sons in what he bitterly described as "the brothers' cursed folly."

Loran was a competent sage and a better person than Urza hoped to be, but she was no match for his jeweled eyes. As she'd heated water on a charcoal brazier, he'd stolen her memories.

The sylex, of course, was gone, consumed by the forces it had released, and Loran's memory of it was imperfect. That was Ashnod's handiwork. The torturer had taken no chances with her many victims. Loran recalled a copper bowl incised with Thran glyphs Urza had forgotten until he saw them again in Loran's memory. Some of the glyphs were sharp enough that he'd recognize them if he saw them again, but most were blurred.

He could have sharpened those memories, his eyes had that power, but Urza knew better than to make the suggestion. Loran would sooner die than help him, so they drank tea, watched a brilliant sunset, then went their separate ways.

Urza had learned enough. The Thran, the vanished race who'd inspired his every artifact, had made the sylex, and the sylex had saved Dominaria from Phyrexia. Although mysteries remained, there was symmetry, and Urza had hoped that symmetry would be enough to halt his dreams. He'd resumed his planeswalking. It had taken five years—Urza was nothing if not a determined, even stubborn, man—before he'd admitted to himself that his hopes were futile. A year ago, he'd returned to Dominaria, to Argoth itself, which he'd avoided since the war ended. He'd found the ruined hilltop where he'd unleashed the land's fury and pain. He'd found Tawnos's coffin.

Tawnos had spent five years sealed in stasis within the coffin. For him, it was as if the war hadn't yet ended and the cataclysm hadn't yet happened. The crisp images on the surface of Tawnos's awakened mind had been battlefield chaos, Ashnod's lurid hair, and the demon from Phyrexia.

". . . if this thing is here . . ." Tawnos had recalled his erstwhile lover's, onetime torturer's words.

Ashnod's statement had implied, at least to Tawnos and from him to Urza, that she'd recognized the demon: a man-tall construction of strutted metal and writhing, segmented wires. Urza recognized it too—or parts of it. He'd seen similar wires uncoiled from his brother's flensed body, attaching Mishra to a dragon engine.

"This one is mine . . ." More of Ashnod's sultry words lying fresh in Tawnos's mind.

Urza's only friend had wanted to argue with Ashnod, to die beside her. She wouldn't grant him that dubious honor. Instead she'd given him the sylex.

Tawnos's memories had clouded quickly as he'd absorbed the vastly changed landscape. While Tawnos had sorted his thoughts, Urza had looked westward, to the battlefield, now replaced by ocean.

Ashnod, as treacherous as she'd been beautiful, had betrayed everyone who fell into her power. Tawnos's back still bore the scars. Mishra had judged her so unreliable that he'd banished her, only to let her back for that last battle.

Or had he?

Had Mishra known Ashnod carried the sylex? Had the traitor himself been betrayed? Which was the puppet and which the master? Why had the demon stalked Ashnod across the battlefield? What was her connection to Phyrexia?

Urza had wrestled with such questions until Tawnos had asked his own. "Your brother?"

"Dead," Urza had replied as his questions converged on a single answer. "Long before I found him."

The words had satisfied Tawnos, who began at once to talk of other things, of rebuilding the land and restoring its vitality. Tawnos—dear friend Tawnos—had always been an optimist. Urza left him standing by the coffin, certain that they'd never meet again.

For Urza, the realization that he hadn't slain Mishra with the sylex had given him a sense of peace that had lasted almost a month, until a new, stronger wave of guilt had engulfed it. He was the elder brother, charged from birth with his younger sibling's care.

He'd failed.

When Mishra had need of an elder brother's help, that elder brother had been elsewhere. He'd failed Mishra and all of Dominaria. His brother had died alone, betrayed by Ashnod, transformed by a Phyrexian demon into a hideous amalgam of flesh and artifice.

Urza had returned to Argoth and Tawnos as the snows had begun, almost exactly one year ago. He'd denied himself sleep or shelter, kneeling in the snow, waiting for Mishra, or death; it hadn't mattered which. But Meshuvel had been correct: Urza had transcended death, and he'd found, to his enduring dismay, that he lacked the will for suicide. A late spring had freed him from his icy prison. He'd stood up, no weaker than he'd been when he'd knelt down.

The left side of his face had been raw where bitter tears had leaked from the Weakstone, but it had healed quickly, within a few moments. He'd walked away with no marks from his season-long penance.

In his youth, when his wife's realm of Yotia had still sparkled in the sun, a man named Rusko had told Urza that a man had many souls throughout his life, and that after death each soul was judged according to its deeds. Urza had outlived his souls. The sylex had blasted him out of judgment's hands. No penance would ever dull the ache of failure.

All that remained was vengeance.

Urza had spent the spring and summer assuring himself that Ashnod had not survived. He'd skipped through the planes, returning after each unreal stride to Dominaria in search of a woman who was too proud to change her appearance or her ways. When fall had arrived without a trace of her, Urza had turned his attention to Koilos, where he and Mishra had come to manhood pursuing relics of the Thran.

His immortal memory, he'd discovered, was fallible. Planeswalking couldn't easily take him to a place he didn't quite remember. In the end, searching for places that had faded from memory, he'd been reduced to surveying vast tracts of barren land from the air, as he and his brother had surveyed in their youth.

He'd have given his eyes and immortality to have back just one of those days he and Mishra had spent in Tocasia's camp.

Sleety wind shot up his sleeves. Urza wasn't immune to the discomforts of cold, merely to their effects. He thought of a felted cloak; it spread downward from his shoulders, thickening as he added a fur lining, then gloves, fleece-lined boots and a soft-brimmed hat that didn't move in the wind. He continued along the path Mishra's workers had left. As before, and despite his new boots, Urza left no footprints.

With each stride, pain ratcheted through his skull. This close to the place where they'd been joined for millennia, his jeweled eyes recalled another purpose. Hoping to dull the pain, Urza turned his back to the cavern. His throbbing eyes saw the snow-etched ruins as shadows painted on gauzy cloth; nothing like the too-real visions he'd suffered the day he'd acquired the Mightstone. Then, the shadows expanded and began to move. They were different from his earlier visions, but not entirely. Where before he had watched white-robed men constructing black-metal spiders, now he saw a battlefield swarming with artifacts, another Argoth but without the demonic disorder.

At first Urza couldn't distinguish the two forces, as an observer might not have been able to distinguish his army from Mishra's. But as he looked, the lines of battle became clear. One side had its back against the cavern and was fighting for the freedom of the plains beyond the hollow plateau. The other formed an arc as it emerged from the narrow defile that was the only way to those plains, meaning to crush its enemy against the cliffs. Blinding flashes and plumes of dense smoke erupted everywhere, testaments to the desperation with which both sides fought.

Urza strained his eyes. One force had to be the Thran, but which? And what power opposed them?

During the moments that Urza pondered, the defile force scored a victory. A swarm of their smaller artifacts stormed the behemoth that anchored the enemy's center. It went down in a whirlwind of flame that drove both forces back. The defile force regrouped quicker and took a bite from the cavern force's precious ground. A mid-guard cadre from the defile brought rays of white light to bear on the behemoth's smoldering hulk. Soot rained and the hulk glowed red.

Caught up in the vision, Urza began to count, "One . . . two . . ."

The hulk's flanks burst, and all-too-familiar segmented wires uncoiled. Tipped with scythes, the wires slashed through the defile cadre, winnowing it by half, but too late. The Thran powerstones completed the destruction of the Phyrexian behemoth.

Millennia after the battle's dust had settled, Urza clenched his jaws together in a grimly satisfied smile. Ebb and flow were obvious, now that he'd identified the Thran and their goal: to drive the Phyrexians into the cavern where, presumably, they could he annihilated.

It was, as the Argoth battle between him and Mishra had been, a final battle. Retreat was not an option for the Phyrexians, and the Thran offered no quarter. Urza lost interest in his own time as the shadow war continued. The Phyrexians assembled behind their last behemoth, charged the Thran line on its right flank and very nearly broke through. But the Thran held nothing back. As ants might swarm a fallen bit of fruit, they converged upon the Phyrexian bulge.

Again, it became impossible to distinguish one force from the other.

Urza counted to one hundred and ten, by which time there was no movement within the shadows. When he reached one hundred and twelve, the shadows brightened to desert-noon brilliance. Reflexively, Urza shielded his eyes. When he lowered his hand, there was only snow. The pain in his skull was gone. He entered the cavern thoroughly sobered by what he had seen.

His eyes had recorded the final battle between the Thran and the Phyrexians. It seemed reasonable to assume that recording Phyrexian defeats was part of their function. From that assumption, it was easy to conclude that the Thran had intended the recording stones as a warning to all those who came after.

Urza had had a vision when he first touched what became his Mightstone. He recalled it as he entered the cavern. Despite his best efforts, the images were dreamlike yet they strengthened his newborn conviction: The Thran had vanished because they'd sacrificed themselves to defeat the Phyrexians.

Within the cavern, Urza gazed up at the rough ceiling. "We didn't know," he explained to any lingering Thran ghosts. "We didn't know your language . . . . We didn't guess what we couldn't understand."

He knew now. The artifact in which they'd found the single stone—the artifact that he and Mishra had destroyed utterly—had been the Thran legacy to Dominaria and the means through which they'd locked their enemy out of Dominaria.

"We didn't know . . . ."

When the stone had split into its opposing parts, the lock had been sprung and the Phyrexians had returned. The enemy had known better than to approach him, the bearer of the Mightstone, but they had—they must have—suborned, corrupted, and destroyed Mishra, who'd had only the Weakstone for protection. The stones were not, after all, truly equal. Might was naturally dominant over weakness, as Urza, the elder brother, should have been dominant over the younger.

But blinded by an elder brother's prejudice and—admit it!—jealousy, Urza had done nothing.

No, he'd done worse than nothing. He'd blamed Mishra, gone to war against Mishra, and undone the Thran sacrifice. Guilt was a throbbing presence within Urza's skull. He closed his eyes and clapped his hands over his ears, but that only made everything worse.

Why hadn't he and Mishra talked?

Through their childhood and youth, he and Mishra had fought constantly and bitterly before repairing the damage with conversation. Then, after the stones had entered into their lives, they hadn't even tried.

Then insight and memory came to Urza. There had been one time, about forty-five years ago in what could be called the war's morning hours. They'd come together on the banks of the river Kar, where it tumbled out of the Kher mountains. The Yotian warlord, his wife's father, had come to parley with the qadir of the Fallaji. Urza hadn't seen or heard from his brother for years. He'd believed that Mishra was dead, and had been stunned to see him advising the qadir.

He, Urza—gods and ghosts take note—had suggested that they should talk, and Mishra had agreed. As Urza recalled the conversation, Mishra had been reluctant, but that was his brother's style, petulant and sulky whenever his confidence was shaken, as surely it would have been shaken with the Weakstone burden slung around his neck, and the Phyrexians eating at his conscience.

Surely Mishra would have confessed everything, if the warlord hadn't taken it into his head to assassinate the qadir as the parley began.

Urza recalled the carnage, the look on Mishra's face.

Back in Koilos, in the first snows of the fifth winter after the cataclysm, Urza staggered and eased himself to the ground. For a few moments the guilt was gone, replaced by a cold fury that reached across time to the warlord's neck. *It was YOUR fault! Your fault!* But the warlord shrugged him away. *He was your brother, not mine.*

If the Phyrexians had not taken Mishra's soul before that day on the banks of the Kor, they had surely had no difficulty afterward.

The blame, then, was Urza's, and there was nothing he could do to ease his conscience, except, as always, in vengeance against the Phyrexians. For once, Urza was in the right place. Koilos was where the Thran had stopped the Phyrexians once and where his own ignorance had given the enemy a second chance. If there was a way to Phyrexia, it was somewhere within Koilos.

Urza left tracks in the dust as he searched for a sign.

The sun had set. Koilos was tomb dark. Urza's eyes made their own light, revealing a path, less dusty than any other, that led deep into the cavern's heart. He found a chamber ringed with burnt-out powerstones. Two sooty lines were etched on the sandstone floor. Marks that might have been Thran glyphs showed faintly between the lines. Urza used his eyes to scour the spot, but the glyphs—if glyphs they were—remained illegible.

He cursed and knelt before the lines. This was the place, it had to be the very place, where the Phyrexians had entered Dominaria. There could be no doubt. Looking straight ahead, past the lines and the exhausted powerstones, there was a crystal reliquary atop a waist-high pyramid. The reliquary was broken and empty, but the pyramid presented an exquisitely painted scene to Urza's glowing eyes: the demon he had seen in Tawnos's memory.

Circling the pyramid, Urza saw two other demonic portraits and a picture of the chamber itself with a black disk rising between the etched lines. He tore the chamber apart, looking for the disk—either its substance or the switch that awakened it—and not for the first time in his life, Urza failed.

When Urza walked among the Multiverse of planes, he began his journey wherever he happened to be and ended it with an act of will or memory. He realized that the Phyrexians had used another way, but it lay beyond his comprehension, as did the plane from which they'd sprung. The Multiverse was vast beyond measure and filled with uncountable planes. With no trail or memory to guide him, Urza was a sailor on a becalmed sea, beneath a clouded sky. He had no notion which way to turn.

"I am immortal. I will wander the planes until I find their home, however long and hard the journey, and I will destroy them as they destroyed my brother."

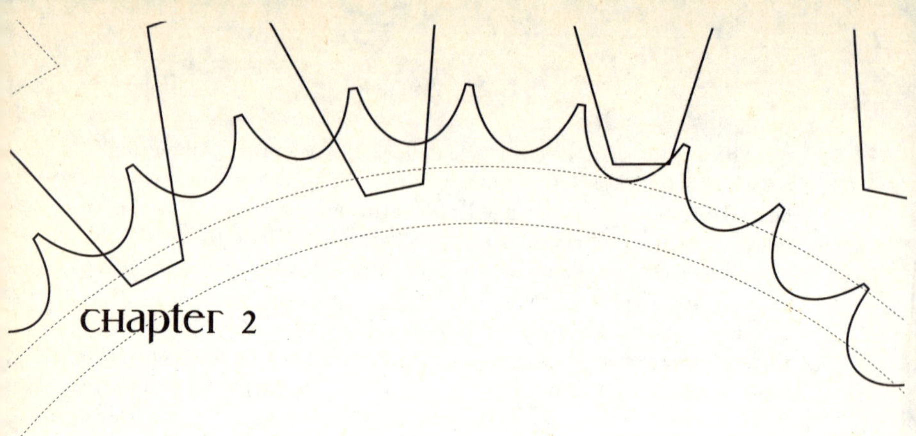

chapter 2

"Nearly five years after Argoth was destroyed and the war between the brothers had ended, Tawnos came to my courtyard. He told me much that I had never known, much that I have written here. He told me that my husband was dead and that he'd died with my name on his lips. It is a pretty thought, and I would like to believe it, but I am not certain that Urza died and, if he did, he would have died calling to Mishra, not me."

Xantcha lightly brushed her fingertips over brittle vellum before closing her tooled-leather cover of *The Antiquity Wars.* It was the oldest among her copies of Kayla Bin-Kroog's epic history, and the scribe who'd copied and translated it nearly twelve hundred years earlier claimed he'd had Kayla's original manuscript in front of him. Xantcha had her doubts, if not about the scribe's honesty, then about his gullibility.

Not that either mattered. For a tale that had no heroes and a very bitter ending, *The Antiquity Wars* had been very carefully preserved for nearly three and a half millennia. It was as if everyone still heeded the warning in Kayla's opening lines: "Let this, the testament of Kayla Bin-Kroog, the last of Yotia, serve as memory, so that our mistakes will never be repeated."

Xantcha stared beyond the table. On a good night, the window would have been open and she could have lost her thoughts in the stars twinkling above the isolated cottage, but Dominaria hadn't completely recovered from the unnatural ice age had that followed the Brothers' War. Clear nights were rare on Xantcha's side of the Ohran Ridge, where the cottage was tucked into a crease of land, where the grass ended and the naked mountains began. Mostly the weather was cool or cold, damp or wet, or something in between. Tonight, gusty winds were propelling needle-sharp sleet against the shutters.

The room had cooled while she read. Her breath was mist and, with a shivering sigh, Xantcha made her way to the peat bin. There were no trees near the cottage. Her meager garden sprouted a new crop of stones every spring, and the crumbling clods that remained after she'd picked out the stones were better suited for the brazier than for nurturing grains and vegetables. She'd had to scrounge distant forests for her table and shutters. Even now that the cottage was finished, she spent much of her time scrounging the remains of Terisiare for food and rumors.

Shredding a double handful of peat into the brazier beneath the table, Xantcha found, as she often did, the squishy remains of an acorn: a reminder of just how much Urza and his brother had changed their world with their war. When whole, the acorn would have been as large as her fist, and the tree that had dropped it would have had a trunk as broad as the cottage was wide. She crumbled the acorn with the rest and stirred the coals until palpable heat radiated from the iron bucket.

Xantcha forgot the table and hit her head hard as she stood. She sat a moment, rubbing her scalp and muttering curses, until she remembered the candlestick. With a louder curse, she scrabbled to her feet. Waste not, want not, it hadn't toppled. Her book was safe.

She returned to her stool and opened to a random page. Kayla's portrait stared back at her: dusky, sloe-eyed, and seductive. Xantcha owned four illustrated copies of *The Antiquity Wars.* Each one depicted Kayla differently. Her favorite showed Urza's wife as a tall, graceful and voluptuous woman with long blond hair, but Xantcha knew none of the portraits were accurate. Staring at the shutters, she tried to imagine the face of the woman who had known, and perhaps loved, Urza the Artificer while he was a mortal man.

One thing was certain, Xantcha didn't resemble Kayla Bin-Kroog. There were no extravagant curves in Xantcha's candlelit silhouette. She was short, not tall, and her hair was a very drab brown, which she cropped raggedly around a face that was more angular than attractive. Xantcha could, and usually did, pass herself off as a slight youth awaiting his full growth and first beard. Still, Xantcha thought, she and Kayla would have been friends. Life had forced many of the same hard lessons down their throats.

Kayla, however, wasn't the epic character who intrigued Xantcha most. That honor went to Urza's brother, Mishra. Three of Xantcha's illustrated volumes depicted Mishra as a whip-lean man with hard eyes. The fourth portrayed him as soft and lazy, like an overfed cat. Neither type matched Kayla's word picture. To Kayla, Mishra had been tall and powerful, with straight black hair worn wild and full. Mishra's smile, his sister-by-law had written, was warm and bright as the sun on Midsummer's day, and his eyes sparkled with wit—when they weren't flashing full of suspicion.

Not all *The Antiquity Wars* in Xantcha's collection included Kayla's almost indiscreet portrait of her husband's brother. Some scribes had openly seized an opportunity to take a moral stance, not only against Mishra, but other men of more recent vintage—as if a princess of ancient Yotia could have foreseen the vices of the Samisar of Evean or Ninkin the Bold! One scribe, writing in the year 2657 admitted that she'd omitted the Mishra section entirely, because it was inconsistent with Kayla's loyalty to her husband and, therefore, a likely fraud—and absolutely inappropriate for the education of the young prince, who was expected to learn his statecraft from her copy of the epic.

Xantcha wondered if that priggish scribe had seen the picture on her table. The Kayla Bin-Kroog of Xantcha's oldest copy wore a veil, three pearl ropes, and very little else. Few men could have resisted her allure. One of them had been her husband. Beyond doubt, Urza had neglected his wife. No woman had ever intrigued Urza half as much as his artifacts. How many evenings might Kayla have gone to bed railing at the fates who'd sent the chaste Urza to her father's palace, rather than his charming brother?

Urza had never questioned his wife's fidelity. At least, Xantcha had never heard him raise that question. Then again, the man who lived and worked on the other side of the wall at Xantcha's back had never mentioned his son or grandson, either.

With a sigh and a yawn, Xantcha stowed the book in a chest that had no lock. They didn't need locks in the absolute middle of nowhere. Urza had the power to protect them from anything. The heavy lid served only to discourage the mice that would otherwise have devoured the vellum.

"Xantcha!" Urza's voice came through the wall; as she contemplated the precious library she'd accumulated over the last two and a half centuries.

She leapt instantly to her feet. The lid fell with a bang. Urza had shut himself in his workroom while she'd been off scrounging, and she'd known better than to interrupt him when she'd returned. Sixteen days had passed since she'd heard his voice.

Their cottage had two rooms: hers, which had begun as a shed around an outdoor bread oven, and Urza's, which consumed everything under the original roof, a dugout cellar and a storage alcove—Urza traveled light but settled deep. Each room had a door to a common porch whose thatched roof provided some protection from the weather.

Wind-driven sleet pelted her as Xantcha darted down the porch. She shoved the door shut behind her, then, when Urza hadn't noticed the sound or draft, took his measure before approaching him.

Urza the great artificer sat at a high table on a stool identical to her own. By candlelight, Xantcha saw that he was dressed in the same tattered blue tunic he'd been wearing when she'd last seen him. His ash-blond hair spewed from the thong meant to confine it at the nape of his neck. It wasn't dirty—not the way her hair would have gotten foul if it went that long between washings. Urza didn't sweat or purge himself in any of the usual ways. He didn't breathe when he was rapt in his studies and never needed to eat, though he spoke in the mortal way and ate heartily sometimes, if she'd cooked something that appealed to him. He drank water, never caring where it carne from or how long it had stood stagnant, but the slops bucket beside his door never needed emptying. Urza didn't get tired either, which was a more serious problem because he remained man enough to need sleep and dreams for the purging of his thoughts.

There were times when Xantcha believed that all Urza's thoughts needed purging; this was one of them.

Mountains rose from Urza's table. All too familiar mountains shaped from clay and crockery. Quicksilver streams overflowed the corners. As melting sleet trickled down her spine, Xantcha wondered if she could retreat and pretend she hadn't heard. She judged that she could have, but didn't.

"I've come," she announced in the language only she and Urza spoke, rooted in ancient Argivian with a leavening of Yotian and tidbits from a thousand other worlds.

Urza spun quickly on the stool, too quickly for her eyes to follow his movement. Indeed, he hadn't moved, he'd reshaped himself. It was never a good sign when Urza forgot his body. Meeting his eyes confirmed Xantcha's suspicions. They glowed with their own facet-rainbow light.

"You summoned me?"

He blinked and his eyes turned mortal, dark irises within white sclera. But that was the illusion; the other was real.

"Yes, yes! Come see, Xantcha. Look at what has been revealed."

She'd sooner have entered the ninth sphere of Phyrexia. Well, perhaps not the ninth sphere, but the seventh, certainly.

"Come. Come! It's not like the last time."

At least he remembered the last time when the mountains had exploded.

Xantcha crossed the narrows of the oblong room until she stood at arm's length from the table. Contrary to his assurance, it was like the last time, exactly like the last time and the time before that. He'd recreated the plain of the river Kor below the Kher Ridge and covered the plain with gnats. She kept her distance.

"I'm no judge, Urza, but to my poor eyes it looks . . . similar."

"You must get closer." He offered her a glass lens set in an ivory ring.

It might have been seething poison for the enthusiasm with which she took it. He offered her his stool. When that didn't entice her, he grabbed her arm and pulled. Xantcha clambered onto the stool and bent over the table with the glass between her and the gnats.

Despite reluctance and reservation, Xantcha let out an awed sigh; as an artificer, Urza was incomparable. What had appeared to be gnats were, as she had known they would be, tiny automata, each perfectly formed and unique. In addition to men and women, there were horses, their tails swishing in imperceptible breezes, harnessed to minuscule carts. She didn't doubt that each was surrounded by a cloud of flies that the glass could not resolve. Nothing on the table was alive. Urza was adamant that his artifacts remained within what he called "the supreme principle of the Thran." Artifacts were engines in service to life, never life itself, and never, ever, sentient.

Bright tents pimpled Urza's table landscape. There were even miniature reproductions of the artifacts he and his brother had brought to the place and time that Kayla had called "The Dawn of Fire."

Xantcha focused her attention on the automata. She found Mishra's shiny dragon engine, a ground-bound bumblebee among the gnats and Urza's delicate ornithopters. When Xantcha saw an ornithopter spread its wings and rise above the table, she was confident that she'd seen the reason for Urza's summons. Miniaturizing those early artifacts had been a greater challenge than creating the swarms of tiny men and women who milled around them.

"You've got them flying!"

Urza pushed her aside. His eyes required no polished glass assistance; he could most likely see the horseflies, the fleas, and the worms as well. Xantcha noticed that he was frowning.

"It's very good," she assured him, fearing that her initial response hadn't been sincere enough.

"No, no! You were looking in the wrong place. Xantcha. Look here—" He positioned her hands above the largest tent. "What do you see now?"

"Blue cloth," she replied, knowing full well that within the tent, automata representing Urza and the major characters of Kayla's epic were midway through a scene she'd observed many times before. At first she'd been curious to see how Urza's script might differ from his wife's, but not any more.

Urza muttered something—it was probably just as well that Xantcha didn't quite catch it—and the blue cloth became a shadow through which the automata could be clearly seen. There was Urza, accurate down to the same blue shirt and threadbare trousers. His master-student, Tawnos, stood nearby, a half head taller than the rest. The Kroog warlord, the Fallaji qadir and a score of others, all moving as if they were alive and oblivious to the huge face hovering overhead. Mishra was in the shadowed tent too, but Urza was peculiar about his younger brother's gnat. While all the others had mortal features, Mishra was never more than wisps of metal at the qadir's side.

"Is it the second morning?" Xantcha asked. Urza was breathing down her neck, expecting conversation. She hoped he didn't intend to show her the assassinations. Suffering, even of automata, repelled her.

Another grumble from Urza, then, "Look for Ashnod!"

According to *The Antiquity Wars*, auburn-haired Ashnod wasn't at "The Dawn of Fire," but Urza always made a gnat in her image. He'd put it on the table, where it did nothing except get in the way of the others. To appease her hovering companion, Xantcha moved the glass slightly and found a red-capped dot in the shadow of another tent.

"You moved her there?"

"Never!" Urza roared. His eyes flashed, and the air within the cottage was very still. "I refine my understanding, I do not ever control them. Each time, I create new opportunities for the truth to emerge. Time, Xantcha, time is always the key. I call them motes of time—the tiny motes of time that replay the past, long after events have passed beyond memory. The more I refine my automata, the more of those motes I can attract. Truth attracts truth as time attracts time Xantcha, and the more motes of time I can attract, the more truth I learn about that day. And finally—finally—the truth clings to Ashnod, and she has been drawn out of her lies and deception. Watch as she reveals what I have always suspected!"

Urza snapped his fingers, and, equally fascinated and repelled, Xantcha watched Ashnod's gnat skulk from shadow to shadow until it was outside the parley tent, very near Mishra's back. Then the Ashnod-gnat knelt and manipulated something—the glass wasn't strong enough to unmask the object—and a tiny spark leaped from her hands. Mishra's wisps and filings glowed green.

The illusion of movement and free will was so seamless that Xantcha asked, "What did she do?" rather than "What did it do?"

"What do you think? Were your eyes open? Were you paying attention? Must I move them backward and do it again?" Urza replied.

Urza was less tolerant of free will in his companions. Xantcha marveled that Tawnos never left him, but perhaps, Urza had been less acid-tongued in his mortal days. "I don't know." She set the lens on a shelf slung beneath the table. "It has never been my place to think. Tell me, and I will stand enlightened."

Their eyes locked, and for a moment Xantcha stared into the ancient jewels through which Urza interpreted his life. Urza could reduce her to memory, but he blinked first.

"Proof. Proof at last. Ashnod's the one. I always suspected she was the first the Phyrexians suborned." Urza seized the lens and thrust it back into Xantcha's hands. "Now, look at the dragon engine. The Yotians have not begun to move against the qadir, but see . . . see? It has already awakened. Ashnod cast her spark upon my brother, and he called to it. It would only respond to him, you know."

Xantcha didn't peer through the lens. A blanket of light had fallen across the worktable, a hungry blanket that rose into Urza's glowing eyes rather than fell from them.

"Mishra, Mishra." Urza whispered. "If only you could see me, hear me. I was not there for you then, but I am here for you now. Cast your heart upward and I will open your eyes to the treachery around you!"

Xantcha didn't doubt Urza's ability, only his sanity, especially when he started talking to his gnat-brother. Urza believed that each moment of time contained every other moment, and that it was possible to not only recreate the past but to reach into it and affect it. Someday, as sure as the sun rose in the east, Urza would talk to the gnats on his table. He'd tell Mishra all the secrets of his heart, and Mishra would answer him. None of it would be the truth, but all of it would be real.

Xantcha dreaded that coming day. She set the lens down again and tried to distract Urza with a question. "So, your side—?"

Urza focused his eyes uncanny light on her face. "Not my side! I was not a party to anything that happened that clay! I was ignorant of everything. They lied to me and deceived me. They knew I would never consent to their treachery. I would have stopped them. I would have warned my brother!"

Xantcha beat a tactical retreat. "Of course. But even if you had, the end would not have changed," she said in her most soothing tone. "If you've got it right, now, then the warlord's schemes were irrelevant. Through Ashnod, the Phyrexians had their own treachery—against the qadir and the warlord, against you and Mishra. None of you were meant to survive."

"Yes," Urza said on a caught breath. "Yes! Exactly! Neither the qadir nor the warlord were supposed to survive. It was a plot to capture me as they had already captured my brother. Thus he was willing, but also reluctant, to talk to me!" He turned back to the table. "I understand, Brother. I forgive! Be strong, Mishra—I will find a way to save you as I saved myself."

Xantcha repressed a shudder. There were inconsistencies among her copies of *The Antiquity Wars* but none on the scale Urza proposed. "Was your brother transformed then, or still flesh?"

Urza backed away from the table. His eyes were clouded, almost normal in appearance. "I will learn that next time, or the time after that. They have suborned him. See how he responds to Ashnod. She was their first creature. They must have known that if we talked privately, I would have sensed the change in him . . . . I would have set him free. If there was still any part of him left that could have been freed. Or, I would have turned my wrath on them from that point forward. They knew I could not be suborned, Xantcha, because I possessed the Mightstone. The stones have equal power, Xantcha, but the power is different. The Weakstone is weakness, the Mightstone is strength, and the Phyrexians never dared my strength. Ah, the evil that day, Xantcha. If they had not driven us apart, there would have been no war, except against them . . . . You see that, Xantcha. You see that, don't you? My brother and I together would have driven them back to Koilos. They knew our power before we'd begun to guess it."

They and them. They and them. With Urza, it all came back to they and them: Phyrexians. Xantcha knew the Phyrexians for the enemies they were. She'd never argue that they hadn't played a pivotal role in Urza's wars. Perhaps they had suborned Mishra and Ashnod, too. But while Urza played with gnats on a tabletop, another wave of Phyrexians, real Phyrexians, had washed up on Dominaria's shores.

"It makes no difference," she protested. "Mishra's been dead for more than three thousand years! It hardly matters whether you failed him, or Ashnod destroyed him, or the Phyrexians suborned him, or whether it happened before "The Dawn of Fire" or after. Urza, you're creating a past that doesn't matter—"

"Doesn't matter! They took my brother from me, and made of him my greatest enemy. It matters, Xantcha. It will always matter more than anything else. I must learn what they did and how and when they did it." He breathed, a slow sigh. "I could have stopped them. I must not fail again." He held his hands above the table. Xantcha didn't need the lens to know that Mishra's gnat shone bright. "I won't, Mishra. I will never fail again. I have learned caution. I have learned deception. I will not be tricked, not even by you!"

Before Urza had brought Xantcha to Dominaria, she'd been more sympathetic to his guilt-driven obsessions. Now she said, "Not even you can change the past," and didn't care if he struck her down for impudence. "Are you going to stand by and play with toys while the Phyrexians steal your birthplace from you? They're back. I smelled them in Baszerat and Morvern. The Baszerati and the Morvernish are at war with each other, just as the Yotians and the Fallaji were, and the Phyrexians are on both sides. Sound familiar!"

Her neck ached from staring up at him and braving his gemstone stare. Xantcha had no arcane power to draw upon, but nose-to-nose, she was more stubborn. "Why are we here," she asked in the breathless silence, "if you're not going to take a stand against the Phyrexians? We could play games anywhere."

Urza retreated. He moistened his lips and made other merely mortal gestures. "Not games, Xantcha. I can afford no more mistakes. Dominaria has not forgotten or forgiven what happened last time. I must tread lightly. So many died, so much was destroyed, and all because I was blind and deaf. I did not see that my brother was not himself, that he was surrounded by enemies. I didn't hear his pleas for help."

"He never pled for help! That's why you didn't hear, and you can never know why he didn't, because you can never talk to him again. No matter what happens in this room, on that table, you can't bring him back! Now you've got Ashnod outside the tent. You've made her into another Phyrexian, pulling Mishra's strings. The Yotians were planning an ambush, the Phyrexians were planning an ambush, and you weren't wise to either plot.

Waste not, want not, Urza—if the Phyrexians had Ashnod before "The Dawn of Fire," how did she manage, thirty years later, to send Tawnos to you with the sylex? Or was that part of a plot, too? A compleat Phyrexian doesn't have a conscience, Urza. A compleat Phyrexian doesn't feel remorse; it can't. Mishra never did."

"He couldn't. He'd been suborned," Urza shouted. "Usurped. Corrupted. Destroyed! He was no longer a man when I faced him in Argoth. They'd taken his will, flensed his flesh and stretched it over an abomination!"

"But they didn't take Ashnod's will? She sent the sylex. Was her will stronger than your brother's?"

Xantcha played a dangerous game herself and played it to the brink. Urza had frozen, no blinking or breathing, as if he'd become an artifact himself. Xantcha pressed her advantage.

"Was Ashnod stronger than you too? Strong enough to double-deal the Phyrexians and save Dominaria in the only way she could?"

"No," Urza whispered.

"No? No what, Urza? Once you start treating born men and women as Phyrexian, where do you stop? Ashnod skulking outside your tent before the Dawn of Fire, Ashnod sending Tawnos with the sylex? One time she's a Phyrexian puppet, the next she's not? Are you sure you know which is which? Or, maybe, she was the puppet both times, and what would that make you? You used the sylex."

Urza folded a fist. "Stop," he warned.

"The Phyrexians spent three thousand years trying to slay you, before they gave up. I think they gave up because they'd found a better way. Leave you alone on a mountainside playing with toys!"

He'd have been a powerful man if muscle and bone had been his strength's only source, but Urza had the power of the Thran through his eyes, and the power of a sorcerer standing on his native ground. His arm began to move. As long as she could see it moving, Xantcha believed she was safe.

The fist touched her hair and stopped. Xantcha held her breath. He'd never come that close, never actually touched her before. They couldn't go on like this, not if there was any hope for Dominaria.

"Urza?" she whispered when, at last, her lungs demanded air.

"Urza, can you hear me? Do you see me?" Xantcha touched his arm. "Urza . . . Urza, talk to me."

He trembled and grabbed her shoulder for balance. He didn't know his strength; pain left her gasping. Her eyes were shut when he made the transition, temporary even at the best of times, back into the here and now. Something happened to Urza when he cast his power over the worktable, not the truth, but definitely real and definitely getting worse.

"Xantcha!" his hand sprang away from her as though she were made from red-hot metal. "Xantcha, what is this?" He stared at the crockery mountains as if he'd never seen them before—though Xantcha had seen even that reaction more times than she cared to remember.

"You summoned me, Urza," she said flatly. "You had something new to show me."

"But this?" He gestured at his mountain-and-gnat covered table. "Where did this come from? Not—not me. Not again?"

She nodded.

"I was sitting on the porch as the sun set. It was quiet, peaceful. I thought of—I thought of the past, Xantcha, and it began again." He shrank within himself. "You weren't here."

"I was after food. You were inside when I returned. Urza, you've got to let go of the past. It's not . . . It's not healthy. Even for you, this is not healthy."

They stared at each other. This had happened so many times before that there was no longer a need for conversation. Even the moment when Urza swept everything off his table was entirely predictable.

"It's started, Urza, truly started. This time there's a war south of here," Xantcha said, while dust still rose from the crumbled mountains, quicksilver slithered across the packed dirt floor, and gnats by the hundreds scrambled for shelter.

"Phyrexians?"

"I kenned them on both sides. *Sleepers.* They take orders, they don't give them, but it's a Dominarian war with Phyrexian interference on both sides."

He took the details directly from her mind: a painless process when she cooperated.

"Baszerat and Morvern. I do not know these names."

"They aren't mighty kingdoms with glorious histories. They're little more than walled cities, a few villages and, to keep the grudge going, a handful of gold mines in the hills between them; something for the Phyrexians to exploit. They're getting bolder. Baszerat and Morvern aren't the only places I've scented glistening oil in the wind, but this is the first war."

"You haven't interfered?"

His voice harshened and his eyes flashed. With Urza, madness was never more than a moment away.

"You said I mustn't, and I obey. You should look for yourself. Now is the time—"

"Perhaps. I dare not move too soon. The land remembers; there can be no mistakes. I must have cause. I must be very careful, Xantcha. If I reveal myself too soon, I foresee disaster. We must weigh our choices carefully."

Retorts swirled in Xantcha's mind. It was never truly we with Urza, but she'd made her choices long ago. "No one will suspect, even if you used your true name and shape. There've been a score of doom-saying Urzas on the road this year alone. You've become the stuff of legends. No one would believe you're you."

A rare smile lit up her companion's face. "That bad still?"

"Worse. But please, go to Baszerat and Morvern. A quarrel has become a war. So it began with the Fallaji and the Yotians. Who knows, there might be brothers . . . . You've been up here too long, Urza."

Urza reached into her mind again, gathering landmarks and languages, which she willingly surrendered. Then, in a blink's time, she was back into her own proper consciousness. Urza faded into the between-worlds. which was, among other things, the fastest way to travel across the surface of a single world.

"Good luck," she wished him, then knelt down.

Crashing crockery had crushed a good many of Urza's gnats. Quicksilver had dissolved uncounted others. Yet many swirled around in confusion on the floor. Xantcha labored until midnight, gathering them into a box no deeper than her finger, but far too steep for any of them to climb. When the dirt was motionless, she took the box into the alcove where Urza stored his raw materials.

The shelves were neat. Every casket and flask was clearly labeled, albeit in a language Xantcha couldn't read. She didn't need to read labels. The flask she wanted had a unique lambent glow. It was pure phloton, distilled from fire, starlight and mana, a recipe Urza had found on the world where he'd found Xantcha.

"Waste not, want not," she whispered over the seething box.

The gnats blazed like fireflies as they fell through the phloton, and then were gone.

Xantcha resealed the flask and replaced it on the shelf, exactly as she'd found it, before returning to her own room. She had a plan of her own, which she'd promised herself she'd implement when the time was right. That time had come when Urza touched her hair.

If Urza couldn't see the present Phyrexian threat because he was obsessed with the past . . . If he couldn't care about the folk of Baszerat or Morvern because he still cared too much about what had happened to Mishra, then Xantcha figured she had to bring the past and Mishra to Urza. She had it all worked out in her mind, as much as she ever worked anything out: find a young man who resembled Kayla's word picture, teach him the answers to Urza's guilty questions, then troll her trumped-up Mishra past Urza's eyes.

A new Mishra wouldn't cure his madness. Nothing could do that, not while those powerstone eyes were lodged in Urza's skull, but if a false Mishra could convince Urza to walk away from his worktable, that would be enough.

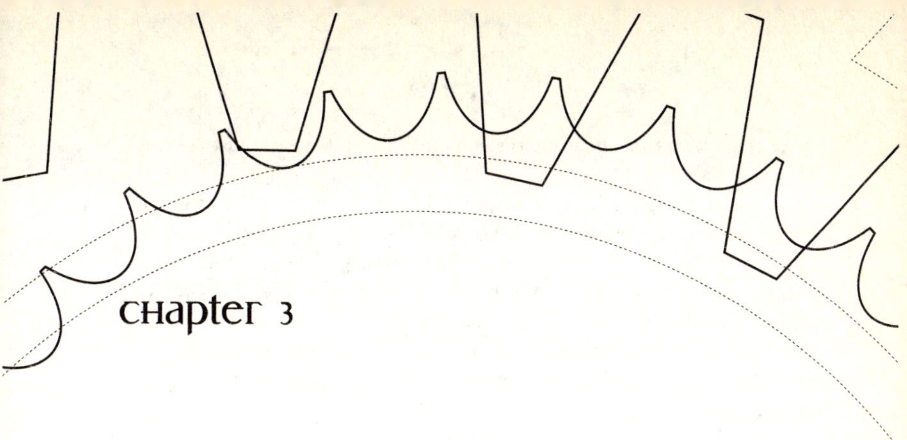

chapter 3

Morning came to the Ohran Ridge, and found Xantcha sitting in the bottom of a transparent sphere as it drifted above springtime mountain meadows. The sphere was as big around as Xantcha was tall and had been a gift from Urza. Or more accurately, the artifact that produced it had been Urza's gift. He'd devised the cyst to preserve her as she followed him from world to world. A deliberate yawn and a mnemonic rhyme drew a protective oil out of the cyst. Depending on the rhyme, the oil expanded into the buoyant sphere or ripened into a tough, flexible armor.

Urza had taught Xantcha the rhyme for the armor. The sphere was the result of Xantcha's curiosity and improvisations. Urza complained that she'd transformed his Thran-inspired artifact into a Phyrexian abomination. The complaint, though sincere, had always perplexed Xantcha. The Thran, as Urza described them, believed that sentience and artifice must always be separate. Xantcha's cyst wasn't remotely sentient, and she supposed she could have dug it out of her stomach, but it had become part of her, no different than her arms . . . or Urza's faceted eyes. Besides, if she hadn't discovered how to make her sphere, Urza would have had to provide her with food, clothing, and all the other things a flesh and blood person required, because Xantcha, though she was almost as old as Urza, was indisputably flesh and blood.

And just as indisputably Phyrexian.

Xantcha willed the sphere higher, seeking the swift wind-streams well above the mountains. She had a long journey planned, and needed strong winds if she wanted to finish it before Urza returned from the south. The sphere rose until the landscape resembled Urza's tabletop, and the sphere began to tumble.

Tumbling never bothered Xantcha. With or without the cyst, she had a strong stomach and an unshakable sense of direction. But tumbling wasted time and energy. Xantcha raised her arms level with her shoulders, one straight out in front of her, the other extended to the side; the tumbling stopped. Then she pointed both extended arms in the direction she wished to travel and rotated her hands so they were both palms up. She thought of rigging and sails, a firm hand on the tiller board, and the sphere began to move against the wind.

It was slow going at first, but before the sun had risen another two hand spans, Xantcha was scudding north faster than any horse could run. Xantcha couldn't explain how the sphere stayed aloft. It wasn't sorcery; she had no talent for calling upon the land. Urza swore it wasn't anything to do with him or his artifacts and refused to discuss the matter. Xantcha thought it was no different than running. The whys and wherefores weren't important so long as she found what she was looking for and got home safe.

But questions lurked where Xantcha's memories began. They crept forward once the sphere was moving smartly, and there was nothing to do but think and remember.

The beginning was liquid, thick and warm as blood, dark and safe. After the liquid came light and cold, emptiness and hard edges, a dim chamber in the Fane of Flesh, the first place she'd known, a soot-stained monolith of Phyrexia's Fourth Sphere. Her beginning wasn't birth, not as Urza had been born from his mother's body. There were no mothers or fathers in the decanting chamber, only metal and leather priests tending stone-gouged vats.

The vat-priests of the Fane of Flesh were of no great status. Though compleat, their appliances were mere hooks and paddles and their senses were no better than the flesh they'd been decanted with. They took orders from above. In Phyrexia there was always above—or within, deeper and deeper through the eight spheres to the center where dwelt the Ineffable. He whose name was known but never spoken, lest he awaken from his blessed sleep.

Obey, the vat-priests said unnecessarily as she'd shivered and discovered her limbs. A small, warm stone fell from her hands. The vat-priests had said it was her heart and took it from her. There was a place, they said—in Phyrexia everything had a place, without place there was nothing—where hearts were kept. Her mistakes would be written on her heart, and if she made too many mistakes, the Ineffable who dwelt at Phyrexia's core would make her a part of his dreams, and that would be the end of her.

Obey and learn. Pay attention. Make no mistakes. Now, follow.

Later, when Xantcha had crossed more planes and visited more worlds than she could easily recount, she'd realized that there was no other place like Phyrexia. In no other world were full-grown newts, like her, decanted beside a sludge-vat. Only Phyrexian newts remembered the first opening of their eyes. Only Phyrexian newts remembered, and understood, the first words—threats—they heard. In her beginning, there was only the Fane of Flesh, and she obeyed without question, writhing across the stone floor because she hadn't the strength to walk.

Xantcha's bones hardened quickly. She learned to tend herself and perform such tasks as were suited to newts. When she had mastered those lessons, the vat-priests led her to the teacher-priests, who instructed the newts as they were transformed from useless flesh into compleat Phyrexians. The teacher-priests with their recording eyes and stinging-switch arms told her that she was Xantcha.

Xantcha wasn't a name, not as she later came to understood names. When Urza had asked, she had explained that Xantcha was the place where she stood when newts were assembled for instruction, the place where she received her food, and the box where she slept at night.

If days or nights had played a part in her early life.

Phyrexia was a world without sun, moon, or stars. Deep in the Fane of Flesh, priests called out the march of time: when she learned, when she ate, when she slept; there was no time for rest, no place for companionship. When she was returned to her box for sleeping, Xantcha dreamed of sunlight, grass, and wind. She might have thought it strange that her mind held images of a place so clearly not Phyrexia, if she'd thought at all.

Even now, more than three millennia after her first awakenings, Xantcha didn't know if she'd been the only newt who'd dreamed of a green, sunlit world, or if the Ineffable had commanded the same dreams and longings for every newt that learned beside her.

You are newts, and newts you will remain, the teacher-priests had taught her. *You are destined to sleep in another place and prepare the way for those who will follow. Listen and obey.*

There were many other newts in the Fane of Flesh, organized into cadres and marched together through their educations. All newts began the same way, with meat and bones and blood-filled veins, then—according to their place in the Ineffable's design—tender-priests excised their flesh and reshaped their bodies with tough amalgams of metal and oil, until they were compleated. After each reshaping, the priests sent the excised flesh and blood to the renderers; eventually it was returned it to the vats. When the newt was fully reshaped, the tenders immersed it in the glistening oil; a Phyrexian's first time in the great fountain outside the Fane of Flesh. When it emerged, the newt was compleat and took its destined place in the Ineffable's grand plan for Phyrexia.

Xantcha remembered standing in her place on a Fane balcony, as fully reshaped newts were carried to the fountain. She remembered the cacophony as newly compleated Phyrexians emerged into the glare and glow of the Fourth Sphere furnaces. To the extent that any newt felt hope, it hoped for a good compleation, a privileged place. The knowledge that she would be forever bound in a newt's body was greater pain than any punishment the priests ever lashed across her back.

Hatred had no place in Phyrexia. Contempt replaced hatred and looked down on the special newts, whose destiny was to sleep in another place. Xantcha looked forward to the moments when she was alone in her box with her dreams.

Once she went to sleep, dreamed her dreams, as she'd always done, and awoke beneath the bald, gray sky of the First Sphere. There were different teacher-priests tending her cadre. The new priests were larger than those in the Fane of Flesh. More metal than leather, they had four feet and four arms. Their feet were clawed, and each of their arms ended in a different metal weapons. They were supposed to protect the newts from the dangers of the First Sphere. Newts had never dwelt on the First Sphere, but the four-armed teachers were not honored by their new responsibilities. They obeyed their orders without enthusiasm, until one of the newts made a mistake.

Newts you are, and newts you shall remain forever, they'd recite as they dealt out punishment with one hand after the other. *You are destined to sleep on another world. Now learn the ways of another world. Listen and obey.*

Xantcha wondered what would have happened if she'd failed to listen or obey. At the time, the notion simply didn't occur to her. Life on the First Sphere was hard enough without disobedience. The newts were taught farming, in preparation for the day when their destiny would be fulfilled, but the slippery dirt of the First Sphere resisted their every effort. The plows, sickles, hoes, and pitchforks that they were commanded to use left their muscles aching, the whiplike razor-grass—the only plant they could grow—slashed them bloody, and the harsh light blistered their skin mercilessly.

Xantcha remembered another newt, Gi'anzha, whose place was near hers in the cadre. Gi'anzha had used a grass sheaf to hack off its arm, then shoved a pitchfork shaft into the bloody socket. Gi'anzha was meat by the time they found it, but Xantcha and the other newts understood why it had done what it had.

Newts were small and fragile compared to everything else that dwelt on the First Sphere. Their uncompleated bodies suffered injuries rather than malfunctions. They could not be repaired but were left to heal as best they could, which sometimes wasn't good enough. Failed newts—meat newts—were whisked back to the Fourth Sphere for rendering. Waste not, want not, nothing in Phyrexia was completely without use, though meat was reviled by the compleat, who'd transcended their flesh and were sustained by glistening oil.

As her cadre was reduced to meat, Xantcha's place within it changed. Another newt should have been Xantcha, she should have become G'xi'kzi or Kra'tzin, but too much time had passed since the vat-priests had organized the cadre. The patterns of their minds were as fixed as those of their soft, battered bodies. Xantcha she was, and Xantcha she remained, even when the cadre had shrunk so much that the priests alloyed it with another, similarly depleted group.

Xantcha found herself face-to-face with another Xantcha. For both of them, it was . . . confusion. The word scarcely existed in Phyrexia, except to describe the clots of slag and ash that accumulated beneath the great furnaces. Together they consulted the priests, as newts were trained to do. The priests judged that as a result of the recombination, neither of them truly stood in the spot of Xantcha. The alloyed cadre's Xantcha was a third newt, who thought of itself as Hoz'krin and wanted no part of this Xantcha confusion. Xantcha and Xantcha were each told to recognize new places within the alloyed cadre or face the lash.

Lash or no, the priests' judgment was not acceptable. Places had become names that could not be surrendered, even under the threat of punishment. The Xantchas stayed awake when they should have slept in their boxes. They slipped away from the priests and spoke to each other privately. Meeting in private with another newt was something neither had done before. They negotiated and they compromised, though there were no Phyrexian words for either process. They agreed to make themselves unique. Xantcha broke off a blade of the razor-sharp grass and hacked off the hair growing on the left side of her skull. The other Xantcha soaked its hair in an acid stream until it turned orange.

They had rebelled—a word as forbidden as the Ineffable's true name and almost as feared. Only the tender-priests could change a newt's shape and only according to the Ineffable's plan. When the Xantchas returned to the place where their cadre gathered for food and sleep, the other newts gaped and turned away, as the teacher-priests came rumbling and clanking from the perimeter.

Xantcha had taken the other newt's flesh-fingered hand. Thirty-three hundred Dominarian years afterward, Xantcha knew that the touch of flesh was a language unto itself, a language that Phyrexia had forgotten. At the time, the gesture had confused the priests utterly and left them spinning in their tracks.

Not long after, the bald, gray sky had brightened painfully.

Xantcha had recalled her heart and the vat-priests' threat: too many mistakes and the Ineffable would seize her heart. Until the other Xantcha had tumbled into her life, she'd made less than her share of the cadre's mistakes, but perhaps one mistake, if it were great enough, was enough to rouse the Ineffable.

She'd thought the shining creature who'd descended from the too-bright sky was the Ineffable. He was nothing like the priests she'd seen and nothing at all like a newt. His eyes were intensely red, and an abundance of teeth filled his protruding jaw. And she'd known, perhaps because of that jaw filled with teeth, that it was he, as the Ineffable was he and not it in the way of newts and priests.

"You can call me Gix," he'd said, using his toothsome jaw to shape the words in an almost newtish way, though he didn't have the soft-flesh lips that were useful for eating but got in the way of proper Phyrexian pronunciation.

Gix was a name, the first true name Xantcha had ever heard, because it couldn't be interpreted as a place within a cadre. Gix was a demon, a Phyrexian who'd looked upon the Ineffable face with his own eyes and who, while the Ineffable slept, controlled Phyrexia. From a newt's lowly perspective, a demon's name might just as well be ineffable.

Gix offered his hand. The only sound Xantcha heard was a slight whirring as his arm extended and extended to at least twice his height. As Gix's hand unfurled, black talons sprang from each elegantly articulated finger. He touched the other Xantcha lightly beneath its chin. Xantcha felt trembling terror in the other newt's hand. The demon's talons looked as if they could pierce a priest's leather carapace or go straight through a newt's skull. A blue-green spark leapt from the demon to the other Xantcha, whose hand immediately warmed, relaxed, and slipped away.

Deep-pitched rumbling came out of the demon's throat. He lowered his hand, his head swiveled slightly, and Xantcha felt a cold, green light take her measure. Gix didn't touch her as he'd touched the other Xantcha. His arm retreated, each segment clicking sharply into the one behind it, then more whirring as his jaw assumed a sickle smile.

"Xantcha."

All remaining doubts about the difference between names and places vanished. Xantcha had become a true name, and confronted with *him*, Xantcha became *her*. The notions for male and female, dominance and submission, were already in Xantcha's mind, rooted in her dreams of soft, green grass and yellow sun.

"You will be ready," the demon said. "I made you. No simple rendering for you, Xantcha. Fresh meat. Fresh blood. Brought here from the place where you will go, where you will conquer. You have their cunning, their boldness, and their unpredictability, Xantcha, but your heart is mine. You are mine forever."

The demon meant to frighten her, and he did; he meant to distract her, too, while a blue-green spark formed on his shiny brass brow. In that, he was less successful. Xantcha saw the spark race toward her, felt it strike the ridge between her eyes and bury itself in the bone. The demon had inserted himself in her mind.

He made himself glorious before her. At least, that's what he tried to do. Xantcha felt the urge to worship him in awe and obedience, to feed him with the mind-storm turbulence no compleat Phyrexian could experience, except by proxy. Gix made promises in Xantcha's mind: privilege, power, and passion, all of them irresistible, or meant to be irresistible, but Xantcha resisted. She made a new place for herself, within herself. It wasn't terribly difficult. If there could be two Xantchas within the cadre, there could be two within her mind, a Xantcha who belonged to Gix and a Xantcha who did not.

She filled the part that belonged to Gix with images from her dreams: blue skies, green grass, and gentle breezes. The demon drank them down, then spat them out. The light went out of his eyes. He turned away from her, to others in her cadre, and found them more entertaining. For her part, Xantcha stood very still. She had denied the demon, rejected him before he could reject her. She expected instant annihilation, but the Ineffable did not seize her. Whatever else she had done, it was not a mistake great enough to destroy her heart.

After sating himself on newtish thoughts and passions, Gix departed. The teacher-priests sought to reclaim their place above the cadre, but after the elegance and horror of a demon, they seemed puny. In time, they became afraid of their charges and kept their distance as the newts began to talk more freely among themselves, planning for their glorious futures on other worlds.

Xantcha maintained her place, eating, sleeping, laboring, and taking part in the discussions, but she was no longer like the other newts. That moment when she'd created two Xantchas in her mind had transformed her, as surely as the tender-priests reshaped newts in the Fane of Flesh. She was aware of herself as no one else—except Gix—seemed to be. She stumbled into loneliness, and, seeking relief from that singular ache, she sought out the Xantcha whose hand she'd once held.

"I am without," she'd said, because at the time she hadn't known a better word. "I need to touch you."

She'd offered both hands, but the other Xantcha had reeled backward, screaming as if it were in terrible pain. The rest of the cadre swarmed between them, and Xantcha was lucky to survive.

Xantcha remembered the newt that had sawed off its arm with the razor grass, but what she wanted was an end to her isolation, not an end of existence. She considered running away. The First Sphere was vast. A newt could easily lose herself beyond the shimmering horizon, but if she placed herself beyond her cadre and its priests, Xantcha would slowly starve, because despite their constant efforts with hoes and plows and sickles, nothing edible grew in First Sphere's soil. Except for the meaty sludge brought up from Fane of Flesh, there was nothing on Phyrexia's First Sphere that a newt could eat.

When the cadre closed ranks to keep her from the simmering cauldrons the priests brought from the Fane, Xantcha picked up a sickle and cleared a path to her place. Five newts went down with the cauldron for rendering; one priest, too. Xantcha went to sleep with a full stomach and the sense that she'd never reopen her eyes. But neither Gix nor the Ineffable came to claim her. Once again, it seemed that she hadn't made a mistake.

Others did . . . newts began to disappear, a few at a time while they slept. Xantcha contrived to make a tiny hole in her box. She kept watch when she should have been asleep, but the Ineffable wasn't consuming newts. Instead, priests picked up a box here, a box there, and took them away. Speaker-equipped priests could spew words faster than soft-lipped newts; sometimes they forgot that newts heard faster than they spoke. Xantcha hid in a place on the edge and listened to chittering, metallic conversations.

The moment she and the others had been promised since their decanting had arrived. Newts were leaving Phyrexia. They were sleeping on another world. One of the priests had gone through the portal. It didn't like what it had found. Its coils had corroded and its joints had clogged because water, not oil, flowed everywhere: in fountains, across the land and in blinding torrents from the sky that was sometimes blue, sometimes black, sometimes speckled, and sometimes streaked with fire. A worthless place, the priest said, rust and dust, fit only for newts.

Xantcha held her breath, as she'd held it before Gix. Although she'd never seen or felt it, she remembered water and knew in her bones that a place where water fell from the sky would be a place where a newt could get lost without necessarily starving. She began to make herself more useful, more visible, to the others, in hopes that the priests would pick her box, but though the disappearances continued, the priests didn't take her.

The cadre withered. Xantcha was certain she'd be taken away. There simply weren't that many left. Then the taking stopped. The newts slept and worked, slept and worked. Xantcha wasn't the only one who listened to the priests. None of them liked what they heard. There were problems in the other world. Newts had been exposed and destroyed.

Thirty centuries after the fact, when she and Urza returned to Dominaria, Xantcha had pieced together what might have happened. Appended to some of the oldest chronicles in her collection were accounts of strangers, undersized and eerily identical, who'd appeared suddenly and throughout what was left of Terisiare, some twenty years after the Brothers' War had ended. The Dominarians hadn't guessed what the strangers suddenly tromping through their fields were or where they'd come from, but ignorance hadn't kept them from exterminating the nearly defenseless newts.

But at the time, in Phyrexia, there'd been only whispers of disaster, thwarted destiny, and newts transformed to meat in a place where not even the Ineffable could find them.

The whispers reached Xantcha's cadre along with orders that they were to move. New cadres were coming, fresh from the Fane of Flesh. Xantcha caught sight of them as she dragged her box through the sharp, oily grass. The replacement cadres were composed of newts who were bigger than her. No two of the larger newts were quite the same and every one was obviously male or female.

Xantcha had lost her destiny. She and the rest of her depleted cadre became redundant. Even the tools with which they'd turned the sterile Phyrexian soil were taken away, and the food cauldrons, which had always arrived promptly between periods of work and sleep, sleep and work, appeared only before sleep . . . if the cadre was lucky.

Luck. A word that went with despair. Denied their promised place, some newts crawled into their boxes and never came out again. Not Xantcha. As regarded luck, Gix was lucky that she didn't know where to find him or how to destroy him. It took time to grow a newt in the vats, and more time to teach it the most basic tasks, and transform it into a Phyrexian. So much time that the male and female newts she'd glimpsed farming her cadre's old place must have been already growing in the vats when the demon had planted his blue-green spark in her skull.

Gix had lied to her. It was a small thing compared to the other hardships she endured, now that her cadre was redundant, but it sustained her for a long time until another wave of rumors swept across the First Sphere. A knife had sliced through the passage that connected Phyrexia with the other world; it had broken and was beyond repair. Half of the larger newts were trapped on the wrong side; the rest were as redundant as she had become.

Without warning, as was usually the case in her Phyrexian life, all the redundant newts, including Xantcha, were summoned to the Fourth Sphere to witness the excoriation of the demon Gix. The Ineffable's plan for Phyrexian glory had been thwarted by the Knife and someone had to be punished. Gix's lustrous carapace was corroded and burnt before he was consigned to the Seventh Sphere for torment. It was a magnificent spectacle. Gix fought like the hellspawn he was, taking four fellow demons into the reeking fumarole with him. Their shrieks were momentarily louder than the roar of the crowds and furnaces, though they faded quickly.

For a while, Xantcha remained in the Fourth Sphere. She had no place, no assignment. In a place as tightly organized as Phyrexia, a place-less newt should have been noticeable, but Xantcha wasn't. She dwelt among the gremlins. Even in Phyrexia, time spent in gremlin town couldn't be called living, but gremlins were flesh. They had to eat, and Xantcha ate with them, as she learned things about flesh no compleat priest could teach her.

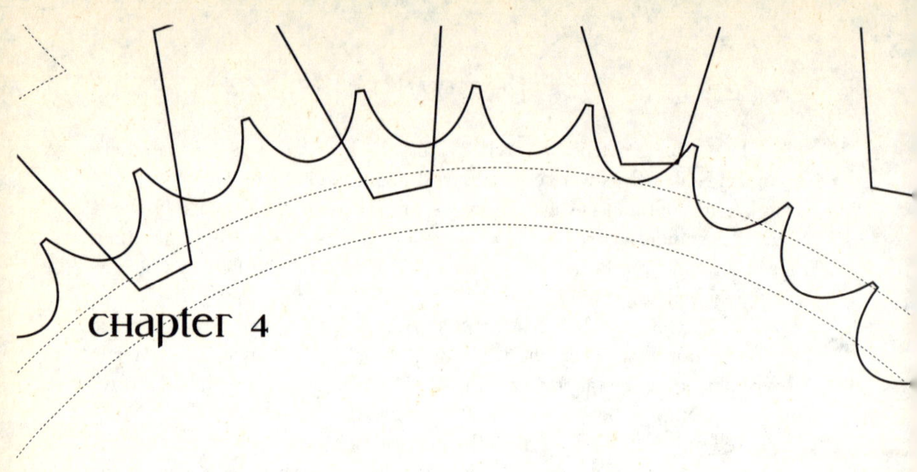

chapter 4

Chaotic air currents rising above a patchwork of cultivated fields seized Xantcha's sphere. For several panicked heartbeats, as she battled the provisions bouncing around inside the sphere, Xantcha didn't know where she was or why. After more than three thousand years, she needed that long to climb out of her memories.

The disorientation had passed before disaster could begin. Xantcha was in control before the sphere brushed the bank of a tree-shadowed stream. It collapsed around her, a warm, moist film that evaporated quickly, as it had countless times before, but thoughts of what might have happened left her gasping for air.

Xantcha hadn't intended to lose herself in her memories. The past, when there was so much of it crammed into a single mind, was a kind of madness. She dropped to her knees and wiped the film from her face before it had a chance to dry. Between coughs, Xantcha took her bearing from the horizons: sun sinking to the west, mountains to the south, and gentle hills elsewhere. She'd come to her senses over inner Efuan Pincar, precisely the place she'd wanted to be. Luck, Xantcha told herself, and succumbed to another round of coughing.

Xantcha never liked to rely on luck, but just then, thoughts of luck were preferable to the alternatives. She'd been thinking of her beginnings, as she rarely did. Worse, she'd been thinking of Gix. She'd never forgotten that blue-green spark. Despite everything, she worried that the demon's mark might still be lurking somewhere within her skull.

She made herself think about Urza and all that they'd survived together.

He could look inside her and destroy her if she became untrustworthy. So long as he didn't, Xantcha believed she could trust herself. But thoughts of Gix were no reason to fear Gix. Nothing escaped the excoriations of Phyrexia's Seventh Sphere. Even if the blue-green spark remained, the demon who'd drilled it into her was gone.

Urza insisted that she steer clear of Phyrexians, once she scented them. He didn't want his enemies to know where he was or that he'd returned to the land of his birth. They both knew that if she ever fell back into Phyrexian hands, they'd strip her memories before they consigned her to the Seventh Sphere, and she knew too many of Urza's secrets to justify the risk.

The Phyrexian presence on Dominaria had been growing over the past fifty years. Morvern and Baszerat were only two among a score of places where Xantcha had once scrounged regularly, but were—or soon would be—off limits. Efuan Pincar was not, however, among them. The little realm on the wrong side of the great island of Gulmany was so isolated and unimportant, that the rest of what had once been Terisiare scarcely acknowledged its existence. It was the last place Xantcha expected to scent a Phyrexian. If she'd succumbed to thoughts of Gix while soaring over Efuan Pincar, it wasn't because a Phyrexian had tickled her mind, but because she'd begun to doubt Urza.

True, he'd go to the places where she'd scented *sleepers*, and he'd find them, but he wouldn't do anything about them. Newts disguised as born-folk weren't enough to goad Urza into action. Xantcha thought it would take death for that. She'd been perversely pleased when she'd found a war in Baszerat and Morvern. She thought for sure that would overcome Urza's obsession with the past, and perhaps it had; he'd never come so close to striking her.

Kayla Bin-Kroog hadn't mentioned Efuan Pincar in her epic. Efuand chroniclers explained that omission by proclaiming that their land had been empty until three hundred years ago, when a handful of boats had brought a band of refugees to Gulmany's back side. Xantcha doubted that there'd ever been enough boats in Terisiare to account for all the living Efuands, but scribes lied, she knew that from her *Antiquity Wars* collection. What mattered to Xantcha was that among any ten men of Efuan Pincar, at least one matched Kayla's word picture of Mishra, and another had his impulsive temperament. To find better odds she'd have to soar across the Sea of Laments, something she'd done just once, by mistake, and had sworn she'd never try again.

Xantcha knew her plan to bring Urza face to face with a dark, edgy youth who might remind him of his long-dead brother wasn't the most imaginative strategy, but she was Phyrexian, and as Urza never ceased telling her, Phyrexians lacked imagination. Urza himself was a genius, a man of great power and limitless imagination, when he chose to exercise it. Once she had him face-to-face with her false Mishra, Xantcha expected

Urza's imagination would repair any defects in her clumsy Phyrexian strategy.

Then Xantcha caught herself thinking about other notoriously failed strategies: Gix and thousands of identical sexless newts.

"What if I'm wrong?" she asked the setting sun; the same question that Urza asked whenever she tried to prod him into action.

The sun didn't answer, so Xantcha gave herself the same answer she gave Urza, "Dominaria's doomed if Urza does nothing. If he thinks his brother's come back to him, he might do something, and something—anything—is better than nothing."

Xantcha watched the last fiery sliver of sunlight vanish in the west. Her sphere had dried into a fine white powder that disappeared in the breeze. By her best guess, she'd been aloft without food, water, or restful sleep for two and a half days. There was water in the stream and more than enough food in her shoulder sack, but sleep proved elusive. Wrapped in her cloak, Xantcha saw Gix's toothsome face each time she closed her eyes. After watching the stars slide across the sky, she yawned out another sphere as the eastern horizon began to brighten.

Xantcha hadn't thought she'd find her Mishra in the first village she visited. Though experience on other worlds had convinced her that every village harbored at least one youth with more ambition than sense, it had stood to reason that she might need to visit several villages before she found the right combination of temperament and appearance. But temperament and appearance weren't her problems.

In the twenty years since her last visit, war and famine had come to Efuan Pincar. The cultivated field in which she'd spent her first sleepless night had proved the exception to the new rules. The first village that Xantcha approached was still smoldering. The second had trees growing from abandoned hearths. Those villages that remained intact did so behind palisades of stone, brick, and sharpened stakes.

She approached the closed gates warily, regretting that she'd disguised herself as a cocky and aristocratic youth. It was an easy charade, one that matched her temperament and appearance, but throughout their wandering, she and Urza had come across very few wars that couldn't be blamed on aristocratic greed or pride.

The war in Efuan Pincar, however, proved to one of the rare exceptions. The gates swung open before she announced herself. The whole village greeted her with pleading eyes. They'd made assumptions: She was a young man who'd lost his horse and companions to the enemy. She needed their help. But most of all, they assumed she'd come to help them. Outnumbered and curious, Xantcha made her own assumption. She'd learn more if she let them believe what they wanted to believe.

"You will go to Pincar City and tell Tabarna what is happening?" the village spokesman asked, once he had offered her food and drink. "We are all too old to make the journey."

"Tabarna does not know," another elder said, and all the villagers bobbed their heads in agreement.

"He cannot know. If Tabarna knew, he would come to us. If he knew, he would help us. He would not let us suffer," A multitude of voices, all saying the same thing.

A man named Tabarna had governed Efuan Pincar twenty years ago. Part priest, part prince, he'd been an able ruler. If the villagers' Tabarna were still the man Xantcha remembered, though, he'd be well past his prime, and beloved or not, someone would be taking advantage of him. Usually, that someone would be a man dressed as she was dressed, in fine clothes and with a good steel sword slung below his hip. Xantcha couldn't ask too many questions, not without compromising her disguise, but she promised to deliver the villagers' message. Red-Stripes and Shratta were terrorizing the countryside.

The village offered to give her a swaybacked horse for her journey. Xantcha bought it instead with a worn silver coin and left the next day, before her debts grew any higher. The elders apologized that they couldn't offer her the escort a young nobleman deserved, but all their young men were gone, swept up by one side or the other.

As she rode away, Xantcha couldn't guess how the Shratta had gotten involved in a war. Twenty years ago, the Shratta had been a harmless sect of ascetics and fools. They preached that anyone who did not live by the two hundred and fifty-six rules in Avohir's holy book was damned, but no one had taken them seriously. She had no idea who or what the Red-Stripes were until she'd visited a few more villages. The Red-Stripes had begun as royal mercenaries, charged with the protection of the palaces and temples that the suddenly militant Shratta had begun threatening, some fifteen years ago.

Oddly enough, in none of the tales Xantcha listened to did she hear of the two groups confronting each other. Instead, they roamed the countryside, searching out each other's partisans, making accusations when nothing could be proved, then killing the accused and burning their homes.

"The Shratta," a weary villager explained, "tell us they are the wrath of Avohir and they punish us if we do not live closely by Avohir's holy book. Then, after the Shratta have finished with us, the Red-Stripes come. They see that the Shratta didn't take everything, so they take what's left."

"Every spring, it begins again," one of the old women added. "Soon there will be nothing left."

"Twice we sent men to Tabarna, twice they did not come back. We have no men left."

Then, as in the other villages, the survivors asked Xantcha to carry their despair to Tabarna's ear. She nodded, accepted their food, and left on her swaybacked horse, knowing that there was nothing she could do. Her path would not take her to Pincar City, Tabarna's north coast capital. She'd begun to doubt that it would take her to a suitable Mishra either. With or without pitched battles, Efuan Pincar had been at war for nearly a decade, and young men were in short supply.

Xantcha's path—a rutted dirt trail because her sphere wouldn't accommodate a horse—took her toward Medran, a market town. A brace of gate guards greeted her with hands on their sword hilts and contempt in their eyes: Where had she been? How did a noble lad with fine boots and a sword come to be riding a swaybacked nag?

Xantcha noticed that their tunics were hemmed with a stripe of bright red wool. She told them how she'd ridden into the countryside with older, more experienced relatives. They'd been beset by the Shratta, and she was the sole survivor, headed back to Pincar City.

"On a better horse, if there's one to be found."

Xantcha sniffed loudly; when it came to contempt, she'd learned all the tricks before the first boatload of refugees struck the Efuan Pincar shore. She'd also yawned out her armor before she'd ridden up to the gate. The Red-Stripes were in for a surprise if they drew their swords against her.

Good sense prevailed. They let her pass, though Xantcha figured to keep an eye for her back. Even with a sword, a slight, beardless youth in too-fine clothes was a tempting target, especially when the nearest protectors were also the likeliest predators.

Xantcha followed the widening streets until they brought her to a plaza, where artisans and farmers hawked produce from wagons. She gave the horse to the farmer with the largest wagon in exchange for black bread and dried fruit. He asked how an unbearded swordsman came to be peddling a nag in Medran-town. Xantcha recited her made-up tale. The farmer wasn't surprised that Shratta would have slain her purported companions.

"The more wealth a man has, the less the Shratta believe him when he says he abides by the book. Strange, though, that they'd risk a party as large as the one your uncle had assembled. Were me, I'd suspect the men he'd hired weren't what they'd said they were."

Xantcha shrugged cautiously. "I'm sure my uncle thought the same . . . before they killed him." Then, because the farmer seemed more world-wise than the villagers, she tempted him with a thought that had nagged her from the beginning. "He'd hired Red-Stripes. Thought it would keep us safe. Shratta never attack men with Red Stripes on their tunics."

The farmer took her bait, but not quite the way she expected. "The Red-Stripes don't bother the Shratta where they live, and the Shratta usually return the favor. But where there's wealth to be taken, every man's a target, especially to the . . ." He fingered the hem of his own tunic. "I won't speak ill of your dead, but it's a fool who trusts in stripes or colors."

Xantcha walked away from the wagon, thinking that it might be better to get out of Medran immediately. She was headed toward a different gate than the one she'd entered when she spotted a knot of men and women, huddled in the shade of a tavern. With a second glance Xantcha saw the bonds at their necks, wrists, and ankles. Prisoners, she thought, then corrected herself, slaves.

She hadn't seen slaves the last time she visited Efuan Pincar, nor had she seen any in the beleaguered villages, but it was a rare realm, a rarer world that didn't cultivate slavery in one of its many forms. Xantcha took a breath and kept walking. She could see that a swaybacked horse found a good home, but there was nothing she could do for the slaves.

Xantcha continued walking, one step, another . . . misery stopped her before she took a third. Looking back over her shoulder, she caught the eyes of a slave who stared at her as if his condition were indeed her responsibility. Though they were at least a hundred paces apart, Xantcha saw that the slave was a dark-haired young man.

I asked my husband's brother how he'd come to lead the Fallaji horde, Kayla had written in *The Antiquity Wars. Mishra replied that he was their slave, not their leader. He laughed and added that I, too, was a slave to my people, but his eyes were haunted as he laughed, and there were scars around his wrists.*

In all the times Xantcha had read that passage, she'd followed Urza's lead and blamed Phyrexia for Mishra's scars and bitterness. But the Fallaji had been a slave-keeping folk, and looking across the Medran plaza, Xantcha suddenly believed that Mishra had told Kayla a simple, unvarnished truth.

Xantcha believed as well that she'd found her Mishra. With Urza's armor still around her, she strode over to the tavern.

"Are they spoken for?" she asked the only unchained man she saw, a balding man with a eunuch's unfinished face.

He wasn't in charge, but after a bow he scurried into the tavern to fetch his master, who proved to be a giant of a woman, garbed, like Xantcha, in men's clothing, though in the slave master's case, the effect was intimidation rather than disguise.

"They're bound for Almaaz," the slave master said. Her breath was thick with beer, but she wasn't nearly drunk. "You know it's against the law to sell flesh here."

By her posture, the slaver was right about the law and ripe for negotiation.

"I have Morvern gold," Xantcha said, which was true enough; money was never a problem for a planeswalker or his companion.

The slave master hawked and spat. "Mug's getting warm."

Xantcha thought fast. "For ransom, then. I recognize a distant cousin in your coffle. You've kept him safe, no doubt. I'll pay you for your trouble and take him off your hands."

"Him!" The slaver laughed until she belched.

There were women in the slave string, and Xantcha was disguised as a young and presumably curious man.

"A cousin," Xantcha repeated, showing more anxiety than she felt. Let the slaver laugh and think what she wanted. Xantcha had the other woman's attention, and she'd have the slave, too. "For ransom." She unslung her purse and fished out a gold coin as big as her nose.

"Five of those," the slaver said, smashing her open hand between Xantcha's shoulder blades. "For ransom!"

If she were truly in the market for a slave, Xantcha would have protested that no one was worth five golden *nari*, but she'd been prepared to split twelve of the heavy Morvern coins between a likely youth and his family. She dug out another four and handed them over to the slaver, who bit each one. Xantcha knew the coins were true but was relieved when they passed the slaver's test.

"Which one's your cousin?"

Xantcha pointed to the dark-haired youth, who didn't blink under scrutiny. The slaver, whose eyebrows remained resolutely skeptical, shook her head.

"Pick another relative, boy. That one will eat you alive."

"Blood's blood." Xantcha insisted, "and ours is the same. I won't leave with another."

"Garve!" the slaver shouted the eunuch to her side. She held out her hand, and Garve surrendered a slender black rod. The slaver took it and turned back to Xantcha. "Another *nari*. You're going to need this."

Would ancient Ashnod be pleased by the all the improvements Dominarian slavers and torturers had brought to her pain-inflicting artifacts in the centuries since her death? Xantcha bought the thing, if only to keep the slaver or Garve from ever using it again.

"Cut him out," the slaver told Garve and added, while Garve walked among the slaves, "Have fun, boy."

"I intend to," Xantcha assured her, then watched as Garve seized the leather band around the youth's neck and jerked him roughly to his feet.

Garve gave the band a vicious twist, so it choked the youth and kept him quiet while the eunuch snapped the rivets that bound Xantcha's new slave to the others. The youth's face became red. His eyes rolled.

"I want him alive," Xantcha warned in a low voice that promised her threats were as good as her gold.

Her new slave dropped to one knee when Garve suddenly released him. Hacking spittle, he got himself upright before the eunuch touched him again. Riveted leather manacles bound his wrists close behind his back; he couldn't clean his lightly bearded chin. A short iron chain ran between his ankles. He could walk, barely, but not run. As he came closer, watching his feet, Xantcha counted the sores and bruises she hadn't noticed while he was staring.

Xantcha hadn't been comfortable owning a horse; she didn't know what she'd do with a slave. The thought of grabbing the arm's length of leather hanging from the band around his neck repelled her, though that was what everyone, including the youth, expected her to do.

"You're too tall," she said at last, though he wasn't as tall as Urza. She hoped that wasn't going to be a problem further along in her plan. "You'll walk beside me until I can arrange something more. . . ." Xantcha paused. Phyrexians might not have imagination, but born-folk certainly did, and there was nothing like silence to inspire the use of it. "Something more appropriate."

She smiled broadly, and her slave walked politely beside her, his chain clanking on the plaza's cobblestones. Xantcha's thoughts were focused on the how she'd get them both out of Medran without attracting trouble from the Red-Stripes. She wasn't expecting any other sort of trouble until the youth staggered against her.

Muttering curses no Efuand had ever heard before, Xantcha got an arm around his waist and shoved him upright. It wasn't a hard shove, but he groaned and made no attempt to start walking again. Sick sweat bloomed on his face. He'd burned through his bravery.

"Do you see that curb beside the fountain?"

A slight nod and a catch in his muscles; he was dizzy and on the verge of fainting.

"Get that far and you can sit, rest, drink some water.

"Water," he repeated, a hoarse, painful-sounding whisper.

Xantcha hoped his problems weren't serious. If Garve had damaged him, Garve wouldn't live to see the sun set. Her slave shoved one foot forward; she helped him with his balance. In five steps, Xantcha learned to hate that treacherous chain between his ankles. He fell one stride short of the fountain curb. Xantcha looked the other way while he dragged himself onto it. Then she drew a knife from the seam of her boot.

The blade was tempered steel from another world, and it made fast work of the wrist manacles. Xantcha gasped when she saw rings of weeping sores. Without a second thought she hurled the slashed leather across the cobblestones. Her slave was already washing his face and slurping water from the fountain. Xantcha thought it was a good sign, but wasn't surprised when her next question, "Are you hungry?" won her nothing more than another cold, piercing stare.

She retrieved a loaf of black bread, tore off a chunk, and offered it to him. He reached past her offering toward the loaf in her other hand.

"You're bold for a slave."

"You're small for a master," he countered and closed his hand over the bread he wanted.

Xantcha dropped the smaller piece and seized his arm. She didn't like the feel of open sores beneath her fingers, and she had every intention of giving him the whole loaf eventually, but points had to be made. She tightened her grip. Appearances, her still nameless slave needed to learn, could be deceiving. In Phyrexia, newts were soft, useless creatures, but on most other worlds, Xantcha was as strong as a well-muscled man half again her size. With a groan, the slave let go of the larger portion, and when she'd released him, picked up the smaller portion from the ground.

"Slowly," Xantcha chided him, though she knew it would be impossible for him to obey. "Swallow, breathe, take a sip of water."

His hand shot out, while Xantcha wondered what she should do next. He captured the unguarded bread and held it tight. Only his eyes moved from Xantcha's face to the black prod she'd tucked through her belt.

"Ask first," she suggested but made no move for her belt.

Even if, by some miracle of carelessness, he stole the prod and struck her with it, Urza's armor would protect her.

"Master, may I eat?"

For a man still short of his final growth, Xantcha's slave had a mature grasp of sarcasm. He definitely had Mishra's attitude in addition to Mishra's appearance.

"I didn't buy you to starve you."

"Why did you, then!" he asked through a mouthful of bread.

"I have need of a man like you."

He gave Xantcha the same look the slaver and Garve had given her, and she began to think she'd gotten herself into the position of a fisherman who'd hooked a fish larger than his boat. Only time would tell if she'd bring him aboard or he'd drown her.

"Your name will be Mishra. You will answer to it when you hear it."

Mishra laughed, a short, snorting sound. "Oh, yes, Master Urza."

Despite what she'd told Urza, the details of Kayla Bin-Kroog's *Antiquity Wars* weren't that widely spread across what remained of Terisiare. Xantcha hadn't expected her slave to recognize his new name; nor was she prepared for his aggressive insolence. I've made a mistake, she told herself. I've done a terrible thing. Then Mishra started choking. He tugged on the tight leather band around his throat and managed to gulp down his mouthful of bread. His fingers came away stained with blood and pus.

Xantcha looked at her own feet. She might have made a mistake, but she hadn't done anything terrible.

"You may call me Xantcha. And when you meet him, Urza is just Urza. He would not like to be called Master, especially not by his brother."

"Xantcha? What kind of name is that? If I'm Mishra and you work for Urza, shouldn't your name be Tawnos? You're a little bit small for the part. Grow out your hair and you could play Kayla—an ugly Kayla. By the love of Avohir, I was better off with Tucktah and Garve."

"You know *The Antiquity Wars*?"

"Surprised? I can read and write, too, and count without using my fingers." He held up his hand but saw something—the stains, perhaps, that she'd already noticed—that cracked his insolence. "I wasn't born a slave," he concluded softly, staring across the plaza at his memories. "I had a life . . . a name."

"What name?"

"Rat."

"What?" she thought she'd misunderstood.

"Rat. Short for Ratepe. I grew into it." Another snorted laugh—or maybe a strangled sob. Either way, it ended when the neck leather brought on another choking spell.

"Hold still," Xantcha told him and drew out her knife again. "I don't want to cut you."

There wasn't even a flicker of trust in Rat's eyes as she laid the blade against his neck. He winced as she slid it beneath the leather. She had to saw through the sweat-hardened leather and pricked his skin a handful of times before she was done. The tip was bloody when it emerged on the other side, but he didn't make a grab for her or the weapon.

"I'm sorry," she said when she was finished.

Xantcha raised her arm to hurl the collar away as she'd hurled the manacles. Rat caught the trailing leash. The leather fell into his lap.

"I'll keep it."

Xantcha knew that in the usual order of such things, slaves didn't have personal property, but she wasn't about to take the filthy collar away from him. "I have a task for you," she said as he worried the collar between his hands. "I would have offered you the gold, if you'd been free. You will be free, I swear it, when you've done what I need you to do."

"And if I don't?"

While Xantcha wrestled with an answer for that question, a noisy claque of Red-Stripes entered the plaza from the east, the direction through which Xantcha had hoped to leave. She and Rat were far from alone on the cobblestones, and she reasonably hoped that despite their mismatched appearance—him in rags and weeping sores, her with her boots and sword—they wouldn't draw too much attention. Rat saw the Red-Stripes as well. He snapped the leather against his thigh like a whip.

Red-Stripes, Xantcha guessed, had something to do with his transformation from free to slave. Considering his apparent education and remembering the farmer's gesture, she wondered if he'd once worn the sort of garments she was wearing.

"Hold it in," she advised him. "You've got a chain. . . ." She left the thought incomplete as a gentle breeze brought her the last scent she ever wanted to smell: glistening oil.

One of the Red-Stripes was a *sleeper*, a newt like her, but different, too. Newts of this new invasion had born-folk ways and didn't clump together in cadres. In truth, they didn't seem to know they were Phyrexian. Xantcha didn't care to test her theory. She hunched on her knees as she sat, catching her breath in her hands, hiding the exhalations that might reveal her glistening scent. She couldn't relax or be too careful.

Beside Xantcha, Rat beat a counterpoint of curses and leather. There was a chance that the Red-Stripe *sleeper* could hear every word.

"Quiet!" Xantcha hissed a command as she clamped her hand over Rat's. "Quiet!" She squeezed until she felt the sores and sinews pop.

"Afraid of the Red-Stripes?"

She took a deep breath and admitted. "They're not my friends. Quiet!"

Rat bent over to match her posture, blocking her view as well. He wouldn't stop talking. "And who are your friends—the Shratta? You keep strange company: Urza, Mishra, the Shratta. You're asking for trouble."

Xantcha ignored him. She hunched lower until she could see beneath Rat's arms. The Red-Stripes were heading into the same tavern where the slaver drank. "We've got to leave. Can you walk?"

"Why? I'm not afraid of the Red-Stripes. I'd join them right now, if they'd have me."

The elders in the first village had warned Xantcha that the young men had chosen sides, one way or another. It figured that her Mishra would have Phyrexian inclinations. She didn't have time to persuade him, so she'd have to out-bluff him. "Want to hobble over and try? You'd better hurry. Or do you think the eunuch's saved you a seat?"

"I'm not that stupid. I lost my chance the moment I got sapped and sold."

"Then stand up and start walking."

"Yes, Master."

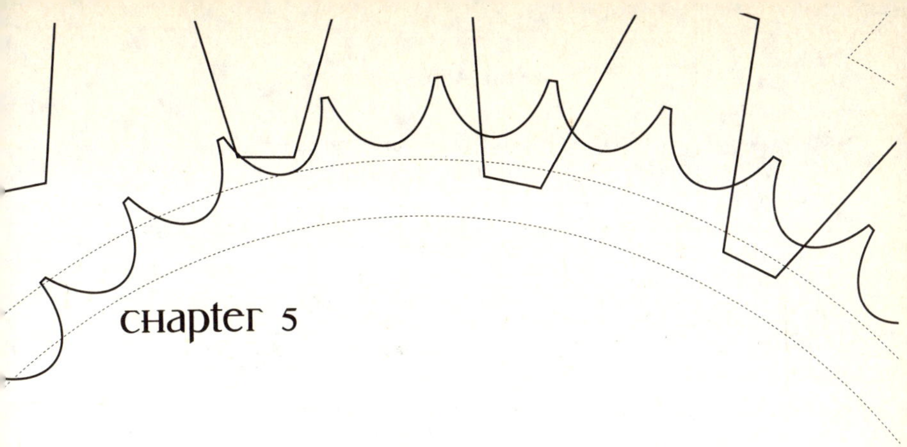

chapter 5

Bread, water, and the absence of tight leather around his neck worked swift wonders for Rat's stamina. He didn't need Xantcha's help as they walked away from the fountain, but his natural pride clashed with the chain between his ankles and guaranteed the sort of attention Xantcha preferred not to attract. They'd never get through the gate without an incident, so once they were clear of the plaza, she chose the narrowest street at each crossing until they came to a long-abandoned courtyard.

"Good choice, Xantcha. The windows are mortared, the doors, too—except for the one we came in." Rat kicked at the rubble and picked up a bone that might have been a child's leg. "Been here before? Is this where you meet Urza?"

Xantcha let the comment slide. "Put your foot up here." She pointed to an overturned pedestal. "I've got to get rid of that chain."

"With what?" Rat approached the pedestal but kept both feet on the ground. "Garve's got the key."

Xantcha hefted a chunk of granite. "I'll break it."

"Not with that, you won't. I'll take my chances with Urza."

She shook her head. "We've got four days' traveling before then. Waste not, want not, Rat—you can't run. You're helpless."

He didn't argue and didn't put his foot on the pedestal, either.

"Do you prefer being chained and hobbled like an animal?'

"I'm your slave. You bought me. Better keep me hobbled and helpless, if you want to keep me at all."

"I need a man who can play Mishra's part with Urza. I give you my word, play the part and you'll be free in a year." Free to tell Urza's secrets to the Red-Stripes? Never. But that was a worry for the future. For the present, "Give me your word."

"The word of a slave," Rat interrupted. "Remember that." He put his foot on the pedestal. "And be careful."

Xantcha brought the stone down with a crash that was louder than she'd expected, less effective, too. Perhaps it would be better to wait. Unfettering a youth who looked like Mishra might be all that Urza needed to free himself from the past.

And maybe they'd have to run from the Red-Stripes.

Xantcha understood how Urza must have felt when they traveled, worried about a companion who couldn't take care of herself: angry and bitter, too. She smashed the granite against the chain. Sparks flew, but the links didn't. Gritting her teeth, Xantcha pounded rapidly but to no greater success. When she paused for breath, Rat seized her wrists.

"Don't act the fool."

She could have dropped the stone on his foot and used both hands to throttle his insolence, and Xantcha might have, if she hadn't been so astonished to feel his warm, living flesh against hers. She and Urza touched each other, casually, but infrequently, and never with particular passion. Rat's hands shook as he held her, probably because slavery had weakened him, but there was something more, something elusive and unnerving. Xantcha was relieved that he released her the instant their eyes met.

"I'm trying to help you," she said acidly.

"You're not helping, you're just making noise. Noise is bad, if you're trying to hide. For that matter, why are we hiding? It's not as if Tucktah's going to tell the Red-Stripes I'm not your ransomed cousin."

"Just trying to keep you out of trouble."

Rat laughed. "You're too late for that, Xantcha. Now, why don't we stop playing child's games and go to your father's house? If Tabarna's laws still mean anything in this forsaken town, it's illegal for one Efuand to own another. You're the one who's in trouble for wasting your father's gold. You paid way too much to ransom me. Is your father a tyrant or can he be reasoned with?"

Given her disguise, Rat's presumptions weren't unreasonable. "I don't have a father. I don't live in this town. I live with Urza and we've got a long—" she considered telling him about the sphere and decided not to, "journey and since I have your word . . ." She brought the stone down on the metal.

"You'll be at that all afternoon and halfway through the night."

Xantcha shrugged. They couldn't leave before then, not if she were going to use the sphere to get them over the walls. She smashed the stone again. A flake of granite drew blood from Rat's shin; the link was unharmed.

Rat rubbed the wound and lowered his leg. "All right. I don't believe you, but if you're determined to play your game to its end, there's an easier way to get out of this town. Do you have any money left?" Xantcha didn't answer, but Rat had seen her purse and presumably knew it wasn't empty. "Look, go back to the plaza and pay some farmer to load me in his wagon . . . or, better, find a smith with a decent hammer and chisel. Get these damn things off the same way they got put on."

With *sleepers* in the town, Xantcha didn't want to go looking for strangers, but there was one farmer in the plaza market who wasn't a stranger.

"I gave my horse to a farmer with a wagon—"

"You had a horse!?"

"I had no further need of it, so I gave it to a man who did and promised to care for it."

"Avohir's mercy, you had no need of a horse, so you gave it away. You didn't even bargain with Tucktah." He swore again. "I've been sold by a beast to a madman! No, a mad child. Doesn't you father usually keep you locked up?"

"I could sell you back," Xantcha said coldly. "I imagine you had a long and pleasant life ahead of you."

She started to retrace their route. Rat followed as quietly as he could with the chain dragging on the ground. Once they were back in the plaza, Xantcha told him to wait in the shadows while she negotiated with the farmer. He agreed, but measured every wall with his eyes and twisted each battered link, in the obvious hope that she'd weakened it, as soon as he thought she couldn't see him.

Well, he'd warned her what his word was worth.

When Xantcha pointed him out to the farmer, he wanted no part of her plan.

"I'll give you your horse back."

"A horse is no use to a slave with a chain between his ankles."

"Imagine if you set the slave free, he'd be willing to travel with you," the farmer countered, still skeptical.

"I forgot to buy the key to his chains."

The farmer hesitated. The slaver and her coffle had moved on, but the farmer had glanced toward the tavern when Xantcha had mentioned slaves. Likely he'd watched the whole scene with her, the slaver, Garve, and Rat.

"Have him come over, and I'll speak to him myself. Alone."

Moments later, Xantcha told Rat. "It's your choice. He wants to know if you're worth the risk."

Rat gave Xantcha a look that said liar, and got to his feet. Xantcha blocked his path.

"Look, I didn't tell him the truth about Urza or Mishra or anything like that, just that we were cousins. And before, when I gave him the horse, I told him that I was alone because I'd been traveling with my uncle. We'd been ambushed by Shratta and everybody but me had been killed. It was good enough at the time, before I'd spotted you, but it's going to make things more difficult now."

Rat frowned and shook his head. "If I was as dumb as you, I'd've died before I learned to walk. What names did you give him?"

"None," Xantcha replied. "He didn't ask."

"You need a keeper, Xantcha," Rat muttered as he walked away from her. "You haven't got the sense Avohir gives to ants and worms."

Rat could have run, or tried to, but chose to get out of the town instead. The farmer waved for Xantcha to join them.

"Not saying I believe you, either of you," he said, offering Xantcha his plain woven cloak to wear instead of her fancier one. "Climb in quickly now. These are strange times . . . bad times. A man doesn't put his trust in words; I put mine in Avohir. I'll get you out of Medran, and Avohir be my judge if I'm wrong."

Xantcha considered stowing her sword in the wagon bed where Rat rode, with straw and empty baskets piled all around him to hide the chain. But her slave had a flair for storytelling. His imagination made her nervous.

"You're not wrong, good man," Rat said cheerfully as he rearranged the baskets. "Not about my cousin and me, not about the times, either. Two months ago, I had everything. Then one night I went carousing with friends who weren't friends and lost it all. Woke up in chains. I told them who I was: Ratepe, eldest son of Mideah from Pincar City, and said my father would ransom me; got a swift kick and a broken rib. I'd given up hope months ago, but I hadn't reckoned on my cousin, Arnuwan."

Xantcha jumped when Rat slapped her between the shoulders. Arnuwan was probably a less conspicuously foreign name than Xantcha, and the moment Rat introduced it, the farmer relaxed and offered his.

"Assor," he said and embraced Rat, not her.

Xantcha was used to following someone else. She'd followed Urza for over three thousand years, but Rat was different. Rat smiled and told Assor easy tales of pranks he and Arnuwan had pulled on their elders. He was very persuasive. She would have believed him herself, if she hadn't known that she was supposed to be Arnuwan. Of course, maybe there was an Arnuwan, and maybe Rat's only lie was that he didn't look at her while he was spinning out his tales. Maybe he was harmless, but Xantcha, who was nowhere near as harmless as she pretended to be, hadn't survived Phyrexia, Urza, and countless other perils, by assuming that anything was harmless.

She kept her sword close and palmed a few black-metal coins that hadn't come from any king or prince's mint. Then, as Assor called *home* to his harnessed horse, she settled in for the ride.

Silence hung thick among them. Ordinary folk going about their late-afternoon affairs looked up as they passed. Xantcha could think of nothing to say except that she longed to be in the air, headed back to the cottage, neither of which were safe subjects for conversation.

Then Rat asked the farmer, "Do you keep sheep in your fallows, or do you grow peas?" He followed that question with another and another until he'd lured the farmer into an animated discussion about the proper way to plow a field. The farmer favored straight furrows. Rat said a sunwise spiral toward the center was better. They were in mid-argument when the Red-Stripes waved the wagon through the gate.

As they cleared the first rise beyond the town walls, even Assor realized what Rat had done and while Xantcha willed away her armor he asked:

"Where are you from, lad? The truth . . . no more of your lies. You're no one's cousin, and I'll wager you're no farmer either, despite your talk. You're too clever by half to be village-bred."

Rat grinned and told a different story. "I read, once, how Hatusan the Blind, had escaped from a besieged city by talking about the weather. It seemed worth trying."

"Read about it, eh?" Assor asked before Xantcha could say that she'd never heard of Hatusan the Blind. "Then, for certain, you're no farmer. I've never seen a book but Avohir's holy book and I listen 'stead of read. Is your name truly Ratepe, eldest son of Mideah?"

Xantcha was watching Rat closely from the comer of her eye. She caught him flinching as Assor sounded out his name. His rogue's grin vanished, replaced by an empty stare that looked at nothing and gave nothing away.

"It is," he answered with a voice that was both deeper and younger than she'd heard from him before. "And Mideah, my father, was a farmer when he died—a good farmer who plowed his fields sunwise every spring and fall. But he was a lector of philosophy at Tabarna's school in Pincar City before the Shratta burnt it down. . . ."

If Rat's second recounting of his life was more accurate than his first, he'd had a comfortable childhood and loving parents. But his cozy world had been overturned ten years ago when the Shratta swarmed the royal city, preaching that any knowledge that couldn't be read in Avohir's book wasn't knowledge at all. They had no use for libraries or schools, so they set them ablaze. Rat's father had been one of many who'd appealed to Tabarna for protection against the Shratta mobs, and to Tabarna's son, Catal, who funded the Red-Stripes to protect them. Then Catal died, poisoned by the Shratta, or so said the Red-Stripes, who'd avenged his death. The city dissolved into carnage and riot.

"We tried. Father grew a beard, Mother made jellies and sold them in the market. I stayed out of trouble—tried to stay out of trouble. But it wasn't any use. The Shratta knew our names. They caught my uncle—I called him my uncle, but he was only a friend, my father's closest friend. They drew his guts out through a hole in his belly, then they set fire to his house—after they'd locked his family inside. Our neighbors came to set our house ablaze, too. Father said that they were afraid of everything, ready to believe anything. He said it wasn't their fault, but that didn't stop the flames. We got away through a hole in the garden wall."

Xantcha wanted to believe her slave. She'd been to Pincar City where simple houses, each with a tidy garden, packed the narrow streets. She could almost see a frightened family running through moonlight, though Rat hadn't said whether they'd left by day or night. That seemed to be Rat's charm, Rat's near-magic. When he took a deep breath and started talking, everything he said rang true.

Mishra never stooped to flattery, Kayla Bin-Kroog had written nearly thirty-four hundred years earlier. *He didn't have to. He had the gift of sincerity, and he was the most dangerous man I ever met.*

"We fled to Avular, where my mother had kin. From Avular, we went to Gam."

Assor grunted; he'd heard of the place. "Good land for flocks and herding, not so good for grain-growing."

"Not so good for city-bred boys, either," Rat added. "But the Shratta didn't bother us. At least they didn't bother us any more than they bothered everyone else. We paid their tithes and lived by the book and thought we were lucky."

Xantcha clenched her teeth. In all the Multiverse, there was no curse to compare with feeling lucky.

"I'd taken two sheep to the next village, to a man who didn't need sheep, but he had a daughter. . . ." Rat almost smiled before his face hardened. "I missed the Shratta as I left, and it was over when I returned. All Gam was dead: butchered, the men with their throats slit, the women strangled with their skirts, the children with their skulls smashed against the walls. . . ." Rat's voice had flattened, as if he were reciting from a dull text, yet that lack of expression served to make his words all the more believable. "I found my father, my mother, my brother, and sister. I shouldn't have looked. It would have been better not to know. Then I ran to the next village, but I was too late there as well. Everybody I knew was dead. I wanted to join them. I wanted to die, or join the Red-Stripes, if I could get to Avular. I knew the way, but the slavers found me the second night."

Either Rat told the painful truth or he was a stone-cold liar. The farmer had no doubts. He cursed the Shratta, then the Red-Stripes, and having already heard Xantcha's false tale earlier in the day, invited them both into his family.

Xantcha declined. "We have family awaiting us in the south." The wagon was rolling west. "It's time for us to take our leave. Past time . . . we should have taken the last crossroads."

Both Xantcha and the farmer looked to Rat, who hesitated before shucking off the straw and baskets that had concealed his fetters.

"Good work," Xantcha whispered while the farmer scuttled about, filling one of the baskets with food.

"He's a good man," said Rat.

The farmer presented them with the basket before Xantcha could challenge her companion's resolve. Xantcha returned the homespun cloak.

"Walk fast," he said, then remembered Rat's fetters. "Try. There's been no trouble this close to Medran, but we all lay close after sundown. The moon's waxed; there'll be light on the road. When you get south to Stezine, ask for Korde. He's the smith there. Tell him you rode with me, with Assor, his wife's brother-by-marriage. He'll break that chain on his anvil. Luck to you."

Xantcha hoisted the basket and started walking, glancing back over her shoulder after every few steps.

"He didn't believe you," Rat chided.

"He didn't believe either of us."

"He believed me because I told the truth."

"So did I," Xantcha countered.

Rat shook his head. "Not to me, you haven't. Urza, Mishra, dead uncles, and ransomed cousins. You're a lousy liar, Xantcha."

She let the provocations pass. They walked until the wagon had rolled from sight, and then Xantcha stopped. She set down the basket and faced Rat with her fists on her hips.

"I saved your life, Ratepe, that's no lie. All I've asked in return is that you help me with Urza. It doesn't matter if you believe me, so long as I can trust you."

"You bought me. You can make me do what you ask, but I'll fight you, I swear it, every step of the way. That's what you can trust."

"I ransomed you."

"Ransom? Avohir's mercy, you said I was your cousin—do you think Tucktah believed that? You're a bold liar, Xantcha. That's not the same as a good one. Tucktah sold me, you bought me. I'm still a slave. Don't bother being kind. I won't love you, and I will escape."

Xantcha sighed and rolled her eyes dramatically. Rat accepted the invitation by lunging for her throat. If it had been a fair fight, Xantcha would have gone down and stayed down. Rat's reach was half an arm longer than hers, and he weighed nearly twice as much. But Rat hadn't been fed enough to maintain the muscles on his long bones, and Xantcha was a Phyrexian newt. Urza said she was built like a cat or a serpent, slippery and supple, impossible to pin down or keep unbalanced.

Rat had her on her back for a heartbeat before she threw him aside. While he rose slowly to his knees, Xantcha sprang to her feet. She snapped her fingers.

"There . . . you're free. As simple as that. You're no longer a slave. I ask you to honor what I have given you, and help me with Urza. When you've done that, in a year, I'll return you to this place. I give you my word."

"You're a moon cow, Xantcha. Your parts don't fit together: fine clothes, a sword, gold *nari* from Morvern, and this Urza of yours. Avohir's mercy—what do you take me for?"

Rat tried to side step around her, but his fetters insured that his strides were shorter than hers. After a few more failed evasions, Xantcha seized his wrists.

"You were going to die, Ratepe."

"Maybe, maybe not—" Rat had the reach, the leverage to free himself, and as soon as he had an opportunity, he grabbed for the slave goad tucked in Xantcha's belt.

"Throw it down," Xantcha warned. "I don't want to hurt you."

Rat laughed and played his fingers over the rod's smooth black surface. A shimmering, yellow web sprang from its tip. "You can't hurt me. You can save yourself from getting hurt by dropping your purse and your sword on the ground, turning around, and following that wagon."

Xantcha eyed the web. She could feel its power where she stood, but it had belonged to Garve. Tucktah wouldn't have given her dim assistant a goad that could seriously damage the merchandise. With a frustrated sigh, she gave Rat one last chance. "You owe me your life. Make peace with me and be done with it."

Rat rushed her, raising his arm for a mighty blow that Xantcha easily eluded. She stomped one foot on his chain, then put her fist in his gut. He tried to move with the punch but lost his balance when the chain tightened. He fell hard, leading with his forehead and losing his grip on the slave goad. Xantcha grabbed the goad and broke it. Despite the numbing, yellow light that oozed over her arms, she hurled both pieces far into the brush beyond the road. She retrieved the farmer's basket.

Rat had levered himself onto one elbow and was trying to rise further, when she shoved him onto his back again. She put the food basket on his stomach then knelt on his breastbone.

"All right, you win. You're a slave, and you'll do what I tell you to do because I can make you."

Xantcha inhaled deeply. She ran through her mnemonic rhyme, then she yawned. The sphere was invisible but not imperceptible. Rat screamed as it flowed around him.

"Don't even think about trying to escape." Xantcha warned.

Weight wasn't a problem. Xantcha could have carried a barrel of iron or lead back to the cottage. Size was another matter. The sphere grew until it was wide as her outstretched arms. Then it stiffened and began to rise. Rat panicked. The sphere lurched and shot up like an arrow, throwing them against each other, the basket, and the scabbard slung at Xantcha's side.

There were too many things competing for Xantcha's attention. She eliminated the largest distraction by punching it in the gut. They were less than a man's height over the ground when she got everything steadied. Rat breathed noisily through his wide-open mouth, even after they'd begun to soar gently westward. He'd pressed himself against the bubble. His arms were sprawled, and his palms were flat against the sphere's inner curve. Nothing moved except his fingers, which clawed silently, compulsively: a cat steadying itself on glass.

Xantcha tried to sort out the tangle of legs, cloak, and overturned basket at the bottom of the sphere, but her least move pushed her companion toward panic. A nearly full moon showed faintly above the eastern horizon; she'd planned to soar through well into the night. That would have been unspeakably cruel, and though she was tempted—her forearms ached where the slave-goad's sorcery had surrounded them—she resisted the temptation.

The sphere swung like a falling leaf in the cooling night air—a pleasant, even relaxing movement for Xantcha, but sheer torture for Rat, who'd begun to pray between gasps. Xantcha guided them slowly to the ground near a twisting line of trees.

She warned him. "Put your hands over your face now. The sphere's skin will collapse against you when it touches the ground. It vanishes more quickly than cobwebs in a flame, but for that moment when it covers your mouth and nose, you'll think you're suffocating."

Rat moaned, which Xantcha took as a sign that he'd heard and understood, but he didn't take her advice. He clawed himself as he'd clawed the sphere. There were bloody streaks across his face before he calmed down.

"There's a stream through the trees. Wash yourself. Drink. You'll feel better afterward." Xantcha stood over him, offering an arm up, which, predictably, he refused. She gave him a clear path to the stream and another warning: "Don't think about running."

He was gone a long time. Xantcha might have worried that he'd thrown himself in if she hadn't been able to hear him heaving his guts out. She'd kindled a small fire before he returned—not something she usually did, but born-folk often found solace in the random patterns of flames against darkness. Rat was shivering and damp from the waist up when he returned.

"You need clothes. Tomorrow, I'll keep an eye out for another town. Until then—" she offered her cloak.

It might have been poison or sorcery by the way Rat stared at it, and he shrank a little when he finally took it.

"Can you eat? You should try to eat. It's been a hard day for you. The bread's good and this other stuff—" she held up a long, hollow tube. "Looks like parchment, tastes like apricots."

Another hesitation, but by the way he tore off and chewed through a finger's length of the tube, Xantcha guessed the sticky stuff might once have been one of his favorite treats.

"There's more," she assured him, hoping food might be a bridge to peace between them.

Rat set the apricot leather aside. "Who are you? What are you? The truth this time—like Assor said. Why me? Why did you buy me?" He took a deep breath. "Not that it matters. I've been as good as dead since the Shratta came."

"I must be a lousy liar, Rat, because I haven't lied to you. I'm Xantcha. I need you because Urza needs to talk to his brother, and when I saw you among the other slaves outside the tavern, I saw Mishra."

Rat stared at the flames. "Urza. Urza. You keep saying Urza. Do you mean the Urza? Urza the Artificer? The one who was born three thousand, four hundred and thirty-seven years ago? Avohir's sweet mercy, Xantcha, Urza's a legend. Even if he survived the sylex, he's been dead for thousands of years."

"Maybe Urza is a legend, but he's certainly not dead. The sylex turned the Weakstone and the Mightstone into his eyes; don't look too closely at them when you meet him."

"Thanks, I guess, for the warning, but I can't believe you. And if I could, it would only make it worse. If there were an Urza still alive he'd kill me once for reminding him of his brother and again because I'm not Mishra. I'm no great artificer, no great sorcerer, no great warrior. Sweet Avohir, I can't even fight you. The way you overpowered me and broke Tucktah's goad . . . and that sphere. That I don't understand at all. What are you, anyway? I mean, there are still artificers—not as good as Urza was supposed to have been, and not in Efuan Pincar, but Xantcha, that's not an Efuand name. Are you an artifact?"

Of all the questions Rat might have asked, his last was one for which Xantcha had no ready answer. "I was neither made nor born. Urza found me, and I have stayed with him because he is . . ." She couldn't finish that thought but offered another instead: "Urza blames himself for his brother's death, the guilt still eats at his heart. He won't fight you, Rat."

They both shivered, though the air was calm and warm around the little fire.

Rat spoke first, softly. "I'd always thought the one good thing that came out of that war was that the brothers finally killed each other. If they hadn't, it never would have ended."

"It was the wrong war, Rat. They shouldn't have fought each other. There was another enemy, the Phyrexians—"

"Phyrexians? I've heard of them. Living artifacts or some such. Nasty beasts, but slow and stupid, too. Jarsyl wrote about them, after the war."

Rat knew his history, as much of it as had been written down, errors and all. "They were there at the end of the war, maybe at the beginning—that's what Urza believes. They killed Mishra and turned him into one of their own; what Urza fought was a Phyrexian. He thinks if he'd known soon enough, he could have saved his brother and together they could have fought the Phyrexians."

"So the man you call Urza thinks that he could have stopped the war." Rat stared at Xantcha across the fire. "What do you think?"

He had Mishra's quick wit and perception.

"The Phyrexians are back, Rat, and they're not slow or stupid. They're right here in Efuan Pincar. I could smell them in Medran. Urza's got the power to fight them, but he won't do anything until he's settled his guilt with Mishra."

Rat swore and stared at the stars. "These Phyrexians . . . Tucktah and Garve?"

"No, not them. They were with the Red-Stripes. I smelled them."

He swore a second time. "I'd've been better off staying where I was."

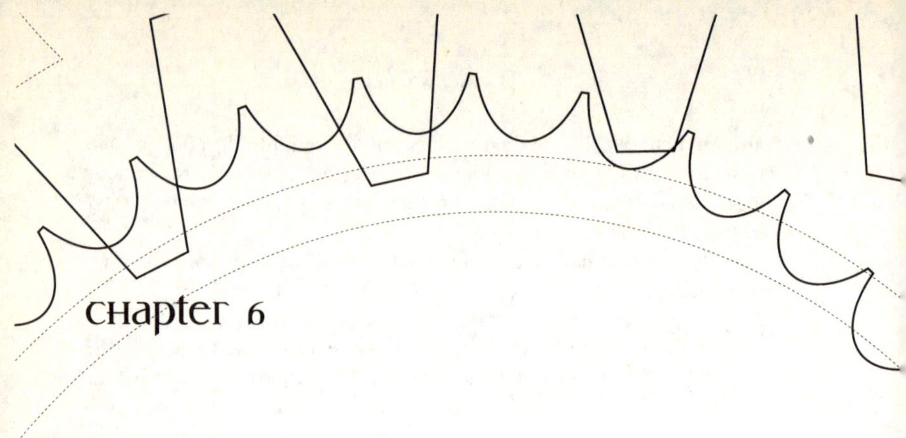

chapter 6

They didn't talk much after that. Xantcha let the fire burn down, and Rat made no attempt to revive it, choosing instead to pull his borrowed cloak tight around his shoulders. As little as he seemed to want to talk, Rat seemed reluctant to give his body the rest it needed. Three times Xantcha watched him slump sideways only to jolt himself upright. Exhaustion won the fourth battle. His chin touched his chest, and his whole body curled forward. He'd find himself in a world of pain when he woke up.

Xantcha touched Rat's arm gently and when that failed to rouse him, eased him to the ground, which was dry and no worse than wherever he might have slept last. He pulled his arms tight against his chest. Xantcha tried to straighten them but met resistance. His fists and jaw remained clenched even in sleep.

She'd thought that kind of tension was unique to Urza, to Urza's madness, but perhaps Rat's conscience was equally guilt-wracked. Whatever lies he'd told her and Assor, he'd been through hard times. His stained and aromatic clothes had once been sturdy garments, cut and sewn so carefully that their seams still held. Not slave's clothing, no more than his shoes were a slave's shoes. They were missing their buckles and had been shredded where the fetters rubbed against them.

If Xantcha were wiser in the ways of mortal misfortune, she might have read Rat's true history in the moonlight. Xantcha knew more about the unusual aspects of a hundred out-of-the-way worlds than she knew about ordinary life anywhere. The two and a half centuries she and Urza had spent in Dominaria was the most time she'd spent in any single place, and though she'd taught herself to read and traveled at every opportunity, all she'd really learned was the extent of her ignorance.

Xantcha's day hadn't been so exhausting as Rat's. She could have stayed awake all night and perhaps tomorrow night, if there'd been any need. But the night was calm, and although Rat's plight proved that there were slavers loose in Efuan Pincar, tonight they were in empty country, far from towns or villages. Xantcha heard owls and other night birds. Earlier she'd heard a wild cat yowling, but nothing large, nothing to keep her from settling down near Rat's feet, one arm touching his chain so she'd know if he moved unwisely during the night.

Were their positions reversed, Xantcha wouldn't have tried to escape. In her long experience, the unknown had never proven more hospitable than the known. She hadn't thought of escape in all the time she was a newt among Phyrexians, although that, she supposed, had been different. A better comparison might be her first encounter with Urza. . . .

After Gix's excoriation, Xantcha had hidden among the Fourth Sphere gremlins, but they'd eventually betrayed her to the Fane of Flesh. The teacher-priests caught her and punished her and then sent her to the furnaces. Xantcha worked beside metal-sheathed stokers. The hot, acrid air had burned her lungs. She'd staggered under the impossible burdens they piled on her back. It was no secret, the remains of Gix's newts were to be used up as quickly as possible, but when Xantcha's strength gave out, it was a burnished stoker who stumbled over her fallen body and plunged into a crucible of molten brass.

The fire-priests wouldn't have her after that, so the Fane sent Xantcha to the arena, where Phyrexian warriors honed their skills against engines and artifacts made in Phyrexia or creatures imported from other worlds. She was assigned tasks no warrior would have dared: feeding the creatures, repairing damaged engines, and destroying those artifacts the warriors had merely damaged. Her death had been expected, even anticipated, but when the fearsome wyverns with their fiery eyes and razor claws went on a rampage that reduced a hundred priests and warriors to oil-caked rubble, Xantcha the newt had survived without a scratch.

Since she wouldn't die and they'd failed to kill her, the planner-priests decided that Xantcha had the makings of a dodger.

Before he'd closed his eyes in sleep, the Ineffable had decreed that Phyrexia must be relentless in its exploration of other worlds and in the exploitation of whatever useful materials, methods and artifacts that exploration uncovered. Exploration was the easy part. A compleat Phyrexian, sheathed in metal and bathed in glistening oil, was thorough and precise. It was incapable of boredom and, when ordered to examine everything, it did exactly that, as accurate at the end as it had been in the beginning.

But confronted with something they'd never seen before, lesser Phyrexians often became confused, and through their rough bumbling they frequently destroyed not only themselves but whatever they'd been examining as well. It was an intolerable situation and necessitated an unpleasant solution. Whole colonies of gremlins were endured, even nurtured, for their canniness and spontaneity, but no gremlin was cannier than the remnants of Gix's newts; the ones that refused to die.

There were twenty of them summoned to the fountain, as identical as ever. They couldn't drink the glistening oil, so they were bathed in it while rows and ranks of compleat Phyrexians watched in silence. A mobile planner-priest described their new destiny:

Go forth with the diggers and the bearers. Gaze upon the creations of born minds. Decipher their secrets so that they may be exploited safely for the glory and dominion of Phyrexia.

There'd been more. Compleat Phyrexians never suffered from fatigue during an endless oration. They had no tongues to turn thick or pasty from overuse. And, of course, they lacked imagination. Never mind that Urza ridiculed Xantcha's imagination; she had more than the rest of Phyrexia rolled together. Standing beside the fountain, slick with glistening oil, Xantcha had imagined a wondrous future.

Her future began on a world whose name she had never known. Perhaps the searcher-priests had known its name when they came to investigate it, but once they discovered something useful to Phyrexia, the name of the place where they'd found it was of little importance to the team of diggers, bearers, and dodgers sent to exploit the discovery.

Once the ambulator portals were configured, it didn't matter where a world truly lay. Just one step forward into the glassy black disk the searcher-priests unrolled across the ground and whoosh, the team was where it needed to be. When the team finished its work—usually an excavation and extraction—they'd pack everything up, stride into the ambulator's nether end (identical to the prime end, except that it lacked the small configuration panel) and whoosh, they were back where they started, waiting for the next assignment.

The ambulators were horrible artifacts: suffocating, freezing, and endless, and a dodger's work was worse than cleaning up after the warriors. The chief digger would lead a newt, and a gremlin or two to whatever artifact had roused the searcher-priests' attention, then sit back at a safe distance while dodgers did the dangerous work. Much of what the teams excavated was abandoned weapons, frequently still primed and hair-triggered; the rest, while not intended as weapons, still had a tendency to explode.

Xantcha quickly realized that gremlins weren't any more imaginative than Phyrexians. They were simply more expendable. That very first time outside the nether end of an ambulator, when she saw blue-gray gremlin hands reaching for the shiniest lever in sight, Xantcha had decided she'd work alone and thrust her knife through the gremlin's throat before his imagination got her killed. The diggers hadn't cared. They only cared that she found and disconnected the tiny wires between that lever and a throbbing crimson crystal deep within the artifact.

After the bearers got the inert crystal back to Phyrexia, a herald had conducted Xantcha to one of the great obsidian Fanes of the First Sphere, where the planner-priests—second only to the demons in Phyrexia's complex hierarchy—interrogated her about the excavation and the insights that had inspired her as she disconnected the wires. They demanded that she attach the crystal to the immense body of one of the planners. Which Xantcha did, having no other alternative to obedience. No one was more surprised than Xantcha herself when both she and the planner survived.

The herald gave her a cloak of golden mesh and a featureless mask before conducting her back to the Fourth Sphere. For the first time, Xantcha looked like a compleat Phyrexian—provided she stood still.

Diggers and hearers had been compleated with scrap: bits of brass, copper, and tin. Their leather-patched joints leaked oil with every move. They were not pleased to have a gold-clad newt in their midst. Her life had never been gentle, but everything Xantcha had endured until then had derived from indifference. It wasn't until she'd been rewarded by the planners that she experienced personal hatred and cruelty.

Beneath Xantcha's arm, the iron chain shifted slightly. Her fingers clamped over the shifting links before her eyes were open, but the movement was merely Rat shifting in his sleep. A blanket of clouds had unfurled between them and the moon. The land had gone quiet; Xantcha sniffed for storms or worse and found the air as empty as before. She loosened her grip on the chain without releasing it completely.

Rat would run. Though he remained fettered and had no hope of survival in the open country, he'd try to run as long as he believed freedom lay somewhere else.

There was no word for freedom in Phyrexian. The only freedom a Phyrexian knew was the effortless movement of metal against metal when each piece was cushioned in glistening oil, and even that freedom was inaccessible to a flesh-bound newt. Battered and starved by the diggers who depended on her for their own survival, Xantcha had taken refuge in endurance. Though none of the worlds she'd visited matched the moist, green world of her dreams—in truth, Dominaria itself didn't match those dreams—the worst of them had been more hospitable than Phyrexia.

And if perversity were a proper measure of accomplishment, then Xantcha took perverse pride in surmounting the challenge she found at the nether end of each ambulator portal. Once an artifact lay exposed in front of her, she'd forget the diggers' prejudice, the bearers' brutality. Every artifact was different, yet they were all the same, too, and if Xantcha studied them long enough—whether they'd been made by Urza, Phyrexia, or some nameless artificer on a nameless world—she'd eventually unravel their secrets.

Xantcha would never be truly compleat, but she had achieved usefulness. She'd become a dodger, the fifth dodger, by virtue of the crimson sphere, which began a revolution in the way Phyrexia powered its largest non-sentient artifacts. A few more finds and she'd become the second dodger, Orman'huzra, though in her thoughts she remained Xantcha. The teacher-priests were right about some things: Gix's newts were too old, too set to change.

There was no Phyrexian word for happiness, and contentment meant glistening oil, yet as Orman'huzra, Xantcha found a measure of both. The others might despise her, but with her gold-mesh cloak she was untouchable. And they needed her. Within their carapaces, Phyrexians were alive; they understood death and feared it more than a newt did because without flesh, compleat Phyrexians could not heal themselves, and scrap-made Phyrexians were almost as expendable as newts.

The next turning point in Xantcha's life came in the windswept mountains of a world with three small moons. The artifact was huge and ringed by the rotting flesh of the born-folk who'd died defending it. Countless hollow crystals, no two exactly alike, pierced its dark, convoluted surface. Flexible wires had sprouted among the crystals, each supporting a concave mirror. When the mirrors moved, sound and sometimes light emerged from the hollow crystals.

The searcher-priests had been certain it was a weapon of unparalleled power. *Disable it,* the searcher had told her. *Prepare it for bearing back to Phyrexia. Do not attempt to dismantle it. The born-folk fought hard. They could not defeat us, yet they did not retreat. They died to keep us from this artifact. Therefore we must have it, and quickly.*

Xantcha didn't need reasons. The artifact—any artifact—was sufficient. Solving each artifact's mystery was all that mattered to her. What the priests did with her discoveries didn't concern her. From a newt's vulnerable perspective, a new weapon meant nothing. Everything in Phyrexia was already deadly.

Ignoring the corpses, she'd approached the artifact as she'd approached all the others.

But the wind-crystal, as she named it, wasn't a weapon. Its crystals and mirrors had no power except what they borrowed from the sun, moons, wind, and rain; then they gave it back as patterns of light and sound. The artifact reached deep into Xantcha's dreams, where it awakened the notions of beauty that couldn't be expressed in Phyrexian words.

Xantcha refused to prepare the artifact as the searcher-priests had demanded. She told the diggers and bearers, *It has no secrets, nothing that Phyrexia can use. It simply is, and it belongs here.* She was Orman'huzra, and the immobile planner-priests of the First Sphere had given her a golden cloak. She'd thought her words would have weight with the scrappy diggers and bearers; and they had, in ways Xantcha hadn't imagined. They stripped away her golden cloak and beat her bloody. They destroyed the artifact, every crystal, every mirror. Then they told the searchers that Orman'huzra was to blame for the loss of a weapon that could reduce whole worlds to dust.

Battered and scarcely conscious, Xantcha had been dragged to the brink of the very same fumarole where Gix had fallen to the Seventh Sphere. One push and life would have ended for her, but Xantcha was made of flesh and the planner-priests had believed that flesh could be punished until it transformed itself. From the fumarole Xantcha was taken to a cramped cell, where she dwelt in darkness for some small portion of eternity, sustained by memories of dancing light and music. When the priests thought she had suffered enough, they dragged her out again. The searchers had found another inscrutable artifact on another nameless world.

Xantcha was Orman'huzra. She was still useful and she had the wit—the deceit—to grovel before the various priests, begging for her life on any terms they offered. They sent her back to work never guessing that a lowly newt, mourning the loss of beauty, had declared war on Phyrexia.

The diggers suspected, but the great priests paid no more attention to diggers than they did to newts, and suspicion notwithstanding, diggers who worked with Orman'huzra lasted longer than those who didn't. As soon as she finished with one extraction, she'd find herself assigned to another team.

Thirty artifacts and twenty-two worlds after being dragged out of her cell, Xantcha's war was going well. She hadn't destroyed every artifact they sent her to unravel, but she'd lost several and rigged several more so that the next Phyrexian who touched it never touched anything again. She grew quite pleased with herself.

The diggers were already in place when Xantcha arrived, alone and nauseous from the ambulator trek, on her twenty-third world. A rattling digger made of metal and leather, all of it slick with oil that stank rather than glistened, led her into a humid cave where rows of smoky meat-fat lanterns marked the excavation.

"They might be Phyrexian," the digger said as they approached the main trench. At least, that's what Xantcha thought it had said. Its voice box worked no better than the rest of it.

Xantcha peered into the trenches, into a pair of fire-faceted eyes, each larger than her skull. She sat on her ankles, slowly absorbing what the searchers had found this time.

"They might be Phyrexian," the digger repeated.

Whatever the artifact was, it wasn't Phyrexian and neither were the ranks and rows of partially excavated specimens behind it. Phyrexians were useful. Tender-priests compleated newt-flesh according to its place in the Ineffable's plan, and then they stopped. Function was everything. These artifacts had no apparent function. They seemed, at first and second glance, to be statues: metal reproductions of the crawling insects that, like rats and buzzards, flourished everywhere, including Phyrexia. And though Xantcha had no liking for things that buzzed or stung, what she saw reminded her more of the long-destroyed wind-crystal than the digger beside her.

"I am told to ask, what will you need to secure them for bearing?"

Xantcha shook her head. Mostly the searcher-priests looked for sources of metal and oil because Phyrexia had none of its own; artifacts were a bonus, but the gems and precious metals that compleated the higher priests came to Phyrexia in the form of plunder.

It didn't take Orman'huzra to secure plunder.

There had to be more, and to find it Xantcha seized a lantern and leapt into the trench where the stronger but far less agile digger couldn't follow. At arm's length she realized that the insects were fully articulated. Whoever made them had meant them to move. She touched a golden plate; it was as warm as her own flesh and vibrated faintly.

Forgetting the digger on the trench-rim, Xantcha ran to one of the second-rank artifacts. It, too, was warm and vibrating, but unlike the first artifact, it had a steel-toothed mouth and steel claws—as nasty as any warrior's pincers—in addition to its golden carapace. On impulse, Xantcha tried to bend the raised edge of a golden plate.

A long, segmented antenna whipped around Xantcha's arm and hurled her against the trench wall, but not before she had the answer she wanted. The plate hadn't bent. It looked like gold, but it was made from something much stronger. Xantcha had another, less wanted, answer too. The artifacts were aware, possibly sentient and at least partially powered.

"Move! Move!" the rattletrap digger shrieked from the rim, less warning or concern for a damaged companion than a reaction to the unexpected.

Sure enough a reeking handful of diggers and bearers came clattering, some through the trenches and others along the rim. One digger, in better repair than the rest, assumed command, demanding quiet from his peers and an explanation from Orman'huzra.

"Simple enough. It moved and I didn't dodge."

A cacophony of squeaks and trills echoed through the cave, as the diggers and bearers succumbed to laughter.

The better-made digger whistled for silence. "They have not moved. They do not move."

Xantcha displayed her welted arm. Sometimes, there was no arguing with flesh. Diggers did not have articulated faces, yet the chief digger contrived a worried look.

"You will secure them," it said, a command, not a request.

"I will need wire—" Xantcha began, and then hesitated as half-formed plots competed in her head.

The searchers must have known that the shiny insects were more than plunder but the diggers and bearers, despite their trench excavations, hadn't known the artifacts could move. She stared at the huge, faceted eyes, fiery in reflected lantern light. The insects weren't Phyrexian; perhaps they could be enlisted in her private war against Phyrexia, if she could get them through intact and without getting herself killed in the process.

"Strong wire," she amended. "And cloth . . . thick, heavy cloth. And food . . . something to eat and not reeking oil."

"Cloths?" the digger whirled its mouth parts in confusion. Only newts, gremlins, and the highest strata of priests draped their bodies in cloth.

"Unmade clothes," Xantcha suggested. "Or soft leather. Something . . . anything so I can cover their eyes."

The digger chattered to itself. The tender-priests could replace a newt's eyes, if its destiny called for a different sort of vision, but diggers had flesh-eyes within their immobile faces. This one had pale blue eyes that widened slowly with comprehension.

"Diggers will find," it said, then spun its head around and issued commands to its peers in the rapid, compleat Phyrexian way that Xantcha could understand but never duplicate. Fully half of them rumbled immediately toward the cave's mouth. The chief digger turned back to Xantcha. "Orman'huzra, begin."

And she did, walking the trenches, examining the insect artifacts already excavated. Xantcha counted the golden, humming creatures that were visible. She climbed out of the trenches and measured the rest of the dig site with her eyes. The cave could easily contain an army. Xantcha hadn't been on this world long enough to know the measure of its day, but it seemed safe to think that she'd need at least a local season, maybe a local year, to get her warriors ready for their war.

Xantcha approached the golden swarm cautiously, starting with those she judged least likely to sever an arm or neck if she made a mistake—which she did several times before she learned what awakened them and what didn't. An isolated touch was more dangerous than a solid thwack to an armored underbelly, and they were much more sensitive to her flesh than to the diggers' shovel-hands.

She foresaw problems inciting her army to fight back in Phyrexia and studied the artifacts by herself, whenever rain drove all but a few diggers and bearers to the shelter beside the ambulator. Rain, especially a cold, penetrating rain, was a poorly-compleated Phyrexian's greatest enemy.

The bearers would retreat all the way to Phyrexia once a storm started. Xantcha could have won her private war with just a few of the mud-swirling, gully-washing deluges that threatened the artifact cave as the world's seasons progressed.

Cold rain and mud weren't Xantcha's favorite conditions either. She commandeered pieces of the digger-scrounged cloth, which was, in fact, clothing for folk generally taller and broader than Xantcha herself. The garments were torn, often slashed, and always bloodstained. They rotted quickly in the wretched weather and when they grew too offensive, Xantcha would throw the cloth on her fire and find something fresh in the scrounge piles. Her need for Phyrexian vengeance hadn't led to any empathy for born-folk.

She successfully dismantled one of the smaller insect-artifacts and learned enough of its secrets to feel confident that they would awaken, as soon as they emerged from the Phyrexian prime end of the ambulator. After that, it was simply a matter of folding their legs and antennae, binding them with cloth and wire, and ordering the bearers to stack them in pyramid layers near the nether end for eventual transfer to Phyrexia.

It never occurred to her that the bearers would act on their own to carry the artifacts with them when they next escaped the rain, and by the time she realized that they had, it was already too late. There was a searcher-priest towering above the diggers and bearers.

"Orman'huzra," the searcher-priest called in that menacing tone only high-ranking Phyrexians could achieve. "You were told to secure these artifacts for Phyrexia. You were warned that inefficiency would not be tolerated. You have failed in both regards. The artifacts you subverted were dismantled before they could cause any damage."

The many-eyed searcher was between Xantcha and the cave mouth. There'd be no getting past it or getting through the massed diggers and bearers, if she'd been tempted to run, which she wasn't. Xantcha might dream of lush, green worlds, but she was Phyrexian, and though she'd learned how to declare war against her own kind, she hadn't learned how to disobey. When the priest called her forward, she threw down her tools and climbed out of the trench.

Diggers and bearers formed a ring around her and the searcher-priest. They chittered among themselves. This time Orman'huzra had gone too far and would not survive the searcher-priest's wrath.

"Dig," the searcher-priest commanded, and she understood what they intended for her.

Xantcha dug the damp ground until she'd scratched out a shallow hole as wide as her shoulders and as long as she was tall. There was nothing worse than a too short, too narrow prison. Her fingers were numb and bloodied, but she clawed the ground until the searcher-priest grew impatient and ordered a digger to finish the job. When it was done, the hole tapered from shallow to waist-deep along its length and was exactly the length and width Xantcha had laid out.

She'd been through this before and, with a sigh, jumped into the hole, her feet landing in the deeper end, ready to be buried alive.

"Not yet," the searcher-priest said as a length of segmented wire unwound from its arm.

Xantcha recognized it as the antenna from one of her insect warriors. She climbed out of the hole prepared for pain, prepared for death, because she was certain that the searcher-priest had lied. Only a few of her warriors had gotten to Phyrexia, and undoubtedly all of them had fallen by now, but at least one had done damage before it fell.

That was victory enough, as Xantcha's wrists were bound by a length of wire slung over a tree limb to keep her upright during the coming ordeal. It had to be enough, as the first lash stroke of the antenna cut through her ragged clothing, and the second cut deep into her flesh.

The diggers and bearers counted the strokes; lesser Phyrexians were very good at counting. Xantcha heard them count to twenty. After that, everything was blurred. She thought she heard the cry of forty and fifty, but that might have been a dream. She hoped it was a dream. Then it seemed that there was a stroke that didn't land on her and wasn't counted by the diggers and bearers. That, too, might have been a dream, except there were no strokes after that, and no one pushing her into what would almost certainly have been a permanent grave.

Instead there was bright light and great noise.

A storm, Xantcha thought slowly. Rain. Driving the diggers, bearers and even the searcher-priest to shelter. Her wounds had begun to hurt. Drowning would be a better, easier way to die.

Without the diggers and bearers to do the counting, there was no way to measure the time she slumped beneath the tree limb, unable to stand or fall. In retrospect, it could not have been very long before she heard a voice speaking the language of her dreams, the language that had given her the words for beauty.

Xantcha did notice that she didn't fall when her arms did and that the rain never fell.

The voice filled her head with comforting sounds. Then a hand, that was both warm and soft like her own, touched her face and closed her eyes.

When she awoke next, she was in a grave of pain and fire, but the voice was in her head telling her that fear was unnecessary, even harmful to her healing. She remembered her eyes and, opening them, looked upon a flaming specter with many-colored eyes. Xantcha thought of Gix, and for the first time in her life she fainted.

The next time Xantcha awoke the pain and fire were gone. She was weak, but whole, and lying on softness such as she had not felt since leaving the vats. A man hovered beside her, staring into the distance. She had the strength for one word and chose it carefully.

"Why?"

His face, worried as he stared, turned grim when he looked down. "I thought the Phyrexians would kill you."

Beyond doubt, he spoke the language of Xantcha's dreams, the language of the place where she had been destined to sleep. He knew the name of her place, too, and had correctly guessed that the Phyrexians meant to kill her, but he hadn't seemed to recognize that she was also Phyrexian. Waves of caution washed through Xantcha's weakened flesh. She fought to hide her shivering.

A piece of cloth covered her. He pulled it back, revealing her naked flesh. His frown deepened.

"I thought they'd captured you. I thought they would change you, as they changed my brother. But I was too late. You bled. There is no metal or oil beneath your skin, but they'd already made you one of them. Do you remember who you were, child? Why did they take you? Did you belong to a prominent family? Where were you born?'

She took a deep breath. Honesty, under the present circumstances seemed the best course, as it had been with Gix, for surely this man was a demon. And, just as surely, he was already at war with Phyrexia. "I was not born, I have no family and I was never a child. I am the Orman'huzra who calls herself Xantcha. I am Phyrexian; I belong to Phyrexia."

He made white-knuckled fists above Xantcha's face. She closed her eyes, lacking the strength for any other defense, but the blows didn't fall.

"Listen to me closely, Xantcha. You belong to me, now. After what was done to you, for whatever reason it was done, you have no cause for love or loyalty to Phyrexia, and if you're clever, you'll tell me everything you know, starting with how you and the others planned to get home."

Xantcha was clever. Gix himself had conceded that. She was clever enough to realize that this yellow-haired man was both more and less than he seemed. She measured her words carefully. "There is a shelter at the bottom of the hill. Take me there. I will show you the way to Phyrexia."

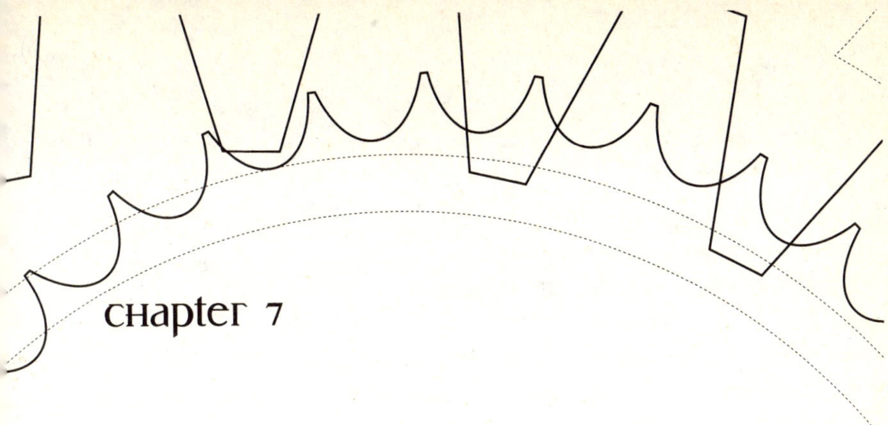

chapter 7

"Wake up!"

Words and jostling ended Xantcha's sleep so thoroughly that for a heartbeat she neither knew where she was nor what she'd been dreaming. In short order she recognized Rat and the streamside grove where she'd fallen asleep, both awash in morning light, but the dreams remained lost. She hadn't intended to fall deeply asleep and was angry with herself for that error and surprised to find Rat clinging to her forearm.

He retreated when she glowered.

"You had a nightmare."

Images shook out of Xantcha's memory: the damp world of insect artifacts, her last beating at Phyrexian hands, Urza hurling fire and sorcery to rescue her. Those were moments of her life that Xantcha would rather not dream about. Between them and anger, she was in a sour mood.

"You didn't take advantage?" she demanded.

Rat answered. "I considered it," without hesitation. "All night I considered it, but I'm a long way from anywhere. I've got a chain between my feet, and even though you may be stronger than me and have that thing that makes us fly, you're still a boy. You need someone to take care of you."

"Me? I need someone to take care of me?" Of all the reasons she could think of to find herself in possession of a slave, that was the last she'd expected. "What about your word?"

He shrugged. "I've had a night to think about it. When I woke up . . . at first I thought you were pretending to be asleep, waiting for me to run. But if I were going to run—walk—" Rat rattled the chain. "I'd have to make sure you couldn't catch me again."

"What were you going to do? Strangle me? Bash my head?"

Another shrug. "I didn't get that far. You started having your nightmare. It looked like a bad one, so I woke you—you don't believe that Shratta nonsense about dreams and your soul?"

"No." Xantcha knew little about the Shratta's beliefs, except that they were violently intolerant of everyone else's. Besides, Urza had said she'd lost her soul in the vats.

"Then why are you so cross-grained? I'm still here, and you're not dreaming a miserable dream."

Xantcha stretched herself upright. Assor's basket was where she'd left it, exactly as she left it, not a crumb unaccounted for. She separated another meal and tossed Rat a warning along with his bread.

"I don't need anyone taking care of me. Don't want it either. When we get to the cottage, your name becomes Mishra, and Urza's the one who needs your help."

Rat grunted. Xantcha expected something more, but it seemed that he'd discovered the virtues of silence and obedience, at least until she told him to sit beside her.

"There's no other way?" he asked, turning pale. "Can't we walk? Even with the chain, I'd rather walk."

Xantcha shook her head and Rat bolted for the bushes. After trying unsuccessfully to turn himself inside out and wasting his breakfast, Rat crawled back to her side.

"I'm ready now."

"I've never fallen from the sky, Rat. Never come close. You're safer than you'd be in a wagon or walking on your own two feet."

"Can't help it—" Rat began then froze completely as Xantcha yawned and the sphere spread from her open mouth.

He started for the bushes again. Knowing that his gut was empty and that she'd be the one who'd be vomiting if she had to bite off the sphere before it was finished, Xantcha grabbed the back of Rat's neck and held his head in her lap until the sphere was rising.

"The worst is over. Sit up. Don't think so much. There's always something to see. Watch the clouds, the ground."

Ground was the wrong word. Cursing feebly, Rat clung to her for dear life. If he couldn't relax, it was going to be a painful journey for both of them. Xantcha tried sympathy.

"Talk to me, Rat. Tell me why you're so afraid. Put your fears into words."

But he couldn't be reassured, so Xantcha tried a less gentle approach. Freeing one arm, she set the sphere tumbling, then yelled louder than his moans:

"I said, talk to me, Rat. You're giving in to fear, Rat." She thought of her feet touching ground, and the sphere plummeted; she thought of playing among the clouds and the sphere rebounded at a truly dizzying speed. "You haven't begun to know fear. Now, talk to me! Why are you afraid?"

Rat screamed. "It's wrong! It's all wrong. I can feel the sky watching me, waiting. Waiting for a chance to throw me down!"

He was sobbing, but his death grip loosened as soon as the words were out of his mouth.

Xantcha thumped Rat soundly between the shoulders. "I won't let the sky have you."

"Doesn't matter. It knows I'm here. Knows I don't belong. It's waiting."

She thumped him again. Rat's complaint was too much like her own in the early days, when Urza would drag her between-worlds. Urza had the planeswalker spark; the fathomless stuff between the Multiverse's countless world-planes bent to his will. Xantcha had been, and remained, an unwelcome interloper. The instant the between-worlds furled around her, she could hear the vast Multiverse sucking its breath, preparing to spit her out.

The planeswalker spark was something a mind either had, or didn't have. Xantcha didn't have it; Urza couldn't share his. The cyst was the only stopgap that he'd been able to devise. It didn't leave Xantcha feeling any less like an interloper, but it did give promise that she'd be alive when the Multiverse spat her out. She'd ask Urza to implant a cyst in Rat's belly—in Mishra's belly—but until then, there was nothing she could do except keep him talking.

The sky above Efuan Pincar wasn't nearly as hostile as the between-worlds. There was a chance he'd talk himself out of his fears. She nudged him into another telling of his life story. The details differed from the second tale he'd told in Assor's wagon, but the overall spirit hadn't changed. When he came to the part where he'd found religious denunciations written in blood on the walls of his family's home, the intensity of his feelings forced Rat to sit straight and speak in a firm, steady voice.

"If the Shratta are men of Avohir, then I spit on Avohir. Better to be damned than live in the Shratta's fist."

That was the sort of fatal, futile sentiment that Xantcha understood, but she was less pleased to hear Rat declare, "When your Urza's done with me, I'll make my way to Pincar City and join the Red-Stripes. They've got the right idea: kill the Shratta. There's no other way. They'd sooner die than admit they're wrong, so let them die."

"There are Phyrexians among the Red-Stripes," Xantcha warned. "They're a much worse enemy than any Shratta."

"They're not my enemy, not if they're fighting the Shratta."

"Mishra may have thought the same thing, but it is not so simple. Flesh cannot trust them, because Phyrexia will never see flesh as anything but a mistake to be erased."

Rat watched her quietly.

"Flesh. We're flesh, you and I," Xantcha pinched the skin on her arm, "but Phyrexians aren't. They're artifacts. Like Urza's, during the Brothers' War . . . only, Phyrexians aren't artifacts. Their flesh has been replaced with other things, mostly metal, according to the Ineffable's plan. Their blood's been replaced with glistening oil. So it should be. Blood cannot trust Phyrexians because blood is a mistake."

His eyes had narrowed. They studied a place far beyond Xantcha's shoulder. Urza talked about thinking, but he rarely did it. Urza either solved his problems instantly, without thinking, or he sank in the mire of obsession. Rat was changing his mind while he thought. Xantcha found the process unnerving to watch.

She spoke quickly, to conceal her own discomfort. "Flesh, blood, meat—what does it matter? Phyrexia is your enemy, Rat. The Brothers' War was just the beginning of what Phyrexia will do to all of Dominaria, if it can. There are Phyrexians in the Red-Stripes, and you'd be wiser, far wiser, to join the Shratta in the fight against them."

"It's just . . ." Rat was thinking even as he talked. His mind changed again and he met Xantcha's eyes with an almost physical force. "You said you smelled Phyrexians among the Red-Stripes. My nose is as good as my eyes, and I didn't smell anything at all. You said 'flesh cannot trust them,' but everybody was flesh, even Tucktah and Garve. On top of all, your talk about me pretending to be Mishra, for someone you call Urza. Something's not true, here."

"Do you think I'm lying?" Xantcha was genuinely curious.

"Whatever you smelled back in Medran, it scared you, because it was Phyrexian, not because it was Red-Stripe. So, I guess you're telling the truth, just not all of it. Maybe we're both flesh, Xantcha, but, Avohir's truth, you're not my sort of flesh."

"I bleed," Xantcha asserted, and to prove the point drew the knife from her boot and slashed a fingertip.

It was a deep cut, deeper than she'd intended. Bright blood flowed in a steady stream from finger to palm, from palm over wrist, where it began to stain her sleeve.

Rat grimaced. "That wasn't necessary," he said, pointedly looking beyond the sphere; the first time he'd done that. Eventually a person would face his fears, provided the alternatives were worse. "You'd know where to cut yourself."

Xantcha held the knife hilt where Rat would see it. He turned further away.

"You were thinking murder not long ago," she reminded him. "Bashing me so you could escape."

Rat shook his head. "Not even close. When my family left Pincar City . . . My father learned to slaughter and butcher meat each fall, but I never could. I always ran away, even last year."

He shrank a little, as if he'd lost a bit of himself by the admission. Xantcha returned the knife to her boot.

"You believe me?" she asked before sticking her bloody finger in her mouth.

"I can't believe you, even if you're telling the truth. Urza the Artificer. Mishra. Smelling Phyrexians. This . . . this thing—" He flung his hand to the side, struck the sphere, and recoiled. "You're too strange. You look like a boy, but you talk . . . You don't talk like anyone I've ever heard before, Xantcha. It's not that you sound foreign, but you're not Efuand. You say you're not an artifact and not Phyrexian. I don't know what to believe. Whose side are you on?"

"Urza's side . . . against Phyrexia." Her finger hadn't stopped bleeding; she put it back in her mouth.

"Urza's no hero, not to me. What he did thirty-four hundred years ago, his gods should still be punishing him for that. You throw a lot of choices in front of me, all of them bad, one way or another. I don't know what to think."

"You think too much."

"Yeah, I hear that all the time. . . ." Rat's voice trailed off. Whoever had chided him last had probably been killed by the Shratta. *All the time* had become history for him, history and grief.

Xantcha left him alone. Her finger was pale and wrinkled. At least it had stopped bleeding. They'd been soaring due west in the grasp of a gentle, drifting wind. Clouds were forming to the north. So far the clouds were scattered, fluffy and white, but north of Efuan Pincar was the Endless Sea where huge storms were common and sudden. Xantcha used her hands to put the sphere on a southwesterly course and set it rising in search of stronger winds.

Belatedly, she realized she had Rat's undivided attention.

"How do you do that?" he asked. "Magic? Are you a sorcerer? Would that explain everything?"

"No."

"No?"

"No, I don't know how I do it. I don't know how I walk, either, or how the food I eat keeps me alive, but it does. One day, Urza handed me something. He said it was a cyst, and he said, swallow it. Since it came from Urza, it was probably an artifact. I don't know for sure because I never asked. I know how to use it. I don't need to know more, and neither will you,"

"Sorry I asked. I'm just trying to think my way through this."

"You think too much."

She hadn't meant to repeat the comment that had jabbed his memory, but before she could berate herself, Rat shot back:

"I'm supposed to be Mishra, aren't I?"

He'd changed his mind again. It was possible that a man, a true flesh-and-blood man, not like Urza, couldn't think too much.

The sphere found the stronger winds and slewed sideways. Xantcha needed full concentration to stop the tumbling. Rat curled up against her with his head between his knees. To the north, clouds billowed as she watched. It was unlikely that they could outrun the brewing storm, but they could cover a lot of territory before she had to get them to shelter. There would, however, be a price.

"It's going to be fast and a little bumpy while we run the windstream. You ready?"

Taking Rat's groan for assent, Xantcha angled her hand west of south-west, and the sphere leapt as if it had been shot from a giant's bow. If she'd been alone, Xantcha would have pressed both hands against the sphere's inner curve and let the wind roar past her face. She figured Rat wasn't ready for such exhilaration and kept her guiding hand sheltered in her lap. The northern horizon became a white mountain range whose highest peaks were beginning to spread and flatten against an invisible ceiling.

"Somebody's going to get wild weather tonight," Xantcha said to her unresponsive companion. "Maybe not us, but someone's going to be begging Avohir's mercy."

She guided the sphere higher. Beneath them, the ground resembled one of Urza's tabletops, though flatter and emptier: a few roads, like rusty wire through spring-green fields, a palisaded village of about ten homesteads tucked in a stream bend. Xantcha considered her promise to replace Rat's rags and, implicitly, to have his fetters removed.

If she set the sphere down, the storm might keep them down until tomorrow. If she kept the sphere scudding, they'd cut a half-day or more off the journey. And by the amount of smoke rising from the village, the inhabitants were burning their fields—hardly a good time for strangers to show up asking favors. Xantcha swiveled her hand south of southwest, and the sphere bounced onto the new tack.

"Wait!" Rat shook Xantcha's ankle. "Wait! That village. Can't you see? It's on fire."

She looked again. Rat was right, fields weren't burning, roofs were. All the more reason to stay on the south by southwest course away from trouble.

"Xantcha! It's the Shratta. It's got to be. Red-Stripes come looking for bribes but don't destroy the villages. We can't just leave—You can't! People are dying down there!"

"I'm not a sorcerer, Rat. I'm not Urza. There's nothing I can do except get myself—and you—killed."

"We can't turn our backs. We're no better than the Shratta, no better than the Phyrexians, if we do that—"

Rat had a real knack for getting under Xantcha's skin, a dangerous mixture of arrogance and charm, just like the real Mishra. Xantcha was about to disillusion her companion with the revelation that she was Phyrexian when he heaved himself toward the burning village. The sphere wasn't Rat's to command. It held to Xantcha's chosen course—as he must have known it would. Rat didn't seem the sort who'd sacrifice himself to prove a point, but he set the sphere tumbling. Everything was knees, elbows, food, and a sword before Xantcha got them sorted out.

"Don't you ever do that again!"

Rat accepted the challenge. This time Xantcha split his upper lip and planted her knee in his groin before she steadied the sphere.

"We're going home . . . to Urza. He's got the power to settle this."

"Too damn late! People are dying down there!"

Rat flung himself, but Xantcha was ready this time and the sphere scarcely bounced.

"I'll drop you if you don't settle yourself."

"Then drop me."

"You'll die."

"I'd rather be dead on the ground than alive up here."

Rat grabbed the scabbarded sword and, with his full weight behind the hilt, plunged it through the sphere. Xantcha reeled from the impact. She hadn't known damage to the sphere meant sharp pain radiating from the cyst in her gut. She could have lived another three thousand years without that particular bit of knowledge. She cocked her fist for a punch that would shatter Rat's jaw.

"Go ahead," he snarled defiantly. "Tell your precious Urza that you killed his brother a second time."

Xantcha lowered her hand. Maybe she was wrong about his willingness to sacrifice himself. By then they were drifting away from the village and nothing but Xantcha's will put them on a course for the flames. The closer they got, the clearer it was that Rat had been right. The north wind brought screams of pain and terror. Born-folk were dying.

When they were still several hundred paces from the wooden palisade, a young woman ran through the broken gate, her hair and hems billowing behind her, a sword-wielding thug in pursuit. Woman and thug both stopped short when they saw two strangers hovering in midair.

"Waste not, want not!" Xantcha muttered.

She thought *Collision* and *Now*! The cyst in her stomach grew fiery spikes, but the sphere plunged like a stooping hawk. It collapsed the instant it touched the gape-mouthed thug, leaving Xantcha to strike with sufficient force to knock him unconscious. She bounded to her feet and crushed the now-defenseless man's skull with her boot heel, deliberately splattering Rat with gore.

If he wanted death, she'd show him death.

The village woman screamed and kept running.

Xantcha seized the sword from the tangle of bodies and spilled baskets. "All right!" She thrust the hilt toward Rat. When he didn't take it up, she poked him hard. "This is what you wanted! Go ahead. Go in there. Save them!"

"I—I can't use a sword. I don't know how. . . . I thought—"

"You thought!" Xantcha angled the sword, prepared to clout him with the hilt. "You think too much!"

Rat got to his feet, stumbling over his chain. He stared at the iron links as if he hadn't seen them before. Whatever nonsense he'd been thinking, he hadn't remembered his fetters.

"I can't . . . You'll have to—"

She shook her head slowly. "I told you, I'm no damn sorcerer, no damn warrior. This is your idiot's idea, your fight. So, you choose: them or me."

It was the same ominous, otherworldly tone Xantcha had used with Garve and Tucktah. She cocked the sword a second time, and Rat grabbed the hilt. He couldn't run, so he skipped and hopped toward the gate.

"Lose the scabbard!" Xantcha shouted after him then muttered Phyrexian curses as Rat stumbled through the gate brandishing a scabbarded sword.

Rat was a fool, and fools deserved whatever harm befell them, but Xantcha's anger faded as soon as her nemesis was out of sight. She reached into her belt-pouch and finger-sorted a few of the smallest, blackest coins. Then, with them clutched loosely in her hand, she yawned out Urza's armor and followed Rat into the besieged village. Not being a sorcerer wasn't quite the same as not having any sorcerous tricks in her arsenal, and not being a warrior was a statement of preference, not experience. There weren't many weapons Xantcha didn't know how to use or evade. On other worlds she'd routinely carried several of them.

But not on Dominaria. She'd given her word.

"I know your temper," Urza had said after they arrived. "But this is home—my home. My traveling years are over. I'm never leaving Dominaria, and I don't want you starting brawls and drawing attention to yourself . . . or me. Promise me you'll stay out of trouble. Promise me that you'll walk away rather than start a fight."

"Waste not, want not—I did not start this, Urza. Truly, I did not."

A gutted corpse lay one step within the gate, but it wasn't Rat's. Xantcha leapt over it. A man bearing a bloody knife ran out of a burning cottage on her left. She slipped a coin into her throwing hand, then stayed her arm as a second, similarly armed, man burst out of the cottage.

Villagers or Shratta thugs? Was one chasing the other? Were they both fleeing? Or looking for more victims?

Xantcha couldn't tell by their clothes or manner. Few things were more frustrating or dangerous than barging into a brawl among strangers. After cursing Rat to the Seventh Sphere of Phyrexia, she entered the cottage the men had abandoned.

The one-room dwelling was filled with smoke. Xantcha called Rat's name and got no answer. Back on the village's single street, she headed for the largest building she could see and had taken about ten strides when an arrow struck her shoulder. Urza's armor was as good as granite when it came to arrows. The shaft splintered, and the arrowhead slid harmlessly down her back.

In one smooth movement, Xantcha spun around and hurled a small, black coin at a fleeing archer. The coin began to glow as soon as it left her hand. It was white-hot by the time it struck the archer's neck. He was dead before he hit the ground, with thick, greenish-black fumes rising from the fatal wound.

A swordsman attacked Xantcha next. He knocked her down with his first attack but was unnerved when she sprang up, unbloodied. Xantcha parried his next strike with her forearm as she closed in to kick him once in the stomach and a second time, as he crumbled, to the jaw. She paused to pick up the sword, then continued down the street shouting Rat's name, attracting attention.

Two more men appeared in front of her. They knew each other and the warrior's trade, giving each other room, exchanging gestures and cryptic commands as they approached. The strategy might have worked if Xantcha had been unarmored or if the sword had been her only weapon. Her aim with the coins wasn't as good with her off-weapon hand. Only one struck its target, but that was enough. The other two exploded when they hit the ground, leaving goat-sized craters in the packed dirt.

Her surviving enemy rushed forward, more intent on getting out of the village than fighting. Xantcha swung, but he parried well and had momentum on his side. Xantcha slammed backward into the nearest wall when he shoved her aside. Elsewhere in the village, someone blew three rapid notes on a horn, and a weaponed quartet at the other end of the village street dashed for the gate. For religious fanatics, the Shratta were better disciplined than most armies. Dark suspicion led Xantcha to inhale deeply, but beyond the smoke and the blood, there was nothing Phyrexian in the air.

A straggler ran past. Xantcha let him go. This was Rat's fight, not hers, and she didn't yet know if he'd survived.

"Ra-te-pe!" She used all three syllables of his name. "Ra-te-pe, son of Mideah, get yourself out here!"

A face appeared in the darkened doorway of the barn that had been her destination. It belonged to an older man, armed with a pitchfork. He stepped unsteadily over the doorsill.

"No one here owns that name."

"There'd better be. He's meat if he ran."

Two more villagers emerged from the barn: a woman clutching her bloody arm against her side and a stone-faced toddler who clung to her skirt.

"Who are you?" the elder asked, giving the pitchfork a shake, reminding Xantcha that she held a bare and bloody sword.

"Xantcha. Rat and I were . . . nearby." She threw the sword into the dirt beside the last man she'd killed. "He saw the roofs burning."

They still were. The survivors made no effort to extinguish the blazes. A village like this probably had one well and only a handful of buckets. The cottages were partly stone; they could be rebuilt after the fires burnt out.

The elder shook his head. Plainly he didn't believe that anyone had simply been nearby. But Xantcha had laid down her weapon. He shouted an all's well that lured a few more mute survivors from their hiding places.

Still no Rat.

Xantcha turned, intending to investigate the other end of the village. The woman who'd fled—the one who'd seen them descend in the sphere—was on the street behind her. Her reappearance, alive and unharmed, broke the villagers' shock. Another woman let out a cry that could have been either joy or grief.

The returning woman replied. "Mother," but her eyes were locked on Xantcha and her hands were knotted in ward-signs against evil.

Time to find Rat and get moving. Xantcha walked quickly to the other end of the village where a whitewashed temple held the place of honor. The door was held open by a corpse.

Given who was fighting in Efuan Pincar, Xantcha supposed she shouldn't have been surprised that the temple had become a charnel house. She counted ten men, each with his hands bound and his throat slit, lying in a common, bloody pool. There were more corpses, similarly bound, sprawled closer to the altar, but she'd spotted Rat staring at a wall before she'd counted them.

"We've got to leave."

He didn't twitch. The scabbard was gone; the sword blade was dark and glistening in the temple's gloomy light. Rat had probably never held a sword before Xantcha made him more afraid of her than death. Odds were he'd become a killer, if not a fighter, in the past hour. A man could crack under that kind of strain. Xantcha approached him cautiously.

"Rat? Ratepe?"

The wall was covered with bloody words. Xantcha could read a score of Dominarian languages, most of them long-extinct, none of them Efuand.

"What does it say?"

" 'Those who defile the Shratta will be cleansed in their own blood. Blessed be Avohir, in whose name this has been done.' "

Xantcha placed her hand over his sword-gripping hand. Without a word, Rat released the hilt.

"If there are gods," she said softly, "then thugs like the Shratta don't speak for them."

She tried to guide Rat toward the door; he resisted, quietly but completely. Mortals, men who were born and who grew old, saw death in ways no Phyrexian newt could imagine, in ways Urza had forgotten. Xantcha had exhausted her meager store of platitudes.

"You knew the Shratta were here, Rat. You must have known what you'd find."

"No."

"I stopped at other villages before I got to Medran. You weren't the first to tell me about the Shratta. This is their handiwork."

"It's not!" Rat shrugged free.

"It's time to leave." Xantcha grasped his arm again.

Rat struck like a serpent but did no harm only because Xantcha was a hair's breath faster in jumping away. She recognized madness on his tear-streaked face.

"All right. Tell me. Talk to me. Why isn't this Shratta handiwork?"

"Him."

Rat pointed at an isolated corpse slumped in the corner between the written-on wall and the wall behind the altar. The man had died because his gut had been slashed open, but he had other wounds, many other wounds, none of which had bled appreciably. Xantcha, who'd fought and sometimes succumbed to her own blind rages, knew at once that this was the man—probably the only man—that Rat had killed.

"All right, what about him?'

"Look at him! He's not Shratta!"

"How do you know?" Xantcha asked, willing to believe him, if he had a good answer.

"Look at his hands!"

She nudged them with her foot. The light was bad, but they seemed ordinary enough to her. "What? I see nothing unordinary."

"The Hands of God. The Shratta are Avohir's Avengers. They tattoo their hands with Shratta-verses from Avohir's holy book."

"Maybe he was a new recruit?"

Rat shook his head vigorously. "It's more than his hands. He's clean-shaven. The Shratta never cut their beards."

Xantcha ran through her memory. Since she'd arrived in Efuan Pincar the only clean-shaven men she'd seen had been in Medran, wearing Red-Stripe tunics, and here where the men she'd fought and the man Rat had killed were beardless.

"So, it's not the Shratta after all? It's Red-Stripes pretending to be Shratta?" she asked.

And knowing that the Phyrexians had invaded the Red-Stripe cadres, Xantcha asked another, silent, question: Had the Phyrexians created their own enemy to bring war and suffering to an obscure comer of Dominaria? If so, they'd learned considerable subtlety since Gix destined her to sleep on another world.

Rat's head continued to shake. "I've seen the Shratta cut through a family like ripe cheese. I saw them draw my uncle's guts out through a hole in his gut: they'd said he'd spilled dog's blood on the book. I know the Shratta, Xantcha, and this is what they'd do, except, this man isn't—and can't be—Shratta."

Keeping her voice calm, Xantcha said. "You said you were gone when the Shratta came through your village. You didn't see any, thing. It could have been the Red-Stripes."

"Could've," Rat agreed easily. "But I saw my uncle get killed, and I saw it before we left Pincar City, and it was the Shratta. By the book, by the true book, Xantcha. Why would Red-Stripes do this? No one but the Shratta support the Shratta. The people here . . . at home, what was home . . . the Shratta would come, real Shratta, and they'd tell us what to do, which was mostly give them everything we had and then some; and they would kill if they didn't get what they wanted," Rat shuddered. "My family were strangers, driven out of Pincar City, but everyone hated the Shratta as much as we did. We'd pray . . . we'd all pray, Xantcha, to Avohir to send us red-striped warriors from the cities. The Red-Stripes were our protectors."

"Be careful what you pray for, I guess. It sounds like the Red-Stripes may have been doing the Shratta's dirty work, and leaving behind no witnesses to reveal the truth."

Rat had reached a similar conclusion. "And if that's true, they're not finished with this place. They're waiting outside. They won't have gone away. Everyone here is dead, you and me, too, unless we can kill them all."

"It's worse than that, Rat. Somebody's gone. Somebody's running a report back somewhere." To a Phyrexian sleeper, saying he'd seen a dark-haired youth hovering in a sphere? No, she'd killed the thug who'd seen them in the sphere. But she'd shaken off an arrow. Phyrexians might lack imagination, but they had excellent memories. Somebody might remember Gix's identical newts, especially since Dominaria was the world Phyrexia coveted above all others, the world of her earliest dreams. Urza was right, as usual. She'd lost her temper, and the price could be very high. "We've got to leave."

"Everyone will die!"

"No deader than they'd be if we'd never set foot here."

"But their blood will he on our hands—on my hands, since you don't seem to have a conscience. I'm not leaving."

"There's no point in staying."

"The Red-Stripes will come back. We'll kill them, then we can leave."

"I told you, there's no point. They'll have sent a runner. This village is doomed."

Rat paced noisily. "All right, it's doomed. So after we kill the Red-Stripes that are still outside the village, you take these people, one by one, to other villages, where they can spread the truth and disappear. By the time the runner leads more Red-Stripes here, this place will be empty. It can be done."

"You can't be serious."

But Rat was, and Xantcha had a conscience. It could be done. First came a long, violent night roaming the fields outside the village with her armor and a sharp knife, followed by three days of burying the dead and another five of ferrying frightened survivors to places where they could "spread the truth about the Shratta and the Red-Stripes then disappear." But it was done, and on the morning of the tenth day, after leaving Rat's fetters draped across the defiled altar, they resumed their journey out of Efuan Pincar.

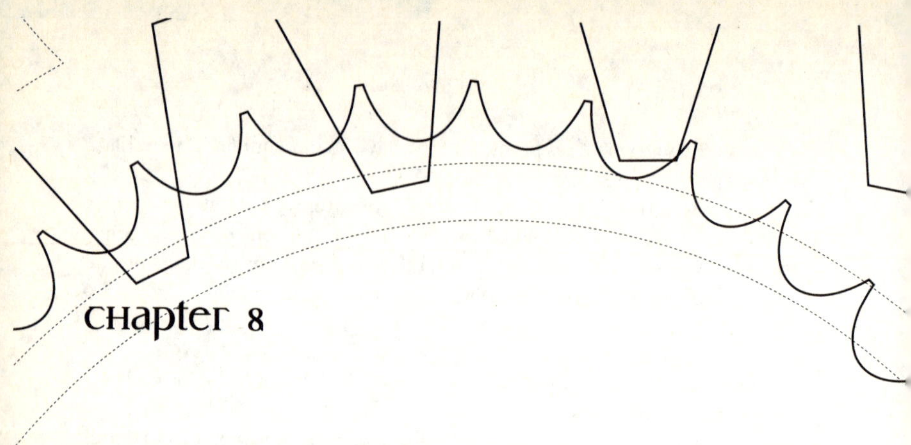

chapter 8

Xantcha guided the sphere with a rigid hand. The Glimmer Moon hung low in the night sky, painfully bright yet providing little illumination for the land below. A dark ridge loomed to the south. On the other side of that ridge there was a familiar cottage with two front doors and the bed in which she expected to be sleeping before midnight.

It was a clear night reminiscent of winter. The air was dead-calm and freezing within the sphere. Her feet had been quietly numb since sundown. Beside her, Rat hadn't said a word since the first stars appeared. She hoped he was asleep.

And perhaps he was, but he awoke when the sphere pitched forward and plummeted toward a black-mirror lake Xantcha hadn't noticed. He'd had nearly two weeks to learn when to tuck his head and keep his terror to himself, but in the dark, with food and whatnot tumbling around them, Xantcha didn't begrudge Rat a moment of panic. In truth, she scarcely noticed his shouts; the plunge caught her unprepared. It was several moments before she heard anything other than her own heart's pounding.

By then Rat had reclaimed his perch atop the sacks. "You could set us down for the night," he suggested.

"We're almost there."

"You said that at noon."

"It was true then, and it's truer now. We're almost to the cottage."

Rat made an unhappy noise in the back of his throat. Xantcha gave him a sidelong glance. Through the dim light she could see that he'd hunched down in his cloak and pulled the cowl up so it formed a funnel around his face. She'd collected Rat's new clothes as she'd ferried Red-Stripe survivors to other Efuand villages. They were nothing like the clothes Mishra would have worn—nothing like the travel-worn silks and suedes Xantcha herself wore—but they were the best she'd been able to find, and Rat had seemed genuinely grateful for them.

He'd cleaned up better than Xantcha had dared hope. Their first full day in the ruined village, while she'd been talking relocation with the elders, Rat had persuaded one of the women to trim his hair. He'd procured a handful of pumice the same way and spent that afternoon scrubbing himself—and being scrubbed—in the stream-fed pool where the women did laundry.

"You didn't have to bother the villagers." Xantcha had told him when she'd seen him next, all pink and raw, especially on the chin. "I could have loaned you my knife."

He'd looked down at her, shaking his head and half-smiling. "When you're old enough to grow whiskers, Xantcha, you'll realize a man doesn't have to cut his own hair."

Xantcha had started to say that with or without whiskers Rat would never be as old as she was, but that half-smile had confused her. Even now, when she couldn't see through the dark or the cowl, she suspected he was half-smiling again, and she didn't know what to say. Once washed and dressed in clothes that didn't reek, he'd proved attractive, at least to the extent that Xantcha understood mortal handsomeness. Rat didn't resemble any of Xantcha's *Antiquity Wars* portraits, and there was a generosity to him that softened the otherwise hard lines of his face.

Rat had healed almost as fast as a newt. His bruises were shadows now, and the sores around his neck, wrists, and ankles shrank daily. Every morning had seen a bit more flesh on his bones, a bit more swagger in his stride. He'd become Mishra: charming, passionate, unpredictable, and vaguely dangerous. Kayla Bin-Kroog would have known what to say—Kayla had known what to say to Urza's brother—but Xantcha wasn't Urza's wife, and, anyway, Rat thought of her as a boy, a deception that, all other things considered, Xantcha thought she might continue after they returned to the cottage . . . if Urza cooperated.

She touched his shoulder gingerly. "Don't worry, we'll be there tonight."

Rat shrugged her hand away. The cowl fell, and she could see his face faintly in the moonlight. He wasn't smiling. "Tonight or tomorrow morning, what difference can it make?"

"Urza's waiting. It's been more a month since I left. I've never been gone this long."

"You'll be gone forever if you don't stop pushing yourself. Even if he were the real Urza, he'd tell you to rest before you hurt yourself."

Rat didn't know Urza. Urza was inexhaustible, indestructible; he assumed Xantcha was too, and so, usually, did she.

"We're almost there. I'm not tired, and I don't need to rest."

The words were no sooner said than the sphere caught another downdraft, not as precipitous as the first one, but enough to fling them against each other.

"You're making mistakes."

"You know nothing about this!" Xantcha shot back. She tilted her hand too far, overcorrected, and wound up in Rat's lap.

He pushed her away. "What more do I need to know? Put it down."

"I didn't argue with you when you said those villagers needed to be rescued."

"I'm not arguing with you. I know you want me to meet Urza. You think there's not a moment to lose against the Phyrexians, but not like this, Xantcha. This is foolish, as foolish as buying me in the first place, only I can't help you keep this damn thing in the air."

"Right—you can't help, so be quiet."

And he was, as quiet as he'd been that first night out of Medran. Xantcha hadn't believed it was possible, but Rat's silence was worse than Urza's, because Rat wasn't ignoring her. He wasn't frightened, either; just sitting beside her, a cold, blank wall even when she pushed the sphere against the wind. There were moments when she could believe that Rat was Urza's real brother.

"You don't have to be Mishra, not yet."

Another of Rat's annoyed, annoying noises. "I'm not being Mishra. Mishra wouldn't care if you killed yourself getting him to Urza and, if you asked me, the real Urza wouldn't either. The real Urza didn't care about anything except what he wanted. The way you're acting, I'm starting to think you believe what you've been telling me. It's all over your face, Xantcha. You're the one who's worried because you're afraid. More afraid of the man you call Urza, I think, than of any Phyrexian."

It was Xantcha's turn to stare at the black ridge on the southern horizon and convince herself that Rat was wrong. The ridge was beneath them before she broke the silence.

"You don't believe anything I've told you."

"It's pretty far-fetched."

"But you've come all this way with me. There were so many times, when I was ferrying the villagers about, that you could have run away, but you didn't. I thought you'd decided I was telling you the truth. Why did you stop trying to run away, if you didn't believe anything I said?"

"Because six months ago I would've sworn on my life that I'd never leave Efuan Pincar, not with some half-wit boy whose got a thing in his belly. I'd've sworn a lot of things six months ago, and I'd've been wrong about all of them. I'm getting used to being wrong and I did give you my word, freely, when you agreed to get those villagers to safety, that I'd play your game. You weren't paying attention, but I was. You saved them because I asked you to, and that makes you my friend, at least for now."

"You've got to believe, Rat. If you don't believe, Urza won't, and I don't know what he'll do—to either of us—if he thinks I've tried to deceive him."

"I'll worry about Urza the Artificer," Rat said wearily.

He was patronizing her, despite everything she'd told him. All the lessons in language and history she'd given to him after dark in the village, Rat didn't believe.

He continued, "You worry about that shadow coming up. I think it's another lake, and I think we're going to go rump over elbows again if you don't wriggle your hand around it."

Rat was right about the lake. Xantcha wove her hand to one side, and another unpleasant moment was averted. It had taken her decades to learn the tricks that air could play on her sphere. Rat was quicker, cleverer than she'd ever been. There was a chance he was right about Urza, too, especially when she saw eldritch light leaking through the cottage windows after the sphere cleared the ridge.

"He's locked himself in," she muttered, unable to keep disappointment out of her voice.

"You didn't think he'd be waiting by the door, not in the middle of the night? A locked door isn't a bad idea, if you're alone and you've got the sorcery to make it stick. A man gets tired," said Rat.

"Not Urza," Xantcha said softly as the sphere touched down and collapsed.

Without the sphere's skin to support them, their supplies rearranged themselves across the ground. It was quicker than the chaos they endured when the sphere tumbled through the air, but quite a bit more painful on the hard ground; a wooden box corner came down squarely on Xantcha's cold ankle.

She was still cursing when the eldritch locks vanished. Urza appeared in the open doorway.

"Xantcha! Where have—?"

He'd noticed Rat. His eyes began to glow. Xantcha hadn't considered the possibility that Urza might simply kill any stranger who appeared outside his door.

"No!" Xantcha wanted to get herself between the two men, but her feet wouldn't cooperate. "Urza! Listen to me!"

She'd no sooner gotten Urza's attention than Rat wrested it away again with a single, soft-spoken word:

"Brother . . ."

Every night in the village Xantcha had sat up with Rat telling him about Urza and Urza's obsessions. She'd warned him about Urza's uncanny eyes and the tabletop where his gnats recreated—refined—the scenes from Kayla's epic. She'd taught him the rudiments of the polyglot language she and Urza spoke when they were alone because it was rich in the words he'd shared with Mishra, when they were both men. She'd taught him the word for *brother* and insisted he practice it until he got it right, but the word he'd said was pure Efuand dialect.

For a moment the space between them was as dark as the space between the stars overhead, then the golden light that had been in the cottage flowed from Urza toward Rat, who didn't flinch as it surrounded him.

"You wished to see me, Brother," he continued in Efuand. "It's been a long, hard journey, but I've come back."

Urza could absorb a new language as easily as a plowed field absorbed the spring rains. Most of the time, he didn't notice the switch, but Xantcha had thought Urza might pay attention to Mishra's language, to the language that anyone pretending to be Mishra spoke during the critical first moments of their encounter. She was ready to kill Rat with her own hands, if Urza didn't do it for her. His eyes hadn't stopped glowing, and she'd seen those jewels obliterate creatures vastly more powerful than an over-confident slave from Efuan Pincar.

"Speak to me, Urza. It's been so long. We never finished our last conversation, never truly began it."

"Where?" Urza asked, a whisper on a cold, cold wind. At least he'd spoken Efuand.

"Before the blood-red tent of the warlord of Kroog. We stood as far apart as we stand now. You said we should remember that we were brothers."

"The tent was not red, and I said no such thing."

"Do you call me a liar, Brother? I remember less, Brother, but I remember very clearly. I have been here all the time, waiting for you; it would have been easier if your memory were not flawed."

Urza's eyes took on the painful brilliance of the Glimmer Moon. Xantcha was certain that Rat would sizzle like raindrops in a bonfire, yet the light didn't harm him, and after a few rib-thumping heartbeats she began to perceive Rat's unexpected brilliance. The real Mishra had been supremely confident and never, even in the best of times, willing to concede a point to his elder brother. Between Urza and Mishra, attitude was more important than language, and Rat had the right attitude.

"It is possible," Urza conceded as his eyes dimmed to a mortal color. "Each time I refine my automata, I learn what I had forgotten. It is a short step between forgotten and misremembered."

Raising his hand, Urza took a hesitant stride toward Rat—toward Mishra. He stopped short of touching his putative brother's flesh.

"I dreamed that in time, through time, I'd find a way to talk to you, to warn you of the dangers neither of us saw when we were alive together. I never dreamed that you would find me. You. It is you, Mishra?"

Urza moved without moving, placing his open hand across Rat's cheek. Even Xantcha, who knew Urza could change his shape faster than muscle could move bone, was stunned. As for Rat himself—Rat, who'd refused to believe her warnings that her Urza was the Urza who'd become more like a god than a man—he went deathly pale beneath Urza's long, elegant and essentially lifeless fingers. His eyes rolled, and his body slackened, he'd fainted, but Urza's curiosity kept him upright.

"They took your skin, Mishra, and stretched it over one of their abominations. Do you remember? Do you remember them coming for you? Do you remember dying?"

Rat's limp arms and legs began to tremble. Xantcha's breath caught in her throat. She'd never believed that Urza was cruel, merely careless. He'd lived so long in his own mad isolation that he'd forgotten the frailties of ordinary flesh, especially of flesh more ordinary than that of a Phyrexian newt. She was certain that once Urza noticed what was he was doing, he'd relent. He could heal as readily as he harmed.

But Urza didn't notice what he was doing to the youth she'd brought from Efuan Pincar. Rat writhed like a stuck serpent. Blood seeped from his nose. Xantcha threw herself into the golden light.

"Stop!" Xantcha seized Urza's outstretched arm. She might have been a fly on a mountaintop for the effect she had. "You're killing him."

Suddenly, Urza's arm hung at his side again. Xantcha reeled backward, fighting for balance while Rat collapsed.

"There is nothing in his mind. I sought the answers that have eluded me: when did the Phyrexians come for him? Did he fight? Did he surrender willingly? Did he call my name? He has no answers, Xantcha. He has nothing at all. My brother's mind is as empty as yours. I do not understand. I found you too late; the damage had already been done. But how and why has Mishra come back to me if he is not himself, if his mind is not alive with the thoughts I know should be there."

Xantcha knew her mind was empty. She was Phyrexian, a newt engendered in a vat of turgid slime. She had no imagination, no great thoughts or ambitions, not even a heart that could be crushed by humiliation, whether that humiliation came from Urza or Gix.

Rat was another matter. He lay face-down in a heap of awkwardly bent limbs. "He's a man," Xantcha snarled. She'd caught her balance, but kept her distance. Another step closer and she'd be a child looking up to meet Urza's eyes. She was too angry for that. "His mind is his own. It's not a book for you to read and cast aside!"

Xantcha couldn't guess whether Rat was still alive, even when Urza put his foot against the youth's flank to shove him onto his back.

"This is only the first. There will be others. The first is never final; there must always be refinements. If I have learned nothing else, I have learned that. I was working in the wrong direction—thinking that I'd have to reach back through time to find Mishra and the truth. And because I was not looking for Mishra, he could not find me, not as he must find me. But his truth will come to me once I have refined the path. I can see them, Xantcha: a line of Mishras, each bearing a piece of the truth. They will come and come until one of them bears it all." Urza headed to his open door. "There is no time." He stopped and laughed aloud. "Time, Xantcha . . . think of it! I have finally found the way to negate time. I will start again. Do not disturb me."

He was mad, Xantcha reminded herself, and she'd been a fool to think she could outwit him. Unlike Rat, Urza never changed his mind. He interpreted everything through the prism of his obsessions. Urza couldn't be held responsible for what had happened.

That burden fell on her.

Xantcha had never kept count of those she'd slain or watched die. Surely there were hundreds . . . thousands, if she included Phyrexians, but she'd never betrayed anyone as she'd betrayed Ratepe, son of Mideah. She knelt beside him, straightening his corpse, starting with his legs. Ratepe hadn't begun to stiffen; his skin was still warm.

"There will be no others!"

Urza turned around. "What did you say?"

"I said, this was a man, Urza. He was a man, born and living until you killed him. He wasn't an artifact on your table that you could sweep onto the floor when you were finished with him. You didn't make him—" She hesitated. Burdened with guilt, she saw that her clever plan to have Ratepe pose as Mishra required confession. "That tabletop didn't reach through the past. I went looking for a man who resembled your brother, I found him, and I brought him here.

"I won't do it again, so there won't—"

"You, Xantcha? Don't speak nonsense. This was my brother—the first shadow of my brother. You could not have found him without me."

"I'm not speaking nonsense! You had nothing to do with this, Urza. This was my idea, my bad idea. His name was never Mishra. His name was Ratepe, son of Mideah. I bought him from a slaver in Efuan Pincar."

Urza appeared thunderstruck. Xantcha leaned forward to straighten Ratepe's other leg. Efuands buried their dead in grass-lined graves that faced the sunrise. She'd helped dig several of them. There was a suitable spot not far from her window where she'd see it easily and lament her folly each time she did.

Unless she left . . . soared back to Efuan Pincar to do battle with the Phyrexians in Ratepe's name. If the cyst would still respond to her whims. If Urza didn't destroy her when his thoughts finally made their way back to the world of life and death.

She reached for Ratepe's crooked arm.

"A slaver? You sought my brother's avatar in a slaver's pens?"

Avatar—a spirit captured in flesh. Xantcha recognized the word but had never consciously used it; it was the right word, though, for what she'd wanted Ratepe to become. "Yes." She straightened Ratepe's elbow. "Mishra was a Fallaji slave."

"Mishra was advisor to the qadir."

"Mishra was a slave. The Fallaji captured him before you got to Yotia; they never freed him—not formally. It's in The *Antiquity Wars.* He told Kayla, and she wrote down his words."

Xantcha had never told Urza about her chest filled with copies of his wife's epic. He hadn't asked, hadn't volunteered any sense of his past here in his home, except what arose from his tabletop artifacts. He didn't appear pleased to hear Kayla's name falling off her tongue. Xantcha sensed she was living dangerously, very dangerously.

She took Ratepe's hand. It was stiff; rigor had begun. Gently, she uncurled his fingers.

They resisted, tightened, squeezed.

Before she could think, Xantcha jerked her hand away—or tried to. Ratepe didn't let go, and she stayed where she was, kneeling beside him, breathless with shock. She looked down. He winked, then kept both eyes shut.

"Waste not, want not," she whispered and cast her glance quickly in Urza's direction but Urza was elsewhere.

"I did not tell you to read that story." His voice came from a cold place, far from his heart. "Kayla Bin-Kroog never knew the truth and did not write it, either. She chose to live in a mist, with neither light nor shadow to guide her. You cannot believe anything in *The Antiquity Wars*, Xantcha, especially about Mishra. My wife saw her world through a veil of emotions. She saw people, not patterns, and when she saw my brother . . ." He didn't finish his thought, but offered another: "She didn't mean to betray me. I'm sure she thought she could be the bridge between us; it was too late. I honored Harbin, but after that, it was all lies between us. I couldn't trust her. You can't either."

Before Xantcha could say that Kayla's version of the war made more sense, Ratepe sat bolt upright.

"I've heard it said that there's no way a man can be absolutely certain that his wife's child is his and only one way he can be certain that it's not. Kayla Bin-Kroog was an attractive woman, Urza, and wiser than you'll know. She did try to become a bridge, but not with her body. She was tempted. I made certain she was tempted, but she never succumbed, which, my Brother, begs one almighty question: How and why are you so certain Harbin was not your son?"

Suddenly, they were all in darkness as Urza's golden light vanished.

"You've done it now," Xantcha said softly and with more than a little admiration. She'd never gotten the better of Urza that way. "He's gone 'walking."

But Urza hadn't 'walked away, and when the light returned it flowed from an Urza that Xantcha had never seen before: a youthful Urza, dressed in a dirt-laborer's dusty clothes and smiling as he reached out to take Ratepe's hands.

"I have missed you, Brother. I've had no one to talk to. Stand up, stand up! Come with me! Let me show you what I've learned while you were gone. It was Ashnod, you know—"

Ratepe proved he was as consistent as he was reckless. He folded his arms across his chest and stayed where he was. "You've had Xantcha. He's not 'no one.' "

"Xantcha!"

While Urza laughed, Xantcha got to her feet.

"Xantcha! I rescued Xantcha a thousand years ago—no, longer than that, more than three thousand years ago. Don't be fooled by appearances, as I was. She's Phyrexian—cooked up in one of their vats. A mistake. A failure. A slave. They were getting ready to bury her when I came along; thought she was Argivian at first. She's loyal . . . to me. She's got her own reasons for turning on Phyrexia. But her mind is limited. You can talk to her, but only a fool would listen."

Xantcha couldn't meet Ratepe's eyes. When they were alone and Urza belittled her, she could blame it on his madness. Now there were three of them standing outside the cottage. Urza wasn't talking to her, he was talking about her, and there were no excuses. All their centuries together, all the experiences no one else had shared, and he'd never conquered his distrust, his disdain.

"I think—" Ratepe began, and Xantcha forced herself to catch his attention.

She mouthed the single word, *Don't.* It didn't matter what Urza thought of her, so long as he stopped playing with his tabletop gnats. Xantcha mouthed a second word, *Phyrexia,* and made a fist where Ratepe could see it. She hoped she'd told him what mattered, and that it wasn't her.

Ratepe cleared his throat. He said, "I think it is not the time to argue, Urza," and made the words sound sincere. "We have always done too much of that. I always did too much of that. There, I've admitted it, and the world did not end. Not yet; not again. You think we made our fatal mistake on the Plains of Kor. I think we made it earlier. After so long, it doesn't matter, does it? It was the same mistake either way. We couldn't talk, we could only compete. And you won. I see the Weakstone in your left eye. Have you ever heard it singing to you, Urza?"

Sing?

Anyone who'd read *The Antiquity Wars* would know that Urza's eyes had once been his Mightstone and his brother's Weakstone. Tawnos had brought that scrap back to Kayla. Ratepe claimed he'd read Kayla's epic several times, and between two stones and two eyes, he could have made a lucky guess. The Weakstone had, indeed, become Urza's left eye. But sing? Urza had never mentioned singing.

Xantcha couldn't guess what had fired Ratepe's all-too-mortal imagination, but as Urza frowned and stared at the stars, she guessed it had propelled him too far.

Then Urza began to speak. "I hear it now, faintly, without word, but a song of sadness. Your song?"

Xantcha was stunned.

Urza continued: "The stone we found—the single stone—was a weapon, you know: The final defense of the Thran, their last sacrifice. They blocked the portal to Phyrexia. You and I, when we sundered the stone, we opened the portal. We let them back into Dominaria. I never asked you what you saw that day."

Ratepe grinned. "Didn't I say that we made our mistake much earlier?"

Urza clapped his hands together and laughed heartily. "You did! Yes, you did! We've got a second chance, brother. This time, we'll talk." He opened his arms, gesturing toward the open doorway. "Come, let me show you what I've learned while you were gone. Let me show you the wonders of artifice, pure artifice, Brother—none of those Phyrexian abominations. And Ashnod! Wait until I show you Ashnod: a viper at your breast, Brother. She was their first conquest, your biggest mistake."

"Show me everything," Ratepe said, walking into Urza's embrace.

"Then we'll talk."

Arm in arm, they walked toward the cottage. A few steps short of the threshold, Ratepe shot a glance over his shoulder. He seemed to expect some gesture from her, but Xantcha, unable to guess what it should be, simply stood with her arms limp at her sides.

"And when we're done talking, Urza, we'll listen to Xantcha."

The door shut without a sound. The light was gone, and Xantcha was left with only moonlight to help her haul the food supplies.

Chapter 9

Cold fog rolled down from the mountains. Xantcha's fingers stiffened, and the rest of her grew clumsy. When she wasn't tripping over her feet, she dropped bundles and cursed loudly, not caring if she disturbed the two men on the other side of the wall.

She didn't disturb them. Urza had a new audience for his tabletop. He wouldn't notice the world if it ended. And Ratepe? Ratepe was playing the dangerous game Xantcha had told him to play and playing it better than she'd dared hope. She'd all but told him not to pay any attention to her; she could hardly begrudge obedience—or fail to notice that Urza's door was unwarded. She could have left the sacks where the sphere had scattered them.

Ratepe—Rat—Mishra—would have defended her right to join them. Xantcha was tempted to walk through the door, if only to hear what the young Efuand would say, which, considering all that hung in the balance was a selfish temptation. She resisted it until the last of the supplies was stowed in the pantry and the fog had matured into an ice-needle rain.

Inside her room, with the shutters bolted against the chill, Xantcha found herself too tired to sleep. Eyes open and empty, she lay on her bed able to hear the sounds of conversation beyond the wall without catching any of the words. She piled pillows atop her face, pulled the blankets tight, then threw everything aside. Before long, Xantcha had wedged herself into the comer at the foot of the bed. With her knees tucked beneath her chin and a blanket draped over her head, Xantcha tried to think of other things. . . .

Of her first conversation with Urza . . .

"There is a shelter at the bottom of the hill. Take me there. I'll show you the way to Phyrexia."

Urza frowned. Xantcha had rarely seen a face creased with displeasure. She expected his jaw to fall to the ground. But her rescuer was flexible—a newt like herself, or one of born-folk, about whom she knew very little. When his frown had sunk as much as it could, it rebounded and became a bitter laugh.

She knew the meaning of that sound.

"It's the truth. I will show you the way. I will take you to Phyrexia—though, it's only fair to tell you that avengers stand guard around the Fourth Sphere ambulator fields and we'll be destroyed on the spot."

"It's gone. It's gotten away," her rescuer said, still laughing.

"The ambulator's nether end should be there—unless you let the searcher get away. The diggers, they don't know how to roll an ambulator, and the bearers can't."

Xantcha tried to rise and felt light-headed, felt light all over. It was not an unprecedented feeling. Every time she stepped into a new world there were changes: a different texture to the air, a different color to the light, a different sense between her feet and the ground. She took a deep breath to confirm her suspicions.

"The hill and shelter are where I remember them, but I am not any place that I remember?"

"Yes, my clever child, I brought you here, and I will take you back. The hill is there, but the shelter and this ambulator of which you speak, alas, is not."

Xantcha thought she understood. "You drew the prime end through itself to bring me to this place?" She hesitated, but this man who had rescued her deserved the truth. "If you unanchored the ambulator, I don't know if I can take you to Phyrexia. I've seen the searcher-priests set the stones for Phyrexia, but I've never set them myself. I don't know what our fate will be if I set them wrong, but I'll go first."

"No, child, you will not go first," he said, grim and serious. "Though you have every reason to condemn Phyrexia, you have become a traitor to them, and traitors can never be trusted, must never be trusted."

Traitor. The word roused a hundred others from Xantcha's dreams. She supposed it was a truthful word, though not as truthful as it would have been if she weren't a newt who'd never been compleated. Insofar as kin pricked her conscience, it was safe to say that she had none.

"I was Orman'huzra when you found me, second of the dodgers. What is my position now? What is yours? What do I do, if I cannot be trusted and I cannot go first?"

The man paced the small, stark chamber in which she'd awakened. His eyes burned as he walked, reminding Xantcha of Gix. She lowered her head when he stopped in front of her. He put his hand beneath her chin to raise it. Her instinct was to resist, to avoid those eyes as she had avoided the eyes of Gix, but he overcame her resistance. Her rescuer had a demon's strength.

"Orman'huzra. That is not a name. What is your name?"

"In my dreams, I am Xantcha."

The answer failed to please him. Fingers tightened on either side of her jaw. She closed her eyes, but that made no difference. The many-colored light from his eyes burnt like fire in her thoughts.

"Your mind is empty, Xantcha," he said after an agonizing moment. "The Phyrexians took it all away from you."

He was wrong. Were it not for what the Phyrexians—Gix in particular—had done to her, Xantcha was sure she would have died right then. She didn't correct her new companion, no more than she'd corrected Gix, and took no small satisfaction in the knowledge that the sanctuary she'd created, when Gix had confronted her, remained intact.

"What is my place? What is yours?" she asked for the second time. "What do you do?"

"My place was Lord Protector of the Realm, and I failed to do what I should have done. You may call me Urza."

There were images for the word *Urza*, hideous images. Xantcha heard the voice of a teacher-priest: *If you meet Urza, destroy him.* The man in front of her didn't resemble the image. Even if he had, Xantcha would have denied the imperative. She wasn't about to destroy an enemy of Phyrexia.

"Urza," she repeated. "Urza, I will show you what I know of the ambulators."

Xantcha tried to rise from her pallet. The ambulator had to be beyond the chamber's closed door. It was too large for the chamber itself. She got as far as her knees. In addition to feeling light, she was weak. But there were no marks on her body. Her wounds had healed. Xantcha didn't understand; she'd been weak before, but never without wounds.

"Rest," Urza told her, offering her the corner of the blanket. "You have been very sick. Many days—at least a month—have passed since I brought you here . . . but not through any ambulator. I did, as you suggest, let the searcher get away. My error, Xantcha. I did not suspect your ambulators and seeing your kind on that other plane, I thought you had 'walked there. My grievous error: the emptiness between the planes is no place for a child without the necessary spark. You were less than a breath, less than a heartbeat, from death before I got you here—which is not where I'd intended to bring you.

"Do not touch that door!" he warned, then had an inspiration and pointed his forefinger at it.

The wood glowed and became dull, gray stone, like the rest of the chamber.

"The Phyrexians changed you Xantcha, and I could not undo their changes, but without what they did, you would not have lived long enough for me to do anything at all. This place is safe for you. It has air and a balance of heat and cold. Outside, there is nothing. Your skin will freeze and your blood will boil. Without the spark, you will not survive. Do you hear me, Xantcha? Can your empty mind understand?"

Xantcha had had no sense of modesty, not so soon after leaving Phyrexia, and the air in the chamber was comfortably warm, yet she'd clutched the blanket tight around her naked flesh—the same as she clutched it millennia later in a cold, dark cottage room while sleet pelted the roof overhead. Her empty mind never had a problem understanding Urza's words. It was the implications that often left her reeling.

"I understand," she assured Urza. "This is my place and I will remain here. But I do not know about *months.* I know days and seasons and years. What is a month?"

Urza closed his eyes and, after a dramatic sigh, told her about the many ways in which born-folk measured time. Xantcha told him that Phyrexia was a place where time went unmeasured. There was no sun by day nor stars by night. The First Sphere sky was an unchanging featureless gray. All the other spheres were nested within the First Sphere. Gix had been dropped into a fumarole that descended to the Seventh Sphere. The Ineffable dwelt in the ninth, at Phyrexia's core.

"Interesting," Urza said. "If you're telling the truth. I have heard the name Gix before, on my own plane, where it was the name of a mountain god before the Phyrexians stole it. In fifty years of searching, I have heard the name Gix many times. I've heard the name Urza, too, and several that sound like *Sancha.* There are only so many sounds that our mouths can make, so many words, so many names. At best, language is confusion. If you are to be useful to me, you must never lie. Are you telling me the truth, child?"

She nodded and added, truthfully, "I am not a child." The image was quite clear in her mind; the world for which she had been destined—the world to which she had not gone—had children. "Children are born. Children grow. Phyrexians are decanted by vat-priests and compleated by the tender-priests. When I was decanted, I was exactly as I am now. I was not compleated, but I was never a child. Gix said he made me."

Urza shook his head sadly. "It is tempting, very tempting to believe that there is only one Gix, but I have made that mistake before. It is just a sound, a similar sound, filled with lies. You do not remember what you were before the Phyrexians claimed you, Xantcha, and that is just as well. To remember what you had lost. . . ." He closed his eyes a moment. "You would not be strong enough. By your face, I'd say you were twelve, perhaps thirteen—" He shook a thought out of his mind and began to pace. "You were born, Xantcha. Life is born or it is not life. Not even the Phyrexians can change that. They steal, they corrupt, and they abominate, but they cannot create.

"You remember the decanting, and I am grateful that you remember nothing before that because I am certain that you were most horribly transformed. In my wanderings I have seen men and women in many variations, but I have never seen one such as you, who is neither."

Urza continued pacing the small chamber. He wouldn't look at her, which was just as well. Xantcha knew many words for madness and delusion, and they all described Urza. He had rescued her—saved her life—and he had strange powers, not merely in his glowing eyes, but an odd sort of passion that left her believing for a few distracted heartbeats that she had been born on the world at the bottom of her memories.

Xantcha ached in the missing places when Urza described her as neither man nor woman. After Gix's excoriation, while she'd hidden among the gremlins, she'd had opportunity to observe the differences between the two types of born-folk: men and women. If Urza was right, she had even more reason to wage war against Phyrexia.

But Urza had to be wrong. He didn't know Phyrexia. He'd never peeked into a vat to see the writhing shape of a half-grown newt. He'd never seen tender-priests throwing buckets of rendered flesh into those vats. Meat-sludge was the source of Xantcha's memories, meat-sludge and Gix's ambition. Nothing had been taken from her. She was empty, as Urza had told her, filled with memories that weren't her own.

Urza confirmed Xantcha's self-judgment as he paced. "Yes, it is better that you don't remember, better that your mind is empty and you have no imagination left that would fill it. Mishra knew what he had become, and it drove him mad. I will keep you, Xantcha, and avenge your loss as I avenge my brother. You will stay here,"

Xantcha didn't argue. She was in a chamber that had neither windows nor doors. Her companion was a man-demon with glowing eyes. There was nothing at all to be gained by argument. Still, there was at least one question that had to be asked:

"May I eat?"

Urza stopped pacing. His eyes darkened to a mortal brown. "You eat? But, you're Phyrexian."

She shrugged and chose her words carefully. "They didn't take that.

I ate from a cauldron when I was in Phyrexia, but I scrounged when I was excavating. I can scrounge here, if you'll show me where the living things are."

"Nothing lives here, Xantcha."

Urza muttered under his breath. His hands began to glow as his eyes had. He strode to the nearest wall and thrust his fingers into what had appeared to be solid stone. The glow transferred to the stone. The chamber filled with the hot, acrid smells Xantcha remembered from the furnaces. She eased backward, blindly clutching the blanket, as if it could protect her. There was a hollow in the wall now, and a radiant mass seething in Urza's hands.

"Bread," Urza said when the seething mass had cooled.

Xantcha had scrounged bread on a few of the worlds the searcher-priests had sent her to. The steaming loaf Urza handed her looked like bread and smelled a bit like bread, a bit more like overheated dust. Its taste was dusty, too, but she'd eaten worse, much worse, and gorged without complaint.

"Do you want more?"

She didn't answer. Want was an empty notion. Newts didn't want. Newts took what they could, what was available, and waited for another opportunity—which might come soon, or might not. Urza faded until he was a pale, translucent shadow; then he was gone. A heartbeat later, the chamber's light was gone, too.

Every world Xantcha had seen had spun to its own rhythms, and though she hadn't acquired an instinctive sense of day becoming night, she'd learned enough about time to be desperately afraid of the dark. She was ravenous when Urza finally returned, exhausted because she'd feared to close her eyes lest she sleep through his reappearance, and bleeding where she'd pinched herself to keep awake. Taking all her risk at once, Xantcha sprang across the chamber. She clung ferociously to Urza's sleeve.

"I won't remain here! Bring back the door. Let me out or destroy me!"

Urza stared at her hands. "I brought you something. Swallow it, and I can, as you say, bring back the door."

He held out his free arm and opened his hand, which held a nearly transparent lump about half the size of her fist. Xantcha had eaten worse meals in the Fane of Flesh, but she didn't think Urza was offering her supper.

"What is it?" she asked, not letting go with either hand.

"Consider it a gift. I went back to the plane where I found you. The Phyrexians were careful to clean up after themselves, but I was more careful looking for them this time. I found a place where the soil had been transformed with black mana, much as you have been. So, I believe you, Xantcha. You are almost what you say you are, almost a Phyrexian. You believe the lies they told because when they transformed you they took your memory and your potential. You are a danger to others and to yourself but not to me. I will unlock your secrets and find answers I need for my vengeance."

"I'll help," Xantcha agreed. She'd agree to anything to get out of the chamber. After that . . .

After that would take care of itself.

Letting go of his sleeve with one hand but not the other, she reached for the lump. Urza swung it beyond her reach.

"You must understand, Xantcha, as much as you can understand anything. This is not bread to be wolfed down like a starving animal. This is an artifact. When you swallow it, it will settle in your stomach and harden into a cyst, a sort of stone that will remain there for as long as you live. Then, whenever we travel between planes or dwell on a plane where you could not otherwise survive, you will say a little rhyme that I shall teach you and yawn mightily at its end. The cyst will release an armor that will cover you completely to keep you alive."

"You will compleat me?"

Urza glowered. Xantcha felt him pursuing her thoughts, her suspicions about the cyst. He rummaged through her memories, yanking on them as if they were the loose ends of a stubborn knot. Did he believe Orman'huzra knew nothing about artifacts? She retreated into her private self.

He sensed her escape. She saw the questions and displeasure on his face. Urza wasn't flesh, no more than Gix, but he had the habits of flesh and all the subtlety of a freshly decanted newt.

"Like a rabbit flees into the brush," he said, and looked beyond the chamber. Tears leaked from Urza's eyes, especially his left eye. Then he shuddered, and the tear tracks vanished. "No, I don't compleat. That is abomination. My artifact will be inside you, because that is the best place for it, but is a tool, nothing more and never a part of you. Never! I cannot erase the memories of Phyrexia from your mind—and would not, because they will prove useful to my vengeance—but you are no longer Phyrexian, and you must not think of Phyrexian abominations."

"Artifacts are tools," she recited as she would have once recited to the teacher-priests. A tool that she would swallow, that would remain in her belly forever but without becoming a part of her. It wasn't reasonable, but reason wasn't important to a Phyrexian, and she would be Phyrexian forever.

Urza let the lump flow into her hand. It was cold and clinging. Xantcha's stomach churned in protest. Gagging, she lost her grip on Urza's sleeve and nearly dropped the artifact as well.

"Swallow it whole. Don't chew on it!"

"Waste not, want not," Xantcha muttered. "Waste not, want not."

She raised her hand to her mouth and nearly fainted. She tried again, breathing out as she raised her hand. The artifact quivered and darkened. Then she closed her eyes and slurped it down without inhaling. It stuck in her throat. She slapped her hands over her lips, fighting the instinct to spit the lump across the chamber.

For something that was only a tool, Urza's artifact felt alive as it oozed down Xantcha's throat, got comfortable in her gut, and hardened into a stone. She was on her knees, banging her forehead on the floor when the horrifying process finally stopped.

"See? All over. Nothing to it."

She rested her head on the floor another moment before pushing herself upright.

"I'm ready."

Her voice felt different. The artifact had deposited a trail as it had moved down her throat. It still clung to her teeth and tongue. She coughed into her hand and studied drops of spittle that glistened briefly then turned to white powder. Urza taught her the rhyme that would release the cyst's power. Pressure built in her gut as she repeated it. The yawn that followed was involuntary, and the sensation of an oily liquid surging from within, covering her completely within two heartbeats, would have driven her to hysteria if it had lasted for a third.

Urza clutched her wrists. The cyst's liquid—her armor—tingled. He began to fade and, looking down, Xantcha saw herself fading as well.

She'd barely begun to scream when her substance was restored, covered by clothing less fine than Urza's, but finer than the rags she'd known all her life. Tempted to fondle the dark blue sleeve, she discovered it was illusion, visible but intangible.

"Later," Urza assured her. "Not long. I won't have a naked companion. Look upon this . . . Tell me: Have you ever seen its like before?"

Xantcha gathered her wits. They stood on a bare-rock plain. The sky was a cloudless pale blue; light came from an intensely white sun-star so high overhead that she thought she should have been hot and sweating. Yet the plain was cold, the wind colder. She could hear the wind and see the dust it raised. When she thought about it, Xantcha wasn't at all sure how she knew it was cold. With Urza's armor surrounding her, she felt nothing against her skin. The sensation, or lack of sensation, so intrigued her that Urza had to clear his throat twice before she saw the dragon.

"With that," he said, pride evident in his voice, "I shall destroy Phyrexia."

The dragon was dead black in the sunlight. Xantcha walked closer until she was certain that it was, indeed, made from a metal, though even when she touched a pillar-like hind leg, she couldn't say which metal. It was bipedal in structure, and her head came barely to its bent knees. Its torso, as yet unfinished, was a maze of tanks and tubes.

"Naphtha," Urza explained before she asked her question. "Phyrexians, the Phyrexians I mean to destroy, are sleeked with oil. They burn."

Xantcha nodded, recalling the Fourth Sphere lakes of slag and naphtha and the screams that sometimes arose from them. Scaffolding struts extruded from the dragon's counterbalancing tail. She seized one. Urza warned her to be careful; she had no intention of being anything else, but he'd asked a question and she meant to give him an honest answer.

The cyst-made armor moved with her however Xantcha contorted herself, even hanging by one knee to get a better look at the claws on the dragon's somewhat short arms. If its arms were short, its teeth were long and varied: sharp spikes, razor-edge wedges, rasps, and crushing anvils, all cunningly geared so that whoever sat in the Urza-sized gap between the dragon's shoulders could bring his best metal weapons to bear on a particular enemy—if a gout of flaming naphtha proved insufficient to destroy them.

More unfinished scaffolding rose above and behind the dragon's shoulders: protection, she guessed, for Urza, but possibly he intended to finish his engine with wings. She judged it little more than half finished and already heavier than anything she'd seen on the First Sphere. Perhaps he'd concocted a more potent fuel than glistening oil. Xantcha finished her exploration without finding the source of the engine's power.

After dangling from the dragon's forearm, Xantcha dropped three or four times her height. She was out of practice, hitting her chin on her knee as she absorbed the impact. Her lip should have been a bloody mess. She was pleasantly impressed with Urza's gift, but as for his dragon . . .

"If you had a hundred of them—" Her voice was definitely thicker, deeper, and distant-sounding to her armor-plugged ears. "You could take one of the Fanes and hold it against the demons, but not against the Ineffable."

"You don't appreciate what this is, Xantcha. I have built a dragon ten times stronger than anything Mishra or I had during our misbegotten war. When it is finished, not even the Thran could stand against it."

Xantcha shrugged. She didn't know the Thran. "It will have to be very powerful, then, when it is finished."

"You have been blinded, Xantcha, by what they did to you, by what you can't remember, but they are not as powerful as they've made you believe. When my dragon is finished—when I've found the rest of what I need—"

"Found?" Her scavenging curiosity had been aroused. "You found this? You did not make it, as you made the bread and tool?"

"I found the materials, Xantcha, and I shaped them to my needs. To make a dragon like this, to make it as I made your bread . . . even for me it would be exhausting, and in the end—" Urza lowered his voice—"not quite real."

Xantcha cocked her head.

"That bread filled your stomach and was nutritious. It would keep you alive, but you wouldn't thrive on it—at least, I don't think you would. When I was a man, I could not have thrived on it. Things that are made, whether they are made from nothing or something else, no matter how well made they are, aren't quite real. It's easier—better—to start with something similar to what you want to have at the end and change it, little by little."

"Compleat it?"

"Yes—" Urza began, then stopped suddenly and stared harshly at her, eyes a-shimmer. "No. Compleation is a Phyrexian taint. Do not use that word. Only artifacts can be made. Everything else must be born, must live and grow."

Xantcha studied her companion with equal intensity, though her eyes, of course, could not sparkle. "We were taught that the Ineffable made Phyrexia."

"Lies, Xantcha. They told you lies."

"I was told many lies," she agreed.

Urza took her wrists again.

"Until now," he said. "I have dwelt here beside my greatest artifact, but now that I have taken charge of you, I will have to have a dwelling in a more hospitable place. It is no great inconvenience. For every hospitable plane there are several out-of-the-way planes such as this. While these plains have supplied me with the ores I needed for my dragon's bones, they aren't where powerstones are to be found."

Xantcha had started to ask what a powerstone was when her armor began to tingle and Urza began to grow transparent in the stark sunlight. They were underway before Xantcha could ask where they were going, and though she'd already guessed that her image for a world was the same as Urza's image for a plane, getting dragged from one world to the next with his hands clamped around her wrists was worse than sinking through the ambulators.

Whether her eyes were open or closed, Xantcha saw the same many-colored streaks whirling around her. Every sense, every perception was stretched to its opposite extreme and held there for what might have been a single moment or might have been eternity. The silence was deafening, the cold so intense she feared she'd melt, the viselike pressure so great she feared she'd explode. And, to complete the experience, when Urza finally released Xantcha, her clinging armor transformed abruptly into a layer of white paste.

Pushed past her limit, Xantcha gave into the panic and terror, clawing the residue as she ran blindly away from Urza. She tripped, as was inevitable, and fell hard enough to knock the wind from her. Urza knelt and touched her. The armor residue was gone in an instant.

"I tested it on myself," he explained. He helped her to her feet and laid his hands on her scrapes and bruises, healing them with gentle heat.

Xantcha had endured much in her unmeasured life, none of it gentle. She pulled away when she could and realized he'd brought her back to the place where she'd been beaten. Parting her lips, she tasted the air; the tang of glistening oil was faint, stale.

"They're gone," she said.

"And not long after I rescued you. The locals would not know the Phyrexians had ever been here. I would not have known, if I had not found them first. This is the place, the very place, where they brought you and where the last of them stood before leaving."

Urza scuffed the ground with his boot. There was nothing visibly different, but movement released the scent of glistening oil to the air.

"It is a familiar place for you, isn't it? You lived here, found food here. Conquer your nightmares, Xantcha. The Phyrexians will not return. They are cowards, Xantcha; they only prey upon the weak. They grasped my brother, but they never came to me. They know me, Xantcha, and they will not return. This will be the place where you can dwell while I complete my dragon, the place where you can layout your wretched memories for my understanding."

Xantcha tried to understand her new companion and failed. He was wrong, simply wrong, about so many things, yet he had the power to walk between worlds. No Phyrexian, not even a demon like Gix, could do that. Urza did not give orders, not in a Phyrexian sense. Still, Xantcha had no alternative but to obey him as she'd obeyed Gix, silently and without grace. She started up the path to the caves.

"Where are you going?"

Let him haul her back; he had that power. Or let him follow, which he did.

The cave was sealed, of course, and carefully, with stones, dirt, and plant life. The locals, as Urza had called them, wouldn't know the treasures of their ancestors had been plundered, but Xantcha knew. She began pulling weeds and hurling dirt with her bare hands.

Urza intervened. "Child, what are you doing?"

"I'm not a child," she reminded him. "They brought me here to extract an army. If it's gone, then you may be right that no Phyrexian will return. If it's not . . ." Xantcha went back to work.

"You'll be digging forever," Urza pulled her aside. "There are better ways."

For a moment, Urza stood stock-still with his eyes closed. When he opened them, they blazed with crimson light. A swirling cloud, about twice his height, bloomed in the air before the cave's sealed mouth. He spoke a single word whose meaning, if it had any, Xantcha didn't know, and the cloud rooted itself where she had been digging.

Fascinated, Xantcha attempted to put her hand in the small, bright windstorm. Urza touched her arm, and she could not move.

"We will come back tomorrow and see what is to be seen. Meanwhile, we will find food—it has been too long since I have enjoyed a meal—and you will begin telling me everything you remember."

Urza took Xantcha's wrists and pulled her into the between-worlds before she could recite her armor-releasing rhyme. The journey lasted less than a heartbeat, less than an airless breath. They emerged in what Urza called a *town*, where Xantcha found herself surrounded by born-folk: all flesh, like her, all different, too, and chattering a language she couldn't understand. He took her to an *inn*, gave orders in the born-folk language, told her to sit in a *chair* as he did, to drink from a *cup* and to use a *knife* and *fork* rather than her fingers when she ate.

It was difficult, but Urza was adamant. Xantcha ate until the knife, at least, was comfortable in her hands.

Later, there was music, exactly as Xantcha had dreamed it would be, and dancing which she would have joined if Urza had not said:

"Too soon, child. Your eyes are open, but you do not truly see."

When the music and dancing had ended, Urza led her from the inn to the night and through the between-worlds to the forest. He was gone when Xantcha awoke, long after sunrise. The scent of glistening oil was stronger, wafting down from the cave. She remembered the knife and wished she still had it in her hand, even though it would have been useless against a Phyrexian . . . or Urza.

Urza was inside the cave, and so were most of the artifacts. Tiptoeing to the brink of an excavation trench, Xantcha watched Urza dismantle one of the insect warriors. He was faster and more powerful. When its mandible claws closed over his ankle, they shattered. Antennae whips burned and melted when they touched his face.

Perhaps one dragon would be enough, if it was Urza's dragon, with Urza sitting between its shoulders.

Xantcha cleared her throat. "They're coming back. They wouldn't have left all this behind. Waste not, want not, that's our way."

Urza leapt into the air and hovered in front of her. "The Phyrexian way is not your way, Xantcha, not anymore, but otherwise, yes, I believe you're right. I'm ready for them tomorrow, though let us hope it isn't so soon. With time to study these automata, I'll be more than ready for them, Xantcha. These could almost be Thran design. They're pure artifice, no sentience at all, but perfectly adaptive. Look!" He held up a pearlescent ring. "A powerstone that isn't a powerstone. There is water in here, light, and simple mana, the essence of all things. I shall call it *phloton*, because it burns without consuming itself. It will give me power for my dragon! More power than I ever dreamed! I shall redesign it!

"Vengeance, Xantcha. I shall take vengeance for both of us. When the Phyrexians return, I will destroy them and pursue them all the way back to Phyrexia itself."

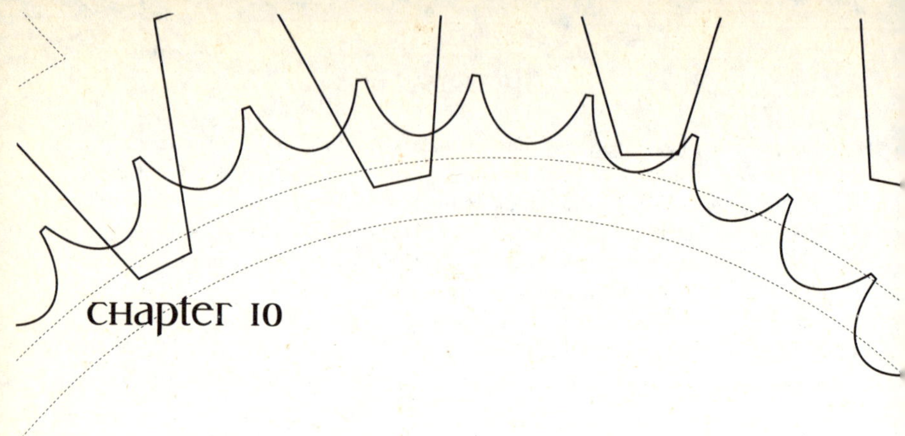

chapter 10

Urza got his wish. The Phyrexians didn't return to the cave the next day, or the next after that. Seasons passed, and years. He dismantled the insect warriors, incorporating their parts into his redesigned dragon, linking their ring-shaped hearts into a single great power source.

Ten years passed, ten *Dominarian* years, according to Urza who claimed his attachment to his birth-world remained so strong that at any time he knew the sun's angle and the moon's phase above the cave he called Koilos, the Secret Heart.

"Come," Urza said one winter morning when Xantcha would have preferred to remain in her nest of pillows and blankets. "It is finished."

He held out his hand and, with a rhyme and a yawn, Xantcha clasped it. No more screaming through the between-worlds. She'd mastered her fears and the cyst in her stomach. Although she dwelt mostly in the forest where the Phyrexian portal had been laid out and where a cottage with a chicken coop and garden now stood Urza had insisted that she accompany him to every new world he discovered. Her nose for Phyrexians was indisputably better than his.

There were no Phyrexians on the world where Urza had built and rebuilt his dragon. There was no life at all and never had been. Urza's new dragon wasn't much taller than the old one, but he'd borrowed from the insect-warriors. The new dragon had a spider's eight-legged body. Any two of the eight legs could be the "front" legs, and any three could be destroyed without unbalancing it.

The many-toothed head remained from the dragon's previous

incarnation, but the short arms had been lengthened, and the torso rotated freely behind whichever pair of legs led the rest. In addition to gouts of blazing naphtha, the new dragon spat lightning bolts and spheres of exploding fire.

"Phloton," Urza said, rubbing his hands together. "Unlimited power!"

Urza demonstrated each weapon, and though Xantcha still thought a hundred lesser war machines would be more effective, she was awed by the destruction Urza's new dragon brought to the barren, defenseless world. The sky was streaked with soot and dust. Slag lakes of amber and crimson pocked the plains. Everything that wasn't molten had been charred. It reminded her of nothing more or less than Phyrexia's Fourth Sphere, and she didn't think even a demon could stand against it. There was only one not-so-small problem.

"It's too big. It won't fit through an ambulator."

"It won't need an ambulator. It can walk the planes directly. Even you could guide it safely."

"I wouldn't know where to go."

Xantcha had conquered her fears, but no matter how hard she tried, she couldn't orient herself in the between-worlds emptiness. Worlds—planes—didn't call out to her the way they called out to Urza. If she lost her grip on Urza's hand, she fell like a stone to whatever world would have her. Urza's armor kept her alive through one failure after another, until Urza conceded that she'd never 'walk the planes.

"You won't have to do anything at all," Urza assured her. "After I've used the ambulator once, I'll know where Phyrexia is, and I'll 'walk the dragon there. You'll wait, safe and snug, until I return. Now, watch!"

Between blinks, Urza shifted from beside Xantcha to the dragon's saddle-seat. It came to life. No, not life, Xantcha reminded herself, never life! The dragon was an artifact, the tool of Urza's vengeance against the abominations of Phyrexia. Never mind that its eyes went from dark to blazing or that a ground-shaking roar accompanied each lightning bolt. The dragon was merely a tool that took aim at an already blackened hill and reduced it to slag in less time than it would have taken Xantcha to eat her breakfast.

"Do you still have doubts?" Urza asked when he'd returned to her side.

"Mountains don't defend themselves."

Urza took her words for a jest. His laughter rang between-worlds as he whisked her back to the forest cottage.

With the dragon finished, there was little to do but wait for the Phyrexians to return, and for Urza, waiting was difficult. Though he'd long since pried every story she was willing to tell from her memory, he continued to quiz her. How high were the First Sphere mountains? Where were the Fanes, the arenas? Which priests were the most dangerous and where did they dwell? Were the iron wyverns solitary creatures or pack hunters? In the Fourth Sphere, were the furnaces clumped together or did each stand alone? And were the fumaroles wide enough to allow his dragon to descend directly to the interior, or would he have to dismantle Phyrexia like a puzzle box?

Worse than the questions were the nights, about one in four or five, when Urza closed his eyes. Urza's terrible dreams were too large for his mind. His ghosts walked the forest when he slept, recreating a silent drama of anger and betrayal. Xantcha had built the cottage to protect herself from his dreams, but no wall was thick enough to insulate her from his anguish.

Urza's call for vengeance was something a Phyrexian could understand. From the beginning Xantcha's life had been full of threats and reprisals, broken promises and humiliation, but Urza needed more than vengeance. When his nightmares reached their inevitable climax, he'd cry out for mercy and beg someone he called *Mishra* to forgive him.

Urza wouldn't talk about his nightmares, which got worse once the dragon was complete. He wouldn't answer Xantcha's questions about the ghosts or their world or, especially, about *Mishra*, except to say the Phyrexians would pay for what they'd done to Mishra, or through Mishra—Xantcha couldn't be sure which. Whenever she dared mention the nightmare name, Urza would fly into a bleak rage. Ten or twelve days might pass without a word, without even a gesture. Then, without warning, he'd rouse from his stupor, and the questions would begin again.

Xantcha began to look forward to the times when restlessness got the better of Urza and he'd head off between-worlds, still hoping to stumble across Phyrexia, or an excavation team with its precious ambulators. He'd be gone for a month, even a season, and her life would be her own.

Long before the dragon was finished, Xantcha had learned how to control the substance that emerged from her cyst and expand it into a buoyant sphere instead of the clinging armor Urza had intended. Seated in the sphere, she'd traveled an irregular circuit of the hamlets and farms surrounding the forest, learning the local dialects and trading with women who accepted her claim that she lived with "an old man of the forest."

She still visited the local women, albeit carefully, lest they notice that she wasn't growing older the way they were, but with Urza gone for longer periods of time Xantcha gradually expanded her horizons. She was, after all, following Urza's orders. He didn't want her to remain near the cave while he was gone. Urza reasoned that Phyrexians might take her by surprise, extract his secrets from her empty mind, then ambush him when he returned. He designed an artifact that was attuned to his eyes. Though small enough to be worn as a sparkling pendant, the artifact could send a signal between-worlds.

"Come back frequently," he'd told Xantcha when he hung the jewel around her neck. "If they've returned, hide yourself far, far away from here, then break the crystal and I will return for my—for our—vengeance. Above all, once you've seen a Phyrexian, stay away from the forest until I come for you. Don't let your curiosity lead you into foolishness. If they find you, they will reclaim you, and you will betray me. You wouldn't want that to happen."

Twelve winters, twelve summers, and Urza still spoke to her as if she couldn't think for herself or hear through his lies. She swore she'd do as he asked. Whatever his reasons were, Xantcha didn't want to come face-to-face with anything Phyrexian, even though she suspected Urza wouldn't come back for her after he dealt with Phyrexia.

Urza's demands weren't a burden. The chaos and subtleties of born-folk societies fascinated her. Giving herself to the world's wind, Xantcha explored whatever struck her curiosity, so long as it didn't reek of Phyrexia's glistening oil. She learned to speak the born-folk languages, to read their writing, when it existed. The warrior-cave had a hundred different names, all of them archaic, all of them curses. In the world's larger towns, where more folk knew their history, she discovered it was better to invent a completely false history for herself than to admit she had roots near the warrior-cave.

After a few narrow escapes and near disasters, Xantcha decided that it was better to disguise herself as well. Born-folk had definite notion about the proper places of young men and women in their societies, and no place at all for a newt who was neither. An incorrigible lad, a rogue in the making, was an easier disguise than a young woman. At best when she wore a young woman's clothes, good-intentioned folk wanted to swallow her into their families. At worst . . . at worst, she'd been lucky to escape with her life. But Xantcha did escape and, hardened by Phyrexia, there was nothing in a born-folks' world that daunted her for long.

The forest world had one moon, which went from full to new to full again in thirty-six days. The born-folk marked time by their moon's phases, and Xantcha did, too, returning to the cave twice each month. Sometimes there was a message from Urza in the ruins of the neglected cottage. Sometimes he was there himself, waiting for her, eager to whisk her between-worlds to witness his latest accomplishment or discovery.

Urza had no one else. Although he said there were others who could walk between planes, he avoided them and born-folk alike. Without Xantcha, there were only ghosts to break his silence. If anything would lure Urza back to her after Phyrexia, Xantcha expected it would be loneliness.

She pitied Urza; it seemed he'd lost more to his nightmares than he believed she'd lost to the Phyrexians. His artifact pendant was her most precious possession, a constant reminder that never left her neck. Yet, she was always a little relieved when she found the forest deserted, and except for one nagging worry, she would not have mourned the loss if Urza never reappeared in her life.

The worry was her heart, the lump Xantcha had held in her hand when the vat-priests decanted her, the lump they'd taken from her moments later, as they took it from every other newt. It had slipped through her memory sometime after she'd become a dodger, but it resurfaced when she encountered the Trien.

The Trien believed that their hearts could hold only so many misdeeds before they burst and consigned them to hell. To defend against eternal torment, the Trien purged their hearts of error through bloodletting and guilt dances. Urza had no more blood within him than a compleated Phyrexian, but she'd thought the guilt dance might defeat his nightmares, so she danced with the Trien—to test her theory—and in the midst of hysteria and ecstasy she'd remembered her own heart.

Xantcha tried to convince herself that the tale the vat-priests had told her was merely another of their countless lies. Her heart hadn't been very big, and no matter who might have done the counting, her or the Ineffable, she'd made a lot of mistakes that hadn't killed her. But Xantcha had never been particularly persuasive, not with Urza nor with herself. For the first time Xantcha's dreams were filled with her own ghosts: newts and priests, a plundered wind-crystal of music and beauty, insect warriors with baleful eyes, and even Gix as the other demons shoved him through the Fourth Sphere fumarole.

Worse than dreams, Xantcha began to worry what would happen if Urza succeeded, and all Phyrexia, including the heart vault beneath the Fane of Flesh, were destroyed.

She conquered her nightmares and worries; obsession wasn't part of her nature. Still, when the time came, after nearly two hundred summers of waiting, that Xantcha found diggers, bearers, and a handful of gremlin dodgers in the forest cave, she didn't retreat before breaking Urza's crystal artifact.

Urza arrived with his dragon less than a day later and caught the Phyrexians by surprise. From her bolt-hole in the hill above the warriors' cave, Xantcha heard the gremlins screaming and counted the flashes as the diggers and bearers exploded.

A handful of diggers made a stand in front of the cave. Urza toyed with them, tossing each again and again before crushing it. It was a display worthy of Phyrexia in its cruelty and single-minded arrogance. Xantcha couldn't watch. She looked away and saw, to her horror, a searcher-priest not ten paces away. She thought it was hiding, though it was difficult to imagine any compleat Phyrexian seeking shelter among living trees and animals.

Then insight struck. The searcher was fulfilling its destiny, watching an artifact Phyrexia would surely covet. Xantcha couldn't guess whether the priest had seen her before she saw it, but a moment later it began to run toward the ambulator, which it could—if it had the time and thought quickly enough—unanchor and suck to Phyrexia behind it.

Xantcha had no means to tell Urza that he was in danger of losing his way to Phyrexia and no reason to think she could stop the searcher-priest or even that she could catch it before it reached the ambulator, but if it paused to unanchor the nether end, she hoped she could delay it until Urza arrived. After a mnemonic yawn, she abandoned her bolt-hole.

The searcher-priest had no intention of unanchoring the ambulator's nether end or even slowing down. It had a score of strides on Xantcha when its brass foot touched the black circle. With its second step, it crossed the midpoint and sank between-worlds. *Too fast. Too fast,* memory warned from the back of Xantcha's mind; the priests had told them to enter the ambulators slowly, lest they get caught between two worlds.

Expecting an explosion, Xantcha skidded off the trail and hid behind the largest tree she saw. There was no explosion, but when she poked her head around the tree trunk fire rippled across the ambulator disk's surface. She had no idea if the priest had survived. For that matter, Xantcha didn't know if the ambulator had survived.

Urza wouldn't welcome the sight of her, not when he'd told her to stay far away, but Xantcha thought it best to warn him. She stepped in front of the dragon when it burnt a path through the trees. Urza shot flame to the left of her and flame to the right. Xantcha ran until she was breathless, then circled back. The dragon sat beside the ambulator; the saddle-seat between its shoulders was empty.

Urza had gone to Phyrexia alone.

Xantcha settled down to wait. Morning became afternoon. The sky darkened, and the dragon's eyes shone red.

Urza returned, not through the ambulator but in a blaze of lightning, and Xantcha did nothing to attract his attention as he remounted the dragon. Moments later they were gone.

The storm ended quickly. The ambulator beckoned. It wasn't broken. For the last rime, Xantcha asked herself:

Was her heart important enough to risk everything to rescue it?

The priests lied about so many things; only a fool could believe they hadn't lied about newt hearts. Try as she might, Xantcha couldn't remember exactly what hers had looked like; mottled amber, perhaps, with bright rainbow inclusions. She'd only seen it that once and never seen another.

Only a fool . . .

And she was a fool.

On hands and knees, Xantcha crept up to the ambulator and was surprised to discover that the searchers had left the prime end in the forest.

She began unanchoring it, careful not to disturb the hard panel where seven jet-black jewels were set in a silver matrix. When the ambulator was loose and rippling, Xantcha yawned. There was a single sharp pain in her gut as the cyst contracted—drawing the armor out twice in a single day wasn't what Urza had in mind when he made the cyst, but she could do it five times, at least, before the process failed. The not-quite liquid flowed beneath her clothes.

She stepped into the unanchored ambulator. It swirled around her, not unlike the armor itself. By the time she'd reached the middle, the black disk had shrunk to half its size and risen to her waist. Xantcha had repressed how much she disliked the ambulators. The sinking and suffocating was worse than following Urza between-worlds, and the cyst made the passage worse. It swelled in her gut; she thought she might explode before her head emerged in Phyrexia.

Because she'd unanchored the prime end in the forest, the nether end in Phyrexia was also loose and shrank as Xantcha emerged. Any Phyrexian would have been suspicious of a newt who rolled up an ambulator behind it. The avengers that normally guarded the Fourth Sphere field, where scores of ambulators were anchored, would have annihilated her on sight, if there had been any left standing. Xantcha assumed that Urza had annihilated them as he emerged; at least, something had.

Waste not, want not, the Fourth Sphere was even uglier than she remembered with acrid air and oily ash drizzling from the soot clouds overhead. The roar of a thousand furnaces was less a sound than a presence, a vise tightened over her ribs. The hollow where the ambulator had been anchored was bright with bilious yellows, noxious greens, and an iridescent purple that was the very color of disease. Nothing was alive, of course; it was just filthy oil, slicked over an eon of detritus not fit for even the furnaces.

There wasn't a living Phyrexian, newt or otherwise, in sight. Grateful, but suspicious of her good fortune, Xantcha retrieved the glossy disk from beneath her feet: the rolled-up ambulator. Holding it by its flexible rim, she twisted her wrists in opposite directions. The disk rippled and shrank until it was scarcely larger than her palm, with the jewels protruding on both sides.

After tucking the ambulator between her belt and her armor, Xantcha took her bearings. There was no sun-star for Phyrexia, especially not here, in the Fourth Sphere. Away from the furnaces, light came harsh, constant and without shadows. But the place was home, or it had been, and it came back to her.

A few strides up the greasy slope, the horizon expanded and Xantcha saw why her return to Phyrexia had been so easy: straight ahead, in the direction of the Fane of Flesh, the soot clouds had turned red and fire fell from the sky.

Urza? Xantcha asked herself and decided it was possible that Urza was burning his way through Phyrexia. The ambulators could be anchored anywhere. Once unrolled, they were tunnels, direct passages from one specific place to another, no detours allowed, but a 'walker made his own path here, there and everywhere. Urza could change his mind between-worlds, but whenever, wherever, he ended his 'walk, he stood on a world's surface. In Phyrexia, the surface was the First Sphere.

When she'd dwelt in Phyrexia, before she'd known the meaning of *silence*, Xantcha had been able to ignore the furnace roar. She reached within herself to remember the trick and realized she'd been gone from Phyrexia several times longer than she'd been a part of it. But the memory was there. Xantcha numbed herself to the ambient rumbling and heard the clanging alarms.

She smiled. Those alarms were struck when a furnace was about to blow. Every Phyrexian had an emergency place, and for newts that place was the Fane of Flesh, precisely where she wanted to go. Of course, the emergency wasn't a furnace, and the closer she got to the sprawled hulks of furnaces, fanes, and gremlin shanties, the clearer it was that in the absence of the expected disaster, panic had replaced plan.

Priests and other compleated types that Xantcha didn't remember, and possibly had never seen, raced through gremlin town. Their voices were shrill enough to hurt. The challenge was staying out of their way; the shambles were already littered with gremlins who'd failed.

Urza's armor protected Xantcha from the sky; her sense of purpose did the rest. The Fane of Flesh wasn't the most impressive structure in the Fourth Sphere, but it stood near the glistening oil fountain, which had become a spire of blue-white flame.

A phalanx of demons made their appearance while Xantcha threaded her way through the maze of furnaces. Narrow beams of amber and orange shot upward from their torsos, into the reddest clouds. Urza answered with lightning. In the Fourth Sphere's filthy skies, the air itself ignited and a web of fire shot to every part of the horizon. Xantcha felt the heat through her armor. Her instinct was to run, but ash quickly followed the fire, and the Fourth Sphere went dark.

For a moment, flesh had the advantage over metal, at least flesh protected by Urza's armor. Neither ash nor smoke irritated Xantcha's eyes, and with a bit of effort she could see a body's length in front of her. As in the gremlin town alleys, the danger came from the panicked and the fallen: no one paid any attention to a stray newt, assuming they could see her.

Then the demons regrouped. A low humming sound began in the distance, followed by a cold wind that scoured the air. As it passed overhead, Xantcha looked up and saw the bottom of the Third Sphere, a sight she'd never seen before. She saw the flames, too, where Urza had burnt through the outer spheres. Another few moments and Xantcha might have seen Urza's dragon, if she hadn't started to run for the Fane.

The rusty doors on the far side of the Glistening Fountain were wide open as Xantcha entered the plaza where newts were compleated. She was in the final sprint for the Fane, when a vast shadow moved overhead. The last time Xantcha had seen Urza's new dragon, she hadn't noticed any wing struts and had assumed the artifact had grown too heavy for flight. She'd assumed incorrectly. Six of the dragon's eight legs supported wings that dwarfed the rest of its body and yet were highly flexible and maneuverable. The dragon swooped sideways to avoid a demon-flung bolt while belching a tongue of flame.

A furnace exploded. Metal shards and slag traced brilliant arcs beneath the Third Sphere ceiling. Impressed by beauty that was also terrifying and deadly, Xantcha considered the possibility that Urza would win. Then a tree-sized clot of slag crashed into the plaza. The flames of the Glistening Fountain sputtered and died while yellow fumes rose from the new crater beside it. Unless Xantcha wanted to die with Phyrexia, she had to find her heart and unroll the ambulator while there was still a solid place left to support the prime end.

Xantcha finished her run with no further distractions.

"Down! Go down!" a jittery vat-priest insisted as soon as she cleared the open doors. "Newts go down!" Its hooks and paddles clattered against each other as it indicated a deserted corridor.

The priests weren't flesh, but they weren't mindless artifacts, either. They might lack sufficient imagination to disobey a fatal command, but they had enough to be afraid.

"I go," Xantcha replied, the first time she'd spoken Phyrexian in centuries. She bungled the pronunciation; the priest didn't seem to notice.

She'd forgotten how big the Fane was. Maybe she'd never noticed; she'd never gone anywhere within it without a cadre of other newts and priests surrounding her. One corridor was as good as another when she had no idea where her heart might be, and the one the vat-priest had pointed toward was the broadest and best lit. She read the glyph inscriptions on the walls, hoping they would provide a clue, but they were only exhortations, lies, and empty promises, like everything else in Phyrexia.

The Fane of Flesh was quieter, cleaner than anything beyond its precincts. Its walls had, so far, resisted the outside flames. But it had taken damage. Turning a corner, Xantcha came upon a pile of rubble from a collapsed ceiling and a defunct vat-priest crushed beneath it. She wrenched one of the priest's long hooks from its shoulder socket and kept going.

A teacher-priest waited at another corner. Its eyes were flesh within a flat, bronze mask. They darted between the hook, Xantcha's face, her boots and her belt. "Newt?" it asked.

Xantcha had taken the hook as a weapon, but the priest assumed it was part of her, that it and her leather garments, were evidence that she'd begun her compleation.

"The hearts. Where are the hearts? I am sent to guard the hearts."

Flesh eyes blinked stupidly. "Hearts? What matter the hearts?"

"We are attacked; they are the future. I am sent to guard them."

"Who sent you?" it asked after another moment's hesitation.

"A demon," Xantcha replied. Small lies weren't worth the effort of defending them. "Where are the hearts?"

The teacher-priest continued to blink. Xantcha feared it didn't know where the hearts were stored, not a confession one priest would want to make to another, especially another under a demon's command. It asked, "Which demon?" as thunder waves pummeled the Fane and rust rained from the ceiling.

Xantcha had no time to wonder whether the strike was for Urza or against him. Gix was dead, thrust through a fumarole centuries ago. Still, any answer was better than none.

"The Great Gix sent me."

Her bluff worked. The teacher-priest just needed a name. It quaked as it gave her detailed directions to a vault so far beneath the Fourth Sphere floor it might actually have been on the Fifth. More blasts shook the Fane. A stairway she was supposed to use was clogged with debris and the scent of fire.

"I'll have to tell Urza that he's wrong," Xantcha complained as she put her hand on the portal artifact tucked beneath her belt. "I wouldn't be standing here, waiting to die, if I didn't have some damn fool useless imagination."

She could have gotten out. The corridor was wide enough to unroll the portal. She'd be back in the forest. Safe. Or not safe. Ambulators could only be rolled up from their prime end. If she left the ambulator's prime end here in the corridor and the Fane collapsed, the rubble might follow her to the forest . . . all of Phyrexia might follow her.

Waste not, want not! I never thought of that.

When she used the ambulator to escape, it would be a three-step process: first to the forest to anchor the nether end, back to Phyrexia to loosen the prime, and then another passage back to the forest. Timing had become even more critical.

Xantcha looked around for an intact stairway. She found one and found the vault, too. Measured by the world she'd left, Xantcha guessed she'd spent a morning in Phyrexia. Looking down at the mass of softly glowing hearts, she guessed it might take a lifetime to find her own.

The Ineffable's plan for Phyrexia was precise, even rigid, but the plan didn't cover every contingency. Vat-priests dutifully brought newt hearts to the vault, then simply heaved the little stones into a pit, one for every newt ever decanted. At the surface the pit was about twice the size of an unrolled ambulator. When she thrust the vat-priest's hook into the chaos, it went in all the way to the shoulder gears without striking anything solid.

The pit seethed. Countless glowing amber fists and a smaller number of dark ones were vibrating constantly against one another. On her knees, Xantcha could hear a steady chorus of sighs and gasps. She wondered about the dark ones and got lucky. She heard a pop! right in front of her, then watched as a glowing heart brightened, then went dark.

Death?

Phyrexians were dying in Urza's assault. Were their hearts, long detached from their compleated bodies, going dark as they did? Xantcha retrieved the newly darkened stone with the vat-priest's hook. Tiny scratches marred its surface: marks left as the heart stone clattered against its companions or a record of errors made by the Ineffable? She read the glyphs on the walls. They repeated the familiar teacher-priest lies.

Xantcha picked up a glowing stone. Its warmth and subtlety was tangible even through Urza's armor. She picked up a second glowing heart and found it just as warm, just as subtle, yet also different. But every dark stone felt as inert as the first she had touched.

The teacher-priests might not have told the whole truth, but they'd told enough. There was a vital bond between Phyrexians and their detached hearts. She hadn't been a total fool. There was good reason to rescue the stone she'd carried out of the vats.

And precious little hope of finding it among all the others.

Tears of frustration rolled down Xantcha's armored cheeks. They fumed when they landed on the glowing stones cradled in her lap. Another shudder rocked the Fane. When it ended, a score of hearts had popped and dimmed. More Phyrexian deaths to Urza's credit, but imagine what his dragon engine could do if Urza brought its weapons to bear where Xantcha sat. Imagine what she could do. The hearts weren't so hard that she couldn't break them, and if her tears could make the stones fume, what might her blood do if she chose to sacrifice herself for vengeance?

She'd been willing to die for much less before Urza rescued her, but she'd come to the Fane of Flesh because she wanted to live. Choices and questions, all of them morbid, paralyzed Xantcha at the edge of the pit, and then she heard laughter. She scrambled to her feet, scattering hearts, crushing them in her frantic clumsiness. There was no one behind her. The laughter hadn't come from the corridor, it came from within . . . within her mind and within her heart.

Throwing the hook aside, Xantcha waded in the pit, sweeping her open hands in front of her, moving toward the laughter. She found what she was looking for not far below the surface, neither in the middle nor at the pit's edge. There was nothing to distinguish it from any other heart stone—a few scratches, but no more than any other stone she'd touched, glowing or dark. Yet it was hers; it had to be hers: Urza's armor absorbed it as it lay in her hand.

Another burst of popping hearts interrupted Xantcha's reverie. A hundred, perhaps several hundred, Phyrexians had died since she entered the vault, and the chamber was as bright as it had been when she entered. Xantcha tried to calculate how many glowing hearts lay on the surface, how many more might lay beneath. She gave up after a few attempts, but not before she'd decided that unless she told Urza about the heart vault, it would be a very long battle before he achieved vengeance.

Her heart was too big to swallow, too risky to carry in her hand. Xantcha tucked it carefully inside her boot before she headed off.

Finding her way out of the Fane was harder than finding Urza. Flames, smoke and sorcery ratcheted through one-quarter of what passed for the Fourth Sphere sky. While she'd been looking for her heart, the demons had mounted a counterattack.

Urza's hulking dragon was surrounded by Phyrexia's smaller defenders: dragons, wyverns and whatever else had been summoned from the First Sphere through the very hole Urza had burnt for himself. As she'd warned him, individually Phyrexia had nothing that could equal his devastating tool, but in Phyrexia, individuals weren't important. For every compleated priest, even for every scrap-made digger or bearer, there were twenty warriors: fleshless, obedient, and relentless. The demons aimed the warriors at Urza's dragon where they died by the score and occasionally did damage.

The dragon's wings were shredded and useless. Two of its legs had been disabled; a third burst into melting flames while Xantcha looked for a path through the Phyrexian lines. Urza could still defend himself in all quarters but if—when—he lost a fourth leg, there'd be gaps, and it wouldn't take imagination to exploit them.

You're lost! Xantcha shouted silently, adding an image of the vault of hearts. *There's a better way! 'Walk away now!* But though Urza could easily extract thoughts from her mind, she'd never been able to insert her thoughts into his.

There were hundreds of Phyrexians on the battlefield and even a few gremlins. All of them were in greater danger of being trampled by the relentless warriors than they were from anything in the dragon's arsenal, but their presence, a thin layer of chaos across the field, was Xantcha's best hope of getting to Urza.

Relying on Urza's armor to protect her from everything except her own stupidity, Xantcha dodged fire, lightning and the distortions of sorcery as she threaded her way through the Phyrexian circle. Once she came face to back with a demon. It was dark and asymmetric, with pincers on one arm and a six-fingered hand on the other, and it had eyes in several places, including the back of its head. Nothing like Gix, except for the malice and intelligence in its shiny red eyes. It studied her from boots to hair and vat-priest hook. Xantcha was sure it knew she wasn't what she was pretending to be, and equally sure Urza's armor wouldn't protect her from its wrath.

Just then a wyvern screamed, and the demon turned away.

A wall of sharp, noxious yellow crystals exploded from the ground between Xantcha and the demon. She staggered back and watched the demon uncoil like an angry serpent, writhing toward the dragon. Urza's armor protected Xantcha from flames and emptiness and corrosive vapors, too. She followed the wall of crystals as it extended across Phyrexia's Fourth Sphere toward Urza and his dragon. If Urza struck down the wall, Xantcha was meat. If he didn't, it would claim the fourth leg from his dragon.

But not before she swung up into the leg's scaffolding, climbing for her life and his.

Xantcha made an easy target, running across the dragon's back, but nothing attacked. The Phyrexians overhead didn't recognize her as an enemy, and Urza's attention was centered on the noxious wall. Xantcha fell hard when the leg collapsed. Worse, there was blood on her hands when she hauled herself back up. Either her armor was weakening, or Urza was.

She swung down between the dragon's shoulders expecting the worst.

Urza reclined in a wire-shrouded couch. Smoke rose from his charred trousers. The dragon's wounds were reflected on his body. Bruises, contusions—bleeding contusions—covered Urza's hands and face.

Xantcha had never seen Urza hurt. She'd assumed he could be destroyed. She hadn't imagined that he could be wounded. She stood, confused and useless, for several moments before she found the courage to touch his shoulder.

"Urza? Urza, it's time to 'walk away from here, if you can."

No response.

"Urza? Urza, can you hear me? It's me, Xantcha." She put some strength into her hand. The whole couch rocked a bit, but there was no response from Urza. He was still in control of the dragon, still fighting. As mindless as any of the wyverns, Urza had abandoned sentience and become the tool. "Listen to me, Urza! Vengeance is slipping away. You've got to leave now!"

Urza's eyes opened. They were horrible to behold. He started to say the one word that would have been more horrible to hear than his eyes were to see, but he didn't finish: "Yawg—"

The Ineffable. The name that must not be spoken. Xantcha knew it; they all knew it. It was with them in the vats. But Urza should not have known it. He'd never gotten anything out of Xantcha's mind that she had not been willing to give him, and she'd never have given him that.

Every instinct said *run, now, alone.* Xantcha resisted. Urza had rescued her when she'd had no hope. She wouldn't leave him behind.

Xantcha reached across the couch and took Urza's wrists as he so often took hers. She steeled her nerves and stared into his seething eyes. "Now, Urza. We've got to leave now. 'Walk us somewhere safe—to the cave where you took me. And leave . . . leave that name behind."

"Yawg—"

"Xantcha!" she screamed her own name at his face.

His hands grasped hers and her vision went black.

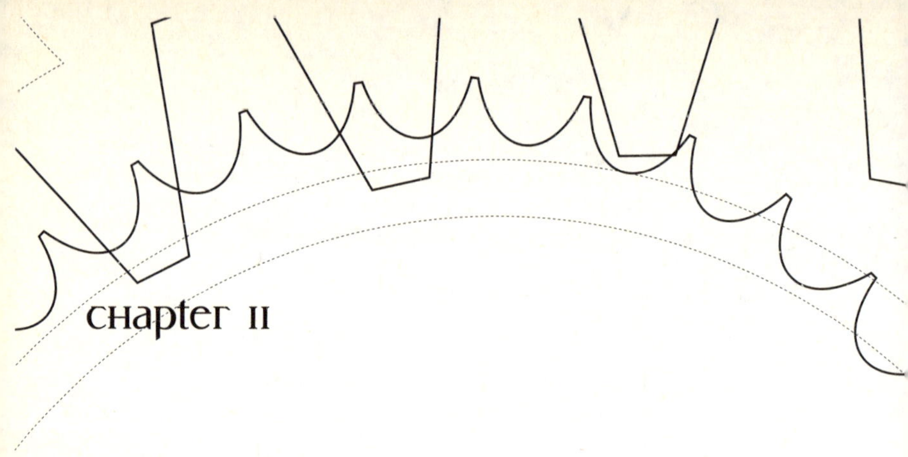

chapter 11

The supplies were stowed, safe against mist, mice, and anything else the changeable climate of Ohran Ridge might drop on the cottage. Xantcha had checked them twice during the interminable night. She'd made herself a pot of tea and drunk it all. The herbs should have helped her relax, but they hadn't. Dawn's golden light fell sideways on the bed where she hadn't slept.

Her door was wide open, inviting shadows. Urza's wasn't. It wasn't warded with layers of "leave me alone" sorcery, but it wasn't leaking sound. The sounds had stopped coming through the wall in the unmeasured hours after midnight. Ratepe, Xantcha had told herself, had probably fallen asleep, and Urza rarely made noise when he was alone. Nothing unusual. Nothing to worry about. So why had she opened her door? Why had she spent the last of the night damp and shivering? Hadn't Ratepe demonstrated, if not an ability to take care of himself, then an inclination to ignore her advice?

And hadn't Urza welcomed Ratepe more enthusiastically than she'd dare hope? Whatever had brought silence to the far side of the wall, it wouldn't have been murder. No matter how annoying Ratepe got, he'd survive.

Xantcha unwound her blankets. Her joints creaked. Phyrexia was easier on flesh and bone than the Ohran Ridge. She broke the ice in her washstand, cleared her head with a few breathtaking splashes, then went outside and listened at the door. She'd give them until midday. If Ratepe hadn't reappeared by then, Xantcha planned to take a chisel to the cottage's common wall. Before that, she had one more gambit to try and put her chisel to work on the hardened ashes underneath her outdoor hearth.

When the fire was just right Xantcha covered it with an iron grate and covered the grate with a rasher of bacon. A friendly breeze carried the aromas into the cottage. She never knew when or if Urza would be in a mood to eat, but if Ratepe was alive, he'd be out the door before the bacon burnt.

Right on schedule Ratepe appeared in the doorway. "By the book! That smells good." He didn't have the cross-grained look of a man who'd just awakened, and he said something—Xantcha couldn't hear what—over his shoulder before closing the door behind him. "I'm starving."

"I see you survived." Xantcha hadn't realized how angry she was until she heard her own voice. "Here, eat. Starting tomorrow, you can cook your own." On his own hearth, too. Xantcha wasn't sharing, at least not until she'd calmed down.

Ratepe had the sense to approach her cautiously. "You're angry about last night?"

Xantcha slammed hot, crisp bacon on a wooden platter and thrust it at him. She didn't know why she was so upset and didn't want to discuss the matter.

"I guess it got out of hand. When I saw him—Urza. He is Urza, the Urza, Urza the Artificer. You were right, you know. Back in Efuan Pincar, I didn't believe you. I thought maybe you thought he was Urza, but I didn't think he could be the Urza, the by-the-holy-book Artificer!" Ratepe paused long enough to inhale a piece of bacon. "I thought I'd been as scared as I could get before I met you, but that was before he touched me. Avohir! I swear I'll never be afraid again."

"Don't make promises you can't keep."

"There can't be anything scarier." Ratepe shook his head and shoved another piece into his mouth.

This time he chewed before he swallowed. She was about to criticize his manners, but he was too fast for her.

"He's Urza. Urza is Urza, the real Urza. And I'm Mishra. I'm talking to a legend, watching things, hearing things I can't imagine, because Urza—Urza the Artificer, straight out of *The Antiquity Wars*, thinks I'm his brother, Mishra the Mighty, Mishra the Destroyer, and we're going to put what's wrong back to rights again."

Another pause. More bacon, more bad manners, but then he hadn't had manners before. His face was flushed and his eyes never stopped moving.

"I'm Mishra. Avohir! I'm Mishra. . . . He tries to trick me sometimes, says things he doesn't believe, things I shouldn't believe. I have to watch him close . . . watch him close. Did you see his eyes, Xantcha? Avohir! I think he's a little touched? But I stay ahead of him, nearly. I have to. I'm almighty Mishra—"

Xantcha had had enough of Ratepe's babbling. She wasn't as fast as Urza, but she was fast enough to seize a would-be Mishra by the neck of his tunic and whirl him against the nearest post. Damp debris from the thatching rained down on them both.

"You are not Mishra, you merely pretend to be Mishra. You are Ratepe, son of Mideah, and the day you forget that will be the day you die, because he is Urza and you cannot hope to 'stay ahead of him.' Do you understand?"

When a wide-eyed Ratepe didn't immediately say yes, Xantcha rattled his spine against the post. His chin bobbed vigorously. She released his tunic and stepped back. The greater part of her anger was gone.

"I know who I am, Xantcha," Ratepe insisted, sounding more like himself, more like the youth Xantcha thought she knew. "I'm Rat, just Rat. But if I don't forget, just a little—when he looks at me, Xantcha—when Urza the Artificer looks at me, if I don't let myself believe I am who he thinks I am—who you told me to be—then . . ." He stared at the closed door. "When I saw his eyes. I never believed that part, Xantcha. It's not in *The Antiquity Wars*. Kayla wrote about Tawnos coming to tell her about how he'd seen Urza with the Weakstone and Mightstone embedded in his skull. She thought it was all lies, nice lies because Tawnos didn't want her to know the truth. The idea that the Weakstone or the Mightstone kept Urza alive, that's not even in Jarsyl. There's only one source for the stuff about Urza's eyes glowing with all the power of the sylex: four scraps of parchment bound by mistake at the back of the T'mill codex. They're supposed to be Tawnos's deathbed confession. My father said it was pure apocrypha. But it wasn't! Urza's eyes, they are the Weakstone and the Mightstone, aren't they? They're what've kept him alive, if Urza really is alive, if he's not just something the stones have created."

Waste not, want not, Xantcha hadn't found Mishra the Destroyer, she'd found Mishra the skeptic and Mishra the babbling pedant! She shot him a disbelieving look. "Don't ask me. Last night, you were the one who said that the Weakstone was singing to you."

Ratepe winced and walked past the bacon without taking any.

"Two eyes, two stones," Xantcha continued. "I thought you'd gotten lucky."

"I heard something, not with my ears, but inside my head." He stopped and faced her, confusion painfully evident on his face. "I called it singing, 'cause that's the best word I had. And it came from his left eye." He sat down on the ash bucket, staring at his feet. "Do you want to know how I knew which eye was which?"

Measured by his expression, she wouldn't like the answer but, "Go ahead, enlighten me."

"It told me. It told me what it was and that it had been waiting for someone who could hear it. When Urza said Harbin wasn't his son, it was, it was . . ." Ratepe made a helpless gesture that ended with his fingertips pressed against his temples. "Not pain, but like the feeling that comes after pain." He stopped again and closed his eyes before continuing. "Xantcha, I heard Mishra. Well, not quite heard him. It was just there, in my mind, from the stone. I knew what Mishra thought, what he would have said. Not his words, exactly. My words." His eyes opened. He stared at Xantcha with only a shadow of his usual cockiness. "I know who I am, Xantcha. I'm Ratepe, son of Mideah, or, just Rat now, 'cause I lost everything when I became a slave. I was born almost eighteen years ago in the city of Pincar, on the sixth day after the Festival of Fruits in the sixth year of Tabarna's reign. I'm me. But, Xantcha, pretending to be Mishra, the way you asked me to—" He broke the stare. "It's not pretend. I could get lost. I could wind up thinking I am Mishra before this is over."

Xantcha bit her lip and sighed. Ratepe wasn't looking, didn't seem to have heard. "Right now, while you're sitting there, can you hear the Weakstone singing Mishra's thoughts in your mind?"

He shook his head. "Only when I'm looking at Urza's eyes, or when he's looking at me."

She began another sigh, of relief this time, but she began too soon.

"I'm worried. Xantcha. It's so real, so easy to imagine him, and that's after just one night. By next year when I'm supposed to go back to Efuan Pincar . . . ? You should've warned me."

Trust Rat—or Ratepe—or Mishra—or whatever he wanted to call himself to go for the guilt. "I didn't know about the singing. I knew about Urza's eyes, where they came from anyway, and I did warn you about that. But singing and Mishra? Beyond *The Antiquity Wars*, I don't know anything but what Urza's told me, and I guess there's a lot he didn't."

The rest of Xantcha's anger went with that admission. She leaned against a porch post, grateful that no one was looking at her. All those times Urza had glowered at her, eyes ablaze—had the voice of Mishra's Weakstone tried to make itself heard in her mind? Why, really, had she gone in search of a false Mishra? What had drawn her to Ratepe? She'd known he was the one to fulfill her plans before she'd gotten a good look at him.

"Can I trust myself?"

Xantcha had no assurances, not for herself or for him. "I don't know."

Ratepe folded his arms tightly across his ribs and shrank within himself. Xantcha had spent all her life with Phyrexians or Urza. She wasn't accustomed to expressive faces and wasn't prepared for the gust of empathy that blew from Ratepe to her. She tried to shake it off with a change of subject and a touch of humor.

"What were the three of you talking about all night?"

Ratepe wasn't interested. "A year from now, will there be anything left of me? Will I be myself?"

"I'm still me," Xantcha answered.

"Right. We talked, some, about you."

She should have expected that, but hadn't. "I haven't lied to you, Ratepe, not about the important things. The Phyrexians are real, and Urza's the only one with the power to defeat them."

"But Urza's wits are addled, aren't they? And you thought you'd cure him if you scrounged up someone who'd remind him of his brother. You thought you could make him stop living in the past."

"I told you that before we left Medran."

"Are you as old as he is?"

Xantcha found the question surprisingly difficult to answer. "Younger, a bit . . . I think. You're not the only one who doesn't know who or what to trust inside. He told you I was Phyrexian?"

"Repeatedly. But, since he thinks I'm Mishra, he's not infallible."

The bacon was burning. Xantcha scraped the charred rashers onto the platter and made of show of eating one, swallowing time while she decided how to answer.

"You can believe him." She took a deep breath and recited—in Phyrexian squeals, squeaks, and chattering, as best she could remember them—the first lesson she'd learned from the vat-priests. "Newts you are, and newts you shall remain. Obey and learn. Pay attention. Make no mistakes."

Ratepe gaped. "That day, in the sphere, when you cut yourself—If I'd taken the knife from you—"

"I'd bleed no matter where you cut me. It would have hurt. You could have killed me, you were inside the sphere. I'm not Urza. I don't think Urza can be killed. I don't think he's alive, not the way you and I are."

"You and I, Xantcha? No one I know lives for three thousand years."

"Closer to thirty-four hundred, I think. Urza believes I was born on another plane and that the Phyrexians stole me while I was still a child then compleated me the way they compleated Mishra. But that can't be true. I don't know what happened to Mishra, but with newts, we've got to be compleated while we're still new. Urza's never accepted that I was dragged out of a vat in the Fane of Flesh."

"So, in addition to everything else, Phyrexians are immortal?'

"To survive the compleation, newts have to be very resilient, immortally resilient. But Phyrexians can die, especially newts, just not of age or anything else that born-folk might call natural."

"And after thirty-four hundred years, Urza still doesn't believe you?"

"Urza's mad, Ratepe. What he knows and what he believes aren't always the same. Most of the time it doesn't make any difference, as long as he acts to defeat Phyrexia and stops trying to recreate the past on a tabletop."

Ratepe nodded. "He showed me what he was working on."

"Again?" Xantcha couldn't muster surprise or indignation, only weariness.

"I guess, if you say so. Funny thing, with the Weakstone, I get a sense of everything that happened to Mishra." He fell silent until Xantcha looked at him. "You're half-right about what happened. Urza's half-right, too. Phyrexians wanted the Weakstone. When Mishra wouldn't surrender it, one of them tried to kill him. The Weakstone kept him alive then and even when they took him apart later, but it couldn't keep him sane." Ratepe strangled a laugh. "Maybe burning his own mind was the last sane thing Mishra did. After that, there're only images, like paintings on a wall, and waiting, endless waiting, for Urza to listen."

"And now Mishra, or the Weakstone, or both of them together have you to speak for them."

"So far, I listen, but I speak for myself."

"What does that mean?"

Ratepe began to pace. He made a fist with his right hand and pounded it against his left palm. "It means I'd do anything to have my life back. I wish I'd never seen you. I wish I was still a slave in Medran. Tucktah and Garve only had my body. My thoughts were safe. I didn't know the meaning of powerless until I looked into Urza's eyes. I'm as dead as he is, as Mishra, as you."

The self-proclaimed dead man stopped beside the bacon platter and ate a rasher.

"I'm not dead."

"No, you're Phyrexian," Ratepe retorted between swallows. "You weren't born, you were immortal when you were decanted. How could you ever be dead?"

Xantcha ignored the question. "A year, Ratepe, or less. As soon as Urza turns away from the past, I'll take you back to Efuan Pincar. You have my word for that."

Silence, then: "Urza doesn't trust you."

That stung, even if Ratepe was only repeating something that Xantcha had heard countless times before. "I would never betray him . . . or you."

"But you're Phyrexian. If I believe you, you've never been anything but Phyrexian. They're your kin. My father once told me not to trust a man who led a fight against his kin. Betrayal is a nasty habit that once acquired is never cast aside."

"Your father is dead." When it came to cruelty, Xantcha had been taught by masters.

Ratepe stiffened. Leaving the last rashers of bacon on the platter, he walked a straight path away from the cottage. Xantcha let him go. She banked the fire, ate the last of the soggy bacon, and retreated to her room. Her treasured copies of *The Antiquity Wars* offered no solace, not against the turmoil she'd invited into her life when she'd bought herself a slave. And though there was no chance that she'd fall asleep, Xantcha threw herself down on her mattress and pillows.

She was still there, weary, lost in time, and wallowing in an endless array of painful memories, when she sensed a darkening and heard a gentle tapping on her open door.

"Are you awake?"

If Xantcha hadn't been awake, she wouldn't have heard Ratepe's question. If she'd had her wits, she could have answered him with unmoving silence and he might have gone away. But Xantcha couldn't remember the last time anyone had knocked on her door. Sheer surprise lifted her onto her elbows, revealing her secret before she had a chance to keep it.

Ratepe crossed her threshold and settled himself at her table, on her stool. There was only one in the room. Xantcha sat up on the mattress, not entirely pleased with the situation. Ratepe stiffened. He seemed to reconsider his visit, but spoke softly instead.

"I'm sorry. I'm angry and I'm scared and just plain stupid. You're the closest I've got to a friend right now. I shouldn't've said what I said. I'm sorry." He held out his hand.

Xantcha knew the signal. It was oddly consistent across the planes where men and women abounded. Smile if you're happy, frown when you're not. Make a fist when you're angry, but offer your open hand for trust. It was as if men and women were born knowing the same gestures.

She kept her hands wrapped around her pillow. "Betrayed by the truth?"

He winced and lowered his hand. "Not the truth. Just words I knew would hurt. You did it, too. Call it square?"

"Why not?"

Xantcha offered her hand, which Ratepe seized and shook vigorously, then released as if he was glad to have the ritual behind him. A suspicion he confirmed with his next remark.

"Urza's gone. I knocked on his door. I thought I'd talk to him and ask his advice. I know, that was stupid, too. But, the door opened . . . and he's not in there."

Xantcha spun herself off the bed and toward the door. "He's gone 'walking."

"I didn't see him leave, Xantcha, and I would've. I didn't go far, not out of sight. He's vanished."

"Planeswalking," she explained, leading the way to the porch and the door to Urza's larger quarters. "Dominaria's a plane. Moag, Vatraquaz, Equilor, Serra's realm, even Phyrexia, they're all planes, all worlds, and Urza can 'walk among them. Don't ask how. I don't know. I just close my eyes and die a little every time. The sphere that I brought you here in started off as armor, so I could survive when he pulled me after him."

"But? You're Phyrexian. The Phyrexians . . . how do they get here?"

"Ambulators . . . artifacts."

Xantcha put her weight against the door and shoved it open. Not a moment's doubt that Urza was gone, but one of surprise when she saw that the table was clear.

"You said you saw him working at the table?"

Ratepe barreled into her, keeping his balance only by grabbing her shoulders. He let go quickly, as he had when their hands had touched. "It was a battlefield, 'The Dawn of Fire.' Can you tell where he's gone?"

Xantcha shrugged and hurried to the table. No dust, no silver droplets, no gnats stuck in the wood grain or stranded on the floor. She tried to remember another time when Urza had cleaned up after himself so thoroughly. She couldn't.

"Phyrexia?" Ratepe asked, at her side again.

"He wasn't ready for a battle, and there'll be a battle, if he ever goes back to Phyrexia. No, I think he's still here, somewhere on Dominaria. "

"But you said 'among worlds.' "

"The fastest way from here and there on Dominaria is to go betweenworlds. Did he mention Baszerat or Morvern?"

Ratepe made a sour face. "No. Why would anyone mention Baszerat and Morvern?"

"Because the Phyrexians are there, on both sides of a war. I told him to go and see for himself. With all the excitement last night, I forgot to ask him what he learned."

"That the Baszerati are swine and the Morvernish are sheep?"

After so many worlds and so many years of wandering, Xantcha tended to see similarities. Ratepe had a one-worlder's perspective, which she tried to change. "They are equally besieged, equally vulnerable. The Phyrexians are the enemy; nothing else matters. It was smelling them in Baszerat and Morvern that convinced me the time was right to go looking for you. Urza's got to hold the line in Baszerat and Morvern or it will be too late."

Ratepe sulked. "Why not hold the line in Efuan Pincar? The Phyrexians are there, too, aren't they?"

"I haven't talked to him about Efuan Pincar."

"I did." He saw her gasp and added, "You didn't say I shouldn't."

When Xantcha had hatched her scheme to end Urza's madness by bringing him face-to-face with his brother, she'd imagined that she'd be setting the pace, planning the strategies until Urza's wits were sharp again. Her plans had been going awry almost from the beginning, certainly since the burning village. While she came to terms with her error, Ratepe attacked the silence.

"He didn't seem to know our history, so I tried to tell him everything from the Landings on. He seemed interested. He asked questions and I answered them. He seemed surprised that I could, because he said my mind was empty. But he paid the closest attention toward the end when I told him about the Shratta and the Red-Stripes. Especially the Shratta and Avohir and our holy book. I told him our family wasn't religious, that if he really wanted to know, he should visit the temples of Pincar and listen to the priests. There are still wise priests in Pincar, I think. The Shratta can't have gotten them all."

"Enough, Ratepe," Xantcha said with a sigh and a finger laid on Ratepe's upper lip. He flinched again. They both took a step back. The increased distance made conversation a little easier; eye contact, too, if he'd been willing to look at her. "It's not your fault."

"I shouldn't have told him about the temples?"

Xantcha raised her eyebrows.

Ratepe corrected himself. "I shouldn't have told him about the Phyrexians. I should have asked you first?"

"And I would have told you to wait, even though there's nothing I want more than to get Urza moving. You did what you thought was right, and it was right. It's not what I would have done. I've got to get used to that. I warn you, it won't be easy."

"He'll come back, won't he? Urza won't just roar through Efuan Pincar, killing every Red-Stripe Phyrexian he can find."

With a last look at the table, Xantcha headed out. "There's no second guessing Urza the Artificer, Ratepe—but if he did, it wouldn't be a bad thing, would it?'

"Killing all the Red-Stripes would leave the Shratta without any enemies."

Xantcha paused beside the door. "You're assuming that there aren't any Phyrexians among the Shratta. Remember what I told you about the Baszerati and the Morvernish—the sheep and the swine? I wouldn't count on it."

She left Ratepe standing in the empty room and had gotten as far as the wellhead, beyond the hearth, before he came chasing after her.

"What do we do now?" Ratepe's cheeks were red above the dark stubble of a two-day beard. "Follow him?"

"We wait." Xantcha unknotted the winch and let the bucket drop.

"Something could go wrong."

"All the more reason to wait." She began cranking. "We'd only make it worse."

"Urza hadn't ever heard of Efuan Pincar. He didn't know where it was. He doesn't know our language."

Xantcha let go of the winch. "What language do you think you two have been speaking since you got here?" Ratepe's mouth fell open, but no sound came out, so she went on. "I don't know why he says our minds are empty. He's willing to plunder them when it suits him. Urza doesn't know everything you know. You can keep a secret by just not thinking about it, or by imagining a wall around it, but in the beginning—and maybe all the time—best think that Urza knows what you know."

Ratepe stood motionless except for his breathing, which was shallow with shock. His flush had faded to waxy pale. Xantcha cranked the bucket up and offered him sweet water from the ladle. Most of it went down his chin, but he found his voice.

"He knows what I was thinking? The Weakstone and Mishra? How I thought I was outwitting Urza the Artificer? Avohir's mercy . . ."

Xantcha refilled the ladle and drank. "Maybe. Urza's mad, Ratepe. He hears what he wants to hear, whether it's your voice or your thoughts, and he might not hear you at all—but he could. That's what you've got to remember. I should've told you sooner."

"Do you know what I'm thinking?"

"Only when your mouth is open."

He closed it immediately, and Xantcha walked away, chuckling. She'd gone about ten steps when Ratepe raced past and stopped, facing her.

"All right. I've had enough . . . You're Phyrexian. You weren't born, you crawled out of a pit. You're more than three thousand years old, even though you look about twelve. You dress like a man—a boy. You talk like a man, but Efuand's a tricky language. We talk about things as if they were men or women—a dog is a man, but a cat is a lady. Among ourselves, though, when you say 'I did this,' or 'I did that,' the form's the same, whether I'm a man or woman. Usually, the difference is obvious." He swallowed hard, and Xantcha knew what he was thinking before he opened his mouth again. "Last night, Urza, when he'd talk about you, he'd say *she* and *her*. What are you, Xantcha, a man or a woman?'

"Is it important?"

"Yes, it's important."

"Neither."

She walked past him and didn't break his arm when he spun her back to face him.

"That's not an answer!"

"It's not the answer you want." She wrenched free.

"But, Urza . . . ? Why?"

"Phyrexian's not a tricky language. There are no families, no need for men or women, no words for them, either—except in dreams. I had no need for those words until I met a demon. *He* invaded my mind. After that and because of it, I've thought of myself as *she*."

"Urza?" Ratepe's voice had harshened. He was indignant, angry.

Xantcha laughed. "No, not Urza. Long before Urza."

"So, you and Urza . . . ?"

"Urza? You did read *The Antiquity Wars*, didn't you? Urza didn't even notice Kayla Bin-Kroog!"

She left Ratepe gaping and closed the door behind her.

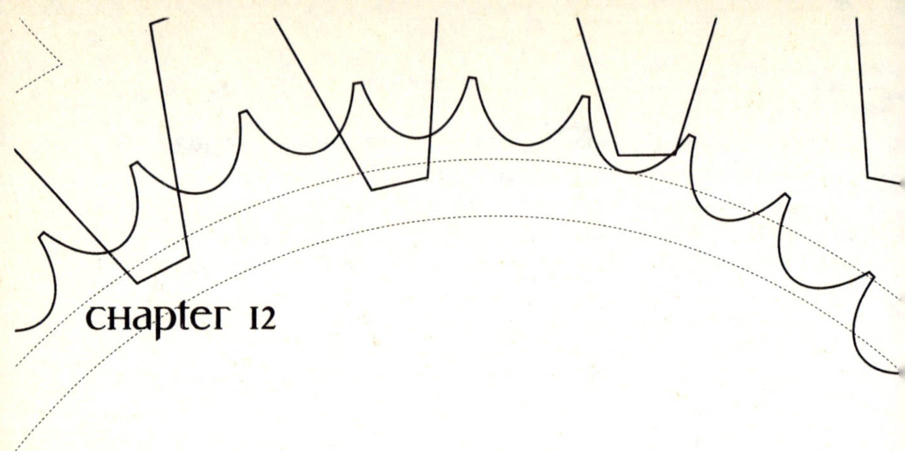

chapter 12

Urza was an honorable man, and an honest one. Even when he'd been an ordinary man, if the word ordinary had ever applied to Urza the Artificer, Urza had had no great use for romance or affection, but he'd tolerated friendship, one friend at a time.

After Xantcha had pushed him out of Phyrexia, he'd accepted her as a friend.

In the three thousand years since, Xantcha had never asked for more nor settled for less.

They'd stumbled through three worlds before the day during which Urza had ridden his dragon into Phyrexia, ended. Xantcha was seedier than Urza by then, which meant they were leaning against each other when Xantcha released her armor to the cool, night mist. There were unfamiliar stars peeking through the mist and a trio of blue-white moons.

"Far enough," she whispered. Her voice had been wrecked by the bad air of four different worlds. "I've got to rest."

"It's not safe! I hear him, Yawg—"

Xantcha cringed whenever Urza started to say that word. She seized the crumbling substance of his ornately armored tunic. "You're calling the Ineffable! Never say that, never do that. Every time you say that name, the Ineffable can hear you. Of all the things I was taught in the Fane of

Flesh, that one I believe with all my strength. We'll never be safe until you burn that name from your memory. "

Sparks danced across Urza's eyes, which had been a featureless black since he'd dragged them away from Phyrexia. Xantcha didn't know what he saw, except it had him spooked, and anything that unnerved Urza was more than enough for her.

Urza took her suggestion to heart. Heat radiated from his face. Waste not, want not, if he could literally burn something from his memory, he could probably survive it, too. Still, she put more distance between them, leading him by the wrist to a rock where he could sit.

"Water, Xantcha. Could you bring me water?"

He was blind, at least to real things. His vision, he'd said, was all spots and bubbles, as if he'd stared too long at the sun. There'd been no sun above the Fourth Sphere, but the dragon had been the target of all the weapons, sorcerous and elemental, that the demons could aim.

"You'll stay right here?" she asked.

"I'll try."

Xantcha didn't ask what he meant. She'd set her feet on enough worlds to have a sharp sense of where she could survive and where she couldn't. Phyrexia and the three worlds after Phyrexia were inhospitable, but this three-moon world was viable. She had her cyst, her heart, and, tucked inside her tunic, an ambulator. If Urza vanished before she returned, it wouldn't be the end of her.

Heavy rains had fallen recently. Xantcha saw water at the base of the hill where they emerged from between-worlds. Carrying it was another matter. She quenched her thirst from her own cupped hands, but for Urza she stripped off her tunic, sopped it in the water, and carried it, dripping, up the hill.

Urza's attempt to remain seated atop the rock had been successful. Silhouetted against the softly lit night sky, his shoulders were slumped forward, and his chin had disappeared in the shadows of his armored tunic. His hands lay inert in his lap.

"Urza?"

His chin rose.

"I've brought you water, without grace or dignity."

"As long as it is wet."

She guided his hand to the sopping cloth. "Quite wet."

Urza sucked moisture from the cloth, then wiped his face. When he'd finished, he let her tunic fall. Xantcha sat at his feet.

"Is there anything more I can do for you? Will you eat? Food might help. I smell berries. It's summer here."

He shook his head. "Just sit beside me. Sleep, if you can, child. Morning will come, a summer morning."

Xantcha fought into her tunic. The night was cool, not cold. The garment was uncomfortable, nothing worse. Discomfort was nothing unfamiliar. She got comfortable against the rock. Urza shifted his hand to the top of her head.

"I told you to stay behind."

"I did, for a little while."

"You could have been hurt. I might have left you in Phyrexia forever."

Urza was Urza, at the very center of his world and every other. On a night like this, after the day they'd survived, his vainglory was reassuring. Xantcha relaxed.

"It went otherwise, Urza. I was neither hurt nor left behind."

"I'd still be there but for you."

"You'd be dead, Urza, if you can die, or in the Seventh Sphere, if you can't, wishing that you could."

"The Seventh Sphere is the place where—" He hesitated. "Where the Ineffable punishes demons?"

"Yes."

"Then I should thank you."

"Yes," Xantcha repeated. "And you should have listened to me when I told you what waited in Phyrexia."

"I will build another dragon, bigger and stronger. I know where Phyrexia is now, tucked across a fathomless chasm. I would never have seen it 'walking. I wouldn't see it now, but I know and I can go back. They will die, Xantcha. I will reap them like a field of overripe grain. The day of Mishra's vengeance is closer today than yesterday."

Xantcha swallowed an ordinary yawn. "You were surrounded, Urza. The fourth leg went right after I climbed it. You'd destroyed hundreds of Phyrexians, and yet there were as many around you at the end as there had been at the beginning."

"I will change my design."

"A thousand legs wouldn't be enough. You can't destroy every Phyrexian by fighting. You'll need allies and an army three times the size of Phyrexia. Tactics. Strategy." Xantcha thought of the heart vault. "Or, the perfect target for a stealthy attack."

"And since when did you become my war consul, child?"

Urza could be disdainful. Strategy and tactics indeed. She'd need to be careful when she mentioned the heart vault. Tonight, while Urza was blind and she was exhausted, wasn't the right time to reveal her discoveries. Another yawn escaped, entirely normal. Without the mnemonic, the cyst was just a lump in her stomach.

"Sleep, child. I am grateful. I underestimated my enemy. I'll never do that again."

Xantcha was too tired to celebrate what little victory she'd achieved. She fell asleep thinking she'd be alone when she awoke.

She was, but Urza hadn't gone far. With nothing more than grass, twigs and small stones, Xantcha's companion had recreated the Fourth Sphere battleground in an area no more than two paces square. His dragon, made from twigs and woven grass, towered over the other replicas in precisely the proportions she remembered. She expected it to move.

"I'm awed," she admitted before her shadow fell across Urza's small wonders. "You must be feeling better?'

"As good as a fool can feel."

It was a comment that begged questions, but Xantcha had learned to tread softly through confusion. "You can see again?"

"Yes, yes." He looked up: black pupils, hazel irises, white sclera. "You had the right of it, Xantcha. Burn that name out of my mind. As soon as I did, I began to feel like myself again, ignorant and foolish. No one was hurt. No planes were damaged."

"A few spheres. The priests will be a long time repairing the damage. And you destroyed a score of their dragons and wyverns. Better than I expected, honestly."

"But not good enough. If I'd come down here—" Urza touched the ground behind the stone-shaped furnaces then quickly rearranged the delicate figures—"I'd have had a wall of fire at my back, and they couldn't have encircled me."

Xantcha studied the new array. "How would that be better? With the furnaces behind you, you'd have been held in one place almost from the start," Urza gave her a look that sparkled. She changed the subject. "Are we staying here while you build another dragon?"

"No. The Multiverse is real, Xantcha. At least every plane I'd ever found before was real, until yesterday when I found Phyrexia. Going there and leaving, those were 'walking strides like I've never taken before. It was as if I'd leapt a vast chasm in a single bound. The chasm, I realize now, is everywhere, and Phyrexia is its far side. No matter where we are, we're only one leap away from our enemy and it from us. Even so, I'll feel better when I've put a few knots in my trail."

She had no argument with that plan. "Then what? Another dragon? An army? Allies? I found something yesterday, Urza, something I thought was probably lies. I found my heart."

Xantcha slid her hand into her boot. The amber continued to glow. She offered it to Urza.

"That is—well, it's not your heart, Xantcha." He didn't take it. "Your heart beats behind your ribs, child. The Phyrexians lied to you. They took your past and your future, but they didn't take your heart." Urza guided her empty hand to her breastbone. "There, can you feel it?"

She nodded. All flesh had a blood-heart in its breast. Newts in the Fane of Flesh had hearts until they were compleated. "This is different," she insisted and described the vault where countless hearts shimmered.

"We are connected to our hearts. We are taught that the Ineffable keeps watch over our hearts and records our errors on their surface. Too many errors and—" She drew a line across her throat.

Urza took the amber and held it to the sun. Xantcha couldn't see his face or his eyes but a strangeness not unlike the between-worlds tightened around her. She couldn't breathe, couldn't even muster the strength or will to gasp until Urza lowered his hand. His face, when he turned toward her again, was not pleased.

"Of all abominations, this is the greatest." Urza held the amber above her still-outstretched hand but did not release it. "I would not call it a heart, yet it falls short of a powerstone. I can imagine no purpose for it, except the one you describe. And you knew where the vault was?"

Xantcha sensed Urza had asked a critical question and that her life might depend on her answer. She would have lied, if she'd been certain a lie would satisfy him. "I knew it was somewhere in the Fane of Flesh,"

"You didn't tell me?"

"I didn't want to die with all the rest of Phyrexia. I wasn't certain, I thought you'd laugh and call me a child again, and I would have been too ashamed to follow you."

Not quite an answer, but the truth and, apparently, satisfactory. Urza dropped the amber into her hand. Without conscious thought, Xantcha clutched it against her blood-heart.

"I wouldn't have—" Urza began, then stopped abruptly and looked down at his grass-and-twig dragon. "No, very possibly your concerns were justified. I do not imagine abominations and have discouraged you, thinking you imagined them. I allowed myself to forget that your mind is empty. Phyrexians have no imagination." He crushed the dragon beneath his boot. "Another mistake. Another error. Forgive me, Mishra, I cannot see when I need most to see and opportunity slips away forever. If only I could relive yesterday instead of tomorrow."

"You can go back as soon as you've restored your strength. If I could find the vault . . ."

Urza shuddered. "They know me now. Your Ineffable knows me, I cannot return to Phyrexia, not without absolute certainty of success and overwhelming strength. For the sake of vengeance, I must be cautious. I cannot make any more mistakes. I would be found out before I set foot on your First Sphere."

Xantcha kept her mouth shut. It wasn't *her* First Sphere. Urza had powers that Phyrexia coveted, but he was oddly reluctant to use them. He had to overwhelm whatever lay before him, and when he made one of his mistakes, that mistake became a fortress.

"I could go. I have an ambulator." She lifted the hem of her tunic, revealing the small black disk tucked beneath her belt. "If you made a smaller dragon, I could turn it loose in the vault."

Urza smiled. "Your courage is laudable, child, but you couldn't hope to succeed. We will talk no more about it," He reached for the portal. Xantcha retreated, folding her arms defensively over her belly. "Come child, you have no need for such an artifact. It is beyond your understanding. Let me have it."

"I'm not a child," she warned, the least incendiary comment seething on the back of her tongue.

"You see, simply having a Phyrexian artifact so close to you taints you, as that name, yesterday, threatened to taint me. You haven't the strength to resist its corruption. You've become willful. Between that and your heart . . . You're overwhelmed, Xantcha. I should take them both from you, for your own safety, but I will leave you your heart, if you give me the ambulator."

"It's mine!" Xantcha protested. "I rolled it up."

She'd seen born-children in her travels and recognized her behavior. Urza didn't have to say another word. Xantcha handed the ambulator over.

"Thank you, Xantcha. I will study it closely."

Urza held the ambulator between his fingertips where it vanished. Perhaps he would study it. Perhaps he would find a way to add its properties to her cyst. Whichever or whatever, Xantcha didn't think she'd see it again, but she kept her heart. Urza could have everything else, not that.

He 'walked through two more worlds that day and two more the next and the next after that, making knots in their trail. After two score worlds in half as many days, Xantcha swore the next would be her last, that she'd let go of his hands and remain behind. Any world would be better than another between-worlds passage. But the next world was yellow gas, wind, and lightning that seemed particularly attracted to her armor, and the world after that had no air. Urza made an underground chamber where Xantcha could breathe without her armor and catch up on her sleep.

They came to a swamp with cone-shaped insects as long as her forearm and an abundance of frogs, not Xantcha's favorite sort of place. It reminded her of Phyrexia's First Sphere, but she could breathe and eat and the water, though brackish, didn't make her sick.

"This is far enough for me," she announced when Urza held out his hand. "I don't need to visit every world."

"Only a few more," Urza protested.

He'd begun to pace. Since Phyrexia, his restlessness had steadily worsened until he could scarcely stand still. He didn't even try to sleep.

"I'm tired," she told him.

"You slept last night."

"Last night! When was last night? Where was last night? The world with the yellow trees or the one with two suns? I want to stay put long enough see the seasons change."

"Farmer," Urza chided her, a distinct improvement over "child" and the truth as well. She'd spent too much time scratching in Phyrexia's sterile soil not to appreciate worlds where plants grew naturally.

"I want a home."

"So do I." An admission she hadn't expected. "It's here, Xantcha. Dominaria . . . home. I can feel it each time we 'walk, but at every step, a darkness blocks me. The darkness was here the last time, before I found you. It was like nothing I'd encountered before. I was sure it would pass, but it hasn't. It's still here, and stronger than before."

"Like a knife?" she asked, remembering the rumors of newts trapped on the nether side of broken portals.

"A knife? No, it is as if Multiverse itself had shattered, as if Dominaria and all the planes that are bound to it have been broken apart. I have 'walked all around, approaching it from every vantage, yet each time it is the same. There is a darkness that is also cold and repels me. I've been making a map in my mind, a shape beyond words. When it's done, I will know that Dominaria is completely sealed from me and Phyrexia.

"It is my fault, you know. It's not merely vengeance that I require from Phyrexia. I require atonement The Phyrexians corrupted and destroyed my brother; that's vengeance. But we, my brother and I, let them back into Dominaria when we destroyed the Thran safeguards. The land itself has not forgiven me, won't forgive me until I have atoned for our error by destroying Phyrexia. Dominaria locks me out, as it locks out the Phyrexians. I cannot go home until I have done what not even the Thran could do: destroy Phyrexia!

"I want to go home, Xantcha. You, who cannot remember where you were born, cannot know true homesickness as I know it. I had not thought it would be so difficult. The land does not forgive. It has sealed itself against me. But it has sealed itself against Phyrexia, too, and though my heart aches, I am content with my exile, knowing that my home is safe."

Xantcha rubbed her temples. There was truth, usually, tangled through Urza's self-centered delusions. "Searcher-priests don't 'walk between-worlds," she said cautiously, when she thought she had the wheat separated from the chaff. When conversation touched Mishra, Dominaria or the mysterious Thran, Urza's moods became less predictable than they usually were. "They use ambulators, but I don't know how they set the stones to find new worlds. Maybe you can't be quite certain that Dominaria is safe?"

"I'm certain," he insisted.

Her thoughts raced along a bright tangent. "You figured out how to set the stones on my ambulator?"

"Yes. I set it for Dominaria, and it was destroyed."

Xantcha's mind went dark. There was much she could have said and no reason to say any of it. She turned away with a sigh.

"When I know, beyond doubt, that Dominaria is inaccessible, then I will look for a hospitable plane. I mean to take your advice, Xantcha. I will build an army three times the size of Phyrexia, and ambulators large enough to transport them by the thousand! I examined your ambulator quite thoroughly before it was destroyed. I can make you another once I find the right materials, and can make it better."

Urza expected her to rejoice, so she tried. She took his arm and followed to a "few" more worlds, thirty-three, before he was satisfied that Dominaria was inaccessible behind what he called a shard of the Multiverse. Urza insisted that, compared to the Multiverse, a thousand worlds could be properly termed a "few" worlds. The Multiverse meant little to her. Urza's efforts to explain the planes and nexi that comprised it meant less. But the fact that Urza did try to explain it meant a lot.

"I need a friend," he explained one lonely night on a world where the air was old and nothing remained alive. "I need to talk with someone who has seen what I have seen, some of it, enough to listen without going numb from despair. And, after I have talked, I need to hear a voice that is not my own."

"But you never listen to me!"

"I always listen, Xantcha. You are rarely correct. I cannot replace what the Phyrexians took away from you. Your mind is mostly empty, and what isn't empty is filled with Phyrexian rubbish. You recite their lies because you cannot know better. Your advice, child, is untrustworthy, but you, yourself, are my friend."

Urza hadn't called her child since they 'walked away from Dominaria, and Xantcha didn't like to think that after so much time together, he continued to distrust her, but an offer of friendship, true friendship, was a gift not to be overlooked.

"I will never betray you," Xantcha said softly, taking his hand between hers.

It was like stone at first, flexible stone. Then it softened, warmed, and became flesh.

"I want nothing more than to be your friend, Urza."

He smiled, a rare and mortal gesture. "I will take you wherever you want, but I would rather you wanted to remain with me until we find a plane that satisfies both of us."

Late that night, when the fire was cold and Urza had gone wandering, as he usually did while she slept, Xantcha sharpened her knife and made an incision in her left flank, the side opposite the cyst. She tucked her amber heart into the gap, sealed it with a paste of ashes, then bound it tightly with cloth tom from her spare clothes.

Urza knew immediately. She'd been a fool to think he wouldn't.

"I swallowed it my own way," she told him, in no mood for a lengthy argument. "It's part of me now, where it belongs. I'll never lose it, no matter where you take me."

Xantcha wanted a world where she could pretend she'd been born. Never mind that by their best guess, she was living near the end of her sixth century and no more than seven decades younger than Urza himself. Urza wanted a plane where he could recruit an army. Their wants, she thought, should not have been incompatible, and perhaps they wouldn't have been, if Urza had been able to sleep. To give him his due, Xantcha granted that Urza tried to sleep. He knew he needed to dream, but whenever he attempted that treacherous descent from wakefulness, he found nightmares instead, screaming nightmares that spread like the stench of rotting fish on a summer's day. Until anyone within a half-day's journey could see the flames of Phyrexia and the metal and flesh apparition that Urza called *Mishra.*

Strangers did not welcome them for long. Recruiting an army was impossible. When she was lucky, Xantcha nursed a single harvest from the ground before they went 'walking again. When they found a truly hospitable world with abundant, rich soil, a broad swath of temperate climates and a wealth of vigorous cultures, Xantcha suggested that Urza build himself a tower on the loneliest island in the largest sea. He could 'walk to such a tower without difficulty and sleep, she'd hoped, without disturbing anyone.

Urza called the world Moag, and it became the home Xantcha had dreamed about. He built a sheer-walled tower with neither windows nor doors and filled it with artifacts. Within a decade, its rocky shores had become a place of prophecy and learning where Urza warned pilgrims of Phyrexian evil and laid the foundations for the army he hoped eventually to raise.

Xantcha built a cottage with a garden, and in the seasons when it didn't need tending, she yawned and went exploring. Urza had made her another summoning crystal, which she wore in friendship hut never expected to use. They met at his island whenever the moon was full, nowhere else, no other time. They'd become friends who could talk about anything because they knew which questions to avoid.

For thirty years, life—Xantcha's apparently immortal life—could not have been better. Until the bright autumn day on Moag's most intriguing southern continent when Xantcha caught the unexpected, unforgettable scent of glistening oil. She followed it to the source: the newly refurbished temple of a fire god with a taste for gold and blood sacrifice.

A born-flesh novice sat beside a burning alms box. For the hearths of the poor, he said, and though it looked like extortion, Xantcha threw copper into the flames. She yawned out her armor before entering the sanctuary. Trouble found her, one Phyrexian to another, before she reached the fire-bound altar.

Wrapped in concealing robes, it showed only its face, which had the jowls and grizzled beard of a mature man and the reek of the compleated. In its gloved hand it carried a gnarled wooden staff that immediately roused Xantcha's suspicion. She had a small sword on her hip. A mace would have been more useful, but out of keeping with the rest of her dandy's disguise.

"*Where have you been?*" it asked in a Phyrexian whisper that could have been mistaken for insects buzzing.

"*Waiting*," Xantcha replied with a newt's soft inflection. Waiting to see what would happen next.

It came faster than she'd expected. There was a priest of some new type inside those robes, and its staff was as false as its face. A web of golden power struck her armor. The priest wasn't expecting surprises, not from a newt. Xantcha kicked it once in the midsection and again on the chin as it fell. Its head separated from its neck, leaving its flesh-face behind. Xantcha understood instantly why Urza could not purge his brother's last memory from his mind. She reached for the not-wooden staff and realized, belatedly, that there'd been witnesses.

Phyrexian witnesses. Four of them were surging out of the recesses to block her path. They all had staves, and she'd lost the advantage of surprise. The sanctuary roof had a smoke vent above the altar. Xantcha grabbed the priest's head instead of its staff as she braced herself for the agony of wringing a sphere from the cyst while the armor was still in place around her. There was blood in the sphere, but it resisted the efforts of the Phyrexians and their staves to bring it down as it expanded and lifted her out of immediate danger.

Willpower got Xantcha drifting silently just above the rooftops south of the temple. But willpower couldn't lift her high enough to catch the winds that would carry her to true safety beyond the walls. The cyst couldn't maintain both the sphere and the armor for long. Already, knife pains ripped through her stomach, and her mouth had filled with blood.

Woozy and desperate, Xantcha went to ground in the foulest midden she could find: a gaping pit behind a boneyard. She thought she'd die when the sphere dissolved on contact with the midden scum, and she found herself shoulder-deep in fermenting filth. With a death grip on the metal-mesh head—if she dropped it, she'd never have the courage to fish it out—Xantcha released her armor as well and hoped that uncontrolled nausea wouldn't prevent the cyst from recharging itself.

By sunset, when swarms of insects mistook her for their evening meal, Xantcha was ready to surrender to any Phyrexian brave enough to haul her out of her hiding place. She thought about gods and the inconvenience of not believing in any of them, then filled her lungs for a yawn. With a single, sharp pain that threatened, for one horrible moment, to fold her in half, the cyst discharged. Xantcha gasped her way through the mnemonic that would create the sphere, and just when she thought she had no endurance left, it began to swell.

She was seen—certainly she was scented—rising above the shambles' roofs, slowly at first, then faster as fresh air lifted her up. There were screams, clanging alarms and, from the open roof of the fire god's temple, a diaphanous gout of black sorcery that fell short of its moving target. The winds blew westward, into the sunset. Xantcha let them carry her, until the moon was high, before she began the long tacks that would take her to Urza's tower.

The moon was a waxing crescent when Xantcha set down on the tower roof five nights later. Urza wasn't expecting her and wasn't pleased to have her within his tower walls. Xantcha had abandoned her clothes and scrubbed herself raw with sand and water without quite ridding herself of the midden's aroma. But Urza reserved his greatest displeasure for the metal-mesh head she stood on his work table.

"Where did you find that?" he demanded and stood like stone while Xantcha raced through an account of her misadventure in the southern city.

"You struck it down, before witnesses? And you brought it here, as a trophy? What were you thinking?"

Urza's enraged eyes lit up the chamber. The air around him shimmered with between-worlds light. Xantcha thought it wise to armor herself, but when she opened her mouth Urza enveloped her in stifling paralysis. Naked and defenseless, she endured a scathing lecture about the stupidity of newts who exposed themselves to their enemies and jeopardized the delicate plans of their friends.

"I smelled glistening oil," Xantcha countered when, toward dawn, Urza released her from his spell. She was angry by then and incautious. "I was curious. I didn't know it came from Phyrexian priests. Maybe it was just a coincidental cooking sauce! I didn't plan to destroy a Phyrexian, but it seemed better than letting it kill me, and as for witnesses, well, I am sorry about that. I didn't notice them standing there until it was too late. And I brought the head because I thought I'd better have proof, because I wasn't sure you'd believe me without it. Should I have let myself be killed? Or captured? Maybe they could have dropped my head on the roof before they attacked! Would that have been better? Wiser, on my part?'

A silver globe appeared in Urza's hand. He cocked his arm.

"Go ahead, throw it. Then what? Make me into another mistake you can mourn? You can't change the past, Urza. The Phyrexians were here before I found them. Empty-headed fool that I am, I thought you'd want to know whatever I could learn, however I learned it. Waste not, want not, I thought you'd be glad I survived!"

The globe vanished in a shower of bright red sparks. "I am. Truly. But they will have found me."

"Phyrexians are here, Urza. It's not necessarily the same thing. How do you suppose they found Dominaria in the first place? Searcher-priests look for more than artifacts. That thing—" Xantcha gestured at the metal-mesh head—"had a face no one would look twice at. The searchers have found a nice, little world, ripe for the plucking. They've set themselves up in the fire god's cult because what Phyrexia needs more than artifacts is ore for its furnaces, and Moag's a metal-rich world."

"They'll destroy Moag, Xantcha. It will all happen again."

"Well, isn't that what you've been waiting for, a chance to right old wrongs?"

"No. No, the price is too high."

"Urza!" Xantcha lost patience with him. "Forget about listening to me, do you ever listen to yourself?"

He stared at her, mortal-eyed, but as if she were a stranger rather than his companion of the centuries. "Go, Xantcha. I need to think. I will come for you at the full moon."

"Maybe I don't want to 'walk away from this. Maybe I want my vengeance!"

"Go, child! You're disturbing me. I must think. I will tell you my decision when I've made it, not before."

They were back to child again, and he *had* made his decision. Xantcha had been with Urza too long not to know when he was lying to her. He'd made a hole in the roof, and she took advantage of it. She gathered the weapons she hadn't discarded and the sack that held her traveling stash of gold and gems, these things the midden hadn't damaged at all. Only the sack desperately needed replacing, so she took one of Urza's and swapped the contents before yawning out the sphere. The hole closed as soon as she'd passed through it.

Morning had come, a beautiful morning with mackerel clouds streaking north by northeast, the direction Xantcha needed, if she were going back to her cottage, which she decided after a heartbeat's thought that she wasn't. Xantcha set her mind south, to the fire god's city. Urza was going to leave Moag, and despite her threats, Xantcha knew she'd go with him, but if he'd intended simply to leave, they could have 'walked already. They'd left other worlds with less warning. No, Urza had something planned, and Xantcha wanted to witness it.

As soon as Xantcha reached the coast, she found a prosperous villa and sneaked into it by moonlight. She left two silver coins and another world's garnet brooch on a night stand, in exchange for her pick of the young heir's wardrobe. His britches were tight and his boots too big, but overall she considered it a fair swap. She didn't linger until sunrise to learn the household's opinion.

Xantcha scuffed up her fine clothes when she reached the southern city and wove a tale of tragedy and coincidence for the apothecary whose shop window had the best view of the fire god's temple. The owl-eyed merchant didn't believe a word Xantcha said, but she could read, count, and compound a script better than either of his journeymen. He took her in with the promise of two meals a day, one hot, one cold, and a night-pallet across the threshold, which was what she'd wanted from the start.

She settled in to wait: one day, two days, three, four. Urza came on the fifth. Or rather, a ball of fire descended from the stars during the fifth night. It struck the temple with hideous force. Masonry, stone and burning timbers flew across the plaza, smashing through shutters and walls. Xantcha got her sword from its hiding place, bid an unobserved farewell to the apothecary, then went hunting for Phyrexians through the smoke.

Xantcha found a few, as terrified as any born-folk, or more so since glistening oil burnt with a hot blue flame. She put an end to their misery and with her armor to protect her from both flames and smoke made her way into the sanctuary. The journeymen had succumbed to her questions, and told her where the fire god's priests had their private quarters. Which was where Xantcha expected to find—and steal—another ambulator.

She found a passage back to Phyrexia, but it was unlike any ambulator she'd seen before. Instead of a bottomless black pool, the flesh-faced priests had a solid-seeming disk that rose edgewise from the stone floor. Face on, it was as black as the ambulators Xantcha was familiar with. From behind, it simply wasn't there. One thing hadn't changed; it still had a palm-sized panel with seven black jewels where the disk emerged from the floor. Since she couldn't roll the standing-portal up and take it with her, Xantcha smashed the panel with her sword.

Smoke and screams belched out of the black disk before it collapsed. Xantcha guessed she'd closed it just in time. A pair of lines gouged into the stone was all that remained when the smoke cleared. She was rummaging through shelves and cabinets, hoping to find a familiar ambulator, when the air grew heavy. The other kind of between-worlds passage, Urza's kind of 'walking passage, was opening.

"It's me!" she shouted as he came into view.

"Xantcha! What are you doing here? I could have killed you."

They never had established whether Urza's armor would protect her from Urza's wrath or Urza's mistakes.

"I came for the ambulator. I knew they'd have one, and I wasn't sure you'd think to roll it." He hadn't when he rode the dragon into Phyrexia. "It was a new kind," she admitted. "I couldn't roll it up."

Urza stared at the lines in the floor. "No, it was a very old kind. Did you destroy it?"

He was so calm and reasonable, it worried her. "Yes. I broke the gems. There were screams, then nothing."

"Well, perhaps it is enough. If not, I have left my mark above, and I will leave a trail. Are you ready to 'walk, or are you staying here?"

"You want the Phyrexians to follow us?"

Urza nodded, smiling, and held out his hand. "I want them to pursue us with all their strength and leave Moag in peace." Xantcha took his hand and said, "I don't think it works that way," but they were between-worlds and her words were lost.

Xantcha never knew if the second part of Urza's plan bore fruit, but the first was successful beyond his wildest dreams. He stopped laying a deliberate trail after the fourth world beyond Moag, but that didn't stop the searcher-priests and the avenger teams they led.

Sometimes she and Urza got a year's respite between attacks, never more. Urza reached into his past for sentries he called Yotians, never-fail guardians shaped from whatever materials a new world offered: clay, stone, wood, or ice.

He'd 'walked her to ice worlds before. They were dark, airless places where the sun was lost among the stars and the ice as hard as steel. Save for the gas worlds, where there was no solid ground at all, ice worlds were the least hospitable worlds in the Multiverse. They never stayed long on ice, no matter how close the pursuit.

Then, years after Moag by Urza's reckoning, he found a world where the ice was melting, and the air was cold but breathable. Once it had been a world like Moag. Whole forests and cities could be glimpsed through the ice when the light was right. Now it was a brutal place, with men who'd forgotten what cities were.

Xantcha thought it was as inhospitable as any airless world, but Urza disagreed and she was disinclined to argue. He hadn't slept soundly since they left Moag. The simple act of closing his eyes was enough to trigger the nightmares—hallucinations of the past, of the Ineffable. To Xantcha's abiding horror, the forbidden name had returned to Urza's memory and came easily to him when he battled through his nightmares.

Years without proper sleep had taken their toll. Urza's restlessness had grown into a sort of frenzy. He was never still, always pacing or wringing his hands. He babbled constantly. Xantcha fashioned wax earplugs so she could sleep. With Phyrexians on their trail, they never strayed far apart.

And Urza needed her. Without her, Urza often didn't know what was real from what was not. Without her gentle nagging, he would have forgotten to carve the Yotians or given them the appropriate orders. Without her willingness to brave his hallucinations he would have gouged the gemstone eyes from his skull and put an end to his misery.

Sitting on the opposite side of a fire, with a score of icy Yotians clanking patrol through the frigid night, Xantcha wondered if she should let him die. They were each over eight hundred years old and though she could still pass for an unbearded youth, Urza looked his age, or worse. The arcane power that enabled him to change his appearance at will had become erratic. On nights like tonight, even though he wasn't hallucinating, Urza seemed to be surrounded by a between-worlds miasma. Viewed from some angles, he had no substance at all, just seething light that hurt her eyes.

"Will you eat? Can you eat?" Xantcha asked gently, trying to ignore the way the hearth flames were visible through his robes. Food was no substitute for sleep and dreams, but it helped keep Urza looking mortal. She'd seasoned the stew pot with the aromatic herbs that had tempted him before. But it didn't work this time.

"I'm hollow," he said, a disturbingly accurate assessment. "Food won't fill me, Xantcha. Eat all you can. Pack the rest. I feel the eyes of the Multiverse upon us."

Xantcha lost her appetite. When Urza thought the Multiverse was watching him, Phyrexians weren't usually far behind. She forced down a small portion—the between-worlds was easier on a near-empty stomach—and filled a waterskin with the rest. The ice-shaped Yotians were almost as restless as Urza. Xantcha slung the waterskin and other essentials from a shoulder harness and checked her weapons. The second-best way to deal with Phyrexians was to batter them apart. She'd long since abandoned her Moag sword in favor of a short club with a jagged chunk of pure iron for its head.

The best way to deal with Phyrexian avengers, however, was to hide, and let Urza demolish them with sorcery and artifice, then wait until he shaped himself into a man again. Waiting was the difficult pan. As the years and worlds and ambushes accumulated, Urza had never had a problem vanquishing the avengers, but increasingly he lost himself in the aftermath. Two ambushes ago, he'd devolved into a pillar of rainbow light that shimmered for three days before condensing into a solid, familiar form. Considering the brutal, backwater worlds they frequented, Xantcha desperately wanted an ambulator and the wherewithal to set its black stones for a hospitable world.

She'd raised the subject as often as she'd dared, which didn't include this night with the ice Yotians clattering like crystals through the shadows.

The ambush came at dawn, in gusts of hot, sour Phyrexian wind. There were a score of them, not counting the two searcher-priests who squatted beside the flat-black ambulator. This time the avengers resembled huge turtles with bowl-shaped carapaces and four broad, shovel-like feet, ideal for churning through snow and ice. Instead of claws or teeth, their weapons were beams of dark radiance that shot through an opening where a turtle's head would emerge from its shell.

Xantcha left the turtles for Urza and the Yotians. Safe in her armor and screaming loudly, she charged the searcher-priests instead, hoping to steal their ambulator. They took one look at her and retreated into the ambulator, rolling it up behind them, abandoning the avengers. She cursed them for their cowardice, but searchers were hard to replace. They were subtle for Phyrexians, far more subtle than avengers who, because they were so powerful, were also stupid.

She supposed the searchers could bring reinforcements, though, so far, once they left, they'd stayed gone. But the other skirmishes had been over sooner. Ice was not the ideal defense when the avengers' weapon was heat. The Yotians had been utterly destroyed without bringing down a single Phyrexian, which meant that Urza had to face them all. He had the skill and power, though the turtles were a bit tougher, a bit nastier they'd been in the last ambush, as if Phyrexia were learning from its failures—a frightening notion in and of itself.

There were only eight of the avengers left. Urza had destroyed two of those with dazzling streaks of raw power from his jeweled eyes. No one learned faster than Urza. He never tired nor depleted his resources. So long as there was substance beneath his feet or stars in the sky overhead, Urza the Artificer could work his uniquely potent magic.

Then, suddenly, his strikes became indecisive.

A turtle scuttled forward unchallenged and knocked Urza backward; the first time Xantcha had ever seen him touched in battle. He destroyed it with a glut of flame, but not before the other turtles pelted him with bursts of darkness.

After that Xantcha expected Urza to make short work of the enemy. Instead he became vaporous, a man of light and shadow. A turtle paw passed directly through him. Xantcha thought it was another of Urza's tactical surprises, until she watched his counter-strike pass through the turtle.

Xantcha had imagined the end many times, but she never thought the end would come from turtles on an ice-bound world.

Her armor would protect her . . . probably. Her club would almost certainly have no effect on avengers meant to destroy Urza the Artificer, but Xantcha would sooner face her personal end right here, right now, than risk capture and return to Phyrexia, or—even worse—eternity on this ice-bound world. She leapt onto the back of the nearest turtle and took aim at the forward gap in its carapace.

The turtle proved quite agile, bucking like an unbroken horse in its efforts to throw Xantcha off. She held on until two of the other avengers began targeting her instead of Urza. The armor held, barely. Xantcha felt the heat of dark magic, front and back, and the crack of her ribs as they began to break, one by one, under the hammer-and-anvil pressure.

The last thing Xantcha saw was Urza, brighter than the sun. . . .

Not a bad sight to carry into the darkness.

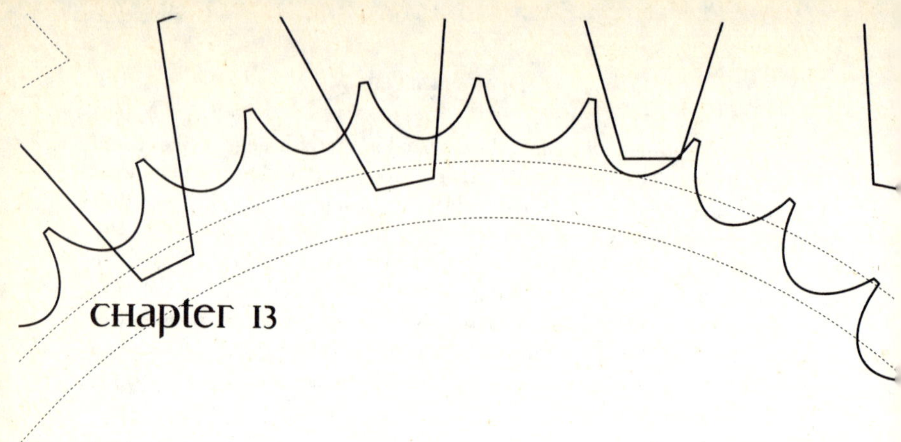

chapter 13

Summer had come to the Ohran ridge some two months after Ratepe arrived. Grass in every shade of green rippled in the wind beneath a blue crystal sky. Xantcha's sphere rose easily, caught a westward breeze, and began the journey to Efuan Pincar.

"Do you think this is going to work?" Ratepe asked when the cottage had disappeared into the folded foothills.

She didn't answer. Ratepe gave her a sulky look, which she also ignored. Still sulking, he began rearranging their traveling gear. Xantcha's head brushed the inner curve. Ratepe, who was a head-plus taller, was at a much greater disadvantage. With a dramatic show of determination, he shoved the largest, heaviest box behind them and upholstered it with food sacks. Although his efforts made the sphere easier to maneuver, if he didn't settle down Xantcha thought she might finish the journey alone.

"I don't think I've ever had cushions up here before," she said, trying to be pleasant, hoping pleasantry would be enough to calm her companion.

"I do what I can," he replied, still sulking.

Ratepe had a flair for solving problems, which didn't seem to depend on the images he gleaned from Urza's Weakstone eye. Even Urza had noticed it and made a point of discussing things with him that he'd never have mentioned to her. Xantcha told herself this was exactly what she'd wanted—an Urza who paid attention to the world around him. Of course, Urza thought he was talking to his long-dead brother, and Ratepe, though he played his part well, wanted more than conversation.

These days, Ratepe's mind swam in the memories of a man who'd been

Urza's peer in artifice. He'd absorbed all the theories of artifact creation, but as clever as he was with sacks and boxes, he was awkward at the worktable. Perhaps if he'd been willing to start with simple things . . . but if Ratepe had had the temperament for easy beginnings, the Weakstone probably would have ignored him, as it had always ignored Xantcha.

He'd tried pure magic where Xantcha had been certain he would succeed. Urza always said that magic was rooted in the land. Ratepe's devotion to Efuan Pincar was the touchstone of his life, and magic often came both late and sudden into a mortal's life, but it wouldn't enter Ratepe's, no matter how earnestly he invited it. The lowest blow, however, had come after he'd badgered Urza into concocting another cyst.

Ratepe had gulped the lump without a heartbeat's hesitation and writhed in agony for two days before he let Urza dissolve it. One artifact poisoning wasn't enough. He'd tried twice more, until Urza—who knew somewhere in the fathomless depths of his being that Ratepe was an ordinary young man and not his brother—refused to brew up another one.

"I don't mind doing the heavy work," Xantcha said. The sphere was moving nicely on its own. She laid her hand on his arm. "I like the company . . . the friendship."

Ratepe was more than a friend, though both of them were careful not to put the difference into words. The cottage had only two rooms. Her room had only one bed. The difference had come suddenly. One moment they were each alone, ignoring another rainy night. The next, they were on the bed, sitting near each other, then touching. For warmth, he'd said, and Xantcha had agreed, as if curiosity had never gotten her into trouble before. As if she hadn't known the difference between curiosity and need and been coldly willing to take advantage of it.

It had been awkward at first. Xantcha was, as she'd warned, a Phyrexian newt, a vat-grown creature whose purpose had never been to love another or beget children. But Ratepe was nothing if not persistent in the face of challenge, and the problems, though inconvenient, had been surmounted without artifice or magic. He was satisfied. Xantcha was surprised—astonished beyond all the words in all the languages she knew—to discover that being in love had nothing to do with being born.

Ratepe laced his fingers through hers. "I could do more. You never made good on your threat to make me cook my own food."

"There's only one hearth. I haven't had time to make another."

"That's what I mean." Ratepe tightened his hand. "You do everything. Urza doesn't notice, but I do. You're the one who makes the decisions."

Xantcha laughed. "You don't know Urza very well."

"I wouldn't know him at all if you hadn't decided to bring me here. I wake up in the morning, and for a few moments I think I'm back in Efuan Pincar with my family and that it's all been a dream. I think about telling my little brother, then I look over at you—"

She made an unnecessary adjustment to the sphere's drift, an excuse to reclaim her hand. "Urza's coming back to life, letting go of his obsessions. That's your doing."

Ratepe sighed. "I hadn't noticed."

Ratepe, like Mishra, had a tendency to sulk. Xantcha had reread *The Antiquity Wars* looking for ways to buoy his spirits. She'd even asked Urza what could put an end to Ratepe—or Mishra's—black, self-defeating moods. Silence, Urza had replied, had always been the best tactic when his brother sulked. Mishra couldn't bear to be ignored. Be patient, out wait him and his quicksilver temper would find another target.

Xantcha had learned endurance without mastering patience. "For the first time in two and a half centuries, Urza's worktable isn't covered with mountains. He's making artifacts again." Xantcha thumped the box behind her. "New artifacts, not the same gnats. He pays attention when *you* talk to him. Why do you think we're going up to Efuan Pincar?"

"To appease me! To keep me in my place?"

Xantcha's temper rose. "Don't be ridiculous."

"No? I've done what you wanted. He calls me Mishra and I answer. I listen to the Weakstone and remember things I never lived, that no one should have lived. When you or he says that I'm so much like Mishra . . . by Avohir's book, I want to go outside and smash my skull with a rock. It's no compliment to be compared with a cold-blooded murderer, and that's what they both are, Xantcha. That's what they always were. They care more about things than people. But I don't do it, because all I've got to replace everything I've lost is you. You asked me to be Mishra, so I am. All I've asked of Urza is that he care enough to send a few of his precious artifacts for Efuan Pincar."

"He does. He has. We're taking these to Pincar City, aren't we?"

"Admit it, you'd both rather be rooting around in Baszerat or Morvern. You've been down there, what, seven, eight times?"

"Six, and you could have come. The lines are clearer there. Urza recognizes the strategies. It's your war all over again, just smaller."

"Not my war, damn it! If I were going to fight a war it wouldn't be in Baszerat or Morvern!"

Xantcha made the sphere tumble and swerve, but those tricks no longer worked. Ratepe had overcome his fear of the open sky. He kept his balance as easily as she did and knew perfectly well that she wasn't going to let them drop to the ground.

"You're wasting your time. Get rid of the Phyrexians in Baszerat or Morvern, and they'll keep on fighting each other. That's what they do."

"And Efuands are so much better than Baszerati swine and Morvernish sheep, or have I got that backward? Are the Baszerati the swine or the sheep?"

"They're all pig-keepers."

Belatedly, Xantcha clamped her teeth together and said nothing. She should have taken Urza's advice, hard as ignoring Rat was when they couldn't get more than a handspan apart. The sphere came around on two long tacks before he saw fit to speak again.

"Do you think it will work?"

The same question he'd asked as they'd risen up from the cottage, but the whiny edge was gone from his voice. Xantcha risked an honest answer.

"Maybe. The artifacts will work. They'll be our eyes and ears and noses in the walls. We'll find out where the Phyrexians are, and if we know that, maybe we'll be able to figure out what they're up to, what can be done to thwart them."

"We know they're in the Red-Stripes and we know the Red-Stripes are doing the Shratta's dirty work. If there are any Shratta left. I want to get to Pincar City and get you into Avohir's temple. I want to know what kinds of oils you smell there. I want you in the palace, so I'll know what's happened to Tabarna. Has he become another Mishra, a man on the outside, a Phyrexian on the inside? Avohir's mercy—I was so certain Urza would listen when I said, 'Brother, don't let the Phyrexians do to another man what they did to me!' And what was his response? Pebbles! We're going to scatter *pebbles* then come back, who knows when, and see if any of the pebbles have changed color!" Ratepe took a breath and began speaking in a dead-on imitation of Urza, "That way I will know for certain if my enemy has come to Efuan Pincar. . . .

"Sometimes I'm not so sure he is Urza. Maybe he was once someone like me, then the Mightstone took over his life. Avohir! If a man's a murderer, what's the use of a conscience? During the war, the real Urza and the real Mishra both made hunter-killers, none of this pebbles-on-the-path, wait-and-see nonsense. They went right after each other."

"Urza doesn't want to repeat his old mistakes." Waste not, want not—she was defending Urza with the very arguments that had infuriated her for millennia. "The situation in Efuan Pincar is different. He's not sure what's going on, so he's being careful."

"And putting all his real efforts into Baszerat and Morvern! Avohir! How many Efuand villages have to burn before they're important?"

"I wouldn't know," Xantcha snarled. "Dominaria's the only world he's ever come back to. Everyplace else, he's just 'walked off and left to its fate. Urza may not be doing what you'd like him to do, but he is doing something. He listens to you, Ratepe. He's never really *listened* to anyone before. You should be pleased with yourself."

"Not while my people are dying. Urza's got the power, Xantcha, and the obligation to use it,"

Xantcha was going to mutter something about men who put ideas first, but resisted the impulse. Prickly silence persisted throughout the afternoon.

She brought the sphere down with the sun. Ratepe made an abortive attempt to help set up their camp, but they weren't ready to talk civilly to each other. Xantcha banished him to nearby trees until she got the fire lit.

The sky was radiant lavender before she went looking for her troublesome companion. Ratepe had seated himself on the west-facing bole of a fallen tree. Xantcha got no reaction as she approached and was rekindling her irritation when she realized his cheeks were wet. Compleat Phyrexians didn't cry, but newts sometimes did, until they learned it didn't help.

"Supper's on the fire."

Ratepe started, realized he'd been weeping, and wiped his face roughly on his sleeve before meeting her eyes. "I'm not hungry."

"Still angry with me?"

He turned west again. "The Sea-star's above the sun. The Festival of Fruits is over."

A single yellow star shone in the lavender.

"Berulu," she said, giving it the old Argivian name that Urza used. It would be another week before it rose high enough to be seen from the cottage.

"I'm eighteen."

Born-folk, being mortal and having parents and usually living their whole lives on a single world, kept close track of their ages. "Is that a significant age?" she asked politely. Some years were more important than others.

Ratepe swallowed and spoke in a husky voice. "You and Urza don't live by any calendar. One day's the same as the next. There isn't any reason . . . I—I forgot my birthday. It must have been three, maybe four days ago. Last year—last year we were together. My mother roasted a duck, and my little brother gave me a honey-cake that was full of sand. My father gave me a book, Suppulan's *Philosophy.* The Shratta burnt it. For them, there is only one book. Or it wasn't the Shratta but the Red-Stripes doing Shratta work who burnt it. It got burnt, that's enough. Burnt and gone." Ratepe hid his face in his hands as memory got the better of him. "Go away."

"You think about them?'

"Go away," he repeated, then added, "Please."

Urza's grief had hardened into obsession. Xantcha understood obsession. Ratepe's flowed freely from his heart and mystified her. "I could roast a duck for you, if I can find one. Will that help?"

"Not now, Xantcha. I know you care, but not now. Whatever you say, it only reminds me of what's gone."

She retreated. "I'll be by the fire until it is good and truly dark. Then I will come back here, if you will not come down. This is wild country, Ratepe, and you're not . . ." The right word, the word that wouldn't offend him, failed to spring into her mind.

"I'm not what? Not clever enough to take care of myself? Not strong enough? Not immortal or Phyrexian? You call me Ratepe now, and you say that you love me, but I'm still a slave, still Rat."

Agreeing with him would start a war. "Come down to the fire. I promise I will not say anything."

Xantcha kept her promise. It wasn't difficult. Ratepe wrapped himself in a blanket and curled up with his back to her. She couldn't easily count the nights she'd spent in silence and alone. None of them had seemed as long. When he stretched himself awake after dawn, Xantcha waited for him to speak first.

"I'm going into the palace when we get to Pincar."

She'd hoped for a less inflammatory start to the day. "No. Impossible. You agreed to stay at an inn with our supplies while I scattered Urza's pebbles in the places where we don't want to find Phyrexians. Your task is to help me find the Shratta strongholds in the countryside once I'm done in the city. We need to know if there are any real Shratta left."

"I know, but I'm going to the palace. Straight to Tabarna, if he's there, whether he's a man or something else. Every Efuand has the right to petition our king. If he's a man, I'll tell him the truth."

Xantcha planned her reply as she set aside a mug of cold tea. "And if he isn't?" She'd learned from Urza, truth and logic were worthless with madmen. It was always better to let them rant until they ran themselves down.

"Then they'll kill me, and you'll have to tell Urza what happened, and maybe then he'll do something."

She grimaced into her tea. "That's a burden I don't want to carry. So, let's assume you survive. Let's assume you're face-to-face with Tabarna. What truth will you tell your king?"

"I will tell him that Efuands must stop killing Efuands. I'll tell Tabarna what the Red-Stripes have done."

"Very bold, but with or without Phyrexians, your king already knows what the Red-Stripes are doing in the Shratta's name."

"He can't . . ." Ratepe's voice trailed off. He'd seen too much in his short life to dismiss her out of hand.

"He must."

"Not Tabarna. He wouldn't. If he's still in Pincar City, if he's still a man, then he thinks what I thought, that it's all the Shratta. He doesn't know the truth. He can't."

Xantcha sipped her tea. "All right, Rat, assume you're right. The king of Efuan Pincar, a man like yourself, still sits on his throne. He doesn't know that there are Phyrexians among his Red-Stripe guards. He doesn't know what those red-striped thugs have done. He doesn't know that, in all likelihood, the Shratta were the first to be exterminated. If Tabarna doesn't know any of this exists, then who else in Efuan Pincar does? And how has this nameless, faceless person kept your king in ignorance all these years?"

Ratepe's whole face tightened in uncomfortable silence. "No." Not a denial, but a prayer, "Not Tabarna."

"Best hope that Tabarna is skin stretched over metal. You'll hurt less, when the time comes, if you're not fighting a man who sold his soul to Phyrexia. In the meantime, until I know where the Phyrexians are and who they are, we will rely on Urza's pebbles and you will stay out of trouble and danger."

Ratepe wasn't happy. He wasn't stupid, either. After a slight nod, he busied himself folding his blanket.

That day's journey was easier and much quieter. Ratepe spent most of their time aloft staring at the horizon, but there were no tears and Xantcha let him be. Most of her journeys had been taken in silence, and though she'd quickly grown accustomed to Ratepe's company and conversation, old habits returned quickly.

She brought them over the Pincar City walls in the darkness between moon set and sunrise six days later. The sky was clear, the streets were deserted, and the guards they could see were more interested in staying awake until the end of their watch than in a dark speck moving across a dark sky. Xantcha decided to risk a pass above the palace. Few things were as useful as a bird's eye view of unfamiliar territory.

A few slow-moving servants were at work in the courtyards, getting a jump on their chores before the sun rose. Sea breezes and frequent showers kept the coastal city livable in the summer, but the air was always moist and if a person had the choice, work was easier done before dawn than in mid-afternoon.

Xantcha was building a mind-map of the royal apartments, servant quarters, and bureaucratic halls when Ratepe tugged on her sleeve and drew her attention to the stables. His lips touched her hair as he whispered.

"Trouble."

Six men, cloaked head to toe but otherwise unmarked, led their horses toward the postern gate—the palace's private gate. Probably it wasn't anything significant. Palaces throughout the Multiverse had similarly placed gates because royal affairs sometimes required the sort of discretion that others might call deceit. But while it was still dark they were in no danger of being seen. Xantcha wove her fingers, and the sphere floated behind the men.

The tide was out, exposing a narrow rocky spit between the ocean and the harbor. The not-unpleasant tang of seaweed and salt-water mud permeated the sphere. Xantcha took a deep breath. No glistening oil. Whoever the six cloaked men were, they weren't Phyrexian.

"Messengers," she decided softly and the sphere began to drift backward with the sea breeze.

"Follow them."

"They're nothing, Rat."

"They're trouble. I smell it."

He knew she detected Phyrexians by scent. She knew his nose wasn't sensitive. "You can't smell trouble, and you can't see it, either. We've got to find an alley where we can set ourselves down without drawing a crowd."

"Xantcha, please? I've just got a feeling about them. I want to know where they're going. I'll stay at the inn. I won't give you any hassle, just—follow them?"

"No complaints when we're stuck hiding in a gully somewhere until after sundown?"

"Not a word."

"Not a sound or a gesture, either," she grumbled, but she shifted her hand and they scooted over the palace wall.

Their quarry stayed along the shoreline, out of sight of the guards on the Pincar walls. Ratepe was likely right. They weren't up to any good, but that could mean almost anything, maybe even a meeting with the Shratta. That would be worth knowing about, but she wasn't prepared for confrontation.

"We're not getting involved," Xantcha warned.

They'd fallen far enough behind the six men that Xantcha wasn't worried about being overheard. She did worry about sun. Dominaria wasn't a world where large man-made objects routinely whizzed through the sky. Urza's ornithopters, like Urza himself, were remembered mostly for their wrongheadedness. She'd followed men for days and never been noticed, but men who were, as Ratepe proclaimed, trouble, tended to look over their shoulder frequently and might notice a shadow where one shouldn't be.

"Not unless we have to."

"No unlesses, Rat. We're not getting involved."

"We've got more than we had when you sent me into a burning village."

True enough. Since she knew there were Phyrexians loose in Efuan Pincar, Xantcha had fattened their arsenal with a variety of exploding artifacts and a pair of firepots. Having protection wasn't the same as using it. She hadn't survived all these centuries by blundering into someone else's trouble.

"We're following them, that's all. In the very unlikely event that they're going to meet with a Phyrexian demon, I'll think about it." She thought about it as long as it took her to spin the sphere around and push it, with all of her might, toward the opposite horizon.

Although Xantcha and Ratepe could still see the city walls, the riders had reached a point where they were beyond the Pincar guards' sight. Accordingly, they mounted and galloped their horses south.

"They're in a hurry," Ratepe said as Xantcha pushed the loaded sphere to its limit. "I wonder where they're going."

"Not far. Not at that speed."

The laden sphere couldn't keep pace. They lost sight of the riders, but not the dust cloud their horses raised. Xantcha took the opportunity to tack behind them and be in the east with the sun when they caught up again.

"You said you'd follow them!" Ratepe said, as the sphere veered sunward.

"You said no complaints."

"If we were on their tails."

"We're on their sun-side flank, it's safer. Trust me."

As expected, the horses slowed, the dust ebbed, and the sphere carried Xantcha and Ratepe close enough to see that the men had reined in at the grassy edge of an abandoned orchard and dismounted.

"That's odd," Xantcha muttered. A warrior's sunrise ceremony? She'd seen far stranger traditions.

Ratepe had no ideas or comments. Perhaps he was feeling foolish or thinking about the long day ahead of him, hunkered down in a gully, forbidden by his honor to complain. Xantcha tapped him on the shoulder.

"See that spot down there on the grass?"

She pointed at a dark splotch in the west. Ratepe nodded.

"That's our shadow. I want you to keep a watch on it, and if I get careless and it gets close to those men or, especially, their horses, I want you to tell me. We're going in for a closer look."

"I concede that you were right, and I'm a fool. Let's find some shade. The sun's just come up, and I'm sweating already."

"Keep an eye on our shadow."

Xantcha kept the sun squarely on their backs as they floated closer. There was no real danger. She'd been seen elsewhere, even shot at with arrows and spears, none of which could pierce the sphere. Sorcerers were more of a problem. But sorcerers—sorcerers with the power to damage one of Urza's artifacts—were almost as easy to detect as Phyrexians and rarer than Phyrexians in Efuan Pincar.

As they approached hearing distance, Xantcha reminded Ratepe to be quiet and brought the sphere into the orchard nearest the men who were trampling the grass in a rough circle about ten paces across. She didn't like what she saw.

"If you sincerely believe in your god," she said softly, "start praying that I'm wrong."

"What?"

She held a finger to her lips.

Ratepe wasn't successful with his prayers, or Avohir, the all-powerful Efuand god, was listening elsewhere that morning. They hadn't hovered among the trees for very long when one of the men pulled something black, shiny, and disk-shaped from his saddlebags.

Xantcha made a fist with her non-navigational hand and swore in the lilting language of a pink-sky world where curses were considered art.

"Trouble?" Ratepe asked.

The six men had each grabbed onto the disk and were beginning to stretch it across the trampled grass, not the way she'd learned to open an ambulator, but it had been nearly two thousand years since she'd last seen one. Undoubtedly there'd been changes.

"Big trouble. We're going to get involved. That's a passageway to Phyrexia that they're rolling out. Maybe they're going to visit the Ineffable, but more likely, there're *sleepers* coming in, and we're going to stop them, or die trying. You understand me?" Xantcha seized Ratepe's shoulder and forced him to look at her. "We either stop those men, or you make damn sure you don't survive, 'cause *sleepers* won't come through alone, and anything else that comes through that ambulator you don't ever want to meet."

He went bloodless pale beneath his sweat and neither nodded nor spoke.

"Understand?"

"W-what can I do?"

"They're not watching their backs. If we're lucky, we can set up the firepots, then you keep dropping Urza's toys into them, one after another."

Ratepe nodded, and Xantcha curled her fingers, raising the sphere slightly, then backing off to the far edge of the orchard, out of sight of the six men, but well within the firepots' range. She brought it down carefully. The thump of their supplies hitting the ground as the sphere collapsed wasn't loud enough to disturb the birds in the nearest trees.

Xantcha kissed Ratepe once before she yawned out a layer of armor that would make affection pointless. The firepots were tubes shaped roughly like men's boots, with the important difference that when Xantcha unlaced them, their phloton linings glowed. She aimed them from memory. Close would be good enough with the canisters they'd be using. After she'd piled the fist-sized canisters at Ratepe's feet and dumped a pair—one filled with compressed naphtha, the other with glass shards—into the rapidly heating firepots, she handed Ratepe her smaller coin pouch.

"Anyone gets too close, don't bother with your sword, just throw one of these at him and duck."

Then the firepots let loose, and it was time to draw her sword and run.

The Efuands were sword-armed but not armored. Xantcha planned to take one, maybe two, of them by surprise, and hoped that the firepots would do the same, but mostly she hoped that the Efuands would abandon the ambulator before it spat out reinforcements. The first part of her plan went well. She met a man charging through the trees, struggling to draw his sword. Xantcha slew him with a side cut across the gut. It was loud and messy but successful.

One down, five to go.

The firepots, whose trajectory was more height than distance, delivered both of Urza's exploding artifacts within twenty paces of the ambulator. They'd spooked the horses; all six had torn free and bolted, but the naphtha had fallen beyond the black pool, and the glass hadn't disabled any of the four men—two still at work anchoring the ambulator, two with their swords drawn and coming after her—that Xantcha could see.

Two more canisters came hissing out of the morning sunlight. One fell on the rippling pool and vanished before it exploded. No time to imagine where it might have gone or what it might accomplish when it arrived. The second spread more glass shards near the two men working on the portal's rim. If she survived, Xantcha planned to tell Urza that glass shards weren't effective against Efuands. Though bloodied and clearly in pain, the pair stayed put.

Four plus one was only five. Xantcha hoped Ratepe remembered the coins. Then she put him out of her mind. The swordsmen positioned themselves between her and the other pair of Efuands. She knew what they saw: an undersized youth with an undersized sword and no apparent armor. She knew how to take advantage of misperception. Her arm trembled, the tip of her sword pointed at the ground, and then she ran at the nearer of the pair.

He thought he could beat her attack aside with a simple parry. That was his last mistake. The other thought he had an easy stroke across the back of her neck. He struck hard enough to drop Xantcha to one knee, but he'd been expecting more and failed to press what little advantage he had. Xantcha pivoted on her knee, got her weight behind the hilt, and thrust the blade up through his stomach to his heart.

She left her sword in the corpse and took up his instead.

Of the two remaining Efuands, one was on his knees fussing with the ambulator while the other stood guard over him. Black on black patterns flowed across the portal's surface. Xantcha didn't dare run across it.

She could smell Phyrexia as the Efuand beat aside her first attack. He was the best of the men she'd faced so far and respectful. He stayed calm and balanced behind his sword, not in any hurry. Xantcha was in a hurry, and led with her empty, off-weapon hand, seizing his sword midway down the blade. It was a risky move. Urza's armor couldn't make her bigger or heavier than she naturally was. She couldn't always maintain her grip, and more than once she'd wound up with a dislocated shoulder.

This time, surprise and luck were with her, at least long enough to plunge her sword in the swordsman's gut before she shoved him backward, off the blade and into the black pool. She kicked the kneeling Efuand in the chin, not a crippling, much less a killing blow, except that he, too, fell backward, into the now seething ambulator.

Two more exploding artifacts arrived. One was simply loud and hurled her backward, away from the ambulator, but still the last direction she wanted to move. The other was fire that spread evenly across the black surface.

Xantcha staggered back to the place where the last Efuand had been kneeling, the place where she expected to find a palm-sized panel with seven black jewels. The priests had changed the design. There was neither panel nor jewels. In their place Xantcha saw a smooth black stone, like Urza's magnifying lens, or like the ambulator itself. The fire still burnt. Nothing had emerged. She brought her sword down on the stone.

The sword shattered.

The fire vanished as if someone had inhaled it.

And the black on black patterns had turned silver.

"Run, Ratepe!" she shouted as loud as the armor permitted, and ignored her own advice.

A Phyrexian emerged from the black pool moments later. It was a priest of some sort. There was too much metal, all of it articulated, for it to be anything less than a searcher, definitely not the scrap-made tender or teacher Xantcha had expected with a band of *sleepers.* It had a triangular head with faceted eyes, a bit like Urza's gemstone eyes, though large enough that she couldn't have covered one with splayed fingers. The design needed improvement. The priest raised a nozzle-tipped arm and exterminated a flying bird an instant after it was fully erupted, but ignored Xantcha who crouched unmoving some three paces from the ambulator's edge.

The nozzle arm was also new to Xantcha. She thought she'd seen a thin black thread reach out to the bird, but the attack had been so quick that she couldn't be sure of anything except the bird had disappeared in a burst of red light. Nothing, not even a feather, had fallen from the sky.

No doubt Xantcha would find out exactly what it could do, and since the priest's arms were mismatched, what surprises lurked on its right side. Urza's armor had never failed.

"Over here, meatling!" Few epithets would get a priest's attention quicker than calling it a newt. Xantcha stood up, brandishing her broken sword.

The nozzle weapon sent something very sharp, very hot at the hollow of Xantcha's neck, and she felt as though it had come out through her spine. Urza's armor flashed a radiant cobalt blue, astonishing both her and the priest.

"What is your place?" the priest demanded through mouth-parts hidden within its triangle head. It was not an avenger, modeled after fleshly predators, it was, despite its weapons, a thinker, a planner.

"Xantcha."

The right arm came up and shot forth a segmented cable, the tip of which was a fast-spinning flower with razored petals. It struck Xantcha's face. She felt bones give, but the flower took greater damage. Steel petals clattered to the ground, and pulses of glistening oil spurted from the still-spinning hub.

Xantcha struck quickly with the broken sword, enveloping the cable and yanked hard. It had two metal legs and a top-heavy torso. In the Phyrexia she remembered, such bipedal priests had a tendency to topple.

And it nearly did, though nearly was worse than not at all. Xantcha had simply pulled it closer, and it lashed the severed cable of its right arm around her waist. It began using its metal arms as clubs. Xantcha could neither retreat nor make good use of her sword. Her right elbow got clobbered and broken within the armor. She managed to get the sword free of the cable and transferred to her left hand before her right went numb within the armor. Xantcha took the only stroke she had, a sideswipe at the priest's right eye.

Two more of Urza's canisters rained down. One was concussive; the other screamed so loud Xantcha's ears hurt through the armor. Together, the canisters jarred something loose inside the priest. Glistening oil poured from the downward point of its triangle head. It struck one final time, another blow to her already mangled elbow—they truly had no imagination—before it expired.

He'd saved her life.

Ratepe, son of Mideah, had saved her life.

The damn fool either hadn't heard her shout or, most likely, had ignored it.

Xantcha writhed free of the cable. Numbness had spread up her right arm to her shoulder. She'd survive. Urza himself had said that a Phyrexian newt's ability to heal itself was nothing less than miraculous, but she wasn't looking forward to releasing the armor and wouldn't consider doing it until she'd dealt with the ambulator.

She got down on her knees and cursed. New designs or no, the black pool in front of her was definitely the nether end of an ambulator, and unless she wanted to poke her head into Phyrexia to loosen the prime end, there was no way Xantcha could destroy it completely. But she could make it very dangerous to use, if she could get it rolled and find some way to break or reset the black lens. She had half the rim unanchored when yet another pair of canisters showered her with glass and fire.

"Enough, already!"

She moved on to the next anchor.

Ratepe arrived moments later. "Xantcha!"

"Stay away!" she warned harshly. The pain was bearable but numbness was making her groggy. She could have used help, but not from someone who was pure, mortal flesh. "It's not done. Not yet. I *told* you to run!"

"Xan—"

Xantcha realized she must look bad, broken bones bruising her face, her right arm, mangled and useless. "Don't worry about me. I'll be fine in a couple of days. Just . . . get away from here. More can come through, even now. Make yourself unnoticeable. I've to create an inconvenience."

"I'll help—"

"You'll hide."

She popped another anchor. The pool rippled, black on black. Ratepe retreated, but not far. She didn't have the strength to argue with him.

"There, by the priest, you'll see a little black glass-circle thing. Don't touch it! Don't touch anything. But think about breaking that glass." Xantcha crawled to the next anchor.

"Priest? Shratta?"

"No." She pointed at the heap of metal that had been the Phyrexian and went back to work on the anchor. Another eight or ten, and she'd have it loose.

"Merciful Avohir! Xantcha, what is it?"

"Phyrexian. A priest. I don't know what kind, something new since I left. That's what we're fighting. Except, that's a priest and not a Phyrexian meant for fighting."

"Not like you, then—"

Xantcha looked up. He was bent over, reaching out. "I said, don't touch it!" He straightened. "And I'm not a fighter. I'm not anything, a newt, nothing started, nothing compleated. Just a newt."

"The six—I killed the last one, myself, with those coins you left me." She hadn't heard the explosions. Well, there'd been other things on her mind. "They called this . . . a priest? They invited it here, to Efuan Pincar?"

"Big trouble, just like you said. And don't kid yourself. Assume they've got more ambulators." She remembered the upright disk in the Moag temple. "Assume they've got worse. Assume that some of the sleepers are awake, that there are priests inside the palace, and that some of your own have been corrupted, starting with your king." Xantcha released another anchor. "Look at the glass, will you? My sword broke when I hit it."

A moment or two of silence. She was down to her last three anchors when Ratepe said, "I've got an idea," and ran into the trees.

He came back with the firepots and the rest of Urza's canisters. "We can put it in one of the pots with the bangers, put one pot on top of the other and let it rip."

All the anchors were up and Xantcha had no better idea, except to send Ratepe to the far end of the orchard before she followed his suggestions.

Afterward, she remembered flying through the air and landing in a tree.

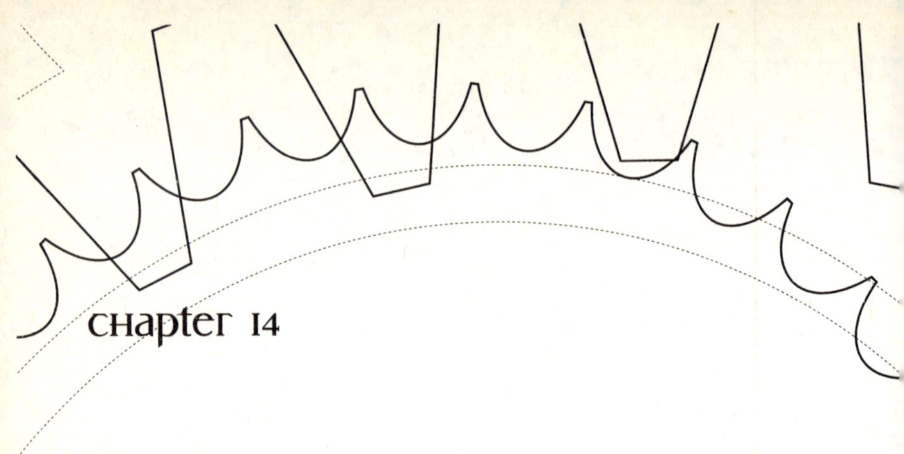

chapter 14

It had happened before in the between-worlds: a sensation of falling that lasted until Xantcha opened her eyes and found herself looking at nothing familiar.

"Ah, awake at last."

The voice was not quite a man's voice, yet deeper than most female voices and quite melodious, though Xantcha suspected that an acid personality powered it. She could almost picture a Phyrexian with that voice, though this place wasn't Phyrexia. Not a whiff of glistening oil accompanied the voice, and the air was quiet. There was music, in the distance, music such as might be made by glass chimes or bells.

Xantcha remembered the wind-crystal on another world.

She realized she was not in a bedroom, not in a building of any sort. The wall to her left and the ceiling above were a shallow, wind-eroded cave. Elsewhere, the world was grass. Grass with a woman's voice?

"Where am I? How did I get here? Urza? Where's Urza? We were together on the ice, fighting Phyrexians." She propped herself up on one elbow. "I have to find him." She was dizzy. Xantcha was rarely dizzy.

"As you were!"

By its tone, the voice was accustomed to obedience.

Xantcha lay flat and returned to her first question. "Where am I?"

"You are here. You are being cared for. There is nothing more you need to know."

She'd been so many places, picked up so many languages. Xantcha had to lie very still, listening to her thoughts and memories, before she could be sure she did not know the language she was speaking. It was simply there in her mind, implanted rather than acquired by listening. Another reason to think of Phyrexia.

Xantcha considered it unlucky to think of Phyrexia once before breakfast and here she'd thought of it three times. She realized she was very hungry.

"If I'm being cared for, I'd like something to eat, if you please."

Urza said manners were important among strangers, especially when one was at a stranger's mercy. Of course, he rarely bothered with such niceties. With his power, Urza was never at a stranger's mercy.

Xantcha remembered the turtles, the Phyrexians they'd been fighting before—before what? She couldn't remember how the skirmish had ended, only a bright light and a sense that she'd been falling for a long time before she woke up here, wherever here was.

"The air will sustain you," the voice said. "You do not need to fill yourself with death."

Another thought of Phyrexia, where compleat Phyrexians neither ate nor breathed but were sustained by glistening oil.

"I need food. I'll hunt it myself."

"You'll do no such thing!"

Xantcha pushed herself into a sitting position and got her first look at the voice: a tall woman, thin through the body, even thinner through the face. Her eyes were gray, her hair was pale gold, and her lips were a tight, disapproving line beneath a large, but narrow nose. She seemed young, at least to Xantcha. It seemed, as well, that she had never smiled or laughed.

"Who are you?" Xantcha asked, though *what are you?* was the question foremost in her mind.

The Multiverse might well contain an infinite number of worlds, but it had no more than two-score of sentient types, if Xantcha followed Urza's example and disregarded those types that, though clearly sentient, were also completely feral and without the hope of civilization. Or nearly four-score, if she followed her own inclination to regard men and women of every type as distinct species.

Urza's type was the most common and with the arrogance of the clear majority. He called himself simply a man where others were elf-men, or dwarf-men, or gremlin-men. His wife, Kayla Bin-Kroog, had been a woman, a very beautiful woman. When Xantcha had asked Urza for a single word that united men and women, as elves united elf-man and elf-woman, he'd answered mankind, which seemed to her a better way of uniting all the men, common and rare, rather than common men with their wives and daughters.

When she'd demanded a better word, Urza had snarled and 'walked away. Xantcha wondered what he'd make of the woman standing in front of her. Wonder sparked a hope he was still alive, and that she'd find him here, but another thought crowded Urza from Xantcha's mind. She and the stranger were both dressed in long white gowns.

Where had her clothes gone? Her sword and knives? The shoulder sack filled with stew and treasure? Except for the gown, Xantcha was naked. She wondered if the stern-faced woman was naked, if she was really a woman after all. Her voice was quite deep, and her breasts were a far cry from generous.

That was very nearly a fifth Phyrexian thought before breakfast, and since the stranger had given no indication that she was going to answer any of her questions, Xantcha got her feet under her and pushed herself upright. Another bout of dizziness left her grateful for the nearby rock.

She rested with her back against the stone and took a measure of the world where she'd awakened. It was a golden place of rolling hills and ripened grasses, all caught in the afterglow of a brilliant sunset, with clear air and layers upon layers of clouds overhead. It was difficult, though, to discern where west lay. Urza had explained it to her in the earliest days. Wherever men dwelt, the sun set in the west and rose in the east. In all quarters the horizon was marked with dazzling amber peaks that might have been mountains or might have been clouds. It was achingly beautiful and almost as strange.

On impulse, Xantcha looked for her shadow and found it huddled close by her feet, where she'd expect to find it at high noon. Curiosity became suspicion that got the better of her manners, "Does this world mark time by the sun?" she asked with a scowl, a sixth Phyrexian thought. "Or do you live in immortal sunset?"

The stranger drew back and seemed, somehow, taller. "We think of it as sunrise."

"Does the sun ever get risen?"

"Our Lady has created all that you can see, each cloud, each breeze, each stone, each tree and blade of grass. She has created them all at their moment of greatest beauty. There is peace here and no need for change."

Xantcha let out a long, disbelieving breath. "Waste not, want not."

"Exactly," the stranger replied, though Xantcha had not intended the Phyrexian maxim as a compliment.

"Are we alone?"

"No."

"Where are the others?"

"Not here."

Xantcha's dizziness had passed. If there were others elsewhere, she was ready to look for them. She took a deep breath, opened her mouth, and yawned.

"Not here!" the woman repeated, an emphatic command this time.

Listen and obey the vat-priests had told Xantcha in the beginning, and despite the passage of time, she still found it difficult to disobey, especially when the cyst felt heavy in her gut, heavy and oddly unreliable. She swallowed the lump that was part unemerged sphere and part rising panic.

"How did I get here?"

"I don't know."

"How long have I been here?"

"Since you arrived."

"Where am I?"

"Where you are."

Panic surged again, and this time Xantcha couldn't fight it down. "What manner of world is this?" she shouted. "The sun doesn't rise or set. You give me answers that aren't answers. Is this Phyrexia? Is that it? Have I been brought back to Phyrexia?"

The stranger blinked but said nothing.

"Can I leave? Is Urza here? Can I find Urza?"

More silence. Xantcha wanted to run. She was lucky she could walk. Her legs had become the legs of a lethargic stranger. Every step required concentration, calculation, and blind faith as she transferred weight from one foot to the other. After ten strides, Xantcha was panting and needed to rest. She didn't dare sit down for fear she wouldn't have the strength to stand again, so she bent from the hips and kept her balance by bracing clammy, shaking hands on her gown-covered knees.

The stranger wasn't following her. Xantcha pulled herself erect and started walking again. She took nearly twenty cautious steps before her strength gave out. The stranger hadn't moved at all.

Urza! Xantcha thought his name with the same precision she used with her mnemonics when she yawned. Urza had never admitted that he was open to her thoughts, but he'd never denied it, either. *Urza, I'm in a strange place. Nothing is all wrong, but it's not right, either and I'm not myself. If you're nearby—?*

She stopped short of begging or pleading. If he had survived their last battle . . . and Xantcha was unwilling to believe that she had outlived Urza the Artificer, and she certainly couldn't have gotten here on her own. If Urza weren't busy with problems of his own, then he would come. Until then, she would walk.

The heaviness and lethargy didn't go away as the dizziness had, but Xantcha became accustomed to them, as she would have accustomed herself to the rise and fall of a boat's deck. Xantcha might not know where she was or where she was going, but when she looked over her shoulder, she'd left a clean line through the ripe grass.

The stranger had told at least one truth. The air was enough. Xantcha forgot her hunger and never became thirsty, even though she worked up a considerable sweat forcing herself across the hills. Up and down and up again. Eventually Xantcha lost sight of the stranger and the rock where she'd awakened. There were other rocks along her chosen path, all dun-colored and eroded into curves that were the same, yet also unique.

Once, and once only, Xantcha saw a bush and veered off her straight path to examine it. The bush was shoulder-high and sprawling. Its leaves were tiny but intensely green—the first green she'd found on this sunset-colored world. Pale berries clustered on inner branches. Xantcha considered picking a handful, then noticed the thorns, too, a lot of them and each as long as her thumb.

The stranger had been appalled when she'd mentioned hunting for her food, as if nothing here needed anything more than air to survive. But if that were true, then why the thorns, and why were there berries only on the inner branches? The stranger had spoken of a Lady and of creation and perfection. Someone somewhere was telling lies.

Xantcha left the berries alone. She rejoined her trail through the grass. If there were predators, they'd have no trouble finding her. The golden grass was ripe and brittle. She'd left a wake of broken stalks and wished she still had her sword or at least a knife. Aside from the stranger, Xantcha had seen nothing living that wasn't also rooted in the ground, no birds or animals, not even insects. A place that had berries should have insects.

Even Phyrexia had insects.

Xantcha walked until her body told her it was time to sleep. How long she'd walked or how far were unanswerable questions. She made herself a grass mattress beside another rock, because habit said a rock provided more shelter than open grass. If the stranger could be believed, night never fell, the air wouldn't turn cold, and there was no reason not to sleep soundly, but Xantcha didn't trust the stranger. She couldn't keep her eyes closed long enough for the grass beneath her to make impressions in her skin and after a handful of failed naps, she started walking again.

If walking and fitful napping were a day, then Xantcha walked for three days before she came upon a familiar stranger waiting beside a weathered rock. Even remembering that she, herself, had been one of several thousand identical newts, Xantcha was sure it was the same stranger. The rock was the same, and a wake of broken grass began nearby.

The stranger had moved. She was sitting rather than standing, and she was aware that Xantcha had returned, following her closely with her gray eyes, but she didn't speak. Silence reigned until Xantcha couldn't bear it.

"You said there were others. Where? How can I find them?"

"You can't."

"Why not? How big is this world? What happened to me? Did I trick myself into walking in a circle? Answer me! Answer my questions! Is this some sort of punishment?" Manners be damned, Xantcha threatened the seated woman with her fists. "Is this Phyrexia? Are you some new kind of priest?"

The woman's expression froze between shock and disdain. She blinked, but her gray eyes didn't become flashing jewels as Urza's would have done. Nor did she raise any other defense, yet Xantcha backed away, lowered her arms, and unclenched her hands.

"So, you can control yourself. Can you learn? Can you sit and wait?"

Xantcha had learned harder lessons than sitting opposite an enigmatic stranger, though few that seemed more useless. Other than the slowly shifting cloud layers, the occasionally rippling grass and the gray-eyed woman, there was nothing to look at, nothing to occupy Xantcha's thoughts. And if the goal were self-reflection . . .

"Urza says that I have no imagination," Xantcha explained when her legs had begun to twitch so badly she'd had to get up and walk around the rock a few times. "My mind is empty. I can't see myself without a mirror. It's because I'm Phyrexian."

"Lies," the stranger said without looking up.

"Lies," Xantcha retorted, ready for an argument, ready for anything that would cut the boredom. "You're a fine one to complain about lies!"

But the stranger didn't take Xantcha's bait, and Xantcha returned to her chosen place. Days were longer beside the rock. Sitting was less strenuous than walking and despite her suspicions, Xantcha slept soundly with the stranger nearby. They had a conversational breakthrough on the fourth day of unrelenting boredom when a line of black dots appeared beneath the lowest cloud layer.

"The others?" Xantcha asked. She would have soared off in the sphere days earlier and over her companion's objections, if the cyst weren't still churning and awkward in her gut.

The stranger stood up, a first since Xantcha had returned from her walk. Gray eyes rapt on the moving specks, she walked into the unbroken grass. She reached out toward them with both arms stretched to the fingertips. But the specks moved on, her arms fell, and she returned to Xantcha, all sagging shoulders and weariness. In this world without night, it finally dawned on Xantcha that she might have leapt to the wrong conclusions. "How long have you been here?" A friend's concern rather than a prisoner's accusation.

"I came with you."

Still a circular answer, but the tone had been less aloof. Xantcha persisted. "How long ago was that? How much time has passed since we've both been here?"

"Time is. Time cannot be cut and measured."

"As long as we've been sitting here, was I lying under the rock longer than that, or not as long?"

The stranger's brow furrowed. She looked at her hands. "Longer. Yes, much longer."

"Longer than you expected?"

"Very much longer."

"The air sustains us, but otherwise we've been forgotten?"

More furrowed brows, more silence, but the language implanted in her mind had words for time and forgetting. Meaning came before words. The stranger had to understand the question.

"Why are we both here, beside this rock and forgotten? What happened?"

"The angels found you and another—"

"Urza? I was with Urza?"

"With another not like you. His eyes see everything."

Xantcha slouched back against the rock. Raw fear drained down her spine. "Urza." She'd been found with Urza. Everything would be resolved; it was only a matter of time. "What happened to Urza?"

"The angels brought you both to the Lady's palace. The Lady held onto *Urza*. But you, you are not like Urza. She said she could do nothing with you, and you would die. The Lady does not look upon death."

"I was stuck out here to die, and you were put here to watch me until I did. But I didn't, and so we're both stuck here. Is that it?"

"We will wait."

"For what?"

"The palace."

Xantcha pressed her hands over her mouth, lest her temper escape. A newt, she told herself. The gray-eyed stranger was a newt. She listened, she obeyed, she had no imagination and didn't know how to leap from one thought to another. Xantcha herself had been like that until Gix had come to the First Sphere, probing her mind, making her defend herself, changing her forever. Xantcha had no intention of invading the stranger's privacy. She didn't have the ability, even if she'd had the intention. All she wanted was the answers that would reunite her with Urza.

And if her questions changed the stranger, did that make Xantcha herself another Gix? No, she decided and lowered her hands. She would not have poured acid down the fumarole to Gix's grave if he'd done nothing more than awaken her self-awareness.

"What if we didn't wait," Xantcha asked with all the enthusiasm of a conspirator in pursuit of a partner. "What if we went to the palace ourselves."

"We can't."

"Why not? Urza gave me a gift once. If you could tell me where the palace is, it could take us both there."

"No. Impossible. We shouldn't be speaking of this. I shouldn't be speaking with you at all. The Lady herself could do nothing with you. Enough. We will wait . . . in perfect silence."

The stranger bowed her head and folded her hands in her lap. Her lips moved rapidly as she recited something—Xantcha guessed a prayer—to herself. No matter. The wall had been breached. Xantcha *was* a conspirator in search of a partner, and she had nothing else to do but plan her next attack.

Within two days she had the stranger's name, Sosinna, and the certainty that Sosinna considered herself a woman. Two days more and she had the name of the Lady, Serra. After that, it was quite easy to keep Sosinna talking, although the sad truth was that Sosinna knew no more about Serra's world than Xantcha had known about Phyrexia when Urza first rescued her.

Sosinna was a Sister of Serra, one of many women who served that lady in her palace. If Xantcha had not walked for three days straight and found herself back where she'd started, she would have laughed aloud when Sosinna described Serra's palace as a wondrous island floating forever among the golden clouds. But it did seem true that Serra's world had no land, not as other worlds where men and women dwelt had great masses of rocks rising from their oceans. Xantcha had already learned that she couldn't walk to the edge of the floating island where she and Sosinna sat in exile, but once she had the thought of a floating island in her mind, Xantcha could see that many of the darker clouds around them weren't clouds at all but miniature worlds of grass and stone.

The others Sosinna had mentioned were angels, winged folk who did Serra's bidding away from the palace. Angels had found Urza and Xantcha, though Sosinna didn't know where, and angels had brought Xantcha and Sosinna to their exile island because the Sisters of Serra were unable to leave the floating palace on their own. The angels' wings weren't like Urza's cyst—the idea of having an artifact reside permanently in her stomach appalled Sosinna so much that she stopped talking for three full days. Nor were the wings added in some floating-island equivalent of the Fane of Flesh. That notion roused Sosinna's anger.

"Angels," she informed Xantcha emphatically, "are born. Here we are all born. The Lady reveres life. She would not ever countenance that—that—Fane. Filth. Waste. Death! No wonder—no wonder that the Lady said you could not be helped! I will have nothing more to do with you. Nothing at all!"

Sosinna couldn't keep her vow. The woman who'd sat silently for days on end could not resist telling Xantcha in great detail about the perfect way in which the Lady raised her realm's children.

Births, it seemed, were rare. Incipient parents dwelt in the palace under the Lady's immediate care, and their precious children, once they were born and weaned, went to the nursery where the Lady personally undertook their education. Sosinna's voice thickened with nostalgia as she described the tranquil cloister where she'd learned the arts of meditation and service. Privately, Xantcha thought Lady Serra's nursery sounded as grim as the Fane of Flesh, but she kept those thoughts to herself, smiling politely, even wistfully, at each new revelation.

On the twentieth day of forced smiles, Xantcha's conspiratorial campaign achieved its greatest victory when Sosinna confessed that she was in love, perfectly and eternally, with one of her nursery peers: an angel.

"Is that permitted?" Xantcha interrupted before she had the wit to censor herself. The notion of love fascinated her, and spending most of her life in Urza's shadow or hiding her unformed flesh beneath a young man's clothes, she'd had very little opportunity to learn love's secrets. "You don't have wings."

Xantcha's curiosity was ill-timed and rude. It jeopardized everything she'd gained through long days of patient questions, but it was sincere. On worlds where mankind lived side by side with elves or dwarves or any other sentients, love, with all its complications, was rarely encouraged, more frequently forbidden. She hardly expected love between the Sisters of Serra and winged angels to flourish in a place where the mere appearance of the sun would have spoilt the perfection of the sunrise.

But Sosinna surprised Xantcha with a furious blush that stretched from the collar of her white gown into her pale gold hair.

"Wings," Sosinna exclaimed, "have nothing to do with it!" A lie, if ever Xantcha had heard one. "We are all born the same, raised the same. Our parentage is not important to Lady Serra. We are all equal in her service. She encourages us to cherish each other openly and to follow our hearts, not our eyes, when we declare our one true love."

More lies, though Sosinna's passion was real. "Kenidiern is a paragon," she confided in a whisper. "No one serves the Lady with more bravery and vigor. He has examined every aspect of his being and cast out all trace of imperfection. There is not one mote of him that isn't pure and devoted to duty. He stands above all the other angels, and no one would fault him if he were proud, but he isn't. Kenidiern has embraced humility. There isn't a woman alive who wouldn't exchange tokens with him, but he has given his to me."

Sosinna removed her veil and, sweeping her hair aside, revealed a tiny golden earring in the lobe of her left ear.

"Beautiful. An honor above all others," Xantcha agreed, trying to imitate Sosinna's lofty tone while she wracked her mind for a way to turn this latest revelation toward a reunion with Urza and escape from Serra's too-perfect realm. "It must be difficult for you to be apart from him. You can't know what he's doing, or where. If something had happened to him, you wouldn't know and, well, if he's given you his token, it's not likely that he'd have forgotten you, so you have to think that he's looking for you, if he can." Xantcha smiled a very Phyrexian smile. Urza would disapprove, although there was no reason for him to ever know. "Of course, sometimes, even paragons get distracted. "

Several long moments of nervous fiddling passed before Sosinna said, "We have our duties. We both serve the Lady. Everyone serves the Lady first and foremost." She sat up straight and looked very uncomfortable. "I have strayed from the path. We will speak of these things no more."

But the damage had been done. Sosinna had lost the ability to stare endlessly at nothing. She watched the clouds. Xantcha supposed Sosinna was looking for angels and hoped, for her own selfish reasons, that they appeared. In the end, though, it wasn't angels that got them moving.

Once she'd learned that Serra's realm was composed of islands drifting in a cloudy sea, Xantcha had quickly realized that each island had its own rhythm and path. With a persistent ache in her stomach, Xantcha wasn't tempted to yawn out the sphere and become her own island, but she thought she could hop from one island to another if a more interesting one drifted near. She dismissed the possibility of a collision between two of the Lady's islands as an unimaginable imperfection, until the ground bucked beneath them. One moment Xantcha and Sosinna were lying flat, clinging to the rooted grass. The next, they were both thrown into the air while the land beneath shattered. For an instant they floated weightless; then the falling began. Without thinking or hesitating, Xantcha yawned and grabbed Sosinna's ankle. The cyst was slow to release its power, and the sphere, when it finally emerged, was midnight black.

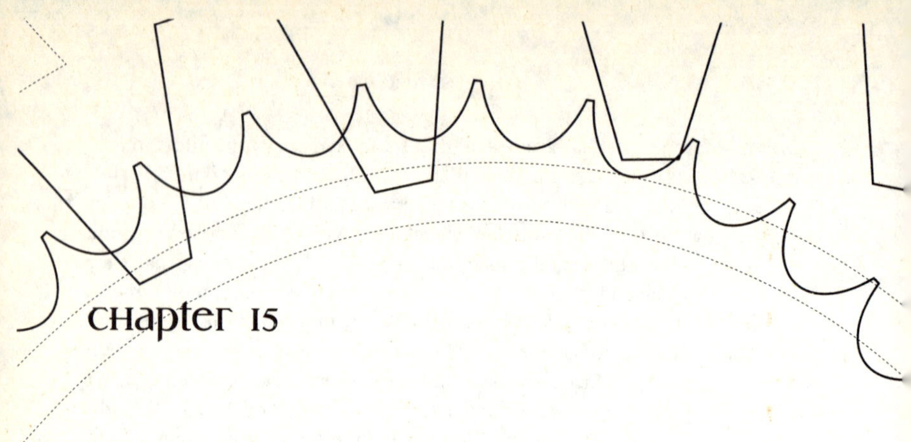

chapter 15

Xantcha and Sosinna both screamed as the darkness sealed around them. Navigation was impossible, and they became one more tumbling object in the chaos raining down from the colliding islands. Sosinna called her lady's name, begging for deliverance. Xantcha hoped Serra could hear. The sphere wasn't like Urza's armor. The armor lasted until Xantcha willed it away, but once the sphere had risen, it collapsed as soon as it touched the ground. At least that was what had always happened. It might do something different this time when it had come out black.

The jostling, which seemed to last forever, ended when they struck a decisive bottom. The sphere collapsed, as it always had, coating Xantcha in soot and leaving them in a shower of rocks. Xantcha was stunned when a stone struck her head. But mind-stars were all she saw through the sticky soot. Sosinna's hand closed over hers. Xantcha let herself be guided to a place where the air was quiet.

"So, what next?" Xantcha asked when she'd wiped away enough soot to open her eyes.

There wasn't much to see. The air was dusty, and the overhead island—the island from which they'd fallen and that continued to rain chunks of itself onto the island where they were standing—remained close enough to keep them in twilight darkness. She feared another collision.

"We can't stay here," she added, in case Sosinna had missed the obvious.

They were both nursing bruises. Xantcha's hand came away bloody when she touched the throbbing spot where the rock had hit her skull.

The left sleeve of Sosinna's gown was torn to rags, and she was dripping soot-streaked blood from a gash on her forearm. Xantcha never worried her own cuts. She healed quickly, and the infections or illnesses that plagued born-folk weren't interested in newt-flesh. She worried about Sosinna, instead.

Although Sosinna had gotten them to safety beyond the rock fall, she was dazed and unresponsive. She held her bleeding arm in front of her and stared at it with glassy eyes. The folk of Serra's realm were born, or so Sosinna had claimed. Despite the strangeness of the floating-island realm and the way Serra's air sustained them, Sosinna might be as fragile as the born-folk usually were. The soot alone might kill her. Blood poisoning wasn't an easy death or a quick one. But unless she had hidden injuries, Sosinna's problem had to be shock and fear.

"Waste not, want not, you're not near dead yet. Pull yourself—"

"It was black," Sosinna interrupted.

"I noticed," Xantcha said with a shrug. "It's always been clear before. But it kept us alive, and we'll use it again."

Sosinna wrenched free. "No! You don't understand. It was black! Nothing here is black. The Lady doesn't permit it." She began to weep. "I told you, you couldn't call on black mana here."

"Black mana? I'm no sorcerer, Sosinna. I've never called to the land in my life." But the cyst had felt wrong since she'd awakened, worse since she'd used it, and the sphere had been black.

"You shattered the land. Shattered it!"

Xantcha didn't demand gratitude, but she wouldn't stand for abuse. "I didn't shatter anything. Two islands collided, and I kept us alive the only way I knew how. Would you rather I'd left you to be crushed by the rocks?"

"Yes! Yes, they'll come for you because of what you've done, and they'll come for me because what you've done is all over me."

"If I'd known that, I'd've done it sooner," Xantcha lied.

Xantcha wasn't in pain. If anything, she was numb. For the first time in centuries, she wasn't aware of Urza's cyst. Her hand felt cloth when she rubbed below her waist, but the rest of her couldn't feel her hand. The numbness wasn't spreading. The part of her mind that knew when she was healthy said that she was numb because she was empty. She didn't know what would happen if she called on the cyst while her gut was numb and didn't want to find out unless she had to.

"How long before your Lady gets here?"

"The Lady won't come. She takes no part in death, even when she knows it must be done. The archangels will come." Sosinna looked up at the still-crumbling underside of their original floating island. "Soon."

Sosinna dried her tears, leaving fresh streaks of blood and soot on her face. Then she did what Serra's folk seemed to do best: she sat down, folded her hands in her lap, and settled in to wait. The gash on her arm continued to bleed. Maybe Sosinna didn't feel pain, or maybe she hoped she'd bleed to death before the dreaded archangels arrived.

If her own life hadn't hung in the balance, Xantcha would have laughed at the absurdity. She grabbed Sosinna below the shoulder and hauled the taller woman to her feet.

"You want to live, Sosinna. You got us both away from the falling rocks and dirt—" She shook the other woman, hoping for reaction. "You want to live. You want to see Kenidiern again."

A blink. A frown. Nothing.

"This is not perfection!" Xantcha shouted and then let Sosinna go.

The taller woman balanced on her own feet a moment, then calmly sat down again. Xantcha walked away in disgust. She'd gone about ten paces before the light of understanding brightened in her mind.

"You knew!" Xantcha shouted as she ran back. "You've known from the beginning! You've been expecting these arch-whatever-angels since I woke up . . . since before I woke up. Your precious, perfect Lady sent me here to be killed and sent you as what? A witness? 'Come back to the floating palace when everything's taken care of'? All this time, waiting for the archangels—"

"I never wanted them to come!" Sosinna shouted back.

It was the first time Xantcha had heard the other woman raise her voice—perhaps the first time Sosinna had raised it. She seemed aghast at her outburst.

"Why not? Didn't you want to get back to the palace and Kenidiern?"

Sosinna gasped and fumbled for words. "Don't you understand? I can't go back."

"Because I saved your life with my black mana." Xantcha thought she understood, perfectly. "If only the archangels had been a little quicker. Is that what you've been doing while you sat all the time. Praying to the archangels: get here soon?"

"I didn't want you to wake up because while you were asleep there was no chance you'd use your black powers, and nothing would draw the archangels to us. Once you were awake . . . You are . . . You are so difficult. I was afraid to tell you anything."

"I'd be much less difficult," Xantcha said with exaggerated politeness, "if I knew the truth." She sat down opposite Sosinna. "The perfect truth."

"Kenidiern—"

Xantcha rolled her eyes. "Why am I not surprised that he is at the heart of the truth?"

"You are very difficult. It is the black mana in you. It rules you. The Lady said so."

Xantcha wondered what the Lady had said about Urza, but that would have been a truly difficult question. "I know nothing about black mana, but I won't argue with your Lady's judgment. Go on . . . please . . . before we run out of time."

"How can you run out of time?"

Xantcha shrugged. "Just talk."

"The Lady smiled on Kenidiern and me. She has never encouraged the divisions between the sisterhood and the angels. We had her blessing to come to the palace, but before we could be together he was sent away, and I was chosen to accompany you. I would not have objected," Sosinna continued quickly and emphatically. "I serve Lady Serra proudly, willingly. We all know how she sacrifices herself to maintain the realm. It would be the worst sort of pride and arrogance to question her decisions. . . . But I could not, cannot believe this was her decision."

"To send me away to die or to send you away to die with me?"

Sosinna had the decency to look uncomfortable. "You are difficult, and you are devious. You imagine dark corners and then you make them real."

That was a criticism Xantcha had never heard from Urza's lips.

"You would never do among the sisters or the angels, but if I were to speak to the Lady, I would tell her that except for your black mana you would make a most excellent archangel, and I think she would agree. I was—am—young among the sisters, but I have—had—the Lady's confidence. I know she would not have sent me away without seeing me or telling me why."

"Then why hasn't she come looking for you? Wouldn't she notice you were missing, you and Kenidiern, both?"

Sosinna shivered. "You ask such questions, Xantcha! I would never think to ask such questions myself." She paused and Xantcha raised her eyebrows expectantly. "Until I met you. Now, I ask myself such questions, and I do not like my own answers! I ask myself if the Lady has been deceived by those who were displeased that Kenidiern had given me his token, and no matter how hard I try to purge my thoughts, I cannot convince myself that she hasn't."

"Or maybe your Lady's not perfect?"

Sosinna's thin-lipped mouth opened, closed, and opened again. "I don't know if she never looked for me or if she could not find me but in either case, yes, there would be imperfection. So you see I cannot go back to the palace, not with these thoughts in my heart. Kenidiern is lost. You mock me, Xantcha, do not bother to lie about it, but Kenidiern is a paragon. He would have looked for me and since he hasn't—"

"Hasn't found you, but maybe he is looking. How many of these floating islands are there? A thousand? Ten thousand? You shouldn't give up. He might be just one rock away. Think of the look on his face when he finds you here dead because you stopped trying to stay alive."

"Difficult."

"But right."

"Half right." A faint smile cracked the dirt on Sosinna's face, then vanished. "We couldn't go back to the palace."

"Seems to me that's exactly the place we should be going."

"We wouldn't be welcomed."

"Waste not, want not, Sosinna, your precious Lady is being lied to, and you'd roll over and die without your lover because your enemies won't welcome you."

"Not enemies."

"Enemies. Anyone who wants you dead, Sosinna, is an enemy, yours and your Lady's. If you're determined to die, let's at least try to find this floating palace where your Lady is surrounded by silent enemies. Urza will support you."

That was a promise Xantcha didn't know if she'd be able to keep, but it had to be made. Anything that would get Sosinna thinking had to be done, because even if the archangels didn't show up, the islands were likely to collide again. The upper island had taken the worst damage in the first collision and might again in the second, but anything on the surface of the lower island was going to get squashed like a bug.

"Difficult," Sosinna repeated.

Xantcha stood up and offered her hand. "But right."

"I don't know where the palace is. Only the angels know."

"Didn't Kenidiern ever tell you how he flew in and out?"

"We never talked about such things."

Xantcha almost asked what did they talk about, but Sosinna might have answered, and she didn't truly want to know. "Come on, let's at least start walking. We've got to walk ourselves clear of what's overhead. Maybe when we get to an edge we'll get lucky and see this wondrous palace."

"We can't."

"Can't what?"

"We can't walk to the edge of an island. I don't think we can walk out from under the one overhead. I tried, Xantcha, before you woke up. I tried to abandon you. I knew when you walked away that you'd have to come back."

"No apologies. I'd've done the same," Xantcha said and offered her hand again. "Come on. I've lived with worlds over my head, but not this close. Makes me nervous."

Sosinna reached, and winced as the gash on her arm began bleeding again. It was ugly now and would only get worse if they didn't find water soon. Xantcha hadn't seen free-running water since she'd first opened her eyes in Serra's realm, but now that Sosinna was moving again, she didn't seem worried about her wounds, so Xantcha said nothing either.

Xantcha kept an eye on the island overhead to measure their progress. The lethargy that had slowed her on her previous walk was worse. They weren't covering ground the way she would have liked. Even so, they were getting nowhere relative to the convoluted underside above them. Sosinna looked at her every time she looked up, a look that expected concessions and defeat, but Xantcha kept walking.

Sosinna's remarks about black mana had confirmed Xantcha's suspicion that Serra's floating-island realm was a magical place, as unnatural in its way as Phyrexia. The forces that made Phyrexia a world of concentric spheres were as inexplicable as the ones that shaped Serra's realm into thousands of floating islands . . . and, perhaps, not all that different from each other. She'd have questions for Urza when they met again. If they met again. If she and Sosinna could walk to a place where the opening between the collided islands was large enough that she'd risk casting them adrift in the sphere.

The thought of waking up the cyst brought an end to gut numbness. Xantcha dropped to one knee.

"The archangels will find us," Sosinna said, not the words Xantcha wanted to hear at that moment. "Every time you call on black mana, it brings them closer."

"I didn't call on black mana," Xantcha insisted.

Xantcha used a mnemonic to awaken Urza's artifact. She didn't know how the cyst made the sphere or armor. Urza knew mana-based sorcery; the necessary insights had come with his eyes. He said the Thran hadn't used mana so he wouldn't either, but the Thran had made Urza's eyes. Sosinna thought Xantcha imagined dark comers. Xantcha didn't need imagination so long as she had Urza.

The pain had faded, and numbness returned. Xantcha's legs were leaden when she stood. She could barely lift her feet when she tried to walk. "There's got to be another way."

"We wait until the archangels find us. There is no other way."

"Is your lady sensitive to black mana, or just the archangels?"

"Black mana has no place here. It hurts. We can all feel it, the Lady most of all. She is aware of the whole realm as you are aware of your body. The archangels patrol the islands looking for black mana and other evil miasmas. They eliminate evil before it can affect the Lady, but when they found you and the other—Urza—together, they called Lady Serra for a judgment. You've already been judged. When the archangels find us, they won't call Lady Serra again. They won't risk her health. None of us would risk it. If the Lady sickened, we would all die."

Another unfortunate choice of words, given the state of Xantcha's gut, but she had an idea. "I'm going to get everyone's attention, the archangels and, with any luck, your Lady herself." Xantcha yawned and thought the mnemonic for her armor. At first there was nothing, and she thought she'd lost the cyst altogether. Then the pain began and she felt something acid rising through her throat. Sosinna screamed, but by then Xantcha couldn't have stopped the process if she'd wanted to. The armor burned as it flowed over her skin. It spared her eyes. When Xantcha looked down what she saw was blacker than the darkest night, as black and featureless as the walls of an unlit cave. She brought her hands together, saw them touch, and felt absolutely nothing.

"You got the archangels, that's all." Sosinna pointed through the narrow opening between the islands. "We're doomed."

Sosinna stood no more than two arm's lengths away, but with the black armor covering Xantcha's ears, she sounded distant and under water. Xantcha looked in the indicated direction. A dazzling white diamond had appeared in the ribbon of golden light between the two islands. A moment's observation revealed that it was growing, moving toward them at considerable speed. From the air, then, the floating islands had edges. It was only from the ground that the horizon never became an edge.

As the diamond grew larger, it became apparent that it had five parts: four smaller lights, one each in the narrow and oblique points, and a much larger light in the center.

"The Aegis," Sosinna said.

The Aegis was also diamond shaped and too bright to look at directly. Xantcha held her black-armored hand in front of her eyes and squinted through the pinhole gaps between her fingers. She saw writhing plumes of yellow fire emerging from a hole that reminded her of a portal, a portal to the sun. Moving her hand slightly she observed the smaller lights, the archangels themselves: radiant, elongated creatures with dazzling wings that didn't move and smooth, featureless faces. They resembled Sosinna the same way many compleat Phyrexians resembled newts. Not an encouraging thought.

Xantcha didn't think Urza's armor, in its present condition, would be proof against the Aegis. She tried to say good-bye to Sosinna and discovered the armor had taken away her voice.

Wind preceded the archangels. It shook boulders loose from the overhead island and lifted the island itself out of the way. One loosened boulder struck the ground so near to Xantcha's feet that she felt the ground shudder. The wind died when the archangels brought the Aegis to a hovering halt. As good warriors anywhere, the archangels tested their weapon before they put it to use. A beam of light as hot as a Phyrexian furnace and many times as bright seared the land directly below the Aegis. Then the beam began to move toward Xantcha and Sosinna.

It made no difference whether Xantcha's eyes were open or shut. She was blind, and it felt as if the back of her skull were on fire. Xantcha had never believed in gods or souls, but facing the end of her life, Xantcha found she believed in curses. She'd roundly cursed Lady Serra's notion of perfection when she was struck down by a sideways wind.

The wind was a word and the word was:

Halt!

A woman's voice. This time there could be no mistaking it, even through Xantcha's blackened armor. The great Lady of the realm reined in her archangels. The heat ebbed at once, but Xantcha remained blind. A more ordinary voice, a man's voice, shouted, "Sosinna!" Xantcha guessed that Kenidiern had found his beloved. She hoped Sosinna was still alive. She'd hoped, too, that Urza might be part of the rescue party, but no one called her name. Someone did lift her to her feet and into the air—at least Xantcha thought that she'd been lifted—she presumed she was being carried by an angel or archangel. Blind and numb as she was, it was impossible to be certain, and she was in no way tempted to release Urza's armor, assuming she could release it.

The journey lasted long enough for Xantcha's vision to recover from its Aegis searing. She was moving through the air of Serra's realm, tucked under the arm of the right side archangel. Craning her neck as much as she dared, Xantcha caught a glimpse of a silver face with angles for nose, chin, and not so much as a slit for vision.

A mask she thought, because the hand she could see at her waist was flesh with stretched sinew and pulsing arteries apparent beneath normal-hued skin. Xantcha could understand why the archangels might choose to cover their eyes. Even when it was shut down, the Aegis—one golden tether to which her archangel held in his, hers? its? other hand—was nothing Xantcha wanted to look at. Easily four times as high as her archangel, it reminded Xantcha of nothing so much as a piece of the sun, that Serra's realm did not otherwise possess.

They left the Aegis behind, shining among the floating island, once the great island that could only be Lady Serra's palace came into view.

The palace was many times the size of any other island Xantcha had seen, and if she'd had to make a guess, she'd have said that it was the very center of the lady's creation.

As all Phyrexia had formed in spheres around the Ineffable?

But Xantcha had seen nothing like the palace in Phyrexia. Lady Serra's home leaped and soared in fantastic curves. Xantcha could think of no stone or brick that would glisten as the palace walls and ribs glistened in the Aegis's light. The underlying color was white, or possibly a golden gray. It was difficult to be certain.

A myriad of rainbows moved constantly along every arch and into every corner. There was sound in all timbres to accompany the kaleidoscopic light, and not an echo of discord.

The total experience, which could have been as overwhelming as the Aegis, was instead subtle and unspeakably beautiful. It was also pushing Xantcha and her archangel away. They were falling behind the others, including the fifth, unmasked angel carrying Sosinna. Xantcha would have preferred to keep her armor, black as it was, around her but she didn't want to be left alone either. Perhaps releasing the armor would be the most foolish thing she'd ever done, and the last, but she recited the mnemonic that made it melt away.

Black dust streamed away from her. It dirtied the archangel's pure white robes, but he regained his right side place in the formation moments before they began a dizzying ascent to the rainbow lace ornament atop the palace's highest, most improbable arch.

With nothing else to guide her eye, Xantcha had misjudged the scale of Serra's palace. She'd seen snow-capped mountains that weren't as high as that single, soaring arch, and mighty temples that were smaller than the deceptively delicate edifice on whose jeweled porch the archangel landed.

Her knees buckled when her feet touched the ground. She was numb the same way the palace was many-colored: awash in shifting waves of sensation. She kept her balance by keeping a close watch on her feet and the floor.

"Follow me."

Xantcha looked up quickly, a mistake under the circumstances. The archangels had already vanished, and Kenidiern, assuming the unmasked angel was Kenidiern, had no hands to spare. Xantcha broke her fall with her arms and stayed where she was, crouched on the glass-smooth floor.

"I can send someone out for you," Kenidiern said in a tone that clearly conveyed the notion that he wouldn't recommend accepting the offer.

He had a friendly, honest voice. Xantcha had never paid much attention to the handsomeness of men, but even she could see that Kenidiern was, as Sosinna had claimed, a very attractive paragon. She guessed he knew how to laugh, although his face was anxious at that moment. If Sosinna wasn't dead, she was clinging to life by a very delicate thread. The Aegis had burned the tall woman badly. Her flesh was seared and weeping beneath its crust of dirt.

"Go," Xantcha told him. "I'll follow." She started to stand and abandoned the attempt. "I'll find a way."

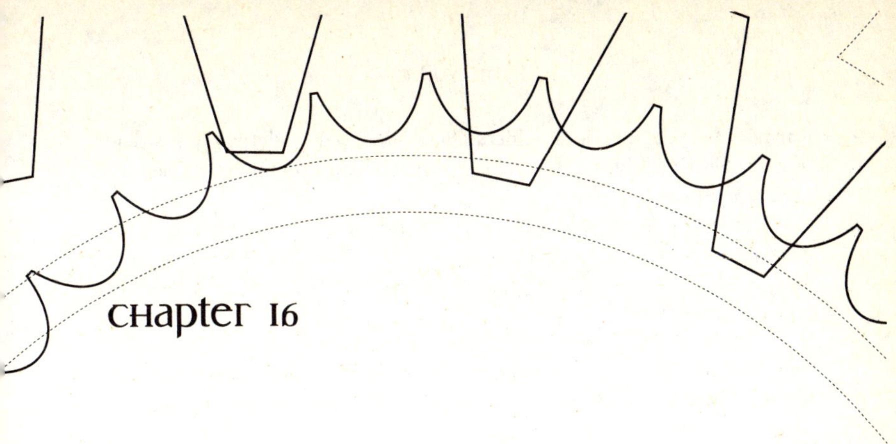

chapter 16

Xantcha watched Kenidiern carry Sosinna through one of the many open doorways, and made sure she'd remembered which one before rising to her feet. Speed, she decided, mattered. The palace didn't like her and especially didn't like her when she moved quickly. Slow, gliding movements, as if she were crossing a frozen pond, offended it least. She made steady progress from the porch through the door and down a majestic corridor. There was no one to stop or question her, at least no one that Xantcha could see, which was not to say that she didn't believe her every step was scrutinized.

The corridor ended in a chamber of breathtaking beauty. Unlike the rest of the palace, which seemed to be made from crystal and stone, this inner chamber was a place of life and growth. A maze of columns that might be trees, all graceful, but asymmetric and entrancing, hid the walls. Each tree or column was taller than her eye could measure.

Xantcha lost her thoughts in the overhead tangle of green-gold branches, and the music, which was no longer the austere interplay of wind and light, but the more playful sounds of water and the bright-feathered birds she glimpsed among the high branches. She was startled witless when someone grabbed her from behind.

"Xantcha! I did not know you still lived!"

"Urza!"

They'd never been much for backslapping embraces or other shows of affection, but any tradition needed its exception. And Urza was more animated, more alive, than Xantcha could remember him. His hands were warm and supple on her shoulders. They banished the lethargy that had plagued her since she'd first awakened and ended the numbness in her gut around the cyst.

"Let me look at you!" he said, straightening his arms. His eyes glittered but only with reflections from Serra's palace. "A bit worn and dirty at the edges—" Urza winked as he tightened his fingers—"but still the same Xantcha."

There was the faintest hint of a question in his statement. The sense that they were being watched hadn't faded with the numbness and lethargy. If anything, Xantcha was more aware than ever that she was in strange, perhaps hostile, surroundings.

"As stubborn and suspicious as ever," Xantcha replied with a wink of her own.

"We will talk, child. There is much to talk about. But, first you must meet our host." His arm urged her to walk beside him.

"I did once, already." Xantcha slipped free and into one of the many, many other languages they both knew. If they were back to child, then she was going to be very stubborn and twice as suspicious. Lowering her voice, she added, "Serra sent me away to die, Urza, and sent one of her own to die with me. That's why you didn't know I was alive."

"We will talk, child," Urza repeated in Serra's language. "This is not a good time to have a tantrum."

She switched to another language. "I'm not a child, I'm not having a tantrum, and you know it!"

Urza could put thoughts into Xantcha's head with only a little more discomfort than when he removed them. *Yes, I know, and I will ask Serra why she misled me. I'm sure the answer will amuse us both. But far now you are safe with me, and it will be better all around if you behave graciously.*

Xantcha replied with a thought of her own. *Graciously be damned! Serra didn't mislead you . . . she lied!*

But Xantcha couldn't put a thought in Urza's mind, and her indignation went unshared. Urza walked away, and faced with a choice between keeping up with him or staying by herself, she caught up, as he'd almost certainly known she would.

He said the chamber was known as Serra's Aviary and that she had seldom left it since creating her floating island realm.

"Then you know this isn't a natural world?" Xantcha asked, still refusing to speak Serra's language.

"Yes," Urza replied, ignoring her choice of language.

"Does it remind you of my home as much as it reminds me?" She was careful not to speak the word Phyrexia.

"There are no abominations here. The angels' wings are no more a part of them than your cyst is part of you. Serra's realm is slow and not without its flaws, but it is a living, natural place."

"For you. I haven't eaten since I got here. That's not natural for me."

"She has paid a price for her creation. Now, be gracious."

Urza took Xantcha's hand as they wound around another organic column. A narrow spiral stairway opened in front of them. Xantcha looked up and up and up.

"There's another way—?"

"We are guests."

Urza began climbing. Xantcha fell in behind him and into a kind of trance. The spiral was a tight one and each step a bit different in height and width than its neighbors. An odd sort of perfection that made each one unique, Xantcha thought, when she dared to think. Each step required concentration lest she lose her balance and tumble to the floor, which through the tangle of branches around them had come to look like twinkling stars on a warm, humid night. Urza surged ahead of her, but a hand waited at the top of the stairway.

Not Urza. Kenidiern. She recognized him by his stained robe.

"She asked me to wait until you were here."

Xantcha was breathing hard, but Urza's embrace had revitalized her. She didn't need anyone's help to follow the angel along a suspended walkway to a somewhat more intimate chamber than any she'd yet seen in the palace. It was only ten or twenty times the size that a room needed to be. Urza was there already, talking with a woman who could only be the lady, Serra, herself.

Having seen angels, archangels and Sosinna, Xantcha had expected a tall, slender and remote woman, but Serra could have walked through any man-made village without attracting a second glance. Her face, though pleasant, was plain, and she had the sturdy silhouette of a woman who'd borne children and done many a hard day's work. She was also one of two light sources in the chamber, surrounded by a gently flickering white nimbus. If she'd created this realm, as Urza said, then, like him, she could change her appearance to suit her whims.

The chamber's other light source was incomprehensible at first glance: a jumble of golden light and angular crystals bound together into two overlapping spheres. An artifact, certainly—Xantcha's dodger instincts had never deserted her—and beautiful, but its purpose, except as a source of light, eluded her.

"Please." Kenidiern offered his hand again. "She is very weak, and she must be alive when the cocoon is closed or there is no reason to close it."

Be gracious, Urza had said, so Xantcha let the angel have her hand, and before she could object he'd swept her up in both arms and carried her into the crystal lights. The wingless sisters of Serra were, perhaps, accustomed to being swooped about the palace, but Xantcha had rarely felt as helpless or as grateful to have her own feet under her once they'd reached a tiny enclosure where the spheres met.

Cocoon, Kenidiern called it, and that was as good a word as any for the vaguely egg-shaped compartment in which Sosinna lay. Her stained gown was gone, replaced by a shining quilt, but the Aegis had seared her face and hair. Her eyes were terrible, frightened and frightening. Sosinna was blind. At least, Xantcha hoped Sosinna was blind.

"Xantcha?" Sosinna's voice was a pain-wracked whisper. Her breathing was shallow and liquid.

Xantcha had seen worse, done worse, though few things in her life had been more difficult than reaching out to touch the quilt-bandaged lump that was, or had been, Sosinna's hand.

"I'm here."

"We made it. You were right."

"Difficult, but right."

Sosinna tried to smile, pain defeated her. "We will name our child for you."

Be gracious, that was easy. "I'm honored." Optimism came harder. "I'll show her, or him, how to be difficult."

Another failed smile on Sosinna's swollen lips and an agonizing attempt to shake her head. "You will go outside where you belong. Kenidiern and I will remember you."

With the sound of his name, Kenidiern came closer. His wings were soft, plumes rather than feathers. He rested his hand on Xantcha's shoulders. A shiver ran down Xantcha's spine, reminding her that, unlike Serra, the Ineffable had decreed that Phyrexians would not be born, and she was neither a man nor woman. Xantcha couldn't know if Kenidiern were a true paragon of anything useful, but she believed he had been looking for his beloved, and she envied Sosinna as she had never envied anyone before.

"We must close the cocoon," Kenidiern whispered, urging her to retreat.

Better call it a coffin. Some hurts were beyond even Urza's healing talents, and Sosinna's would be among them. It wasn't just her skin that had been charred and blistered, Sosinna had breathed fire and her insides were burnt, as well. Xantcha took a backward step.

"Good-bye . . . friend," Sosinna whispered.

"Good-bye, friend."

The upper sphere had begun to descend. Sosinna might be blind, but the cocoon wasn't silent. Surely she knew it was closing around her. She met her end without a whimper.

"Until you rise again," Kenidiern added, a euphemism, if ever Xantcha had heard one, though Sosinna managed a trembling smile just before the spheres blocked Xantcha's view.

There was a click, the golden light intensified, and, through her feet, Xantcha felt the whir of a distant engine. She thought of the Fane of Flesh, of the vats where discarded flesh was rendered and newts were decanted.

"You didn't say good-bye," she said to Kenidiern.

"Sosinna will rise again. The Lady does not offer her cocoon to everyone, but when she does, it never fails."

He swept Xantcha up again before she could protest and brought her down to Urza and Serra, whose conversation died as they approached.

"Sosinna is a special child to me," Serra said before Xantcha's feet were on the floor. "I didn't know what had become of her. I'm grateful that you showed us where she was, even though I'm not grateful for your methods!"

The lady had Urza's voice, the voice of someone who treated everyone as children, someone whom mortals might mistake for a god. Xantcha had never been mortal, never believed in gods, and she'd used up all her graciousness.

"Sosinna didn't believe in mistakes, she never lost faith in you. All the time we were together on that forsaken, floating island, she was hoping you or Kenidiern would rescue her before the archangels came to kill her. If that was you who called the Aegis off, then when it comes to rescuing your special children, you cut very close to the edge." Urza was appalled. His eyes glowed dark. Kenidiern stared at his sandaled feet. "Things here aren't as perfect as she believed they were."

"You are Phyrexian, are you not?" Serra asked, a tone short of accusation.

Urza's displeasure rumbled through the empty part of Xantcha's mind. The important part, the part she'd kept for herself since Gix had taught her how to build mental walls, remained unbowed. "You know I am."

"Your leave, my lady," Kenidiern interrupted. "My love is in your hands now. There is no need for me to stay."

Serra dipped her chin. Kenidiern was in the air before she raised it again. There were only three of them left in the branch-framed chamber: a man and a woman with the powers of gods, and a Phyrexian newt. Well, Xantcha was used to being overmatched.

"There is no need for this, Xantcha." Urza attempted to impose peace. "I think Lady Serra will concede there have been certain imperfections in our condition here." He turned toward Serra.

"Your arrival was so unexpected—" Serra began.

Xantcha cut her off. "That reminds me. How did we get here? The last thing I remember was beating on the shell of a Phyrexian turtle."

"I destroyed that abomination and all the others," Urza answered quickly. "But my enemies were lurking, watching from nether places, and before I could escape, they sent through reinforcements. It threatened to become the Fourth Sphere battle all over again, so I decided to retreat. I 'walked away, grabbing you as I left. But you were badly injured, and my grasp was not firm. I sensed the chasm to Phyrexia, of course—it is always there—but I sensed another, too, and threw myself across it. It was a terrible passage, Xantcha. I lost you. I would not have survived myself if Lady Serra had not found me and put me inside that cocoon you just saw.

"Such a marvelous artifact! If there is life, any life at all, the cocoon will sustain it and nurture it until the whole is healed. I am well again, Xantcha, well and whole as I have not been since I left Phyrexia, since before Phyrexia . . . since I met you. The principle is ingenious. To make her plane, Serra has treated time itself as a liquid, as a stream where water flows at different speed. . . ."

Xantcha swallowed hard. It didn't help. She stopped listening to Urza ramble about the wonders of Serra's cocoon. His recounting of events was laced through with simplifications that were no better than lies: *so I decided to retreat* and *I 'walked away* didn't accurately describe what she remembered of Urza's Phyrexian invasion and was probably no better at describing how the skirmish with the turtle-avengers ended or how they'd come to Serra's realm, but Urza remembered what he wanted to remember and forgot the rest.

He had rescued her from the turtles. Never mind asking if he'd cared about anything beyond keeping her away from Phyrexian scrutiny. His grasp might not have been firm. He might have lost her by accident. And he had been ill . . . since Phyrexia, but not before.

Xantcha was relieved to see Urza looking vigorous again, pleased to see him talking and moving in a mortal way, but she could not escape the implications of those few words: *since I met you.* They echoed ominously in her own thoughts. Had Urza decided something, perhaps everything, was her fault?

That warm greeting in the lower hall had been less relief or enthusiasm, than guilt.

Xantcha glanced at Serra, wondering what role she had played. Romance? That seemed unlikely with Urza . . . unnecessary, too, when she could distract him with the cocoon. After she'd gotten rid of Urza's annoying, Phyrexian companion?

"You want to know what I did when you were found?" Serra asked, an indication that she was sensitive to thought and, perhaps, did not find Xantcha's mind as empty as Urza did.

"I know what you did, why did you do it? What had I done to you or your perfect realm?"

"All things, natural or artifact, are created around a single essence. Your essence is black mana. When I created my plane, I created it around white mana, because the underlying essence plays a pivotal role in determining the character of a thing. White mana is serene, harmonic. It has the constancy that allows my plane to be the safe haven I desired. Black mana is discord, suspicion, and darkness. There is black mana here—it was not possible to eliminate it entirely—but it is only the small remainder that balances the rest—"

"I told you it is not so simple," Urza interrupted their host. "Lady Serra turned away from all that was real to make this place. She created it out of sheer will. But it seems there is a flaw, a fallacy, in willful creation. Outside, in the Multiverse that is unbounded, balance simply is and all planes are balanced among all the essences. Inside, when a plane is created by an act of single will, balance is impossible. One essence must dominate and another become the odd fellow."

"I knew this place reminded me of Phyrexia!" Momentarily forgetting everything else, Xantcha savored the satisfaction of solving a thorny puzzle. "The teacher-priests said the Ineffable made Phyrexia. I thought they meant that we all answered to him, that we were all part of his plan, but it was more than that. The Ineffable created Phyrexia. It was nothing, nothing at all, before he made it."

"Precisely," Urza agreed. "I had reached the same conclusion. A created plane, cut off from the rest of the Multiverse by an unfathomable chasm, no wonder it was so hard to find! But, inherently unbalanced! Think of it, Xantcha. Lady Serra retreats to her cocoon where she adds her will to her plane's flux, constantly keeping it almost in balance, but never quite and never for long. It always slips away. She prunes it to keep it small—"

"Small's never been a part of the Ineffable's plan—"

"Excuse me!" Serra said firmly and in her own language, which neither Xantcha nor Urza had been using.

The air in Xantcha's lungs became so heavy she couldn't speak and even Urza seemed to be at a loss for words.

"As I was saying." The lady's tone implied she'd tolerate no more interruptions. "The only black mana here is here because it cannot be eliminated. Nothing here has black mana as its underlying essence. Such a thing, natural or artifact, would disrupt everything around it. When the archangels found you and Urza, both near death and unable to speak for yourselves, they—I—determined that you had swallowed a piece of him. You were clinging to him. And your essence was black—is black.

"They have standing orders. Safe haven cannot be extended to anything with an underlying black mana essence. Because you had a piece of him, and we did not know then if it was a vital piece, I sent you away—put you in quarantine—while my cocoon restored Urza. His underlying essence is white mana, the same as ours. There was no risk. The cocoon purged him of a black mana curse."

The Ineffable, Xantcha thought. The Ineffable had placed a spark in Urza's skull as surely as Gix had placed one in hers all those centuries ago. She said nothing, though, because Serra would object, and because she wanted to hear Urza's version of events before proposing her own.

If black mana was suspicion, then Xantcha had become black mana incarnate.

"It was not a vital piece, of course," Serra continued. "Urza explained how he'd enabled you to survive the journeys between planes when he emerged from the cocoon, but by then . . ."

By then, *what*! Xantcha asked silently, eager to hear how Serra would wriggle free of the truth.

The lady hesitated and Urza plunged into the silence. "By then, her plane needed tending. She needed tending! Your presence alone had been enough to disrupt the balance more than it had ever been disrupted. You were well and truly lost by then, and I had no idea that you'd survived at all. My grasp had been weak to begin with. I asked the elders here, and they said I'd been alone when archangels brought me to the palace."

"They lied," Xantcha snapped, unable to stifle her indignation. She wished Kenidiern had not taken his leave. She'd liked to have seen his face when he'd heard that remark.

"Misinformed," Urza prevaricated. "I was alone. The archangels separated us, took us in different directions. The sisterhood had no idea what I was talking about."

"They knew, Urza. They sent Sosinna to die with me—" At least that was what Sosinna had assumed. But there were other possibilities. Serra said she had decided what would be done with her and Urza both. Xantcha looked straight at Serra. "Someone sent Sosinna to die with me."

"I cannot keep up with you!" the lady complained. "Either of you. You should hear yourselves, switching languages every other phrase, every other word. You have been together too long. No one else could possibly understand you." She took Urza's hand. "My friend, my offer stands, I will take her wherever you think best, but this is something for you to work out between yourselves. That piece of you she holds within her, surely it is a vital part of your memory, Urza. You should consider carefully before abandoning it."

Serra faded, 'walking somewhere else within her realm, leaving Urza and Xantcha alone in the golden light from the cocoon.

"What offer, Urza? Abandon it? Abandon me?"

But Urza was staring at the place where Serra had stood. "She was angry. I had no notion, no notion at all. You should not have done that, Xantcha. It was very ungracious to speak your mind in a way that Lady Serra couldn't understand. She doesn't understand that the Phyrexians emptied your mind. I must find her and apologize."

He started to fade as well.

"Urza!" Xantcha called him back. "Waste not, want not—you don't hear the words or their meanings! She said both of us. We were both speaking whatever words fit best. We do that, we've done it from the beginning. We've been too many places and seen too many things that no one else has seen. We have our own way of talking. We might just as well be one mind with two bodies."

"No! That can't be," he insisted. "Lady Serra is a Planeswalker. You aren't. She saw great tragedy, as I did on Dominaria, and she made this place, this plane, as a memorial to what she'd lost. She understands me, Xantcha. No one else has understood me. I've been happy here with her."

"Who wouldn't be happy in a world of their own making? The Ineffable is happy. The Ineffable understood you."

Urza whirled around. "Don't try to tempt me. That trap is sprung, Xantcha."

"What trap?" she retorted, but beneath the surface her fears and suspicions had intensified. "What offer, Urza? What's happened to you while I was floating on that island? What changed your mind about me?"

"Lady Serra healed me. Her cocoon healed me of all the taint and curse that Phyrexia has laid on me since Mishra and I let them back into Dominaria."

He reached for her. Xantcha eluded him.

"It's not your fault, Xantcha. No one is blaming you, least of all me. The one you call the Ineffable used you. He could not tempt me directly, so he made you to tempt me, to lead me to him. Oh, I knew you were dangerous, I've known that since I rescued you. I knew you could never be completely trusted, but I thought I was strong enough, clever enough to use you myself.

"Your Ineffable has lost his power over me, Xantcha. You were merely his tool, his arrow aimed at my heart. All these centuries that you've been beside me, I have been obsessed with simple vengeance. I didn't see the larger patterns until you were gone. It is all Lady Serra can to do keep her plane balanced. She knows that some day she will grow tired and it will fail. She does not let it expand. Created planes fail. They cannot evolve. They dare not grow. They are doomed from the moment of their creation. I understand that now, only natural planes endure. Yawg—"

"Don't—"

"Your Ineffable was exiled from some other plane before Dominaria. He thinks of Phyrexia not as a safe haven, as Serra thinks of her realm, but as a place to build a conquering army. Twice he has tried to conquer Dominaria, and he will try again. I know it. And I have wasted all my time looking for Phyrexia, trying to conquer Phyrexia—"

"I told you it couldn't be done."

"Yes. Yes, you did. Your creator knew I would not believe you. He is mad, but he is also cunning and clever. That is why he emptied your mind. That is how he tempted me off the path."

And if the Ineffable was mad, but cunning, what did that leave Urza? There was truth and logic wound through Urza's argument. Phyrexia was the Ineffable's creation as this world of floating islands was Serra's creation, and Phyrexia was the rallying point for a conquering army.

If all had gone according to plan, Xantcha would have been part of that army, at least as the demon Gix had conceived the army while the Ineffable slept. . . .

Serra slept in the cocoon to keep her world alive. Had the Ineffable slept for the same reason? Was that why the priests warned the newts, *Never speak the Ineffable's name lest he be awakened*?

"You awoke him," Xantcha said incredulously, interrupting Urza's diatribe, which had gone on while she asked herself questions. "When you rode your dragon into Phyrexia you must have awakened the Ineffable."

"No, Xantcha, you will not lead me astray again. I know what must be done. Yawgmoth is a Planeswalker, like Serra and me. Only Planeswalkers can create planes, and Planeswalkers are born in natural worlds. No one born here can 'walk, no Phyrexian can 'walk. So Yawgmoth was born on a natural plane and driven out. I will find that plane where Yawgmoth was born, and when I do, I will know his secrets and his weaknesses. I will find the records of those who cast him out, and I will learn how they won their victory. I will find the tools that I need to build the artifacts that will keep Yawgmoth away from Dominaria and away from any other natural plane he might covet."

"That's reasonable," Xantcha conceded. "If we knew when the Ineffable created Phyrexia—"

"No! I have said too much already! You have no thoughts of your own, Xantcha. Whatever you think, whatever you say, comes from Yawgmoth. It is not your fault, but I dare not listen to you. We must go our separate ways, you and I. Lady Serra discussed this before you arrived. She is willing to take you to a natural plane she knows. That's the offer she mentioned. I have not seen it, but she says it is a green plane, with much water and many different races. I think it must be like the Dominaria of my youth. You will do well there, Xantcha."

Xantcha was a breath short of speechless. "You can't mean that. You can't. Look at me, Urza. I am what I am, what I've always been. What would a newt like me do forever on a single world?" Never mind that it had been her destiny to sleep on such a world. . . .

Urza reached for her and this time caught her. "You've always done very well for yourself. You trade, you travel, you learn all their languages, you scratch a little garden in the dirt. When I rescued you, I never imagined we'd be together as long as we have been."

"I've never imagined anything else."

"Xantcha, you don't imagine anything that Yawgmoth didn't put inside your skull. I will win your vengeance, trust me. You cannot climb into the Lady's cocoon. Black mana is your underlying essence. The cocoon would destroy you, or you would destroy it. I'm sorry, but it has to be this way."

"You can't just abandon me . . . not to Serra! Who will you talk to? Who else understands, truly understands."

"I will miss you, Xantcha, more than you can imagine. You have been my ward against loneliness and, yes, even madness. You have a good heart, Xantcha. Even Lady Serra admits that. She finds no fault with your heart."

Heart.

Xantcha wriggled out of his embrace. "Give me your knife." She had nothing but her ragged, dirty robe and a pair of sandals. Urza had a leather sheath slung from his belt. If it wasn't real, he could make it real with a thought. "Please, Urza, let me have your knife, any knife."

"Xantcha, don't be foolish. You were always happiest when we settled in one place."

"I'm not going to be foolish. I just want to borrow your knife! I'll find something else that's sharp—"

She eyed the cocoon's golden crystals, and Urza relented. The knife he handed her had a blade no longer than her longest finger—which would have been plenty long enough to slash her throat, if she'd been determined to bleed to death. But Xantcha had never in her life wanted to die. She wasn't fond of pain, either, when there were other alternatives, which, at that moment there weren't.

Xantcha put a few paces between them. Then, with a steady hand, she plunged the short knife into her flank where she'd tucked her heart away. Her hand was shaking as she lengthened the incision. Urza tried to stop her. Panic gave her the strength to reach inside.

"My heart," she said, offering him the bloodstained amber. "If you think I'm untrustworthy, if you think I belong to the Ineffable, crush it and I'll die. I swore I'd never betray you. I'd rather die than live knowing that you've abandoned me."

"Xantcha!" Urza reached for the wound, which he could heal with a touch.

She staggered backward. "Take it! If I am what you say I am, I don't want to live. But if you won't kill me, then take me with you."

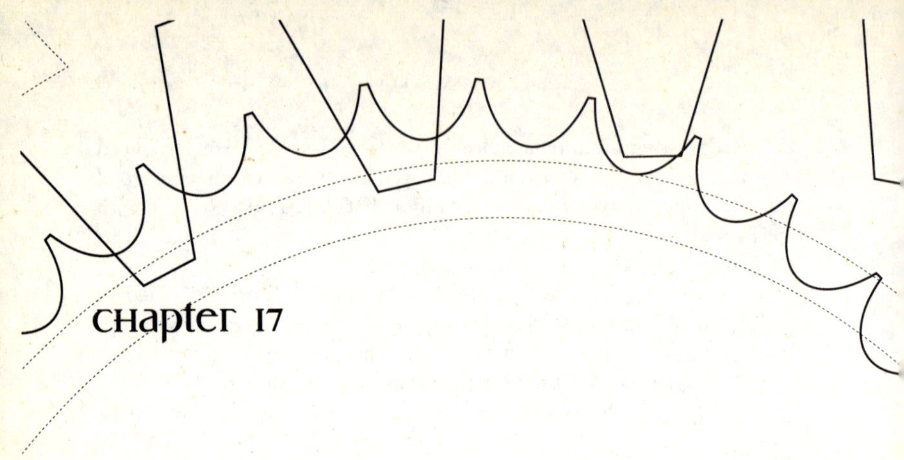

chapter 17

Xantcha awoke with her butt on the ground and her back against an apple tree's broken trunk. Torn branches with upside-down leaves blocked her view of the world. There were green apples piled in her lap and the crook of her throbbing arm. The portal explosion had thrown her so hard she'd shattered a tree when she fell, but Urza's armor had kept her whole.

Ratepe stood among the branches, looking anxious, but not at her.

"How long was I out?" she asked, reaching for the waterskin he dangled with her good arm.

"A bit . . ."

He dropped the waterskin in her lap. Whatever had his attention wasn't letting it go. She pulled the cork with her teeth and took a swallow before asking:

"What's out there?"

"He came out of nowhere, as soon as you'd fallen. His eyes blazed lightning and fire."

Xantcha imagined the worst. "Another Phyrexian?"

She tried to stand but armor or no armor, Phyrexian or no Phyrexian, she'd taken a beating, and her body wasn't ready for anything. Latching onto the hem of Ratepe's tunic, Xantcha dragged herself upright.

The awe-inspiring invader had been Urza, not another Phyrexian. Garbed in stiff armor and looking like a painted statue, he contemplated the metal-and-oil wreckage. He carried an ornate staff, the source of the lightning web that ebbed and flowed around him. Xantcha thought Urza had lost that staff ages ago when they were dodging Phyrexian ambushes. She wasn't entirely pleased to see it again.

Her battered arm wanted out of the armor. Xantcha would have preferred to wait until she had a better sense of Urza's mood, but there wasn't time for that. She silently recited the mnemonic that dissolved the armor. Her arm swelled immediately.

"Has he said anything?" she asked.

"Not a word. The way he looked, I got out of his way. Might've been better if there had been another Phyrexian for him to fry?"

"Might've," Xantcha agreed.

If there'd been an upright Phyrexian in the vicinity, Urza would have had another target besides her. She couldn't remember the last time he'd come charging to her rescue. In point of fact, she didn't think he had come to her rescue. Since they'd gotten to Dominaria, Xantcha's heart had sat gathering dust on a shelf in Urza's alcove. She didn't think Urza had given it a second thought in over a century, but she wasn't surprised that he'd been watching it closely while she and Ratepe were away. She imagined it had flashed when she hit the tree.

Best get it over with, she decided and said to Ratepe, "You wait here," though there was no chance that he'd pay attention, and she was grateful for the help clambering through the tangled branches.

"Been a long time since I've seen a compleat one," she said casually, starting the conversation in the middle, which was sometimes the best way when Urza was rigid and wrapped in power.

"You should have known better than to engage a Phyrexian with my brother beside you!"

Urza was angry. His eyes were fire, his breath sulfur smoke and sparks. Xantcha winced when they landed on her face. He either hadn't noticed, or didn't care that she wasn't encased in his armor. She was groping for the words that would calm him when Ratepe spoke up.

"This was my idea. We wouldn't have gotten into trouble if I hadn't badgered her into tracking the riders away from Tabarna's palace."

Urza turned without moving. "Palace?" He'd followed her heart between-worlds and didn't know where, precisely, they were.

"Pincar City's a short, hard ride for six men on good horses," Xantcha said and pointed northwest. "We spotted the riders going out a sea gate at sunrise. It was my decision to get involved when I saw them laying down an ambulator's nether end."

"An ambulator, here?"

Urza turned his head, looking for one. He was in the here and now again. Xantcha relaxed.

"We blew it up in the firepots. They had the nether end here. I sure didn't want to go through to get the prime, and I didn't want to risk carrying a loose nether around with me, especially not after what came out. I swear I was expecting *sleepers* and, at the outside, a tender-priest. Nothing like this."

Urza rolled the wreckage with his staff. Bright, compound eyes looked up at the sun, metal parts clattered, and Ratepe leapt a foot in the air, thinking it was still alive.

"They've sent a demon," Urza mused, slipping out of Efuand, into his oldest language, pure ancient Argivian.

"Not a demon," Xantcha corrected, sticking with Efuand.

"Some new kind of priest. Not as bad as a demon, but pretty bad when you were expecting a cadre of *sleepers*."

"How do you know what it was if you've never seen it before?" Ratepe asked. A reasonable question, though Xantcha wished he hadn't been staring at Urza's eyes as he asked it.

"Yes," Urza added, back to Efuand. "How can you be sure?" He tipped his staff toward one of the two Efuand corpses lying near the Phyrexian. "Are they *sleepers*? They have the smell of Phyrexia around them."

Xantcha swallowed her shock. Urza had long admitted that she was better at scenting out Phyrexians, but he'd never hinted how much better, and she'd never tried to put the distinctions into words, any words from any language, including Phyrexian. "This is a priest—" she nudged the wreckage with her foot—"because it looks like a priest."

"That's not an answer," Ratepe chided.

"I'm not finished!"

Xantcha got on her knees and with her good hand attempted to loosen the Phyrexian's triangular face-plate. It was a struggle. The tenders had compleated it carefully, and it had recently received a generous allocation of glistening oil to bind what remained of its flesh to its metal carapace. Once she'd got her fingertips under one sharp corner, Ratepe helped her pry it off.

Shredded leather clung to the interior of the plate, matching the shreds of a skinless but still recognizably childish face that it had covered.

"It had compleated eyes," Xantcha explained, indicating the coiled wires emerging from the empty sockets. "Only the higher priests and warriors have compleat eyes. And it had an articulated mouth; that's definitely priest-compleat. Diggers and such, they just have boxes in their chests. And all the metal's the same, not scraps. That's priest-compleat, too. It's got no guts, just an oil bladder. A priest's got muscles and nerves, compleated, of course, joined with gears and wire, but it's got the brain it was decanted with. The brain makes it go. That's why most Phyrexians have two arms, two legs, its brain knows two arms, two legs—"

"You said they weren't flesh," Ratepe interrupted, a bit breathless and green-cheeked. He'd told her once that he hadn't been able to help with the butchering on his family's farm. Probably he wished he hadn't helped her now.

"This isn't flesh." She tore off a shredded bit. Not surprisingly, he wouldn't take it from her hand, but Urza did. "This is what flesh becomes when it is compleated."

"They start with a living man and transform him into this," Urza's voice was flat and cold as he ground the shred between his fingers.

"They start with a newt," Xantcha said flatly.

"So, this is what would have happened to . . ." Ratepe couldn't finish his thought aloud.

"If I'd been destined to become a priest."

She could remember the Xantcha who'd waited, hope against hope, for the tender-priests to come for her. Would she have been happier if they had? There was no Phyrexian word for happiness.

"And my brother?" Urza flicked the shred into the weeds. "Did he become a priest? Is that what I fought in Argoth? His skin had been stretched over metal plates, over coiled wire. What was he?"

"A victim," Ratepe answered before Xantcha had a chance.

"What about the demons and the *sleepers*?"

She chose to answer the easy part first. "*Sleepers* are newts, uncompleated, the way we came out of the vats. But there's oil in the vats, and the smell never goes away. That's how I spot them."

"This one recognized you?" Ratepe always had another question.

Xantcha shrugged. "Maybe, if I hadn't gotten its attention first." She rubbed the hollow of her neck. "That left arm, Urza. It shot something new at me. Your armor barely stopped it, and for a moment I was glowing blue. And those canisters you made for the firepots? The glass shards are worthless, but the shrieking ones, they brought this priest to its knees."

Urza snapped the wreck's left arm at the shoulder with no more apparent effort than she'd need to break a twig. He angled it this way and that in the sun as glistening oil poured over his hand.

"Do *sleepers* know what they are?" Yet another question from Ratepe.

"I was destined to sleep and I knew, so I assume they know, but I think, lately, that I'm wrong. The *sleepers* I've seen don't seem to recognize one another, don't seem to know they weren't born. And if you were going to ask—" she pointed to the Efuand corpses—"they're not sleepers."

"How do you know?" Urza demanded. "How can you be certain? They're man-shaped, not like you. And they smell."

Xantcha rolled her eyes. "Gix corrected the man-woman mistake before they excoriated him. *Sleepers* were men and women before I left the First Sphere. Phyrexians know about gender, Urza, they've just decided it's the way of flesh and not the way they're going to follow. These Efuands, they've got oil on the outside from handling the ambulator. Right now, you smell of glistening oil. *Sleepers* have oil on the inside, in their breath."

"So you cover your mouth?" Ratepe asked.

She nodded. He'd watched her do that more than once. "If they're not breathing, you might have to cut them open to be sure."

"Have you cut them open, to be sure?" Urza asked.

Xantcha answered. "I've always been sure."

She met Urza's eyes, they were mortal-brown just then. How many times in the past two hundred years had she sent him out to confirm her sightings? He always said she'd been correct, always told her never to risk encountering them again, but had he ever scented a Dominarian *sleeper*?

"I have cut them open," Urza confessed. "I've killed and eviscerated men and women because they smelled, faintly, of Phyrexia. But when I examined them outside, I saw only men and women, not what you have become, what my brother became. Even on the inside, there was nothing unusual about them. They had a black mana essence, but essence isn't everything. It doesn't make a man or woman a Phyrexian."

Xantcha didn't know what to say and was grateful when Ratepe asked,

"What about demons?"

"The demons are what they are—and that is an answer. They're as old as Phyrexia, as old as the Ineffable. They're powerful, they're evil. They smell of oil, of course, but, in Phyrexia, I knew a demon when I saw one because I felt fear inside me."

"Mishra met a demon." Ratepe's eyes were glazed. His attention was focused between his ears where he heard the Weakstone sing. "Gix."

The bees in the orchard were louder than Ratepe's whispered declaration, but he got Xantcha's attention and Urza's too.

"Names are just sounds," Urza said, the same as he'd said when Xantcha told him—long before she read *The Antiquity Wars*—the only demon's name she knew. "The Brotherhood of Gix was ancient before I was born. They venerated mountains, gears, and clockwork. They were susceptible to Phyrexian corruption after my brother and I inadvertently broke the Thran lock against Phyrexia, but neither they nor their god could have been Phyrexian."

"Gix promised everything. He knew how to bring metal to life and life to metal." Ratepe's voice remained soft. It was hard to tell if he was frightened by what he heard in his mind or dangerously tempted by it.

"Ratepe?" Xantcha reached across the wrecked priest to take Ratepe's hand. It was limp and cold. "Those things didn't happen to you. Don't let Gix into your memory. Gix was excoriated more than three thousand years ago, immersed in steaming acid and thrown into the pit. He can't touch you."

"You cannot seriously think that there is a connection between the memories placed in your mind and those in Mishra's," Urza argued. "At best there is a coincidence of sound, at worst . . . remember, Xantcha, your thoughts are not your own! Haven't you learned?"

Still clinging to Ratepe's hand, Xantcha faced Urza. "Why is it that everything you believe is the absolute truth and anything I believe is foolishness? I was meant to sleep here—right here in Dominaria. I dreamed of this place. I was decanted knowing the language that you and Mishra spoke as children. There is something about this world, above all the others, that draws Phyrexia back. They tried to conquer the Thran. That didn't work so they tried to get you and Mishra to conquer each other. Now they're trying a third time. Big wars didn't work, so they're trying lots of little wars. If you would listen to someone else for a change instead of always having to be the only one with the right answers—"

Ratepe squeezed Xantcha's hand and helped her to her feet.

"Xantcha's got a point, Urza. Why here? Why do the Phyrexians come back to this world?"

Urza 'walked away rather than answer, and this time he didn't come back.

"I shouldn't have challenged him." Xantcha leaned against Ratepe, grateful to have someone to share her misery with, and aware, too, that she would have spoken much differently if there hadn't been three of them gathered around the Phyrexia wreckage. "I always lose my temper at the wrong time. He was so close to seeing the truth, but I had to have it all."

"You're more like Mishra than I am." Ratepe wrapped his arms around her. "Must've been something Gix poured in your vat."

He was jesting, but the joke made Xantcha's heart skip a beat. What had Gix said on the First Sphere plain? She remembered the spark and walling herself within herself, but the words hung outside of memory's reach. What had happened to Mishra's flesh? Flesh was rendered, never wasted. Had she been growing in the vats while Urza and Mishra fought? She'd thought she had.

Xantcha leaned back against Ratepe's arms and saw the thoughtful look on his face.

"Don't," she said, a plea more than a command. "Don't say anything more. Don't think anything more."

Arms tightened around her, one at her waist, the other cradling her head. She couldn't see his face, but she knew he hadn't stopped thinking.

Xantcha hadn't either, though there was neither joy nor satisfaction in any of her conclusions.

"We've got to leave," she said many silent moments later. "Someone's going to wonder what happened to the riders."

"If we're lucky, someone. Something, if we're not."

Xantcha grimaced. Ratepe's humor was missing its mark, and her arm, compressed between them, kept her edgy with its throbbing. "Whichever, we're going to have to leave this for someone else to sort out. I should've shoved the priest through before we destroyed the ambulator."

"Then there wouldn't have been anything for Urza to look at."

"Not sure whether that was good or bad."

Ratepe let her go and did most of the work assembling their supplies in a pile for the sphere to flow around. One look at his face and Xantcha knew he was disappointed that they weren't returning to Pincar City, but he never raised the subject. Her elbow had swollen to the size of a winter melon and her arm, from the shoulder down, looked as if it had been pumped full of water. Her fingers resembled five purple sausages. Her arm was rigid, too. It had been centuries since she'd had an injury Urza hadn't healed. She'd almost forgotten how newts stiffened when they broke their bones.

If Xantcha had the nerves Ratepe had been born with, she would have been curled up, whimpering, on the ground. As it was, she was grateful for Ratepe's company, sought the calmest wind, streams through the air, and brought them down frequently.

Twice over the following several days they spotted gangs of bearded men riding good horses through the summer heat. She gritted her teeth and followed them, still hoping to find a Shratta stronghold, but both times the men ended their treks peaceably in palisaded villages. Either the religious fanatics had gone to ground or they'd gone from dreaded to welcome in little more than a season. She thought of going up to the gates and inviting herself into their councils, as she had scarcely a season earlier. Her arm kept her from acting on those thoughts.

"It was your idea to disperse those villagers, let them spread the word that it was Red-Stripes who were killing and burning in the Shratta's name," Xantcha reminded Ratepe as she guided the sphere to its prior course. "You're the one who told me that I was a friend because I was the enemy of your enemy. What did you expect?"

"Not this," Ratepe replied with a scowl. "Maybe I'm wiser now. The enemy of my enemy still has his own plans for me."

Xantcha let the provocative comment slide.

High summer was a season of clear, dry weather on Gulmany's north coast. They rounded the western prong of the Ohran Ridge without excitement and hit the first of the big southern coast storms at sunrise the next day. For three days they camped in a bear's hillside den waiting for the rain to stop. Xantcha's arm turned yellow. Her fingers came back to life, knuckle by spasmed knuckle.

Xantcha was in no hurry to get back to the cottage. Once her elbow recovered from its battering, she could enjoy Ratepe's company, and his attentions. There was always a bit of frustration. She simply didn't have the instincts for romance, or even pleasure, that Ratepe expected her to have. They loved and laughed and argued, walked as much as they soared the windstreams. They didn't see the cottage roof until the moon had swung twice through its phases, and there was a hint of frosts to come in the mountains' morning air.

"He's there," Ratepe said, pointing at the lone figure.

Xantcha blinked to assure herself that her eyes weren't lying, but it was Urza, tall, pale-haired and stripped to the waist beside the hearth, vigorously stirring something that bubbled and glowed in her best stew pot.

She'd always thought of Urza as a scholar, a man whose strength came from his mind, not his body, though Kayla had written that her husband built his own artifacts and had the stamina of an ox. Over the centuries, Urza had become dependent on abstract power, using sorcery or artifice rather than his hands whenever possible. The sight of a tanned, muscular, and sweating Urza left Xantcha speechless.

She would have preferred to approach this unfamiliar Urza cautiously from the side, but he spotted the sphere and waved.

"He seems glad to see us." Ratepe's voice was guarded.

Maybe it wasn't that Phyrexians had no imagination, but that their imaginations never prepared them for the truth. Xantcha reminded herself that Urza had her heart on a shelf. He'd followed it to Efuan Pincar. He could have found her again or crushed the amber stone in his fist.

She brought the sphere down beside the well. Urza ran toward them—ran, as a born-man might run to greet his family. He embraced Ratepe first, slapping him heartily on the back and calling him "brother." Xantcha turned away, telling herself she'd learned her lesson in the apple orchard. Urza didn't have to be sane, he didn't have to see anything except as he wished to see it, as long as he fought the Phyrexians. She hadn't quite finished the self-lecture when Urza put his hands on her shoulders.

"I've been busy," he said. "I went back to all those places I'd been before. I trusted my instincts. If I thought it was Phyrexian, I believed it was Phyrexian. I didn't need outside proof. They have a new strategy, Xantcha. Instead of fighting their own war, or pulling the strings on one big war, they've stirred a hornet's nest of little wars just in Old Terisiare alone. I have no notion what they might be doing elsewhere.

"But I'll find out, Xantcha. I know Dominaria less well than I know a score of other planes, but that's going to change, too. Come, let me show you—"

He pulled Xantcha toward the cottage. She dug in her heels, a futile, but necessary protest.

"No, Xantcha. This time—this time I swear to the Thran, it is not like before." He gestured to Ratepe. "Brother! You come too. I have a plan!"

Urza did have a plan, and it truly was like nothing he'd done before. He'd drawn maps on his walls, maps on the floor, a map on the worktable, and maps on every other reasonably smooth surface in the workroom. No wonder he was working outside. The many-colored maps were annotated with numerals she could read and a script she couldn't. None of them made particular sense until she recognized the crescent-shaped capital of Baszerat on their common wall. After that she recognized several towns and cities, drawn upside down by her instincts, but accurate, so far as she could remember. She guessed the annotations included the number of *sleepers* he'd found in each city and asked,

"Are you going to drive the *sleepers* back to Phyrexia?"

"Yes, in proper time. The first time no one was left and the message was lost. The last time, no one knew what we faced until the very end and as you pointed out—" Urza included Ratepe in the discussion—"nobody believed the message. This time I will take no chances. The Phyrexians have chosen to fight a myriad of wars. I will fight them the same way, with a myriad of weapons. I will expose them! Watch!"

Urza left her and Ratepe standing in the middle of the room while he fussed with a tattered basket. His eagerness and delight would have been contagious, if Xantcha hadn't watched too many times before. She'd exchanged a worried-hopeful glance with Ratepe when the world erupted into chaos.

The chaos was a sound like Xantcha had never experienced, sound more piercing than the howling winds between-worlds. She tried to draw breath to yawn out her armor, but the sound had taken possession of her body. It shook her as a dog shook its fur after the rain and threw her to the floor. Her bones had turned to jelly before it reached into her skull and shook her mind out of her brain.

Control and reason returned as suddenly as they had departed. Except for a few bruises and a badly bitten tongue, Xantcha was no worse than dazed. She knew her name and where she was, but the rest was muddled. Ratepe stood a little distance away. Xantcha realized he hadn't been affected by the attack, but before she could consider the implications, Urza was beside her, cupping her chin in his hands, taking the pain away.

"It worked!" he exalted before she could stand. "I'm sorry, but there was no other way, and I had to be sure."

"You? You did that to me?" She propped herself up on one elbow.

"Wind, words, they're both the same. Sound is merely air in motion, like the sea. You said the priest collapsed because of the whistling shot. I have made a new artifact, Xantcha, a potent new weapon. It has no edge, no weight, no fire. It is sound."

Urza opened his hand, revealing a lump roughly the size and shape of a ceiling spider. Xantcha couldn't accept that something so simple had laid her low.

"It's too small," she complained. "Nothing so small could hurt so much."

"You gave me the idea when you said the oil was inside the *sleepers*. Sound, if it is the right sound, can move things, break things. The sound this artifact makes is one that shakes glistening oil until it breaks apart."

Xantcha would have said oil could not be broken if she had not just endured a sound that had proven otherwise.

"Do we throw them at the *sleepers*?"

"We plant them in all the places where Xantcha's scented *sleepers,*" Ratepe said from the wall where he had studied several of the maps.

"Yes! Yes, exactly right, Brother!" Urza left Xantcha on the floor. "We will scatter them like raindrops!"

"What will set them off? They're too small for a wick or fuse."

"Ah, the Glimmer Moon, brother. A strange thing, the Glimmer Moon. It has virtually no effect on tides, but on sorcery—white-mana sorcery—it is like a magnet, pulling the mana toward itself, sometimes strong, sometimes not so strong, but strongest when the Glimmer Moon reaches its zenith. So, very simple, I make a spindly crystal and charge one end with white mana. I put the crystal inside the spider, in a drop of water where it floats on its side. When the Glimmer Moon goes high, it tugs the charged end of the crystal, which stands up in the drop of water, and my little spider makes the noise that affected Xantcha, but not you or I. It is as good as an arrow!"

"But just a bit more complicated," Ratepe warned.

"Geometry, brother," Urza laughed. "Astronomy. Mathematics. You never liked mathematics! Never learned to think in numbers. I have done all the calculations." He gestured at the writing-covered walls.

Xantcha had pulled herself to her feet. Her anger at being tricked had vanished. This was the Urza she'd been waiting for, the artifacts she'd been waiting for. "How powerful are they? I was what, maybe four paces away? How many will we need to flush out all the *sleepers* in a city? Hundreds, thousands?"

"Hundreds, maybe, in a town. Thousands, yes, in a city. The more you have, the greater the effect, though you must be very precise when you attach them to the walls. Too far is bad, too close is worse. They'll cancel each other out, and nothing at all will happen. I will show you in each town we pass through. And I will continue to refine them."

Ratepe's face had turned pensive. Xantcha thought it was because he'd play no part in Urza's grand plan, but he proved her wrong, as usual.

"We could just make things worse. I know Xantcha's Phyrexian, but when she fell just now I didn't guess she fell because she was Phyrexian. You're going to have something make a noise born-folks can hardly hear, but a few are going to collapse on the ground. People won't know why. They don't cut up corpses, they've never seen a Phyrexian priest. They'll think it's a god's doings and there's no guessing what they'll think after that."

"The *sleepers* will be gone, Brother. Dead. Lying on the ground. Let men and women think a god has spoken, if that's their desire. Phyrexia will know that Dominaria has struck back; and that's what matters: the message we send to Phyrexia. It is as good as saying that the Thran have returned."

"I'm only saying that if no one knows why, no one will understand, and ignorance is dangerous."

"Then, Brother, what would you have me do?" Urza demanded. "Handwriting in the sky? A whisper in every Dominarian ear? Would you have another war? Is that what you want, Mishra—another war across Terisiare? This way there is no war. The land is not raped. No one dies."

"The *sleepers* will die," Xantcha said.

In her mind's eye she saw the First Sphere and the other newts, the other Xantcha with its orange hair. She'd slain newts herself—she'd slain that other Xantcha when it got between her and food—but when she thought about vengeance against Phyrexia, she thought about priests and demons, not newts or *sleepers.* Her head said they had to be eliminated—killed. The artifact-spider's sound had gripped her. She believed it could kill, but not quickly or painlessly, and if her hunch was correct, that many of the *sleepers* didn't know they were Phyrexian, they wouldn't know why they suffered.

Ratepe and Urza were watching her.

"They have to die," she said quickly, defensively. "There's no place for them. . . ." A shiver ran down her back. Place, one of the oldest words in her memory. Her cadre never had a place. They were oxen, deprived of everything except their strength, used ruthlessly, discarded as meat when there was nothing left. "I'll do it," she snarled. "Don't worry. Waste not, want not. I'll do whatever has to be done until Phyrexia is rolled up like an ambulator and disappears." Her voice had thickened as it did when she yawned, but her throat was tight with tears, not armor. "But it's not true that no one will die."

Urza strode toward her. "Xantcha," he said softly, insincerely.

The open door beckoned. She ran through it. Urza tried to call her back:

"Xantcha, no one's talking about you . . . !"

She ran too far to hear the rest.

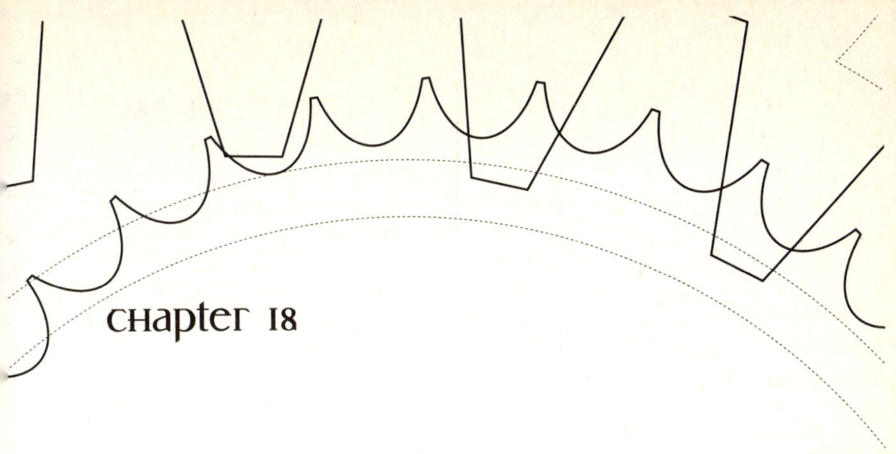

chapter 18

There were other discussions, some less volatile, a few that had the three of them storming off in different directions, but in the end Ratepe and Xantcha fell in with Urza's plan to broadcast the screaming spiders—Ratepe named them—throughout Old Terisiare and anywhere else that Urza or Xantcha might sniff a Phyrexian in the air.

They had about three seasons to get the spiders arrayed on dusty walls and ceilings. By Urza's calculations the Glimmer Moon would strike its zenith above Old Terisiare a few days short of next year's midsummer's eve. Xantcha had little time for visiting unfamiliar places or searching out new Phyrexian infestations. The windstreams weren't fast enough. Urza 'walked her to realms where glistening oil tainted the air. Then he left her with a cache of spiders while he 'walked on with several thousand more. Nine days later, he'd examine her glowing amber heart, find her, and take her back to the cottage where Ratepe waited for them.

In a compromise between delusion and practicality, Urza had decided his brother's talents were uniquely suited to constructing spiders. Ratepe had tried to argue his way out of the responsibility, but Urza's instructions were clear and aside from charging the white mana crystals, making the small artifacts was more tedious than difficult. Every nine days, when they were together at the cottage, Urza banished Ratepe and Xantcha from his workroom while he grew and charged the crystals.

Summer ended, autumn vanished, winter came, all without disrupting their cycles.

"Not that you couldn't do it," Urza would say, the same words every time he and Xantcha returned, as if they were written on the instructions he'd given Ratepe. "But you've been alone all this time, and Xantcha likes to talk to you. And I've got another idea or two I'd like to tinker with. I can make them better, make them louder, wider, more powerful So, you two go on. Let me work. Go next door. Talk, eat, do as you like. I'll be busy here until tomorrow night."

"He's as mad as he ever was." Xantcha said as Ratepe put his weight against the workroom door, cracking the late-winter ice that had sealed it since Urza and Xantcha had left nine days earlier.

"He was mad long before the real Mishra died," Ratepe said lightly and regretted his nonchalance as he lost his footing on the slick wood. "You didn't really think anything was going to change that, did you!"

Like Urza, the two of them had fallen into habits and scripts, at least until they'd lit the oil lamp and the brazier and warmed the blankets of Xantcha's old bed. They seldom talked much or ate after that until the lamp needed replenishing.

"I want a favor from you," Ratepe said while Xantcha re-lit the lamp with a coal from the brazier.

Xantcha looked up silently.

"It's getting on toward a year."

She'd been expecting that. Winter lingered on the Ridge. It was spring in the lowlands, a bit more than two months shy of the year she'd asked of Ratepe in Medran. She and Urza were three-quarters through the workroom maps, but their chances of finishing the job before midsummer were nil, and none if Ratepe demanded the freedom she'd sworn to give him.

"You want to go back to Efuan Pincar." A statement, not a question. She made tea from the steaming water atop the brazier.

"No, I can count as well as you—better, usually. Urza needs me here until midsummer, at least. I have my doubts, so do you, but nobody knows what happens next. We agreed to take the risks."

"So, what's the favor?"

"I want you to go back to Efuan Pincar,"

"Me?"

"Everywhere else the Phyrexians are all *sleepers*—everywhere, except Baszerat and Morvern, and they'll keep fighting each other with or without Phyrexian meddling. But I'm still worried about Efuan Pincar and the Shratta. We never went back—"

She interrupted. "I did. I plastered the walls of Medran and seven other towns while Urza did Pincar City. You said midsummer's the biggest holy day of Avohir's year and everybody goes to the temples, so I put a few spiders in the sanctuaries, just in case, but I didn't smell anything suspicious. My guess is that the Red-Stripes wiped out the Shratta years ago. Maybe they had Phyrexian help, maybe not. It's history now."

"I figured that, and that's why I want a favor. I've tinkered with the spiders—studied the changes that Urza's made since last summer, even made a few of my own and tested them, too."

Xantcha raised her eyebrows as she strained the tea.

"It's not like you didn't experiment with the cyst after Urza gave it to you," Ratepe retorted.

Xantcha decided not to pursue the argument.

"Urza doesn't count the crystals. I think he expects me to damage a few—and, anyway, we know the crystals work. It's the other part that I modified."

"You're not trying them out on me." She slammed the straining bowl on the table for emphasis.

"No, they're not like that, but I did change the sound they make. The way Urza had them set, the sound makes things boil. What I did makes solid things like rocks and especially mortar break down into sand and dust. And I want you to plant my spiders in the foundation of the Red-Stripe barracks and under the high altar of Avohir's temple in Pincar City. When the Glimmer Moon passes overhead, the sound will rattle the stones until they come apart."

It would work, but "Waste not, want not—why? Even if I could do it, why? Not that I care, personally, but Avohir is your god. Why would you want to turn Avohir's altar into rubble?"

"And the Red-Stripe barracks. Both. I want to make a sign for every Efuand to see that whatever strikes down the *sleepers* strikes down the Shratta, too. If there's any left anywhere, I don't want some bearded fanatic to take advantage of what we've done. All right, the Shratta didn't kill my family, but they drove us out of the city. They burnt the schools and the libraries. If the Phyrexians got rid of them, well, that's a mark in their favor, but I don't want to take the chance. Will you do it, Xantcha? For me?"

She followed the steam rising from her mug. "I'll talk to Urza."

"Urza can't know."

"Ratepe! I'm not just wandering out there. I 'walk out of here with Urza and nine days later I 'walk back with him. What am I supposed to do, yawn and hightail it up to Efuan Pincar the moment he sets me down and then hightail it back again?"

"That's what I thought you'd do."

"And when he asks about the spiders I was supposed to be planting?"

"I thought of that. You'll tell him they didn't feel right so you didn't spread 'em around. I've learned how to make duds, too. If he gets angry, he'll be angry at me for being careless."

"Wonderful."

"You'll do it?"

"Let me think about it. Lying to Urza. I can get angry with him,

I can yell at him and keep secrets, but I don't know if I can outright lie to him."

Ratepe didn't push, not that night, but he asked again the next time they were together and alone. If he'd gotten her angry, just once, she'd have put the whole cockeyed notion behind her, but Ratepe was too canny for that. Passionate, yet totally in control. Xantcha wondered what Kayla Bin-Kroog would have thought. She wondered whether Kayla would have stood under the stars as she herself did a few visits later and said:

"We're getting to the end. He's taking me to Russiore tomorrow. It's not infested with *sleepers.* More important, it's not far from Efuan Pincar. I can get down the coast to Pincar City, plant your spiders and cover Russiore, too."

Ratepe lifted Xantcha off the ground and, before she had a chance to protest, spun on his heels, whirling her around three times while he laughed out loud. She was gasping and giddy when her feet touched down.

"I knew you would!"

He kissed her, a kiss that began in joy and ended in passion as he lifted her up again.

he next evening, when Urza took her wrist for 'walking, Xantcha was sure that he knew she had extra spiders in her sack and deceit in her heart. She couldn't meet his eyes at their most ordinary.

"There is no shame to it, Xantcha," Urza said moments later when they stood on a hillside above the seacoast principality of Russiore. "He is a young man and you prefer yourself as a woman. I heard you laughing with him last night. I racked my memory but I don't think I've ever heard you or him so happy. It does my old bones good. After Russiore, I shall go off and leave you two alone together."

Urza vanished then, which was just as well, Xantcha needed to breathe and couldn't until he was gone.

Urza's bones, she thought with a shudder. Urza doesn't have any bones, she chided herself and yawned out the sphere.

The sphere rose swiftly through the ground breezes until the ocean windstreams caught it and threw it south, an abrupt reminder—as if Xantcha needed one—that she made mistakes when she was distracted. She wove her hand through the wind, pushing the sphere to its limit. Dawn's light revealed Efuand villages. Morning found her walking the market road into Pincar City.

Xantcha had scattered spiders all winter without once breaking a sweat, but she was damp and pasty-mouthed when a Red-Stripe guard asked her particulars at the city gate. He had a mortally unpleasant face, a mortally unpleasant smell.

"Ratepe," she told him, "son of Mideah of Medran." Despite anxiety, Xantcha's accent was flawless, and the coins of Russiore were common enough along Gulmany's northern coast that she could offer a few as a bribe, if needs be.

"Here for?"

"I've come to pray before Avohir's holy book on the fifth anniversary of my father's death."

Ratepe had said there was no more solemn obligation in a Efuand son's life. No born Red-Stripe would question it, and no Phyrexian would last long if it did.

"Peace go with you," the Red-Stripe said and touched Xantcha on both cheeks, a gesture which Ratepe had warned her to expect. "May your burdens be lifted."

Xantcha went through the gate in peace, her burdens hung from her shoulder, exactly as she'd packed them. She knew where the garrison barracks were and that they'd be swarming with Red-Stripes most of the day. That left the temple, which might be just as busy but was open to anyone who needed Avohir's grace. Ratepe had taught her the necessary prayers, when and where to wash her hands, and not to jump if anyone sprinkled seawater on her head while she was on her knees.

Three thousand years, more worlds than she could count, and always—always—an outsider.

The square altar was as tall as a man and stood on a stairway dais that was almost as high. Xantcha could barely see the holy book laid open atop it, although it was the largest book she'd ever seen—bigger than her bed. A huge cloth of red velvet covered the altar from the book to the dais. As Xantcha watched from the back of the sanctuary, an old man climbed the dais steps on his knees. At the top he lifted the velvet over his head and shoulders. He was letting Avohir dry his tears; she would be affixing Ratepe's spiders.

Xantcha claimed a space at the end of the line of mourners, petitioners, and cripples shuffling along a marked path to the dais where a red-robed priest guarded the steps. She was under the great dome, halfway to the altar, when a second priest came to take the place of the first. The second priest also wore a red robe with its cowl drawn up. His beard, as black as Ratepe's hair, spilled onto his chest.

Shratta, Xantcha thought, remembering what Ratepe had told her in the burning village.

He'd been at his post a few moments before the air brought her the scent of glistening oil.

Xantcha tried to get a look within the priest's cowl as her turn on the dais stairway neared. The oil scent was strong, but no stronger than with other *sleepers.* She didn't expect to see glowing or lidless eyes and his—its—hands, which she tried unsuccessfully to avoid, had a fleshy feel around hers.

"Peace be with you," he said, more sincere than the guard. Xantcha held her breath when he touched her cheeks. "May your burdens be lifted."

The path was clear, as simple as that, as simple as Ratepe had promised it would be. She hobbled on her knees, like everyone else, raised the velvet drape and flattened an artifact against the dark stone. A second spider on the opposite side would be a good idea, four would be better. Xantcha gazed up into the dome as she left, looking for a sphere-sized escape hole.

There were no holes in the roof, but there was one in the wall—an archway into a cloister where a few laymen in plain clothes appeared to be continuing their prayers. Xantcha took the chance and joined them. No one challenged her, and after she bruised her knees a while longer, she yawned out Urza's armor and left the cloister through a different door.

The smell of oil was stronger in the corridor beyond the cloister. Not a great surprise. She was in the priests' private quarters now. The corridors were poorly ventilated, and under such circumstances she'd expected the taint to thicken, but there was something more. Xantcha palmed a handful of screaming spiders from her sack, affixed them to the wall, and pressed deeper into the tangled chambers behind the sanctuary. The scent grew stronger and more complex. She suspected there was an ambulator nearby, or perhaps one of the vertical disks she'd seen so long ago in Moag.

We call them priests, she reminded herself, although there were no gods in Phyrexia, only the Ineffable, and blind obedience wasn't religion.

Midway down a spiral stairway, Xantcha encountered a priest rushing for the surface. Without a gesture or apology, he shoved her against the spiral's spine. She slipped down two, treacherously narrow, steps before catching her balance. The scent of glistening oil was heavy in his wake, but except in rudeness, he hadn't noticed her.

In her mind, Xantcha heard Ratepe muttering, *Phyrexians: no imagination!* Ratepe was young. He hid his fears in sarcasm. She put one of his stone-shattering spiders on the spiral's spine.

The stairway ended in a vaulted crypt. Light came from a pair of filthy lanterns and Phyrexian glows attached haphazardly to the stone ribs overhead. The sight of Phyrexian artifacts answered a wealth of questions and left her feeling anxious within Urza's armor. Xantcha thought again of Moag and wondered if she shouldn't scurry back to Russiore, confess her deceit when Urza came for her, and let him explore the crypt instead of her. But the truth was that Xantcha feared Urza's anger more than she feared Phyrexia.

Tiptoeing forward, Xantcha silently apologized to Ratepe. The crypt's air was pure Phyrexia. Not only was there some sort of passageway in Avohir's temple, it was wide open. She might have to tell Urza what she'd found, after she knew what it was, after she'd shared her discoveries with Ratepe, with Mishra.

Xantcha came to another door, the source of a fetid Phyrexian breeze. She hesitated. She had her armor, a boot knife and a handful of fuming coins, a passive defense and no offense worth mentioning. Wisdom said, this is foolish, then she heard a sound behind her, on the spiral stairs, and wisdom said, *hide!*

Three steps beyond the door the corridor jogged sharply to the right and into utter darkness. Xantcha put one hand behind her back and finger-walked into the unknown. The loudest sound was the pulsing in her ears. She had a sense that she'd entered a larger chamber when the breeze died.

She had a sense, too, that she wasn't alone; she was right.

"Meatling."

Thirty-four hundred years, give or take a few decades, and Xantcha knew that voice instantly.

"Gix."

Light bloomed around him, gray, heavy light such as shone on the First Sphere, light that wasn't truly light, but visible darkness. Xantcha thought the demon was the light's source and needed a moment to discern the upright disk gleaming behind him.

Gix had changed since the last time she'd seen him, corroded, crumbling, and thrust into a fumarole. He'd changed since the first time, too—taller. She looked at his waist when she looked straight ahead; symmetric, altogether more man-shaped, though his metal "skin" didn't completely hide the glistening sinews and tubes—like a born-man's veins only filled with glistening oil—that wound over his green-gold skin. Gix's forehead was monumental and framed a rubine gem that was almost certainly a weapon. His skull seemed to have been pivoted open along his brow ridge. A black-metal serrated spike ran from the base of his neck to the now-raised base of his skull. From the side, it looked like the spike was rooted in his spine and attached to a red, blue, and yellow fish.

In another circumstance, the demon would have been ludicrous or absurd. Far beneath Avohir's altar, he was the image of malignity and horror. Xantcha stood transfixed as a narrow beam of blood-red light shone between her and Gix's bulging forehead. She felt surprise, then a command:

Obey. Listen and obey.

"Never." Urza's armor wasn't perfect protection against the demon's invasion of her mind, but added to her own stubbornness and to the walls she'd made ages ago. Xantcha defied the demon. "I'll die first."

Gix grinned, all glistening teeth and malice. "Your wish—"

He probed her mind again, brutally. Xantcha fed him images of his excoriation. The demon withdrew suddenly, his metallic chin tucked in a parody of mortal surprise.

"So old!"

Light sprang up in the portal chamber, a catacomb with desiccated bodies heaped here and there, all male, all bearded. The Shratta, if not all of them, then at least a hundred of them, and probably their leaders. Replaced with Phyrexians or simply exterminated? Like as not, she'd never know. Whatever their crimes, Xantcha knew the Shratta would have suffered horribly before they died; that would have to suffice for Rat's vengeance.

"Yes, I remember you," Gix whispered. "One of the first, and still here?" His metal-sheathed shoulders jerked. "No. Not sent. I saved you back . . . Waiting. Waiting . . ." The demon's voice faded. The light in its forehead flickered. "Xantcha." He made her name long and sibilant, like a snake sliding over dried leaves. "My special one. Here . . . in Dominaria?"

Before Gix had needed cables and talons to caress Xantcha's chin. Now he used light and encountered Urza's armor.

"What is this?"

The light bored into her right eye, seeking Xantcha's past, her history. Defiantly, she threw out images of Urza's dragon burning through the Fourth Sphere ceiling.

"Yes. Yes, of course. Locked out of Dominaria, where else would you go? I gave you purpose and you pursued it. You pursue it still."

The light became softer. It caressed Xantcha's mind. She shivered within Urza's armor.

"I'll tell Urza that the demon who destroyed his brother has returned."

It was a guess on Xantcha's part, Ratepe had seen Gix in Mishra's Weakstone recordings, but he'd never said anything about the Phyrexians who'd undertaken Mishra's compleation. But it was a good guess.

"Yes," Gix sighed. "Tell Urza that Gix has returned. Tell him the Thran are waiting for him."

Xantcha didn't understand. The Phyrexians had fought the Thran. Her mind swirled with echoes of Urza's lectures about Koilos and a noble race that sacrificed itself for Dominaria's future.

Gix laughed. All the raucous birds and chittering insects of summer couldn't have equaled the sound. "Did he tell you that? He knows better. He was there."

The statement made no sense. Urza had found his eyes at Koilos and through them, remembered the final battle between the Thran and the Phyrexians, but he hadn't been there. Gix was toying with her, feeding on her confusion and terror, waiting for her to make the mistake that would let him into her secret places.

"You have no secrets, Xantcha." More laughter. "I made the stone the brothers broke, and I made the brothers, too, and then I made you."

"Lies," Xantcha shot back and remembered standing beside a vat. A body floated below the surface: dark haired, angular, sexless . . . her. "There were a thousand of us," she shot back.

"Seven thousand, and only one like you. I looked for you . . . after."

After he escaped the Seventh Sphere? "I have my own heart."

"Yes. You have done well, Xantcha. Better than I hoped. I had plans for you. I still have them. Come back. Listen and obey!"

Gix pulled a string in Xantcha's mind. She felt herself begin to unravel. Newts had no importance. Newts did what they were told. Newts listened and obeyed. She belonged with Gix, to Gix, in Phyrexia, her home. Gix would take care of her. The demon was the center. She would do as he wished.

Urza's armor was in the way. . . .

Xantcha was about to release the armor when she thought of Ratepe. Suddenly there was nothing else except his face, laughing, scowling, watching her as she walked across the Medran plaza with a purse of gold on her belt. The sensations lasted less than a heartbeat, then Gix was back, but Xantcha hadn't needed a whole heartbeat to retreat from the destructive folly she'd been about to commit.

"So, you found him," Gix said after he'd retreated from her mind. "Does he please you?"

The red light continued to shine in her eye. Gix would pull another string, and this time there'd be no Ratepe, son of Mideah, to surprise the demon. Ratepe had given Xantcha a second chance, but she had to seize it. And Xantcha did, diving to her left, toward the corridor. Something hard and heavy struck her back. It threw her forward. She skidded face-first along the floor-stones, surrounded by red light, but the armor held. Xantcha scrambled to her feet and ran for her life. Demons weren't accustomed to defiance. They had no reflex response to stop a newt's desperate escape. Gix chased her, but he didn't catch her before she reached the spiral stairway.

He howled and clawed the stones, but the passage was too tight, too narrow. A fireball engulfed Xantcha in an acid wind. She clung to the spine until it passed, then ran again, through the corridor, the cloister and into Avohir's sanctuary.

Night had fallen on the plaza. Xantcha wasted no time asking herself where the day had gone. She released the armor, yawned out the sphere as soon as she dared, and headed up the coast to Russiore.

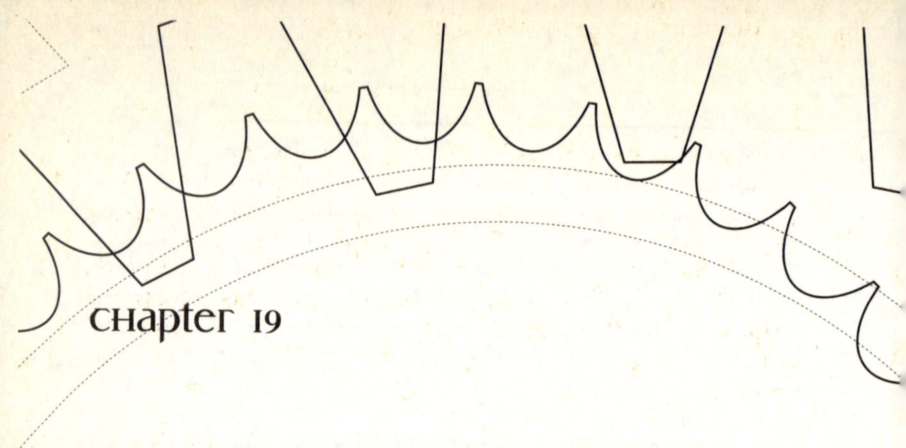

chapter 19

Urza and Xantcha 'walked away from Serra's realm not long after Xantcha gave him her heart. Xantcha was scarcely wiser about the imperfections of Serra's creation than she'd been when she'd walked into the palace, though it was clear that her presence, so close to the Cocoon, affected not only the realm as a whole but Sosinna's recovery from the Aegis burns. For Sosinna and Kenidiern, Xantcha would have accepted Serra's offer of transit to another, natural and inherently balanced world, but the offer was not made a second time. Urza accepted Serra's judgment. Even though he distrusted Xantcha as a Phyrexian, he'd been through too much with her to go on alone.

He held Xantcha in his arms for that first terrible step across the chasm that separated a willfully created plane from the natural Multiverse. She held a sealed chest nearly filled with gifts from Lady Serra. The gifts included a miniature cocoon that was the perfect size for Xantcha's amber heart.

Their first natural world was a tiny, airless moon circling another world that appeared to be one vast blue-green ocean, though Urza said otherwise. He made a chamber beneath the moon's surface and filled it with breathable air, his usual course in a place where he could survive indefinitely but Xantcha could not.

"A terrible thing, this," he said, removing Xantcha's heart from the chest and placing it in a niche he had just finished. "I believe it contains everything they took away from you, even your soul."

Despite his incursion into Phyrexia, and Lady Serra's assertion that Xantcha wholly and entirely differed from any born man or woman, Urza wouldn't surrender his belief that she'd been stolen from her parents and abominably transformed by her Phyrexian captors. She no longer bothered arguing the point with him. It was reassuring to be treated as he had always treated her.

"I would destroy it, if I could find a way to return what it has taken. But that mystery does not solve itself easily, and I cannot devote my energies to it until I have determined the first plane of the Phyrexians and my vengeance has feasted on their entrails. You will understand that vengeance must come first."

Xantcha nodded unnecessarily. Urza had not asked her a question. His concentration did not extend beyond his own thoughts, and he didn't notice her head moving.

"Serra and I determined that the true number of natural planes in the Multiverse cannot be counted, even by an immortal. If one started at the beginning, new planes would have emerged, and old planes would have disappeared before the count was concluded. This is not, however, an insurmountable problem, as we can be certain that the Phyrexians were not driven away from a freshly engendered plane, and while it would be a tragedy if their keystone plane had succumbed to entropy and reorganization, we need not blame ourselves for the loss. Thus, it is only necessary that I start somewhere and proceed with great precision until I reach the end, which, with the Multiverse, is also the beginning. Do you understand what this means?"

Xantcha nodded again, confident that Urza would continue explaining himself until her answer was truthful.

"Good. I will, of necessity, 'walk lightly. I had thought of creating my own plane, since such planes are always accessible across the chasm, but I would have to create a plane in which both you and I could thrive, and Serra told me that such a creation would be quite difficult to manage. Black essence, which is to say your essence, and white, which is mine, are deeply opposed to each other and virtually impossible to balance in the microcosm of a created plane. Now, I do not shirk challenges, but I must avenge my brother before I allow myself the pleasures of pure research, thus I have put creation out of my mind. I will make do with bolt-holes such as this, which I will forge and relocate as I have need of them. There is an element of proximity in the Multiverse, and eventually one is within an easy 'walk of a particular plane.

"This should be an especial relief to you, Xantcha, since I will keep your heart in such a place where it cannot be lost or disturbed. It is also useful for me, since when I know where you are, I also know where your heart is, and contrariwise as well. And Serra has returned that crystal pendant I gave you while I was fleeing Phyrexia." He fished it out of one of the many boxes and draped it around Xantcha's neck. "You, I, and your heart and my pendant together make a single unit, a triangle, the strongest of angled structures. None of us can get lost."

Triangles . . . triangles with four points? It had to be mathematics. . . . Of all the lessons Xantcha had been taught in the Fane of Flesh, mathematics had come hardest. She'd long since learned that she didn't need to understand the why of mathematics if she simply followed all the rules. If the rules turned her heart into one of a triangle's four parts, she'd keep quiet about it. And she'd survive with her heart in a niche on an airless moon the same way she'd survived the centuries when it had lain in the Phyrexian vault.

"What do you need of me?" she asked, hoping to forestall any further discussion of unimaginable triangles.

"You are good at sniffing out Phyrexians. When we reach a plane, I want you to explore it, as you would anyway, looking for infestations."

"I'll need to use the sphere, is that all right?" The modifications remained a sore point between them. "You'll fix it so it isn't black anymore?"

Urza ignored her questions. "For me, being somewhere quickly is easier than getting there slowly. I will search for the victors, the folk who drove the Phyrexians out and forced them to create Phyrexia."

You will do what you want, Xantcha thought in the most private corner of her mind. Of course, so would she. Life was never better than when she was soaring the windstreams, chasing her curiosity, trading trinkets with strangers, and collecting the stories that born-folk told.

"What do I do if I find a Phyrexian infestation?" She liked the word, her mind filled with possible ways to drive out an infestation.

"You run away. The moment you are aware of Phyrexians, you hide yourself in the meeting place I'll point out to you, and you wait for me. I'll take no more chances with you and Phyrexians. You are vulnerable to them, Xantcha. It's no fault of yours—you're brave and good-spirited—but they tainted you. You are a bell goat and after you followed me to Phyrexia, my enemies were able to use you to find me—much as I will use your heart to find you."

I never told you the Ineffable's name. That's how they found you. Xantcha thought, but said nothing. She'd made her choice to stay with Urza, even knowing his obsessions and madness. If he reordered his memories of the past to absolve himself of blame or responsibility, well—he'd done it before and he'd do it again. Xantcha believed in vengeance against Phyrexia and believed that Urza, with all his flaws, stood a better chance of achieving it than she.

So they began their quest for the victors, the folk who'd driven the Phyrexians out of the natural Multiverse. Urza set his mark on each world they visited, regardless of its hospitality. That way, he said, they would know when they'd come full circle. Xantcha wasn't certain about the full circle notion; it raised some of the same problems as a four-pointed triangle, but the marks kept them from accidentally exploring the same world twice.

It was no surprise to Xantcha that they found very few hospitable worlds where the Phyrexians had not made an appearance. She'd been a dodger. She knew about the relentless explorations carried out by the searcher-priests. The first few decades after leaving Serra's realm, she'd spent most of her time huddled up at whatever meeting place Urza designated, then gradually Urza had relaxed his rules. She could wander freely, provided she encountered no *active* Phyrexians.

Thus began a long, golden period of wandering the Multiverse. Every handful of worlds held one that was hospitable enough for Xantcha to exchange Urza's armor for the sphere. Every ten or twelve handfuls of hospitable worlds revealed one that was interesting, at least to Xantcha. She became the tourist who delighted in minor variations, while Urza was on a single-minded quest.

"They were here," he said when they rejoined each other. They met in a white stone grotto of a world where elves were the dominant species and civilization was measured by forests, not cities.

"I know," Xantcha agreed, having found the spoor of two searcher expeditions and heard tales of demons with glistening, metallic skin in several languages. "Searchers came through a good long time ago. They're remembered as demons and the bringers of chaos. They came through again, maybe a thousand local years ago, but only in a few places. They collected beasts both times, I think. There's metal here, but no mines. The searchers will come back again. They're waiting for the elves to do the hard work of opening the ground."

Urza nodded though he wasn't happy. "How did you learn such things? There are no centers of learning here, few records in the ground or above it. I have found it most frustrating!"

"I talk to everyone, Urza. I trade with them," she explained, handing Urza a sack filled with trinkets and treasures, her profits from three seasons' wandering. He'd take them to the bolt-hole where he kept her heart. "Everyone has a story."

"A story, Xantcha—what I want is the truth! The hard-edged truth."

She squared her shoulders. "The truth is, this is not the victor's world. I could have told you that before the sun set twice."

"And how could you have done that?"

"No one here knows a word for war."

Urza stiffened. A planeswalker didn't have to listen with his ears. He could skim thought and meaning directly off the surface of another mind and drink down a new language like water. As a result, Urza seldom paid attention to the actual words he heard or spoke. He handled surprise poorly, embarrassment, worse. His breathing stopped, and his eyes shed their mortal illusion.

"I have encountered a new world," he snapped after a pensive moment. *Equilor.* His lips hadn't moved.

Xantcha didn't disbelieve him, although Equilor wasn't a word that she remembered hearing on this or any other world. "Is it a name?" she asked cautiously.

"An old name. The oldest name. The farthest plane. It belongs to a plane on the edge of time."

"Another created world, like Phyrexia or Serra's realm?"

"No, I think not. I hope not."

She'd wager, if she'd ever been the wagering sort, that Urza hadn't learned of Equilor from the elves of the forest world but had heard of it years ago and forgotten it until just now when she'd challenged him.

They set out at once, with no more preparation than Urza made for any between-worlds journey. He explained that preparation and, especially, directions weren't important. 'Walking the between-worlds wasn't like walking down a path. There was no north or south, left or right, only the background glow of all the planes that were and, rising out of the glow, a sense of those planes that a 'walker could reach in a single stride. By choosing the faintest of the rising planes at each step, Urza insisted they would in time arrive at Equilor, the plane on the edge of time.

Xantcha couldn't imagine a place where direction didn't matter, but then, for her the between-worlds remained as hostile as it had been the first time Urza dragged her through it. For her the between-worlds was a changeless place of paradox and sheer terror.

At first, the only evidence she had that Urza was doing anything different was indirect. Her armor crumbled, the instant Urza released her, in the air of the next, new world. There was breathable air in each new world they 'walked to, as if he'd at last given up the notion that the Phyrexians could have begun on a world without air. And Urza himself was exhausted when they arrived. He would go into the ground and sleep as much as a local year while she explored.

They were some thirty worlds beyond the elven forest world when Urza announced, as Xantcha shook herself free of flaking armor:

"Here you do not need to look for Phyrexians. Here we will find others of my kind."

Urza didn't mean that he'd brought her to Dominaria. Every so often, he journeyed alone to the brink of his birth-world to assure himself that it remained safe within the Shard they'd discovered long ago. Urza meant, instead, that he'd broken an age-old habit and set them down on a plane where other 'walkers congregated.

He'd never insinuated that he was unique, at least as far as 'walking between-worlds. Serra was a 'walker and so, Xantcha suspected, had been the Ineffable. But Urza had avoided other 'walkers until they came to the abandoned world he called Gastal.

"Be wary," he warned Xantcha. "I do not trust them. Without a plane to bind them, 'walkers forget what they were. They become predators, unless they go mad."

Knowing Urza fell in the latter category, Xantcha stayed carefully in his shadow as they approached a small, fanciful, and entirely illusory pavilion standing by itself on a barren, twilight plain, but the three men and two women they met there seemed unthreatening. They knew Urza—or knew of him—and welcomed him as a prodigal brother, though Xantcha couldn't actually follow their conversation: planeswalkers conversed directly in one another's minds.

But Urza was not the only 'walker who tempered his solitary life with a more ordinary companion. Outside the pavilion, Xantcha met two other women, one of them a blind dwarf, who braved the between-worlds on a 'walker's arm. Throughout the balmy night, the three of them sought a common language through which to share experience and advice. By dawn they'd made progress in a creole that was mixed mostly from elven dialects from a hundred or more worlds. Xantcha had just pieced together that Varrastu, a dwarf, had heard of Phyrexia when Urza emerged to say it was time to move on.

Xantcha rose reluctantly. "Varrastu said that she and Manatarqua have crossed swords with folk made from flesh and metal—"

Words failed as a second sun, yellowish-green in color, loomed suddenly high overhead. The air exploded as it hurtled toward them. Xantcha had the wit to be frightened but hadn't begun to guess why or to yawn Urza's armor from the cyst, when the pavilion burst into screaming flames, and Urza seized her against his chest. He pulled her between-worlds. Without the armor to protect her, she was bleeding and gasping when they re-emerged.

Urza laid her on the ground then cradled her face in his hands. "Don't go," he whispered.

It seemed an incongruous request. Xantcha wasn't about to go anywhere. The between-worlds had battered her to exhaustion. Her body seemed to have already fallen asleep. She wanted only to close her eyes and join it.

"No!" Urza pinched her cheeks. "Stay awake! Stay with me!"

Power like fire or countless sharp needles swirled around her. Xantcha fought feebly to escape the pain. She pleaded with him to release her.

"Live!" he shouted. "I won't let you die now."

Death would have been preferable to the torture flowing from Urza's fingers, but Xantcha hadn't the strength to resist his will. Mote by mote, he healed her and dragged her back from the brink.

"Sleep now, if you wish."

His hand passed over her eyes. For an instant, there was darkness and oblivion, then there was light, and Xantcha was herself again. She exhaled a pent-up breath and sat up.

"I don't know what came over me."

"Death," Urza said calmly. "I nearly lost you."

She remembered the yellow-green sun. "We must go back, Varrastu—Manatarqua—"

"Crossed swords with the Phyrexians. Yes. Manatarqua was the pavilion. She died on Gastal."

A shudder raced down Xantcha's spine. There was more that Urza wasn't saying. "How long ago?"

"In the time of this plane, nearly two years."

Xantcha noticed her surroundings: a bare-walled chamber with a window but not a door. She noticed herself. Her skin was white. It cracked and flaked when she moved, as if her armor clung in dead layers around her. Her hair, which she always hacked short around her face, hung below her shoulders. "Two years," she repeated, needing to say the words herself to make them true in her mind. "Long years?"

"Very long," Urza assured her. "You've recovered. I never doubted that you would, if I stayed beside you. You'll be hungry soon. I'll get food now. Tomorrow or the next day we'll move on toward Equilor."

Already Xantcha felt her stomach churning to life—after two empty years. Food would be nice, but there was another question: "At Gastal, Manatarqua—you said she 'was the pavilion.' Do you mean that she was Phyrexian and that you slew her?"

"No, Manatarqua was a 'walker like myself, but much younger. I have no idea why she presented herself as an object. I didn't ask, it was her choice. Perhaps she hoped to hide from her enemies."

"Phyrexians?"

"Other planeswalkers. I told you, they—we—can become predatory, especially toward the newly sparked. I was nearly taken myself in the beginning—Meshuvel was her name. She was no threat to me. My eyes reveal sights no other 'walker can see. Until Serra, I avoided my own kind. They had no part to play in my quest for vengeance. I'd been thinking about 'walkers since leaving Serra's realm. I thought I might need someone more like myself."

"But they died."

"Manatarqua died. I suspect the others escaped unharmed, as I did. They prey on the young and the mortal because a mature 'walker is no easy target. But I had made up my mind almost from the start. I don't need another 'walker. I need you. To finally realize that and then feel you die so soon afterward—it was almost enough to make me worship the fickle gods."

Xantcha imagined Urza on his knees or in a temple. She closed her eyes and laughed. He was gone when she reopened them, and she was too stiff yet to climb through the window. Her saner self insisted that Urza wouldn't abandon her, not after sitting beside her for two years, not after what he'd just said about needing her. Then this world's sun passed beyond the window. Sanity's voice grew weaker as shadows lengthened. Of all the ways Xantcha knew to die, starvation was among the worst. She had dragged herself to the window and was hauling herself over the sill when she felt a breeze at her hack. The breeze was thick with fresh bread, roasted meat, and fruit. Urza had returned.

He called the meal a celebration and ate with her, at least until a more ordinary sort of tiredness drove Xantcha back to the bed where she'd lain for so long. She awoke with the sun. There was a door beside the window, more food and, somewhere beyond the sun, near the edge of time, a world called Equilor.

Later, after they'd gotten to Dominaria, when Xantcha sorted through her memories, the largest pile belonged to the years they had searched for Equilor. Every season, for much more than a thousand Dominarian years, she and Urza wandered the Multiverse, taking other worlds' measure. There were surprises and excitement, mostly of the minor variety. After Serra's realm, Phyrexia seemed to lose interest in them—or, at least, had lost their trail. Though they sometimes found evidence of searcher-priests and excavations. Eventually, everything they found was long abandoned.

"I'm headed in the right direction," Urza would say whenever they came upon eroded ruins no one else would have noticed.

"I'm headed toward the world that cast them out."

Xantcha was never so confident, but she never understood how Urza found anything in the between-worlds, much less how he distinguished hospitable worlds from inhospitable ones, near from far. She was content to follow a path that led endlessly away from the Phyrexia she knew and toward the vengeance that seemed equally distant. Until the day when they came to a quiet, twilight world.

"The edge of time itself," Urza said as he released Xantcha's wrists.

She shed her armor and filled her lungs with air that was unlike any other. "Old," she said after a few moments. "It's as if everything's finished—not dead, just done growing and changing. Even the mountains are smoothed down, like they've been standing too long, but nothing's come to replace them," She gestured toward the great, dark lump that dominated the landscape like a risen loaf of bread. "Somehow, I expected an edge to have sharp angles."

Urza nodded. "I expected a plane where everything had been put to use, not like this, neglected and left fallow."

Yet not completely fallow. As twilight deepened, lights winked open near the solitary mountain. There was a road, too: a ribbon of worn gray stone, cut in chevrons and fitted so precisely that not a blade of grass grew between them. Urza insisted he had no advance idea of what a new plane was like, no way at all of selecting the exact place where his feet would touch the ground, yet, more often than not, he 'walked out of the between-worlds in sight of a road and a town.

They began to travel down the road.

A carpet of bats took flight from the mountain, passing directly over their heads. When their shrill chirping had subsided, other noises punctuated the night: howls, growls and a bird with a sweet, yet mournful song. Stars appeared, unfamiliar, of course, and scattered sparsely across the clear, black sky. No moon outshone them, but it was the nature of moons to produce moonless nights now and again. What surprised Xantcha was the scarcity of stars, as if time were stars and the black sky were itself the edge of time.

"A strange place," Xantcha decided as they strode down the road. "Not ominous or inhospitable, but filled with secrets."

"So long as one of them is Phyrexia, I won't care about the rest."

The light came from cobweb globes hovering above the road and the three-score graceful houses of an unfortified town. Urza lifted himself into the air to examine them and reported solemnly that he had not a clue to their construction or operation.

"They simply are," he said, "and my instinct is to leave them alone."

Xantcha smiled to herself. If that was Urza's instinct then whatever the globes were, they weren't simple.

A man came out to meet them. He appeared ordinary enough, though Xantcha understood how deceptive an ordinary appearance could be, and it bothered her that she hadn't noticed him leave any one of the nearby houses, hadn't noticed him at all until he was some fifty paces ahead and walking toward them. He wore a knee-length robe over loose trousers, both woven from a pale, lightweight fiber that rippled as he moved and sparkled as if it were shot with silver. His hair and beard were dark auburn in the globe light and neatly trimmed. A few wrinkles creased the outer corners of his eyes. Xantcha placed him in the prime of mortal life, but she'd place Urza there, too.

"Welcome, Urza," the stranger said. "Welcome to Equilor. We've been waiting for you."

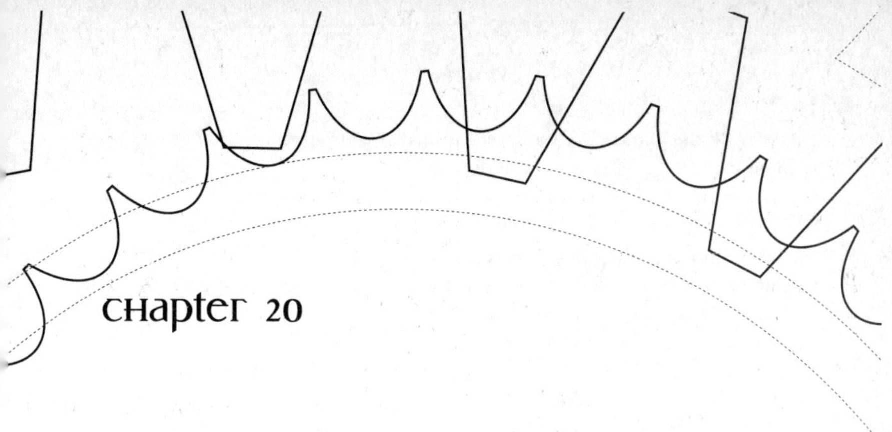

chapter 20

Xantcha had understood every word the auburn-haired man had said, an unprecedented happening on a new world. She dug deep into her memory trying to recognize the language and missed the obvious: the stranger spoke Argivian, the sounds of Urza's long-lost boyhood and of her newt-ish dreams, the foundation of the argot she and Urza spoke to each other. But if this were Dominaria, then Urza would have recognized the stars, and if the stranger were another 'walker with the power to absorb languages without time or effort, then why had he said, We've been waiting?

The stranger touched his forehead, lips, and heart before embracing Urza, cheek against cheek. Urza bent into the gesture, as he would not have done if he were suspicious.

"And you're . . . Xantcha."

The stranger turned his attention to her. He'd hesitated before stating her name. Taking it from her mind? Not unless he were much better at such things than Urza was; she'd felt no violation. Once again the stranger touched himself three times before embracing her exactly as he'd embraced Urza. His hands were warm, with the texture of flesh and bone. His breath was warm, too, and faintly redolent of onions.

"Waiting for us?" Urza demanded before asking the stranger's name or any other pleasantry. "Before sunset I was elsewhere, very much elsewhere. And until now, I did not know for certain that I had found the place I have been seeking for so long."

"Yes, waiting," the stranger insisted, keeping one hand beneath Xantcha's elbow and guiding Urza toward one of the houses with the other.

"You 'walk the planes. We have been aware of your approach for quite some time now. It is good to have you here at last."

Xantcha glanced behind the stranger's shoulders. Urza had devised a code, simple hand and facial movements for moments when they were among mind-skimmers. She made the sign for danger and received the sign for negation in response. Urza wasn't worried as the stranger led them through a simple stone-built gate and into a tall, open-roofed atrium.

There were others in the atrium, a woman at an open hearth, stirring a pot of stew that was the source of the onions Xantcha had smelled earlier, two other women and a man, all adults, all individuals, yet bound by a familial resemblance. An ancient sat in a wicker chair—wrinkled, toothless, and nearly bald. Xantcha couldn't guess if she beheld a man or a woman. Beyond the ancient, in another atrium, two half-grown children dangled strings for a litter of kittens, while a round-faced toddling child watched her from behind the banister at the top of a stairway.

Of them all, only the toddler betrayed even a taint distrust of uninvited guests. Where moments earlier Xantcha had warned Urza of danger, she now began to wonder why the household seemed so unconcerned. Didn't they see her knives and sword? Had they no idea what a 'walker could do—especially a 'walker named Urza?

"There is a portion for you," the hearth-side woman said specifically to Xantcha, as she ladled out a solitary bowl and set it on the table that ran the length of the atrium. Like the man who'd met them on the road, she spoke Argivian, but with a faint accent. "You must be hungry after your journey here."

Xantcha was hungry. She caught Urza's eyes again and passed the general sign that asked, What should I do?

"Eat," he said. "The food smells delicious."

But a second bowl wasn't offered—as if they knew a 'walker never needed to eat.

Xantcha sat in a white chair at a white table, eating stew from a white bowl. Everything that could have had a chosen color, including the floors and the walls, was white and sparkling clean. Except for the spoon in the bowl. It was plain wood, rubbed until it was satin smooth. She used it self-consciously, afraid she'd dribble and embarrass herself—both distinct possibilities, distracted as she was by conversations between Urza and the others that she couldn't quite overhear.

The stew was plain but tasty. If there was time, she'd like to see the garden where they grew their vegetables and the fields where they harvested their grain. It was a meatless stew—somehow that didn't surprise her—with egg drizzled in the broth, and pale chunks, like cubes of soft cheese, a bit smaller than her thumb, taking the place of meat. The chunks had the texture of soft cheese, but not the taste; indeed, they had no taste that Xantcha could discern, and she was tempted to leave them in the bowl until the woman asked her if the meal was pleasing to a wanderer's palate.

The auburn-haired man's name was Romom, the cook was Tessu, the other names left no impression in Xantcha's mind, save for Brya, the toddler at the top of the stairs. When Xantcha had finished her second bowl of stew and a mug of excellent cider, Tessu suggested a hot bath in an open, steaming pool. Xantcha had no wish to display her newt's undifferentiated flesh before strangers and declined the offer. Tessu suggested sleep in a room of her own—

"Facing the mountain."

It was a privilege of some sort, but Xantcha declined a second time. She pushed away from the spotless white table and took a cautious stride toward the pillow-sitting knot of folk gathered around Urza. Opposition never materialized. The family made room for her between the two women whose names Xantcha couldn't remember. Urza gave her the finger sign for silence. The family discussed stars and myths. They used unfamiliar names, but all the other words were accented Argivian with only a few lapses of syntax or vocabulary. It wasn't their native language, yet they'd all learned it well-enough for an esoteric conversation that couldn't, in any meaningful sense, include her or Urza.

Xantcha twisted her fingers into an open question, and Urza replied with the sign for silence. Silence wasn't difficult for Xantcha, unless it was imposed. She fidgeted and considered joining the youngsters still playing with the kittens until Tessu shuttled them upstairs. The conversation began to flag and for the first time since they'd entered the austerely decorated atrium, the air charged with anticipation. Even at the edge of time there were, apparently, conversations that could be held only after the children had gone to bed.

Tessu and Romom together brought the ancient to what had been Romom's place on Urza's right. Then everyone shuffled about to make room for the pair—who Xantcha had decided were husband and wife, if not lord and lady—on the opposite side of the circle.

"You have questions," the ancient said. The voice gave no clues to the grizzled figure's sex, but the accent was thick. Xantcha had to listen closely to distinguish the words. "No one comes to Equilor without questions."

Urza made two signs, one with each hand, silence and observe, before he said, "I have come to learn my enemies' weakness."

The two men exchanged glances, one triumphant, an ongoing dispute settled at last. Against all reason, these folk had been expecting them, exactly them: Urza from Argive and a companion who'd been glad of a hot meal at the end of a long day. But they hadn't known for certain why, and that made less sense. If you knew Urza well enough to know his name and where he was headed, then surely you knew what had driven him through the Multiverse to Equilor.

The men, however, said nothing. Like Xantcha, they seemed relegated to silence, waiting for the ancient to speak again.

"Equilor is not your enemy. Equilor has no enemies. If you were an enemy of Equilor, you would not have found us."

Another created plane like Phyrexia and Serra's realm, accessible only across a fathomless chasm—which Urza hadn't mentioned?

"I am a seeker, nothing more," Urza countered, as formal and constrained as Xantcha had ever heard him. "I sensed no defenses as I 'walked."

"We would not intimidate our enemies, Urza. We would not encourage them to test their courage. We knew you were a seeker. We permitted you to find what you sought. The elders will see you."

By which the ancient implied that he, or she, was not one of the elders. Perhaps the term was an honorific, not dependent on age. Xantcha would have liked to ask an impertinent question or two, but Urza's fingers remained loosely in their silence and observe positions.

"And I will ask them about Phyrexia. Have you heard of it?"

There was considerable movement in the circle. Xantcha couldn't observe it all, but Phyrexia was not unknown to the household.

The ancient said one word, "Misguided," which seemed sufficient to everyone but Urza and Xantcha.

"More than misguided," Urza sputtered. "They are a force of abomination, of destruction. They have set themselves against my plane, and I have sworn vengeance against them in the name of my brother, my people, and the Thran."

That word, "Thran," also brought an exchange of glances, less profound than what had followed Phyrexia.

"Misguided," the ancient repeated. "Foolish and doomed. The elders will tell you more."

"So, you know of them! I'm convinced that they were banished from their natal plane before they created Phyrexia. I am looking for that plane. If it is not Equilor, I hope that you can tell me where it is. I have heard that whatever is known in the Multiverse is known to Equilor."

The ancient nodded. "The ones you seek have never come to Equilor. They are young, as you are young. Youth does not often come to Equilor."

"They fought the Thran over six thousand of my years ago, and I myself have walked the planes for over two millennia."

The ancient fired a question to Romom in a language Xantcha couldn't understand.

Romom replied, in Argivian, "Shorter, Pakuya, by at least a third."

"You are old, Urza, for a young man, but compared to Equilor, you are scarcely weaned from your mother's breast. In Equilor, we began our search for enlightenment a hundred millennia ago. Do not wonder, then, that you could not see our defenses as you passed through them."

"You will think differently when the Phyrexians arrive!"

"They are a small folk with small ambitions, smaller dreams. We have nothing to offer them. Perhaps we were wrong about you."

The ancient added something short and decisive in the other language. Watching Urza as closely as she watched the household, Xantcha realized that Urza couldn't skim the thoughts of these deceptively simple folk.

"It is late," Tessu said, putting a polite, yet unmistakable end to the discussion. She rose to her feet. Romom rose beside her. "Time to rest and sleep. The sun will rise."

The rest of the household stood and bowed their heads as Romom and Tessu helped the ancient from the atrium. Moments later, Urza and Xantcha were alone.

"This is the place!" Urza said directly in her mind.

"The old one said not."

"She is testing us. Tomorrow, when I meet with these elders, I will have what I have long wished to learn."

In her private thoughts, Xantcha wondered how Urza knew the ancient was a woman, then chided herself for thinking he could be right about such a small thing when he seemed so wrong about the rest. The ancient had talked to Urza as Urza often talked to her, but he hadn't noticed the slights.

"They have secrets," Xantcha warned but no reply formed in her mind, and she couldn't know if Urza had retrieved her thought.

Tessu and Romom returned. Romom said there was a special chamber where those who would speak to the elders waited for the sun to rise. For Xantcha, who was just as glad not be included, there was a narrow bedchamber at the end of a cloistered corridor, a change of clothes, and a worried question:

"You will bathe before sunrise?"

She answered in the same tone, "If I may bathe unobserved?"

"The mountain will see you."

There were no roofs over any of the chambers. Xantcha wondered what they did when it rained, but, "The mountain is not a problem."

"You have customs that inhibit you?"

Xantcha nodded. If that explanation would satisfy Tessu, she'd provide no other.

"I will not interfere, but I cannot sleep until you have bathed."

"Your customs?"

Tessu nodded, and with her clean clothes under her arm Xantcha followed her host to the dark and quiet atrium. If Tessu failed to contain her curiosity, Xantcha was none the wiser. As smooth and hairless as the day she crawled out of her vat, Xantcha eased herself into the starlit, steaming pool. A natural hot spring kept the water pleasantly warm. A gutter—white, of course, and elegantly simple—carried the overflow away.

She'd scrubbed herself clean in a matter of moments and, knowing that Tessu waited in the atrium, should have toweled herself off immediately, but the mountain was watching her and she watched back.

It had many eyes—Xantcha lost count at thirty-three—and, remembering the bats, the eyes were probably nothing more than caves, still, the sense of observation was inescapable. After staring so intently at shades of black and darkness, Xantcha thought she saw flickering lights in some of the cave eyes, thought the lights formed a rippling web across the mountain. Xantcha thought a number of things until she realized she was standing naked beside the pool, at which point all her thoughts shattered and vanished. She grabbed her clothes, both clean and filthy, and retreated into the atrium.

"You are unwell?" Tessu asked discreetly from the shadows as Xantcha wrestled with unfamiliar clasps and plackets.

"It did see me."

Tessu failed to repress a chuckle. "They will not harm you, Xantcha."

Urza was right. They were being tested. Xantcha hoped she had passed.

Xantcha slept well and awoke to the unmistakable sounds of children being quiet outside her door. They were not so fluent in Argivian as the household's adult members, but the tallest of the three boys—who understandably took himself to be older than Xantcha and therefore entitled to give her orders—made it clear that sunrise was coming and it was time for guests to come outside and join the family in its morning rituals.

The eastern horizon had barely begun to brighten when Xantcha settled into what was evidently a place of honor between Tessu and the ancient. They faced west toward the mountain, which was as monolithic black in the pre-dawn light as it was during Xantcha's bath. There were no prayers, a relief, and no Urza or Romom or Brya, either. Brya's absence could be explained by the motionless serenity with which the household awaited the coming of daylight. No toddler could sit so still for so long.

Xantcha herself was challenged by the discipline. Her mind ached with unasked questions, her nose itched, then her toes, and the nearly unreachable spot between her shoulder blades. She was ready to explode when light struck the mountain's rounded crest. As sunrises went, it was not spectacular. The air was clear. There were no clouds anywhere to add contrast or movement to the surprisingly slow progression of color and light on the mountainside.

But that, Xantcha realized, was Equilor's mystery and revelation. Those who dwelt at the edge of time had gone past a need for the spectacular; they'd learned to appreciate the subtlest differences. They'd conquered boredom even more effectively than the perfect folk of Serra's realm. They could wait forever and a day, which Xantcha supposed was a considerable accomplishment, though nothing she wished to emulate.

Find what you're looking for! she urged the absent Urza, moments before the dawn revealed two white-clad figures moving among the mountain's many caves.

The ancient rapped Xantcha sharply on the back. "Pay attention! Watch close!"

Guessing that some rite of choosing or choice was about to take place, Xantcha did her best to follow the ancient's advice, but it proved impossible. Brilliant lights suddenly began to flash from the cave mouths, as if each contained a mirror. She blinked rapidly and to no useful effect. Each cave mouth had its own rhythm; no matter how Xantcha tried, her eyes were quickly, painfully blinded by reflected sunlight.

"You'll learn," the ancient chortled, while tears ran down Xantcha's cheeks.

The dazzle ended.

Tessu embraced Xantcha with a hearty "Good morning" and pulled her to her feet before releasing her. Xantcha had scarcely dried her face on her sleeve before the rest of the household followed Tessu's example and greeted her with the same embrace they used with one another. She had never been so carefully included in a family gathering, and seldom felt so out of place. Her vision was still awash in purple and green blobs when she and Tessu were alone in the atrium.

"You aren't used to it yet," Tessu said gently. "You'll learn."

"That's what the ancient said."

"Ancient? Oh, Pakuya. She'll go up the mountain herself, I think, after you and Urza leave. We've been waiting quite a long time, even for us, for you to arrive."

The certainty in Tessu's voice was an unexpected relief. "Urza's in one of the caves, right?"

"Keodoz, I think. Romom will say for certain when he returns this afternoon."

Keodoz, the name of the cave or the elder who occupied it? Xantcha stifled idle curiosity in favor of a more important question: "Do you know when Urza will return?"

"Tomorrow or the next day. Whenever he and Keodoz have finished."

It was nearly twenty days before neighbors spotted a white-robed man coming down the mountain. By then Xantcha knew that there was no difference between the cave and the elder—or more accurately, elders—who dwelt within it. Romom, Tessu, and the rest of the Equilor community—and there was only the one community at the edge of time—lived their mortal lives in expectation of the day when they'd climb the mountain one last time to merge with their ancestors.

Despite their focus on their cave-dwelling ancestors, the folk of Equilor weren't a morbid people. They laughed with one another, loved their children, and took genuine delight in the small events of daily life. They argued, held grudges, and gossiped among themselves and about the elders, who, despite their collective spirits, were not without individual foibles. Keodoz, Xantcha learned, was known to be long-winded and supremely self-confident. As Urza's time in the caves had lengthened, the household began to joke that Keodoz had found a soulmate—a notion that distressed Xantcha. Idyllic ways notwithstanding, Equilor was not a place where she wanted to spend eternity.

When she heard that Urza had been spotted, she left the house at once and jogged along the stone road until she met up with him.

"Did you get your answers?" she asked, adding, "I can be ready to leave before sundown."

"I have only scratched the surface, Xantcha. We are young compared to them. We know so little, and they have been collecting knowledge for so long. A thousand years wouldn't be enough time. Ten thousand, even a hundred thousand wouldn't be too much. You cannot imagine what the elders know."

Of course she couldn't imagine. She was Phyrexian. "Remember why we came here. What about vengeance? Your brother? Dominaria? Phyrexia!"

He grabbed her and lifted her into the air. "Keodoz knows so much, Xantcha! Do you remember, after we left Phyrexia, how I was unable to return to Dominaria? I said it was as if the portion of the Multiverse that held Dominaria had been squeezed and sealed away from the rest. I was right, Xantcha. Not only was I right. but I was the one who had squeezed and twisted it when I emptied the sylex bowl! It wasn't evident at first—well, it was. Dominaria was cooler when I left, but I didn't understand how the two were related. But it was in my mind, when I used the sylex, to protect my home for all time, and the bowl's power was so great that my wish was granted. No artifact device, nor planeswalker's will, can breach the Shard that the sylex created. The elders here at Equilor could not breach it."

"You turned your home into Phy—" Xantcha caught herself before she finished the fatal word and substituted, "Serra's realm?" instead.

"Better, Xantcha. Much better! The Shard is more than a chasm, and Dominaria is an entire nexus of planes, all natural and balanced. Dominaria is safe, and I saved it with the sylex."

"But the Phyrexians? Phyrexia? The Ineffable?"

"They are doomed, Xantcha. Accidents and anomalies, not worth the effort of destroying them, now that I am sure Dominaria is safe. There are more important questions, Xantcha. I see that now. I've found my place. Equilor is where I belong. Keodoz and the others have so much knowledge, but they've done nothing with it. Look around us, Xantcha. These folk need leadership—vision!—and I will give it to them. When I am finished, Equilor will be the jewel of the Multiverse,"

Xantcha thought of Tessu and Romom waiting to merge with all their ancestors. She wriggled free and said, cautiously, "I don't think that's what anyone here wants."

"They have not dreamed with me, Xantcha. Keodoz has only begun to dream with me. It will take time, but we have time. Equilor has time. They are not immortal, but they might as well be. Did you know that if Brya, Romom's youngest, had been born where I was born, she would be an old woman in her eighties?"

Xantcha hadn't known and wasn't comfortable with the knowledge. Urza, however, was radiant, as intoxicated by his ambitions as she would have been by a jug of wine. "Urza, you haven't found your place," she said, retreating into the grass. "You've lost it. We came here to find the first home for the Phyrexians. They've never been here, and if the elders don't know where they're from, then we should leave . . . soon."

"Nonsense!" Urza retorted and started walking toward the white houses.

Nonsense was also the first word out of Pakuya's toothless mouth when Urza regaled the household with his notions over supper. Tessu, Romom, and the others were too polite—or perhaps too astonished—to say anything until Urza had 'walked back to

Keodoz's cave, and then they spoke in their own language. Xantcha had learned only a few words of Equiloran—she suspected they spoke her Argivian dialect precisely to keep their own language a mystery—but she didn't need a translator to catch that they were unhappy with Urza's plans or to decide that their politeness masked a strong, even rigid, culture.

Tessu confirmed Xantcha's suspicions. "It might be best," she said in a supremely mild tone, "if you spoke with Urza."

"I've already told him but Urza doesn't listen to me unless I'm telling him what he wants to hear. If I were you, I'd send someone up the mountain to talk with Keodoz."

"Keodoz is not much for listening."

"Then we've got a problem."

"No, Xantcha, Urza's got a problem, because the other elders will get Keodoz's attention, sooner or later."

"Is Urza in danger? I mean . . . would you . . . would they?" Tessu was such a calm, rational woman that Xantcha had difficulty getting her question out, though she knew from other worlds that the most ruthless folk she'd ever met were invariably calm and rational.

"Those who go up the mountain, do not always come down," Tessu said simply.

"Urza's a 'walker, I've seen him melt mountains with his eyes."

"Not here."

Xantcha absorbed that in silence. "I'll talk to Urza, the next time he comes down . . . assuming he comes back down."

"Assuming," Tessu agreed.

Urza did return to the white houses after forty days in Keodoz's cave. He summoned the entire community and made the air shimmer with visions of artifacts and cities. Xantcha had learned a bit more Equiloran by then. When she spoke to Urza afterward, her concerns were real.

"They're not interested. They say they've put greatness behind them and they're angry with Romom and Tessu for letting you stay with them so long. They say something's got to he done."

"Of course something's got to be done! And I'll get Keodoz to do it. He's on the brink. He's been on the brink for days now. I left him alone to get his thoughts in order. They're a collective mind, you know, each elder separately and all the elders together. They've become stagnant, but I'm getting them moving again. Once I get Keodoz persuaded, he'll give the sign to the others, and the dam will burst. You'll see."

"Tessu said, those who go up the mountain don't always return. Be careful, Urza. These people have power."

"Tessu and Romom! Forget Tessu and Romom, they might as well be blind. Yes, they've got power. All Equilor had undreamed power, but they turned their back on power and they've forgotten how to use it. Even Keodoz. I'm going to show them what greatness truly is!"

Xantcha walked away wondering if Tessu had enough power to take her between-worlds once Urza stayed in the mountains with Keodoz. The adults were missing, though, and the children wouldn't meet Xantcha's eyes when she asked where they'd gone, not even eighty-year-old Brya. Xantcha went outside, to the place where they gathered to watch sunrise light the mountain each morning. The skies were clear. It had rained just four times since she'd arrived—torrential downpours that soaked everything and recharged the cisterns. During the storms they'd taken shelter in the underground larders. She'd thought the adult community might be meeting there, or outside one of the other houses. Xantcha listened closely for conversation but heard nothing, and though she'd never heard or seen anything to suggest that the gardens and fields beyond the white houses were dangerous at night, she decided she was safest near the children.

Tessu's children took harmless advantage of her absence. They raided the larder, lured the kittens onto the forbidden cushions and, one by one, fell asleep away from their beds. Xantcha guessed they'd slipped into the long hours between midnight and dawn.

She decided to try another conversation with Urza, but he was gone, 'walked back to Keodoz, most likely. She sensed that the Equilorans didn't approve of skipping between-worlds to get from the house to the cave. They didn't say anything, though; they weren't inclined toward warnings or ultimatums. Not that either would have mattered with Urza.

Xantcha went outside again. She paced and stared at the mountain, then paced some more, stared some more. The sky brightened: dawn, at last.

The adults would come back for the sunrise. She'd talk to Tessu. They'd work something out.

But the brightening wasn't dawn. The new light came from a single point overhead, a star, Xantcha thought—there weren't so many of them in the Equilor sky that she hadn't already memorized the brightest patterns. She'd never seen a star grow brighter before, except on Gastal when the star had been a predatory planeswalker.

Xantcha ran inside, awakened the children, and was herding them to the larders when Tessu raced through the always-open door.

"I was sending them to shelter, before that thing—" Xantcha pointed at the brightness overhead—"crashes on top of us."

The children had rushed to their mother, babbling in their own language—offering apologies and excuses for why they weren't in bed, Xantcha guessed, and maybe blaming her, though there were no pointed fingers or condemning glances. Tessu calmed them quickly. If the youngest was indeed eighty, Tessu had had several lifetimes in which to learn the tricks of motherhood. She didn't urge them into the larder, however, but outside to the sunrise gathering place.

"Thank you for thinking first of the children," Tessu said. It wasn't what she'd come running home to say, but the words seemed sincere. "Nothing will crash down on Equilor. A star is dying."

Xantcha shook her head, unable to comprehend the notion.

"It happens frequently, or so the elders say, but only twice when we on the ground could see it, and never as bright as this." Tessu took Xantcha's hands gently between hers. "It is an omen."

"Urza? Is Urza—?"

"There will be a change. I can't say more than that. Change doesn't come easily to Equilor. We will go outside and see what the sunrise brings."

Xantcha freed herself. "You know more. Tell me . . . please?"

"I know no more, Xantcha. I suspect—yes, I suspect the elders have gotten Keodoz's attention. The problem with Urza will be resolved, quickly."

Xantcha stared at her hands. She didn't grieve or wail. Urza had brought this on himself, but when she tried to imagine her life without him she began to shiver.

"Don't borrow trouble," Tessu advised, draping a length of cloth over Xantcha's shoulders. "The sun hasn't risen yet. Come outside and wait with us."

No night had ever been longer. The dying star continued to brighten until it cast shadows all around. It remained visible after the other stars had dimmed and when the dawn began. Xantcha worried the hem loose from her borrowed shawl and began to mindlessly unravel it.

There was change, more noticeable than anyone had imagined. As dawn's perimeter moved down the mountain, the caves flashed in unison and in complex rhythm that could only be a code. Xantcha tugged on Tessu's sleeve.

"What does it mean?" she whispered.

"It means they've come to their senses," Pakuya snapped. "If that fool wants to change a world, let him change his own!"

To which Tessu added, "You'll be leaving soon."

"Urza's alive?"

"No more than he was yesterday, and I'd be surprised if he's learned anything. Keodoz certainly hasn't. But that's for the best, isn't it, if they both think they've made the changes for themselves?"

Xantcha thought a moment, then nodded. Urza 'walked up a few moments later.

"The future's ended before it began," he began, talking to her, talking to the household and talking to himself equally. "I cannot stay to lead you, and Keodoz has already begun to waver in the face of stagnant opposition. But they have lifted me into the night and shown me a frightening sight. The fortress I made around the planes where I was born has been brought down by a misguided fool! As my brother and I undid the Thran, so I have been undone by ignorance. But I can go back, and I will go back.

"Equilor, however, is on its own. You will have to complete my visions without my guidance."

The household made a fair show of grief. From Pakuya to Brya, they said how sorry they were that they wouldn't get to live the future Urza and Keodoz had promised them. The entire community flattered Urza's righteousness and strength of character. They wished him well and offered to make him a feast in honor of his departure for Dominaria. Xantcha was relieved when Urza declined. She didn't think she'd have the stomach for an extended display of insincerity.

Tessu had been right. It was for the best that Urza left Equilor thinking the decision had been his own.

It took them a hundred Dominarian years to 'walk the between-worlds from Equilor to Dominaria, but in the spring of the 3,210th year after Urza's birth, Xantcha finally stood on the world where she'd been destined to sleep.

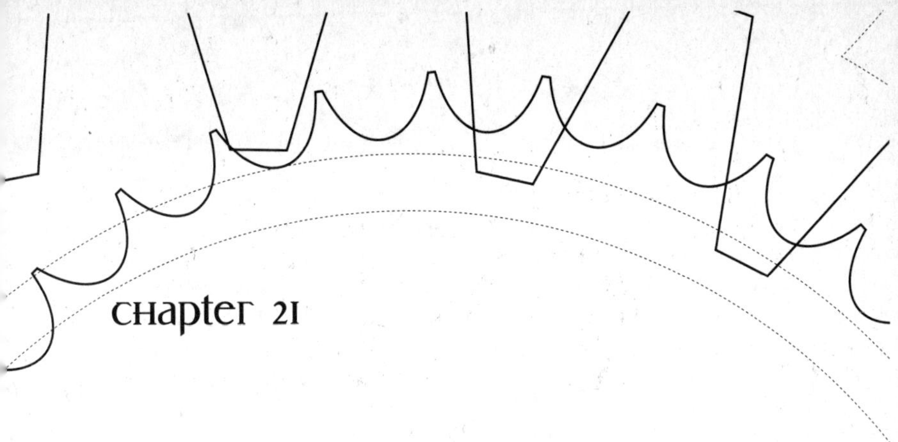

Chapter 21

"If Gix could find me, he would find me. He would have found me before I left Pincar City. He would have come for me while I slept. If he didn't want to be seen, he would have sent *sleepers* after me."

Eight days after her narrow escape, Xantcha sat in the branches of an oak tree. The sun would set sometime during the thunderstorm that was bearing in from the ocean. She'd been watching the clouds pile up all afternoon, watching the lightning since she left Russiore with the day-traders. Her armor tended to attract lightning even as it protected her from the bolts, and a big, old tree, standing by itself on a hillside, wouldn't be a good hiding place much longer.

Once the storm struck, Xantcha figured she'd find a saner place to wait for Urza. With all that metal and exposed sinew, Gix wasn't apt to come looking for her in the rain.

"He didn't know we were here. He didn't recognize me until he found the spark in my mind."

The spark. She'd had a headache the first day away from Pincar City, but her back had ached, too, along with her neck and jaw and every other part of her body: the aftermath of total terror.

There were uglier beasts in the Multiverse, meaner ones, and possibly more dangerous ones. None of them had a demon's malignant aura. Bornfolk had a word, rape. It occurred on every world, in every language. In Phyrexian, as Xantcha understood it, the word for rape was Gix.

Xantcha had scrubbed her skin raw even though Gix hadn't touched her because she couldn't scour her mind. She'd rehearsed a score of confessions, too, and her greatest fear as the wind whipped the branches around her wasn't that Gix would find her but that he'd already found Urza . . . or Ratepe.

Urza could take care of himself. Xantcha had to believe that; she couldn't let herself believe, even for a heartbeat, that Gix had told the truth when he'd said "I made the brothers, too, and then I made you." And if she believed that Urza's mind was his own, then she could be confident it would take the Ineffable to challenge him in single combat. But whatever she managed to believe about herself and Urza, it didn't help when she thought of Ratepe, alone and unsuspecting on the Ohran ridge. Rat wouldn't have a chance, whether Gix came to kill or corrupt.

And when all those memories of Ratepe's face had freed her from Gix's thrall, surely some of them had given away the cottage's location, if Gix were inclined to find the man who went with that face.

"Gix doesn't care," she told the oak tree. "Phyrexians have no imagination."

Rain pelted, driven by the wind, and Xantcha was drenched in an instant. Urza's armor was strange that way. It would protect her from fire or the complete absence of breathable air, but it was entirely vulnerable to plain water. Xantcha clambered down a branch or two, then dropped straight to the ground. She found an illusion of shelter among the briar bushes tangled at the bottom of the hill.

Urza would find her no matter where she hid. Her heart, he said, pulled him between-worlds. He'd grumble about the rain, if he arrived before the storm died out. Not that any weather affected him; Urza simply didn't like surprises. He wouldn't like her confession.

The storm moved south without clearing the air. A steady rain continued to fall, as a starless night closed in around the briars. Xantcha tried to stay awake, but it was a losing struggle. She hadn't slept much in Russiore. She'd been busy, for one thing, distributing nine days' worth of screaming spiders in less than eight and afraid to close her eyes for the other. The briars were secure and friendly by comparison and the rain's patter, a lullaby.

Xantcha had no idea how long she'd been asleep when Urza awoke her with her name.

"Over here!" she called back.

The rain had stopped, save for drips from the leaves around her. A few stars shone through the thinning clouds, silhouetting Urza as he strode down the hill.

"Ready to go home?" He sounded cheerful. Xantcha told herself that confession would be easier with Urza in a good mood. "No sacks?" He cocked his head at her empty hands and shoulders. "You couldn't get his food and such?" Urza generally avoided choosing a name for Ratepe.

"Urza, I have to talk to you—"

"Problems in Russiore? Are they in the midst of a famine?"

"Not exactly. I didn't have time to scrounge supplies. Something came up—"

"Not to worry. I have other plans, anyway. We'll talk at the cottage."

He seized Xantcha's wrist, and before she could protest they were between-worlds. The journey was swift, as always. Two strides through nothing, and they were on the Ohran ridge. It was also, as always, disorienting. Urza stepped out several hundred paces from the cottage to give Xantcha a chance to gather her wits before they greeted Ratepe.

Xantcha's nerves reassembled themselves slowly, in part because she had to assure herself that the cottage was unharmed. Urza had gotten ahead of her. She ran to catch up.

"Urza, I said we have to talk. There's a problem. You. Ratepe. Your brother. The spiders—" All her carefully rehearsed statements had vanished in the between-worlds.

"I've thought it through. I can do the work of all three of us for the next nine days. I'll distribute the artifacts that he's made for us, yours and mine together, and get the next batch assembled. It's another aspect of time: I'll live a little faster. It's good practice, crawling before walking. The spiders won't end this war, Xantcha. They'll only buy time until I solve the Phyrexian problem at its source."

Urza had gotten over his obsession with righting his brother's fate, but he still talked of traveling back in time, much further back in time. Urza wanted to meet the Thran and fight beside them in their final battle against the Phyrexians. He thought they might know his enemy's true home and, although he didn't say it, Xantcha believed Urza hoped go behind the Thran, all the way to the Phyrexians' first world to annihilate rather than exile them.

Gix had said the Thran were waiting. The demon could have rummaged the name out of her memories or out of Mishra during the war. Almost certainly Gix wasn't telling the truth; at least not the important parts of it, but Urza needed to know what had happened in the catacomb beneath Avohir's temple in Pincar City.

"I met . . . I found . . ." She was still tongue-tied. Had the demon left something in her that left her able to think but not to speak? It wasn't impossible. Gix savored fear spiced with helplessness and frustration. She didn't know the measure of the red light's power, but she'd lost an entire afternoon in the catacomb, and when Ratepe burst out of memory to save her, she'd been doing the unthinkable: walking toward Phyrexia.

"Xantcha?" Urza stopped. He faced her and gave her his full attention.

"We have to go back to Pincar City."

"No, Efuan Pincar is out of the question. Anywhere we've found *sleepers* is out of the question. You and he have to go someplace, of course. I don't want anyone around while I'm working this time. I could wait. I should wait until after the Glimmer Moon rises. We can never know the future, Xantcha. I'm sure of that. Only the past is forever, and only now gives us choices. I choose to give the next nine days to you and him so you will always have them. Tell me where you want to be, and I'll 'walk you both there in the morning."

Nine days. Nine days in hiding while she sorted out her tangled thoughts? It was the coward's way, but Xantcha seized it. "I'll talk to him." A lie. Xantcha could feel that confessing to Ratepe would be no easier than confessing to Urza. "We'll decide where we want to go."

Ratepe welcomed them with the enthusiasm and relief of any talkative youth who'd kept company with himself for entirely too long. He cast several inquiring glances Xantcha's way. She pretended not to notice them while Urza announced his intention to reclaim his workroom for the next nine days.

"You told Urza," Ratepe snapped to Xantcha the moment they were alone together. "Now he's taking over everything! Just tell me, did you get my artifacts attached to Avohir's altar?"

"One," Xantcha answered truthfully. "There were *sleepers* in the temple, made up as Shratta. And Shratta dead in the catacombs. They were finished years ago, Ratepe. If there are Shratta left, they're like the Efuands in the Red-Stripes. They're in league, consciously or not, with Phyrexia." She thought of Gix; this wasn't the time to tell him, not when they were both angry. "I put your shatter-spiders, and screamers, too, in places where the glistening scent was strong. I didn't get to the barracks."

Ratepe threw his head back and swore at the ceiling. "What were you thinking! I don't want to bring Avohir's sanctuary down—not while the Red-Stripe barracks is still standing!" He shook his head and stood with his back to her. "When it wasn't what I expected, you should've waited. Sweet Avohir, what did you tell Urza!"

Xantcha's guilt and anxiety evaporated. "I didn't tell him anything!" she shouted.

"Then keep your voice down!"

"Stop telling me what to do!"

They were on opposite sides of the table, ready to lunge at each other, and not with the passion that normally accompanied their reunions. Ratepe seemed to have outrun himself. Jaw clenched, eyes pleading, he looked across the table, but Xantcha was similarly paralyzed. It was her nature, created in Phyrexia and shaped over time in Urza's company, to back down or explode when cornered. This was a moment when she couldn't see a clear path in either direction.

The door was at her back. Xantcha ducked and ran out, leaving it open behind her, listening for the sounds that never came. She settled in the darkness, wrestling with her conscience, until the lamps in her shared room had flickered and died. Approaching the door through starlight, she saw a dark silhouette at the table, where Ratepe had fallen asleep with his head on his arms. She crept past him, as silently as she'd crept toward the Pincar catacomb. Her bed was strung with a creaking rope mattress. Xantcha quietly tucked herself in a comer by her treasure chest.

Ratepe was sprawled on the bed when she awoke. Urza was in the doorway, the golden light of dawn behind him.

"Are you ready to 'walk?" he asked.

Urza never came into her side of the cottage. Perhaps he thought she'd been sleeping in the comer since Ratepe arrived. They weren't ready to 'walk anyway; Ratepe wasn't ready to wake up. He was cross-grained from the moment his eyes opened. Xantcha expected him to start something they'd all regret, but instead he just said, "You decide," as he slipped past Urza on his way to the well.

"We don't need you to 'walk us anywhere," Xantcha said to Urza as she stretched the kinks out of her legs. Her foot felt as if her boot was lined with hot, sharp needles.

"I don't want you near here while I work."

"We won't be."

"Don't dawdle, then. I want to get started!"

Ratepe stayed away while Xantcha rearranged her traveling gear. She packed a good deal of gold and silver, which could be traded wherever they went, but included copper, too, in case they got no farther than their closest neighbors along the frontier between the ridge and the coast. She threw in flour for journey bread, as well, and thought about the hunter's bow suspended from the rafters. Nine days could be an uncomfortably long time to live off journey bread, but a bow could be troublesome in a city. In the end Xantcha put a few more coins in her belt purse, left the bow on its hook, and met a sulking Ratepe beside the well.

Urza either didn't notice or didn't care that Xantcha and Ratepe were scarcely speaking to each other. He'd been away from his workroom for nearly a half-year and didn't wait to see the sphere rise before sealing himself in with his ideas.

The morning sun was framed with fair weather clouds against a rich blue sky. Prairie wildflowers blanketed the land above which the sphere soared. It was difficult, in the face of such natural beauty, to remain sullen and sour, but Xantcha and Ratepe both rose to the challenge. A northwest wind stream caught the sphere and carried it toward Kovria, southeast of the ridge. There was nothing in the Kovrian barrens to hold Xantcha's attention, no destinations worth mentioning, but changing their course meant choosing their course, so they drifted into Kovria.

By mid-afternoon, the tall-grass prairies of the ridge had given way to badlands.

"Where are we going?" Ratepe asked, virtually the first full sentence he'd uttered since the sphere rose.

"Where does it look like we're going?"

"Nowhere."

"Then nowhere, it is. Nowhere's good enough for me."

"Put us down. You're crazed, Xantcha. Something happened in Efuan Pincar, and it's left you crazed. I don't want to be up here with you."

Xantcha brought them down on a plain of baked dirt and weedy scrub. They were both silent while the sphere collapsed and powdered.

"What went wrong?" Ratepe asked as he brushed the last of the white stuff from his face. "It's not just *sleepers*. *Sleepers* wouldn't frighten you, and you're afraid. I didn't think there was anything that could do that."

"Lots of things frighten me. Urza frightens me, sometimes. You frighten me. The between-worlds frightens me. Demons frighten me." Xantcha tore a handful of leaves off the nearest bush and began shredding them. Let Ratepe guess; let him choose, if he could.

"There was a demon in Avohir's temple? In the catacombs with the dead Shratta? A Phyrexian demon?"

Ratepe was uncommonly good at guessing and choosing.

"I don't know any other kind."

"Avohir's mercy! You and Urza didn't find demons anywhere else, did you?"

"I didn't."

"Why Efuan Pincar? If a Phyrexian demon was going to come to Dominaria, why come to Efuan Pincar. We keep to ourselves. When our ancestors left Argive, they never looked back. They settled on the north shore of Gulmany because it's so far away from everywhere else. We're not rich. We don't bother our neighbors, and they've never bothered us. We don't even have an army—which is probably why we had trouble with the Shratta and the Red-Stripes, but why would that interest Phyrexia? I don't understand. Do you?"

"I told you, demons frighten me. I didn't ask questions, just . . . just got away." She stripped another handful of leaves. Xantcha wanted to tell Ratepe everything, but the words to get her started weren't in her mind.

"The day you bought me, I told you that you were a lousy liar. You may be three thousand years old, Xantcha, but my eight-year-old brother could fib better than you. When he got into trouble, though, I could guess what he was hiding, 'cause I'd hidden it myself. I can't guess about demons."

Xantcha scattered the leafy bits and faced Ratepe. "It was Gix. I smelled *sleepers* in the sanctuary, I followed the smell, planting spiders as I went, yours and Urza's both. I wound up way underground, in the dark. There was a passageway, one of the big, old, upright ones, and there was Gix."

"You said Gix had been killed in the Sixth Sphere."

"The Seventh. He was excoriated, consigned to endless torment. We were taught that nothing escapes the Seventh Sphere."

"Another Phyrexian lie? You're sure it was Gix, not some other demon?"

"Yes." One answer for both questions.

"Did he hurt you?"

Ratepe never failed to ask the question Xantcha wasn't expecting. "I'm here, aren't I?"

"Then, what's got you so riled? Why were we headed 'nowhere'? Unless . . . wait, I get it now. Urza's sent you off with the mere mortal. He's not that crazed. He knows what I am, who I'm not. He's going back after Gix, and you're here with me instead of—"

"I didn't tell Urza." The words belched out of her.

"You found a Phyrexian demon under Avohir's temple and you didn't tell Urza?"

She turned away in shame.

"Of course," Ratepe sighed. "He'd yell at you and blame you, just as I've yelled at you and blamed you. And you are a lot like my little brother when you get accused of something that's not your fault. And Gix. Gix was the one who got Mishra. Mishra didn't know—not until it was too late. Strange thing. They fought over those two stones that are Urza's eyes now, but I don't think either brother could hear the stones sing."

Xantcha took a deep breath. "Do you wonder why you can hear them?"

"I can't hear them. I only hear Mishra's stone. I don't know for sure that the Mightstone sings, but—yes, I do wonder. I think about it a lot, more than I want to. Why? Did Gix say something about the stones?"

"Yes. He said he made them, and then he said something about you." And Urza. Xantcha's mind added, but not her tongue.

Ratepe was pale and speechless.

"He could have gotten your name out of my mind. I was careful what I gave him, enough to keep him from digging too deep. But I got in trouble. Serious trouble." Xantcha's hands were shaking. She clasped them together behind her back. "He had me, Rat. I was walking toward the passageway. I would've gone into Phyrexia, and that would've been the end of me, I'm sure. Then, suddenly, all I could think of was you."

"Me?"

"You're the first 'mere mortal' I've gotten to know. You've . . ." Blood rushed to Xantcha's face. She was hot, embarrassed, but she stumbled on. "Thinking about you pulled me back. But Gix was in my mind when I did, so he could have taken your name and made a lie around it. Everything he said could've been lies . . . probably was lies." And why share Gix's lies with anyone? "He didn't tell me anything I didn't know, except, maybe, about the Thran. And, well, Mishra knew some things about the Thran."

Though Xantcha could feel the blood draining from her own face, Ratepe's was still dangerously pale.

"Tell me what Gix said about me, then what he said about Mishra and the Thran. Maybe I can tell you if it's lies or not."

"Gix said he wondered if I'd found you, as if he'd planned that we were supposed to meet."

"And about the Thran?"

"When I said that Urza would finish what the Thran had started against the Phyrexians, he laughed and said the Thran were waiting for Urza and that they'd take back what was theirs. Gix was thinking about Urza's eyes—at least, I started thinking about Urza's eyes and how they were the last of the Thran powerstones. Gix laughed louder, and the next thing I knew, I was thinking about you and not walking toward the portal. What he said about you and what he said about me, they're lies. Even if Mishra was compleated in Phyrexia . . . even if his flesh and blood were rendered for the vats . . . I was one of thousands. We were exactly alike. We don't even scar, Ratepe. We couldn't tell ourselves apart!"

"Lies," Ratepe said so softly that Xantcha wasn't sure she'd heard him correctly and asked him to repeat himself. "Lies. The Weakstone's a sort of memory. Mostly it's Mishra's memory, but I've been hit with some Thran memories and some of Urza's, too, though not as strong. With Mishra, there's personality. I'm thankful I never met him while he was alive. He'd've killed me for sure. With the Thran and Urza, it's like faded paintings. But if you were Mishra—if any part of you was Mishra—the Weakstone would have recognized him in you, even though you're Phyrexian. And if I'd been touched by Gix, I'd be dead. The Weakstone doesn't like Phyrexians, Xantcha, and it especially doesn't like Gix."

"Urza's eye doesn't like me?"

Ratepe shook his head, "Sorry, no. It sees you, sometimes, but if Urza doesn't trust you, the Weakstone could be responsible because it doesn't trust you."

"The Weakstone has opinions?"

"Influence. It tries to influence."

Xantcha considered Urza's eyes watching her and Ratepe each time they retreated to her side of the wall. "It must be overjoyed when we're together."

Color returned to Ratepe's face in a single heartbeat. "I'm not Mishra. I make my own opinions."

"What do you know from Mishra and the Weakstone about the Thran and the Phyrexians?" Xantcha asked when Ratepe's blush had spread past his ears.

"They hate each other, with a deep, blinding hate that gives no quarter. But I'll tell you honestly, in the images I've gotten of their war, I can't tell one side from the other. The Thran weren't flesh and blood, no more than the Phyrexians. Even Mishra's just something the Weakstone uses. Urza's notion that the Thran sacrificed themselves to save Dominaria, maybe that's the Mightstone's influence, but it's not true. My world's better off without both of them, Thran and Phyrexians together."

They'd wandered away from their gear. Xantcha headed back. "Maybe Urza will succeed someday in 'walking between times as easily as he 'walks between worlds. I'd like to know what really happened back there at Koilos. I'd like to see it for myself. It's a shadow over everything I've ever known, all the way back to the vats."

Ratepe corrected her pronunciation of Koilos, reducing the three syllables to two and moving the accent to the first.

"I heard it from Urza and he's the one who named it," she retorted.

"I guess language drifts in three thousand years. It's still there, you know—well, it was three hundred years ago when the ancestors left Argive."

Xantcha stopped short. "I thought it wasn't recorded where the first Efuands came from. That's part of your myth."

"It is . . . part of the myth, that is. But Father said our language is mostly Argivian and the oldest books, before the Shratta burnt them, had been written in Argivian. And, if you look at a map, Efuan Pincar is about as far away from Argive as you can get without sailing right off the edge."

"And Koilos?" Xantcha stuck with Urza's pronunciation. "It's still there in Argive?"

"It's not in Argivia. It never was, but folk knew where it was three hundred years ago. It's like *The Antiquity Wars*, something that's not supposed to be forgotten. I guess it was inaccessible for most of the Ice Age, but when the world got warmer again, the kings of Argivia and their neighbors sent folk up on the Kher to make sure the ruins were still ruins."

"Urza's never mentioned them. I just assumed Koilos vanished with Argoth."

"You've seen a map of what's left of Terisiare?"

Xantcha shrugged. There were maps in her copies of The *Antiquity Wars*. She'd assumed they were wrong and paid no attention to them.

"We'd have to go over the Sea of Laments. We'd never make it there and back in nine days," Ratepe said with a smile that invited conspiracy. Waste not, want not. If Gix hadn't lied about the young Efuand, they were all doomed.

"We'd make landfall on Argivia in two very cold days and colder nights. Getting back would be more difficult, but it's that or go back to the cottage and tell Urza that I saw Gix in Pincar City."

"He wouldn't be pleased to see us."

The journey over the Sea of Laments was as uneventful as it was unpleasant. They'd traded for blankets and an oil-cloth sail in a village on

Gulmany's south coast. The fisherman who took Xantcha's silver thought she was insane; a little while later, both Ratepe and Xantcha agreed with him, but by then it was too late. They were in the wash of a roaring wind river and remained there until they saw land again. For two days and nights there was nothing to do but huddle beneath blankets and the sail.

"Don't you have to keep one hand free?" Ratepe had shouted early on, as they struggled to wrap the blankets evenly around their feet.

"Tack across this?" she shouted back. "We're here for the ride."

"How many times have you crossed the sea?"

"Once, by mistake."

"Sorry I asked."

Misery ended after sunrise on the third day. There was land below, land as far as the eye could see. Xantcha thought down and thrust her hand through the sphere for good measure. Her hand turned white as they plummeted down to familiar altitudes.

As her hand began to thaw, Xantcha asked, "Now, which way to Koilos?"

"Where are we?"

"Don't you recognize anything from your maps?"

"Avohir's sweet mercy, Xantcha, maps don't look like the ground!"

They found an oasis and a goatherd who seemed unfazed by the sight of two strangers in a place where strangers couldn't be common. He spoke a language neither of them had heard before but recognized the word Koilos in its older, three-syllable form. He rattled off a long speech before pointing to the southeast. The only words they recognized, beside Koilos, were Urza and Mishra. Xantcha traded a silver-set agate for all the food the youth was carrying. He strode away, whistling and laughing.

"What do you think he said?" Xantcha asked when they'd returned to the gulch where their gear was hidden. "Other than that we're fools and idiots."

"The usual curses against Urza and Mishra."

The sphere flowed over them and they were rising before Ratepe continued.

"Haven't you ever noticed how empty everything is? Even in Efuan Pincar, which was as far from Argoth as it could be, it's nothing to ride through wilderness and find yourself in the middle of ruins from the time before the ice and the war. Here in Argivia, according to the books the Ancestors brought to Pincar, they were still living in the shadows of the past—literally. They didn't have the wherewithal to build the buildings like the old ruins. Not enough people, not enough stone, not enough metal, not enough knowledge of how it was done. Urza talks about the mysteries of the Thran. The books my father studied talked about the mysteries of Urza and Mishra. They all talk about Koilos. It's the place in Terisiare, new or old, where everything comes to an end. It's a name to conjure darkness."

Xantcha caught a tamer wind stream and adjusted their drift. "Does everyone in Efuan Pincar talk about such things? Are you a nation of storytellers?"

Ratepe laughed bitterly. "No, just my father, and he taught me. My father was a scholar, and both my grandfathers, too. The first things I remember are the three of them arguing about men and women who'd died a thousand years ago. I was ashamed of them. I hated lessons; I wanted to be anything but a scholar. Then the Shratta came. My grandfathers were dead by then, Avohir's mercy. My father did whatever he had to do to take care of us. When we got to the country, he learned farming as if it were a Sumifan chronicle, but he missed Pincar. He missed not having students to teach or someone to argue with. My mother told me to sit at his feet and learn or she'd take her belt to me. I never argued with my mother."

Xantcha stared at Ratepe who was staring at the horizon, eyes glazed and fists clenched, the way he looked whenever he remembered what he'd lost. Urza had buried Mishra beneath layers of obsession, and there was little enough in Xantcha's own life worth cherishing. Looking at Ratepe, trying to imagine his grief, all she felt was envy.

The winds were steady, the sky was clear, and the moon was bright. They soared until midnight and were in the air again after a sunrise breakfast. By midday they saw the reflection of a giant lake to their south, and by the end of a long afternoon they were over the foothills of the Kher Ridge. There were no villages, no roads, not even the bright green dot of an oasis.

Ratepe closed his eyes and folded his hands.

"Now what?" Xantcha asked.

"I'm praying for a sign."

"I thought you knew!"

"I do, somewhat. The landscape's changed a bit since Mishra was here last. But I think I'll recognize the mountains when I see them."

"We're fools, you know. At most we'll have a day at Koilos—if we find it."

"Look for a saddle-back mountain with three smaller peaks in front of it,"

"A saddle-back." Xantcha muttered, and lowered her hand to get a better look.

The setting sun threw mountain-sized shadows that obscured as much as they revealed, but there was nothing that looked like a double-peaked mountain, and the wind streams were starting to get treacherous as the air cooled. Xantcha looked for a place to set up their night camp. A patch of flat ground, a bit lighter than its surroundings and shaped like an arrowhead, beckoned.

"I'm taking us down there for the night," she told Ratepe, dropping the sphere out of the wind stream.

He said something in reply. Xantcha didn't catch the words. They'd caught a crosswind that was determined to keep her off the arrowhead. She felt like she'd been the victor in a bare-knuckle brawl by the time the sphere collapsed.

Ratepe sprang immediately to his feet. "Avohir answers prayers!" he shouted, running toward a stone near the arrowhead's tip.

Time had taken a toll on the stone, which stood a bit taller than Ratepe himself. The spiraled carvings were weathered to illegibility, but to find such a stone in this place could only mean one thing.

Ratepe lifted Xantcha into the air. "We've found the path! Are you sure you don't want to keep going?"

She thought about it a moment. "I'm sure." Wriggling free, she explored the marks with her fingertips. Here and there, it was still possible to discern a curve or angle, places that might have been parallel grooves or raised dot patterns that struck deep in memory. "Koilos isn't a place I want to see first by moonlight."

"Good point. Too many ghosts," Ratepe agreed with a sigh. "But we will see it—Koilos, with my own eyes. Seven thousand years. My father . . ." He shook his head and walked away from the stone.

Xantcha didn't need to ask to know what he hadn't said.

The desert air didn't hold its heat. They were cold and hungry before the stars unveiled themselves. Xantcha doled out small portions of journey bread and green-glowing goat cheese, the last of the dubious edibles they'd traded from the goatherd. The cheese and its indescribable taste clung to the roof of Xantcha's mouth. Ratepe wisely stuck to the journey bread. He fell asleep while Xantcha sat listening to her stomach complain, as she watched the sky and the weathered stone and thought—a lot—of water.

The sphere reeked of cheese when she yawned it at dawn. Ratepe, displaying a healthy sense of self-preservation, said nothing about the smell.

It was all willpower that morning. The wind streams flowed out of the mountains, not into them. She'd been about to give up and let the sphere drift back to the desert when Ratepe spotted another stone, toppled by age. Xantcha banked the sphere into the valley it seemed to mark. They hadn't been in it long when it doglegged to the right and they saw, in the distance, a saddle-back mountain overshadowing three smaller peaks.

With Mishra's memories to guide them, they had no trouble weaving through the mountain spurs until they came to the cleft and hollowed plateau Urza had named Koilos, the Secret Heart. Xantcha could have sought the higher streams and brought them over the top. She chose to follow the cleft instead and couldn't have said why if Ratepe had asked. But he stayed silent.

Seven thousand years, and the battle scars remained: giant pockings in the cliffs on either side of them, cottage-sized chunks of rubble littering the valley floor. Here and there was a shadow left by fire, not sun. And finally there was the cavern fortress itself, built by the Thran, rediscovered by two brothers, then laid bare during the war: ruins within ruins.

"That's where they hid from the dragons," Ratepe said, pointing to a smaller cave nearly hidden behind a hill of rubble.

"I didn't expect it to be so big."

"Everything's smaller now. Smell anything?"

"Time," Xantcha replied, and not facetiously. The sense of age was everywhere, in the plateau, the cleft which had shattered it, the Thran, and the brothers. But nowhere did she sense Phyrexia.

"You're sure?"

"It will be enough if I know that Gix lied."

Xantcha started up the path to the cavern mouth. Ratepe fell behind as he paused to examine whatever caught his eye. He jogged up the path, catching her just before she entered the shadows. "There's nothing left. I thought for sure there'd be something."

"Urza and I, we're older than forever, Ratepe, and Koilos is older than us."

Her eyes needed a moment to adjust to the darkness. Ratepe found the past he was looking for strewn across the stone: hammers and chisels preserved by the cavern itself. He hefted a mallet, its wood dark with age but still sturdy.

"Mishra might have held this."

"In your dreams, Ratepe," Xantcha retorted, unable to conceal her disappointment.

Koilos was big and old but as dead as an airless world. It offered no insights to her about the Thran or the Phyrexians or even about the brothers, no matter how many discarded tools or pots Ratepe eagerly examined.

"We may as well leave," she said when the afternoon was still young and Ratepe had just found a scrap of cloth.

"Leave? We haven't seen everything yet."

"There's no water, and we don't have a lot of food with us, unless you want to try some of that cheese. What's here to see?"

"I don't know. That's why we have to stay. I'm only halfway around this room, and there's an open passage at the back! And I want to see Koilos by moonlight."

Urza's idea, in the beginning, had been to get her and Ratepe away from the cottage, to give them some time together. Koilos surely wasn't what Urza had in mind, but Ratepe was enjoying himself. Whether they left now or in the morning wasn't going to make much difference in the return trip to Gulmany, and considering what that journey home was going to take out of her, Xantcha decided she could use some rest.

"All right. Wake me at sunset, then."

Xantcha didn't think she'd fall asleep on the stone but she did until Ratepe shook her shoulder.

"Come see. It's really beautiful, in a stark way, like a giant's tomb."

Sunset light flooded through the cavern mouth. Ratepe had stirred enough dust to turn the air into ruddy curtains streaked with shadows. They walked hand in hand to the ledge where the path ended and the cavern began. The hollowed plateau appeared drenched in blood. Xantcha was transfixed by the sight, but Ratepe wanted her to turn around.

"There are carvings everywhere," he said. "They appeared like magic out of the shadows once the sunlight came in."

Xantcha turned and would have collapsed if Ratepe hadn't been holding her.

"What's wrong?"

"It's writing, Ratepe. It's writing, and I can read it, most of it. It's like the lessons carved into the walls of the Fane of Flesh."

"What does it say?"

"Names. Mostly names and numbers—places. Battles, who fought who. . . ." Her eyes followed the column carvings. She'd gone cold and scarcely had the strength to fill her lungs.

"What names? Any that I'd recognize?"

"Gix," she said, though there was another that she recognized: Yawgmoth, which she didn't—couldn't—say aloud. "And Xantcha, among the numbers."

"Phyrexian?"

"Thran."

"We know they fought." Ratepe freed his fingers from her death grip.

Xantcha grabbed them again. "No, they didn't fight. Not the Phyrexians against the Thran. The Thran fought themselves."

"You can't be reading it right."

"I'm reading it because it's the same writing that's carved in the walls of every Fane in Phyrexia! Some of the words are unfamiliar, but—Ratepe! My name is up there. My name is up there because Xantcha is a number carved in the floor of the Fane of Flesh to mark where I was supposed to stand!" She made the familiar marks in the dust then pointed to similar carvings on the cavern walls.

Ratepe resisted. "All right, maybe this was the Phyrexian stronghold and the Thran attacked it, instead of the other way around. I mean, nobody really knows."

"I know! It says Gix, the silver-something, strong-something of the Thran. Of the Thran, Ratepe. If Urza could go back in time, he'd find Gix here waiting for him. That's what Gix meant! Waste not, want not, Ratepe. Gix was here seven thousand years ago! He wasn't lying, not completely. Those are Thran powerstones that you and Urza call the Mightstone and the Weakstone. The stones made the brothers what they were, Ratepe, and Gix might well have made the stones!"

"The Phyrexians stole powerstones from the Thran?"

"You're not listening!" Xantcha waved her arms at a heavily carved wall. "It's all there. Two factions. Sheep and pigs, Red-Stripes and Shratta, Urza and Mishra, take your pick. 'The glory and destiny is compleation'—compleation, the word, Ratepe, the exact angle-for-angle word that's carved on the doors of the Fane of Flesh. And there." She pointed at another section. " 'Life served, never weakened' and the word Thran, Rat, is the first glyph of the word for life." She recited them in Phyrexian, so he could hear the similarities, as strong as the similarities between their pronunciations of Koilos. "If language drifts in three thousand years, imagine what it could do in seven, once everyone's compleat and only newts have flesh cords in their throats."

The sun had slipped below the mountain tops. The marks, the words, were fading. Xantcha turned in Ratepe's arms to face him.

"He's been wrong. All this time—almost all his life—Urza's been wrong. The Phyrexians never invaded Dominaria! There was no Phyrexia until Gix and the Ineffable left here. Winners, losers, I can't tell. We knew that. We spent over a thousand years looking for the world where the Phyrexians came from, so we could learn from those who defeated them . . . and all the time, it was Urza's own world."

Xantcha was shaking, sobbing. Ratepe tried to comfort her, but it was too soon.

"Urza would say to me, that's Phyrexian, that's abomination. Only the Thran way is the right way, the pure way. And I always thought to myself, the difference isn't that great. The Phyrexians aren't evil because they're compleat. They'd be evil no matter what they were, and those automata he was making, he was growing them in a jar. Is it right to grow gnats in a jar but not newts in a vat?"

Ratepe held her tight against his chest before she pulled away. "The Red-Stripes and the Shratta were both bad luck for everybody who crossed either one of them," he said gently. "And so were Urza and Mishra. Any time there's only one right way, ordinary people get crushed—maybe even the Morvernish and the Baszerati."

"But all our lives, Ratepe. All our lives, we've been chasing shadows! It's like someone reached inside and pulled everything out."

"You just said it: the Phyrexians are evil. Urza's crazed, but he's not evil, and he's the only one here who can beat the Phyrexians at their own game. We wanted to find the truth. Well, it wasn't what we expected, but we found a truth. And we've still got to go back to Urza. The truth here doesn't change that, does it?"

"We can't tell him. If he knew his Thran weren't the great and noble heroes of Dominaria . . . If he knew that the Thran destroyed Mishra . . ."

"You're right, but Mishra would laugh. I can hear him."

"I can't believe that."

"It's laugh or cry, Xantcha." Ratepe dried her tears. "If you've truly wasted three thousand years and you're stuck fighting a war that was stupid four thousand years before that, then either you laugh and keep going, or you cry and give it up."

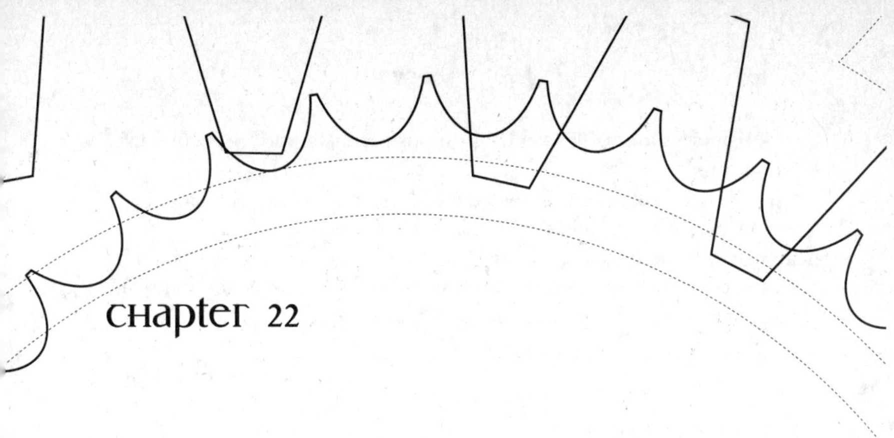

chapter 22

There was no laughter three days later over the Sea of Laments. The weather had been chancy since Xantcha had put the Argivian coast at her back. From the start, thick clouds had blocked her view of the sun and stars. She navigated against a wind she knew wasn't steady and with an innate sense of direction that grew less reliable as she tired. They hadn't seen land for two days, not even a boat.

Xantcha would have brought the sphere down on a raft just then and taken her chances with strangers. A black wall-cloud had formed, leaking lightning, to the northeast. The waves below were stiff with cross winds and froth. She knew better than to try to soar above the impending storm, didn't have the strength to outrun it, and didn't know what would happen to the sphere if—when—downdrafts slammed it into the ocean.

Ratepe had his arms around her, keeping Xantcha warm and upright, the most he could do. He'd spotted the storm but hadn't said anything, other than that he knew how to swim. Ratepe was one up on Xantcha there; the long-ago seamen who'd taught her how to sail had warned her never to get friendly with the sea. If—when—they went down, she'd yawn out Urza's armor. Maybe it would keep her afloat, though it never had kept her dry.

The storm was bigger than the wall-cloud, and fickle, too. In a matter of minutes it spawned smaller clouds, one to the north, the other directly overhead. The first wind was a downdraft that hit the sphere so hard Xantcha and Ratepe were weightless, floating and screaming within it. Then, as Xantcha fought to keep them above the waves, a vagrant wind struck from the south. The south wind pushed them into sheets of noisy, blinding rain.

The squall died as suddenly as it had been born. Xantcha could see again and wished she couldn't. The distance between them and the storm's heart had been halved and, worse, a waterspout had spun out. Rooted in both the ocean and the clouds, the sinuous column of seawater and wind bore down on them as if it had eyes and they were prey.

"What is that?" Ratepe whispered.

"Waterspout," she told him and felt his fingers lock into her arms like talons.

"Is it going to eat us?'

The waterspout wasn't alive and didn't really have an appetite for fools, but that scarcely mattered as they were caught and spun with such force that the sphere flattened against them. It flattened but held, even when they slammed into the raging waves. At one point Xantcha thought they were underwater, if only because everything had become dark and quiet. Then the ocean spat them out, and they hurtled through wind and rain.

Wind, rain, and. above all, lightning. Whatever the cyst produced, whether it was Urza's armor or the sphere, it attracted lightning. Bolts struck continuously. The air within the sphere turned acrid and odd. It pulled their hair and clothes away from their bodies and set everything aglow with blue-white light. Xantcha lost all sense of north or south and counted herself lucky that she still knew up from down.

Every few moments the storm paused, as if regrouping its strength for the next assault. In one such breather, Ratepe leaned close to her ear and said, "I love you."

She shouted back, "We're not dead yet!" and surrendered the sphere to an updraft that carried them into the storm's heart.

They rose until the rain became ice and froze around the sphere, making it heavy and driving it down to the sea. Xantcha thought for sure they'd hit the waves, sink, and drown, but the storm wasn't done playing with them. As lightning boiled off the ice, the winds launched them upward again. Xantcha tried to break the cycle, but her efforts were useless. They rose and froze, plummeted, and rose again, not once or twice, but nine times before they fell one last time and found themselves floating on the ocean as the storm passed on to the south.

The pitch and roll among the choppy waves was the insult after injury. Ratepe's grip on Xantcha's arms weakened, and she suffered nausea.

"I can't lift us up," she said, having tried and failed. "I'm going to have to let go of the sphere."

"No!" Ratepe's plea should have been a shout; it was a barely coherent moan instead.

"I'll make another—"

"Too sick. Can't float."

She tried to ignite his spirit. "A little seasickness won't kill you."

"Can't."

"Waste not, want not. I'm the one who can't swim! I'm counting on you to keep me afloat until I can make another sphere."

Ratepe slumped beside her. His face was gray and sweaty. His eyes were closed. Whatever strength he had left was dedicated to fighting the spasms in his gut. A little bit of seasickness would kill them both if she released the sphere. And if she didn't release it?

Xantcha tried to make it rise, but lifting the sphere had always been something that simply happened as it formed and not anything she'd ever consciously controlled.

"Urza," Ratepe said through clenched teeth. "Urza'll come. Your heart."

Urza had come when she'd nearly blown herself up with the Phyrexian ambulator, but now she wasn't in any immediate danger. The sky overhead was a brilliant blue, and the sphere bobbed like a driftwood log.

"Sorry, Ratepe. If he didn't pull us out of that storm we were riding, then he's not going to pull us out of here. I'm not close enough to dying to get his attention."

"Gotta be a way."

Xantcha peeled Ratepe's sweat-soaked hair away from his eyes. He'd said he loved her, in a moment of sheer panic, of course, but there was a chance he'd been telling the truth. Sexless, parentless newt that she was, Xantcha didn't imagine she could love as born-folk did, but she felt something for the miserable young man beside her that she'd never felt before, something worth more than all her books and other treasures.

"Hold on," she urged, grasping his hand. "I'll think of something."

Xantcha couldn't think of anything she hadn't already tried, and the sphere remained mired in the water. The waves had lessened, and she enjoyed the gentle movement, but Ratepe was as miserable as when the storm had dropped them, and by the way he was sweating out his misery, he'd be parched before long, too.

"Come morning, we'll be late," she said as the sky darkened. "Maybe Urza will come looking for us, but maybe not right away."

"Can't you . . . do something . . . to make him look?" Ratepe asked.

A whole sentence exhausted him. He rested with his eyes closed. Xantcha tried to tell Ratepe that the motion would bother him less if he sat up and looked at the horizon, as he'd learned to do when they were soaring. Ratepe insisted the motions were totally dissimilar and refused to try.

"How does . . . Urza know when you . . . need him?"

"He doesn't," Xantcha answered. "When we were dodging Phyrexians we stayed close, but the rest of the time, I never gave much thought to needing Urza, and he certainly never needed me."

"Never? Three thousand years . . . and you never . . . needed each other?"

"Never."

Ratepe sighed and curled around his knees. He began to shiver, a bad sign considering how warm the Sea of Laments was in the summer. Xantcha tucked their blankets around him, then, because she'd worked up a sweat herself, and stripped off her outer tunic. It got tangled in her hair and in the thong of a pendant she'd worn so long she'd forgotten why she wore it.

"You can hit me now," she said, breaking the thong.

"What?"

"I said, you can hit me now . . . or you can wait until after we find out if this thing still works."

"What?"

"A long time ago—and I mean a long time ago—Urza did make me an artifact that would get his attention. I used something like it just once, before Urza invaded Phyrexia. I have to break it."

That time Xantcha had crushed the little crystal between two rocks. This time she tried biting it and broke a tooth before it cracked. Waste not, want not. At least she'd been farsighted enough to use her back teeth which grew back quicker than the front ones.

That time, between the rocks, there'd been a small flash of light as whatever power or sorcery Urza had sealed within the crystal was released. This time Xantcha neither saw nor felt anything, and when she examined the broken pieces, they were lined with a sooty residue that didn't look promising.

"How long!" Ratepe asked.

"A day before he got there with his dragon."

Ratepe groaned, "Too long."

Xantcha was inclined to agree. Urza must have come back to the forest before he went after the dragon. He wouldn't have taken the chance that the Phyrexians might get away, and after he'd finished with the diggers, he'd known where the ambulator was. If Urza was going to haul them out of the Sea of Laments, they'd be on dry land before moonrise. If the crystal hadn't lost its power. If Urza recognized its signal and remembered what it meant.

Those were worries Xantcha kept to herself. The stars came out. Xantcha began to fear the worst, at least about Urza, and for Ratepe. They had enough food and water for two more days. Taking advantage of her newt's resilience, Xantcha could get to land either way. She wasn't sure about Ratepe.

It would be a stupid way for anyone to die, but the same could be said about most deaths.

Ratepe fell asleep. His breathing steadied, his skin grew warmer and drier. He might be over his seasickness by morning; he had adapted to soaring, and there was nothing to be gained by premature despair. Xantcha settled in around him. It was remarkable that two bodies could be more comfortable curled around each other than either was alone. She closed her eyes.

Xantcha woke up with a stabbing pain in her gut, water sloshing against her armpits, and Urza shouting in her ear:

"What misbegotten scheme put you in the middle of an ocean!"

He had her by the nape of the neck, like a cat carrying a kitten, and held Ratepe the same way. The sphere was burst, obviously. Xantcha knew she should yawn out the armor, but Urza moved too fast. They were a split instant between-worlds, a heartbeat longer in the wintry winds of a nearby world, then back through the between-worlds to the cottage. Xantcha was gasping, mostly because Urza dropped her before turning his attention to Ratepe who'd turned blue during the three-stride 'walk. She knew his color because they'd traveled west and the sun wasn't close to setting behind the Ohran Ridge.

A bit of healing and a few sips from a green bottle off Urza's shelves brought Ratepe around.

"Change your clothes, Brother," Urza commanded in a tone that had surely started battles in their long-ago nursery. "Wash. Get something to eat. Xantcha and I need to talk."

Mishra, of course, stood his ground. "Don't blame Xantcha, and don't think you can ignore me . . . again. I'm the one who wanted to see Koilos."

Ratepe pronounced the word in the old-fashioned way. Xantcha dared a glance at Urza's eyes, thinking her lover was getting advice from the Weakstone. Both of Urza's eyes were glossy black from lid to lid. She hadn't seen them like that since they'd left Phyrexia, which made her think of Gix and the Thran and a score of other things she quickly stifled. Xantcha tried to catch Ratepe's eye and pass him a warning to tread cautiously, if he couldn't figure that for himself.

With his bold remark, Ratepe had effectively changed the landscape of recrimination. If Xantcha could have seized control of the argument at that moment, she could have guaranteed there'd be no revelations about the fate of the Thran. If she could have seized control. She didn't catch Ratepe's eye, and Urza had lost interest in her as well.

"Koilos is dead. There's nothing left. We took it all, Brother. Us and the Phyrexians," Urza said, leaving Xantcha to wonder if he'd visited the cave since his return to Dominaria.

"I needed to see it with my own eyes," Ratepe replied, a comment that, considering the circumstances, could have many layers of meaning. "You told me to go away for a while, so I did."

"I never meant you to go to Koilos. If it was Koilos you wanted, we could have gone together."

"That was never a good idea, Urza," Ratepe said with finality as he walked out the open door, following the near-orders Urza had already given.

"You should have stopped him," Urza hissed at Xantcha when they were alone. "My brother is . . . fragile. Koilos could have torn him apart."

"It's just another place, Urza," Xantcha countered, resisting the urge to add that Ratepe was just another man. Neither statement was true. After a year on the Ohran Ridge, Ratepe might not be Mishra, but he'd become more than a willful, onetime slave.

" 'Just another place,' "Urza mocked her. "For one like you, yes, I suppose it would be. What would you see? A cave, some ruins? What did my brother see? He isn't quite himself yet. The next one will be better, stronger. I expected it would be several Mishras before I'd take one back to Koilos."

"There won't be another Mishra, Urza."

Urza turned away. He puttered at his worktable, scraping up residues and dumping them in a bucket. He'd been working on something when the crystal struck his mind. Xantcha's anger, always quick to flare, was also quick to fade.

"Thank you for picking us out of the ocean."

"I didn't know at first. It took me a moment to remember what it was that I was hearing. I made that crystal for you so long ago, when I still thought I could invade and destroy Phyrexia. My ambitions have grown smaller. Since Equilor, it's all I can do to protect Dominaria from them. I'll make you another."

"Make it easier to break. I lost a tooth on this one. Make one for Ratepe, too."

"Ratepe?" Urza looked up, puzzled, then nodded. "When this is over, when I've exposed the sleepers and put Phyrexia on notice that Dominaria is prepared to fight them, it will be time to talk about the future. I've thought about it while you were gone. This cottage isn't big enough. I've begun to envision permanent defenses for all Dominaria, for Old Terisiare and all the other great islands. Artifacts on a scale to dwarf any that I've made before. I'll build them in place, and when I've finished one of my new sentries, I'll move on to the next. I'll need assistants, of course—"

"Other than me and . . .?" Xantcha left her thought dangling.

"What I've planned will take a generation, maybe ten before it is complete. And the assistants I have in mind will become the guardians of my sentries. They'll become the patriarchs and matriarchs of permanent communities. You understand that can't include you. As for him, he is mortal, not like you or me. We are what the Phyrexians made us. I can't change that, or him. I wouldn't, even if I could. That would be adding abomination to abomination. But he—Ratepe, my brother—will age and die. I thought, I hoped you would choose, while you were together these last few days, to remain together, with him—"

"Somewhere else?"

"Yes. It would be best. For me. For what I have to do."

Urza wasn't mad, not the way he'd been mad and locked in the past for so long. Bringing him face-to-face with Mishra had set him free to be the man Kayla Bin-Kroog had known: self-centered, self-confident, and selfish, blithely convinced, until the world came to an end, that whatever he wanted was best for everyone else.

Xantcha was too weary for anger. "We'll talk," she agreed. Maybe she'd tell him what she'd learned at Koilos. More likely, she wouldn't bother. Urza was immune to truth. "Do you still need either of us, or should we make ourselves scarce again?" she asked.

"No, not at all! I have work for you, Xantcha." He gestured toward one wall where boxes were piled high. "They've all got to be put in place. I'll 'walk you there. You know, it's quite fortunate, in a way, that you broke that crystal. I'd forgotten them completely; I'll make up a score by dawn. Think of it, no more waiting, no more wasted time. As soon as you're finished, you can summon me, and I'll 'walk you to the next place!"

"Tomorrow," she said, heading for the door. Xantcha had gotten what she wanted; if she'd been born with true imagination, she would have known that getting what she wanted wouldn't be the same as what she had expected. "Tonight I've got to rest."

Ratepe was waiting for her in the other room. "Did you tell him?'

Xantcha shook her head. She sat down heavily on her stool. The chest with her copies of *The Antiquity Wars* caught her eye. What would Kayla have said? Urza never really changes. His friends never really learn.

"There wasn't any need to tell Urza anything. He's got his visions, his future. Nothing I'd tell him would make any difference, just like you said. We're going to be busy until the Glimmer Moon goes high. I am, at least. He's got a pile of spiders for me to plant and great plans for that crystal I broke. Watch and see, by tomorrow Urza will have decided that it was his idea for us to get stuck in the Sea of Laments."

Ratepe stood behind her, rubbing her neck and shoulders. It had taken only a year, after more than three thousand, to become dependent on the touch of living fingers. She'd miss him.

"I should've stayed?" he asked. "I hoped if I took the blame—if I made Mishra take it—he'd calm down quicker. Guess I was wrong."

"Not entirely. You had a good idea, and you handled it well." She shrugged off his hands and stood. "Has Urza ever told you that he thinks you're the first of many Mishras who're going to walk back into his life?"

"Never in those words, but, sometimes I know he's frustrated with me. Scares me sometimes, because if he decided he didn't want me around, there'd be nothing I could do about it. But I've gotten used to not having charge of my own life. I've forgotten Ratepe. I'm just Rat, trying to live another day and not always sure why . . . except for you."

Xantcha studied her hands, not Ratepe's face. "Maybe you should think about taking charge of your life again."

"He's decided it's time for a new Mishra? Do I get to help find my replacement?"

"No." That didn't sound right. "I mean, I'm not going to look for another Mishra." She took a deep breath. "And I won't be here if another Mishra comes walking over the Ridge."

Ratepe pushed air through his teeth. "He's sending us both away because we went to Koilos?"

She shook her head. "Because my plan worked. Urza's not thinking about the past anymore, and you and I, we're part of his past."

"I'll go back to Efuan Pincar, to Pincar City," Ratepe spoke aloud, but mostly to himself. "After we expose the *sleepers* and all, Tabarna's going to need good men. If Tabarna's not a *sleeper* himself. If he is, I don't know who'll become king, and we'll need good men even more. What about you? We could work together for Efuan Pincar. You're smarter than you think you are. You leap sometimes, when you should think, as if a part of you is as young as you look. But you know things that never got written down."

Xantcha walked to the window. "I am part of the past, Ratepe, and I'm tired. I never realized just how tired."

"It's been a too-long day and the worst always falls on you." He was behind her again, rubbing her shoulders and guiding her toward the bed.

Xantcha's weariness wasn't anything that sleep or Ratepe's passion could cure, but she wasn't about to discuss the point.

Urza 'walked her to Morvern shortly after dawn. He left her with two sacks of improved spiders, explicit instructions for where they should be placed, and a plain-looking crystal he promised wouldn't break her teeth. Four days later Xantcha took no chances and crushed the crystal between two stones. Urza 'walked her to Baszerat, then to other sleeper-ridden city-states on Gulmany's southern and eastern coasts. There wasn't time, he said, for side trips to the cottage. They had eighteen days until the Glimmer Moon struck its zenith.

"What about Efuan Pincar?" she asked before he left her and a sack of spiders in the hills beyond another southern town. "Will there be time to put the new ones there?"

"You and him!" Urza complained. "Yes, I've taken care of that myself. When the night comes, that's where you'll be, in the plaza outside the palace in Pincar City. I wouldn't dare suggest any place else! Now, you understand what has to be done here? The spiders in that sack, they're for open spaces, for plazas, markets, and temple precincts. You've got to put them where there are at least twenty paces all around. Less and the vibrations will start to cancel each other out. And make sure you put them where they won't attract attention or be trampled. You understand, that's important. They mustn't be trampled. They might break, or worse, they'll trigger prematurely."

They'd come a long way from screaming spiders. Xantcha supposed she'd find out exactly how far in Pincar City. Until then, "Twenty paces all around, no attention, no big feet. How long?"

"Two days, less, if you can. There are some places in the west that we've missed, and it wouldn't hurt to put a few across the sea in Argivia—"

"Urza, we've never even looked for Phyrexians there!"

"It couldn't hurt, if there's time."

With that, Urza 'walked away.

Seventeen days later, the eastern city of Narjabul in which Xantcha was planting spiders had begun to fill with revelers for the coming mid-summer festival. Finding the privacy she needed to plant them was becoming more difficult by the hour. At last a tall, blond-haired man stepped out of the crowd and said, "I think there's nothing more to be done. Let's 'walk home."

The man was Urza, looking like a man in his mid-twenties and dressed in a rich merchant's silks that felt as real as they looked.

Xantcha hadn't expected to see him for another day. She hadn't felt she could break the crystal before then. "I'm nowhere near finished," she confessed. "There aren't enough rooms. The crowds just stay on the streets. It's been difficult, and it's getting worse. They sleep in the plazas where I'm trying to plant the spiders."

"No matter," Urza assured her. "One spider more or less won't win the day, or the night. There's always next month, next year."

He was in one of his benign and generous moods. Xantcha found herself instantly suspicious.

"Has something gone wrong?" she asked. "With the spiders? At the cottage?" She hesitated to say Ratepe's name.

"No, no . . . I thought you and he might want to celebrate. I thought I'd 'walk you both to Pincar City and leave you there tonight."

Urza had his arm draped across Xantcha's shoulder and was steering her through the crowd when they were accosted by three rowdy youths, considerably worse for the wine and ale that flowed freely in the guild tents pitched across the plaza. The soberest of the trio complimented Urza's wide-cuffed boots while one of his companions grabbed Xantcha from behind and the third tried to steal Urza's coin pouch. Xantcha stomped her boot heel on her attacker's instep and rammed her elbow against his ribs to free herself.

The youth, remarkably sobered by his pain, immediately shouted, "Help! Thief! He's taken my purse and my father's sack! Help! Stop him before he gets away!"

Xantcha had no intention of running or of surrendering the spider-filled sack. She had a fighting knife and could have put a swift end to her attacker, but they'd drawn attention, and the middle of a mob was a dangerous place to make a defensive stand, even with Urza's armor. If she'd been alone, Xantcha would have used her sphere and made a spectacular exit. She wasn't alone, though, Urza was a few steps away in the midst of his own fracas, so she yawned out her armor instead and hoped he'd get them free before too many revelers got hurt.

Justice was swift and presumptive. A bystander grabbed her from behind again and put a knife against her throat. He'd probably guessed that something wasn't quite right before she stomped and elbowed him as she'd done with her first attacker, but everyone knew she was more than she seemed when they saw that the knife hadn't drawn blood. Most folk retreated, making ward-signs as they went, but a few rose to the challenge. One of challengers, a thick-set man in long robes and pounding a silver-banded ebony staff against the cobblestones, was also a sorcerer.

"Urza!" Xantcha shouted, a name that was apt to get everyone's attention anywhere in Dominaria. It didn't matter what language she used after that to add, "Let's go!"

The sorcerer cast a spell, a serpentine rope of crimson fire that fizzled in a sigh of dark, foul-smelling smoke when it touched the armor. He'd readied another when Urza ended the confrontation.

Urza had abandoned his merchant's finery for imposing robes that made him seem taller and more massive. He didn't have his staff—it was absolutely real and couldn't be hidden—but Urza the Artificer didn't need a staff. Mana flowed to him easily. Even Xantcha could feel it moving beneath her armored feet, in such abundance that he could afford to target his spells precisely: small, but not fatal, lightning jolts for the three troublemakers and a mana-leaching miasma for the sorcerer who'd intervened on the wrong side of a brawl.

Then Urza clapped his hand around Xantcha's and 'walked with her into the between-worlds.

"Between us and the spiders, everyone in Narjabul's going to remember this year's mid-summer festival," Xantcha laughed when her feet were on solid ground outside the cottage.

Urza grimaced. "They'll remember my name. The *sleepers* and who knows what else might get suspicious before tomorrow night. I didn't want to be connected with this, not yet. I want Phyrexia to know that Dominaria is fighting back, not that Urza has returned to haunt them."

"I'm sorry. I'd had a knife at my throat, there was a sorcerer taking aim at me, and a crowd about to get very unpleasant. I wasn't thinking about consequences."

"I never expect you to."

Ratepe came out of the workroom. They hadn't seen each other for seventeen hectic days, but when Xantcha kept her greeting restrained, he caught the warning and did likewise until they were alone in the other room.

"Did Urza tell you, we're going to watch the spiders from Efuan Pincar!" He lifted Xantcha off the floor and spun her around.

"He said he was going to leave us there."

Ratepe set her down. "I told him that you'd given me your word that I could go back to my old life. I called it 'the life I had before Mishra awoke within me.' He'd started talking about making big artifact-sentries, just like you'd said. He didn't quite come out and say that he wanted to make room for a new Mishra, too, but I understood that's what he meant."

"I keep thinking about the Weakstone."

Ratepe shook his head. "If Urza paid attention to the Weakstone, he'd have an aching head, but he's less attuned to it now than he was when I got here. He is putting the past behind him. I decided to make it easier for myself. If he leaves me in Pincar City, I'm no worse off than I was a year ago. Better, in fact, since I've learned some artifice." Ratepe tried to sound optimistic and failed.

Xantcha opened the chest where she kept her supply of precious stones and metals. "Wouldn't hurt to be prepared." She handed him a heavy golden chain that could keep a modest man in comfort for life.

"He'll change his mind about you, Xantcha. He's never going to send you away," Ratepe insisted, but he dropped the chain over his head and tucked it discreetly beneath his tunic.

Xantcha hauled out coins as well and a serviceable knife with a hidden compartment in its sheath.

"It's the Festival of Fruits," Ratepe protested, refusing to accept the weapon.

"There's going to be chaos for sure and who-knows-what for us afterward." She took his hand and lightly slapped the knife into it.

"What about a sword, then?" he asked, eyeing her rafter-hung collection.

"I was wrong to have a sword in Medran. Efuan Pincar doesn't have a warrior cult, and your nobility averted its eyes about ten years ago. We'll try to be part of the crowd. Knives are a common man's weapon."

"You're nervous?" Ratepe asked with evident disbelief.

"Cautious. You and Urza, you're acting as if this is going to be some victory celebration. We don't know what's going to happen, not in a whole lot of ways."

"You don't want to go?"

"No. I want to see what happens, and Urza's made up his mind. I haven't survived all this time by being careless, that's all."

"You're nervous about being with me? About taking care of me, 'cause you think I can't take care of myself?"

Xantcha pulled up her pant leg and buckled an emergency stash of gold around her calf. She didn't answer Ratepe's question.

"I know Pincar City," he said petulantly. "It's my home, and I can keep my own nose clean, if I need to. Avohir's mercy, it's the damned Festival of Fruits—seven days of berries! All music and bright colors. Parents bring their children!"

Unimpressed, Xantcha handed him a smaller knife to tuck inside his boot, then closed the chest on her treasures wondering if she'd ever look at Kayla's picture again.

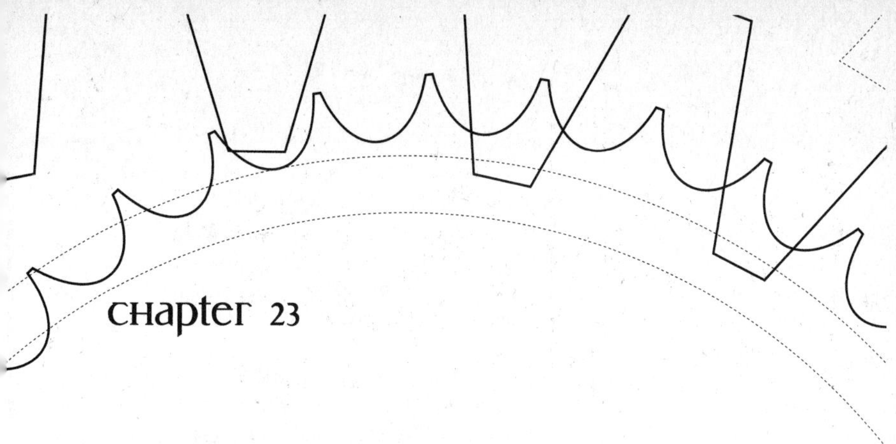

chapter 23

Urza 'walked them to the royal city shortly before sundown. Knowing that Pincar was crowded with revelers and that the journey would leave Ratepe incapacitated, Urza strode out of the between-worlds near the orchard where Xantcha had battled the Phyrexian priest. Other than birds and insects, there were no witnesses to the trio's arrival. Few signs of the previous year's skirmish remained. Trees still sported scorched and unproductive branches, and there was a gap in the geometric rows where a broken tree had been removed.

Ratepe was stunned and shivering. Urza knelt beside him, healing him with warm, radiant hands and saying nothing about the small fortune in gold hung around his neck.

"You'll be careful getting over the walls," Urza said to Xantcha while Ratepe finished his recovery.

"Of course," she replied, irritable because she was suddenly anxious about entering the city.

Neither of them had asked her if she wanted to watch the spiders scream from the plaza of Avohir's great temple, not far from the catacomb where she'd encountered Gix. Xantcha knew she would have lied even if they had. She'd never told Urza about the demon before, and events had moved too swiftly since Narjabul to tell him now. Besides, she hadn't expected to be anxious. If the demon had wanted to find her, he could have found her. Phyrexian demons were many terrible things, but they weren't shapechangers the way Urza was. If Gix hadn't pursued Xantcha to any of the out-of-way places she'd been since their encounter, she didn't expect him to simply appear in the middle of Pincar City's crowded plaza.

"You'll need these," Urza offered her two lumps of milk-white wax.

She hesitated before taking them and asked the question, Why? with her eyes.

"You're vulnerable, and the armor might not be enough protection. Plug your ears first. You'll know when, and you'll have time. Don't fret about it."

He must think the spiders themselves were what made her jumpy, and he might have been right, if it weren't for Gix. "I won't worry," she lied and tucked the wax in the hem of her sleeve. Then she asked the question she'd been avoiding. "Afterward? Should I break the crystal?" She still had the one he'd given her for Narjabul.

"I'll find you."

Xantcha dipped her chin. After three thousand years, it would end without even a good-bye. She could see Kayla frowning in her mind's eye. *The Antiquity Wars* should have prepared her for this.

Urza 'walked away. She and Ratepe waited silently for sundown. Their lives were unraveling, pulled apart between the past and future. Xantcha wanted to hold the present tight. This past year with Ratepe was as close as she had ever come to forgetting that she hadn't been born. She sensed that once the present became the past, regardless of whatever lay in the future, these moments wouldn't be recaptured.

But when Xantcha looked at Ratepe, staring northwest, toward the city of his past and future, she had nothing to say to him until the sky darkened and the first stars had appeared.

"It's time," she said.

They sat together as Xantcha recited her mnemonic and the sphere formed around them.

Country folk who didn't want to pay for a room within the city had pitched tents in the fields and fairgrounds beyond the walls. Between the smoke from their cookfires and a scattering of clouds overhead, Xantcha had no trouble getting the them over the walls and above the southeast quarter of the city. Ratepe said he knew the area and provided directions to a quiet street and the long-abandoned courtyard of a burnt-out house.

"You lived here?" Xantcha asked when the sphere had collapsed.

He pointed at a gaping second-story window. "Last I saw, it was burning. My mother was yelling at my father, telling him to carry me and forget about his precious books."

"Did he?"

"Yes." Ratepe put his arm on a charred door. It opened partway, then struck a fallen roof beam. "We weren't poor. I'd've thought that by now someone would've taken advantage of our misfortune."

Xantcha took his hand, tugging him toward the alley that led back to the street. "Remember how you said everything was smaller since Urza's war? Everything's even smaller in Pincar City."

She and Urza weren't the only ones letting go of their pasts. Xantcha could almost hear Ratepe's disillusionment as they made their way to the wide plaza between the royal palace and Avohir's temple. There were as many empty houses as occupied ones, and those that were inhabited had shuttered windows, despite the summer humidity. Their doors were strapped with iron.

Ratepe didn't see anyone he might have recognized because they didn't see anyone at all. The sounds of the festival came filtered over the rooftops, along with the faint scent of *sleepers,* but the neighborhoods were locked tight.

When they got to the great plaza between Tabarna's palace and Avohir's temple, they understood why, and saw why so many festival-goers had chosen to pitch tents outside the city walls. The crowd was sullen and mean-spirited, looking for fights and, by the sounds of it, finding them with each other. Most of them were men dressed as Ratepe and Xantcha were dressed in the nondescript garments of the countryside. The few women whom Xantcha could see didn't appear to be anyone's wife, mother, daughter, or sister—not quite the family gathering Ratepe had promised.

He didn't say a word when the crowd surged and parted, giving them a glimpse of eight grim-faced men coming through a palace gate, headed for Avohir's temple. The men were uniformed in black-dyed leather and chain mail, except for their sleeveless surcoats, which bore a broad red stripe above the hem. Two of them carried torches that could double as polearms, the other six carried short halberds—wicked weapons with a crescent ax facing one direction and a sharpened gut-hook going the other way. Xantcha knew the kind of damage such weapons could do against a mostly unarmored mob; she hoped she wasn't going to witness it again.

The crowd reformed in the Red-Stripe wake, watchful and not quite silent. Someone muttered fighting words, but not loud enough for Red-Stripe ears. That would come later. Xantcha figured her hopes were futile. Both sides wouldn't be satisfied with anything less than bloodshed.

"I—I don't know what's happened," Ratepe stammered. "*Sleepers?*"

He wanted an affirmative answer, which Xantcha couldn't give. There was oil in the air, the smell faint and mostly coming from the temple or the palace, both still secure within their separate walls. "We happened," Xantcha replied, as grim as the Red-Stripe faces. "We made sure the truth got out, didn't we? These are all your folk, Ratepe, ordinary Efuands, the ones who got caught up with the Red-Stripes and the ones who didn't. Now everybody's got a grudge."

Screaming spiders and Phyrexians would just get in the way.

"I was afraid of what would happen if we just took out the Red-Stripes and the Phyrexians, but this is worse than I imagined it could ever be," Ratepe said. His hand rested momentarily on her shoulder, then fell away.

Closer to the temple, the plaza erupted in shouts and screams. Ratepe succumbed to gawking curiosity as he eased past Xantcha for a better look at the skirmish. She grabbed his arm and rocked him back on his heels.

"Unless you know a better place with food and beds," she snapped, "I say we go to ground in your family's old courtyard." They were traveling light on everything but gold. "This will be calmer come daylight, or the whole city could be in flames," she added.

Without much confidence, Ratepe said that the better inns were on the western side of the plaza. Xantcha, who hadn't eaten since the previous night in Narjabul, was game, though she had to grab Ratepe's arm again to keep him from striking off through the middle of the plaza.

"Forget you ever knew this place, all right? Pay attention to what you see, not what you remember," she advised as they headed north, toward the sea and the palace.

They were on the cobblestones near the Red-Stripe barracks, doing their best not to attract attention, when the temple gongs rang out. This time Xantcha expected the worst and would have bolted for any shadow large enough to contain the sphere if Ratepe hadn't held her back.

"There's a procession every night," he said. "That's what everyone's here for, what they're supposed to be here for. The high priests march the Book around and put it on the dais until midnight."

Xantcha noticed the hulking white-draped platform in the middle of the plaza for the first time. "Every night?" she asked, thinking of tomorrow night when the spiders would scream.

Ratepe nodded.

She nodded, too, seeing to the heart of his requests. "You've been thinking about this from the moment Urza started talking about exposing the *sleepers* with the Glimmer Moon! So, why, exactly, put shatter spiders on the altar?"

"Because the Book won't be there when the altar's destroyed. I figured it would shame the Shratta, whatever's left of them, and I wanted the Shratta shamed at the same time the Red-Stripes were exposed. I didn't expect Red-Stripes to be leading the procession."

He cocked his head toward the temple where what he'd described was happening: the same eight armed men they'd seen earlier marched at the head of a short parade whose focal point was an ornately shrouded litter bearing Avohir's holy book. The tome's container was borne on the shoulders of four priests, at least one of whom reeked oil. Xantcha glanced up at the sky.

The Glimmer Moon had risen, hut though she knew the habits of the larger moon and its phases, she'd always regarded the smaller moon as a nuisance, sometimes there, sometimes not, never welcome. She didn't know if it rose earlier or later each day and wasn't completely clear on the whole "striking its zenith" moment that Urza was counting on.

"They just carry the Book out to the dais and then carry it hack at midnight? A couple thousand paces. You're not hoping for something to happen while they're carrying it, are you?" If Ratepe had wanted to shame the Shratta, she couldn't imagine anything more effective than having a *sleeper* collapse while the holy book's litter was sitting on his shoulder.

"No," Ratepe replied, but before he could specify which question he'd answered, the nearest palace gate swung open. More armed and armored Red-Stripes emerged.

A *sleeper* marched in the second octet. He passed so close that Xantcha was sure she knew which of the eight it was: a clean-shaven young man, not apparently much older than Ratepe and not handsome either. His mouth and nose were too big for his face, his eyes too small. When he turned and stared, Xantcha's blood cooled. She forced her head to remain still and her eyes to lose focus. He might not be able to tell she'd been watching him. Xantcha held her breath, too, though that surely was too late. When the octet had passed, she started walking again.

The dais was still unburdened when they reached the western plaza where the guild inns, each a little fortress, stood behind their closed-gate walls. Ratepe handled the negotiations with the guild guards while Xantcha watched the procession go round and round the plaza. The joint guild of barbers and surgeons had a room behind the kitchen for which they wanted an exorbitant amount of copper and silver but not in any of the forms Xantcha or Ratepe carried it. Fortunately—but not, she suspected, coincidentally—there was a money changers' booth butted up against the barber's watchtower.

"Festival robbery," Ratepe said dramatically as he collected the devalued worth of a golden ring. "Tabarna shall hear of this!"

"Avohir, he knows," the money changer replied, pointing to the lead seals dangling from a silk ribbon overhead.

The room behind the kitchen had been let to another traveler. They wound up in a dust-choked garret that Xantcha was sure had been home to a flock of pigeons earlier in the day.

"The food will be good," Ratepe promised once they'd claimed their quarters.

"Don't say another word. You've been wrong about everything else. If you keep quiet now, the meal may at least be edible!" She was jesting, resorting to the rough humor that worked well on the Ohran Ridge and floundered here in the city.

But the food was good. They devoured roast lamb with sweet herbs, a thick grainy paste that tasted of nuts and saffron, honey-glazed bread, and an overflowing jug of the berry wine served only for the Festival of Fruits.

It wasn't worth the silver they'd paid for it, but it was good nonetheless, and they hauled the remaining wine up to the top of the stairs when they were finished.

The garret overhung a blind alley, but a bit of acrobatics put them on the roof and gave them one of the better views of the plaza that Pincar had to offer. A breeze stirred the humid air, making it pleasant. In the plaza, Avohir's book remained open on the dais. Red-Stripes stood guard while priests took turns reciting Shratta verses from memory—or so Ratepe said. Their voices didn't reach the top of the guild inn.

The crowd had thinned, and what remained had settled in around ten or fifteen campfires scattered across the cobblestones. Red-Stripes stood guard outside the palace and the temple. Xantcha wondered who held the allegiance of the men who guarded the inns. Not that it mattered overmuch. The sky was open to her sphere if they had to get away in a hurry.

"This is a good place," she decided. "We can see everything that's important, and there's nothing to block the sphere if we need it. We'll watch tomorrow night from here."

They stayed on the roof until the temple gongs sounded again at midnight and the Red-Stripes escorted the huge holy book into Avohir's sanctuary.

"What do they do if it rains?" Xantcha asked as they swung and slipped back to the garret.

If the roof had been pleasant, their rented room was a prison. Leaving the windows open had attracted swarms of buzzing, biting insects without improving the air. The excuse for a bed smelled as if its last occupant had been a corpse, and a summertime corpse at that. Xantcha seriously considered yawning out the sphere, if only for Ratepe's sake. She'd breathed Phyrexian air, the ultimate standard by which foul air should be judged, and survived without a wheeze or cough. Poor Ratepe was sneezing himself inside out and short of breath. In the end they dragged the best of the blankets up to the roof and bedded down beneath the stars.

The day they'd been waiting for began before dawn with more gongs clanging from the temple as the Festival of Fruits started its fourth day. When the city gates opened, the tent encampments disgorged their pilgrims who were, on the whole, far less hardened than the men who'd held sway in the plaza at night. There were children and flower sellers and all the other things Ratepe remembered from his own childhood. He coaxed Xantcha out of the garret for bowls of berries and a second visit to Avohir's great sanctuary.

The line of petitioners waiting for Avohir to dry their tears was prohibitively long and the cloister passage to the priests' quarters and, ultimately, the crypt where she'd confronted Gix was closed off and guarded by the burliest Red-Stripes she'd seen since arriving in the city. They glistened with oily sweat, but they weren't Phyrexian.

"I can't believe they're all gone but that one I scented last night with the litter," Xantcha mused when Ratepe had finished taking her on a brief tour of the sanctuary. "Maybe Gix had pulled the sanctuary *sleepers* back. It doesn't take much practice to be a bully like a Red-Stripe, but a priest has to do things right."

"You put the spiders where they live—"

"I'd feel better if I'd seen that they were still in place."

"We'll find out soon enough," Ratepe replied with the sort of fatalism Xantcha herself usually brought to any discussion.

They were on the temple porch, looking down at the plaza from a different angle and gazing north at an afternoon storm. There was time for one more bowl of berries before the storm swept over the palace. Xantcha was indifferent to sweets, but Ratepe would have eaten himself sick. She saw what they did with Avohir's book when it rained. A team of priests who'd obviously worked together before scrambled to get the great book closed and covered with a bleached sail.

"It's going to get wet and ruined sooner or later," she pointed out as she and Ratepe climbed the five flights of narrow, rickety stairs to the garret.

"Sooner."

"But isn't it too precious to be mistreated like that?"

"It used to be there was a new Book every five years. I think the one they've got is maybe older than that. But it's not any one, specific copy of the Book that matters, it's the idea of Avohir's book and the wisdom it contains. When a new Book's brought into the temple, the old one is cut up and passed out. Some people say if you burn a piece of the Book on New Year's Day, you'll have a better year, but some people—my father, for one—kept his scraps in a special box." Ratepe fell silent and stared out the window at the rain.

"Lost?" Xantcha asked.

"We brought it with out of the city. I didn't even think about it after the Shratta." He went back to staring.

"Should I buy a duck?' Xantcha asked, quite serious.

"A duck?"

"Six days after the Festival of Fruits, you'll be nineteen. I made sure I remembered. You said your mother roasted a duck."

"We'll see after tonight."

The festival crowds never recovered from their afternoon soaking. Hundreds of Efuands had returned to their tents beyond the walls, and the rowdy, mean-spirited element took over the plaza long before the midsummer sun was ready to set. Xantcha and Ratepe were spotted standing on the roof, silhouetted by the sun. The innkeeper, a man as burly as the sanctuary Red-Stripes reminded them in no uncertain terms that they'd rented the garret. For an additional two silver hits they rented the roof as well. The innkeeper offered to send up supper and another jug of berry wine.

Xantcha had had her fill of berries. They ate with the other guests in the commons, another leisurely, overpriced meal, then retreated to the roof for the spectacle. The western sky was blazing, and there were two brawls in the plaza, one strictly among the revelers, the other between the revelers and what appeared to be a cornered pair of Red-Stripes. A different, more strident set of gongs was struck, and a phalanx of mounted warriors thundered out of the palace, maces raised and swords drawn.

She couldn't decipher the details of the skirmish from the rooftop, but it wasn't long before three corpses were dragged away and a handful of men, bloodied and staggering, were marched into the palace. One of the prisoners wore an empty sword belt. He wasn't a Red-Stripe; that besieged pair had vanished back into the cadres. By his straight posture and arrogant air, even in defeat, the prisoner looked to be a nobleman, the first of that breed Xantcha had seen since arriving in Pincar City.

The nobleman's appearance crystallized a conclusion that had been lurking in Xantcha's thoughts. "Efuan Pincar has lost its leaders," she suggested to Ratepe. "Wherever I look, whether at the Red-Stripes, the temple, or that mob down there, I don't see anyone taking charge. If there are leaders, they're giving their orders in secret and then watching what happens from a distance, but they're not leading from in front."

Ratepe had an explanation for that absence. "Efuan Pincar's not like Baszerat and Morvern and places like that where every man, woman and child answers to a lord. Our Ancestors left that way behind at the Founding. It's written in Avohir's book. We have a season for making decisions, wintertime, when the harvest's been gathered and there's time to sit and talk—"

"Where's your king? Where's Tabarna? When I came here twenty years ago, he was visible. If there'd been riots outside his palace, the way there've been last night and tonight, he'd have been out here. If not him, then someone, a high priest, a nobleman, even a merchant. There were men and women who could speak louder than the mob. Look down there. Folk have been killed, and there's no true reaction. There's anger everywhere, but nobody's gathering it and turning it into a weapon,"

"Efuands aren't sheep. We think for ourselves," Ratepe countered quickly, a reply that had the sound of an overlearned lesson.

"Well, it's strange, very strange. It's not like anything I've seen before, and that doesn't happen very often. And it's not the way Efuand Pincar was twenty-odd years ago. Your king or someone would be visible. Efuands may not be sheep, Ratepe, but without leaders to stop them. I don't wonder that the Red-Stripes and Shratta were able to cause such trouble for you."

"Are you saying Phyrexians were with the Shratta and the Red-Stripes from the start?"

Ratepe was incredulous, sarcastic, but as soon as Xantcha thought about her answer, she realized, "Yes, I am. I found Gix in Avohir's crypt, but I probably could have found him in the palace just as easily."

"Do you think he's still here?"

"He might be. That passageway I saw wasn't like an ambulator. But Gix was too big to chase me up the stairs. If he's here, he's not going to come walking through the sanctuary doors."

Ratepe said nothing as the sunset aged from amber to lavender. Then, in little more than a whisper, he said, "In the war, Urza and Mishra's war, the Brotherhood of Gix made themselves useful to both sides. They pretended to be neutral. Neither Mishra nor Urza questioned them, but they answered to Gix, didn't they? The Gix in Avohir's temple. The Gix who made you. He controlled the brotherhood, and the brotherhood manipulated the brothers. Avohir's sweet mercy, Gix—the Phyrexians—did control that war. Kayla Bin-Kroog said never to forget the mistakes we made, but she didn't suspect the real rot . . ." His voice trailed off, then returned. "It's happening again, isn't it? Here and everywhere. And nobody's seeing it come."

"Urza has." Xantcha let out a pent-up breath. "Urza's mad in a thousand different ways, but he does remember, and he has learned. He knows to fight this war differently. He knows not to make the old mistakes. I've been listening to him, but I wasn't watching him. Urza lies to himself as much as he lies to you or me, but that hasn't stopped him from doing what has to be done. Until now. I've got to go back, Ratepe, after tonight. I've got to find him and tell him about Gix and about the Thran. There's a part of him that needs to know—deserves to know—everything that I know."

"You won't go alone, will you?"

"Efuan Pincar's going to need true leaders."

"True, but for Efuan Pincar's sake. Urza needs a Mishra that I can trust."

The Glimmer Moon was the evening star this midsummer season, far brighter than the star Ratepe called the Sea-Star and Xantcha called Berulu. It pierced the deepening twilight like a faintly malevolent diamond. Every world that Xantcha remembered where sentient races came together to talk and create societies, folk looked overhead and recited myths about the stars, the moon, and the wanderers.

Gulmany was no exception, but the Glimmer Moon was. It was bright, it wandered, everybody saw it, everybody knew it, and by some unspoken agreement, nobody included it in their myths. Like a loud, uninvited guest, the Glimmer Moon was acknowledged across the island with averted eyes and silence.

Even knowing what an important part it would play this evening, neither Xantcha nor Ratepe could look at it for long, and the pall it cast effectively ended their conversation.

Other, friendlier stars made their nightly appearance. Avohir's gongs clanged to announced the holy book's procession from the sanctuary altar to the white-draped dais. Xantcha found herself breathing in painful gasps, expecting the spiders to scream while the litter was in transit. She clutched Urza's waxen lumps in her fists and had the mnemonic for his armor on the edge of her mind. But the Glimmer Moon didn't strike its zenith in the night's early hours.

She couldn't truly relax after the book was on the dais and the priests had begun to recite whatever passages tradition declared appropriate for the fourth night of the Festival of Fruits. The memory of her one exposure to the spiders kept her nerves jangled. Urza had been steadily increasing the range and power of his tiny artifacts. What if the combination of wax and armor weren't enough? The level part of the roof where they stood was a small square, three paces on a side, twelve in all, which she traced, first to the left, then to the right.

"Stop pacing, please!" Ratepe begged. "You're making me nervous, and you're making me dizzy."

Xantcha couldn't stand still, so she slid over the edge of the roof and into the garret, where the usable pacing area was somewhat smaller. She'd worked up a clinging sweat before thousands of insects got between her ears and her mind. She put the wax plugs into her ears and got Urza's armor out of the cyst within a few heartbeats, but not before she was gasping on the floor.

Ratepe appeared in the garret window just as she'd recovered enough to stand. He grabbed her hand. Xantcha could feel his excitement, but she'd become deaf even to her own voice. They didn't need words, though, to return to the roof where Ratepe's swinging arm showed her where to look for already fallen *sleepers.*

They'd gotten lucky, she thought, observing in sterile silence. Some of the Efuand Red-Stripes must have known there were Phyrexians within their cadres. How else to explain the swiftness with which the standing Red-Stripes distanced themselves from their fallen comrades or, in one instance that unfolded in the torch-lit area in sight of the guild inn's roof, turned their weapons on one of their own?

From the beginning Ratepe had been concerned with the problem of how unaffected folk might interpret the *sleepers'* collapse. The issue seemed to be resolving itself more favorably, if also more violently, than either he or Xantcha dared hope.

She could see men and women whose mouths were moving, and she wished she could ask Ratepe what they were shouting. Probably she could have asked; it was the hearing of the answer that no wish could grant her.

The first of the shatter spiders did its damage as a section of the Red-Stripe barrack collapsed. She could see the destruction from the roof, which was higher than the first of several walls that encircled the palace. The folk in the plaza wouldn't have seen anything, but they might have heard the walls fall, or the inevitable shouts as flames poked through the rubble. Overturned lamps and such finished what the shatter-spiders had begun.

In all, Xantcha thought, it was going very well. She was surprised that Ratepe wasn't visibly jubilant. She tried to ask him with gestures and the old hand code that she and Urza had devised and that, lacking foresight of this moment, she'd failed to teach him. Ratepe pointed toward Avohir's temple, where the shatter-spiders had yet to produce any obvious damage and no priests, *sleeper* or otherwise, were visible in the pools of torchlight.

Could Gix have ordered a search that had removed her handiwork? The Phyrexian presence in Avohir's temple had been noticeably less tainted with the glistening oil scent when Xantcha had made her second visit to Pincar City and all but absent this past afternoon.

But if the demon had scoured the temple walls, wouldn't he have checked the Red-Stripe barracks, too, or the plaza itself? Were compleat Phyrexians truly lacking in suspicious imagination?

There was a flurry around the dais. The holy readers were no longer reciting, and other priests had joined them, getting in one another's way as they closed the great book and made haste to get the litter poles beneath it. That would explain Ratepe's distress. He didn't want Avohir's book inside the sanctuary when—if—the altar collapsed.

But there was more she should worry about: Red-Stripes cadres had spilled from the barracks and the temple. They began, ruthlessly, to restore order in the swirling crowd. Their only opposition came from those other Red-Stripes who'd turned on the disabled *sleepers* when the spiders began to scream. It seemed that some *sleepers* and Phyrexians hadn't been affected by Urza's artifacts or, even more incredibly, that some Efuands had so embraced Phyrexian aspirations that they pursued them even after the Phyrexians had fallen.

Xantcha grabbed Ratepe's sleeve and made him face her.

"What's happening down there?" she demanded. "Is it over? Can I unplug my ears?"

He shrugged helplessly and, consumed by frustration, Xantcha stuck a finger in one ear.

The spiders hadn't stopped screaming, and breaking the seal that protected her from their power was an instant, terrible mistake. Xantcha lost all awareness and sense of herself until she was on her back. Ratepe knelt over her, pressing his fingers against her ears. One hand was bloody when she felt strong enough to push them both away. Ratepe helped her stand.

The situation had changed in the plaza. Some of the second wave of Red-Stripes had succumbed to the spiders' screaming. They were literally torn apart by the Efuand mob, and gruesome though that was to watch, it was also instructive. The resistant Red-Stripes were more compleat than Xantcha or the already fallen *sleepers.* Beneath their seemingly mortal skins they had bones of metal, wired sinews, and veins that spilled glistening oil onto the cobblestones.

The oil did truly glisten in malevolent shades of green and purple until someone discovered, as Urza had discovered a very long time ago, that glistening oil burned.

A slow-moving question that was not her own passed through Xantcha's mind, and Ratepe's, too—he staggered and might have fallen from the roof, if Xantcha hadn't grabbed him. Across the plaza, most Efuands were not so fortunate, though they had less far to fall. All whom Xantcha could see shook themselves back to their senses and stood up unharmed. None of the Efuands, including Ratepe, could know what had happened, but Xantcha, who knew a demon's touch when she felt it, looked for a strand of ruby red light and found it sweeping through the smoke above the burning oil.

Gix.

Xantcha's hand rose to her throat. She broke the crystal. Ratepe watched her do it; he asked questions she couldn't hear, and she answered with the demon's name.

Avohir's sweet mercy! She read the prayer from Ratepe's lips.

In the plaza, the frantic priests of Avohir had finally slung the litter poles beneath the holy book in position to carry the volume back to the sanctuary. That building had still to show any signs of damage from the shatter spiders. The sanctuary might not show such damage to observers on the guild-inn roof. They hadn't expected or intended to bring the great outer walls down, merely the altar and a dormitory cloister behind the sanctuary. And, of course, the spiral stairway down to the crypt.

Xantcha didn't know whether to relax or ratchet her apprehension tighter when the priests successfully navigated through the plaza throng, and Avohir's holy book disappeared into the sanctuary. Ratepe was obviously more anxious, but his lips moved too quickly for her to read his words, even after she'd asked him to slow down and speak distinctly.

Then something happened to make Ratepe put his hands over his ears. All across the plaza, Efuands hitherto unaffected were reacting to a painful noise, but there were no Red-Stripes—no Phyrexians—to take advantage of them. All of them, *sleepers* and compleat, those already dead and those still alive, simply exploded, bursting like sun-ripened corpses. Sound, as Urza had promised, with the power to shake glistening oil until it pulled apart. The Glimmer Moon had struck its zenith. Everything until that moment had been mere forewarning.

Xantcha's whole body tingled from the inside out. If Urza's armor failed, she'd be dead before she knew she was endangered. She tried to imagine the scenes in all the other cities where she and Urza had planted the spiders.

Born Dominarians on their knees, as Ratepe was, perhaps spattered with blood that glistened malevolently in the moonlight. All of them wondering if it were their turn to die.

The Red-Stripe barracks collapsed and, through her feet, Xantcha heard the ground wail. A cloud of dust as large as the guild inn billowed through the sanctuary doors, a cloud that rose quickly to hide the temple and half the plaza from Xantcha's view. When dust had settled some, she and every Efuand saw that the great dome above the altar and the gong tower—shadows in the night moments earlier—were both missing.

From his knees, Ratepe lowered his hands and pounded the roof with his fists. A god who couldn't protect his book or his sanctuary was apt to lose the faith of his worshipers. Xantcha didn't know the depth of Ratepe's faith, but she guessed it had been shaken to its roots.

It was shaken further when an intense red glow filled Avohir's sanctuary, overflowing through the open doors, the windows, and the roof. Xantcha saw the word fire on Ratepe's lips, but the light wasn't fire. It was Gix.

Xantcha broke the chain that had held Urza's pendant around her neck. She held the crystal up in the crimson light. Very clearly, it was broken and, just as clearly, Urza wasn't coming. He hadn't said where he'd go to watch the Glimmer Moon strike its zenith. He could have gone to the Glimmer Moon itself or he could have remained in the Ohran Ridge cottage.

Or Urza's absence could mean that Gix was not the only demon on Dominarian soil and that Urza was already in a desperate brawl. Urza could 'walk anywhere, but even he couldn't be in two places at once.

The red light within Avohir's sanctuary grew brighter, larger. It fluctuated and emitted serpentine flares that faded slowly in the night. The smell of Phyrexia grew steadily stronger. Xantcha imagined Gix burning and battering his way up from the catacombs. She wondered if he had the power to destroy a city and didn't doubt for a heartbeat that the demon would, if he could.

There was nothing Xantcha could do to stop Gix, and until she was sure that the spiders were exhausted, there was nothing she dared do to spirit herself and Ratepe away.

Vast crimson fingers leapt from the roofless sanctuary. They soared into the sky, then arched toward the plaza. Looking up, Xantcha and everyone else saw that the fingers were hollow, filled with darkness and fanged like serpents. The darkness resembled the upright passageway to Phyrexia that she'd seen in the crypt. Xantcha feared they'd all be sucked into the Fourth Sphere. Ratepe put his arms around her, and Xantcha wrapped hers around him. She wanted to feel his warm, mortal flesh with her fingers and wouldn't have cared if the spiders killed her, except that she wouldn't force Ratepe to watch her die.

She saw a ribbon of silvery light emerge from the center of the palace.

Diving and soaring, the palace light pierced each serpent and drew them all together with a choking knot before dragging them over the north wall and out to sea.

Xantcha shouted, "Urza!" at Ratepe who needed a few more heartbeats before he could shape his lips around the name.

Gix fought back, but as Xantcha had always suspected, Urza was more than a match for a Phyrexian demon . . . or a Thran one. Neither duelist was visible from the plaza or the roof, though they each knew exactly where the other was. They fought with light and fire, with artifacts and creatures that defied naming in any language Xantcha knew. Gix would have lost quickly if the demon had not aimed most of his destruction at the Efuand survivors in the plaza and thereby forced Urza to defend the innocent.

Then Urza loosed two weapons at once: bolts of lightning to counter Gix's last cowardly thrust and a dragon shaped like the one he'd ridden into Phyrexia, but shaped from golden light. Stars shone through the dragon's wings, but its power was anything but illusory. A jet of intense blue fire shot from its mouth as it began a stoop that would take it into Gix's sanctuary lair.

Gix didn't die fighting; nor did he retreat to Phyrexia. Instead he abandoned Pincar City altogether: a relatively small green-gold streak racing to the south, a half-breath ahead of the dragon's flame.

Xantcha expected the dragon to pursue Gix over the horizon, but it continued its stoop into the ruined sanctuary. She braced herself for the physical shock wave of a crash that never came. A heartbeat, and another, and the dragon lifted into flight again, showing first its wings, then its spidery torso, and at last, clasped in a pair of legs, a book that recently had seemed very large and now looked quite small. The dragon beat its translucent wings twice for altitude. Then it stooped again and set Avohir's holy book on the battered dais before climbing back into the sky.

The dragon circled out to sea—Avohir's home according to myth—and the Efuands still standing, including Ratepe, set up a cheer in its wake, but Urza wasn't finished. He brought the dragon back (Xantcha would have sworn he shrank it just a bit, too) for a gentle glide over the palace roofs. Through its bright, shifting light, Xantcha wasn't sure it had picked something up until it was almost overhead and she could see a frail old man getting the ride of his life.

It was a miracle of another sort that Tabarna's heart didn't fail before the dragon set him down beside Avohir's book. The dragon flew straight up after that and disappeared among the stars.

The Efuands who'd cheered the survival of their book, went wild when they saw their king. Xantcha couldn't get Ratepe's attention no matter how hard she pounded his back or how loudly she shouted, "Is it over? Can I release Urza's armor?"

Yes, it's over, Xantcha. Urza's voice spoke to Xantcha's thoughts.

You heard! she replied, releasing the armor and pulling the wax out of her ears. *You came!* The cheers of the crowd, after total silence, were as deafening as the spiders.

Xantcha had trouble hearing Urza when he said, still in her mind, *I've been here all along, keeping my eyes on Gix. I didn't want to frighten you.*

Waste not, want not. How long had Urza known?

Xantcha hadn't kept her thoughts private. Urza pulled the question from her mind and answered it. *Since the priest in the orchard. I went back to all the haunted places. I saw how the Phyrexians had crept into my world again. I found Tabarna in a cell beneath the palace—he was quite mad, but still himself. The Phyrexians needed to trot him out periodically, and they could only do what they did to Mishra because he carried the Weakstone. So I stole Tabarna from them and hid him on another plane.*

That, I confess, was the act that brought Gix here to Pincar City. Since then, everything I've done—everything I've had you do—has been building toward this moment. I healed Tabarna. Madness, you know, sinks deep roots in a man's soul once he's seen sights and thought thoughts no man should see or think. There are some moments he'll never remember again, moments such as I wish I could forget, Xantcha. The Shratta could not be deceived, so they were killed while Tabarna watched. But he'll live another ten years and sire another son or two. I guarantee it.

Xantcha had warned her slave, assume that if you've thought about it Urza knows it. Then she had failed to remember her own advice.

"You've had reason to be suspicious, Xantcha. There's never been anyone who could do for me what I've done for Tabarna."

Urza was on the roof with them, looking very ordinary. He had no trouble getting Ratepe's attention but was unprepared when Ratepe threw himself into a joyous, tearful embrace.

The affection Efuands had for their elderly king—whose speech none of them could hope to hear through their shouting—was nothing Xantcha wanted to understand, though it was also clear that Urza had done exactly what was necessary to insure that the realm would recover from its long battering.

Xantcha stood a bit apart from Ratepe and Urza, giving herself a few moments to consider all that she'd just learned. She stayed apart when Urza extended his hand.

"What happens next?" she demanded thinking deliberately of Gix.

"I go to Koilos."

She folded her arms. "Not alone. Not if you're going after Gix."

Urza frowned, then sighed. "No, I suppose not." He turned to Ratepe. "And you, Brother, I suppose you'll want to come, too."

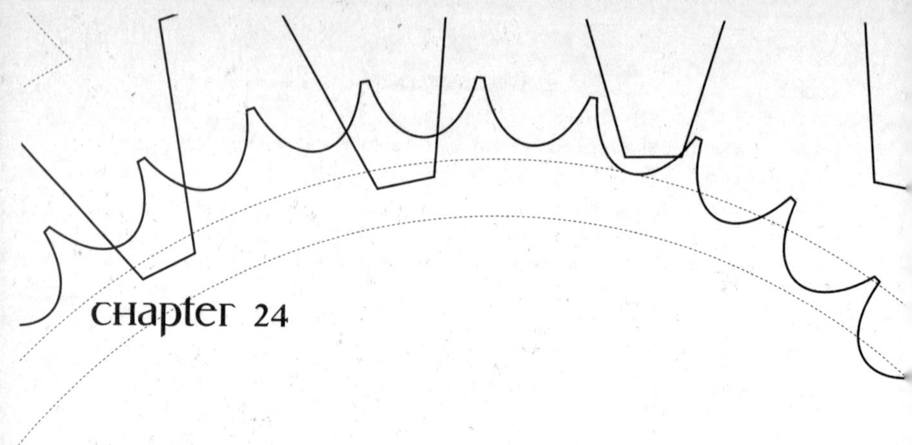

chapter 24

The sun just had risen over the Kher Ridge, far to the east of Gulmany island and Efuan Pincar. It would be a summer day with clear air and high clouds that wouldn't come close to raining on these desert-dry stones. Koilos, the Secret Heart, was on the other side of the mountain where Xantcha and Ratepe rested, waiting for Ratepe to recover from the three-step 'walk from Pincar City. Urza was already at the cavern. He'd sworn he wouldn't go looking for Gix until they arrived, unless Gix came looking for him. Ratepe sat on the ground, chafing his arms and legs against the morning chill and the shock of healing.

"You think he knows everything?"

Xantcha had just finished telling him what had passed between her and Urza on the guild inn roof not an hour earlier. She was impatient to yawn out the sphere and get into the air, even though she knew there'd be no part for her or Ratepe to play in the coming fight. More than three thousand years ago she'd watched as other demons thrust Gix down a fumarole to punishment that had proved less than eternal. She expected Urza to do a better job and wanted to watch him doing it.

"He's still calling you Mishra."

Ratepe nodded several times. "True enough. But he was something in the sky last night over Pincar City—a little while ago—whenever. I got used to the idea that he was the crazed, foolish man who lived on the other side of the wall. I let myself forget what I knew he was, through the Weakstone. He was the man who came within an hour of destroying the world."

"You weren't the only one," Xantcha confessed. "You ready to finish this?"

"All in a morning's work," Ratepe joked grimly as he stood. "Avohir's mercy, I should be happy. I am happy, but inside, I feel like I felt after I saw my father dead, or when we were falling through that storm over the ocean and we were floating in your sphere. I don't feel a part of anything that's around me. If I ask myself what happens next, there's nothing there, not even a sunrise."

Xantcha replied, "Urza 'walked us under the sun. That's why we missed the sunrise, and I'll try not to drop the sphere through a storm again." She left Ratepe's other observations behind on the ground as the sphere flowed around them and lifted them into the air.

Urza waited not far from the place where Xantcha had read the Thran glyphs. He was taller than any mortal man and clad in his full panoply with robes armored in the colors of sorcery. His hand circled the gnarled wood of a war staff capped with a peculiar blue-gray metal. His eyes were hard and faceted, as if he'd see nothing so puny as flesh, but his voice was strong and vibrant when he greeted them.

"Gix is here, waiting for me."

The scents of Phyrexia were indeed in the air: glistening oil, Fourth Sphere fumes, and the malevolence Xantcha recognized as Gix. She yawned out her armor while Urza laid hands on Ratepe's shoulders. The young Efuand glowed like swamp water once they entered the cavern. Sunlight ended ten paces into the upper, glyph-covered chamber. Urza's war staff emitted a steady light from the edges of its many blades. The light reached to the glyph-covered walls.

"Phyrexian, you say?" Urza asked.

"Close enough. Do you want to read them through my eyes?"

"Not yet. After. I've waited too long to taste vengeance against the Phyrexian who destroyed my brother. It's hard enough to know that Gix is one of the Thran, one of the ones who got away; I don't want to know the rest, not yet. And once I know it, then I'll decide if it's worth remembering. I have much to do, Xantcha. I cannot always embrace the truths that might be written on stone walls. I know that's been hard for you, but it's been even harder for me."

The ultimate confession from the crazed and foolish man who lived on the other side of the wall?

They continued to the rear of the chamber, where Ratepe had spotted a passage. Without torches or powerstone eyes, he had been unable to explore it. The passage sloped steeply downward and was marred by deep gouges in the stone. Xantcha walked on Urza's left, a half-pace behind. Ratepe held a similar place on Urza's right.

"We took everything," Ratepe whispered, softly, but in Koilos a whisper carried like a shout. Urza didn't tell him to be quiet, so Ratepe continued.

"The chamber below, where we found the stones, we stripped it bare. We needed the metal. At the end we were so desperate for metal, any metal, that we opened tombs and took the grave goods from our dead and fueled our smelters with their bones."

"So did we," Urza assured him. "So did we."

Xantcha saw light ahead, the harsh, gray light of Phyrexia.

The second chamber of Koilos was as large as the first and empty, except for Gix who stood somewhat behind dead center. Xantcha expected some preliminary taunting and boasting, but neither Urza nor Gix was a young mortal with an itch for glory. They'd come to kill or be killed. All their whys had been buried long ago.

Gix attacked first as they emerged from the passageway. He didn't waste time or effort with side attacks against Xantcha or Ratepe. They weren't innocents with rights to Urza's protection. They'd come of their own free will, and they'd be meat, at best, if Urza failed to win.

The rubine gem in the demon's bulging forehead shone bright. A thumbnail-sized spot of the same color appeared on Urza's breast. Heartbeats later, a boulder, Urza-high and Urza-wide, bilious green and glassy, stood where Urza had stood between Xantcha and Ratepe. The boulder blew apart an instant later. Fists of stone hammered Xantcha from face to toes and threw her back against the chamber wall. Ratepe was on the floor, covered in a thick layer of dust. Two counterspinning coils of fire and light whirled around the demon until he spread his arms to vanquish them.

An ambulator took shape, closer to Urza than to Gix. The ambulator heaved and rotated upward, sprouting a toothy hole of a mouth and many viscous, reaching arms. An arm came close enough to Xantcha that she judged it prudent to put a little distance between herself and the duel. She scuttled crabwise along the curving chamber wall and was relieved to see Ratepe do the same on the other side.

Urza spoke a word, and the ambulator-creature became a sooty smear. He did nothing at all that Xantcha could see, and yet Gix was slammed against the chamber's far wall. A crystal sarcophagus surrounded the demon. Xantcha thought that might be the end, but purple fumes rose from the crystal, and Urza disappeared as manic wailing filled the barren chamber. Gix shook off the dissolving crystal and clambered to his metallic feet.

Xantcha took heart from the fact that the demon wasn't claiming victory by targeting her or Ratepe. His oddly shaped head swiveled frantically. The rubine light danced over the naked stone, leaving a trail of smoke as Gix sought a target. Twice the demon blew futile craters in the rock, but he was ready when ghostly blue arms seized him from behind. Urza landed on his back in the middle of the chamber. The impact shook jagged stones the size of a man's torso from the ceiling.

Both combatants righted themselves and backed away from each other.

The testing phase was over; the duel began in earnest with flurries of attacks that ebbed and flowed too fast for Xantcha's eyes. The demon was stronger, cleverer, and much more resilient than she'd believed after seeing him flee the dragon in Pincar City. She thought of the excoriation. It had taken a clutch of demons to wrestle Gix into that fumarole. She suspected that he was the only one who'd survived.

Urza succeeded in melting away one of Gix's legs, though that was little more than inconvenience in a battle that wasn't about physical injury. And though Urza seemed to have the advantage more often than not, he couldn't deliver a killing attack. Not that he didn't try a in a hundred different ways from elemental ice to conjured beasts and the ghosts of artifacts he and Mishra had wielded against each other. Gix countered them all, sometimes barely, with an equally bewildering assortment of arcane memories and devices.

Eventually, when it had become apparent that neither flash nor guile was going tilt the balance, Urza and Gix locked themselves in a contest of pure will that manifested itself in an increasingly complex web of blue-white and crimson light. The spindle-shaped web stretched between Urza's eyes and Gix's gem-studded forehead. At its widest, which was also its middle and the middle of the chamber, the web did not descend to the floor. Sparing nothing for effect, the web gave off neither heat nor sound and endured, without really changing, until Xantcha had to breathe again.

How long, she asked herself, could they remain enrapt in each other? Her best answer: for a very long time. She got up on her feet.

"Look at Urza's eyes!" Ratepe shouted from the other side of the chamber.

Xantcha had to walk closer than she considered wise before she found a slit in the web that let her look down the spindle to Urza's face. She didn't see anything strange—nothing stranger than two specks as bright as the sun—but she didn't have Ratepe's rapport with the Weakstone. And, as Ratepe's voice had seemed to have no effect on the duel, she asked, "What am I looking for?"

"You can't see everything changing . . . coming back from the past, or going back to it?"

She started to say that she couldn't see anything changing and swallowed the words. Shadows were growing in the Koilos chamber. Not shadows cast by the web's light, but shadows cast by time, growing more substantial as each moment passed. Metal columns grew along the walls. Great machines, worthy of Phyrexia, loomed up from the floor.

Beneath the widest part of the light-woven spindle a low platform came into being. Mirrors sprang up in a circle behind both Gix and Urza, behind Xantcha and Ratepe, as well. An object similar to Avohir's great book, but made from metal like Urza's staff, grew atop the platform. As Xantcha watched, Phyrexian glyphs formed on the smooth metal leaves.

Xantcha was waiting for those glyphs to become legible when dull-colored metal sprang out of the central platform. The metal shaped itself into four rising prongs, like uplifted hands.

"His eyes, Xantcha! His eyes! They're going back. Gix is dragging them back through time!"

The Weakstone and the Mightstone had pulled out of Urza's skull and were advancing through the spindle.

Gix had said, The Thran are waiting. . . .

And when the powerstones merged into the prongs, Urza would be in the hands of the Thran.

Ratepe shouted, "We can stop them."

"No."

"We can!"

"Not if you're getting influence from the Weakstone. It's Thran. It belongs to Gix. No wonder he was waiting here." Xantcha would have sobbed, if the armor had let her.

"We can stop this, Xantcha. Gix is sending the powerstones into the past. All we have to do is get there first."

Xantcha shook her head—never mind that she couldn't see Ratepe. "That's the Weakstone influencing you," she shouted. "Gix. Phyrexia." Her gut said anything she did would only make things worse, if anything could be worse than watching Urza become a tool of the Phyrexian Thran. She was paralyzed, frightened as she had never been before—except, perhaps, at the very beginning when the vat-priests told the newts *Listen, and obey.*

"Meet me in the light, Xantcha!"

On the other side of the spindle, Ratepe thrust his hands into the web. From Xantcha's side, looking into the spindle, his flesh had become transparent and his bones gleamed with golden light.

"Now, Xantcha!"

The powerstones had traveled half the distance to the prongs. The etched-metal glyphs were legible, if she could have concentrated and read them. She walked to the right place, the place opposite Ratepe, then hugged herself tightly, tucking her hands beneath her arms, lest she move without thinking.

"I need to be sure!" she shouted.

"Be sure that Gix wants the Weakstone and Mightstone, not you and me. At least we can give him what he doesn't want. It's all we've got to give."

Xantcha reached for the spindle. The light repelled Urza's armor. A good omen or a bad one? For whom? She didn't know and tucked her hands beneath her arms again.

"I can't, Ratepe. I'm Phyrexian. I can't trust myself. I'm always wrong."

The powerstones were three-quarters of the way. The devices beyond the ring of mirrors thrummed to life.

"I'm not! And I'm never wrong about you. Meet me in the light, Xantcha. We're going to end the war."

Xantcha shed her armor and thrust her hands into the spindle.

Begone! Listen and obey. Begone! Do not interfere.

The demon's anger, roaring through Xantcha's mind could have been deception. Gix should have known that she would, in the end, disobey his command, in which case Gix had outwitted them all and wanted her to reach into the light. But, on the chance that he wasn't quite that imaginative, Xantcha extended her arms to their fullest reach.

Time and space changed around her. She'd left her body behind. To the right, the Weakstone and the Mightstone, two great glowing spheres, rolling toward her, fighting, losing. To the left was the unspeakable, blood-red maw of Gix, calling the stones, sucking them to their doom.

Straight ahead stood Ratepe, son of Mideah, with a radiant smile and outstretched arms.

Their fingers touched.

Gix turned his wrath on her and on Ratepe. It was the last thing the demon did. Xantcha felt the stones free themselves to destroy the enemy they'd been created to destroy.

As for her and Ratepe, they were together.

Nothing else mattered.

And Rat's face, joyous as they embraced, was a glorious sight to carry into the darkness.

For Urza, the battle had ended suddenly, in a matter of moments and without easy explanation. One moment Mishra and Xantcha had been blocking the light, arms outstretched and reaching toward each other, not him. The next moment—less than a moment—a fireball had filled the lower chamber. Once again his eyes had lifted him out of death's closing fist. His Thran eyes had guarded this cavern for four thousand years before he and his brother found them, and they still preferred to see it in its glory, filled with engines, artifacts and powerstone mirrors.

Or should he say his Phyrexian eyes?

It scarcely mattered. Urza's borrowed eyes preserved him as the fireball raged like a short-lived sun.

The sun-ball consumed itself . . . quickly, Urza thought, though he remembered Argoth and that the time he'd spent completely within the powerstones could not be measured. As his eyes recorded it, there was fire and then the fire was gone, two edges of the cut made by an infinitely sharp knife, without a gap between them.

There'd been no visions, as there had been the other times when the Mightstone and Weakstone had held him in their power. No explanations, however cryptic. Nothing, except a dusty voice that said, *It is over.* He had a sense, much less than a vision, that Mishra had grasped Xantcha's hand just before the explosion consumed them.

In the aftermath silence reigned. A natural silence: Urza wasn't deaf, but there was nothing left to hear. Urza thought light, and it flowed outward from him.

"Xantcha," he called, because he'd been without his brother before.

Her name echoed off the chamber's scorched walls. He was alone.

At the end, she'd chosen Mishra, charming, lively Mishra. Urza wished them joy, wherever they'd gone. He wished them peace, far away from any Phyrexian or Thran design. They had earned peace, vanquishing their shared enemy: Gix.

The demon had vanished within the powerstone-derived fireball. There was nothing left. Urza's eyes told him that. He could hear them now, faint and smug in his skull.

The truth was written on the upper chamber ceiling. The Thran had fought among themselves, fought as only brothers could fight, with a blindness that transcended hatred. Remembering the battle the Weakstone and Mightstone had shown him the last time he'd come to Koilos. Urza realized he truly did not know which army had escaped to Phyrexia, if, indeed, Xantcha's Ineffable hadn't slipped away to create Phyrexia before that fatal day.

Standing in the Koilos cavern, Urza concluded that he'd have to continue his experiments with time because he'd have to go back himself, not to a moment in his own lifetime, but to the Thran, Gix and all the others. . . .

"Not yet," Urza cautioned himself.

This would be a cunning war. Gix was still extant in the past; Yawgmoth and the other Phyrexians were in the past, the present, and the future, too. The battle—the real and final battle for Dominaria—had, in a sense, just begun. It would be fought in the past and in the future.

And Urza would have no allies, none at all: not Tawnos, not Mishra.

Urza recalled light and moved along the blackened corridor to the surface. No real body. No real need for light, or anything else.

A weight tugged against him.

Xantcha's heart, which the powerstones, his eyes, had preserved.

He wasn't alone.

Urza would never be alone.

TIME STREAMS
J. ROBERT KING

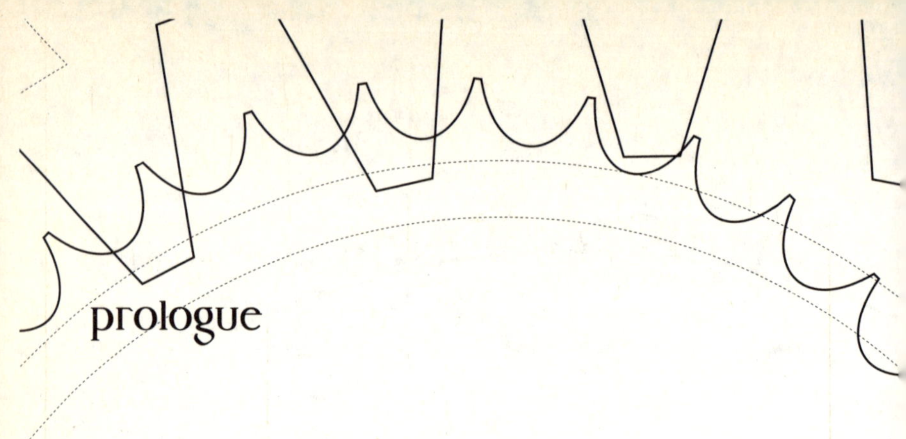

prologue

Urza says he's sane. Perhaps he is. Measures of sanity among planeswalkers are hard to come by. He has lived for over three thousand years. He heals by merely willing it. With a thought, he steps from world to world to world. His very appearance is a matter of convenience, clothes and even features projected by his mind. How can conventional notions of sanity apply to a planeswalker?

Perhaps they cannot, but his madness began before he was a planeswalker. Three thousand years ago, a mortal Urza battled his mortal brother. Their sibling rivalry turned fratricidal. So began the Brothers' War. In his rage to kill Mishra, Urza enlisted the armies of the world, sank the isle of Argoth, gutted the continent of Terisiare, and wiped whole nations from the globe. He ushered in an ice age. In repayment for all this madness, he became a planeswalker.

Urza says he regrets the destruction. True regret would be a good sign.

It wasn't regret that later sent Urza on his own private invasion of Phyrexia. It was revenge for his brother. Somehow, Urza convinced himself he hadn't killed Mishra, that the Phyrexian Gix had done it. True, Gix seduced Mishra with promises of awesome power and in the end transformed him into a monstrous amalgam of flesh and artifice. But Urza was Mishra's slayer. Not in his mind, though. In the mind of madness, Urza blamed Gix and plotted to get even. His motive was mad, and his invasion madder still. Urza attacked Phyrexia—one planeswalker against armies of demonic monstrosities. He lost, of course. He couldn't defeat a whole world and was nearly torn to pieces trying.

Tail between his legs, Urza retreated to Serra's Realm, a place of angels and floating clouds. There he convalesced, but he never truly recovered. Madness still haunted him, and so did Phyrexia. Gix followed on his tail. No sooner had Urza left Serra's Realm, thinking himself whole and hale, than Gix and his demons arrived. A war began in heaven. That place, like any other where Urza had chosen to dwell, was decimated. Centuries later, it is still shrinking in its long collapse.

When I point out these mad indiscretions, Urza shrugs. He claims he regained his sanity after all that. He credits his newfound perspective to Xantcha and Ratepe—"two dear friends who sacrificed themselves to slay the demon Gix, close the portal to Phyrexia, and save my life. To them, I am forever grateful."

True gratitude would be a good sign, too.

Urza has never, in his three millennia of life, shown true gratitude nor had a "dear friend." I have known him for three decades. For two of those, I have worked side by side with him at the academy we established here on Tolaria. I am not his dear friend. No one is. Most of the tutors and students at the academy don't even know his real name, calling him Master Malzra. The last person who was close enough to Urza to be a dear friend was his brother, and everyone knows what happened to him.

No, Urza is incapable of regret and gratitude, of having dear friends, not that there haven't been folk like Xantcha, Ratepe, Serra, and me, who genuinely love the man and would give our lives for him. But he seems incapable of returning our affection.

That's not enough to declare him insane, of course. As I said, measures of sanity among planeswalkers are hard to come by, but there is something mad about Urza's blithe belief that Xantcha and Ratepe sacrificed themselves, that Serra's Realm and Argoth sacrificed themselves, that Mishra sacrificed himself. . . . It seems everyone and everything Urza claims to care about gets destroyed.

And what does that mean for me, his newest dear friend?

—Barrin, Mage Master of Tolaria

PART I

SCHOOL OF TIME

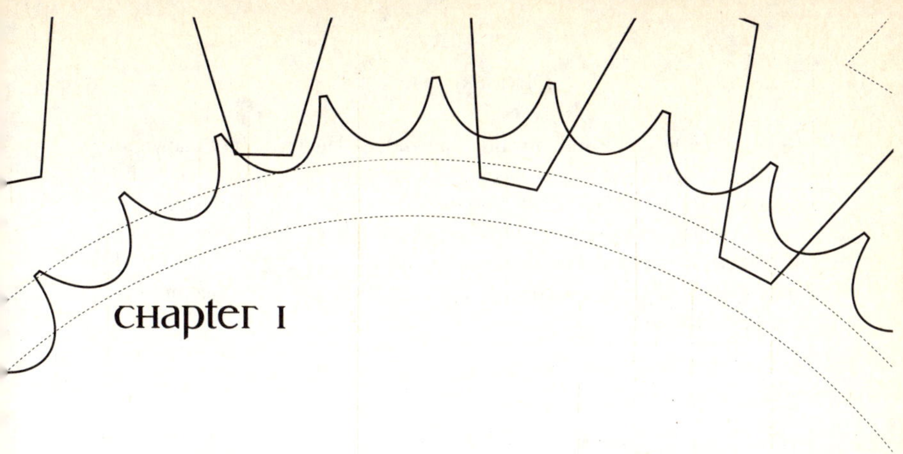

Chapter 1

Jhoira stood at the edge of her world. Behind her lay the isle of Tolaria, its palm forests and lecture halls overrun with magical prodigies and clockwork creatures. It was a realm of ceaseless tests and pointless trials and worries and work, lots of work.

Before her lay the blue ocean, the blue sky, and the illimitable world. Clouds piled into empyrean mountain ranges above the shimmering sea. White waves broke on the ragged rocks below. Beyond the thin, brilliant line of the horizon, the whole world waited. Her soul mate was out there somewhere, she dreamed. Everything was out there—her homeland, her parents, her Shivan tribe, her future.

Jhoira sighed and slouched down to sit on a sun-warmed shoulder of sandstone. Sea winds sent her long black hair dancing about her thin shoulders. Breezes coursed, warm and familiar, through her white student robes. She'd spent many hours in this sunny niche, her refuge from the academy, but lately the hideaway brought her as much sadness as joy.

She'd been at the academy for eight years now, learning all she could of machines. A prodigy when she arrived, Jhoira was now a formidable artificer. She was also a woman, or at eighteen nearly so, and was weary of the school and the kids, of brimstone and machine oil. She was sick to death of artifice and illusion and wanted something real—some*one* real.

Jhoira closed her eyes, drawing a deep breath of salty air into her lungs. Her soul mate would be tall and bronze-skinned, like the young Ghitu tribesmen back home—keen-eyed and strong. He would be smart, yes, but not like Teferi and the other boys who tried to get Jhoira's attention through juvenile antics and unsubtle innuendoes. He would be a man, and he would be mysterious. That was most important of all. She could not be in love with a man unless, at the core of his being, there was mystery.

She opened her eyes and shifted her weight, one sandal sending up a puff of dust. "I'm a fool. There's not a man like that in the world." Even if there were, she'd never get to meet him, not while she was stuck on this blasted island.

Standing, the silver man awoke. He had moved before, had walked and spoken before. He had occupied this enormous body of metal, peered out of its silvery eyes, and lifted things in its massive hands. Before it had been always as if in a dream. Now he was awake. Now he was alive.

The laboratory around him was bright and clean. Master Malzra liked it clean—clean but cluttered. One wall held hundreds of sketches and refinements of sketches, some in ink, some in lead, some in chalk. Another bristled with specialized implements—metal lathes, beam saws, injection molds, presses, rollers, bellows, drills. A third wall bore racks of cogs and struts and other mechanical castings. A fourth held ranks of assembled mechanisms. A fifth—very few of the school's rooms were square—allowed egress into the room. In the center of the space, a great black forge rose. Its smokestack climbed up and away through the dome above. A second-floor gallery ringed the fringes of the room. Up in those balconies even now, young eyes peered down on the result of Master Malzra's latest experiment. They peered down on the silver man.

The silver man peered back. He felt frightened, awkward, shy. He wondered what they thought about him—wondered and cared in a way he never had before. Everything was like that. He had seen this laboratory many times before, but he never would have used terms like clean and cluttered and bright to describe it or the man who had created it. Now the silver man perceived more than just things. He perceived the organization of things, their disposition, and what they implied about their creator. The laboratory was a study in the mind of Master Malzra—ancient, obsessed, brilliant, tireless, preoccupied, short-sighted, grandiose. . . .

Master Malzra, meanwhile, studied him. The man's gaze was penetrating. Folds of aged skin drew up skeptically beneath one eye. His nostrils flared, but he didn't seem to breathe at all. One soot-blackened hand trembled slightly as he raised it to scratch his ash-blond beard. He swallowed, blinking—but with eyes like that, as hard and sharp as diamonds, it seemed he didn't need to blink at all.

"Any noticeable change in the probe's energy profile, Barrin?" Malzra asked over his shoulder.

It was a strange greeting. The silver man felt somewhat offended.

"A reasonable enough question," came the response—from Malzra's second, a master mage. Barrin stepped from beside an injection mold. He wiped grit from his hands with a white cloth. "Why don't you ask him?"

Malzra blinked again. "Ask whom?"

"Ask *him*," the mage repeated, quirking one corner of his mouth. "The probe."

Malzra pursed his lips. He nodded. "Probe, I am Master Malzra, your creator. I wish to know if you notice any change in your energy profile."

"I remember who you are," responded the silver man. His voice was deep and resonant in his metal form. "And I notice a very definite change in my energy profile. I am awake."

A sibilance of voices came from the balcony.

Malzra seemed almost to smile. "Ah, you are *awake.* Good. As you are doubtless aware, we've made some modifications to you, hoping to enhance your performance, your intellect, and your capacity for social integration." He ground his teeth and could not seem to come out with anything else. Malzra glanced back to Barrin for help.

The mage—lean, middle-aged in a white work smock—approached. He patted the silver man's shoulder. "Hello. We're glad you've woken up. How do you feel?"

"Confused," the silver man heard himself say, then in a voice of wonder, he went on. "Everything seems to have a new dimension. I am filled with conflicting information."

Barrin asked, "Conflicting information?"

"Yes," replied the silver man. "I sense, for example, that though Master Malzra is your superior in rank and age, he often defers to you due to his social disinclinations."

"Social disinclinations?" Barrin prompted.

"He prefers the company of machines to that of people," clarified the silver man.

Titters of humor came from the gallery. Malzra's expression darkened as he glanced up.

The probe continued, "Even now, I perceive that my observation, though accurate, displeases Master Malzra, amuses the students, and embarrasses you."

Barrin flushed slightly. "True enough." He turned to Malzra. "I could run some magical tests, but even without them, it's clear the intellectual and emotional components of the implant are functioning."

"Only too well," responded Malzra ruefully, to the delight of the watchers in the gallery. "Still, I would be just as glad for further tests of these components to occur outside of my company."

"In other words—?"

"Send out the probe. Let it interact with the students. We can monitor its progress," Malzra instructed.

Barrin looked levelly at the probe. Wisdom and magic danced in the man's brown eyes. "You heard what he said. Go out. Explore. Meet some people. Make some friends. We will recall you when we are ready for more experimentation."

The silver man acknowledged these instructions by moving toward the door. As he shuffled past lathes and drill presses, the probe marveled at the resentment he felt toward his creator. Malzra had referred to him as an "it." Barrin had referred to him as "you."

As if reading his mind, Barrin approached the silver man and patted his shoulder once again. "You were right about Master Malzra's 'social disinclinations,' that he likes machines better than people. What you didn't seem to recognize is that he got flustered in dealing with you."

The silver man's response was sullen. "I recognized that all too clearly."

"Yes," Barrin said, "but that means he doesn't think of you as a machine, not any longer. To him, you are becoming a person."

As the probe and the students filed out of the laboratory, Barrin drew Urza to a wall of sketches. There, in diagrams of lead and ink, the silver man was detailed, inside and out.

"Well, you were right," Baffin said quietly. "Xantcha's heart was the key. Her affective and intellectual cortexes must be intact, as you had thought. We can be thankful that none of her memories remain, or her personality—apparently. Still, I have to wonder about the wisdom of placing what amounts to a Phyrexian matrix into the head of your most powerful and advanced creation. I could have achieved the same effect with an animation spell—"

The master waved off the comment. "I wanted to achieve sentience through purely mechanical means. Besides, there is nothing Phyrexian about the heart crystal anymore. There is not even anything of Xantcha left in it—just enough of a matrix to allow logical, emotional, and social learning."

Barrin winced slightly at the man's choice of words. "Yes, well, that's the other matter. What we've got here is no longer just a machine. You know it, and I know it. So does the probe. You gave him emotions. You need to acknowledge those emotions. You need to *respect* those emotions." Only a blank stare answered him. "Don't you see? This is not just a probe anymore. He is a man—no, more than that—he is a child. He'll need to be guided, nurtured—"

The master looked stern. "I wish you had brought this up before. We could have devised a rubric for handling this aspect of the probe's development."

"That's just it," replied Barrin. "You can't devise rubrics for this kind of thing. You can't chart it out in blueprints. You have to stop thinking like an artificer and start thinking like a—well, like a father."

"I was an orphan at twelve. Mishra and I both. We turned out all right."

The mage snorted just slightly at that. "If you wish, I will act as the probe's mentor in your place, but in time you are going to need to create that bond yourself. And that will mean telling him who you really are—telling him he was created by Urza Planeswalker."

Master Malzra's laboratory had been daunting enough for the silver man and his new intellectual cortex. The corridors and spaces beyond the lab—tutorial rooms, lecture halls, surgical theaters, wind tunnels, test chambers, and countless more laboratories—were overwhelming. In gazing at these elaborate structures, the probe understood at last what a school was: a building designed to aid in gaining new knowledge, communicating it to others, and applying it in invention. This was a revelation. His creators needed to learn. They were not all-knowing angels, driven by logical necessity and an apprehension of the ascendant good. They were ignorant animals, ennobled only by their insatiable curiosity, and some were less ennobled than others.

"I'm Teferi," offered a boy who capered into the silver man's path and stopped stock still, as if daring the half-ton creature to walk over him. "I'm the magical prodigy." He followed the introduction with a snap of his fingers, sending blue sparks bursting through the air.

The probe stopped in his tracks and crouched slightly to get a better look at the young scholar. Teferi's face was small, dark, and impish. Tousled black hair jutted wildly about his gleaming eyes. He wore the manifold white robes of a Tolarian student. At his waist, a leather sash held his personal array of crystals, wands, and fetishes. His feet were bare, in defiance of school policy, though his toenails bore strange legends in bright, glossy paint. He held one of his hands out formally toward the probe.

The silver man extended his own massive hand and lightly shook the boy's whole arm. "I am Master Malzra's Probe." No sooner had he taken the boy's hand than the probe noticed a strange, stinging jolt in his silver hide. "Your handshake is shocking."

The lad pulled his hand away and shrugged, seeming somehow disappointed. "Just a spell I've been working on. Knocks people on their butts. Not golems, I guess. Say, what kind of a name is Master Malzra's Probe, anyway?"

"It is the only name I have," replied the probe truthfully.

Teferi's face rumpled, and he shook his head. "Not good enough. You've got a personality now. You need a real name."

Other young students were gathering in the corridor behind Teferi, and they leaned inward, anticipating something.

"I am unfamiliar with naming procedures."

Teferi gave a confident smile. "Oh, I'm quite familiar. Let's see. You're big and shiny. What else is big and shiny? The Null Moon. Why don't we call you the Null Man?"

The students laughed at this suggestion.

The probe felt a sense of irritation. "That sounds unsatisfactory. Null means nothing. Your suggestion would imply I am a nothing man."

Teferi nodded seriously, though a smirk played about his mouth. "We can't have that. Anyway, you aren't really a man. You're an artifact. Arty would be a nice name for you. Arty the Artifact."

The probe could not determine any reason to reject this suggestion—aside from the chuckles of the students. "Arty is a name used among humans?"

"Oh, yes," replied Teferi enthusiastically, "as a first name, but most humans also have a last name. Let's see, you are silver. What else is made of silver? Spoons are, and since you are large, we ought to name you after the largest spoon—a ladle, or perhaps a shovel. Thus, your full name should be Arty Ladlepate or Arty Shovelhead."

These young folk seemed to giggle at any and every suggestion made to them. The silver man became less concerned about their amusement. "Whichever name sounds more pleasant to human ears—"

"Oh, either name will bring a smile to anyone who hears it. Still, Ladlepate sounds a little too uppity, as if you were putting on airs. Shovelhead is much more accessible. I vote for Arty Shovelhead. What say the rest of you?"

The gathered students cheered excitedly, and the silver man could not help being swept up in the mood. At the moment, any name seemed better than no name.

"I shall then be Arty Shovelhead," the probe said solemnly.

"Come along, then, Shovelhead," said Teferi grandly, gesturing down the corridor with his boyish arm. Streamers of conjured illumination fanned out from his fingers. "I have much to show you."

The crowd of students surged up around the probe and dragged at his cold metal hands with their warm fingers. He plodded along among them, careful not to step on their feet.

The entourage of children led the probe along as though he were a visiting dignitary. They arrived first at a large dining hall with ivory rafters and soaring walls of alabaster. Beneath this white vault were long, dark tables crowded with more students who bent above bowls of gruel and platters of hard crackers and cheese.

"This is the great hall," narrated Teferi. "This is where we students eat. The food is specially prepared so that nothing about it could distract us from our studies. Notice the bland colors and mean consistency of it all? The flavors are even more indistinguishable. No one could gnaw on one of those crackers and spend even a moment to contemplate its nonexistent virtues."

The probe could tell that this boy had an acute grasp of the truth behind appearances. "Master Malzra must care greatly about your studies."

Teferi laughed, though the sound was rueful. "Oh, yes. He nurtures our minds like a farmer nurtures grain. He heaps manure on our heads, knowing we will rise up through it, despite it, to bear richly, and then he comes along—with a scythe and cuts our heads off to nourish his own appetites. It is a fine arrangement, depending on who you are." He had said this last bit while leading the probe and his companions down the passageway to another chamber, similar to the first, except that the vault overhead was dark, and the students at the long tables were crouched over sheets of paper, quill pens scraping fitfully across them. "Here is part of that diet of manure I spoke of. These students are copying plans and treatises of Master Malzra, Mage Barrin, and other scholars. It is in sedulously copying the scribbles of our betters that we become consummate scribblers ourselves."

The probe was appreciative. "What do these plans and treatises describe?"

"Machines, such as yourself. Gadgets, mainly. He's got a whole mausoleum—um, that is, museum—filled with artifact creatures. You'll be there too, soon enough. Master Malzra has a very active imagination and puts it to great use devising elaborate means to save himself a little bit of labor. He has created numerous devices to more quickly and efficiently cook the gruel and crackers, to more effectively limit the freedom of those under his command, to more completely defend all of us against external foes so that he alone can torment us."

The silver man felt uncomfortable with this new line of thought. "External foes? What foes does Malzra have?"

"Oh, everyone is against him, or didn't you know?" said Teferi lightly as they moved farther down the hallway. He idly conjured a small knife, whirled it deftly between his fingers, and then dispelled it. "At least that's what Malzra thinks. He's got clockwork creatures and actual warriors roaming the walls around the academy at all hours, and clay men tramping through the woods by the sea, and gear-work birds that spy on the island. I myself have never heard of a single real enemy, but Malzra spends so much time creating these machines and recreating them and perfecting them, there must be something more than psychotic paranoia at the root of it, wouldn't you think?"

"I suppose so," the silver man answered.

They came to another room, this one filled with dissected hulks of metal, leaning clockwork warriors, dismantled machines, piles of rusted scrap iron, and at the far wall, a great open furnace. Workers on one side of the blazing forge shoveled coal into the flames and pumped massive bellows. Workers on the other side dumped bins of spare parts into great vats of molten metal. Throughout the rest of the grimy chamber, students moved among the ruined machines like vultures picking at a battlefield of dead. A shiver of dread moved through the probe.

Teferi noticed the impulse and smiled grimly. "See, Arty, even if Malzra has no other enemies, his old creations could easily turn on him. They should. They certainly have reason to hate him. Malzra quickly tires of his playthings. I can imagine a legion of metal men such as yourself learning that Malzra planned to melt them down. They could escape across the sea. I can imagine whole nations of clockwork creatures who have fled their creator only to muster themselves in hopes of returning and killing him."

The silver man was aghast. "How could an artifact creature ever seek to destroy the artifact creator?"

"Give it a year, Arty," Teferi said lightly, though none of the students laughed this time. The boy patted the golem's arm. "Give it a year—two at the outside, and you'll be facing that fiery furnace. It's the way of artifice. When you're in pieces in that room, then ask yourself what you think about Master Malzra."

Jhoira was again in her rocky haven from the world. She spent less and less time in the academy and more and more time here, dreaming of far-off places and futures—

A white flapping motion caught her eye. There along the shore, between two fingers of stone, something was moving. It looked like a seagull's wing, only too large. A pelican? A white sea lion? Jhoira blinked, rubbing her eyes. The sea and sky were dazzling here. Maybe it was only a glaring bit of foam.

No, it was more than that. It looked like fabric—perhaps another student? Jhoira slid from the sandstone ledge and eased herself down the tumbled hillside. One edge of the white fabric was tied to something rigid—a spar. It was a sail. Jhoira descended more quickly. Her sandal soles slid on pea-gravel and sand. She thrashed past a brake of grass and clambered down the cleft between two wind-carved stones.

The space gave out onto a wide beach of beige sand, broken by rills of craggy black stone. Above one such rill, a lateen-rigged sail jutted flaglike from a shattered wooden hull. The impact had staved the boat's prow and splintered the timbers amidships. Since then, the rocks had chewed away at the frame, each new wave grinding the hull again on the ragged stones.

Jhoira approached cautiously. So few ships arrived at Tolaria. Most were the academy's own supply vessels, captained by seamen hand-picked by Master Malzra. The island was too remote, too removed from trade routes to attract other ships. This boat must have drifted for some distance off course before crashing. Perhaps it was abandoned. Perhaps its crew had been washed overboard. Jhoira craned her neck as she neared, looking for signs of life in the ruined hulk. Her sandal prints filled with salty water behind her. She reached the stony outcrop and climbed up above the pitching wreck.

It was a small craft, the sort that might have been manned by a crew of five or a crew of one. The deck was in disarray—lines lashing loosely, small barrels rolling with each sea surge. The hatch was open, and in the dark hold Jhoira glimpsed gulls fighting over bits of hard-tack that had spilled from broken crates. The mainmast was cracked, though it still held aloft the raked sail, and the mainsail's sheet was cleated off, as if the boat had been at full sail when it struck the stone. It must have run aground last night, when the Glimmer Moon had been obscured by a midnight storm. The bow was gone entirely, but the stern remained. A narrow set of stairs led downward to a small doorway. The captain's quarters would lie beyond.

"What are you doing?" Jhoira asked herself worriedly as she clambered down the boulder where the ship was impaled, lifted one leg over the starboard rail, and hauled herself onto the pitching deck. "This thing could come loose any moment and roll over and drag me out to sea."

Even so, she crawled forward, reached the set of stairs that led down to the captain's quarters, and descended. She pulled open the red door and cringed back from the hot, stale air within. The space was dark and cramped. With each wave surge, the floor clattered with junk—a map tube, a lodestone, a stylus, a wrecked lantern, spanners, a slide rule, and other indistinguishable items. To one side of the cabin, a small table hugged the wall. To the other was a pair of bunks. The bottom bed held a still figure.

Dead, Jhoira thought. The man lay motionless, despite the tossing sea. His face was tanned beneath curls of golden hair. His jaw was shaggy with a week's growth of beard. His hands, large and strong, were laid across his chest in the attitude of death. Jhoira backed away. Perhaps this was a plague ship, this man the last to succumb, with no one to throw him overboard. She'd been a fool to climb aboard.

Then he moved. He breathed, and she knew, even if he was plagued, she could not abandon him. Without another moment's hesitation, Jhoira crossed the crowded cabin, stooped beside the bunk, and lifted the man. She had always been strong. The Ghitu of Shiv had to be strong. Shifting the man to her shoulder, she struggled out of the cabin and up the stairs. Navigating the rubble-strewn deck with a man on her shoulder was difficult, and Jhoira stumbled twice. Gritting her teeth in determination, she made the rail. With a heart-rending leap, she reached the rock and clung there.

As if shifted by her jump, the broken craft heeled away from the crag. A wave crashed into it, lifting it up, and with a briny surge, the boat scraped up toward Jhoira and her charge. She clambered to a higher spot on the rock. The wave tumbled back from shore, taking the hulk with it. The mast rolled under and snapped like a twig. Shroudlike, the sail wrapped the splintered boat as it heaved outward on the retreating wave. Broken barrels and other debris boiled in the wake of the boat.

Panting, Jhoira watched the broken mass of wreckage bob out into deeper water. The next wave rolled it once more, and then the ship disappeared. For some time she could see it, moving in the undertow like some white leviathan.

Jhoira waited for a break in the waves and climbed down from the stone. She crossed the sandy berm, tempted to set the man down there. A darting glance up at the hilltop told her that no other students or scholars had seen the shipwreck or knew of the man, but others might come soon. The man would be as good as dead. Malzra did not suffer the arrival of strangers on his island paradise, and the students were sworn to report any such castaways they discovered. Jhoira planned to report this one, of course, but she didn't want anyone else to know about him—not yet.

Strong though she was, the climb from the shore to her hideaway was a hot labor. When she arrived, she laid the man down on the sunny stretch of sandstone where she had spent so many afternoons. She checked for breath and pulse, found both, and set a hand on his brow to check for fever. He felt warm, though that might have been only from the sunlight. There was a better test for fever. Her heart pounding, she leaned over and kissed his forehead.

"Hot. Yes. Very hot," Jhoira said breathlessly.

She removed her outer cloak, snagged a bit of scrub, and propped the fabric up over his face, shielding him from the sun. She retrieved a small canteen from her belt, parted the man's lips, and poured a cool trickle of water into his mouth.

He was beautiful—tan, strong, tall, and mysterious. That was the most important thing of all. The last drops fell from the canteen.

"You stay here," she whispered, patting his shoulder. "Don't let anybody see you. I'll go get more water and blankets—supplies. I'll take care of you. Stay here."

Heart fluttering in her breast like a caged bird, Jhoira hurried away from her secret spot and her secret stranger.

Her footsteps had hardly faded beyond the rocky rise when the stranger's blue eyes opened. There was a gleam in them, something vaguely metallic.

It might have been only the silver shimmer of clouds reflecting there, but there might have been something else to that gleam, something mechanical, something menacing.

Monologue

At last, Urza has done it, making a machine that really lives. He's been working for three thousand years to devise such a thing. Now that he has one, he doesn't know what to do with him.

The silver man is engineered to let Urza return in time, even farther back than those three thousand years, to the time of the ancient Thran. Urza hopes the probe can reach the time of that ancient race, some six millennia in the past. If Urza himself could reach such a time, he could prevent the Thran from transforming into the race of half-flesh, half-machine abominations that seek to destroy life on Dominaria, thereby rectifying the error he and his brother Mishra made in opening the doors to Phyrexia.

I've pointed out that unmaking the Phyrexians is tantamount to slaying all of us who have lived in this world since their creation. Still, Urza would rather wipe the slate clean than deal with his past—just as he did at Argoth.

The disturbing thing is, he is making all the same mistakes over again. If he could only have embraced his brother instead of attacking him—if he could only have apologized for his arrogance and obsession and been reconciled—the Brothers' War would never have been fought, the brotherhood of Gix would never have gotten a foothold in the world, and Argoth and most of Terisiare would not have been destroyed. If he had worked with his brother instead of against him, combining their genius and the power of both halves of the stone they had discovered, the pathway from Phyrexia might have been cut off the very day it was accidentally opened.

Reconciliation is not in the man any more than regret or remorse or friendship. Every sin of omission Urza committed against his brother, he repeats now against his own students . . . and his newborn silver man.

—Barrin, Mage Master of Tolaria

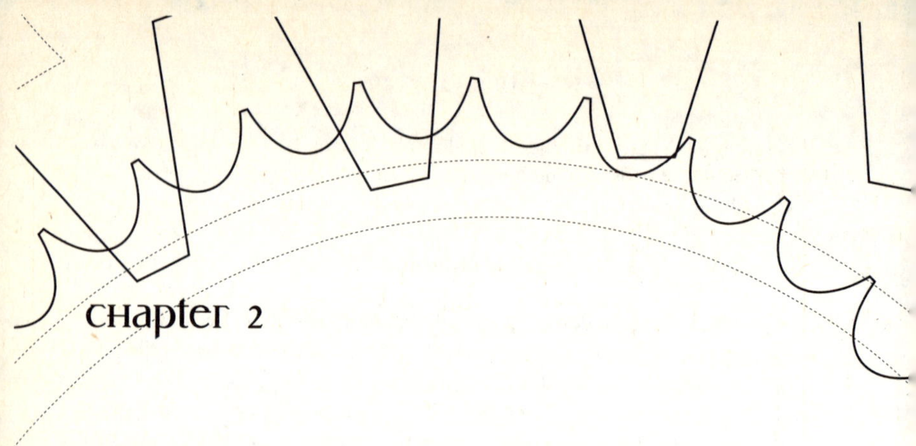

chapter 2

The students were gone from the laboratory. Only Master Malzra, his trusted associate Barrin, and the silver man remained among the dark implements and ubiquitous sketches.

"You've learned much in your first day," said Barrin gently. "We have been observing, remotely. You have interacted well."

"I have a friend," the silver man volunteered.

A creased smile played across Barrin's face. "Yes. Teferi, my prodigal prodigy—we know about that."

"He told me many things," the probe continued. His voice was edged with suspicion. He explained the academy to me. He has named me Arty Shovelhead."

The mage sighed in irritation. "Teferi is a brilliant young mage—my most promising student—but he likes to stir up trouble. He makes things twice as hard for himself, and three times as hard for everyone else—"

"Teferi is a good first friend," interrupted Malzra with uncharacteristic alacrity. He glanced between the silver man and the man of flesh, then seemed to withdraw behind his glimmering eyes. "After all, Barrin, you said the probe has emotions—needs friends."

"Yes," the mage said, diverting the conversation at its awkward turn. "Master Malzra is eager for you to begin the experiments you were created to carry out. That's why we called you back this evening."

Barrin moved to one wall, opened a small hatch, and drew forth a long pole three times his height. At the tip of the pole was a small hook. Barrin hoisted the hook to the ceiling, engaged it in a hidden slot, and pulled downward once. A large panel in the dome shifted and then slowly separated from the smooth curve. On hydraulic rods, the panel eased downward from the dome. A large, complex machine of glass cylinders, metal casings, and snaking tubes emerged. Lamplight glowed from the descending apparatus, ten times more massive than the silver man himself.

"This is a time field distortion device," Master Malzra explained. "It is powered by four separate sources of energy—thermal, mechanical, geomagnetic, and of course, Thran. The thermal component provides a molecular time clock, an exact measure of the temporal vector, calibrated in atomic vibration per second. The mechanical component rotates the unit about its axis, thus creating beneath the device a cone of radiation within which the temporal distortion will manifest. The geomagnetic component provides precise coordinates of longitude, latitude, and altitude for the origin and destination points. Thran powerstones, of course, provide the main drive of the machine."

The silver man wondered aloud, "What is this . . . machine?"

"A time machine," Barrin explained. "Actually, it provides travel through time and space both. Tonight we plan to test only the temporal components."

"You wish me to operate this machine?" the probe guessed.

"We wish you to travel in it," Master Malzra replied. "The current design plays havoc with biological creatures. Any organism with a heartbeat, respiration, a sequential digestive tract, and a network of neural pathways that rely on chemical reactions is ill-adapted to time-field distortions."

"They die," Barrin explained. "Metals are much less susceptible to temporal stresses. Silver, of all metals, showed the least resistance. That is why you are made of silver. That is why you were made—to travel through the portal and report back what you have discovered."

The silver man approached the dangling device. His eyes traced out a circle on the floor beneath the massive machine. "Teferi told me about this. Every machine is made for a specific purpose. Every machine is made to defend you and the academy against . . . external foes."

Master Malzra's eyebrows rose. "Teferi knows that much?"

"Everyone seems to," the silver man said.

"Well, then—yes," the artificer said. "This is part of that defense. You must not divulge the information we are relating to you—"

"Of course not—"

"We intend, in time, to send you or another probe or perhaps eventually a person back to the time of the Thran, to divert them from the path that led to these—external foes."

"Send me or another probe . . ." echoed the silver man, thinking of the fiery furnace, heaps of scrap metal, and workers with shovels.

"This is all utterly secret, of course," Malzra said.

"Yes," replied the silver man.

"Tonight's regression will be nothing so grand," assured Barrin, apparently sensing the probe's hesitancy. "If things go well, you will return in time perhaps as far back as this morning."

"What must I do?" the probe asked.

"You must stand here, within the circle," said Master Malzra. "That is all. You will stand and wait while the machine does its work. When the time regression slows, you must step from the circle to arrive in the former time. You will remain somewhat out of phase in the former time—you will be able to see your surroundings, but no one will be able to see you. This is to protect the time continuity. As the particles of your being gradually align themselves with your surroundings, this out-of-phase effect will lessen, and you will become visible. Whether in phase or out, you will be able to affect your environment, but we ask that you make no significant alterations, again for sake of temporal integrity. We will control your return trip from this end. When you are drawn back to the present, you will make a report of what you have discovered. Do you understand?"

"I understand," the silver man said flatly. "It is my purpose. It is why I was made."

Barrin eyed the silver golem narrowly and shook his head. He turned to Malzra and spoke quietly in his ear. "I don't like it. He's been traumatized by Teferi."

Malzra laughed quietly. "*You* are traumatized by Teferi."

"His emotional cortex is too new."

"He exhibits the correct emotional response to Teferi."

"I tell you, I don't like it."

"He understands. He knows this is the reason he was made."

"What if he meddles in the time stream?"

"Then we'll draw him back through, and we'll know he isn't sufficient to the task."

The silver man stood silent while the men spoke, his acute senses picking up every word.

"I understand you are eager, Malzra, but we have time. If our experiments work, we'll have all the time in the world. Testing a living creature is not like testing a machine. You can't just dismantle a creature, insert new parts, and start him up again—"

"On the contrary, that's what we did just this morning," Malzra finished, turning away from his associate. With a curt gesture, he said to the silver man, "Into the circle then. The power-up phase will take us a few moments."

Wordless, the probe stepped into the circle and stood. He could feel the silent, magnificent weight of the time machine hanging above his head. From the precise center of the floor, he watched Malzra and Barrin.

Barrin used the same hooked pole to trigger a hidden panel in the floor. A trefoil section of stone shifted aside, and an array of consoles rose into the room. Copper coils and pulsing tubes spilled from beneath the control panels. Barrin checked the various conduits where they connected with the floor. Malzra meanwhile worked adjustments to levers and switches.

Fluids began to move through the tubes. A low hum started among the great glass cylinders. Brass fittings buzzed. Even the dome itself rumbled with the mounting sound.

A high-pitched whine rose to echo through the lab, and a thin red beam stabbed from the base of the machine. It lanced through the charged air, just past the silver man's shoulder, and neatly struck the circle scribed on the floor. The ray fluttered a moment before sweeping in an arc. It looped the golem once and sped in its course. In moments, the single spinning beam had widened into a crimson cone that enveloped him.

The silver man stood there, bathed in lurid light, watching his creators. The men were busy at their consoles, drawing up one energy source and leveling off another, directing the beam in its spiraling crescendo, configuring the coordinates of space and time. . . . Light intensified. The artificers' endeavors slowed. The whining hum reached a peak. Master Malzra and Barrin soon moved not at all, frozen in space . . . or time.

The probe understood. The roaring machine and its whirring cone of light had teased the cord of time down to a frayed nub, and then to nothing. With rising fury, the device plucked at the packed skein of past moments. They too began to unravel. No longer motionless, Master Malzra and Barrin moved backward, undoing all they had done. Their arms darted with strange jabs like scorpion tails. More than that, the silver man also moved, or his past self moved. It trudged backward out of the circle just as he had trudged forward into it, only minutes before.

Within the cone of regression, the present-time silver man watched in amazement. His doppelganger conferred with Malzra and Barrin. Their words were lost to the hum of the machine, but the sense of them was clear—reversed syllables that did not inform or enlighten but rather disinformed and obscured. All the while they spoke, the ghost golem knew less and less, and the ghost time machine retracted into the dome above. When the brief conference was done, the past-time golem staggered backward toward the door, ignorant of the hidden machine and all that had been said.

The regression accelerated. Barrin and Malzra scuttled backward about the room, dismantling things, forgetting conversations, reducing conclusions to hypotheses, surrendering step by step the whole march of time. Soon they moved too quickly to seem anything but man-shaped blurs, then were gone entirely. The lab was dark and empty for some time, except the occasional jag of a mouse backing fitfully across the floor.

Eventually the two scholars returned, drawing after them a backwash of assistants and tutors. The galleries above flooded with eager, watchful eyes. The past-time golem trudged backward into the midst of it all. His return was heralded by nodding heads and hands coming sharply away from each other, drawing a brittle ovation from the air. The artificers themselves formed a retreating pocket of space into which the golem walked. He reached a designated spot and settled into immense inertia. There was another time of questions.

Malzra, with a suddenness that seemed almost savage, reached toward the probe's neck, performed some quick manipulation, and shoved the creature's head back on its shoulders. In a moment more, he lifted the metal skull-piece cleanly away.

Within the time machine, the silver man stared, stunned to see his own being so quickly and easily dismantled. The body yet stood, though the casing of the head lay now, as if discarded, on a side table. The inner workings of the golem's head were laid bare. Cogs and cables gleamed beneath a low set of struts. Light leaked through the whole mass. Malzra was busy tugging at a central silver case, the movements of his fingers awakening twitches in the creature's vivisected frame. Another two jiggles and Malzra drew forth the case. He opened it. Inside lay a dark stone the size of a child's fist. He removed the crystal. All final signs of life fled the creature.

The silver man watched in amazed dread as Malzra held high the stone. Gulping backward laughter came from the gallery. Malzra shouted something that ended the jollity and retreated to a table where he positioned the stone in a metal case.

The students in the gallery began to move. Malzra and Barrin busied themselves setting tools into cases and rubbing smears of oil from rags onto their hands. As the room slowly emptied, the dissected golem merely stood, lifeless and headless in the midst of it all.

The regression slowed. The time-traveling silver man's hulk smoldered—heat from temporal stress. He stepped from the coruscating beam. Around him time resumed its forward march. The students headed back into the gallery. The scholars unpacked their tools and wiped their hands clean.

Out of phase and unnoticed by them all, the silver man approached his headless predecessor. He stared into the vacant silver case jutting from the golem's neck. He reached up to his own neck, wondering where the catch was that would allow his skull-piece to be lifted away. His mind, his emotion, his very essence could be hauled up like a hunk of coal and displayed. He was a mere amusement for children. They had called him friend, but in truth he was only Shovelhead. Without that dark stone, he was not even that. The silver man stared into the undeniable image of his own death.

The regression was done. He was suddenly yanked from the time stream and back again, bathed in that rapacious red glow. Master Malzra summoned him to the present.

The silver man arrived. The beam skittered and danced away, withdrawing into the machine overhead. It too withdrew, trailing gray tendrils of smoke from the temporal stress it had endured.

Barrin and Malzra stood, blinking, at their consoles. Tentative, the two scholars released the controls beneath their fingers and approached the probe.

Barrin spoke first. "Are you well—?"

"Are you capable of rendering a report?" Malzra interrupted.

"My frame is quite hot," the silver man responded, "but I am capable, yes."

"How far back did you go?" Malzra asked.

"Back to this morning, to the time of my awakening."

"Excellent," Malzra said as Barrin noted the response on a sheet of paper. "And did you touch or move anything in that time?"

"I touched only the floor, with my feet, and moved only myself."

"Were you approached by anyone, or was there any other indication that your presence was noted?"

"No."

"What did you observe?"

This answer would not come as readily as the others.

"I observed myself dismantled. I observed the core of my being removed. I observed the small, dark, fragile thing that is my mind and self and soul."

Monologue

The first day of life is always the hardest, to be dragged from whatever warm, safe womb in which one is conceived and then thrust into the cold glare of the world. There is much to adjust to—breathing air instead of liquid, for one; being naked and prodded and scrubbed, for another. Worst of all, there is that moment when the cord is cut, and one is suddenly and irrevocably alone.

It is in recognition of such traumas that mothers' arms are made.

You have no mother. You have no father, either. You have a pair of creators, but that is not the same. Neither of us knows how to comfort and protect you. If you need too much nurturing, we may even consider you defective. Perhaps it is because you were designed to be a tool, a weapon—not a person. Perhaps it is because we have not expected to have to save you. We were hoping you would save us.

—Barrin, Mage Master of Tolaria

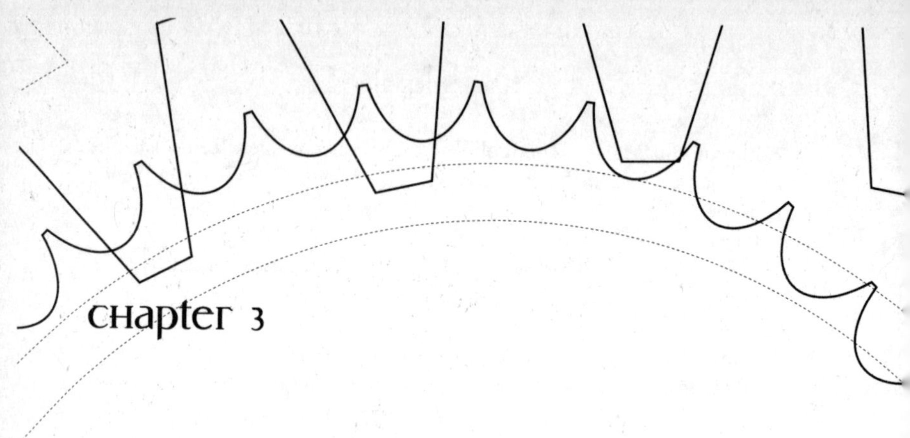

Chapter 3

It had been nearly a month since Jhoira had observed the lab session in which the silver man awoke. She could remember each detail of Master Malzra's technique. She'd spent the intervening time studying powerstones, like the one placed in the golem's head, and poring over the artifact's design sketches. All of it was preparation for the design debrief she would be required to give. It was the price paid by all the elite students invited to observe the procedure. There remained only one more task before she was ready to write her report—actually interviewing the machine.

She sighed with dread and tapped her fingers idly on the plans. She had hoped to derive a satisfactory description of the golem's intellectual and emotional performance from these plans, her research on Thran powerstones, and first-hand observation of the refit. None of these things explained its—his—apparent logical and affective capacities though. She would have to interview him.

Jhoira glanced in surrender at the ceiling of her dormitory cell. Interviewing the machine meant winning past his self-appointed wrangler, Teferi. The boy—and at fourteen, he was *only* a boy—was one part prodigy, one part prankster, and one part pervert. Unfortunately all three parts were madly infatuated with Jhoira. She had done her best to discourage his advances, but he didn't notice subtle rebukes, and he considered unsubtle ones only affectionate horseplay. If she told him she wasn't interested, he would pledge to make her interested. If she said she hated him, he would respond that hate and love were only a hair's breadth apart—and speaking of hair's breadths, could he have a breadth of hers? She had the inkling that he had made several attempts to devise a magical love potion to win her over.

Just thinking about the young man—the *boy*, he was only a boy—exasperated Jhoira. She stood up from her desk and paced the small, spare room she occupied in the academy. If only Teferi could glimpse a real man, could glimpse the man she had found at the seaside and had provisioned and kept secret in her stony hideaway . . . No. Nobody could know about Kerrick except for her. That's the way it was and the way it should be. Jhoira sat down on her cot and stared out the window of her cell. Beyond the pitching treetops and the tumbled boulders lay the shore and her secret love.

She shook her head to clear it. The sooner she interviewed the silver man, the sooner she could finish her report, and the sooner she could rejoin Kerrick. Snatching up a sheaf of paper and a lead nib, Jhoira made her way through the door and out into the academy to hunt down the silver man.

She found him in the great hall, crouching to sit on a stump that had been hauled in specifically for him after he had broken three of the academy's benches. He looked dejected, hunkered down at the end of a table. Teferi held court beside him, and a passel of the prodigy's devotees clustered in a laughing bunch around. Carrots were on the menu today, and Teferi had discovered that by levitating them into various holes in the golem's skull, he could create comical ears and a long twisted nose. To these alterations came others—oily lettuce in an improvised head of hair, and large, bulging eyes made of hard biscuits rammed into the machine's eye sockets.

Jhoira shook her head as she approached. If reports were right, this machine was fully aware. He knew what was being done to him, and he cared.

"Does Master Malzra know what you are doing, Teferi?"

The boy looked up, his impish features lighting up when he caught sight of her. "Hello, Jhoira! Have you met Arty Shovelhead?"

"Does Master Malzra know what you are doing?" she repeated angrily.

The fourteen-year-old affected a smug superiority. He nodded toward the mirrored loft where Malzra and Barrin often took their lunch. "Master Malzra is keenly interested in all of my adventures. I'm Barrin's magical prodigy. Of course they know what I am doing."

"This artifact creature is self-aware, Teferi. He thinks. He has feelings. You can't just toy with him like this."

"I can, and I do," replied Teferi. He levitated a pair of radishes to make them hover like earrings on either side of the golem's head. "What fun is it to toy with someone who doesn't have thoughts and feelings?"

Exasperated, Jhoira flung out her hands. "Anyway, I need to interview him."

Teferi smiled. "Go right ahead. I'm his interpreter—right, Shovelhead?"

Behind his mask of biscuits and carrots, the silver man remained silent.

Reaching out distastefully, Jhoira drew a dripping leaf of lettuce from the creature's head, slug-trails of salad oil glistening across his shiny brow. "Did you ever think you might be damaging him, might be destroying him? This is sensitive machinery."

"Master Malzra wants it tested," Teferi replied glibly. He laced his fingers behind his head and leaned back on the bench. "I'm just giving it a rigorous exam. If you're jealous, I could arrange a rigorous exam for you, back in my cell." His friends chorused a thrilled *oooh* at the suggestion.

Jhoira flushed. "I'm not interested in little boys—" she countered, savagely knocking the biscuits from the silver man's face. The golem sent her a look of lost misery. "—not interested in tiny, mean, little boys who cut the eyes out of sparrows and stomp roses into the ground and empty their bladders on anything beautiful and good. That's what you are, Teferi—you're not even a nasty little boy, but an infant who can't control his own body, can't recognize anybody else as real, can't do anything but whine and cry and soil yourself and everybody around you. You're going to have to do lots of growing up before you'll be anything more than a squalling baby." Jhoira punctuated this tirade by yanking forth the variously placed carrots. Teferi was silent. His face grew pale, as though the flush of Jhoira's features sucked the color out of his. By the time she was finished, his lip was quivering. His eyes were as wide and staring as the biscuits on the floor.

Jhoira reached down, gently, regally, and took the silver man's hand. "Let's go. I have a lot of questions to ask you."

The probe rose, as though his half-ton bulk could have been lifted by her one slender hand. Looking back over his shoulder, the silver man followed Jhoira, dejection and confusion in his bowed shoulders.

Barrin was nettled. He let go of the rail that overlooked the great room and paced in front of it. Through a one-way glass enchanted by the mage himself, they had both witnessed the incident with the carrots and biscuits—and hundreds of other pranks Teferi had played on the hapless golem. These occasions seemed only to mildly amuse Urza. They made Barrin furious.

"I can't understand why you allow it!" he stormed. "Here is the first truly living artifact creature you have created, and yet you surrender him to the depredations of that . . . that vulture!"

"Living things have to live, Barrin," Urza said calmly. "If Teferi breaks down the probe, we'll know it needs to be redesigned."

"Breaks down? Redesigned?" Barrin raged. "That's not what you do with living things. They have to live—as you said. This golem of yours is only a month old. Give him time—"

"Time is all I give him. We'll attempt another regression at the end of this month," Urza said, heading toward the chamber door.

"Meanwhile," said Barrin grimly, "I'm going to ask Jhoira to look after him, to keep him away from Teferi. I really don't understand why you refuse to let me expel that troublemaker."

Urza turned back in the open doorway. "I keep him here because he is a magical genius—driven and destined to greatness. He may be a social nuisance, yes, but I was one, too."

"You still are," Barrin observed tartly, "but Teferi's more than a nuisance. Jhoira said it best. He's selfish. He's dangerous. He hurts people without thought or apology. He takes no responsibility for his actions. I don't care about his potential. Until he grows up, he will leave a path of destruction in his wake."

"You have said the same of me before." Urza blinked, considering. "Yes, I keep Teferi here because he reminds me of me."

Jhoira ushered the silver man into her room. He had to turn sideways to fit through the arched doorway, and once within, merely stood there, as stiff and fearful as an adolescent boy.

"It's all right. I'm not going to bite," Jhoira assured him. She gestured the golem in so that she could swing the door closed behind him.

The click of the latch made the room feel even smaller. Despite his stooped shoulders and silent demeanor, the probe seemed especially massive in that moment.

Jhoira skirted around him and busied herself tidying the room. "It's not much, I know, but it's all I need and private." She snatched up a conspicuous undergarment and secreted it within a basket in one corner. "Here's my bed," she continued, nervously straightening the slate-gray blanket on it and fluffing the pillow, as though she expected the silver man to lie down on it. "Here's where I keep my clothes—the student robes hanging in that bone-inlaid wardrobe there, and my knockabout clothes here in this drawer. That's one drawback to being made of skin. You've got to cover it all the time."

That felt forced. Jhoira reminded herself this was a man of metal, no more interested in her undergarments than a doorknob would be.

"Here. Here's something you'll like." She reached up to a low shelf above her drafting desk and drew down a small metal pendant. It was fashioned to resemble a lizard-man dressed in heavy robes. "This is from my homeland, Shiv. It's metal—not just metal, but Viashino metal. That's some of the hardest stuff in the world." Unthinking, she tossed the trinket to the golem.

One massive hand snatched the item from the air—the first movement the golem had made since settling into stillness. He stared down at it. "It is hard," he agreed in a voice like the distant rumble of a waterfall. "It scratched me."

Jhoira's brow furrowed. She crossed the floor to look. Two small scratches marked the silver man's palm. "Oh, no. I'm sorry. Let me get something for—" She broke into laughter, backed up, and slumped onto the bed.

The silver man leaned forward. "What is it? Did I say something stupid?"

"No, no," Jhoira assured. "I did. It's me. If one of my other friends had gotten scratched, I'd have pressed a rag on it to stop the bleeding, but you can't bleed. Still, I was going to get a rag."

"One of your *other* friends—?" the golem echoed.

"Oh, I'm just nervous. I don't know why." She sat up soberly on the bed. "I don't really have a lot of friends. I don't usually let anybody else in here, and I know you're just a machine, but you seem so real, so much like a person."

"So much like a person—"

She shook her head and fetched a rag from among her drafting supplies. "Still, you could use one of these. I've been going on and on, and there you stand, vinegar dripping from your head." Flipping the rag in one hand, she walked to the golem and began wiping away the liquid. "You know, in my tribe back home in Shiv, they put oil on somebody's head to honor him. It's called anointing. Ghitu do it when you are born, and when you set out on a vision quest, and when you need healing, and when you've just been saved from death." She patiently daubed away the streams of liquid and polished the creature's shiny pate.

"Maybe that's what happened to me," said the silver man. "Maybe I've just been anointed."

"You're lucky it was just oil and vinegar. Knowing Teferi, it could have been something much worse."

"It wasn't Teferi who anointed me," the silver man rumbled. "It wasn't Teferi who saw that I needed healing."

Jhoira smiled sadly, wiping the last of the oil away. She gestured at the pendant. "You can keep it. They're supposed to be lucky. They're good to have with you on a vision quest." She wiped her hands on another cloth and tossed both into the basket in the corner. "Anyway, I'm doing a treatise on you, and I have some questions—if you don't mind?"

The silver man said solemnly, "You are the first person to ask whether I minded anything."

Jhoira nodded distractedly. She drew a large folio of sketches from beneath her drafting table and selected a number of rattling sheets from it. She spread them out on the workspace.

"These are drawings of me," observed the golem.

"Yes. This is the final set of plans for you before the powerstone was implanted—front, back, left, right, top, and bottom views. There's a detail of your torso. You've got lots of room in there. And here's your head," she said as she pointed to each matrix of gray lines and gear-work.

"This legend names me only 'PROBE 1,' "the golem indicated.

"Yes," responded Jhoira. "Master Malzra is not very imaginative when it comes to names. Still, it's a better name than Arty Shovelhead."

One of the golem's massive fingers traced out a bracket that indicated the whole frame of the construct. Beside it was a callout that said simply, "KARN."

"I like this name better. What does it mean?"

Jhoira looked up from the sketch. Her eyes narrowed intently as she studied the golem's gleaming features. "That's Old Thran. I don't know much of the language—even Master Malzra doesn't know much of it—but I know that word. It means 'mighty.' "

"Karn," the golem repeated thoughtfully.

Jhoira smiled again. "Yes. That's a good name. That's your name.

Karn." She turned back to the table. "Now these sketches on this side show the powerstone and its integration into the superstructure. The point of my treatise is to explain how an automaton becomes a thinking, feeling creature, simply through the addition of a crystal. I haven't been able to figure it out by looking at these diagrams, even by watching the operation. I can't imagine how a powerstone—especially one that looked dead, like the one inside you—could give a creature thought and life and soul."

"Perhaps it isn't a powerstone," offered Karn quietly.

"Not a powerstone?" Jhoira wondered. "Then what would it be?"

"I don't know, but without it, I am nothing," Karn observed. "I've seen myself without it. I'm just a pile of metal."

"Seen yourself?" Jhoira asked. She turned toward the silver man and took his hand conspiratorially. "Karn, just what is it they have you do in there? I know Master Malzra has been running secret experiments with you at the center of them. He's been building some kind of big machine—I've worked on parts of it—but none of us can guess what it does. And there's been something strange about the school since you arrived, something about the air. It feels like waves moving through a tidal pool or something. Do these experiments have anything to do with that?"

An insistent knock came at the door.

Jhoira's face hardened. "It's Teferi, the little rat." Then, to the door, "Just a moment."

The knock came again. "It's Mage Barrin. I've come for the probe. And I have a request to make of you, Jhoira."

Jhoira hurried to the door, opened it, and bowed slightly. "We were just in the middle of an interview, but we can talk later. Would you mind, Karn?"

"Not at all," replied the silver man, "I would like that." He turned sideways to slide out the arched doorway.

Barrin backed up to make room. "Karn?"

"Yes," responded Jhoira. "That's his name. What was your request?'

Night drew down around Tolaria. The dying sun burnished rooftops of blue tile, giving them a bronze patina. The Glimmer Moon peered palely over the treetops. Hot, dense breaks of jungle chittered with the final choruses of day birds, and night birds raised their first ululating songs. White waves along the shore glowed golden over burgundy seas. Throughout the afternoon, a hot, still column of air had stood upon the isle, but now, before evening breezes, it shifted and uncoiled until trees and students and all shivered in relief.

Jhoira was among them. She crouched in the shadowy lee of the academy's eastern wall, breathing slowly. The culvert where she lurked had been designed as runoff for garderobes, but the building it served became a lab instead of a dorm. A series of grates fastened into the passage and a main sluice gate were meant to secure the passage against invaders. Jhoira first noticed the unused duct in plans of the buildings; she had quite an eye for details on a page. The prospect of having her own entrance and exit to the academy had been enticing. It would allow her to skirt strict curfews. She didn't actually remove the bolts until she had devised replacements that would hold the passage secure to all but her. She was not selfish enough to jeopardize the security of the whole school for the sake of her own private amusements.

Private amusements. She smiled. Kerrick would have been flattered by the title. Their liaison had lasted for two months—surely more than a passing amusement.

Before she reached him, Jhoira had to slip past the guards, both human and clockwork. They would be more vigilant now in the shifting air than they had been in the hot, still afternoon. She dared not open the grate until she heard her friend above. . . .

"There it is again!" one of the men shouted overhead. "Look out!"

"Damned bird!" cursed another.

"Bird, my eye," a third yelled. "They make them in there. They're wind up toys."

She heard her shrieking toy bird dive and harry the men on the wall. It was a simple construction, weighing the equal of two pieces of paper, but it was fast and shrill. She'd discovered the plans in some ancient designs by none other than Tawnos, legendary assistant to legendary Urza. It didn't matter who actually designed the feathery flying machines. It mattered only that she could make them easily and—

"Arghh! It's in my hair!"

"Bash it with a glaive!"

"No! It's in my *hair*, damn it!"

"Hold still!"

"They banned the things. They circulated a memo! That's what they said! Let them guard up here and get these damned things stuck in their—"

The little mechanical birds were as adept at mischief as Teferi himself. During the next exclamation, Jhoira swung the grate outward, rolled from the sluice, closed the metal, set her special pins, and crawled away into the underbrush. There, breathless, she paused. There was a hammering noise above and the sickly flapping of ruined wings. Someone stomped a final time, and there was silence. Then—

"See, it's not a real bird at all. See where the quills are folded into this paper loop? And here, this hard part? That's what smells your sweat. They make these things to dive on us! The twerps are too young, too pasty-faced and frail, to sweat."

"If I ever catch the little prodigy that's making these—"

"He's watching us right now, I'll wager."

"There! There! That's what I do to your invention, you little twerp!"

Jhoira tried not to giggle as she made her way through the dense forest. She knew the path perfectly. It was narrow and shaded, exposed only after the hillsides below the western bank. She moved without breaking twigs or tearing leaves. They were her allies in this deception. As long as no one found the forest path, no one would find the rocky niche she kept above the shifting sea. As long as no one discovered the rocky niche, no one would know about Kerrick.

In an hour's time, she topped the final shoulder of parched earth above the niche. Already the sun had quit the sky. A russet blanket of clouds covered the world. The hooded lantern she had brought to the spot glinted faintly through a crevice. Peering through the crack, she saw the bookshelf Kerrick had improvised from stones and flat slabs of driftwood. The shelf burgeoned with volumes on loan from the academy: Kerrick was an avid reader. He had little else to do during his days and said he hoped to gain enough knowledge of artifice that he could apply for admittance. He was a good reader, a better trapper, and a superior cook. Even now, Jhoira could smell the savory aroma of salt-marsh hare sizzling on a skillet. Kerrick had dressed the creature with wild spearmint and scallions. Jhoira's knees melted.

What the academy served could not even be considered food next to fare like that.

Drawn by those aromas, Jhoira tiptoed around the corner. Beside the sizzling skillet was a pair of slim, bronzed feet crossed over each other. As she approached, she saw the long, muscular legs attached to those feet, the man's ragged trousers, his tattered shift, his strong hands, clutching yet another book. Then there was his handsome face, his beautiful golden curls. Jhoira's knees melted again.

What the academy had to offer could not even be considered manhood next to fare like this.

He looked up, saw her, and smiled.

Jhoira leaped into his lap and wrapped him in eager arms and kisses. "I've been waiting all day to see you."

Laughter danced in his eyes. "Rotten day?"

"You have no idea," she said between kisses. "There's a little tyrant prig who thinks his job is making everyone miserable—"

"Yes, Teferi," Kerrick replied.

"I've mentioned him before?"

"Often," Kerrick said. "You've said he has a crush on you, but you're the one always talking about him."

"He's a child!" she replied indignantly. "I talk about him like I would talk about a goblin infestation."

Kerrick shrugged. He shifted toward the fire to turn the hare meat, and Jhoira caught a whiff of his musky scent. It was not the reek of worry but the strong animal smell of a man who works beneath the sun.

Over his shoulder, the man said idly, "Teferi seems one of your only friends."

"Oh?" Jhoira replied archly. "I spend too much time out here to have any other friends. And I don't hear you complaining."

"No, you don't."

"Besides, I have made a new friend. He's stronger than you, taller than you, younger than you, more polite . . . definitely more polite."

A delicious flash of jealousy showed in Kerrick's eyes. "Then why are you here?"

"He's a machine!" Jhoira said, rolling the man into another embrace. "He's a thinking, feeling machine, and I think he also has a crush on me."

"Really?" Kerrick replied. "Is the feeling mutual?"

"It is," Jhoira teased brightly, "and a little jealousy will do you some good. You've gotten quite comfortable living here in my secret place."

"Stronger than me, taller than me, younger than me? If you want me to be really jealous, bring out the plans so I can obsess over them."

"You'll have them tomorrow—if you return your overdue books," said Jhoira. "Now, come back over here. Those steaks need another few moments, and so do I." She dragged him with her onto the pallet and drew the scent of him and sizzling steaks into her chest.

Ah, she could put up with a hundred Teferis as long as she had her escape route, her paper birds, and her wild, secret love.

Monologue

What does Urza see in Teferi? The little monster is nothing like Urza at any age. For one thing, Teferi has a sense of humor. That is perhaps his only redeeming trait—aside from his undeniable brilliance. Still, Teferi uses his brilliance only to tear things apart, not to build them up. Urza has always been a builder and a serious one.

On the other hand, Urza's creations—his clockwork men, his war towers, his powder bombs and power armor—have always been used to destroy. The sum of Urza's constant creation is always destruction. Ironic, isn't it?

Do I dare to hope that, in the end, Teferi's constant destruction will bring about a new creation?

—Barrin, Mage Master of Tolaria

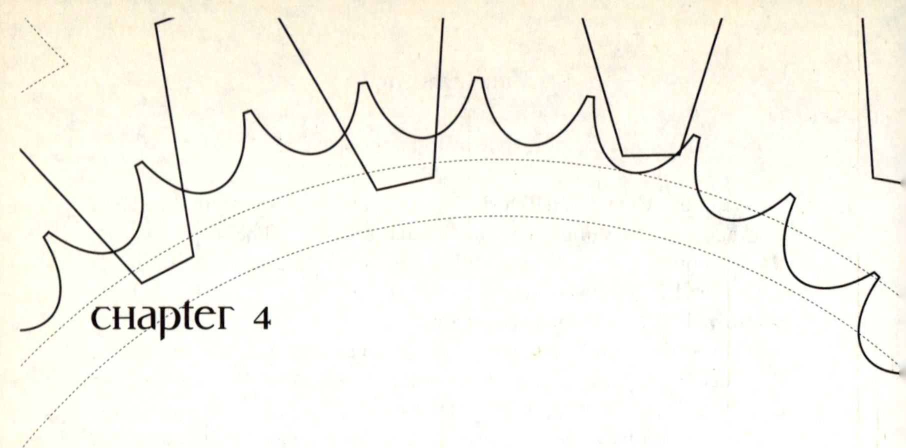

chapter 4

Karn stood in the whirling red beam. Overhead, Malzra's machine turned back the tide of time. It was Karn's third trial in as many months. Each test reached only hours farther back in time. Each produced greater temporal stress across his frame. The current envelope was a regression of eighteen hours, beyond which lay almost certain meltdown.

Karn told himself he should be getting used to the vertiginous moment when the gear-work of the universe ground to a halt and then began slowly to turn backward. There was an instant of spinning wheels and whines of protest before time's conveyor reversed. Then came a sudden acceleration: Barrin and Malzra were freed from their immobility. An alien physics took hold. Effect became cause, memories became prophecies, and silver men were disassembled to gulping laughter.

Now as the spool of time rewound, space shifted as well. Within his red cone of light, Karn slid slowly sideways. He jittered through steel engines and furnace casings, his physical form out of phase with the atomic synchronicity around him. In moments, he slipped past the laboratory wall and out into the corridor. He saw himself strolling backward down the hall beside Jhoira. She had accompanied him to the lab, talking of her volcanic home island and how she missed her tribe.

Jhoira and Karn had become fast friends in the last months. She was a mental giant, and he a metal one. Whenever Karn was not in the lab and Jhoira was not studying or sleeping, the two were together. She had taught him to skip stones, which he could do with rocks the size of bread loaves. He had let her ride on his back as he climbed the eastern pinnacles. From the top of the jutting stones, they had seen ships so distant that only their topsails showed above the horizon. Jhoira had shared with Karn her many impressive clockwork inventions—toy birds and frogs and leafhoppers—and fixed a finger servo that had burned out after one of his secret tests. He had borrowed her drafting tools one evening when she fell asleep mid-conversation and had drawn a crudely elegant portrait of her. Best of all, they had made a home for each other, a refuge from the grueling rigors of their posts at the academy—and from the depredations of a certain fourteen-year-old menace.

Karn and his pool of red light drifted out the other side of the corridor. He moved through a set of tutorial rooms. Some were dark and vacant. Others were crowded with tutors, students, and artifact constructs. Many of these structures were basic forms meant to teach the principles of artifice to young scholars. More advanced devices could make beds, tie bootlaces, or scuttle like cockroaches. The most mobile of these creations were used by some of the senior students in elaborate off-hours stakes races. Some elite machines were designed to slither into the cells of opposite-sex students to spy for their makers. For every such offensive device, there were three defensive ones that could detect, disable, or outright destroy the offender. The highest-level creations, though—the sort Jhoira spent her days designing and building—were complex components for Master Malzra's time-travel device. He had dozens of his oldest and most promising students working on the project, though none of them knew the ultimate end of the devices they designed.

Onward went the time traveler in his vessel of light. He saw into lecture halls, slid through a sleeping student lying sick and alone in her cell, tore past a pyrotechnic display on the properties of coal dust, and drifted through Malzra's private study. Books and models lined the walls, diagrams and studies hung on stands. In their midst, across a table piled with ancient manuscripts, Barrin and Malzra argued heatedly.

Karn drifted beyond those walls as well. He emerged into early morning in the academy's gardens and passed the twelve-foot-thick outer wall, then he moved through forests. Leaves twirled in odd backward spirals to sucking winds. The sun retreated to disappear below the horizon. Through a vast and settling darkness, Karn glided out toward the distant western shore. It was a place he and Jhoira never explored on their rambles, keeping themselves to the pinnacles and the east. Karn slid through tree trunks and boulders, even long low shoulders of earth at the edge of the island. Afterward, the ground fell away. A series of rough steppes rambled down to the sea.

In what seemed mere moments, the foamy verge of ocean passed some fifty feet beneath Karn's dangling feet. The water seemed to boil, ever receding from the toothy shore. He floated outward. Morning deepened into night. The Glimmer Moon quit the sky. Black midnight shimmered with twilight.

He was hot. He was nearing the edge of the envelope, eighteen hours back and five miles in space. The plan had been for Malzra and Barrin to monitor the temporal stresses on the portal device and recall Karn before he reached meltdown. That wasn't happening. Already his silver chest plates ground against each other in feverish expansion.

Still he drifted outward—

The red pool of light suddenly shimmered out of existence around him. Flailing to stay upright, Karn plunged, as massive and hot as a meteor. Overhead, the sky was starry but moonless. The ocean below was black with night and deep. It roared up to meet him. Flecked waves seized his legs, sent jets of steam from the golem's sizzling hide, and dragged him under. For several long moments Karn was enveloped in a fine cloud of steam bubbles, and then he slipped down out of the foamy stuff and sank through cold, viscous dark. Sandy silt sifted up around him, and then his feet struck the benthos at the bottom.

For a few moments he simply stood there feeling salt water wriggling past all his plates and into the interior spaces of his being. Surely they would recall him now. He needed only to wait. Still, with each creeping moment, he felt his temporal displacement draining away. He would soon be in phase with the particles of this time continuum, solid and seeable to anyone who might look. Best not to give anyone a chance. He would remain where he was until recalled.

An hour passed. The last pockets of air in him had seeped out and escaped to the surface some fifty feet above. He'd been bumped three times by an inquisitive serpent and had given up hope of being automatically recalled. Perhaps he was out of range. He would have to find his own way out.

Luckily, among his capacities were an internal clock, compass, and sextant—not that he could see any stars. Even so, with the various improvements Malzra had made to all these systems, Karn had an almost foolproof direction sense. He set out, slogging toward the island.

It took longer than he had anticipated. There were numerous submerged sandbars to climb and other pits to descend into. There was also a coral reef that was too fragile to climb over and too extensive to circumnavigate. He ended up having to smash through, the sharp animal accretions scarring his silvery knuckles.

It was midnight when his head finally cleared the water. Constellations spangled the sky over the black island. In the extreme distance, the academy glowed, a collection of ivory jewel boxes. Within those walls, his other self, his historic self, would be spending the night in voluntary deactivation. Within those walls, Jhoira and Teferi slept, and Malzra and Barrin no doubt pondered the upcoming spatial-temporal trial. The wrapping walls of that school held everything in the world to Karn, and the rest of the island was dark—

Save for that one dim glint near the brow of the sea cliff. The light was so small he had first taken it to be a distant star. Marking its position, Karn emerged from the water and strode up the sloping shore. Water disgorged itself by the gallon from his sloshing innards. He stood and let the purge continue.

What about that light? No one was allowed beyond the walls after dark. Who could be in that niche?

Karn climbed. The rocky cliff side before him was all too easy to ascend after the dragging depths of the sea. In sliding, scraping moments, he had reached the peak. Ahead, in a deep, narrow cleft of stone, the light shone tepidly forth. Karn strode toward it.

It suddenly went out.

He paused, allowing his eyes to adjust to the starry darkness. Something moved in that space—something warm. Karn made out a peering, squinting face and the glint of stars from a small, steel blade. The figure withdrew again into the cave. Karn started forward, his massive feet grinding quietly over the gravel-covered ground.

The person in the cave reappeared, hoisting a curved stick. There came a thrumming sound. Something—a crude arrow—darted swiftly out to strike Karn's hide. Metal rang with the sound of stone cracking. A shattered shaft tumbled away to one side.

A hostile act. A caveman living on the edge of Tolaria. An intruder.

Karn set his jaw and marched toward the cave. Two more arrows struck the golem and cracked off into the rocks. He came on, furious. The man abandoned his bow for a large, stone-tipped club. He bounced it in his hand, growled out a wordless warning, and squinted into the night.

Karn strode to the figure and swiped out to capture him, but the man was too fast, spinning from his grasp. The club descended. Its stone tip shattered and sprayed outward. The hardwood handle jangled in the man's grasp. Karn whirled. He caught the man with the back of one hand and flung him to the ground. The body sprawled against an outcrop of rock and lay still.

Light flared to Karn's side. He spun. Flames roared over him. Fire sizzled away the water in his joints. He lunged past the flame at the second attacker. Arms limned in flame, Karn surged into the cave.

"Karn!" came a shout of surprise and relief. "What are you doing here?"

"Jhoira?" Karn asked. His eyes quickly adjusted to the darkness.

Jhoira trembled in her nightclothes, a smoldering torch butt held in her hand. She must have used the brand to ignite airborne coal-dust, as the students were taught at the academy.

Karn blurted, "What are you doing here?"

Jhoira's face grew resentful and desperate. "You followed me. I can't believe you followed me."

"I didn't follow you," Karn protested.

"Why did you leave the school grounds at night then? What about the curfew?" Jhoira challenged.

"I could ask the same of you," countered Karn.

"Where is Kerrick? What have you done?" she demanded suddenly, and stumbled past Karn to the mouth of the cave. She felt around blindly in the dark until her hand settled on the leg of the man. She shook him. "Are you all right? Can you hear me?" The man did not move.

Karn approached. "I'll carry him inside—"

"No," insisted Jhoira, shoving past him and clambering into the cave. "His neck might be broken. Moving him might kill him." She lit the lantern, gathered gauze and supplies from a shelf, and hurried back out. Kneeling beside the fallen man, she let out a moan of worry. One hand reached to stroke his curly golden hair. "No blood, and he's breathing." She gritted her teeth as her fingers encountered a large lump on his forehead. "You banged him up pretty good."

"Who is he?" Karn asked suspiciously. "What's he doing here?"

"He is Kerrick," said Jhoira with a sigh. She probed his neck to check for injury or swelling. "He was trying to protect me."

"He's not a student," Karn observed.

"No. He's a castaway, and he's my friend." She slipped her arms under the man, lifted him, and carried him inside. "Get the lantern, will you, Karn?"

The golem complied, following like a dejected dog. "You never told me about him."

Jhoira settled the man onto the pallet in one corner of the niche. "I never told anyone. Master Malzra would have him killed."

"But we are friends. We have no secrets from each other," Karn said. He set the lantern on the makeshift table.

"We have secrets. You won't tell me what experiments you are involved with."

"Master Malzra forbade me."

Jhoira smiled grimly, dipping a cloth in a pitcher of water and applying it to the lump on Kerrick's head. "Master Malzra forbade me—or anyone—from harboring castaways, too, so it all comes down to Master Malzra. I keep secrets from you because of him, and you keep secrets from me because of him. That's just the way he wants it. He doesn't want any of us to have friends, to have lives."

Karn felt a wave of sick dread move through him. He remembered what his existence had been like before meeting Jhoira, caught between the quiet apathy of Malzra and the loud antipathy of Teferi. This moment could ruin things between him and Jhoira. This moment could cost Karn the only friend he had and turn him back into Arty Shovelhead.

"Time travel," Karn blurted, his voice anguished. "That's what Master

Malzra is testing. That is why I am here. He is testing a device that will send me back centuries or millennia, that will transport me anywhere across the planet."

Jhoira stopped her ministrations and stared in amazed wonder at the golem. "That's why he called you a probe. . . ."

"It is the whole reason I have been created," Karn said soberly. "He instructed me to tell no one about this on pain of being dismantled."

"If he can do this, he can change history—"

"He doesn't want me to change history." Karn suddenly realized he might be changing history even at that moment.

"There's much more to Master Malzra than meets the eye," Jhoira noted, amazed.

"Well," said Karn, kneeling before Jhoira in the wan light of the lantern. "That is the only secret I have kept from you. You know everything else about me. You have studied all my plans. You have watched Malzra assemble me. You even gave me my name, my life. Can you forgive me? Can we still be friends?"

A smile that was one part joy and one part pity broke across her face. "Of course, Karn. You know my greatest secret now, too. I've always trusted you, and I still trust you. Karn, you're my only real friend in the world."

"What is he?" Karn asked, indicating the unconscious man.

"He is my love."

She had no sooner spoken these words than the shimmering tug of temporal displacement laid hold of Karn. He shuddered, shifted out of phase, turned incorporeal, and felt the sudden swift sliding of the red light.

Just before he spun away through the stone wall of the niche, he glimpsed, behind the wondering face of Jhoira, one of Kerrick's fingers draw inward and his eye slit open.

"It's worth the effort," Urza insisted where he sat in his high study. "The Thran became the Phyrexians. If we can divert them from that course, keep them on the path of artifice rather than mutation, we can save the whole world."

Barrin held his hand out and paused, seeming to sniff the air. "What was that? Did you feel that?"

"A temporal anomaly," Urza said. "They have been occurring since we first sent the probe through the time-travel portal. That one was stronger than most."

"A temporal anomaly," Barrin repeated, stunned. "This is what I am talking about. We get anomalies like this when sending someone back eighteen hours. What will happen beyond that?"

"We must stop the Thran from becoming the Phyrexians."

"But millennia? If we could reach that far back in time, you could take a few side trips and rectify all your own past mistakes—leading the Phyrexians to Serra's plane, attacking Phyrexia, blowing up Argoth, killing your brother . . . why, you could even decide to undiscover the powerstone at Koilos and keep the Phyrexians from reentering Dominaria at all."

Urza's look was sober. "That is what my life's accomplishment amounts to in your eyes? One grand failure after another?"

"Of course not," assured Barrin. "You have done much good, and I do not begrudge you your mistakes. Mages also learn through trial and error. What I begrudge you is the fact that you never take responsiblity for your errors. You don't learn from your mistakes. You never clean up after yourself."

"That's what I am trying to do now. I brought the Phyrexians back into the world. Now I am doing all, I can to find out how to drive them from it forever," Urza said. "I have learned, but I have much more to learn before I can right this greatest wrong."

"Yes," agreed Barrin, "you have much more to learn."

Missing the intent of this comment, Urza said, "I have seen one piece of the puzzle, but I don't know where it fits yet. Have you noticed the pendant Karn wears?"

Barrin gave a wave of his hand. "A little lizard on a chain."

"Have you noticed how hard the metal is? I tested its hardness. It scratched steel and adamantine and diamond. What's more, it doesn't heat up at all from temporal stress."

Barrin blinked, considering. "What are you saying? That we should build another probe made of this metal?"

"Perhaps. Perhaps," Urza's eyes glinted with possibilities. "I'll have to ask Karn where he got it. If we could forge a probe of it—"

"Should we work out a treaty with the makers of the metal," Barrin asked sarcastically, "or just take over their homeland and drive them out?"

"Start with a treaty, of course. There's always time for conquest later."

Barrin was grim. Under his breath, he said, "Yes, you have much to learn."

In a few months, the spatial displacement capacities of the time machine had been perfected. On one journey, Karn arrived in the Adarkar Wastes, thousands of miles from Tolaria. The place was little more than a brittle blue sky above a brittle white land. Snow and ice covered most of the ground. Bare spots revealed sand that had fused together into great, thin slabs of glass, left from a long-ago battle of fire. Where Karn arrived—this time without the disconcerting fall from the sky—the land was a cracked sheet of glass, sand fused in furnacelike heat. At Malzra's request, Karn gathered shards and brought them back with him.

Malzra tested the samples. He declared them indeed to be from the Adarkar Wastes. He was very pleased with this result and planned to go even farther with the next trial.

Meanwhile, the rills of temporal distortion grew worse. At first these disturbances were subtle and few, slight time-lags passing through the air like mild tremors. The frequency of the episodes gradually increased, from once a week to once a day. The severity went from mere hiccoughs to lapses that spanned four or five heartbeats. Words lagged behind lips. Music lurched up and out of tune. Carillon crews became hopelessly jangled. Goblets were overfilled or dropped. Unbound folios turned traitor in the fingers of tutors and fanned out on the floor. Flames devoured hunks of meat on the grill while neighboring steaks remained raw.

These were minor annoyances only, especially to a creature like Karn without heartbeat or breath to get tangled up. Some of the more infirm tutors, though, had to ride out these time storms by folding to their knees and gasping for breath. As the bands of distortion deepened and grew more common, the school infirmary filled up.

It disturbed Karn. The next time he was called for a time trial, two months later, he brought up his concerns.

"I am not like you," Karn noted. "That's why you made me, because creatures like you cannot safely move through time distortions. Each time I regress through the machine, more time leaks occur, and bigger ones."

Master Malzra studied the golem keenly. The founder of the academy always had a strange intensity in his face and a scintillating focus in his eyes, as though he could see centuries of time crystallized into mere moments.

"Are these . . . time leaks harming you?"

Barrin glanced up from the console he prepared. He nodded approvingly at Karn, nudging him to continue.

"Not me," Karn replied, "but everyone else. They're not safe. You have a lot of aging scholars here and a lot of young children. You are responsible—"

"Have there been any serious injuries?" interrupted the master, his eyes flashing like twin gemstones.

"Not yet, but if we continue these experiments, there will be injuries, and perhaps deaths, across the whole island."

Another nod came from the mage.

Malzra blinked, astonished. "If we don't continue these experiments, there will be injuries and deaths across the whole world. You don't understand, Karn. You have lived mere moments. You have seen only a hundred square miles of land. I have lived millennia. I have seen worlds and worlds of worlds. There are evils at the door, Karn, evils beyond anything you can imagine. I alone know they are there and are knocking. I alone am devising a way to keep them forever out or destroy them when they get in. I alone stand between this world and utter destruction, and you come to me like a nurse-maid for these children and old dotards and demand they get goat's milk and nap times?"

Mage Barrin dropped his gaze, head wagging softly.

Karn stood for some moments without responding. He believed, at long last, what Teferi had said about Malzra's paranoia. An impulse urged Karn to confront the man with his own tortured insanity, but the past months had taught him much about dealing with these strange, irrational creatures of flesh.

"Yes. It is a lonely, dangerous struggle."

Barrin looked up, impressed. "One that might, one day, kill us all," he said in quiet reproof.

Malzra took the comments as accord. "Good. I'm glad you both agree. Now, Karn, before you get into the machine, I want you to leave that pendant with me. It may be interfering with the regression."

Suspicious, Karn slowly lifted the pendant from his neck and surrendered it.

Malzra looked it over keenly. "Where did you get it?" There was a greedy gleam in his eye.

Karn opened his mouth to speak, but the words caught short. Malzra's mad ravings still rang in his head. If the master started poking around in Jhoira's room, he might find out her secret. She might be expelled—or worse.

"I found it. It was snagged on a piece of driftwood that washed ashore."

"Driftwood," Malzra said dubiously.

"Driftwood," Karn repeated.

Shaking his head in irritation, Malzra said, "Into the machine then, Karn."

This time the regression took him to a scene of great carnage. The place was evil beyond Karn's imagining. Men, or what had once been men, lay in broken death across the grassy ground. Some were nearly complete, marked only by telltale roses of blood on their hearts or bellies. Others were missing limbs, likely dragged away by the wild dogs that loped shamelessly among the dead. Even less remained of some warriors. They had been torn in half by unimaginably sharp blades or blasted into fragments by fireballs. Smoldering war machines hulked on the horizon. The smell of waste, smoke, offal, maggots, and disease filled the air.

Surely this devastation has been caused by the horrors and evils Malzra spoke of, the silver man thought.

Karn had never felt sick before, but now his silver bulk quivered as with a tarnish that reached to the very core of him. He had been asked to gather some sign of his journey, but he could not bring himself to pry a sword from the hand of a fallen man or pull loose the helm that had failed to save a life. Instead Karn found a single shield, lying alone and bloodless on a windblown tuft of glass. This he lifted and held against him, waiting miserably for the master to recall him.

When Karn returned, he sorrowfully presented the shield to Malzra. The master identified it—a bracer from New Argive. To the silver man's description of the battle, Malzra merely nodded grimly—a battle had occurred in that spot only two days before. Karn had regressed only a day and a half. The master was frustrated and angry. He brusquely handed the pendant back.

"If these are the atrocities you spoke of, Master Malzra," Karn said solemnly as he donned the amulet, "I understand now why you fight so hard."

Malzra's smile—an unusual sight—was sardonic. "These atrocities are nothing, the result of human hatreds. What I fight is the hatred of demons."

Monologue

Sometimes I forget all Urza has seen, all he has done.

The silver man returned from New Argive. We debriefed him and shut down the laboratory. That night, during the reading session in Urza's study, he let the volume he was reading slide down to lie open on his lap. He stared straight ahead for some time. I lowered my book as well and waited. Urza's eyes had that faraway look, and I glimpsed the halves of the Mightstone and Weakstone showing through. Beyond the high windows, sea winds argued among the palms.

"I was fighting a whole world, not just Gix, but a whole world," he murmured.

Cautiously, I ventured, "Fighting a whole world?"

In Phyrexia. I had gone to fight Gix, but there was a whole world of Gixes. Demons, witch engines, dragon engines, the living dead and the dead living. And at the heart of it all, a god. A dark, mad god."

I wryly imagined the same description coming from an invader of Tolaria.

"I fought to destroy a whole world, but Xantcha—she fought only to regain her heart."

I drew a deep breath of sea wind. "Yes. That one stone was a whole world to her. It is a whole world to Karn."

A gleam of sudden realization shone in Urza's dark, ancient eyes.

"That's why they act the way they do."

"Who?"

"The students, the tutors—even you and Karn. Every one of you is defending your own heart, your own world."

He is not mad, not wholly. He is ancient and inhuman, transformed by the millennia, but he is not wholly mad.

"Yes," I agreed. "Don't you remember how it feels? It is a lonely, dangerous struggle, one that will, one day, kill us all."

—Barrin, Mage Master of Tolaria

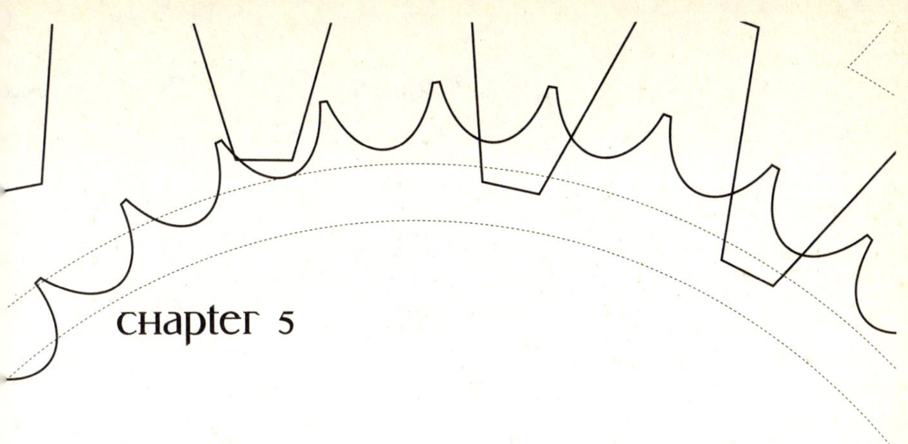

Chapter 5

Teferi sat on a wind-blasted crest of rock above the restless nighttime sea.

It had been quite a feat, reaching this point. Jhoira was lithe and athletic. She had moved quickly and soundlessly from her room after lantern-call that evening. Despite Teferi's invisibility enchantment, she sensed she was being followed. Twice, as she made her way through the empty corridors of the school, she looked back. The first time, Teferi fetched up against a recessed doorway to the forge room. The handle of the door rattled. She peered a long time back in the feverish night, and Teferi dared not breathe. When at last he looked again, she was already gone. He caught up to her in the Hall of Artifact Creatures—a museum where Malzra placed important but obsolete inventions. The place was unnerving enough by day. It was filled with statuesque creatures of metal plate and guy wire, each posed with limbs extended as if beseeching the viewer to reactivate them. At night the museum was downright frightening. Wiry, dog-headed Yotian warriors menaced in their crouches. Backward-kneed *su-chi* lifters seemed behemoths from some far-off world. At the far side of the mechanical menagerie, Jhoira was no more than a fleeting triangle of cloth. The door she exited led to the western laboratory—a half-used structure that was beastly hot in the height of summer and dank in the drear of winter.

Once again, he almost lost her. There was no sign of her in the lab. He cast a spell, seeing the fading heat of her footprints on the floor. They disappeared as he followed. She'd gotten away. Teferi stepped on a slightly skewed grating. It rang with possibilities. He knelt and stared down into the darkness below the grate. Jhoira's tampering had been evident even in the dark—at least to a mage's eye—and the trick of her specially engineered bolts took only minutes to divine. After that, it was easy enough reach the wall. He saw her slip from the channel as the guards overhead cursed some nocturnal bird. Teferi conjured a real bird to do the task for him, a skycaptain that nearly spooked the men into jumping. With the bird and his invisibility, the young prodigy followed with ease.

Jhoira was not so cautious thereafter. Perhaps, once away from the school, she thought no one would be around to detect her. Perhaps, once near her hideaway, she was too eager to be careful. Even in the patchy light of the Glimmer Moon, Teferi made good time through the steaming woods and to this spot, just above the sea, just beside the mouth of the dimly flickering cave. He dispelled his invisibility, drew a deep breath, and with a smug smile, started into the niche. He stopped just in time.

Teferi saw what lay within, *who* lay within.

In a fit of disgust, he withdrew, unable to bear any more. He'd expected to find something to use against Jhoira, something with which he could extort a kiss from her, perhaps—but not this, another man. Even if Teferi mentioned that he knew her secret, he could not win her heart with it. She would only hate him all the more. He sat there while the sea toiled ceaselessly below and the wind dug its claws into the clouds overhead. He rose and headed back toward the academy, his mind abuzz with questions.

As he pushed past the pawing undergrowth of the western isle, a new thought occurred to him: it was possible there were certain things in life that could not be attained through manipulation and trickery. Nothing he had done had won Jhoira to him. No amount of misdirection, cajoling, humiliation, artifice, boasting, or innuendo had convinced her he was great. Teferi was honestly confused. He had never met a person so resistant to the obvious truth of his supremacy. She couldn't see any of his overwhelming virtues, determined to focus on the difference in their ages. "Grow up," was all she could ever think to say to him. He *was* growing up. How could he grow up faster? He didn't have a time machine. . . .

That's when he felt the hand seize his shoulder and thrust his face to the ground.

"Teferi knows about Kerrick," Karn said to Jhoira. The silver man hunched just outside the doorway in the nervous light of morning.

Drowsy, Jhoira blinked at her friend. She had gotten back only an hour before, during the sunrise change of the guard.

"What are you talking about?"

"They caught him outside the academy this morning. He was coming back from the western shore."

Her stomach sinking, Jhoira motioned Karn into the room and closed the door behind him. She ran her hand through her tousled hair.

"Now, what's all this about?"

"Teferi's been watching you," Karn said with quiet intensity. "He probably followed you. They caught him on his way back from the shore. He must have seen—"

"Who caught him?" Jhoira interrupted.

"The guards from the western wall. One had seen something rustling in the jungle when he left. The guard followed until she lost the trail but waited on the path for him to return. They interrogated him for hours—they're angry about your mechanical birds and think Teferi conjured them. They got nothing out of him, though, not even the route you used out of the school, and half an hour ago they turned him over to Master Malzra himself."

Shaking her head in irritation, Jhoira swung wide the bone-inlaid doors of her wardrobe and rifled among her clothes. She chose her most formal white cloak, trimmed in gold piping, and slipped it on. Shedding her nightclothes beneath the robe, she selected a belt of gold rope and cinched it angrily around her waist.

"What are you going to do?" Karn asked, stunned.

"I'm going to go defend myself."

"Teferi hasn't said anything yet," Karn pointed out.

"Teferi?" Jhoira asked, angry. "He's holding out for the right price. He'll sell me out as soon as he has Master Malzra twisted around his finger." She shook her head again. "I want to beat him to the punch. I want to confess what I've done, so at least I have honesty on my side." With a final snort of surrender, she turned and bent over her cot, her hands drawing up the covers over a lump Karn had not noticed before. "Let's go."

As the two turned to leave, Karn glanced back at the cot, where he saw the curly golden hair of Kerrick.

Master Malzra was in a state. His face, always alight with a golden inner glow, was bright as a candle. His eyes seemed to cast twin red beams of hellfire. He paced, his blue robes crinkling all about him. In the dim light of the small study he was enormous and powerful, as though he wore one of the suits of power armor he had on display in the Hall of Artifact Creatures.

Before him, fourteen-year-old Teferi looked as small as a sparrow.

"Who are you, then? What are you? A spy? You're too young to be a Phyrexian sleeper. You don't smell like glistening oil. But you are smart and ambitious and incorrigible, just the sort of person the Phyrexians choose. What were you doing beyond the wall? Who were you meeting? Phyrexian negators?"

Teferi kept his eyes averted on the blackwood tabletop where he sat. "I don't even know what you mean by a Fire Ex—Fry Egg—Friar Ecclesian—"

"Don't mock me!" demanded Malzra, pounding the tabletop with his fist.

Tapping an inner reserve of strength, Teferi raised his eyes to meet the glowing orbs of the master, which looked like the multi-faceted eyes of an insect. Teferi drew a deep breath and roared right back at the man, "You're mad, Master. Everyone knows it. You're also a genius, of course. None of us would come here to study if we didn't know that. You know more about artifice and magic than any man for millennia, but you are mad. Fire-Eaters and Fanatics, Demons and Dog-Faced Men, Invaders and Conspirators and Spies—the only invaders that ever come to this island are fish stupid enough to get stranded by the tide or seagulls who have lost their sense of direction and flown away from everything and into nothing. No one wants to get in here, Master Malzra, but I can think of about two hundred students and forty scholars who want out, and that's what I was doing beyond the wall, believe it or not."

In the sudden, stunned silence, a knock came at the door. Mage Barrin shifted from the shadows and went to the door.

While the latch sounded and hushed voices spoke, Teferi and Malzra stared into each other's eyes. There was recognition between them. Despite the vast difference in their ages, the two knew in that moment that they were more alike than different—brilliant, driven, selfish, unstoppable, obsessive, irrepressible, and as deeply flawed as they were gifted. But there was something more to it, an undeniable spark of greatness—unmistakable among those blessed, or cursed, by it.

Malzra's eyes intensified. Teferi felt a *presence* in his mind. Sinuous as a snake, Malzra slithered through his thoughts. The master sniffed among skittering memories, snapped and swallowed them. Fear like a mouse went first into that maw, then jealousy and timid insecurity. The master's mind snapped down images of the forest and the Glimmer Moon. The truth lay beyond. It smelled sour and strong. Malzra wound forward. In moments, he would know. He would know.

Teferi's eyes intensified, too. A cat came prowling among his thoughts—righteous indignation and pride—and it leaped on the snaking mind of Malzra. Fangs and claws, spitting and hissing, fur and scale, they fought in the young man's mind. The battle was ferocious, though only their beaming eyes gave outward sign of it.

Barrin discreetly cleared his throat to break the tension. "Jhoira and Karn are here."

"Another time," Malzra growled.

"She says she's come to confess," Barrin said, gesturing the young woman and the silver man into the small study.

Malzra ended the staring match. His eyes flashed as he marked the Ghitu woman. She was dressed in her formal academy robe, the one she wore when inducted into the ranks of his senior students.

"Confess to what?"

"I am to blame for all this," Jhoira said evenly. "I am the reason Teferi was outside the walls last night."

The young man goggled for a moment at her and then jumped in. "She dared me." All eyes in the room turned quizzically on him. "I'm always trying to impress her, but she thinks I'm too young for her. Finally, she said she didn't want to talk to me again until I did something brave and grown-up."

"That's not what—" Jhoira began.

"You thought sneaking out of the academy would be grown-up?" Malzra demanded.

"I thought if I could get out into the woods at night, I could maybe catch a night loon. They have a beautiful song. They sing to the Glimmer Moon. I made those mechanical birds to impress her—she's not interested in my magic, and I wanted to show her I was an artificer too—but she said only, 'they're fake, just like you.' So I thought, if I caught a real bird, a rare nighttime songbird, and did it without magic, did it by going myself—"

"To catch a loon?" Barrin asked, astonished.

"I had a little chain with a metal collar. I was going to clip it around the bird's leg and put a hood on his head, but they got knocked out of my pocket when the guard tackled me."

"A night loon?" Barrin repeated, incredulous. He turned to Malzra. "I don't believe him. Malzra, I think in this case we could suspend the school's moratorium against mind probes. I could cast a truth spell on him—"

"No—" Something had changed in Malzra's eyes, not a softening, but a hardening, a keen calculation. "No, this was no crime great enough to warrant such drastic measures." A guilty look passed between him and Teferi. "He found a night loon all right, himself, but I daresay this stunt wasn't enough to impress Jhoira. It was not brave or grown-up. It was foolhardy and stupid."

Teferi swallowed and bowed his head. "Yes, sir."

Stunned, Jhoira realized her mouth was moving, but nothing was coming out.

"What do you have to say, Jhoira?" Malzra asked. "Are you impressed by such exploits?"

She took a deep breath and said, "Well, in a way, yes."

After the students and the silver man had left, Barrin lurked among the book shadows of Urza's library. For his part, the planeswalker sat, silent and brooding, at the blackwood desk.

How to say this, wondered Barrin, how to say any of this? "There's more to this, Urza. You know that."

"I know," came the calm response.

"You shouldn't allow the truth of Teferi's words—all that business about genius and madness and paranoia—to distract you from the fact that he was outside the school for more than night loons."

"Yes," agreed Urza wearily. He drew a long, conscious breath, not something he needed to do to live, being a creature of pure energy. Simple acts such as breathing brought him an invaluable connection to the world around him. "There is a Phyrexian in the school. I smell it. It is warded, shielded, wary. Its smell is faint and diffuse, but it is here. A Phyrexian in Tolaria."

The ruby light of the time-travel portal pulsed around Karn. He saw none of it. His mind's eye was turned inward, to the confrontation among Malzra, Teferi, Barrin, and Jhoira. The outcome of that episode a week ago still boggled him. Kerrick should have been exposed, Jhoira and Teferi reprimanded and expelled, and the animosity between them become an unbreachable wall. Instead, the castaway had gained access to the academy by way of the secret passage, Jhoira and Teferi had only risen in Malzra's estimation, and the young prodigy had won respect in the eyes of the woman he always sought to impress. How any of this had transpired, Karn still didn't understand. He had the distinct sense that much of what had taken place in that strange meeting lay in words unspoken and deeds undone.

Time slowed and stopped. Malzra and Barrin stood statue-still at their consoles. The whine of the machine reached a peak. Beyond was dead calm. Then the turbines of time reversed and began rolling backward. It was a dreadful instant, and in it Karn always felt utterly alone. With slow deliberation, Malzra and Barrin moved again, their hands withdrawing along the consoles, undoing all they had done and powering down the machine. The light deepened around Karn. This time, the pool did not shift. Malzra had achieved proficiency in spatial displacement—he seemed to have an especial grasp of that arcane endeavor—and so had set it aside to try to push the temporal envelope. With this trial, all the power of the machine was shunted to the temporal vector.

It began, the dizzy spooling of time. Karn had gotten used to seeing himself withdraw from the pool of light and slump along backward, listen attentively to the two men, and retreat through the door. In the time prior to that, Malzra and Barrin were often busy, breaking down portions of the time machine, removing shiny new components and replacing them with burnt-out hunks of metal and glass. One day, their alterations would reshape this machine so that it could carry Karn back centuries or millennia. . . .

He let his mind drift. On that journey, he would see his own creation and the dead pile of plates and cogs he had been before. He would pass through the time when Barrin was young, was a baby, was in the body of his mother, was nothing at all. It would be a longer journey back to Malzra's beginnings, of course. How much longer, Karn could not have guessed. En route, he would see the man being disassembled piece by piece, just like the time machine before him. He would see each component removed from Malzra—his mania, his paranoia, his obsession, his brilliance, his constant abiding regret and misery. Some of it was part of his original design, perhaps. Much of it, though, the worst of it, must have come from suffering, centuries of it.

The laboratory grew dark. Barrin retreated around it. He drew from each light orb the enchantment that made it shine. He backed out the door, closed it, and locked it. Then came a period of deepening darkness. Karn could almost feel the sun diving silently below the world, a leviathan swimming backward beneath the sea.

It was twenty-two hours now, the extent of their previous success.

In the dead of that recoiling night, someone entered the laboratory. It was not Barrin or Malzra. Whoever it was neither cast light spells nor lit the mundane oil tapers around the walls. There were workers assigned to cleaning the labs, but who would clean in the dark? The intruder moved along the wall of plans, studying them as though he could see without light. He sorted briefly among the piles of parts and drew from his pockets glimmering stones to lay among the others.

A thief.

Karn almost stepped from the circle of light but remembered Malzra's instructions—to travel back in time until his frame neared the melting point. He was nowhere near that now, and in moments, the figure was gone. He thought he glimpsed, in the gray wedge of hallway light, golden curls.

Evening came, in the form of an unnatural dawn. The regression accelerated. Karn waited through the spooling hours as students and tutors jittered through the space, bees in a hive. Morning came. Shadows lengthened and puddled into vast pools of darkness. It was night again.

Karn's hide heated until it steamed.

The thief returned.

It was forty-six hours into the past. Long enough. Karn stepped from the ruby light. His frame fairly sizzled as the silver plates met the air of the former time. The man who had been opening the door closed it. The silver golem made a rapid and quiet passage to the door and eased it open. He peered out, seeing Kerrick withdraw beyond a corner of the corridor.

Kerrick. Jhoira had allowed him into the school, and he was stealing from Master Malzra. There would be more powerstones or plans or parts in his pockets. What use did a castaway have for artifact technology? He must have been delivering these items to someone else. To whom?

There are evils at the door, Karn, evils beyond anything you can imagine.

Karn pursued. He would be out of phase and invisible only so long, and his metallic footsteps would soon give him away. If he didn't catch the thief soon, he never would.

Kerrick fled down a series of curving corridors. At the end of the snaking route lay the Hall of Artifact Creatures. Perhaps he planned on stealing one of the devices in it or copying its design. He slipped the latch and entered the chamber.

Karn hurried to catch the door before it swung closed. He eased inward. His quarry darted away among a cluster of dog-headed Yotian warriors. The silver man followed. His frame was already slipping into phase—he was fading into being. He made his way forward under cover of the mechanical menagerie.

He crouched beside a delver. Its sloping backbone was a vast conveyor designed to bear ores up from mines. Beyond it stood a weathercock topped with a collection of whirring instrumentation—anemometer, thermometer, barometer, cyclonometer. The next beast was wiry and configured like a hunting dog, with long thin legs, a sleek head, and a whiplike tail. Adjacent to it, *su-chi* lifters crouched in their backward-kneed massiveness. It was unsettling to stalk among these metallic brothers, deactivated and nearly discarded, made to stand like statues in this mausoleum. Karn wondered if he would one day be among them, when Malzra's mania had turned to some pursuit other than time travel, or when he had made a better probe to do it.

He was only halfway across the chamber when Kerrick slipped away through the far door, toward Jhoira's secret passage. Karn could not have followed through the tight duct work, but perhaps he could intercept the thief beyond the wall.

Turning, Karn headed for a different door, one that led to the courtyard. He slid the bolt, eased it open, and scanned the yard. Beyond lay a hot and windy night. The Glimmer Moon was a cataracted eye burning behind sultry clouds. Karn was hotter still, his frame smoldering with heat stress. He emerged and stole across the courtyard. Malzra might recall him at any moment. Karn reached the western wall and climbed the inner buttresses. He rose to the battlements.

Beside the turrets, guards stood in lazy clumps. A pair of clockwork watchers perched on adjacent towers, their optics turning in slow fans along the outer wall.

Deep darkness swathed the wall's footing. The grate at the end of Jhoira's passage lay halfway between the mechanical guards, obscured by tall grasses. Metal shifted slightly in the murk. A glint of hair like gold coins showed beneath.

Above, the guards still lounged, conversing in their quiet knot.

Kerrick slipped from the grate. He scrambled up the weedy embankment and entered the thick wall of jungle beyond. He had not been seen.

Silver skin sizzling with heat, Karn rose to crouch on the battlements and hurled himself into the wheeling night air. He dropped and landed with a thud that brought the heads of the guards around. Karn crouched, half-visible in the silvery moonlight. In time, the guards' attention turned elsewhere. Masked by a rising wind, Karn ambled quietly up into the woods, after Kerrick.

More noises came, necessarily, ahead—the thrash of leaves, the crackle of sticks, the hiss of dew on red-hot silver. Karn feared to alert Kerrick, but speed was the thing. The thief had moved quickly and soundlessly over Jhoira's path, taking with him whatever plans or powerstones or artifacts he had stolen.

Karn followed. His energy stores were taxed by the rapid movements. Heat stress made his joints grind, but anger lent him strength. He topped a rise just as light from the Glimmer Moon lanced through a patch of cloud. Kerrick and two strangers stood beyond. Karn paused, attuning his ears to the whispered conversation.

The golden-haired young man held out a large roll of paper and pointed, saying, "The passage is here. Bring the full company of negators. I will be sure the way is open. I will be sure the guards on the wall are dead—"

That was all Karn heard or saw.

Malzra's machine reached back through time and laid hold of him—every smoldering mote of his being—and dragged him forward. In angry whips of red energy, the jagging light whirred into a solid cone of radiation. The hillside vanished and with it Kerrick and his conspirators. Only the lurid light remained. Roaring in frustration, Karn waited to reemerge in the time stream. Eventually the fabric of the future formed itself around Karn. The cone whirred once more, winked, and was gone.

Smoldering and red-hot, Karn stood in the midst of Malzra's time laboratory. The master looked up from his console. He and Barrin both wore expressions of awe, their eyes tracing the tendrils of smoke that snaked up from the massive metal man and tangled themselves hotly around the time machine. Its own fuselage streamed gray soot and crackled fragilely as it cooled.

Karn stepped out of the transport circle. It was a breach of protocol: he was supposed to wait until Master Malzra summoned him. He further offended by speaking before being spoken to.

"There is an invasion coming."

Barrin approached and gestured the silver man back. "There is a danger of contamination if you step out of the ring—"

"What sort of invasion?" Malzra asked from the console.

"I do not know. I did not see who he spoke to, but he talked of negators—"

"Phyrexians," Malzra replied in grim confirmation.

The mage asked, "*Who* spoke of negators?"

"Kerrick," Karn said. In that moment, he realized he must betray Jhoira's secret, for the safety of the whole academy and her safety as well. Still, the necessity of the crime made it no easier to commit. "He is a castaway, washed up on shore nearly a year ago. Jhoira found him and saved his life. He has discovered a way into the academy and now has taken floor plans of the academy to whoever is in charge of these negators."

Malzra began pacing again, the old fury resurfacing. "They must have a portal to a nearby island or perhaps merely a Sargasso or boat. They knew I would have defenses against portals directly into Tolaria. They are massing somewhere for this attack."

"How do you know all this?" Barrin asked Karn.

"I followed him out of the academy, out of this very room. He took the plans from here," Karn reported. "Beyond the wall, he met with two figures. They talked of the negators."

Malzra was reeling, his face livid. "Damn. Then they know of my time tampering. They could not have chosen a more crucial time to attack."

"When did this Kerrick hand off the plans? How far back did you go?"

"Forty-six hours."

"They could be arriving any moment," Barrin said. "I will alert the guard." He rushed for the door and down the hall.

"It's too late," Malzra said quietly, breathing for the first time in perhaps hours. He caught a whiff of the air that wafted from the open door. "They are already here."

Still sizzling, Karn charged for the door and bolted into the corridor. It was empty and silent, but a smell of oil and metal and death tinged the air. He thought but one thought—Jhoira—and hurled himself down the clattering hall. Malzra called out, but Karn paid no heed. Down a set of stairs, around a long slow bend, and up a rise, he reached the small, round-topped door to Jhoira's room.

He tried the handle, but it was locked. He pounded. The wood jumped in its frame. He bellowed a call, but no answer came from within. Lifting a massive foot, Karn kicked the splintering mass inward and, turning sideways, won through.

There was blood everywhere.

Jhoira had struggled, that much was clear. Now the struggle was done forever. She lay facedown in the center of the floor, and a red pool extended from her matted hair out to the edges of the room. Her sodden robe rested over a body that was half the size it should have been.

There were footprints in the blood, iron shod and spike toed. One led into the wardrobe where Jhoira's robes hung. The door was slightly ajar, and from the darkness within peered a feverishly glowing eye.

Monologue

He is not mad. I should never have doubted him. The madness is what he knows is coming, is what is already here. It surrounds me. Its fangs sink into me. Its claws rend my guts. I can somehow feel the warmth of them splatter my feet in the moment before I die.

—Barrin, Mage Master of Tolaria

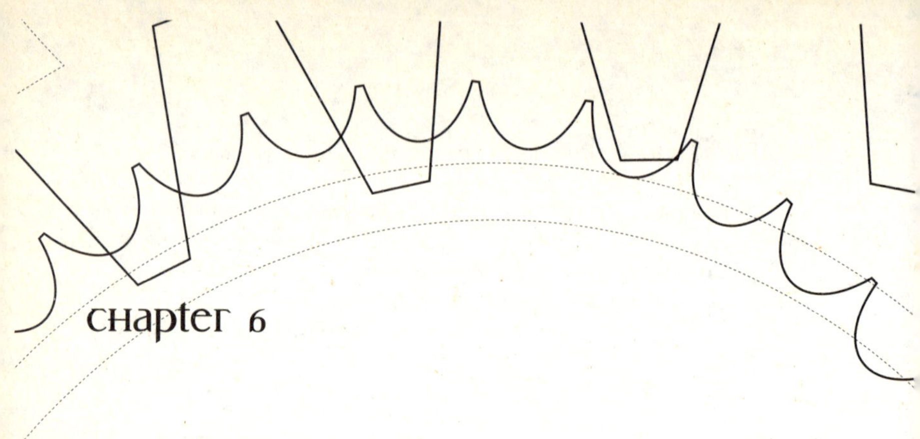

chapter 6

The creature in the wardrobe flung back the bone-inlaid doors, ripping them from their hinges, and emerged.

It was a huge thing, in general configuration human, though with its armor implants, protruding bone spikes, and barb-edged legs, it seemed almost an insect. A pair of steel struts extended its lower jaw, which was tipped with glimmering metal tusks that dripped Jhoira's blood. Its nose had been replaced with another spike, the task of breathing being accomplished through a series of holes bored through the creature's sternum and directly into its bronchia. Its eyes seemed to glow, bedded deep in mirrored sockets, and its horn-studded brow ridge rose into a sagittal crest that also ran with blood. Sharpened tips of bone protruded from shoulders, elbows, fingertips, knees, and toes.

The creature rasped, "Disarm and deactivate yourself, and you will be taken intact. Otherwise, you will be destroyed."

Karn answered by hurling himself at the thing. It was fast, sliding from beneath his descending bulk with all the speed of a snake. Karn clutched one shoulder, but the creature melted away.

It was suddenly on his back. Its scissor-fingers jabbed beneath Karn's headpiece. He remembered how easily Malzra had flung back his skull and removed the powerstone within—

Karn pivoted and toppled, hoping to smash the bug between the hammer of his frame and the anvil of the floor. The monster shifted again, elusive as water, and landed atop him. A red spray went up from the puddle of blood where Karn landed. Gore sizzled on his hot skin. He brought his fists together, pounding the invader's sides.

With a growl and a heave, the beast worked the mechanism at Karn's throat and flung back his skull. Karn could see nothing more, could move little, his limbs jangling around him, but he could feel the spike-tipped fingers slide in around the silver case where his powerstone lay. One yank and the whole assembly would spill forth, and Karn's life would be gone—a fragile crystal clutched in the claw of a Phyrexian killer.

It paused, its fingers catching first upon a small trinket hanging about the golem's neck, the Viashino medallion.

The beast lifted it, looked it over, and softly purred a single word: "Thran."

Karn spoke a different word: "Jhoira."

Gathering together his shattered will, Karn caught up the Thran-metal trinket, broke the silver chain that bound it, and impelled the bauble into the Phyrexian's skull. A gush of hot oil-blood streamed over him.

Screaming, the creature fell back. Karn managed to knock closed his skull-piece and felt his power, his will, reassembling from fragments on the floor. In the next instant, he rose above the crouching killer, the Viashino trinket half-sunk in its frontal lobe. He flung the beast to the ground, and with one stomp of his massive foot, reduced the thing's head into an oily mass of slumped skin, brain ooze, and bone meal. The body trembled for a few moments afterward, but Karn kicked the sloppy corpse aside and knelt beside his fallen friend.

Dead. Jhoira was dead. The rage Karn had felt at his discovery melted now into anguish and sorrow. The silver man crumpled before her. This ached worse than a red-hot frame or a skull-plate peeled back like the rind of a melon.

"They are everywhere," came a stern voice from the doorway. "They are killing everyone. Barrin is dead already. Teferi too."

Karn looked up to see Master Malzra arrayed in battle armor that made him look not unlike the machine-implanted Phyrexian.

"It is too late to stop them. We mustn't thrash at the branches of evil, but chop the root. I will send you back. This whole attack can be averted. Return in time. Return forty-eight hours. Intercept Kerrick and kill him before he can relay the plans. I will guard the machine and fight all corners. I must have Mage Master Barrin back. Let the portal destroy itself, if it must. Let your own frame melt into nothing, but stop Kerrick and his negators."

If I kill him, thought Karn as the smoky beam of the portal danced around him, if I even delay him, detain him, Jhoira will live again.

Beyond the fitful circling of that red ray, Master Malzra worked feverishly at both consoles, his associate lying dead somewhere in the ravaged school.

If I kill Kerrick, thought Karn, it all will be as it was.

Even then, a brace of negators burst through the door. Huge and trussed with steel armor, much like the Phyrexian Karn had already slain, each of these creatures was unique. One had a lupine head and limbs, though its shoulders and torso were human—or once were before they had been pierced in a thousand places by seeking tubes and conduits. Another was a lurching ogre with massive, infolded features, deep, malevolent eyes, and arms as huge as other men's legs. A third was lithe and quick and spidery. These three emerged among spinning shards of the shattered door and plunged toward Malzra.

Karn staggered, almost lurching from the light to drive back the creatures.

Without even looking up from the machinery around him, Malzra lifted a hand and sent out a shocking blast. Three bolts separated from the main surge and caught the monsters mid-chest. Lightning blasted holes where the hearts would have been in humans and raced in crackling fury across the steel frames. Eyes lit from within. Fangs danced with sparks. Muscles glowed eerily where neurons ran, but still the Phyrexians converged.

For the next sorcery, Malzra did not even raise his hand. The spell blossomed full-formed from his mind even as his fingers danced across the consoles. Each of the three creatures abruptly froze, midstride, and fell to the floor, shattering like black ice.

Karn saw no more. In the next moment, all the rest of the world froze. It stood for a shuddering instant, as if on the verge of cracking, and then time began scrolling backward. Broken bits of Phyrexian slid together on the floor and rose up, assembling themselves in midair and retreating toward the door. A gathering spell formed flesh from ribbons of smoke and thrust it into the holes in the creatures' breasts. They obligingly fled outward, rebuilding the door from wood fragments before they departed.

And then time scrolled faster still. The dancing beam shrieked in its frenetic spinning. The world jittered and shook. Master Malzra had harnessed the full power of the device, of its four vectors and its sea-cave turbines, to power this regression. Karn would likely not survive this journey, and even if he did, the machine might not remain to bring him back. But Jhoira would survive, and that would be enough. Jhoira and Teferi, Barrin and the school. If saving them meant losing himself, Karn did not mind. Better to end that way than as a statue in the Hall of Artifact Creatures.

Morning brought darkness to the world; Kerrick entered the laboratory on his last visit and was gone; and evening brought light. Karn waited anxiously through another day and into the morning-twilight beyond. He was already quite hot, his bulk steaming and his plates grinding against each other in expansion. Night deepened. The regression slowed. The light faltered. Karn clenched his hands at his sides and felt the strange, very human impulse to pray—to what god he did not know, perhaps to the time machine itself.

With a light more beautiful than any true dawn, the laboratory door cracked slowly open, and the gray corridor glimmered beyond.

Karn heaved himself from the dissipating pool of light, his own silver bulk glowing a dull red to match that color of the beam. Without pause, he raced toward the now-closing door, grappled the handle, and flung it wide. He barged into the hall just behind the golden-headed Phyrexian sleeper.

Kerrick whirled when he heard the door bang raggedly against the corridor wall. Though Karn was still out of phase, his superheated shell sent wisps of smoke into the air in an aura around his body, and Kerrick saw the shape of the void within.

He turned and bolted. Karn followed. He had not been built for speed, and running taxed his frame. Kerrick darted ahead down the corridor, quickly pulling away.

Perhaps another regression, Karn thought desperately. Perhaps I should be withdrawn for another regression—except the machine may destroy itself to accomplish this one.

Karn was not as fast as the Phyrexian, but he knew the academy and knew where Kerrick headed. Launching himself down a side passage, Karn reached the Hall of Artifact Creatures. He entered quickly, closing and bolting the door behind him.

Karn stalked past deactivated creatures two and three times his size—mechanical mammoths, rovers with the form of steel crickets, spidery devices with hands at the end of each leg. The killer was there, too. Kerrick had entered the chamber from the far end, and he stalked cautiously forward. He was on his way to the west laboratories and would need to pass through the door behind Karn. The silver man eased himself onto a nearby platform and crouched beside the metal skeleton of a clay warrior. There, camouflaged among dead metal creatures, he waited.

Kerrick came. Cautious and quick, he came. A sneer jagged across his lip as he set his hand on the doorknob and pulled, certain he had evaded his pursuer.

Karn fell upon him.

There is an unmistakable sound when bones—whether human or Phyrexian—snap. Kerrick's lower right leg folded below the knee. Shrieking in agony, the man crumpled to the floor.

It was a piteous noise, and Karn, fists balled and ready to finish the man, hesitated. Perhaps breaking Kerrick's leg was enough to stop him, to keep him from escaping the wall and meeting with the Phyrexians. He would be found here by the guard and recognized as a spy. He would be dealt with harshly by Malzra and Barrin, and perhaps they would learn from him who he was, and how many Phyrexians massed, and where. To kill this man insured the Phyrexians would come again, another day, but leaving him alive to interrogate—

Still only half-visible in his phase shift, Karn hoisted the angry man to his shoulders and marched past rank upon rank of artifact creatures. Kerrick arched away from the silver man's burning skin and gave little cries of agony. Prisoner and captor reached the far doorway, passed through it, and started down the corridor beyond.

"I have a spy, a Phyrexian spy!" Karn called out. "Guards! Mage Barrin! Master Malzra!"

Before an answer came, every particle of Karn's being was seized by Malzra's future hand. The machine was drawing him back. There was something different about this summons—its tearing insistence. The silver man jolted under the assault and almost fell. He clutched his captive all the tighter. His frame became griddle-hot. Kerrick thrashed and wriggled. The long dark hallway whirled.

With a shriek of fury, the Phyrexian rammed his fingers beneath Karn's jaw, fumbling for the release mechanism. In reflex, Karn seized the man's hand and flung it violently away. The wrenching movement hurled Kerrick free. He landed, a leg-broken mass, on the stony floor of the hall. Karn staggered back.

The red beam came, a chaotic, stabbing light. The hallway began to dissolve. Karn swung a massive hand toward the Phyrexian, but his fingers closed on wheeling chaos and nothing. Shards of reality slid past in mirror moments. Karn plunged through raveling time.

Something was wrong with the machine, terribly wrong.

The lashing pulses of temporal energy formed a vortex around him, drawing him downward, forward, toward the dark future and its disintegrating mechanism.

The laboratory took fitful shape outside the cone. It winked into and out of existence. A tumbling chaos of red forms blossomed around Karn. For a second time that day, he felt the impulse to pray. The laboratory returned. Malzra's consoles flickered through a shroud of rolling smoke. The master and Barrin labored mightily at the sparking controls. Over Karn's head the time machine swayed ominously, its side panels bleeding soot into the air.

It was disintegrating.

The light orb at the base of the device cracked, sending jabbing rays out in all directions. Where red beams struck, walls turned to dust, machines to slag. Each ray carved a jagged rent in whatever it hit, tearing through the laboratory and the corridors beyond, through the dormitories and the wall itself, reaching out to rend all of Tolaria.

Karn stood in the center of it, shielded beneath the coruscating cone of light.

Then came the explosion.

Red was suddenly gone, red and all other color and all darkness. There was only light in that moment, light like the center of the sun. It came with a fragile shattering sound, as though a crystal had been sundered. A bell-tone keen followed and what might have been thunder if a lightning bolt could be large enough to encompass a whole world.

The air was solid for a moment, an amalgam of gas and energy, then rushed outward. Walls were gone, just as color was before. The rushing inferno rolled out in an incandescent ring from where Karn stood, pulverizing stone and steel and glass. Farther out, the ring devolved into lines of blast as raw energy gathered in radiating avenues. The holocaust obliterated whole sections of the academy and scoured the earth down to bedrock. Other areas remained untouched. Buildings were torn in cross section.

The shock wave pelted outward. It bore a storm of shattered stone and rent metal that consumed with a million gnashing teeth anything it struck. Millennial trees toppled. Stony pinnacles were eaten right through. Green leaves burst into flame. Clouds of dust and ash boiled up from the shuddering forests.

The blaze reached even the sea, and in mile-long arms it boiled water to a depth of five fathoms. It reached to the clouds overhead, flinging some aside and bringing fiery hail from others. It shook the oceans, awakening tidal waves that destroyed coastal villages two hundred miles distant. It was a blast like none felt on Tolaria since the dark days of Argoth.

It was a blast awoken by the same follies of the same man.

Urza stood beyond it all. He had been beside the time portal in the white-hot instant that it exploded. It had taken every ounce of his metaphysical might to gather the particles of his being against the massive waves of power. As mote by mote of matter was blown away from him, he slowly became a being of pure energy. He resolved himself again and again in the first heartbeat of that hailing storm.

In the second heartbeat, he risked it all by reaching out beyond the rolling envelope of destruction and snatching them up, one by one—perhaps not his best and brightest, but those nearest, those who could be saved. Mage Master Barrin was first (yes, the silver man, Karn, had done what he was sent to do, had averted the Phyrexian invasion, though even the facts of that other time loop were as difficult to hold to and reassemble as Urza's own body was), then five other scholars, and eight students. He whisked them up with him in a sudden, spontaneous planeswalk. They would not survive the journey in human form, he knew, and took a moment to transform them all into stone. It could be undone later, when there was time, when there was strength. . . .

Ravening beams streamed past Urza and his company of statues. The death throes of his latest dynamo flung out shrapnel of every conceivable thing. Metal and stone and bone and brain and even mind tore repeatedly through them. Urza held fast against the storm. He rose. He took the others with him.

Now they were . . . where?

The hillside was sunny and green. A gentle, heather-smelling wind strolled easily past the fourteen statues. Urza had saved himself and fourteen others—which meant that more than two hundred were left to die. He had saved himself and Barrin and thirteen others. The negators might have done less damage, but they would have killed Barrin and captured all of Urza's devices and the time machine itself. It had been a reasonable trade. Urza had saved fifteen, and kept his work from Phyrexian claws. Yes, it had been a very good trade.

The Tolarian survivors stood frozen and silent in that caressing wind. There was a single, broad-crowned tree at the top of the grassy hill, and it alone moved, breathing the balmy air.

Urza cast the last enchantment he held. It was his final saving act on that afternoon, for he was spent. He would not be able to maintain his physical coherence much longer. It was a feat of will to cast that last spell, to transform Barrin back into flesh.

Stone became bone and muscle and blood. Barrin awoke.

Brows knotted darkly above his intense brown eyes, the man staggered through tall grass to reach Urza.

"Where are we?"

Urza achingly shook his head. "I do not know."

Nodding, Barrin took a calming breath and looked out over the rolling hills, chartreuse beneath the cloud-cluttered sky. "Why are we here?"

A shadow passed over Urza's features. "Tolaria is gone. The time machine exploded. We are the survivors."

The younger man's mouth dropped open, and he gazed with angry appraisal at the other thirteen, arrayed like tombstones in a forgotten graveyard. "Just us? Just fourteen?"

"Fifteen," Urza corrected solemnly. "You and I, five scholars, and eight students."

Barrin crouched suddenly, clutching his knees. "And the rest?"

Urza blinked. He did not need to blink, but it was an old habit that came with disturbing thoughts. "Most are dead. Some may live, sheltered by rubble, but most likely not."

His assistant remained on his haunches. He panted like a dog afraid of thunder. "We have to go back. We have to get them."

"Teleport, if you have such a spell ready. I can do nothing more for a time," Urza replied grimly. "I am spent. As it is, I cannot anchor myself here much longer."

"I have no teleport spells. I had no thought I would need one," Barrin spat. "Then a boat or something. We have to go save whoever may remain."

Already Urza's form faded, his features shifting. The gemstones that had become his eyes flickered. The fire in them guttered near death. "We will find them in time, any who escape the island tonight. Any who do not will be dead by morning."

Karn heaved on the slanting slab of limestone. It creaked. Its far end ground massively against the edges of the rubble field. The voices beneath cried out in hope and terror as light appeared above—not sunlight, but firelight from the raging flames of the explosion. Karn levered the edge of the stone a foot off the ground, and two young students scrambled out. The silver man hauled the block higher. An aged scholar with a bloody head clawed his way free.

"That's all of us," gasped the man raggedly.

"Head for the jungle," Karn ordered as he let the stone grind back downward. "Go through the ruins, not the clear paths. Move through the deep jungle. Get to the sea. Stay away from the clear paths. They are time gashes, and if you enter them, they will kill you."

The aged scholar was still on his knees, cradling a broken arm. His two young students huddled shivering beside him. The man looked about at the devastation. Here and there ragged remains of buildings towered precariously. Between crumbling stacks of stone, the ground had been scoured to bedrock. Bodies littered the smashed edifices, but in the clear paths nothing at all remained but fire-scarred rock. The old man scratched his silver hair just beneath a bubbling gash. He blinked, and blood droplets leaped from his eyelashes to spatter his cheeks.

"Once we reach the sea, what then?" the man rasped.

"Find others," Karn advised as he moved toward the next sounds of screaming. "Find something that floats. Malzra kept boats on the east shore."

It was all he had time to say. He'd rescued seventeen so far, though most of those would die of their wounds or wander into wild time storms that would tear their bodies apart. Karn had already encountered a few such destructive regions, and even his silver bulk, engineered to survive temporal fluxes, had been nearly destroyed. Any creature of flesh needed only to catch his head in a different time stream from his heart, and his veins would burst. Karn had seen it happen many times already today, too many times.

The screaming came from ahead. Karn found a guard pinned under a boulder. The man's upper body had been burned to resemble the purple-black flesh of a date. His lower body was smashed beneath the giant stone.

"Get it off me! I can't feel my legs. Lift it off me."

Grim-eyed, Karn knelt by the boulder, set his shoulder against its bulk, and heaved. The moment the stone eased up from the man's crushed pelvis and legs, a great tide of blood fled out of his belly, and he sank immediately into death.

Karn let the boulder back down. He stood. He could not imagine a worse fate for these folk—half of them only children and the other half fragile old men and women. He could not imagine how an invasion of Phyrexians could have been worse than this. It was a second Argoth, this destruction, and Malzra was a second Urza, more willing to destroy the whole world than let another creature rule it.

If only Jhoira still lived . . . that might make all this carnage less bitter. If only, but her shattered cell was buried beneath tons of rubble, and no pleading had come from it. Perhaps she had escaped. Perhaps she was still out there, somewhere, in the ruined, burning place.

Another shout came from just ahead, where a tower had fallen atop a corner of the north dormitory. Karn marked the swirling temporal storm that roiled in the space between him and the spot, and he strode out to circumnavigate it.

Perhaps she is still out there.

It was near to midnight when the ship slid slowly from its dock and out into the black, rolling sea. Its masts had burned away along with its sails. About three feet above waterline, its bow bore a gaping, man-sized hole where a red-hot chunk of iron had struck it. The boat was slowly taking on water, but Karn and a few of the other survivors were healthy enough to man the bilge pumps.

The rest—only thirty-three in total—huddled together on the singed deck and watched fearfully as the burning island slid silently away behind them. Fires blazed across the island, and weird lights danced in veils that reached through the clouds overhead. Waves surged in fits against the rocky shores, and a hellish moan of tortured winds made the place seem haunted by the ghosts of the fallen. The Glimmer Moon, near to sinking into the hungry waves, watched the whole display with bald accusation.

Thirty-three survivors, mused Karn grimly as he pumped. The light of the burning isle faded behind them, and only turgid cold blackness lay ahead, the sky and sea indistinguishable and menacing. Thirty-three survivors, and Jhoira nowhere among them. How could a Phyrexian invasion have been worse than this?

"It was a terrible trade," Karn said to himself, "terrible and unforgivable."

Monologue

Urza says he did it to save me. He says he let the time machine explode in order to save me and a handful of others . . . and keep his precious designs from Phyrexian claws. In another time continuum, he claims, I was slain by Phyrexian negators, and the school was overrun. Urza diverted that time stream so we could end up here, or so he says.

He is not truly mad. I know that now. He may be lying—a terrifying possibility, for what dark motive would make Urza lie to me? He may be telling the truth—all the more terrifying. But he is not truly mad.

Tolaria is gone, just like Argoth. And why? To save me? Of course not. I was saved from Tolaria just as Tawnos was saved from Argoth, as a side thought.

Tolaria is gone because if Urza could not have it, no one would. Urza is still Urza. I doubt he will ever return to the island he has destroyed, return to rebuild, to declare himself father to the scholars he has orphaned. I doubt it.

Mad or sane, he does not learn from his mistakes.

—Barrin, Mage Master of Tolaria

PART II
Times Returning

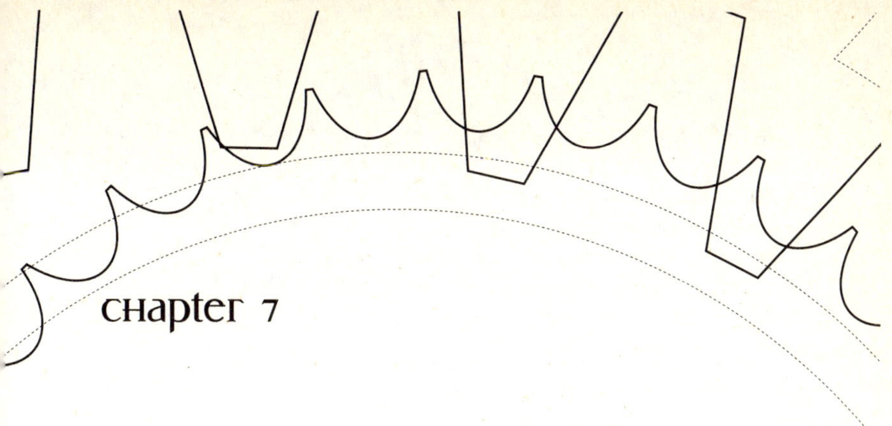

chapter 7

Karn stood at the prow of a very different ship—large and golden and fully regaled—when he next saw Tolaria. The isle was only a dark shoulder above the heaving sea. Sky and water scintillated with life and daylight, but that jag of land on the horizon was as dead and dull as a dried bloodstain. Karn shuddered. He remembered that horrible night among the raging fires and toppled walls and time fissures.

The scratches he had suffered that night had all been polished away. Other improvements had been made in the ten years since the destruction of Tolaria. Master Malzra had completely replaced the finger mechanism that Jhoira had repaired. He had also redesigned the latch and coupling device that held Karn's skullpiece in place, lest other foes learn the trick of it as easily as had Kerrick or the negator in Jhoira's room. In his tinkering way, Malzra had worked a piecemeal overhaul of the power conduits throughout the golem's frame, making his reflexes somewhat quicker. Outwardly Karn seemed a new creature.

Inwardly he felt very old. His intellectual and affective cortex—the dark power matrix—remained, and with it sad memories of his first friends. He thought often of Teferi, the young and brilliant mage. He thought even more often of Jhoira, Malzra's best and brightest artificer and Karn's only true friend. Every day that dawned after that hopeless night, Karn remembered his friend and mourned for her.

"What are you thinking?" came a kindly voice at the silver man's shoulder. It was Barrin. He squinted against the bright sea and sky, and strands of silver glimmered in his hair. His eyes reflected thc dark wedge of distant Tolaria. "You have been standing here all morning."

Karn turned back to face the approaching isle. "I am thinking of lost friends."

Barrin's voice softened. "It is a difficult return for all of us. But one long overdue."

"It is a place of ghosts," Karn observed. He could feel Barrin's intense eyes focused on the side of his face but did not look at him.

"You never cease to amaze me, Karn," the mage master said incredulously, "a machine that sees ghosts all around."

"Don't you remember the lost students, the lost friends?" Karn asked.

Barrin took a long breath. "Oh, yes, I remember them, and I will be sad to be back where they perished. But I have mourned. It has been ten years. There are new flowers rising among your ghosts."

"I still ache over my friends," Karn replied. "It is as raw as on that first day."

"Perhaps it is something to do with flesh. Mourning is healing. You cannot heal. You cannot truly mourn. You can only ache forever," Barrin thought aloud. He sounded pensive. "We'll have to devise some means to keep you from aching forever."

At last Karn turned toward the man. Beyond Barrin he saw the golden ship, manned by a whole new contingent of students and scholars. Gold-painted rails glimmered in the sea-shine, and, white sails reached eagerly toward the isle. At the helm stood Malzra himself, at once ancient and young. The ship's name even told the tale—*New Tolaria*—and for the last eight years, it had been laboratory and tutorial hall and dormitory to all of them, vessel for all of Malzra's pursuits.

It was the genius of humans to discard the old and embrace the new, but flesh was malleable. Silver was not.

"How can I forget this ache and still be me?"

Jhoira stood at the edge of her world. Behind her lay Tolaria, desolated by the blast of Master Malzra's time machine. Before her lay the illimitable sea. She was caught between. Her secret trysting spot had become her home. It was a small place, but dry and clean, appointed with furniture, books, and implements scavenged from the academy.

Most of the old school lay in ruins. The walls that remained were leaning hazards. The walls that had fallen were cairns for the dead. Many of the living had been buried in them too.

Jhoira herself had had to dig for three days to escape the secret passage where she had been when the inferno began. She spent the next three days digging up the final few others who were trapped alive. She and eight others—all young students, resilient, canny, and agile—withdrew from the death-smelling place to Jhoira's secret niche. They, of course, made forays back into the ruins, to bury the dead and salvage equipment and food stores. These trips were far from safe. On the first such excursion, the group lost four of its members who wandered into extreme time rifts and were torn apart. Jhoira and the remaining four learned to avoid such rankling crevasses of time.

Some zones were dark and dry, their flora withered away. These were fast-time areas, where a week might pass in a day. Such places received perhaps a day's worth of sunlight and rainwater in a week and so became chill deserts. The darker and drier the zone, the faster the time in it and the more extreme the rent between it and the temporal flow of the rest of the island. Other zones were bright and wet—steamy swamps. These were slow-time areas, where a day took perhaps a week to pass. In such areas, the sun was intensely bright, moving visibly across the sky, and rain came in constant, short, drenching downpours. Most slow-time areas had not had time to adjust to their new climactic conditions, flooded to their edges and filled with drowned trees. In others, time moved so slowly, the fires of the original blast still stood in orange curtains.

Extraordinary time shifts proved impassable to Jhoira and her companions. Crossing such verges boiled blood and shredded skin, caused some limbs to die of deprivation and turn gangrenous and others to burst as interstitial tissues swelled. Such were the fates of the first four who died. The survivors were careful to map and avoid the violent time rifts. They ventured with trepidation into more moderate time fissures and found them difficult to enter and leave. Changes in inertia caused walking into a slow-time area to feel like wading forward into hardening cement. Emerging from slow time to fast time often resulted in extreme dizziness and sometimes loss of consciousness.

Even so, the final survivor of the school came from an extreme fast-time peak, which fused inexplicably with a slow-time slough beside it. From the normalized zone stepped an old man named Darrob. He had been only a child of twelve at the time of the blast but, five years later, he emerged a gray-haired madman.

There was only one true benefit Jhoira and her companions discovered from these time shifts—slow-water. Water resisted temporal change, retaining the speed of its former milieu awhile before gradually absorbing a new pace. Water that flowed from a certain extremely slow-time zone had preserving qualities, slowing and even stopping the aging of anyone who drank the thick stuff. Jhoira had no real idea how it worked, but she knew it did, at least for the short term. It was by drinking slow-time water that she had stayed young—seeming only twenty-two.

Despite this rejuvenating drink, death stalked the survivors of Tolaria. In the sixth year, their numbers were dwindled from six to five. Out hunting snakes, a fifteen-year old boy fell down the sea cliff, broke his neck, and was dragged out to sea, even as the others swam helplessly after him. Two years later, a pair of eighteen-year-old lovers carried out a suicide pact, leaving only Jhoira, old Darrob, and another young woman. This last withered soon after, wasted by some interior disease. Her ashes nourished the rose bushes she had so patiently planted and pruned and nurtured. In the two years since her death, the roses had gone wild, spreading across the nearby boulders in a savage, fragrant blanket.

Old Darrob was dead now, too. Three months back, he had succumbed to the rattle in his chest. Jhoira had buried him beside the slab of sandstone where Darrob had loved to lie, a great silver lizard soaking up sunlight. His years in the dim depths of fast-time had taught him to love the sun. He had been Jhoira's last companion and, though mad himself, her final hold on reality. Since the day of his death, Jhoira had felt her own soul going wild, like the thorny rose.

She was alone now, yes, but she always had been. The nine who had lived with her had been companions, not friends, not confidantes. The only true friend she had ever had was Karn, and he was not even human. Jhoira often wondered what was wrong with her. Perhaps she had been taken from her people too young. Among Ghitu, a girl was not a woman until she had gone on a vision quest. Jhoira had never gone. She was twenty-eight chronologically and twenty-two by all appearance, but her soul was still the foolish and frightened soul of a child. That child had made one desperate lunge toward adulthood, had opened her secret heart to one man, believing love could not be fooled. It could be. It always would be. The man had proven a monster. Now, forevermore, Jhoira would be alone. It was a miserable way to live, but it was at least that—a way.

The island had become hers. At some point in the forty mad seasons since the blast, her fierce desire to escape the forsaken land had become a fierce desire to protect it from invaders. At first she referred to this new mania as Malzra's Malaise—a fear of invaders, destroyers. Now she was beyond such light and self-conscious word-play. She was the island's protector, its guardian spirit. She was the ghost woman on the western shore, forever watching for nearby ships, forever fashioning arrows as Kerrick had taught her, forever designing and building whatever mechanisms she could for the defense of the land.

And now, with unmistakable intent, a white-bellied sailing ship sliced through the spitting billows, making straight for the eastern ports of the island. Jhoira had not forgotten her dream of glimpsing her soul mate on a ship such as that one, but such were the fantasies of a child. Love could and would and forever must be fooled.

Jhoira watched the ship a moment more before withdrawing into the niche, fetching up her bow and quiver of arrows and heading out to intercept the landing party. With the whole of the island between her and the docks, and over a hundred time rifts slicing through the center, Jhoira would not beat them to the shore. It didn't matter. The island's natural defenses were formidable enough.

Barrin inhaled the salty scent of the eastern bay, remembering the smell of saw grass and palm. He sensed nothing of death or decay in the air and was glad. Perhaps time did heal all wounds. Perhaps Tolaria had forgiven—or at least forgotten—its despoiler.

Barrin glanced back toward Urza, who helmed the golden galley *New Tolaria*. It had become his floating workshop, mobile and elusive, beyond the reach of any petty government. From the moment the refitted and renamed ship had slid out of dry dock, Urza had been its unquestioned master. Captain Malzra, the students called him, and he proved a deft helmsman. Somewhere in his three and a half millennia, the man had learned to sail. Better still, Urza's knack for teaching seamanship equaled his talent for teaching artifice. He did not so much instruct as demonstrate and inspire. The young scholars needed only watch the master hoist the main or scale the ratlines before they all wanted to do it as well and as quickly as he.

Of course, being a functional immortal with a body of pure energy can make even the oldest planeswalker a marvel in feats of strength, agility, and speed.

As *New Tolaria* rounded the stone jetty at the mouth of the bay, Urza manned the helm, and his young crew worked their posts with a quiet ease that allowed them long looks at the land ahead. Barrin, too, studied his erstwhile home.

The eastern docks remained largely intact, though the pilings were desiccated from neglect, and thorny weeds had volunteered in the rotting planks. Two ships of the former Tolarian complement lay half submerged dockside, their upper portions scored with burn marks; and their lower portions so covered in barnacles they seemed made of stone instead of waterlogged wood. As each wave rolled, long and even, across them, they rocked indolently in the basins they had hollowed for themselves.

On the opposite edge of the bay, a sinister slough of dark water lay, its surface churning as though it boiled. A time rift, Barrin realized. Urza had described such phenomena after returning from one of his planeswalking scouting excursions. He had spoken in depth about the physics of the rents but could answer none of the important questions, such as—what happens to mortal flesh that ventures into or out of one? Urza's only response to such queries was, "We'll have to find out when mortal flesh encounters one." Barrin had made sure the students were taught how to recognize temporal anomalies and warned what dangers might surround them. He had even devised illusory models and magical simulations to prepare the explorers, but all he could offer was supposition. The experiments with mortal flesh were yet to come.

Urza steered clear of the time rift and the other hazards in the bay and brought *New Tolaria* smoothly into the deep-water inlet. He shouted orders, and one by one the last few sails were taken in. Released by the wind, the ship lounged aft and piled up glassy mounds of water before it. It slowed to a near stop, Urza leaned on the rudder, and students eagerly crowded the starboard rail, each wanting to be the first to leap to the dock and tie off the ship. Two young women were the first with the strength and daring to jump, and three young men followed shortly after. Their laughing comrades hurled to them thick coils of line, which they swiftly hitched onto the pilings. The great vessel lulled once to the fore with the last of its lazy motion and then settled in on its moorings.

More students leaped to the dock and received the gangplank hoisted down to them. It no sooner boomed into place than the five ensigns and their five exploratory parties were trooping in orderly fashion onto the dock. The ensigns were the oldest students—in their mid-twenties—left from the school at Tolaria, and their parties were picked from late-teens who had volunteered knowing the dangers they would face. These groups debarked with the easy strides of conquerors. The white robes of the former academy had been replaced by rugged canvas cloaks and capes, with leather leggings, knee-high putties, and iron-edged shoes. In moments, the explorers filed off the dock and gathered in clusters, receiving orders. Then, to north, south, west, and the angles in between, they set out.

Barrin watched it all, apprehension knotting the muscles in his neck. If it was Urza's island and he felt so safe on it, why were mere children being sent out to explore it? The touch of Urza's hand on his back made the knots redouble.

"We are home again, Barrin," Urza said, deep satisfaction in his voice.

"We are at the door, knocking," Barrin replied. "We aren't inside yet."

Urza studied his longtime associate and friend. "After all your lectures about owning up to my mistakes, returning to right the wrongs I have done, how can you criticize me today?"

"They're only children, Urza—" Barrin began.

"They are grownups. They have been thoroughly trained. They know what to expect. They know what they risk," Urza replied evenly.

"They're only children. Not grownups, not probes, not machines," Barrin finished.

"If anything should go awry, I am linked to them and can reach them at a moment's notice." Urza paused, seeming to hear a voice speak to him out of the wheeling blue sky. "In fact, the first party of explorers is summoning us. They have discovered a time rift." He reached out and grabbed Barrin's hand, saying simply, "We go."

Barrin felt the world fold in around him and Urza. They were planeswalking.

After complications had arisen with Urza's trick of turning planeswalking mortals to stone (four of them had been cracked en route and hemorrhaged massively when returned to flesh), he had devised better spells for keeping mortal flesh alive through a planeswalk. The enchantment currently in effect reduced Barrin from a three-dimensional construct to a two-dimensional one. In this compacted form, he was protected against the trials of sudden vacuum, volcanic heat, and absolute cold encountered in a planeswalk. Barrin's lungs could not explode because they were no more than flat sheaves of paper. Urza hung there beside him, attached and pulling him through to where the world opened up again.

When it opened, the two scholars stood suddenly on a bald brow of sand. Before them, the land dipped away into a grassy swale. There three students stood, staring in astonishment toward a sharp-edged ravine. The air in the ravine looked dusky and turgid, tiny flecks of dust catching and scattering the rays of the sun. Beyond the deep furrow stood an old-growth forest, but within it, the ground held only short, scrubby plants with tender purple blossoms. Small white rocks lined the base of the valley. At the lip of the ravine crouched the team ensign, a powerfully built blonde woman. Beside her hovered a young man with long black hair. They spoke to each other in hushed tones and gestured into the yawning rift, which emitted a sound like a breathing giant.

"Let's see what they have found," Urza suggested.

He released Barrin's hand and started down the hillside. With each step, puffs of dust rose from his feet, making him seem to walk inches above the ground.

That's the way he would prefer it, Barrin mused to himself as he followed. The two scholars passed the group of whispering students, who startled back, lost the thread of their conversation, and receded into watchful silence. Urza and Barrin continued until they stood behind the crouching ensign and her comrade.

"You summoned me?" Urza said by way of introduction.

The ensign stood and snapped to attention, "Yes, Captain."

"What have you found, Ensign Dreva?"

"A time rift, Captain, just as Master Barrin had indicated in his reports." Dreva's eyes were a bit wider than normal, and she stared into space. "A fast-time rift, I would suggest, judging from the apparent darkness and the lack of water. We have conducted a few experiments. I can repeat them. Rehad?"

She reached out to the young man next to her, gesturing for something, and received a long, leafy branch he had gathered in a nearby forest. Despite her formal demeanor, the affection between ensign and student was obvious in the lingering way the branch was passed, hand to hand.

Ensign Dreva turned her attention back to the captain. "Watch the foliage on the end of this bough."

She raised the branch and swung it slowly into the air above the ravine. Something invisible seemed to take hold of the dangling end, making it jitter and sway, and the ensign dug her feet in and tightened her grip on the bow to keep it from being yanked out of her hand. The leaves quickly grew brown and curled into dry crescents. Next moment, they rushed downward from the branch to the floor of the ravine, where they lulled before turning to dust. Meanwhile, the leafless twigs twisted, their bark peeled away, their wood cracked and grayed, and the entire branch came to resemble the hoary claw of a forest hag. The ensign withdrew the stick and laid it beside two others, similarly transformed.

Urza's smile, small and unaccustomed, showed his delight at these findings. "Excellent work. Using a living branch to probe the rift was an insightful innovation."

The ensign flushed. "Thank you, Captain Malzra."

"There are some who doubted whether you would be equal to the task—" Urza turned his mysterious smile toward Barrin "—but I was confident."

"Thank you again, Captain," Dreva replied. "I suggest we continue probing the edges of this time rift and set warning markers. Though most likely the blast that created the geographic ravine also created the temporal anomaly, we shouldn't assume the boundary of the one will be the exact boundary of the other."

"Well reasoned, Ensign," Urza said. "Continue. Report in if you discover anything else of note." He turned, shouldering Barrin toward the privacy of a nearby hilltop as the ensign sent Rehad and the other students to the forest eaves to gather more branches. "It seems to me they are doing quite well, these children you speak of."

Barrin stared down at the tangled grass at his feet "The dangers here are your doing and my doing, not theirs."

"If they will live here with us, build here and study here, they must inherit all the evils of the past," Urza replied. "It is the responsibility of every new generation to understand what has come before, if only to decide what to keep and what to discard."

The philosophical debate was interrupted by a warning shout from the verge of the forest. Barrin and Urza turned. Ensign Dreva stood at the edge of the wood, grasping something in one arm and urgently summoning her comrades with the other. The students flung down the branches they had chopped loose and ran. Urza and Barrin ran too.

Dreva pulled savagely on a tree limb. Other students, two young men and a woman, reached her and added their muscle to the task. Moments of shouted orders and position-jockeying gave way to groans as the students hauled hard on the limb.

Barrin pelted toward them, wondering what could be so urgent about pulling the branch from a tree, and then he saw.

It was no tree they pulled on, but Rehad, standing just within the forest edge. One hand rested on a fat green bole, just beside a branch he had been intending to cut off. He was trapped in a slow-time rift, one arm extending beyond, and his companions were doing all they could to pull him out.

"Wait!" Barrin ordered. He struggled to form a spell but was too late.

Rehad's arm, bloodless from being trapped beyond the time continuity of his heart, was no match for the pulling might of the ensign and the three others. It dislocated. The tissues caught in the lacerating edge of the time stream tore and gave way. The arm came off in their grasp. Gore dribbled slowly from the ruined shoulder. Ensign Dreva and the students landed in a sloppy heap on the grass, the severed arm among them.

Barrin and Urza came to a stop just before the temporal rift. Rehad's face was slowly twisting in pain as the initial shock of the injury gave way to rending agony. Urza lifted a hand and pressed it into the wall of slow time. His fingers trembled as they sank into the hot, thick air. Had he blood in him, that limb might well have become stuck, like Rehad, but the master inhabited a body of focused energy. Even so, the time difference tugged at him, sending crazings of energy in twisting spirals along the surface of the distortion. With an effort of will, he maintained the forward motion of his hand and slowly gripped the man's bleeding shoulder.

All the while, Rehad was turning, eyes wide and mouth dropping open in a scream. He shied instinctively back from Urza's grasping hand, but the master anticipated the move. He caught the grisly joint and clamped down hard, stanching the killing blood flow, then, with grim deliberation, slowly drawing the young man toward him.

Behind Urza, Ensign Dreva and the students had risen. The severed arm lay on the ground at their feet. Rehad's blood painted their leather leggings and canvas cloaks. Two of the students were crying, and the third gaped in terrified disbelief. Dreva herself was closemouthed and dry-eyed, though her face was bone-white. She shook her head in raw regret.

Barrin moved to comfort her.

She ducked away, grabbed the fallen arm, and pushed up beside Urza.

"Put it back, Captain. You have to put it back," she implored, jabbing the limb toward him.

Gritting his teeth, Urza gently pushed her aside. He was pivoting Rehad around so the man would emerge with brain and heart aligned, so that he could escape the time trap as gradually as possible.

Dreva staggered back. She blinked at the sanguine thing in her grip and tenderly kissed the back of the hand. Her lips patted in quiet words: "Oh, Rehad, forgive me." She laid the limb at her feet and, in a sudden rush like a panicked deer, darted away.

"Ensign Dreva!" Barrin shouted, seeing where she headed.

"Come back!"

She was deaf to it, already hurling herself past the toothy edge of the fast-time ravine. There came a splash of energy as she plunged into the time shift. Rings of temporal flux whirled on the air around her. Waves sank into the ground and rose into the arcing sky. Within their dancing midst, Dreva's airborne form withered. Flesh wrinkled and dried. It cleaved to atrophying muscle and showed bone beneath. Once she had completely entered the envelope, she fell to earth in a sudden rush and was lost to sight beyond the rim of the ravine.

Barrin bolted after her, down the grassy swale and to the verge of the fast-time rift. There he staggered to a halt and gaped.

She was dead already, her dry, deflated skin teeming with vermin.

Barrin turned away, sickened. When he at last mastered his gut, there was nothing left of Ensign Dreva but scraps of canvas and leather and a bleached skeleton.

They sat aboard *New Tolaria* that night. Urza had planned a banquet to celebrate the island's reclamation. Trenchers of salt-pork stew steamed beside vast loaves of marbled bread and mounds of fresh oranges.

The mood was anything but festive. The day had been a chastening failure.

Rehad was below-decks, bandaged extensively and lying in a drugged sleep. Rejoining his arm was beyond the skill of the crew's best healers and beyond the power of even Urza Planeswalker. It lay now in a wooden case within a pocket of extreme slow time in the vain hope it might be rejoined in the future. Meanwhile, Rehad's leader, his love, lay in a pocket of extreme fast time, her skeleton perhaps even now scattered by the tiny scavengers of the ravine.

These two were not the only casualties. Each exploratory party lost at least one member, and one party was wiped out entirely. Urza performed two other rescues like the one he did for Rehad, and Karn assisted in shepherding a young woman from the recursion loop she found herself in. The only non-organic members of the crew, Urza and Karn, had the best resistance to time distortions, though their systems were greatly stressed by these operations.

The crew ate their victory dinner not in Old Tolaria, as Urza had hoped, but on *New Tolaria*. They ate in near-silence. The waters of the bay lapped, black and thirsty, at the gunwales of the great ship, and beyond the beam of the lanterns, the island and sky were black with night.

From the darkness came a woman. She was tan, keen-eyed, and mysterious. A savage skein drew her dark hair back sharply over her head. Garbed in ragged but regal clothes, she seemed an avatar of the isle itself—alien, angry, and forbidding. She strode up the gangplank and onto the deck, pushing past the stunned guards.

Urza stood.

Barrin rose, his mouth dropping open in recognition.

It was Karn, the silver man, who first spoke her name, in a voice like a rain-swollen waterfall. "Jhoira!"

"Master Barrin. Master Malzra," the woman said in a greeting that combined awe and animosity. "I never thought you would return. I wish you hadn't. After today, you probably wish you hadn't, either."

Monologue

I was overjoyed to see Jhoira. Her death had weighed heavily on me and on Karn as well. She was much changed, of course, hard-muscled and hard-eyed. The impulses of wonder and forgiveness had been winnowed out of her. She had ceased to be a student of the academy, becoming a native of the island.

As the island's native advocate, Jhoira spoke strongly in its defense. There, before Urza's new passel of students, she laid out all his past sins, planted like thistles across the island and grown up now into great killing forests. Quite openly, she berated him for his time machine. The tampering that had brought about the blast had riven the tapestry of days on the island and left it a jumbled mess. She talked of the other survivors who had, one by one, perished, leaving her alone.

Even more powerfully, she spoke of how life here had continued. Fast-time forests had died and fallen away, giving place to new plants and animals, to an arid tundra ecology with its own balance of predator and prey. Slow-time forests had turned into swampy jungles, hot and steamy—refuges for thousands of creatures that could not have survived on the island before. Within all these details, I sensed how the years had changed her too.

"We are, Master Malzra—" she had said at the end of it all "—we are your children of fury, orphans who have grown up in your absence, no longer yours, no longer beholden to you. Many of us hate you, Master Malzra."

He listened through it all. I'll give him that much. And then, into the unhappy silence that settled, Urza spoke, and what he said filled me with even more admiration.

"I understand. But I am committed to return, and I don't want to fight you, my children of fury. I want to be reconciled. It will be a thorny way, I know, charged with the thistles I myself planted. But I am committed to return."

"You'll need an advisor," I said, "a guide. Jhoira, I can think of no one better than you to help Master Malzra understand the mistakes of the past and avert them in the future."

There was one final, anxious moment, and then something in her broke.

The mad sheen of defiance cracked, and I saw beneath it a lonely woman fearing but needing to be among others.

"Only because if I refused, every last one of you would die."

I tried to look grimly chastened, but I was elated. Urza was pleased too. The fearful students and scholars were both jangled and relieved. Someone—even this frightening wild woman—had to guide them through the terrors of Old Tolaria.

—Barrin, Mage Master of Tolaria

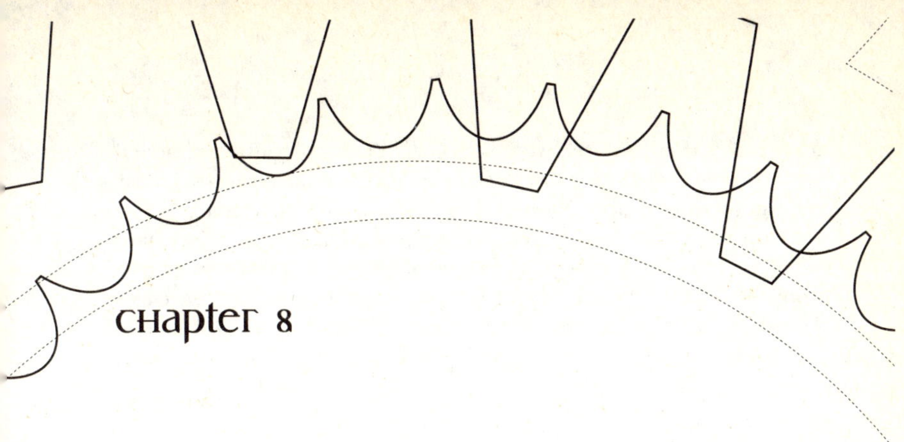

chapter 8

When most of the crew awoke the next morning, Jhoira was already on deck. She had drawn aside to trade stories with Karn. Though fierce and formidable around other humans, Jhoira laughed and spoke easily with the golem. They were an impressive pair—the wild woman and the silver man. Her flesh was as smooth and brown as the sandstone shoulders around the bay, and his as mirror-bright as the sea they had crossed.

Karn told her of all the students and scholars he had rescued, and how he had searched late into the night for her, allowing the refugee ship to leave only as the Glimmer Moon sank in the sea. Jhoira told her own stories of rescue and loss. All of this passed without the long, awkward silences of the night before, as though not a moment had gone by between these long-separated friends. They walked along the shore and reminisced, skipping stones in the choppy waves, until the deck was teeming with crew, and the smell of freshly brewed tea drew them back aboard.

Jhoira drank eagerly, burning her lip with the piping stuff. She smiled at Karn and said, "There are certain drawbacks to being a 'wild woman' and among them are forgoing real tea from a porcelain cup."

The crew broke their fast with a second feast, those going ashore knowing the meal would have to last them until they made camp at the center of the isle. Jhoira predicted that with a caravan of fifty, it would take the whole day to thread their way past the worst time rifts and through the mildest ones.

Jhoira's tone of gloom returned as she described to the crew the temporal distortions of the island. They resembled the physical topography after the blast. At the detonation point was a wide temporal basin like a blast crater, where the explosion uniformly ripped away the natural flow of time. Near the edges of this slow-time crater were a series of concentric rills of time, tightly packed fast-zones. The center would be unreachable except for avenues of force that radiated spoke-like from it and joined the outer island with the inner. Many of these avenues were deep slow-time rents, though others allowed a gradual descent into the crater. Others still had admixed with the fast-time shells nearby to make bridges of normal time. Beyond these concentric fast-time rings were large, irregular regions of extreme time shift, many contiguous square miles of territory unreachable to those outside—sheer time plateaus and deep time canyons. In these areas, whole new ecologies had evolved and cultures with them.

Bearing only the clothes on her back and a long walking staff, Jhoira led a pack-laden parade of scholars and students up the winding forest paths between temporal canyons and plateaus.

Urza followed just behind her. He carried a large wooden case with ornate inlays of brass and ivory. It looked terrifically heavy, but his strides were weightless, and his questions came easily despite the panting of others. Perhaps he had cast an enchantment that let his feet glide among the gorse, or perhaps microscopic machines did the walking for him.

Barrin came next, carrying the stowed tent that would hold him and Urza, as well as clanking pots and an assortment of swaying parcels.

Behind him, Karn carried the burden of ten men. Throughout the line, other, smaller automata ambled beneath heavy packs. The rest of the company consisted of aging scholars and young students, at once eager and fearful about what lay ahead.

"Karn, come up here. I want you to see this," Jhoira said.

She gestured toward a wide, glaring, and desolate swamp filled with the ghost-gray corpses of drowned and burned-out trees. The water in it was black and seemed infinitely deep. Insects hung in static suspension above the mirror waters. Some were poised just before death, the goggle eyes and gaping mouths of fish stretching the surface tension below.

"I call this Slate Waters. Here the fires from the original explosion went out only seven years ago, after drenching rains. Before then, a pillar of smoke rose above the spot. By my calculations, in Slate Waters the equivalent of ten days have passed since the blast. Step in there, and you'd need a time machine to get back out."

Karn stared at the spot. It reflected darkly in his hide. "My time-traveling days are done. Master Malzra is intent on other pursuits. I'm not much needed these days." The words sounded at once relieved and disappointed.

Jhoira studied her old friend. Provisions hulked up from his massive shoulders.

"Don't worry, old friend. *I* need you." She patted his side and pivoted. "Now look over on this side of the path. That's a temporal plateau. I call it the Hives because of the domed mud huts that its residents build across it." She pointed to a region that was forever in twilight, the land sunk in a vast pall.

Scattered forests of short, scrubby trees clung to the hillsides, a gray and torn fabric of woodlands that looked all the more spectral because of the blur of their wind-rattled leaves and rapidly growing boughs. Here and there, in clear patches among these stern woodland copses, rounded hovels took rapid shape, proliferating like chambers in a mud-daubers' nest until whole dim villages could be discerned in spots, and slender footpaths marked the ground between them. The villagers themselves moved with unseeable speed. As quickly as a particular settlement would mound into being, it would dissolve away again, ephemeral as bubbles atop boiling water.

"Five of their generations are born and die during one of our years," Jhoira said levelly to Urza, who had taken the occasion to stop and stare.

Barrin, coming up behind, asked breathlessly, "Five generations of whom? There were no natives on this island."

Jhoira's eyes were keenly fastened on Urza's face. "I can only assume these were students of the academy, caught in extreme fast time, as unable to escape their rift as we are to enter it. They are fifty generations removed from your school. They have lived a thousand years of tribal history since then."

Barrin was stunned silent for a moment. Then he said, "They see us right now, don't they? The hour it will take us to march past their land will be four days of their time. We are statues to them."

"Yes. Unreachable, inexplicable, nearly immobile statues," Jhoira affirmed. "They can hear us, too, but our speech is deep and long and meaningless, like whale-song. Haunting and otherworldly. They've become a different race from us. Soon they'll be a different species." She began walking again, and the line of students and scholars stretched out behind her. "There's an even more fearsome sight in another time plateau ahead. But first, paradise."

All down the lines, scholars and students traded intrigued looks and hunkered down beneath their burgeoning packs. Jhoira led them up a meandering hillside, past stands of cypress and creeping vines on the left and a gray place of tumbled downs on the right. For some time, the hives of mud and stick were still visible, boiling and receding among the trees.

Eventually, the party reached a new place, a highland with rolling green embankments and thick forest growth. The native flora of Tolaria thrived here on the bright hillsides. Fat-boled trees were green from root-clusters to crowns. Vines like vein work coiled along every stem. Broad leaves lay in a series of dense canopies above.

"This is a mild slow-time area, where sunlight and rainwater are gently enhanced, where creatures and plants live in abundance, where the heat of the canopy is matched by the cool of the forest floor. The hills allow enough runoff to keep the land from becoming deluged, and the hollows where water collects are deep and clear and cool. It is paradise. I call it Angelwood, after the fireflies that light it at night. Whenever I have grown exhausted from my cliff-side vigil. I have come here to swim and climb and breathe again. That is perhaps the best part, breathing again."

Eyes all around the group turned hungrily toward the garden of delights. Sweat-dotted brows eased.

Among the vast tree trunks, large bright birds flew dreamily through curtains of light and shadow. Beneath them, water bounded down a sloping face of stone and emptied into a clear brown channel. After coiling among the forest's seeking roots, the waterway slid into a nearby vale, forming a deep, cool pool before spilling into another stream at the far side. Beneath the surface of the water, the silvery gleam of fish shone.

"Why didn't you make this your home?" one student asked, pushing brown hair back from her eyes. "The game is plentiful, the nights are warm, the water is pure, and you would live longer there than anywhere else."

Jhoira was grim. "You can't live in paradise."

She set out again. The company behind her lingered, a few sipping on canteens, but most just standing and staring. One student made a point of scrawling a crude map on a piece of paper, apparently intent on returning to this spot when time allowed.

Jhoira led the group up toward a wide level place where an outcrop of ancient granite had been worn down like a filed tooth. Aside from the eastern pinnacles, this summit was the highest point on the island. Its gray crown was scoured clean by the blast, dead trees lying in parallel lines all about the peak. Young trees sheltered by the fallen logs rose in the midst of the devastation, a future forest. From the top of the rock, the views were clear from the pinnacles in the east to Jhoira's niche in the west.

There, atop that worn-down stone, the company of fifty paused to catch breath and shake out weary legs. The intimate vistas of Angelwood were replaced by the panorama of what Jhoira called the Giant's Pate. In the east, the sea was a quicksilver curtain streaming down from the white-rising sun. *New Tolaria* was a dark and tiny silhouette against it, crew resting about the deck in the quiet of morning. The shore was a beige ribbon, silky and coiling. Inland, forest and briar, marsh and meadow made shifting patterns of green and gray, shade and daylight. It was a verdant land.

Not so the westward Isle. Its distant shore was a bright orange pile of rankled rocks, among which Jhoira's niche nestled. Closer to the Giant's Pate, the ruins of Old Tolaria lay. They were gray and blighted. The onetime logic of walls and paths was still obvious in the maze-work of foundations, but most of the buildings had been razed by the blast. Here and there part of a structure remained, sometimes in gutted, unnatural towers with open sides and decrepit backbones of stone. Though not an actual crater, the slow-time field of Old Tolaria was noticeable in the bright shimmer of the air over those ruins and the water that lagged in cellars and leaning doorways.

Nearby the glaring section that was Old Tolaria was another district, a place of deep darkness in a literal canyon. It lay in the morning shadow of the Giant's Pate, but its gloom was intensified by the high, leaning walls of the canyon and the vast time shift within it. The floor of the space was indistinguishable, and some of the students whispered it was a crack right through to the underworld.

"It looks like a good place for ghosts," one said.

"If I were dead, I'd choose a home like that," another answered lightly.

"It looks like a scar in the world," ventured a third with awe, "a bad scar, one that tried to close and heal but only festered and grew deeper."

"You are more right than you imagine," Jhoira said. "That is a very deep chasm and a sheer fast-time precipice. But there is a bottom to it, and there are creatures trapped in it."

"Like the tribes in the Hives?"

"No," Jhoira said flatly. "Look there. You may not be able to see it while the Giant's Pate casts its shadows—sometimes it can't be seen even at the height of midday, but there is a fortress down there."

Urza's brow furrowed in concern. "A fortress?"

"Perhaps it is only a kind of commune, but what I have seen of it looks savage and braced against attack."

"What have you seen?" Barrin asked.

"Spiked battlements, for one, a causeway of suspension bridges between high guard towers, flying buttresses that look like they are fashioned of dragon bone, windows as: black and smooth as onyx, fiendish adornments, and thick-cast tiles of clay. I have the notion they would prefer to make everything of steel, if they could make it, but iron is the best they have and not much of it. It has taken many hours of distant observation to piece that much together. I would not suggest close scrutiny: I've seen harpoons fly from that space, spear deer, and drag them in."

Barrin blinked in confusion. "This barbarous culture arose from refugees from the academy? Students of ours?"

"Again, no," Jhoira said. "You remember that man, Kerrick, whom you found with the broken leg, whom you interrogated as a Phyrexian sleeper? The man I had let into the academy? Remember that he escaped an hour before the blast? He must have been trapped in that fast-time gash—he and whatever Phyrexian negators he had summoned to Tolaria."

Through a two-story-tall window of polished obsidian, K'rrik watched the new arrivals. They stood atop the gleaming peak at the height of the island, a summit always visible to K'rrik and his retainers here in the depths of the abyss.

Jhoira was among them. She seemed, in fact, to be leading them. She had been a canny foe during the century of his imprisonment in this timegash. She never entered range of the harpoon crews, and more's the pity. He had much to repay her for. Betrayal to Urza Planeswalker was chief among the offenses. Putting a harpoon through her gut and hauling her across the jagged lip of the chasm to burst like a fist-clutched skull—that would have been glad repayment of her debts.

She probably still called him Kerrick. She probably, still thought of him as a golden-haired boy, but a hundred years had turned Kerrick to K'rrik, had made the smooth-skinned Phyrexian sleeper into a hoary warrior.

If there were some way to bring Jhoira over alive, not masticated like the goat and deer carcasses they feasted on, K'rrik would at last consummate their "love." That was her other great offense, her persistent virtue in the face of his advances. It was galling that flimsy chastity should stand against the might of Phyrexia.

Of course, if he could drag her across whole, he himself could have escaped this abyss. It had taken the death of half his negator minions—twelve of the twenty-four—to finally convince K'rrik to suspend his escape attempts. Even so, with each new generation decanted, he sent one in ten out to seek escape—a tithe to his eventual return to Tolaria, to Dominaria.

This ten percent attrition was no great loss. He still commanded a mighty nation of two hundred Phyrexians. They filled every corner of the chasm. Generations of them worked in the deep dank of the waters at the base of the canyon. They hatched, netted, and gutted the various species of blind scavenger fish that were their major diet. Other Phyrexians, for generations, drilled deep into the chasm walls in search of buried veins of obsidian and the basalt stones the palace was built of. Scant resources had been the only real limit to K'rrik's inventive genius. If he could make steel or powerstones, his artifact creatures would have overrun the isle eighty years ago. As it was, what little iron the miners found was more precious than gold. It was constantly oiled with Phyrexian blood to prevent rust. An iron sword like K'rrik's was a kingmaker. It made him unopposable in the arena and maintained his power. Thus the miners who found scant veins of iron were essential to his power base, the figurative foot soldiers of his regime. By carefully distributing these slivers of iron among real foot soldiers, K'rrik controlled a private army engineered to be loyal only to him. These killers used draconian measures to ensure the compliance of all the others. K'rrik presided over the army and the nation because he had created both and was the smartest, strongest, and most vicious of them all.

To these native talents, the Phyrexian sleeper had added enhancements to himself of bone and steel and, eventually, even spawned tissue implants. He was indomitable in the arena. His once-smooth shoulders were now adorned with tusks hollowed out to inject scorpion-fish poison in anyone he fought. Similar spikes jutted from his elbows and knees. The spikes were back-barbed like arrows so that once they sunk into flesh, they ripped it out in great chunks. His torso was braced by a black-steel frame that prevented his spine from being broken and allowed him to break the spines of others. He himself had wielded the cleaver that removed his outer two fingers of each hand, making room for more venom spikes. The century of imprisonment in the abyss had done much to perfect his form.

Now, gazing through the thick, dark glass of his upper throne room, K'rrik saw the means by which he would at last escape his prison—the power of his old foe, Urza Planeswalker.

It was a bitter pill for Master Malzra, Jhoira could tell. The man stood there, gazing into that black jag in the ground. His eyes saw more than most eyes did—they gleamed with an acute, penetrating judgment. Surely they saw past the shrouding murk to the Phyrexian colony that lay within it. Surely Malzra peered into that black pile of basalt and obsidian to the wretched creature at the heart of it—malicious and brooding, growing a year in strength for every month outside.

Kerrick was the man. Even without preternatural sight, Jhoira knew that. Of course, he was no man, but a monster wearing the skin of a man. She knew he was at the nexus of that vast infection and that he would be powerful now, perhaps the equal of Malzra himself, perhaps his superior.

Karn's eyes, too, saw more than most. He drew Malzra, Barrin, and Jhoira aside from the others.

"It is no secret to any of you what I was made for—to travel down the throat of time. Perhaps I have found my new purpose here, to enter that place and destroy them." The suggestion was made with a mild, matter-of-fact tone, but in a voice like the myriad whisper of trees before a summer storm.

A knowing glance passed between Malzra and Barrin.

The mage said through a grim smile, "I seem to remember just such a journey, from my study of arcane lore. There was once upon a time a planeswalker who went into Phyrexia to destroy it. He was armored much as you are, Karn, but was nearly destroyed in the attempt."

Malzra nodded. "It is a good analogy. What we have here is a pocket Phyrexia. And in Tolaria." His all-seeing eyes were suddenly hooded beneath angry brows. "Jhoira, you spoke last night of the children of fury

I have left in my wake—the orphaned mistakes that have, in my absence, grown up to defy me, to hate me, to harry me and slay me if they can. I see now just how true your words are." He blinked and drew a deep breath, two actions that signaled a powerful shift in the mind of the man. "Better not to create such foes than to be forever fighting them."

Barrin looked with admiration at him.

The sun glinted from Malzra's lifted eyes as he marked its march across the sky. "Already the sun begins its descent. Come, take us to Old Tolaria, to a place where we can safely make camp. Somewhere outside the slow-time slough in the center of the blast. Preferably on high ground nearby, where time follows its normal courses."

A solemn look crossed Jhoira's face. "I know just the place."

She turned, heading for a path down from the Giant's Pate toward the decimated academy below. Squinting in tired amazement, the students and scholars on the hilltop watched her go. Many of them were worn out from staring into the impenetrable blackness of the Phyrexian rift and exhausted from the nettling worry that the cleft awoke in them. They had unpacked meals of press-bread and jerky. When Jhoira marched on, they glanced a question at Master Malzra and Barrin. The two men took their last survey of the spot and started after her. Flashing on the brow of the hill, Karn also set his feet to the path. With angry sighs, the students jammed their half-eaten lunches back into their packs, hauled the parcels to their shoulders, and stomped onward down the trail.

Jhoira took a path that had been carved out by her own feet during her rambles. It passed a number of other time rifts, these small and severe, some as narrow as an arm's breadth but a mile in length. Jhoira called these the Curtains of Eternity because anyone who ventured into them would be instantly torn to pieces. There was no need to instruct the party to stay strictly to the path.

Beyond loomed the labyrinth of riven buildings that had once been the Tolarian Academy. The march line stilled to silence as they approached the necropolis. The older members of the company had lived in these gutted hulks, had had friends who died in the cross-sectioned towers and lay even now, skeletal, beneath the piles of cut stone. To the natural dread that came upon them all in descending into that dead place, there was added the drag of slow time on their hearts and lungs. To step onto those ravaged and rubble-strewn streets was to sink into a nightmare made real in stone and bone and ash. Eerily, the sun shone bright and merciless in that flagging place. Those who glanced up toward it saw the fiery ball fleeing visibly toward the horizon.

During their tour of the old town, Jhoira led the group to a particularly disturbing sight. It was the statue of a young man running. Both feet hovered impossibly above the ground. His mouth was wide in despair. His eyes were clenched tight. His hands groped out madly. His white robes were lit with a diffuse orange glow that enwrapped him and rose into an onion-shaped dome over his head. The young man was ensconced in a pillar that shone with fiery light. Just ahead of him, floating still in air, was a heavy cloak, caught in the moment before descending to enfold him.

Jhoira watched the faces of Malzra, Barrin, Karn, and the older students and scholars, looking for recognition. They stared bleakly for some time, their minds unraveling the mystery before them.

At last, Karn breathed the name: "Teferi."

"Yes. He was caught in flames when the blast occurred. Only a moment of time has passed for him in these ten years. When I discovered him here seven years ago, I fetched a heavy cloak, soaked it in water, and flung it into the air to engulf him. In another few years—a split second of his time—he will be wrapped in it, his burning robes extinguished. Perhaps a few years later, he will tumble to the ground. Perhaps in ten years, he will see the *New Tolaria* and strive to reach it. Then, of course, he will be torn to pieces." Her face hardened. She gnawed at one lip. "That damned cloak is all I can do for him. I've studied the time fissure, performed experiments, tried everything I could imagine, but he's caught and cannot be saved."

Stunned silence followed this revelation. Fifty sets of eyes traced out the doomed figure, frozen in fire, unreachable, but only an arm's length away.

At last, Malzra spoke words that comforted them all. "The first area of study for our new academy will be techniques to rescue this young man."

Jhoira wore a grim expression as she turned away. She led onward at a stern pace. The young students, some only children of twelve or thirteen, followed close behind. Older marchers paused at Teferi's Shrine, as some were already calling it. Master Malzra, Barrin, and Karn themselves brought up the rear of the procession.

The marchers felt their sunken spirits and slowed hearts rise again as they climbed the headlands on the southern verge of the ruins. Beyond lay a wide, level place covered with tall, dry grass. The parched blades made a familiar and soothing noise in the warm afternoon winds.

Despite Jhoira's steady pace, evening deepened across the hilltop by the time Malzra, Barrin, and Karn reached the summit. There the master looked about with his piercing eyes. He marked the closeness of Old Tolaria, of the Curtains of Eternity, and beyond it the Phyrexian canyon where his foes, even then, multiplied.

"You were right, Jhoira," he said simply. "This is just the place." He walked to the pack of one of his young, tired hikers, drew a tent spike from the gear stowed there, and, with the sheer force of his hand, drove it deep in the dry ground. "Just here, we will build our new academy."

Monologue

I was bone-weary and soul-weary that first night when, by lantern light, we erected our tent city. We cleared fire circles, set stones to hem them in, gathered firewood and water for the evening, and sat down to dried meat, press-bread, and a little hot broth. I had been the one all along telling Urza he must return to Tolaria, must rectify his past mistakes and embrace the children of fury. But in glimpsing those children for the first time—whether the tribal folk of the Hive, the unseeable Phyrexian hordes in the gorge, or the ghosts of the dead that almost palpably haunt the ruins of the academy—I fear I was perhaps wrong.

Forgetting the past, fleeing the death it holds, shrugging off the wounds—this is the way mortals live. Yesterdays are supposed to remain dead. It is the gift of time. Each new generation is supposed to be born ignorant of the horrors that came before. How else can any of us live?

And, yet, perhaps I was right after all. Urza is not mortal. He cannot afford to forget, any more than time can afford to forget. The world is not large enough to let him go from mistake to mistake, leaving destruction in his path. He has to clean up after himself. In a way, his mania to return in time was a desire to remember, to own up to the past. He likely would have come to this conclusion with or without me. Of course, now that Urza has decided, we might as well assist his every endeavor, for he won't change his mind for another millennium or so.

I only hope, after all this temporal fiddling, I have the blessing of dying after a normal human span—not before and certainly not after.

—Barrin, Mage Master of Tolaria

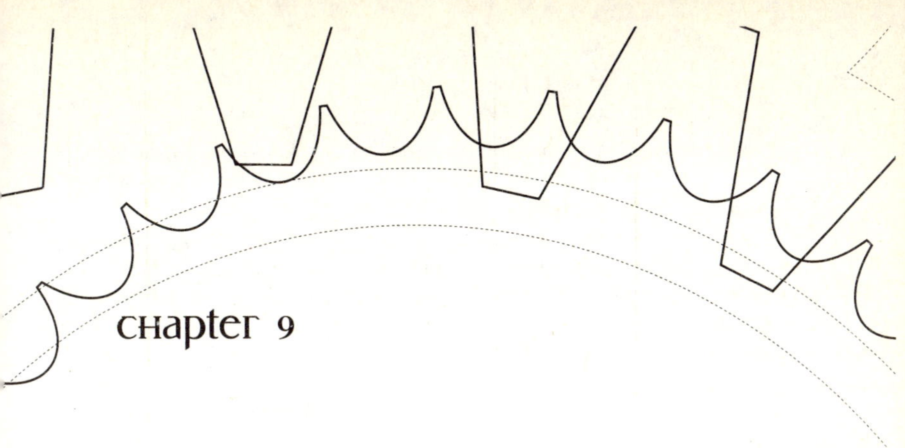

chapter 9

The heavy wooden case Malzra had borne on his back turned out to be an elaborate desk. He unfolded it next morning to the surprise and delight of the breakfasting students. The surface of the thing was smooth ebony composed of various panels. Each black wood panel slid out of the main compartments on hidden joints and fused seamlessly with its counterparts. The end result was an extensive, smooth tabletop, as wide as Malzra's arm span and twice as long. The work surface rested on cabinets with many small drawers and compartments. By some ingenious trick, the whole thing—cabinets and drawers and all—had collapsed easily into a compact box. More marvelous than even these capacities: no sooner was the desk fully set up, than Malzra drew open drawer after drawer, producing styluses, spanners, rule rods, compasses, protractors, a set of angle edges, and roll after roll of plans. He smoothed the last down atop the workspace, struggling to get them to lie flat until Barrin set a stone on each comer of the sheets.

Barrin and Malzra stepped back, allowing the gathering crowd of students to look on grand vistas in lead and ink. There was a soaring central hall, with room to seat four hundred students and scholars, a series of balconies overlooking the grand space, and an empyrean vault open on one side to show the dense forest canopy. There were fanciful towers, rounded and lean like exotic gourds, some topped with guard stations, others with fire towers, and others still with observatories that bristled with optical paraphernalia. The outer wall was an enormous bulwark of earth and stone, with a notable absence of sewage grates and duct work.

Long, curved corridors, great hanks of jeweled-glass windows, an aviary, aerial docks, a gymnasium, a large, rock-lined pond, gardens and groves. The dormitories provided private rooms that were bright and open—no longer the cells of the previous prison. Every aspect of the design was marked with imaginative ornamentation—octopodal figures, fantastical sea prawns, Tolarian drake-head appointments, four-winds motifs, devices drawn from the naval architecture of *New Tolaria*, gulls and kingfishers, anvil-headed storm clouds, tridents and coral and nautilus shells.

This was not the stern infirmary of the previous Tolaria. This was not a prison. Asceticism had given way to aestheticism, strict artifice to fanciful art.

"Of course," Malzra said to no one and everyone at once, "we will have to move the eastern gate from there—" he pointed to a place on the plans, and the corresponding location on the topography before them, "—to there, allowing easier access to the safe path and Angelwood beyond."

Barrin assessed his friend. "I'm glad to see you've not turned the school into a fortification after seeing the Phyrexian rift."

Malzra smiled tightly, drawing a new plan to the fore. "They are the ones to be imprisoned, not us. Look, here. This is the first building. It will be everything to us to start with—great hall and sleeping quarters and tutorial space. In time it will be my private lab." He indicated a large lodge with walls of stone rubble and a peaked roof held up by tree boles felled and lashed together. According to the schematics, the initial roof would be thatch, but in time it could be converted to shake and eventually to slate. "It will stand there, on that rocky ridge at the edge of the tent city. We start building it today."

Breakfasts were forgotten in the ink-and-parchment visions of a bold, bright future. The whole encampment gathered around to hear their assignments.

One ensign and his contingent were given guard of the camp, charged with setting up posts, building palisades, organizing a day-and-night patrol schedule, and assembling an arsenal. The guard group's duties would include the investigation and marking of temporal danger zones, as well as exploration into techniques for rescuing Teferi from his pillar of frozen time.

Another ensign and her team were sent out to thoroughly survey the ruins of the old academy, cataloguing whatever could be salvaged—block and brick, wood and steel, furnishings and artifacts. She was also charged with making recommendations for a site and structure that would be a memorial to the students and scholars who had died in the blast. Barrin volunteered to join this group, as he was keenly interested in the proper disposition of any remains the group might encounter.

A third group—called the food commission—was sent out with Jhoira. They sought glades where they could set rabbit snares, ponds in which to string lines for fish, and verdant fields for planting. Malzra urged Jhoira to make the best use of mild fast-time areas, where hares and fish and crops could mature in weeks instead of months.

Another team took up picks, shovels, levels, stakes, and twine. They began clearing the location of the new lodge and excavating a foundation per Malzra's plans and elevations. Karn accompanied this group, intent on lending his strength to the earth-moving tasks.

The last group accompanied Malzra himself on a return trip to the Giant's Pate. There they initiated further study of the Phyrexian gorge and suggested strategies and devices for the extermination of their century-old foes. Malzra spoke of an ancient and minute device, a tiny crystal attuned to the Glimmer Moon and suspended like a lodestone in a drop of water. When the moon rose, the crystals were drawn upright and emitted a high-pitched tone that dismantled Phyrexian blood, breaking glistening oil to its component parts. By mass-producing these "spiders," as he called them, and introducing them into the gorge though one of the rivers that flowed into it, they could hope to slay the whole army of Phyrexians before any of them knew what had happened.

With the quiet and determined efficiency of refugee ants digging a new hill, Malzra's company marched out across the strange and hostile hillsides of Old Tolaria. The tents that had sheltered them the night before fluttered, empty and clean, in the hot, shifting air of summer. The columns of fire that had held up the black vault of night now smoldered in gray slumber. There was a sense of expectant hope in the air. Around axe-wielding arms and bent shoulders and shovel-prodding feet, there arose the airy vision of a new academy taking shape all around them.

As the last sharpened logs were set in place about the tent camp and the foundations of the new lodge, a cool breeze moved through the surrounding forest. The summer's labors were done. Autumn had arrived. Workers paused. They breathed deeply, straightened their tired backs, and lifted grimy, streaming faces toward the sun. Life at sea had been no idle existence for the crew of *New Tolaria*, but at least it had not held the daily back breaking task of wrestling the earth—piercing it, digging it, lifting it, hauling it, dumping it, compacting it. The grit at sea had been largely salt, which washed easily enough away and provided the skin certain natural protections against insects. This grit was good, black earth. It coated everything evenly, never completely washed away, and smudged the books and scrolls that the scholars and students studied in their off-hours. They were a brawny, tanned, industrious lot after their long months of labor, starting to look like Jhoira, like natives of the island.

The cool breeze riffled tents where students rested or studied. It fanned flames where a midday meal of fresh-water fish sizzled. It kicked up dust from wheeled litters that dragged dressed tree boles into place for the lodge's nearly complete vault. It rattled the roll of animal skins that would, when complete, become a great dirigible to lift Malzra's Phyrexian war machine. The breezes seemed all too eager to bear the dismantled machine into the air. Most of all, the refreshing wind buoyed heat-weary workers, promising of cooler days and more rain.

Barrin drank in the air as he marched up the hill that led into the palisades. Autumn would mean tall, dry grasses, ready to be scythed and sheaved and draped into a roof for the lodge. The place would be warmer and drier than the tents and more resistant to mosquitoes and snakes. The prospects of real beds and real pallets was enticing, too.

Even so, Barrin's uplifted mood came not from hopes of future comfort but from the completion of long labors. The ruins were fully scavenged. Every bit of useable stone had been hauled to the site of the new academy, many of the rougher pieces already incorporated in the mortared lower walls of the lodge. Barrin's team had also discovered the wreck of the Hall of Artifact Creatures and rescued from that shattered place many operable pieces of machinery. These Urza had used to construct five *su-chi* lifters, units designed to perform the heavy tasks of the construction projects.

The most important result of these scavenging efforts culminated today, though, and Barrin had climbed into the encampment to gather Urza, Karn, Jhoira, and any others not immediately employed to come see the result.

"It's finished," Barrin said simply, brushing dust from his hands as he stood before Urza.

The planeswalker glanced up distractedly from the plans for his war machine, nodded, and gestured to a pair of students to remove the face plate they had just attached to the metal framework. One of the young men gave him a look of consternation, to which Urza replied sternly, "We have to deepen the belly of that piece or the incendiary devices won't slide smoothly from the payload chamber. They might get jammed, they might explode within the superstructure.

"Now do it!"

As the students set to work, Barrin repeated, "It's finished. I'd like you to come see it."

Urza turned back toward his plans, which showed a fuselage of thinly tapped metal. The device, shaped like a horseshoe crab, hung beneath a great sack of heated gasses.

"I'm in the middle of something. Can't it wait? Schedule a formal ceremony. I'll attend."

Barrin's eyes hardened slightly. "Two hundred students and scholars died in that blast, Urza. Another twenty have worked long and hard among the ghosts of those two hundred, trying to find a way to honor them and remember them. If you won't come for my sake, come for theirs."

"While you are mucking about in the past," Urza snapped, flinging a hand out toward the half-built war machine, "I have been devising a means to save the future. Just this morning we learned why the spiders didn't work—not enough moonlight in the cleft to activate them. This is our only hope. I have to complete this machine, or your monument might stand for all of us. I'm thinking about our future."

In a gesture he rarely made, Barrin took hold of the master's arm. He felt the hot surge of power beneath the man's skin. "Come see the memorial. It is why we are working for the future."

Urza took one more exasperated look at the fuselage, where the students swore quietly over their turning wrenches. He waved them off.

"Come along, you two. Set those tools aside, and come along. We are going to look into the past."

They stared at him for one uncertain instant before his stormy brows convinced them to drop their wrenches in the dirt and rise to follow.

Urza issued a similar command to all the students and scholars he and Barrin passed on their way out of the encampment. Scores of tasks were abandoned half finished, and the folk of Tolaria flocked up behind their two masters. They had specialized in those long, hot months of summer, the guards different in dress and demeanor from the gardeners and hunters, who were different in turn from the artificers working on Urza's war machine, and so forth. In that spontaneous parade down into the time-slough of Old Tolaria, all the scholars and students were one again, as on the day they had marched into the island. Jokes and laughter flowed out in the stern-faced master's wake, the sound of it not deadened or dragged down by the steady decrescendo of time.

Barrin wondered about this happy spirit. He and his scavengers had always adopted a solemn demeanor among the ruins, not that much ruin remained. Despite the short days in that slow-time spot—Barrin and his crew had only ten hours of sunlight during the sixteen-hour summer days—they had been diligent. The foundations of most of the buildings were still there, rectilinear crazings of stone moving through the hard-packed earth. Rainwater had gathered in the exposed basements of a number of buildings. Grasses had volunteered in many of the cleared areas. A few short walls remained intact, but most of the structures that had survived had been reverently pulled down. The cut stones were carefully sorted and stacked for use in the new buildings. Even the field-stone rubble lay in piles in the new camp. As a result, the old school now seemed almost a parkland, with quiet meadows, wandering paths of stone, and placid pools. The ruins were ruins no longer. Barrin's mood, too, lifted as he felt the final leveling of the temporal descent, and the parade wound its way into the heart of the place.

A plaza had been laid, dressed stones set into an even mosaic between the two stunning sights there. On one side was Teferi, mouth still gaping and eyes still screwed tight, the eternal flames of his robes enveloping him, and the wet cloak descended only a finger's-breadth. The leaning corner of a building remained behind Teferi, helping to shield him from the intense sunlight.

As Urza and Barrin paused beside this living shrine, Jhoira emerged from the throng. She stepped up beside them and stared bleakly at her imprisoned friend.

"He is trapped, like me. Alone. Abandoned. Neither dead nor alive."

"We'll save him, Jhoira," Barrin assured. "We'll find a way.

"He can't reach us. We can't reach him." Her voice held desperate anger. "If he tries to emerge, he will die."

"Yes. We must save him before then," Barrin replied.

"Every night I wrack my brain. I can't sleep, thinking about him. There must be a way," she insisted. A trembling hand traced across her jaw.

Barrin took her hand and led her away from the spot. "Come. I have something else to show you."

On the opposite side of the courtyard stood the memorial to the others slain in the blast. The base of the monument was the old foundation stone of the former academy. Urza had wanted the stone brought to the new school, but Barrin was adamant. He said it should mark the beginning and the end of what came before. The side of the giant block of stone bore both its original inscription—Academy Tolaria, Established 3285 AR—a new inscription—Destroyed 3307 AR. The front of the block bore the names of the dead. On the other side was an inscription in the ancient tongue of Yotia, which meant in translation:

The souls of a man who dies
Standing in the teeth of fate
Are the souls of all men,
Gone on ahead that we may remain.

The hollow interior of the stone held all the bones unearthed by Barrin and his team, interred as they lived and died—together.

The stone was surmounted by a sculpture from the sketchbook of old Darrob—Jhoira's final companion in the months before Urza's return. Though his mind had been too fragmented to allow him to communicate well in words, Darrob was an accomplished artist. Perhaps the most common image in his drawings was a seeking figure, gaunt and wind-torn, holding out a lantern and peering toward the future with eyes like twin, hopeless pits in his skull. Barrin had taken the metal remnants of ruined artifact creatures and welded them, one to another, into a statue of that bleak, searching soul, leaning ever against a ceaseless and silent gale.

Jhoira stared sadly. Barrin stood beside her still holding her hand. Urza took in the whole sight at once. The long caravan behind spread out in a semicircle to either side. All of them—student and scholar, artificer and guard—grew silent as they studied the memorial. Soon, only the wind spoke.

Barrin stood in that awed hush and felt an emotion swell through him, something that was as much joy as it was despair, something that darkened his eyes and made his lips clamp in a tight line.

"On behalf of all of us left here after the blast, Master Malzra," Jhoira said at last. "I want to thank you for this. It is right that this is the first finished building of the new school."

"Yes," replied Urza with a decisive nod, "yes, it is right."

The new lodge was completed just before the wet drear of winter, and the embers in its two great fireplaces did not go out until spring was warm on the hillsides. Though better than the tents, the accommodations were still tight. The finished fuselage of Urza's flying war engine took up one corner, sitting atop the rolled animal-skin balloon that was to haul it into the sky. The nighttime floor beyond it was filled to its edges with sleeping mats and the daytime floor with tables of food being prepared and eaten. Books and plans were crammed into cobbled nooks in one corner, and artifact experiments crowded another. So cramped were these accommodations that Jhoira and her food-gatherers chose to sleep and eat on *New Tolaria*, where hammocks and bolt-head meals seemed almost luxuriant. Aboard the ship, she also had more room to pace the nights away, designing and discarding means of saving Teferi. It was a long, wet winter, and the only saving grace of it was the drive of Urza and Barrin to push forward all of the projects begun.

By the first breezes of spring, a second building was half completed—a round-walled dormitory with each room opening outward to the forest splendors of Tolaria and inward to a central courtyard. Even without doors on the rooms and shutters on the windows, many of the scholars and students opted to move into the structure and brave the first days of spring. By the middle of that season, most artifact study had migrated to the central courtyard of the dormitory, and there was room for all in the lodge.

Today the winds were right. Mild and even, they flowed from the east, past the harbored *New Tolaria* up the very path they had taken back into Tolaria. Breezes coursed over the Giant's Pate and straight out above the Phyrexian gorge.

"Ten years have passed in that gorge since our enemies first saw us, our return." said Urza, sniffing the sea breeze as it breathed through the new academy. "Surely they have not been idle in that time. They are tenfold stronger than they were on that first day and perhaps twice as numerous. Every day we wait gives them another week to prepare. It is time."

He spoke these words to Barrin, but everyone who took breakfast in the lodge that morning heard him, and they all knew what he meant.

"Today, we attack," Urza said.

Most of those breakfasts went unfinished. Students rushed to their posts, excited and terrified by what the day might bring.

Moments after this announcement, crews hoisted the balloon of animal skin and the metal fuselage from the corner and bore them up toward the crest of the Giant's Pate. Behind them went more workers with massive bellows hooked to specially designed forges meant to heat air. Ropes borrowed from the docked *New Tolaria* followed in their turn, and crates of dark orbs carried gingerly by pairs of workers.

"It is crude, I know," Urza said with chagrin as he sat across from Barrin, who was rapidly filling his mouth with too-hot forkfuls of fried loon eggs, "but until we have full laboratory capacity, I am not willing to cobble together an ornithopter. Besides, this floating behemoth can hold one hundred times the number of powder bombs as an ornithopter."

"Even four thousand bombs may not be enough to destroy them. And if any Phyrexians remain in the gorge, we will be in grave danger," Barrin pointed out, hissing between scalding sips of tea.

"They are working on something, Barrin, a way to escape," Urza replied. "They've been searching for an escape for a hundred ten years of their time. They mustn't have the metals or powerstones for anything but a few crude artifact creatures, or they would be sending them out after us. They must be developing some new mutation, some new strain of Phyrexian that can escape their time rift. If one of the four thousand bombs penetrates to their bio-labs and destroys generations of research, we will have bought ourselves another few years."

"Yes," Barrin agreed. He brushed off his hands and rose. "Yes, today is a good day for this. I'll go brief the flight team."

Urza caught the man's shoulder and shook his head. "No, let me do it. I'll be the one on board with them."

By midmorning, the great war machine of skin and metal was fully inflated atop the Giant's Pate. Its air-bag shone in the sunlight gold and brown, crossed in a thousand places with sewn seams. Beneath, the metal fuselage gleamed, its base spotted with dew from its early morning trek. Strong winds up from the bay tugged and teased the dirigible, and its anchor lines moaned. The ground team worked busily among these ropes as well as the three long tethers that would guide the machine out over the rift. Barrin led the team through checks of the capstans bolted into the stone. Karn was there as well, prepared to lend his titanic strength to haul on the lines.

Meanwhile, the flight team of five was receiving its final instructions from Master Malzra. One team member was assigned to each vector of the balloon's movement—an officer of altitude, another of radius, and a third of tangent. Through a system of signals, these officers would instruct the ground team to accomplish the desired movement through a combination of rope trim and wind utilization. As Malzra's most accomplished artificer, Jhoira was made officer of altitude, in charge of the elaborate onboard forge bellows that provided the machine its lift. The final two fliers, a scholar and her protégé, were the school's best cartographers. They would lie prone in belly-holds on opposite ends of the device and would each make maps of what they saw. Their work would prove invaluable in determining what sites to bomb, what resources the Phyrexians likely had, and what strategy to use in future strikes against the stronghold. Malzra, the final member of the team, was captain. Receiving information from the mappers, he would send instructions to the flight officers to position the machine and, at the precise moment, release salvos of incendiary devices.

"The sixth bay is full, Master Malzra," reported a dark-haired, young woman, breaking in to Master Malzra's briefing. "Five hundred powder bombs. Two more bays. and the full complement of four thousand will be loaded."

"Good," Malzra responded. His eyes seemed especially dark this morning in the gleaming sunlight. With a nod, he dismissed the woman and turned back to his anxious team. "Jhoira, remember, at all times we must remain at least a thousand feet above the top of the gorge—at the same height as the Giant's Pate. Even there some Phyrexian projectiles might be able to reach us. Fifteen hundred feet will be safer. The bomb bays and mapper bays are shielded, but projectile penetration is possible and could cause a chain of explosions that would destroy the machine."

The crew had known all these facts before, but their repetition in the shadow of the leaning, leaping device widened eyes and brought uncomfortable gulps.

"If a projectile pierces the air sac, we will release all bombs and ballast and signal to be brought back. Escape will be impossible until we reach the Giant's Pate. Any who fall atop the time rift will die immediately. The scarp below the Giant's Pate is too sheer and littered with fallen trees to allow any safe landing," Malzra said. He studied the grave young faces arrayed around him. "I hope you have said your good-byes, should we not return. If not, I have brought a messenger." He indicated a fleet-footed girl, who obligingly tapped a shoulder satchel with quills and parchment. "Avail yourselves in the next moments. We must be aboard once the final bomb bays are full."

Four of the five crew members turned quickly to the girl, selecting quills and nibs and beginning to scrawl what might be their last words.

Only Jhoira stood, resolute and ready. "Karn is here, and we have already spoken," she said by way of explanation to Malzra. "The only other person I would send a note to is Teferi. Of course, any note to him would burn up before he could read it."

Malzra's eyes narrowed in assessment of the young woman. "You must concentrate on the task at hand, Jhoira."

"Teferi never leaves my mind," she replied. "If I could trade places with him, I would. We needn't both be forever alone. He saved me once, you know."

"I did not. But if you cannot maintain focus, I shall have to find a different officer of altitude—"

She dropped her gaze. "I'll fight all the harder, thinking of him."

"Good," he replied. "Let's take our positions."

Malzra laid a hand lightly on her shoulder, directing her with him toward the waiting craft. His touch felt almost searing.

Jhoira walked beside him.

Shiny and glowing in the morning, the craft loomed up before them. It bucked slightly under the restless winds. Reaching the machine, Mama drew back a rope slung across the doorway. He gestured inward and gave a gentle bow.

Jhoira preceded him into the vessel. She crouched as she scuttled down the tight passage. Her feet made small pings on the plate armor below. The bomb bays crowded either side of the passage. Ahead, the tangent-officer's crawlways cut across the main corridor. The radius-officer would remain in a seat on one side of the craft, monitoring the lengths of rope anchoring them to the Giant's Pate. Jhoira's post was in the exact center of the vessel at the juncture between the fuselage and the balloon. She had sight lines in every direction and had memorized the height of the various landmarks. She also had an open shaft downward for a visual check of the ground position. A harness of hemp held her suspended in this empty column of air. The rig was designed to pivot in a complete circle but otherwise provide a stable base. To one side of it was the forge bellows that Jhoira would stoke and tend to keep the machine aloft. To the other side were a set of instruments—anemometers, barometers, compasses, spyglasses . . . Jhoira climbed into the seat and strapped herself in.

Malzra, in a similar rig in the belly of the craft, ordered through the speaking tube, "Stoke the forge for liftoff."

"Aye." Jhoira complied, feeling small shudders in the fuselage as the other team members clambered into their positions.

She faintly heard instructions spoken into tubes that went elsewhere. Beyond the superstructure, anchor lines were one by one drawn loose, and the ground crew took up the three lines that snaked around the capstans.

"Cast off," came the order in all the speaking tubes.

The craft lurched up from the rock. The nervous chitter of metal against stone was gone and the rattling resistance with it. Jhoira pumped the bellows before her, fueling the fire in the black box. A hiss of red air roared up from the forge. The vessel rose farther, heeling away from the stone. Beyond snapping lines and stretched skins, the bright brow of the hill retreated. The folk clustered thickly atop it, toiling at the capstans, were diminished. Soon their faces were only knots of exertion. Then there were no features at all, only bent backs and sinewy arms like extensions of the stout ropes themselves. A shadow-painted face of stone slid by below, descending suddenly into vast distance. An immense bowl of land opened up. The Giant's Pate became only a ground-down prominence on one edge of the basin. Lines that had once seemed massive now looked all too thin, stretched across the plummeting spaces.

"Take us up three hundred feet to thirteen hundred," Malzra's voice came. "Let's come in from above, give us time to survey the pit and choose our targets."

"Aye," Jhoira responded.

She slid back the door to the coal chute, allowing a few more shards into the firebox. A lever spread the black stones across the embers. She pumped repeatedly on the bellows. Hot air jetted into the vast air sac above, and more tepid air spilled from the lips of the balloon. Impatient, the machine rose higher, its lines tugging it in an arc back toward the Giant's Pate.

Malzra issued course adjustments, signaled to ground crews by the tangent and radius officers. The tethers slackened, and the machine swooped out on new winds over the black wound of the Phyrexian pit.

"We're getting clear visuals," the map scholar said into her speaking tube. "A main fortification at the center of the cleft, perhaps a hundred yards square, with many turrets and towers, elevated battlements, and scores of heavy ballistae, each targeted on the rim of the gorge."

"Thirty-three ballistae, by my count," the student broke in.

Jhoira peered down the shaft. She could make out the black form of the main structure and the bristling array of spear throwers atop the towers and rooftops. Even as she watched, the long shafts foreshortened.

"They are redirecting them at us," she noted urgently.

"Maintain altitude," Malzra ordered. "Remember, they have ten seconds to our every one. They can respond, regroup, and regear quickly."

"The main fortress seems to be perched on a rock prominence in the center of a deep lake. I cannot make out the contours of the bottom," the chief cartographer reported. "I'm surprised by all that water. Fast-time rifts tend to have little water. It looks as though numerous streams empty into the gorge."

"Any sign of structures that might be laboratories?" Urza asked. "I'm looking specifically for spawning facilities."

"There seem to be fish hatcheries in various places in the lake," replied the mapper. "I can make out figures moving among the sluices and nets. As to laboratory structures, I could not begin to guess."

The assistant cartographer said, "There are various caves and what might be mines in the walls of the gorge—"

He broke off as the tip-tilted ballistae flickered in sudden, violent motion. Before any of the crew could blink, a flight of thirty-three massive shafts leaped into being twelve hundred feet below. They raced up with preternatural speed, going from being wickedly barbed jags to being large as lightning. They rose to within a hundred feet of the ship's belly before slowing and curving off. The ballistae bolts lingered a moment on the winds and then tumbled. Their heavy heads drew them quickly back downward, and they sank toward the temporal envelop where the Phyrexians were trapped. Striking the verge of the fast-time gorge, the bolts accelerated to blinding speed.

The crack of those thirty-three shafts smashing through rooftops was like manifold thunder. A cheer went up from the flight and the ground crews.

"Excellent," Malzra said. "Maintain tangent, radius, and altitude. Stay directly above them. They'll think twice before sending another salvo. I am dropping the payload of bomb bay five."

There came a great ratcheting sound as the doors of the bay swung slowly downward. Out tumbled the powder bombs. Just such devices had been employed with devastating effect at Koilos three millennia before, though they had been dropped in tens on marching troops instead of in hundreds on a stationary fortification. Now the black objects, which seemed merely tumbling stones, rolled slowly in their swarm, gathered speed, and pelted down into the fast-time rift. They struck the envelop *en masse*, making a distant, ominous patter. Accelerating to the speed of the rift, they struck.

Light leaped from the cleft. Orange flares in their hundreds illuminated the previously veiled depths. Jagged rooflines and battlements shone in sudden relief. The cartographers scribbled frantically. Then smoke obscured everything in a deeper shroud, and blackness settled again.

The sound of the attack lagged a moment behind this brief, pure flash, but when it came, the roar was amplified by the basalt fort, the glassy water beneath it, and the rocky cliff faces all around. It seemed a great beast had awakened, furious, from sleep. The noise filled the air for some moments, and then all was silent. Smoke—gray and white and black in curdled rills—bled from the gap.

"That got their attention," Jhoira shouted, giving a whoop.

"Cartographers," came Malzra's call, "target acquisition?"

"Too much smoke," replied the scholar. "Give it a few minutes to clear."

"That will give them a few hours to regroup," Malzra responded. "Altitude, radius, tangent—has our position held?"

"We've gained height," Jhoira said, "after the bombs went. We're up to about seventeen hundred feet."

"Bring us down to twelve," Urza commanded, "and anticipate the next payload drop."

"Radius is steady."

"Tangent is steady."

"Down to about twelve hundred feet."

"Payload six away."

The first wave of attacks slew over a hundred and fifty of K'rrik's minions, toppled three towers, blasted away the roof of the upper throne room and, worst of all, sent blazing death into the spawning lab. Vials of brain and placenta burst and oozed, recombination matrices ended in tatters on the floor, vats of glistening oil ignited in enormous jets, mutant stock burned to cinders, and the decanted, half-mature killers that K'rrik had been breeding to survive the time rift were roasted alive. The destruction was almost total. Almost.

Out of chaos came order. The fires from the initial onslaught were already extinguished, the dead and dying thrown to the fishes, and the ballistae recalibrated for greater distance. K'rrik ordered all able-bodied beasts to salvage whatever specimens, equipment, and plans had survived from his breeding laboratories. The remains were taken below the castle, into the caves. Urza's crude bombs might have blasted holes in roofs and walls, but they would not crack the basalt extrusion on which the castle sat and would not completely wipe out a century of research. All hope of escape and victory rested in that ragged refuse, in the half full jars of cracked glass with their skittish placental inhabitants. Some of the creatures would survive, and K'rrik's clawed and tentacular horrors carried them as tenderly as human mothers with their babies.

All of this had happened in the hour after the first attack. As the smoke cleared enough to make out the dim line of the airship above, guards spotted more of the bombs resting in the air below it. They looked like pepper on a white piece of paper. It was an easy thing to predict where they would strike and evacuate the areas.

K'rrik stood, furious and humiliated, among his folk. Sizzling chunks of fire struck the roof of one guard tower and the adjacent section of wall. The resultant chorus of flares and pops shook the rest of the fortress and echoed through the chasm. Hunks of stone pelted outward and hailed across the Phyrexian host, who flinched away. The tower came to pieces, pulverized by the attack. The weakened wall crumbled away, crushing an armory lower down. Fires flared up wherever there was wood or cloth or skin to burn, and the armory ignited. A cloud of flame and soot shot up in a vast column, its top rolling and boiling.

K'rrik watched. The filed teeth in his enhanced jaw ground into their opposite gums, cutting bloody rents in the flesh.

"What are you going to do?" barked a creature next to him. It seemed more a giant flea than a man, its head three times the size of K'rrik's and its pale, naked body humpbacked and twisted. "You can't let this go on!"

"Yes," K'rrik responded grimly. Pus-colored blood was suddenly jetting from the creature's severed back as K'rrik withdrew his sword. The monster tumbled from the wall where they stood, its body bouncing twice along the buttresses before striking the black foundations of the fortress and bursting in a white mass. "Yes, I cannot let you question my authority."

K'rrik turned to another Phyrexian, this one more manlike, though he had the infernal head of a haggard goat. The commander ordered, "Tell two ballistae crews to fire three rounds every half hour, half-cocked rounds that will fall short. Have crews ready in the water to retrieve the shafts. Cover the rest of the ballistae with dead bodies. I want Urza to think he has destroyed most of our ballistae, and nearly disabled those that are left. I want to draw him downward. Once they are in range, fling the dead from the ballistae and fire all simultaneously. Aim for the flying machine's bomb bays."

Nodding his understanding, the goat-faced man headed off on his mission.

K'rrik snarled at the minions around him, "As for the rest of you, put out those fires. And keep watching for more onslaughts. Anyone injured will be killed. Anyone killed will be defiled. It is your duty to fight and to live."

The third, fourth, and fifth drops went as well as the first. Bombs hailed down. Fire and smoke came up. The sound of tumbling towers and shrieking beasts rose to meet them. On the second drop, Jhoira had learned the trick of spilling heat from the air sac at the moment the bombs were released, thereby preventing the machine from lurching upward. This technique allowed for quicker follow-up attacks, greater accuracy, and less time spent reeling.

Until the sixth drop. The gorge below was a gray scar, so full of smoke that no fortification was evident within. Still, the cartographers had picked out landmarks on the edges of the cliff and could, from memory alone, pinpoint important sites to strike. They were above just such a site now—what had looked like a throne room or great hall—and Malzra issued the now familiar warning.

"I am opening bay two."

Jhoira paused a breath and then bled the air from the forge. She knew immediately that something was wrong. There came no grating ratchet. There was no sound of tumbling bombs. There was only the sudden loss of height as hot air spilled from the sac.

"The mechanism is jammed," came a shout over the speaking tube.

Jhoira ground her teeth as she struggled to shut off the bleed and pump the bellows. The dirigible sagged on its lines, dipping below the crest of the Giant's Pate. The deflated sac rattled in a sudden downdraft. Jhoira heaved at the bellows, and jets of red air roared into the sac. It began to reinflate.

Loud shouts of metal came below, ballistae shots hammering into the fuselage. The speaking tubes were flooded with screams. Then came another wave of ballistae shots only a breath after the first. They penetrated. Spearheads struck powder bombs. With a dull roar, they ignited. The explosion spread. Bomb bay two blasted away. The metal fuselage fragmented. The machine mounted up on a wave of fire. What remained of the fuselage rammed up beneath the air sac.

Jhoira was suddenly inside the balloon, the air around her baking her skin and burning in her lungs. She was aware of a great emptiness beneath her. Half of the fuselage was gone. The rest was shoved in a tangle of lines inside the skin sac. The other crew members were dead—the officers of tangent and radius, the cartographers, even Master Malzra. She was about to die too.

"I'm sorry, Teferi," was all she could think to say.

The ragged metal fuselage dropped from the air bag and slewed sideways. It tugged the deflated dirigible down behind it. The whole mass plummeted toward the Phyrexian gorge below.

Coals from the tilted forge sprayed out around Jhoira. Cursing, she clawed her way from the harness and climbed into the tangle of ropes. She clambered over them, seeing through their webwork as the vast gray gorge rushed up to swallow her. One of the ropes was fatter than the others and tighter. She grabbed it and felt the insistent tug of life on the other end.

"Karn is up there," she gasped to herself. Karn and the rest of the ground crew.

She fought her way out of the flapping folds of skin and the taut net of ropes and clambered up that one fat line, the one that pulsed with life. Hand over hand, she dragged herself up the rope, toward the Giant's Pate and away from the Phyrexian fortress.

There was too much rope, too little air, too much rock.

The world roared up with crushing weight. She climbed.

The ruined dirigible was about hundred feet behind her now. It struck the fast-time envelope. Waves of time-distortion roiled out around it. The war machine plummeted in a sudden preternatural rush. The rope snapped taut. It flung Jhoira free. The capstan ripped from its mooring and surged through the air. There came a white-hot explosion within the rent. The sky and ground fused into a single sheet.

"I'm sorry, Teferi." Jhoira struck earth, and all went black.

Monologue

We do not make machines, I now realize. We make only fire and death.

The blast surprised all of us, even Urza. He survived through a great concentration of will, holding his corporeal form together, but unlike the explosion that tore apart Tolaria, or that which tore apart Argoth, Urza had not anticipated this one. He was struggling to keep his body solid even as his crew members were no more than red particles on the wind.

And there is no time machine for bringing them back.

The blast surprised all of us. I summoned a wall of air, trying to catch the falling craft, but only slowed its descent. In the midst of the fumbling hopelessness of it all, I saw Jhoira ambling spiderlike up the main line toward safety. That was the greatest surprise of all, though it shouldn't have been. Jhoira's force of will equals that of Urza.

—Barrin, Mage Master of Tolaria

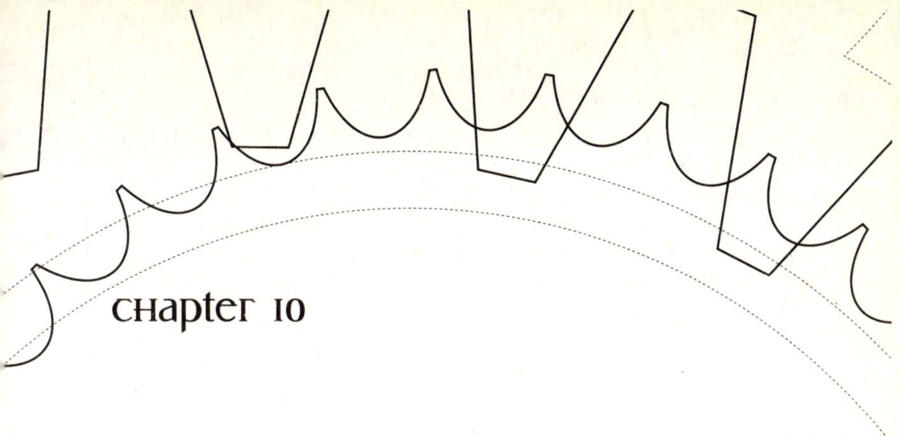

chapter 10

They sat at Jhoira's bedside in the makeshift infirmary. No pallet, no cot—here she had an actual bed—Barrin's, volunteered by him for the purpose. The infirmary was soon to be a kitchen attached to one end of the great hall, but now, amid newly mortared fireplaces and stacks of iron-worked spits and grills and pots, she lay in coma. She was the only one injured in the wreck of the dirigible. All the others were killed.

Except Urza. He and Barrin sat on cook stools just next to the bed, and they spoke in low tones.

"She's become another Teferi," Barrin said sadly. "Three months, and still no response. Lying there, an arm's length away but unreachable."

Urza watched the still woman, his eyes glimmering darkly. "Physically, she is well. You saw me lay hands on her. You saw the wounds close and the breath begin again. She was whole the moment I laid hands on her. I can't understand why she does not awaken."

"Her wounds are deeper than you can reach, my friend," Barrin replied.

He fondly brushed her hair back from her forehead. Her face was losing its olive patina after all this time beneath roofs and blankets. Her hair was darkening from the roots outward. It was as though the years were being one by one revoked from her, and she was becoming again a mere child.

"She survived Old Tolaria, through ten years of abandonment, isolation, and want. Then we came back, and we all thought she would return to us. But she didn't. Karn was her only friend. She was withdrawn and haunted. Every time she saw Teferi—spoke of him, thought of him—the horror of those ten years came welling back. She felt trapped, like him. An arm's length away from us but always alone."

"She could stay in this coma forever," Urza said.

"No. She is fighting. Either she will win or lose. It will not be forever, but it may be a long time. Last time, she fought for a whole decade."

Urza lifted his eyes, seeming to see straight through the wall and even through an oblique curve of the world to some dazzling place that lay beyond it all.

"Serra's Realm had once restored my health. I would take her there at once if Serra remained, if the place weren't shrinking, if I hadn't led Phyrexia to it. . . ." A cloud passed over his features and they grew iron-hard. "We have to keep up the fight. Everywhere I have gone, those monsters have followed. Everyone I have befriended has been wounded or killed by them. I would destroy myself if I knew it would stop them, but they will never quit. I must fight them as long as I live."

"And what if you die before they are defeated?" Barrin asked soberly. "Who will fight them then?"

All light fled Urza's face, and it was as black as a mask. "Yes, who then?"

Karn heaved the massive keystone into position atop the archway. The stone grated against its neighbors. Sand sifted down from its settling bulk. Silver hands lingered in uncertainty on the huge block.

"Does it look straight?"

Behind him, Barrin looked up from Malzra's field table and squinted along a sight line. The keystone gleamed like a jewel in the morning sun, its polished edges reflecting the Tower of Artifice and the Tower of Mana in the background.

"Yes, Karn. It looks straight."

The silver golem nodded and then asked, "Will it stay put?"

This time, Barrin was too busy with his sketches to look up. "Of course it will stay put."

He sighed. The stack of floor plans and elevations before him were the latest creations of Urza for his new academy. Already, after five years of intensive, year-round building, the school was nearly as extensive as it had been in its previous manifestation: dormitories, lecture halls, laboratories, great halls, guard towers, curtain walls, gates, gardens, and now a new infirmary. Not that many of the academy's hundred and ninety students were ill or injured. Most were too young to have any serious health problems aside from homesickness. Whatever injuries or illnesses occurred were treated with placebo pills, gauze, and Urza's healing touch. No, this grand new two-story infirmary was not so much a necessity as it was a monument to the school's perpetual patient.

Jhoira had not awakened. She had indeed become another Teferi. For his part, the young man was now wrapped in the wet cloak and beginning a tumble that would take him another handful of years to complete. Jhoira had meanwhile grown pale, her hair dark brown again. She did not awaken. Barrin had discovered that water from slow-time rifts helped to sustain her health, and Urza provided his healing touch daily. Nothing improved. Urza had devised a machine that liquefied whatever food was offered in the great halls and pumped it into her stomach. Karn, meanwhile, had developed the habit of picking wildflowers for her from the hillsides of Angelwood and bringing them to her bed. He too often stood vigil there, choosing to spend his nights in her company instead of deactivated.

Her plight weighed heavily on Barrin and Karn as they worked on the new building. Both moved sadly and slowly, as though building a mortuary rather than an infirmary. There was anger in them too, frustration at their inability to save her.

Karn trudged up beside the desk and stood, gleaming in the bright, hot sun.

Barrin shielded his eyes from the glare and said irritably, "Can't you let yourself tarnish a little?"

"Master Malzra forbids it," Karn replied truthfully. Then, with a tone of sarcasm he had been slowly developing over the last fifteen years, he said, "It would bother you less if you wore a sack over your head."

Barrin cast a reproachful look at the golem. "I think maybe it's time to design a new helper—one with a thicker skin, if that is possible."

"If you're after compatibility, try a helper with a thicker skull."

"Thicker than Arty Shovelhead's?"

"Teferi was a better companion than you—"

"An old shoe is a better companion than you—"

A sudden buzz tore through the air between the two. They shied instinctively back, gaping at empty space. Something darted, the size and speed of a falcon, above the treetops. It circled and dived down toward them again. It glinted metallic.

Barrin swore, stepped to the desk, and hauled a sword from it. As the thing swooped by again, he swung the blade. It cracked against the silvery shoulder of the device, but the metal bird soared again, ripping leaves from their boughs as it shot through the forest. The rattle of its passage faded briefly and then returned with a swift crescendo. Growling, Barrin hefted his blade again and watched the mechanism shriek inward.

Karn stepped into the path of the attacker. He reared back, balled a fist, and hurled the massive thing at the flying target. It crashed amid a jangle of slivered struts and sprung coils. The artifact creature fell back in the dirt. Its metallic wings glinted, shuddering to either side. Spikes thrust outward all across it. An assortment of round, rending blades emerged, whirling violently.

Astonished, Barrin and Karn gazed at the broken mass as it whined furiously. They were so amazed by the display that neither noticed Master Malzra approach from behind. The artificer watched with amused interest. It was only when the mechanism had nearly spent itself and shimmied into stillness that the master spoke.

"It was only a prototype. The final falcons will stoop at hundreds of miles an hour on the gorge—arriving even before the sound they make. They will smell Phyrexian glistening-oil blood, home in on it, penetrate the beast's hide, and begin a shredding procedure."

Panting heavily, Barrin turned toward the man. "How many of them will you build?"

As many as I can, given our supply of Thran powerstones. If I could only design and build my own stones, I could fill the skies with these creatures, could perhaps protect the whole world. With the stones we have—and the ones I hope to uncover at three Thran sites I have found—I can make perhaps a thousand."

"Three Thran sites?' Barrin asked, eyebrow canted. "You are planning on sending students to dig!"

"Yes," Malzra replied. "They'll be taken aboard *New Tolaria*, and the ship will return with a new load of students, whom I've chosen from the best and brightest the world has to offer. I have the itinerary right here. And since I, myself, need to remain for research—"

"Yes, yes," Barrin replied irritably. "How many years will I be away this time!"

"Teferi is covered in your robe, now," Karn said gently. He sat by Jhoira's bedside in the completed infirmary. "He's not being burned anymore. You've saved him." He didn't add that the boy would likely rise, now, and make his way toward the outer world and be killed in the curtain of time.

Jhoira was too fragile to bear that sort of news. She looked pale and small in the bed. Her arms and legs were weak from years of stillness, her eyes were lost beneath lids forever closed, her mouth was red where the tube of Malzra's feeding machine descended.

"The new students are arriving today," Karn said, changing the subject. "Barrin has been out collecting them the last three years."

Karn glanced up at the rafters of the building. The academy was at last complete. Malzra had ceased his new building designs. He now poured all his energy in the arsenal he was creating to eradicate the Phyrexians in the gorge. He spoke of the battle as a "dress rehearsal for global conflagration." It was his new mania. The minds of all the scholars and students were trained on the task. One team had developed a battery of long-range ballistae, which were stationed in a ring around the site and were employed in a day-and-night peppering of the fortress. Another crew had devised a set of catapults, which delivered powder bombs as quickly as they could be concocted. Rivers had been dammed and diverted away from the gorge to empty the Phyrexian fish hatcheries and starve them.

Meanwhile, every student spent hours every day assembling the delicate and complex clockwork falcons Malzra had designed. He would do just about anything to slay Phyrexians.

On the other hand, in these ten years, what had he done to save Teferi or Jhoira?

Reaching in delicately, Karn grasped the tube that ran from Malzra's feeding contraption into Jhoira's stomach. Bracing himself, the silver man hauled slowly on it, withdrawing the hose. It emerged with a jolting, sucking motion.

Karn set the tube aside and said gently, "Come with me." He lifted her limp form in his arms and, with reverent step, carried her out the door.

It was a long walk past the towering buildings of the new academy and through the western gate. No one stopped him, though everyone stared. Karn was well known among the students and scholars, the ever-present builder and guardian. Jhoira was known too, the never-present ghost of the former island. In all accounts, they were dear friends, and half of those who glimpsed the pair believed she had died at last, and he was taking her to be buried. The other half assumed Karn was acting at the bidding of the inscrutable master.

Karn carried her away for his own purposes, and hers. Bypassing the killing time pits and pinnacles, the silver man bore Jhoira through the thick forests of Tolaria, across tan shoulders of sandstone, and to the secret niche she had kept on the western edge of the island. Her things were still there as she had left them ten years ago, as she had left all of Tolaria ten years ago.

"It is time for you to come back." Karn said heavily.

He brought her to the sunny ledge of sandstone where she had loved to stand and gaze out to sea. He climbed onto the stone and sat down. Jhoira was small and cold, cradled in his lap. Salty air rose warmly around them, lifting and gently tossing Jhoira's hair. The laboring waves below worried stones to pebbles and pebbles to sand. The sky was endless in blue. Mountain ranges of cloud slid in slow panorama through it. On the horizon of the vast ocean, a tiny white sail shone—the returning *New Tolaria.*

"You always said you would be here, on this stone, when you would first see your soul mate arrive." He glanced down at her unmoving form, and desperate sadness welled in his voice. "Wake up, Jhoira. You have slept too long."

Only her hair moved, lifted by the caressing breeze.

"You have to come back, Jhoira. Despite his best intentions, Master Malzra has turned the school into a fortification, the students into a young army. He's bringing more students, to do the same with them." Karn gazed desolately at the pounding waves. "You wouldn't have allowed that. You were the soul of this place. Remember how I was before Master Malzra gave me that dark crystal—what he called an intellectual and affective cortex? Remember what I was like before I had a soul? That's what the island is like without you."

Still, there was only the slow shift of breath in her, the arms and leg in languid repose.

"Look out on that huge dark sea. You see that scrap of white. It is Tolaria's hope, returning. I know you have been far away. I know your soul feels tiny, lost amid rolling breakers and heaving gales, but it is our best hope. Return."

There came a fluttering at her eyelids. Karn held still, not daring to believe. Jhoira's breath deepened, and she seemed to settle against him. Her eyes again were closed.

"If you don't wake now, you may miss your soul mate."

"I've . . . dreamed—" a voice came, as thready and elusive as the wind, "—I've . . . quested. . . . I know how to break through. . . ."

"What?" Karn blurted stupidly. He peered at her, but she was unconscious again, her figure as limp as the wet cloak she had thrown over Teferi.

Karn stood up, the woman in his arms. He felt as though he had a heart in his chest, for all the thrumming ache of it. Was she awakening, or was it only the wishful thinking of a silver man given to fantasy? Feeling as though his burden had doubled, he staggered back toward the distant academy. Which healer would know how to waken her again? What if she never woke again? How had he lived these ten years without her?

K'rrik stood in the midst of his deep mutant lab, sunk in the lightless bedrock beneath his castle. For twenty years, the spot had been exposed, no longer shielded by water—ever since Urza Planeswalker had diverted rivers from the gorge to kill off the fish they ate. K'rrik had dammed the far end of the gorge, thereby making a shallow, stagnant lake, where at least scavenger fish could be bred from the waste poured into the pool. For forty years, powder bombs and ballistae bolts had rained down on their heads. Urza must have been clearing the island's forests as fast as he had cleared Argoth's. None of it, not brimstone hail, lightning shafts, flood nor famine, had reached this deep cavern and its precious contents.

In great vats of obsidian, melted and cast for this very purpose, K'rrik's latest generation of negators was gestating, maturing. Vast, pulpy heads, hideously distorted bodies, arms as sharp and thin as swords, legs that could lope at the speed of jackals, clawed feet that could crush a man's skull as if it were merely a melon. In two years, this sixth batch of modified negators would be ready to emerge from their vats, full-formed, ready to scale the walls of the gorge and struggle through the vast rending curtain of time that surrounded them. Perhaps they would die, like the five previous harvests. Perhaps they would win through, too weak to hunt down the man at the heart of K'rrik's torment.

The man? The god!

Whatever happened, K'rrik had already harvested their flesh, sampled it, improved on it. The seventh batch would be stronger yet and ready in another decade. In no more than twenty years of Urza's time, his beautiful garden academy would be overrun with Phyrexians, bred to walk uninjured through the worst time storm, and—this was the best part—bred to be utterly faithful to their master, K'rrik. To them, he was more than an ancient sleeper, more than an indomitable and unkillable warlord. To them, he was a god—

He was Yawgmoth incarnate.

It had been six months since Jhoira had first reawakened in the silver arms of her old friend. The healers and Malzra himself had been incapable of reviving her, despite their intense and sometimes rigorous interventions.

Karn's touch had worked the magic their hands could not, bringing her around again a week after the first occasion. The moment of lucidity had been brief and feverish, but Jhoira again said she had been on a vision quest and had seen a way to "break through." To this cryptic revelation, she added that she knew how to save herself—and Teferi—then she lapsed back into unconsciousness.

Since that time, Karn had refused to aid in any more war efforts. He spent his time sitting at her side, gently speaking to her through the long hours of night, telling her anything he could think of, even reading stories of Shiv from the academy's library. It was just as in the old days, the two of them making a home for each other, withdrawing from the ignorant outside world that recognized and welcomed neither of them. Jhoira responded. Soon she had awakened every hour or so and remained awake for minutes at a time. Karn forced broth and bread into her on these occasions, refusing to allow Malzra's tube to be in her throat anymore. In another month, she had been able to sit up, and her arms and legs had grown stronger.

At that point, she had called for paper and writing implements and tools. She sketched out a complex machine that even Malzra could not quite visualize—long tubes and pump chambers, with large gears bearing huge sails of gauze windmilling up from wide troughs, a massive turbine driven by teams of workers. . . . When Barrin and other scholars expressed their reservations about the large, costly design, none of them spoke of dream delirium, but the thought lingered in their words.

Karn gathered a passel of young, bright students from the new batch that had arrived on the island. He brought them to the infirmary and equipped them with whatever tools and resources Jhoira directed. They worked tirelessly, these children, forever guided by Jhoira and her vision.

Three months later, their creation was wheeled to the center of the slow-time slough where the Teferi monument stood. The creature was also wheeled to the spot, on a cart Jhoira had had modified for the purpose. The whole of the academy gathered as the woman's young protégés rolled long, flexible tubes out of the slow-time area, over the hills, to a nearby rift of extreme fast time. While they worked, discreet murmurs of dubiety circulated among the crowd.

Jhoira rolled herself up beside the hulking machine she had first glimpsed in her coma. She rapped on the side of a metal reservoir. The thunderous sound drew the attention of the group.

As they quieted, she began to speak, "The principle is simple. Water resists time change. We have witnessed this. We survivors of the first academy used the properties of slow-time water to stop aging. So, too, fast-time water is reluctant to give up its pulse. This machine draws fast-time water from a nearby rift that contains an underground spring. The pumps here fill the reservoirs with water. These sets of cranks then power the wind turbine and the gauze sails. The windmill blades dip into the reservoir, drawing water into the gauze. Wind from the turbine blows through the gauze and produces a thick fog of fast-time water. The saturated fast-time cloud will create a safe corridor of passage into the time pit where Teferi is, and safe passage back out again."

Silent doubt gave way to silent admiration.

"Have any organic creatures successfully passed into and out of this fast-time cloud?" Barrin asked sensibly.

Jhoira's countenance sagged. "This machine is the result not of artifice alone but of vision—Ghitu vision. We have not tested the device on living creatures, no."

"I will enter it," Karn said, his voice like the quiet rumble of gravel in a breaking wave. "I was made to withstand temporal distortions that would kill any living thing, and I believe in Ghitu vision."

Barrin, looking chagrined, continued his objections. "Yes, Karn, but just because you might be able to walk safely into the pocket that holds Teferi does not mean he could walk safely out again."

It was Karn's turn to stare downward in defeat.

"I will go with him," came another basso voice, and all attention turned to the bright-eyed and bearded speaker.

"Master Malzra?" Barrin protested. "It's out of the question. We need further tests, animal tests, before any of us steps into the cloud—"

"I believe in this machine," Malzra responded simply. "It is a fine design. It is the first glimmering that any of us have had about crossing severe rifts. I believe in this machine, and—-" he paused to send a mocking wink in Barrin's direction "—since I am the reason Teferi is caught there anyway, I owe it to the lad to help get him out." He gestured toward Jhoira's protégés, clustered in an anxious knot beside the pump mechanism. "Fill the reservoir."

Brightening, Jhoira nodded toward the students, who began plying the pumps with all their might. The tubes hissed and gurgled for a time before the first brown splashes of water entered the reservoir. The liquid spattered the base of the trough and immediately evaporated, leaving a residue of dry dust.

Jhoira was distressed to see this, but Malzra crossed to her and patted her shoulder. "It just shows that the water retains its fast-time properties. Be patient. The pumps will do their work. It is a very good design."

Water flooded up from the pump tubes and rushed out along the base of the trough. It shimmered and splashed with preternatural speed, rectangular waves coursing over its rising surface. The students continued their work at the cranks. The water level rose. It seemed to be teeming with fish, so energetic was its surface. It reached the halfway point along the wall of the reservoir and crept upward. The crowd around the tank watched in anticipation.

Malzra stood beside Karn as the gauze-covered blades began to windmill through the trough. After a complete revolution of the blades, workers manning the turbine began cranking. A hot, unnatural wind jetted from one end of the device, striking wet gauze and sending a thin spray outward. Wind bore the vapor along, spotting flagstones between the machine and the alcove where Teferi huddled beneath his soaked robe. The spray entered the slow-time pit and crept slowly over him. Those gathered near the shrine strained forward to make out any movement across the crouched figure—the shift of wet fabric, the quickening of drip lines. As the crank teams set up a powerful rhythm, the mist thickened into a white wall of fog, opaque and dazzling in the sunlight.

Jhoira nodded to Malzra.

He studied the roiling wall of fog before him. It churned in a dizzy dance, the suspended particles of water as vital as they had been in the trough.

"Well, Karn, it seems creature and creator will step together into this time machine."

The silver man stared at the turgid mist. "I can precede you and provide report."

Malzra flung away the suggestion with a simple shake of his head. "We go, side by side." With that, the two strode to the rolling edge of the fog and stepped inside.

The mist enveloped Karn with sudden force. It felt like the rush of sea water when he had fallen into it from his time-travel cone. He could sense the wet flagstones beneath his feet, but the fog tore over him like a gale.

Bracing himself against the rolling blast, Karn reached a hand outward to make certain Malzra was beside him. Through the impenetrable white air, as thick as paint, it was impossible to see the man. The buffeting wind coursed around something solid. Karn's hand swayed outward and struck another hand, reaching. Malzra took hold of the silver man's fingers and clung tightly.

The winds slackened. The violent forces tearing along Karn's armor plating diminished to a washing flood, and then a gentle caress.

Malzra's voice sounded pinched, as though he were caught in a great vise. "The time differential . . . is leveling . . . off."

Karn responded easily. "You are having trouble breathing."

"I don't need . . . to breathe," came the reply. Again the winds softened. "We should walk. We are nearly . . . time adjusted now. Hours will pass on the outside for every few minutes we spend . . . in here."

Shoulder to shoulder, they pressed forward, in line with the sifting fog. Though time in the fog was compacted, space remained constant. In only five steps, white mist turned to gray, and they could sense the looming corner behind the Teferi shrine. The boy himself lay in a barely distinguishable huddle on the ground. Karn was thankful he hadn't stepped on him. It might not have mattered. Teferi didn't appear to move beneath that wet cloak.

Except that he was panting. . . .

"Teferi," Malzra said, the old roundness returned to his voice, "rise. We have come to take you out of here."

A small shiver moved through the cloak, and a young, breathless voice emerged, "Who are you? Angels?"

Malzra laughed, but it was Karn who replied, "It's me, Teferi. It's Arty Shovelhead. I'm here with Master Malzra."

The boy tugged the cloak back from his head and stared into the thick darkness. He could not have seen more than a pair of towering figures wrapped in dense fog.

"What is happening? There was a big lightning bolt out of the clear air, and thunder so loud I couldn't hear it, and then everything was flying and burning, even me. Once I could get my feet under me, I ran. Everything was blinding and boiling hot, and then all of a sudden comes this darkness and you two."

"We've come to take you out of here," Malzra repeated.

The gray cloud around them suddenly dimmed and grew black. Night had fallen in the world outside. Only the Glimmer Moon, streaking bright beyond the fog, lit the niche.

Feeling a new urgency, Karn reached down, drew off the cloak, and lifted Teferi by his hand. "Come along. Hurry now. Jhoira is waiting."

"Jhoira?" the boy said as he staggered to his feet. "I'll be glad to see her."

"Come along."

Monologue

After the first hour of cranking, I moved among the crowd, organizing the students into teams that took shifts powering the pumps, windmills, and turbines. If the flow of fast-time fog had ceased for only a moment, Urza, Karn, and Teferi could have been torn to shreds on the verge of their time pit. The teams worked all through the night. I fortified them with a number of white-mana spells I know. All the while, Jhoira and I remained beside the machine to monitor it for stresses and possible breakdown. No crises came—as Urza had said, it was a good design.

The real crisis was one of hope. It had occurred to me after the first hour that Urza and Karn might have been torn to pieces by the time cloud only moments after entering it. They might be lying dead just within the wall of steam, unseeable to us. How long would we keep up our labors? Days? Weeks? Months? I could tell that these same dark musings were plaguing Jhoira, though neither of us voiced our concerns. It was the middle of the next morning before I overheard these questions muttered among the crank teams. It had been a weary and sleepless night for all of us—the fatigue of labor overlaid with the fatigue of welling doubt.

"How long do we keep this up?" I asked Jhoira quietly during the blazing afternoon.

"We keep it up until the machine breaks or the master and Karn emerge."

I felt heartened by her words. Here was a woman who had struggled out of a ten-year coma to design a machine worthy of Urza himself.

A quick march up over the hill told me our labors would soon end. The water in the fast-time rift would not last into the night.

I was coming down the slope to report this grave news to Jhoira when I saw a terrifying sight. The windmills ground to a halt, the turbines ceased their whining, and the thick, life-giving wall of fog roiled and dissipated on the wind. I started to run until I saw Urza, Karn, and Teferi standing there, having just emerged, alive, from the time pit. The crowd of students let out a spontaneous whoop and surged up around the three refugees. I hurried down toward them until I saw another knot of young folk, clustered quietly around Jhoira's wheeled cart. In the next moments I reached her side. Her eyes were shut, her hands limp at her sides, but blessed breath coursed smoothly in her chest.

"She stayed awake until they emerged," one of the students said with quiet reverence, "and then, a moment later—"

"Rest, dear girl," I said fondly, stroking the sweaty hair from her forehead. "Sleep awhile more. We'll wake you again. We'll always wake you again."

—Barrin, Mage Master of Tolaria

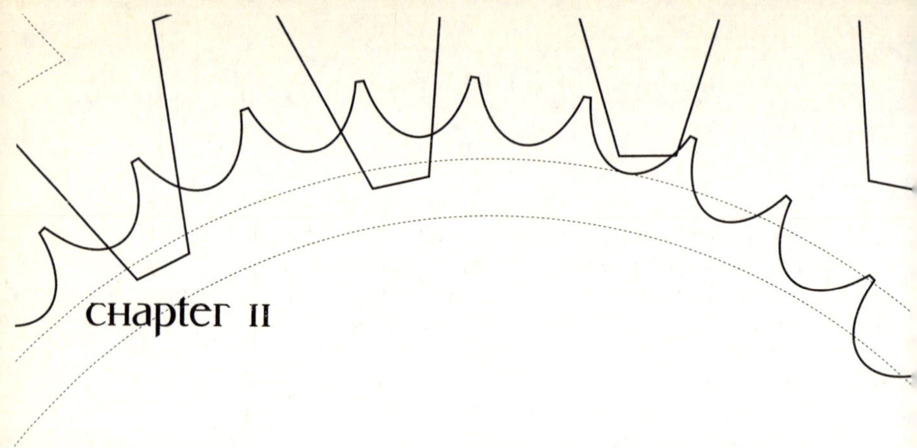

Chapter 11

Teferi had not adapted well in the months after his rescue. The explosion had been horrible, of course, and the fire afterward, but he had been utterly devastated by the fact that the world and all his former friends were nearly twenty-five years older. Teams of healers had gingerly counseled the victim about his ordeal, focusing on his slow-time isolation.

"What isolation!" he asked. "I was alone for three seconds! When you're on fire, you don't care if you're alone. The fourteen years before the explosion were more traumatic. Talk about isolation! I had no peers. Every equal of mine was five years older than me. Now they're almost three times my age! Jhoira's forty. Malzra's probably five hundred and forty. What about Teferi? Oh, he's still fourteen!"

It was another wound Urza couldn't heal.

Neither, apparently, could Teferi. After weeks of counseling, Teferi told the healers to leave. When they wouldn't, he cast an itching enchantment on them. They struggled to maintain their decorum but soon were scratching like a pack of mongrels. They fled.

Teferi stalked out of the infirmary. He marched across the finished academy.

"That wall wasn't here before," he growled, and flung a spell at it. Green coils of energy leaped from his fingers and lashed into the grass at the base of the wall. Ivy grew rampantly up from the ground, overwhelming the limestone wall. In moments, the redoubt was buried deep beneath a riling green mound. "Look at these lovely towers." His hand flung out again. Moss sprouted all along the rooftops of blue slate and hung down in gray beards.

Teferi's tantrum began to attract a crowd of students. Heads popped from behind shutters. Faces appeared in doorways. Students emerged to follow the tempestuous lad. They all knew him from the Teferi monument and excitedly crowded up to see the teenage hermit in action.

Teferi whirled. "Get out of here. I'm tired of being stared at! You've had nearly fifteen years! Look at something else!"

The students shied back from him, but the moment Teferi stalked onward, they followed.

Drawing a deep breath, Teferi bellowed. "Then look at this!"

The student robes of Old Tolaria opened obligingly down their back panel, allowing for various necessary functions—and this unnecessary one.

A new generation of students glimpsed Teferi's infamous "Breech of Etiquette." Many of them turned in disgust. Others laughed, some even checking to see if their work suits would allow a similar display.

Teferi was apparently dissatisfied with this response and added to his visual display an olfactory one. He cast a spell that sent a stink cloud through the whole academy. The crowd shut their mouths and squinted their eyes and ran. Doors and shutters slammed closed. The community that had stared at Teferi continuously for over a decade at last closed their eyes to him.

And he disappeared.

Eventually, the squelching cloud dissipated enough that students and scholars ventured back into the streets.

Barrin and Malzra were livid, a week-long experiment ruined. Their anger only deepened when the prankster was nowhere to be found.

"Look everywhere," Barrin commanded the students in the streets. He hissed to Malzra. "We've not saved him from fire and time only to lose him to stupidity."

The whole school was mobilized. It seemed they were being invaded. It was too bad Teferi was gone, for he would have loved the sight.

Jhoira emerged into the din. Students and scholars trooped like army ants through the academy, opening every door, looking beneath every bed, poking at every curtain and tapestry. Her brow was creased in consternation.

"Teferi, where are you hiding?"

A smile came to her face. It was as though she could read his mind.

"I knew I would find you here," Jhoira said quietly as she approached her niche on the western edge of the isle.

Teferi didn't look up. He sat on a sunny slope of sandstone and stared out at the glimmering sea. He had come to this spot once before, ages ago, and discovered Kerrick and Jhoira trysting within. Teferi's heart must have broken, but he hadn't betrayed her secret, even in the face of Malzra's questions.

Jhoira remembered the time. To her it was ages ago, but for Teferi, it had been only a matter of months. Ages. Months. What did they mean on Tolaria? Jhoira herself seemed little older than in those days. Slow-time water had kept her outward age around twenty-two, and the coma had left her seeming younger still. Her inward vision quest had restored her. It had saved Teferi and her as well. She had discovered a way to break through the temporal wall that isolated him and the social wall that had isolated her. They were perhaps not soul mates, she and Teferi, but they were meta-physical twins.

Jhoira eased up to the rock and slid into position beside him. It was as though she were reenacting that low moment ages ago, though now Kerrick was gone. It felt right to sit beside Teferi instead.

"I'm glad you're here. It's a good place to be, when you're feeling trapped between Tolaria and the world."

The muscles along Teferi's jaw clenched. He stared out to sea.

"If you have to be alone, it's the best place in the world."

"You don't understand," Teferi broke in.

"Yes, I do," she said. "Yes, I do." She reached a hand out to him.

He didn't take it. "We're farther apart than ever. When you were eighteen, you always told me to grow up. Well, look, now you're forty, and I still haven't taken your advice."

"This is Tolaria," Jhoira said philosophically. "Time doesn't matter. You'll see. In a few years, we'll be the same age."

He heaved an angry breath. "A few years—an eternity, a horrible eternity."

"Not so horrible," Jhoira said, "when you've got friends."

At long last, he took her hand. "Thanks, Jhoira. Thanks."

Seven years had passed since Teferi was released from his temporal prison. In that time, he had at last become a man—a young man, to be sure, but at twenty-one, he and Jhoira seemed the same age. She had been partaking of slow-time water for two decades. Most of the scholars and students over the age of thirty were also allowed to drink slow-time water once a year—the frequency required to halt aging. More frequent drinks caused strange illnesses. Since no one understood the long-term effects of the stuff, its use was strictly regulated. Those younger than thirty were forbidden the drink at all. Teferi, at one point, had to be reprimanded by Barrin for drinking fast-time water in hopes of growing up sooner.

In the seven years that he had been free, young Teferi had distinguished himself among the pupils and shown a new maturity. His pranksome nature eventually played itself out, though he still had a sharp wit and, occasionally, a sharp tongue.

Among Teferi's most ingenious innovations was organizing a squad of "temporal spelunkers"—students interested in studying the effects of movement into and out of steeper time gradients. They modified Jhoira's machine to create longer-lasting artificial bridges into drastic time shifts. Teferi even pioneered using existing rivers to cross temporal curtains. By submerging oneself completely in water and holding a large glass jar of air inverted over one's head, a spelunker could be carried along by the current and, cushioned by the water, slowly readjust to a different time. Through such discoveries, the academy was able to establish laboratories in moderate fast-time areas, where a month of experimentation could occur in a week.

The most visible effect of these accelerated laboratories was the rapid proliferation of Malzra's falcon attackers. Their intricate mechanisms were manufactured more quickly than powerstones could be found. The crystals came in only sporadic numbers aboard *New Tolaria* as it made its rounds from Thran site to Thran site.

Meanwhile, Malzra had been busy designing another set of guardians. He took the sensor systems from the guards he had built for the walls of Old Tolaria and merged them with various locomotor apparatuses—bipedal structures modeled after long-legged and fleet-footed emus, preferentially quadrupedal frames based upon the feline physiology of panther-warriors, and even octopedal devices made for ambling over any terrain type and up even the sheerest surfaces. Each of these devices was armed with specially designed pincers and blades for piercing Phyrexian flesh, an array of sight-targeted quarrel launchers, and a core packed with explosive powder, to be activated when all other systems are spent and an engaged foe has incapacitated the sensory or locomotor systems.

The resulting machines were collectively known as the Guardian class—a fearful assortment of artifacts. The two-legged variety were Tolarian runners, capable of great bounding speeds, their mirrorlike torsos bearing eight quarrel ports up each side. Where wings would be on emus, scythe blades emerged to snap together before them. These artifact creatures were meant to fight on open fields. The four-legged machines were known as pumas, sleek stalkers that would patrol the forests from the treetops and drop soundlessly onto any intruders. Their daggerlike claws could bear them swiftly up even sheer tree trunks and could take off a man's head with one swipe, slicing his neck into three equal disks. These claws sharpened themselves each time they were withdrawn into the machine's pads. The final type—eight-legged beasts—were called scorpions, with pincers fore and aft and the dexterity of any spider. As yet only half a dozen of each of these beasts existed, but their gleaming hides and dark, gemstone eyes were enough to frighten even the older students.

Given the need—and given Teferi's fast-time laboratories—armies of these creatures could be created in a single year.

With patrols of runners, pumas, and scorpions on the ground and flights of falcons in the sky, Malzra felt he could ensure the safety of his isle. In addition to these forces, Malzra instructed students on the creation of ornithopters. Five were currently being built.

The academy had become an armed fortification, despite the efforts of Barrin and Jhoira. They had ensured, however, that it was still a human place. They emphasized learning and experimentation over arms production and scheduled celebrations and festivals to help break the tedium of work. Even so, the black blight of the Phyrexian gorge never went away, and every tender thing that came into being in the walls of the new academy did so in the shadow of that horrid threat.

Then they found it—the dead Phyrexian lying at the top of the gorge, having clawed its way up the cliff. It had used the properties of normal-time river water to help cushion its passage, climbing a thin waterfall. Even so, the beast was macerated from the crown of its bony head. to the last spike in its scourgelike tail. The fiend's pink skin was ripped, revealing mounds of gray muscle over a hulking skeleton. Its once-long claws had been worn to bloody nubs in its tortured climb to the top of the chasm. It had passed through the shredding blades of time and somehow survived to reach the top. After two hundred years of experimentation and mutation, the Phyrexians had bred a beast resistant enough to time change to climb five hundred feet through the curtain of fast time. In two more generations, they would be strong enough to escape the gorge and fight. In four more generations, there would be hundreds of them. With their fast-time advantages, the Phyrexians could produce four generations of hybrids in eight years of time outside.

This was why Malzra planned the Day of Falcons. Even as he geared up for all-out war, he devised a swift, preemptive air strike. The attack had two objectives. Minimally, it would slay Phyrexians, perhaps even the new generations, and buy time for Malzra to complete his arsenal. Maximally it could exterminate every last beast in the gorge and thereby end its threat forever. Barrin approved the plan, which required no risk to students or scholars and employed the seven hundred fifty falcon mechanisms already created.

At long last, the Day of Falcons arrived.

Atop the Giant's Pate, Barrin and Karn watched Malzra climb into the framework of his newly completed ornithopter. This command-class mechanism carried remote sensors that were linked to the prototype runners, pumas, and scorpions deployed in a circle around the gorge. It also bore a payload of fifty powder bombs, a complement of sixteen quarrel ports, and wings capable of being swept back alongside the main struts to allow for swift diving. From this aerial command seat, Malzra would monitor and direct the coming attack.

Barrin squinted into the bald morning sun. He held his hand visorlike over his eyes and peered from the Giant's Pate out toward the edges of the island. Thin tendrils of red smoke appeared on the western rim of the isle and frayed out on the sea winds.

"Jhoira and her three squads have reached the shore and set up their posts. They are the last of the thirty-eight launch squads. The falcon fleet is ready to be deployed."

Urza strapped himself into the command seat. His usual blue robes were replaced by a charcoal-gray suit replete with pockets, tool belt, and armor at the shoulders. He wore boots laced to the knee, and his gemstone eyes were shielded by a dark crescent of polished obsidian.

"If this works today, perhaps we can send millions of these beasts into Phyrexia itself, and not a single Dominarian will have to fight."

"What about you?" Barrin asked levelly. "You are a Dominarian."

"Don't you ever stop worrying?" Malzra asked. "I will fly over the gorge, drop my payload of bombs, and rise out of reach of anything they could hurl my way. It'll be just like flying over the deserts of the Fallaji. Besides, I'm only a diversion, a smoke screen to hide the assault."

"The falcons themselves will hide their own assault. That's why we're taking the trouble of launching them at the edge of the island. They'll outrun sound itself in their dive. The Phyrexians will neither hear nor see them until they are torn apart by them. Your bomb salvo only risks you and your new ornithopter."

"We both know I might possibly survive a fall through the temporal bubble around the Phyrexians—"

"Could you survive the moments afterward, surrounded by hundreds, perhaps thousands, of the beasts? Planeswalking cannot save you when the distances are temporal."

With a snort, Malzra activated the great Thran device. It shivered to life. Its wings accordioned out and began to beat. The machine rose, slow and animated, into the skies.

"This is a battle I must fight and win." Malzra soared away from the Giant's Pate.

Just before the wings' whirring drowned out all sound, Barrin shouted, "There is another battle, a much bigger battle, you must fight and win."

Karn watched the machine climb into the sky, beyond the reach of words. The silver man said, "The crews have prepared your ornithopter, Mage Master, as you requested. They included a payload of fifty bombs."

After a long, drawn breath, Barrin said, "I hope I will not need it. Master Malzra might survive a fall into the time bubble, but I am quite—" he broke off, as though he thought better of what he was about to say.

"You are quite human, yes," Karn agreed. his eyes still focused on the shrinking ship, "and I have been near him long enough to know Master Malzra is not."

The not-human in his not-bird spiraled upward above their heads in a maneuver designed to catch the attention of every beast in the gorge—and to signal the falcon crews at the edge of the isle.

"There's the signal," Jhoira said to herself. She peered into the rising sun, where Malzra rode in bold spirals. "He'll start his bombing run any moment." Turning, she called to her three squad captains, "Falcons ready?"

"Squad Fifteen ready," replied Teferi, who stood beside an array of twenty falcon creatures.

Each bird occupied a small metal launch platform, anchored by a foot-long spike driven into the wet sand. The small creatures shimmered in the early light, their metal pinions folded against their legs, and their eyes glinting with predatory hunger.

"Squad Sixteen ready," carne the report of its captain.

"Squad Seventeen ready."

Jhoira paused a moment, surveying the gleaming rows of bird creatures, fifteen rows of four each. They and their six hundred and ninety comrades could well save the isle. "Loose falcons!"

Sixty pairs of wings flashed out. Sixty artifact creatures crouched a moment, gathering themselves to leap into the air. Then the wind was filled with the sharp slap of metal wings. The falcons rose in a great glittering cloud, camouflaged against the silvery work of the sea. The great rush of them upward, of wings and cogs and seeking probes, was something horrific.

Jhoira glimpsed another mass of glimmering wings along the shore in either direction. In moments, though, even her own three squads had ceased to be individual birds and become only a writhing swarm, an amorphous swirling monster, and then it too was gone, through the ceiling of clouds. All across the island, there was no more sign of the flocks of killer raptors.

"Gods speed you," Jhoira said to the cluttered sky. "Gods speed you."

Urza reached the peak of his spiral into the sky. He folded the wings of his ornithopter back beside the struts. The nose of the craft lost lift and dropped toward the black rift below. Urza blinked placidly behind the obsidian crescent that shaded his gemstone eyes. Wind shrieked over the triangular wings. The isle rushed up to meet him. Easing the airfoils outward, he caught lift and corkscrewed low above the black cleft. The craft leveled into a furious strafing pass.

Black ballistae bolts soared out in a spiky forest all around him.

Urza triggered the hold, pouring powder bombs down onto the much-scarred fortification below. Each tumbling incendiary device plunged into the fast-time envelop and rushed fiercely to impact. Shrapnel and smoke belched out in a line below Urza. He banked, soaring away from another barrage, and stared with delight at the boiling cloud of destruction. They would not see the doom that rose at the edges of the island, rose to descend and pierce the walls of their time prison and slay them.

Nor did he see the bolt that rose with fiendish speed and smashed through his port wing and dragged him down into the Phyrexian pit.

Amid rolling clouds of smoke, shrieks of glee arose. Every throat and air sac and proboscis in the Phyrexian Tent hooted as the ballistae bolt transfixed Urza Planeswalker's flying machine. It dragged on the wing. The ornithopter listed with agonizing slowness. Would the man have time and sense to planeswalk from the falling wreck? The smoke thickened, obscuring the view of all beasts below.

K'rrik surged to the tail of his observation tower and grasped it. Even as he gripped the metal, he saw one wing of the machine dip into the fast-time envelop and send rings of distortion ripping out from it. The sudden inertial change hurled the rest of the ornithopter, rider and all, into the gorge. That was all he saw, smoke boiling up to obscure anything else.

K'rrik spun to shout down into the riot of dying Phyrexians and burning buildings, "To the south wall! Capture the planeswalker!"

Stunned, Barrin and Karn saw the ballistae bolt lunge up from the black gorge like a darting fish, lance the wing of Urza's ornithopter, and drag the listing thing down into the lashing currents of fast time. The flying machine whirled once, hung up on the surface of the envelop, and then, before Barrin could send out a saving spell, slid down into the vast murk of the gorge. Smoke and darkness obscured all else.

Barrin turned, darting down the slope of the Giant's Pate.

Karn called after him, "Where are you going?"

"You said my ornithopter was prepped," came the shouted response, flung over Barrin's shoulder as he ran.

"What should I do?" Karn asked.

"Do anything you can, but be quick. Minutes are hours."

The silver man suddenly wished he had the controls that would summon the runners, pumas, and scorpions.

That useless thought was swept away by a sudden shrieking roar, descending from everywhere and nowhere at once. Karn had hardly lifted his brow when, from every corner of the heavens, shooting stars fell in a great converging ring. The whistle of their flight rattled the silver plates across Karn's body. With a series of booms that came so close to each other as to sound like a ceaseless peal of thunder, the lightning-swift creatures lanced down the sky. They punched through the time ceiling and accelerated to blinding speed. They seemed to ricochet between the rock walls of the gorge.

Do anything you can. The words rang in the resounding air.

Karn shifted his silver bulk. He lifted the Viashino luck charm to his mouth for an awkward kiss, and bolted down the steep slope of fallen trees between the Giant's Pate and the gorge. In clumsy moments, he reached the black lip of the space. Without pause or thought, he hurled himself within.

It happened too quickly, the impossible ballistae bolt through the wing, the sudden unresponsive stick, the listing turn, the tug of fast time, yanking Urza and his machine down into the envelope. Before he could think to planeswalk, he was immersed in the vast, churning field of the gorge. Then all of thought and will and power were channeled into holding himself together against rending, dispersing distortion.

His hands turned to protoplasmic mush. His feet evaporated. The wave of destruction clambered up his limbs, to knees and elbows, hips and shoulders, until heart and head both were melting into air. The temporal field tore not merely particle from particle, but wave from wave. The core of his being dissolved. Urza had to think his body and mind and soul, had to plan them and stare at the immutable design of them to force chaos back into order. Again and again, he resolved himself, red clouds of pulverized meat accreting into the figure lashed in the ornithopter's sear. All the while, the ruined bird-machine and the ruined man wrangled in a tangle between worlds of light and darkness.

Suddenly he was free and falling. The last angry torrents of flesh recombined, and he plummeted. The air was dark and dank and foul. The scent of glistening oil was overwhelming. Sulfur smoke roiled from the bombs he himself had just dropped, and beneath those ropy columns, armies of monsters converged. They slithered in gray-skinned masses, slime and bone and horn, clambering over each other like swarming roaches.

Urza fell.

There was not enough strength left to planeswalk. Even if there were, his powers would not allow him to step through the gates of time. There were spells, though.

With a weary thought, Urza cast a flying enchantment on himself and stopped his descent. Ragged, panting if only as a reminder of the physical form he cast, Urza hung for a moment in midair. With another effort of will, he began to rise toward the surface of the gorge. It was like ascending through great pressurized depths toward the air and light above.

The first ballista bolt was a surprise, ripping through his liver and tearing out his right lung before pulverizing his sternum and snagging in his rib cage. Pain was a sensation like any other, useful for orienting him in his physical form, but this screaming, hopeless pain shattered his concentration for a moment. He shut off the claxon of agony, reshaped his body with a thought, letting flesh shrink away from the shaft until the bolt tumbled free. He grew a new liver and lung from the pulverized muck of the old ones.

But this was work, and it distracted him a few moments. He fell again. The air rushing up around him was a flashing mass of smoke, oil-reek, and black shafts. Two more bolts pinioned him in his plummet. By the time they, too, were out and the organs they had skewered were regrown, Urza Planeswalker came splashing down in five feet of foul water.

From a nearby causeway of carved basalt, hordes of gibbering monsters—star-shaped eyes and great shags of barbed hair and curved claws and teeth indistinguishable from each other in their scythelike savagery—hurled themselves into the water. The horrid splashing of their deformed figures seemed the slap of shark tails in frenzy. In moments, Phyrexians surrounded Urza and rushed in, biting great chunks from him.

He thrashed against them. Lightning roared out from his hands beneath the water. Phyrexians died in scores, but more came. Whenever he fought free of them and began to rise through the air, arrows and ballista bolts ran him through, and he sank again into the churning flood.

They would not kill him, though they could. They would only harry him until every sorcery was spent, every last trick gone to the graveyard, then they would net him like one of their scavenger fish and haul him up to be flayed alive by the man standing there on that smoke-wreathed bridge.

K'rrik.

K'rrik's vast host gathered in the arena at the center of the city. It was an elevated circle of black basalt, carved out like a giant funnel, rings of balconies and seats converging on the small, central platform. Though used most often for gladiatorial contests—many of which featured K'rrik himself—the central space was not bounded by any rails, walls, or gates that might contain the warriors. Battles began on this stage but ranged the whole arena. Competitors were not only expected but encouraged to use the topography, weaponry, and even citizenry of the arena in their fight. The outer rim of the stadium was lined with a variety of barbed and spiked weapons provided by the state—bone, stone, and horn, but of course no iron. To get a metal weapon, a gladiator would have to wrest it from the claws of a spectator. Often obnoxious crowd members lost arms or tails, taken up as makeshift cudgels and whips, and sometimes smaller beasts were used whole.

It was not a gladiatorial battle scheduled today, though. This crowd had assembled for a state execution. They still brought their weapons in hopes that they might get a chance to join in the fun.

In the center of the arena, Urza Planeswalker hung, lashed to a much-scarred column of obsidian. The pillar was traditionally used to execute traitors, who were mauled to death by gibbering horrors. With Urza, the mauling hordes were needed to keep him weak and defenseless while K'rrik flaunted his new prize. The largest of his three executioners was little more than a massive fist of flesh, with two tiny eyes positioned under a pair of jagged pincers. At intervals, the beast lunged in and eviscerated Urza, dragging his steaming entrails onto the polished basalt. The other two beasts were jackal-headed spiders, waiting to leap in should Urza overpower the other killer.

K'rrik paced before the knot of them, hissing with laughter. Though given to excited ovations whenever the planeswalker was assaulted, the gathered throng of beasts was otherwise silent, straining to hear every word of their ruler, their god. He spoke to them not in the dulcet tones he had used to ply Jhoira all those years ago. He spoke to them in no human language at all, but rather in the growling, crackling tongue of Phyrexia.

Urza, who could drink down languages like water, knew what he said.

"Children of Phyrexia, scions of the greater god Yawgmoth and his son K'rrik, newts and negators and spawn of time, behold the man who brought us here. Behold the man who opened for us the gateway to this new paradise, to Dominaria—"

This statement was punctuated by a brutal lunge from the pincered beast. Rent viscera spilled in a fetid flow on the floor. A throaty howl erupted from the gathered throng. Even as the monster withdrew and K'rrik began again to speak, Urza's innards writhed on the floor. They drew themselves by force of will back into the murdered man.

"He has a long, honorable history of aiding our coming domination. In the caves of Koilos, he and his brother Mishra sundered the powerstone that had locked us away from Dominaria, thus opening the way for us. During Urza's subsequent war against his brother Mishra, followers of our patriarch Gix were welcomed into both armies, and Gix even made a Phyrexian out of Mishra. When Urza learned of his brother's conversion, he was so delighted, he loosed a catastrophe across Dominaria to slay its greatest armies, sink its mightiest nations, and soften the way for us to invade. He forsook his world, his trusted associate Tawnos, and even his own son, Harbin, all of which we have inherited."

"Harbin!" Urza cried out in despair, just before his gut was ripped open again and there was no breath left to scream.

"Allying himself with our comrade—the newt Xantcha—Urza traveled to Phyrexia under the pretense of war. In truth, he was drawn to us like a gnat to a great lantern. He desired to join us, to become one of us. To show his good faith, he led an army of us to the Realm of Serra, where we initiated a war of conquest that brings the angel realm to its knees even now. He betrayed the woman who healed him and gave us her plane as a trophy,"

The hisses and groans of delight almost drowned out the sound of spilling blood.

"Now, our eternal champion, our spy in Dominaria and through, out all the planes has come to us. He has come to pay homage to Yawgmoth and the Son of Yawgmoth—K'rrik. He has come to grant us the world! He has given us his brother, his associate, his son, his best friend, and now, he gives us himself. Once he is dead, no one on Dominaria can stand against us."

Into the roaring ovation came a high-pitched whistle. The keen was omnidirectional and ear-splitting. Those Phyrexians with ears clutched them in sudden reflex. Those with knees crumpled to them. Even the massive pincer beast fell back, its fistlike head clenching and flexing beneath the onslaught. Only two creatures remained upright—K'rrik and his captive. Together they saw a vast silver corona slice through the time envelope and shriek toward the rim of the arena.

For one flashing moment, the machines were etched vividly in the sky—a circle of razor beaks and raptor talons and wings that glared like lightning. They crossed paths in a vast spiral and, in precise succession, punched one after another into the beasts at the base of the arena.

One monster's inch-thick skull shattered like glass as a falcon smashed into it. Another was split open from neck to navel and spilled gray-blue organs out over its shag-furred lap. Beside that creature, a crane-necked monster was undone when a falcon bit through its neck in a shrieking pass. The creature's eyes darkened, and its head tilted and dropped away like the crown of a felled tree.

Whenever a falcon tore cleanly through a beast, it would continue on to attack the next one, killing two or three in progression. Whenever a falcon was caught in a particularly resistant ball of muscle or cage of ribs, its wings stabbed outward. Spinning saw blades emerged from its frame to mince whatever meat lay about. Phyrexians penetrated by falcons jittered in death spasms, their punctured bowels or chests or brainpans boiling with vicious motion.

In an instant, the three hundred beasts in the lower seats were slain. They crumpled and jittered and spilled downward in a wave of death that crept visibly up the arena. Falcons darted like electrical jags from beast to beast, dropping them wherever they stood. More metallic birds roared in and impacted.

In the second instant, the remaining seven hundred Phyrexians took up their own defense. They swung blades and clubs to bash the birds from the skies. The tide of slaughter slowed but did not stop. The shriek of silvery wings was joined by a manifold roar of fighting and dying Phyrexians.

In the midst of it, tied to the obsidian post, Urza at last recovered fully from the pincer beast's attacks. His abdomen reassembled. His flesh knitted in glowing health. He lifted his head. The jackal-headed spiders cowered back from the quicksilver cyclone that ravaged the stands all around. With a summoning of will, Urza reached out to the mountains of Tolaria and drew from them the power for four spells. A red flare arced out from Urza, burning away his ropes and impacting the pincer beast. He amplified the kindled blast with his own mounting fury. The massive monster went to shreds of meat before him, blood extinguishing the fires there.

The jackal-spiders pivoted in sudden amazement.

Urza flung out two other spells, fireballs splashing across them and sizzling them away. His own figure steaming with the rage of the moment, Urza stalked past the smoldering heaps of his attackers, seeking the Phyrexian at the heart of all this.

But K'rrik was already gone.

Karn plummeted.

He passed the ravening time envelope. It tore futilely at his wires and conduits. Heat sparked across his frame. His orientation meters went haywire, and he could not distinguish up from down, past from future. Then, in a sick rush, he was through and plunging into the fast-time gorge.

That was the worst feeling of all. Something in Karn responded to that place, something at the core of his being. Though he sensed the reek of oil-blood and decay in the air, though he saw the wicked outline of the monstrous city below and knew Urza was there somewhere, trapped or dead—still there was a harsh rightness to it all. It was a vast, desolate beauty that he could not help being drawn to. At first, he could not imagine from where rogue feeling arose, but then he knew. It was the core of his being. The powerstone that provided him mind and heart and soul, it had come from these monstrous creatures. Karn had come from here.

Karn landed in a brackish lake. Filthy water coursed into every seam and hollow of his body. He struck the muck bottom—bones and decay over bedrock. Heaving himself upward, Karn stood and discovered his head cleared the surface. The rock wall of the gorge towered before him. He turned, for the first time clearly seeing the demon city Kerrick had built.

From a volcanic outcrop at the base of the canyon rose a bristling collection of towers, walls, spikes, and battlements. The gorge walls all around the city stared out at it with deep, black mines, like mourning faces, twisted and dribbling. The waters where Karn waded teemed with ravenous creatures, many of which even now converged and nipped at his silver frame. Above the city, clouds of mechanical falcons circled in a great storm.

Urza would be at the center of that storm.

Ignoring the snapping jaws and battering tails, Karn trudged toward the city.

The tide had turned. Most of the falcons were spent. Many Phyrexian negators remained. Urza's enchantments were used up. The artifact creatures he had summoned were being dismantled in the claws and fangs of his foes. Over grisly steppes of dead, K'rrik's nation converged on the center of the arena to slay Urza.

He could perhaps muster the strength to planeswalk, though the trip would merely take him to some other dark corner of the time rift. There he would die when K'rrik returned. Better to fight now and decimate his forces.

Suddenly, into the bleeding, black arena came a silver figure—Karn. He advanced in his slow and ceaseless way, casually tearing arms and stingers and tails from his assailants and continuing on. They swarmed him, but he carved a path through them. They piled on him, but he dug his way out.

An infernal court came with him. Smoke bombs struck among the advancing circle of Phyrexians. Shrapnel sprayed out in a killing ring. More glistening oil mixed with what already painted the seats, and here and there it caught fire.

Urza gazed up through the rising ring of sulfur smoke. There frozen in time above the gorge was the figure of an ornithopter. It hovered low over the temporal envelop. Urza thought he could make out the shadowy figure of its pilot. Better still, uncoiling in silvery promise from the craft came a slender metal cord. It looped down into the time rent, unwrapped, and swayed within paces of Urza.

Suddenly, the silver man was there, too. He clasped the strand in one powerful arm and caught up his master in the other.

How slowly they rose above the shrieking hordes. Thrown scythes and arrows pinged from Karn's skin or buried themselves in Urza until he could will them outward again. Soon, though, they were beyond reach of any thrown weapons, and then beyond even the few ballistae that were still operational. They took one final glance at the shrinking city of devils, littered with the remains of his falcon engines.

"I've only given them more metal . . . more powerstones . . . to fight us," Urza gasped out grimly.

Then the coruscating edge of the rift enveloped them.

Monologue

Even as I flew them from that vile gorge, I knew this meant full-scale war. We would have ten or twenty years to ready our arsenal. K'rrik would have one or two centuries. But all-out war would certainly come.

And this time, the battlefield would be all Tolaria.

—Barrin, Mage Master of Tolaria

PART III

Journeys

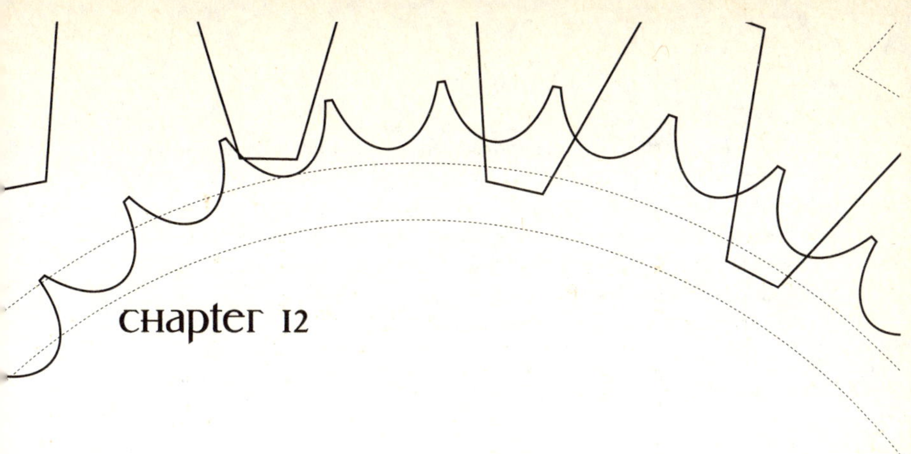

chapter 12

It was a decade later when Malzra called them together in the new Hall of Artifact Creatures.

This hall was no mausoleum and no mere museum. It was a working laboratory, a robotics infirmary, an assembly line, a military staging ground, and a tutorial hall that offered instruction to humans and artifacts alike. Karn's touches were apparent throughout the place. No machines were interred here. The exhibits contained only living, active mechanisms, which spent periods of voluntary deactivation on view. The plans of the various inventions were stored in an archive along one end of the huge chamber, available to scholars, students, and artifacts themselves.

The command center for Malzra's island defense lay here as well. As a result, the place bustled even in the depths of night. Some of Malzra's runners and scorpions were stationed here permanently, and a puma reported in each afternoon, but the main body of machine defenders was stationed remotely around the island. A hundred of the troops were posted in fast-time curtains around the academy. They could leap from cover even before an assault could commence. These machines were rotated into and out of service every day, due to the ravages of fast time. Another hundred served in slow-time curtains—the long-term defenses. They were rotated into and out of service twice a year.

"Between them and our corps of sorcerers, led by Mage Master Barrin, the island's defenses are complete," Malzra said as he paced before the wall of schematics. Mechanical and biological troops were laid out in ink and paper in this private corner of the Hall of Artifacts. "Five hundred large-scale artifact creatures, seven hundred and fifty new falcon engines, a fleet of thirty ornithopters, and even a new dirigible."

Barrin, Jhoira, Teferi, a handful of senior scholars, and Karn sat in the tutorial space and studied the layouts, though the island's defensive systems were well known to all of them. Malzra's presentation was quickly becoming a tedious review.

"In the past five years, we have repelled five Phyrexian incursions and slain over a thousand negators."

"We know," Jhoira reminded him impatiently. "We were the ones who fought those battles."

Malzra turned from his pacing and glanced up, blinking. "There will be more. The creatures will be deadlier and more numerous. With ingenuity, foresight, and grit, the systems we have developed should be enough to repel these attacks. For the time being, the island is safe—"

"Master Malzra," Jhoira interrupted, "we know all this."

"I hope so, since I am going away," the man said quietly.

That brought back the attention of everyone but Barrin. The mage master leaned back in his seat in appraisal, watching the response of the others.

Jhoira stood, alarm in her voice and on her face. "You're leaving? Again? What about the Phyrexian gorge? What about concluding all the business of the academy?"

Barrin rose as well. "He is going on academy business. As to the Phyrexian gorge, Malzra has spent the last half hour reviewing the defenses and our tasks in maintaining and upgrading them."

"That's not what I am talking about," Jhoira said, crossing arms over her chest. "He has unfinished business—"

"Our senior student is reminding me of the 'children of fury,' " Malzra said, cutting through Jhoira's objections and Barrin's apologies. "She is reminding me of my pledge to clean up the messes of my past—chief of which would seem to be this time-torn isle and the monsters I brought here—"

"And the children you brought here—"

"And," added Karn quietly, "the machines you brought here—"

"Thank you," Malzra said not unkindly to the added comments, "but in the way of young folk, you have underestimated my capacity for pernicious destruction. No, the ills I have done here are nothing next to the ills I have done elsewhere, in the world at large."

He walked back to the drawings, reached up with hands that seemed almost to glow in that dark corner of the Hall of Artifacts, and drew down a large pallet. Behind it lay a map of the Phyrexian gorge. Lines of lead detailed the woundlike fissure—dark and narrow, overrun with evil.

"This is our most up-to-date rendering of the gorge." With a sword-sized pointer, Malzra gestured at the drawing. "Here is the gladiatorial arena, and here, the palace of K'rrik, and here, the breeding laboratories. In these hovels beside and beneath the water, K'rrik's minions dwell, nearly a thousand strong, the number growing by ten each day. Unless extinguished, they are fomenting a threat that will one day overrun the whole island."

With a swift and fierce gesture, Malzra tore down the map, revealing beneath it a much larger schematic—what looked like a series of nesting dolls in cross section.

"This is Phyrexia—nine stacked planes, one within another. This top layer is the only one where a human might survive, for a few hours. It is inhabited by dragon engines, some five hundred feet in length, and creatures discarded as useless, creatures that would make our runners and pumas and scorpions seem like mechanical fleas. The dense forests in this region are made of semimetallic plants—poisonous, with razor-edged leaves—that grow in the light of the ceaseless lightning storms that fill the soot-black sky. Each layer downward grows worse—with mutilated priests, demon hordes, witch engines, titanic worms, poison and acid and fire. At the base of it all, there is a figure deeper, darker, more hideous than any Dominaria has ever known."

To himself, Barrin whispered a name. None heard that name, but the look of solemn dread on his face made the others wince.

"I have awakened this creature. I have drawn him here. That is how deep and ancient my mistakes are. I am responsible for the plague of Tolaria, yes, but also for the gradual collapse of a realm of angels, the long ice age of this world, the destruction of Argoth, and the very introduction of evil into the world. That is the scale of my failures. All of that is what I strive to undo. K'rrik is a nightmare, yes, but one man's nightmare. K'rrik's lord is the nightmare of a whole world—a corporate, unconscious, and universal terror. As certainly as K'rrik is arming himself to take over this isle, the creature I will not name is arming himself to take over our whole world."

There were no interruptions now, only sober eyes.

"To fight such a creature and his millions of minions, I need . . . we need a much different arsenal. I go to begin work on it," Malzra said.

At last, Jhoira had regained her voice. "How can you be responsible for all that? How could anyone be responsible for all that? Even if you were responsible, how could you—or any mortal man—hope to undo all those evils? You would have to be Urza Planeswalker to have any hope of—" She broke off mid-sentence, her horrified glare of comprehension bringing paralysis to her whole being.

"Nevertheless, I must go," Malzra said, "and I go alone, for now. It is a very dangerous place I am going. In time, if I am successful, I will bring all of you with me to help."

Trembling, Jhoira had regained her seat. "You're not going . . . you're not going to Phyrexia."

"No," said Malzra fondly.

He crossed to Karn and reached out toward his neck. For a moment, the silver man withdrew as if fearing the master would unlatch his skull piece and deactivate him. Instead Malzra lifted a pendant from the golem's neck and held it out before them all. A lizard-shaped trinket of very hard metal dangled, glinting, in the dark air.

"Not Phyrexia. I'm going to your homeland, Jhoira. I'm going to Shiv."

Urza descended. It felt nice not to have to walk. It felt nice to indulge himself in the luxuries of being a planeswalker, to forget about the worrisome business of feigning breath and blinking, of being asked to join in dinners. For him, eating was only a nuisance. Despite his many almost limitless powers—stepping plane to plane with little more than a thought, casting all colors of magic at high levels, living beyond the terrors of ravaging time, seeing to the essence of things, smelling Phyrexian blood at a hundred paces—portraying a convincing human was a task that was at once vexing in its minutiae and exhausting in its limitations. It was a small and tedious job, but a necessary one.

Except in times like these.

Urza descended past great rafts of sulfuric cloud and banks of rusty steam. His ceremonial robes shrank inward about him, becoming a suit marked with drake-feather pads to deflect the volcanic heat of the landscape. His sandals transformed into thick leather boots that laced to the knee. Hair braided itself tightly to his head, proof against stray fingers of flame. He needn't enter a landscape this way, dropping from such a height, but he wanted to survey this land before alighting upon it. And, frankly, he enjoyed the ride.

Urza had descended once before this way, returning to the ancient, ruined wasteland where he and Mishra had first discovered the Thran site of Koilos. That landscape, blasted by a force that sank continents and brought a millennium of winter to the world, could not have been more tortured than this one.

Backlit mountains jutted in a devilish ring against the sooty horizon. At their tilted tops, steamy lakes glowed evilly in haloes of brimstone. Twisted piles of rock slumped down the sides of these silent sentinels, and rivers of stone pulsed and glowed like arteries. Among them, black courses formed networks of cool veins. Black and red alike, the rivers plunged into a great steaming ocean of bubbling lava, beside which sat twisted columns of stone like dejected statues. The magma vented gasses in mile high jets, rock-spitting coronas, and foamy, belching chunks that sizzled nastily along the shore.

Urza descended. He landed atop a knob of stone that overhung this seething sea of fire. Beneath his feet, the rock was maroon and warm and rumpled, like a glob of blood pudding. All around him, the air was hot and thick with noxious fumes. Urza breathed and reminded himself what a good thing it was to be immortal.

He lifted his gaze. There, above him, magnificent in the dead glare of the place and the roiling gloom of the sky, was what he had come to see: the mana rig.

It crouched on a massif of basalt, vulturelike on broad talons of stone and cast clay. These talons ended in myriad claws that reached in a webwork down the rock face to the boiling caldera below. The extrusion looked like a gigantic heart, and once it had functioned that way. In ancient times, the tubes that crisscrossed it drew lava up from the boiling pit and pumped it into the immense facility above.

The rig was a thing to behold. At either end of it, a pair of bowl-shaped heat shields each held aloft a great city. One, tucked back from the ocean of fire, was an ancient monastery, its conic temples and towers stacked in a decorous hive into the sky. The other, hanging out over the brimstone sea, was a colossal forge of Thran design. It was from here that the incredibly hard Thran metal had come. Urza had arrived in Shiv to explore this site. Between the two cities extended a long storage and production facility with high, cathedrallike walls and tapered archways. In that spot, Urza would begin to assemble the weapon that would turn back the Phyrexians forever.

Jagged script crawled along the base of the bowl-shaped heat shields. Within the structure would be more script, perhaps undisturbed libraries of it. The rooms and halls, the mechanisms and walls themselves would be chronicles in metal and stone of the minds of the builders. He would learn to forge Thran metal, yes, but more, he would plumb secrets of the greatest artificers the world had ever known—secrets that had made them into the very enemies he now faced.

Urza strode from the warm shoulder of stone, making his way past ropy lines of cooled magma. His gemstone eyes scanned the eroded edges of the volcano. He would have to circle north and east, past a giant steaming fissure and a pair of twin cliffs washed by tides of superheated rock. It would be a five-mile walk to reach a structure one mile away—an uncomfortable walk. He was immune to the destruction of fire and poison but not inured to the pain they would cause.

To his clothing, Urza imagined a silver-gilt wrap that flung back the red heat assailing him on all sides. The wrap took form, and he felt his other clothes cool and sigh, venting heat. A veil of fine-ringed metal mesh assembled itself before his face. Thus garbed, Urza climbed the difficult mountain passes.

Of course, he could simply have wished himself into the structure, but to walk a land was to know it. Geography would force him to trace the same paths as generations of others, perhaps as the Thran themselves.

He would approach the rig as they had, would see it the way they had. It was much like holding a book upright when learning to read, though it is perfectly possible to read upside down and backward.

Already the alien script of this place was beginning to resolve into meaningful words. There were trails here—broad, smooth, patient trails. The stone over which they ran was etched with claw marks. Paths led to various prominent points—lookout posts. If they were currently manned, Urza could see no sign of it. Whoever used these trails moved in the open and at a measured pace. They were man-sized creatures. They ruled this place and routinely defended it. Urza lifted the pendant about his neck and stared at the robed lizard dangling there.

Other creatures frequented the hillsides too. They had made various rank nests beneath tilted stones and within lava tubes. Though hidden from sight, these spots reeked of furtive movements, worry, and quick death. Spies. Some of the sites were burned out from within. The bones of their inhabitants lay in ruin at their entrances in warning to others. Other spots, invisible to mortal eyes but plain to Urza's all-seeing gaze, were yet occupied. Tiny eyes gleamed, ratlike and blinking, beneath dark brows of stone.

Goblins. Urza smiled gently. Poor, wretched monsters, vermin more accursed than rats. Once he had taken hold of the facility, he could bring a few dozen scorpion engines to clear out the infestation.

Until then, he had a long walk. Unless a goblin emerged to bar his way—and descending from the clouds had probably done much to convince all watchers to merely watch—Urza would not engage any of the beasts.

He entered a vast defile and wandered the length of it. In blackeyed cave mouths, goblins crouched. They whispered to each other and blinked in resentful appraisal but did not emerge. Urza's instinctual mind marked their positions while his higher mind analyzed the structure that hung overhead.

A third part of his psyche roamed a different defile, one glimpsed long years before. In it, two vast armies engaged in a death match. Urza had believed the vision to show the Thran driving the Phyrexians from the world. It took him millennia to realize the Thran had willingly become the Phyrexians, that Mishra had willingly transformed himself too. Only in that bitter realization had Urza begun to regain his sanity, to recognize the enemy in himself.

Something emerged from the lip of stone at the mouth of the defile. Many somethings. Their rust-red robes melded so naturally with the cliff sides that Urza had not seen them until they were rising from every crevice and steam vent across the stone. They moved with a silent, sinewy grace. Some slid out on all fours, clutching the ground with four-clawed hands and feet. Others strode out on hind legs and brandished thin, wickedly barbed polearms. They posted themselves in Urza's path and planted muscular tails behind them. The nearest ones drew back mottled hoods from their heads. They were reptiles, lizard men, with short, toothy snouts, small, bright eyes, and craggy skulls. Their scaly skin gleamed gray-green and red in the fiery light of the caldera.

Jhoira had called them Viashino.

The largest Viashino in the party of thirty-some approached Urza. It held its hook-edged polearm out before it. The creature glared into the planeswalker's eyes. Slivered pupils stared, unblinking. There was intelligence in that alien gaze, but also fear and resentment. It hissed angrily.

Urza's mind scrolled through all the languages he had learned in three millennia, many of them only written, never spoken. This tongue was not among the ones he had heard before, but for Urza to know a language was only for him to breathe it in.

"Ghitu are forbidden this high," the lead creature hissed.

To understand an alien language was one thing; to frame a response in it was something else. Urza wondered if he should have brought Jhoira with him as a native liaison. He could planeswalk and snatch her up even now, but the rattle of polearm butts on volcanic scree convinced him not to endanger her. He kept his constructions simple.

"Do I look Ghitu?"

"Who are you, then?"

"I am Malzra of Tolaria. I have come to see the rig."

"It is forbidden."

"I must see the rig. You cannot stop me."

"Perhaps I cannot," the warrior said, his eyes glinting like metal, "but our champion can."

From the rear ranks of the Viashino, eight lizard men emerged—not eight, but one the size of eight. It was not a Viashino, though, but a young Shivan drake. The massive creature slithered forward on hands and feet, tail lashing viciously behind it. A predatory grin drew black jowls back from rows of daggerlike teeth. The thing's eyes were small and keen beneath homed brows. Scaly spikes rose across its shoulders. In place of the robes of the others, this brute wore a leather harness, as though it were often used to haul heavy machinery.

No dumb beast, though, the drake reared up and snorted, "I am Rhammidarigaaz, champion of the Viashino. Feeling so arrogant now?"

Urza tilted his head in admission. Were he a mere man, he would be terrified at the prospects of battle, but Urza could sidestep the fastest blows of this creature, could shock the drake mercilessly until it fell dead, could enervate it so it could not attack, could summon armies of artifact creatures to swarm the hillside and dismantle these creatures. Subtlety in dealing with such creatures was a lesson hard learned over the last few thousand years. It was not fear that informed his next actions, but a concern that he not reveal too much about his powers—just yet.

"Arrogant? No. Confident? Yes." Urza waved the monster forward.

Rhammidarigaaz came on. The shouldering might of the drake was like a mountain moving. Urza did not flinch away. Without changing appearance, his robes hardened into armor that would bend only when he willed it to. The creature clutched him in one massive claw, nails clamping down. Urza did not struggle. Rhammidarigaaz hoisted him into the air and snorted hot breath over him.

It regarded the unmoving man. "Shall I bear you to the dungeons or kill you now?"

"You will let me go," Urza replied placidly, "and take me to your king."

"Our bey does not entertain vagrants," Rhammidarigaaz sneered, "and I cannot let you go. You have seen our homeland. You will remain our captive or die."

"I foresee a different future."

The beast clenched its claw. Urza's robes crumpled in slowly around him, but he gave no gasp of pain. The Viashino watched in awe, half-expecting blood to rim the man's eyes and lips.

Instead, Urza repeated his request. "Release me, and take me to your bey."

Enraged, Rhammidarigaaz opened his jaws in a roar and lifted Urza into the gap. Teeth dripped hot saliva across his head. The monster shoved him inward.

As placid as ever, Urza reached up into the drooling jowls of the thing. One hand clutched a great, slimy tooth above him, and the other a tooth below. He flexed his shoulders.

The drake's jaw distended. Like a dog with a stick rammed in its mouth, Rhammidarigaaz gagged and rolled his head. He hissed a cloud of acidic breath. Lizard-men scattered, but the man in the maw did not relent. Rhammidarigaaz tried to clamp his jaws together. A great clacking sound answered. He howled with pain. Yanking Urza from his mouth, he hurled the man to the ground. The beast clutched one jowl with a twitching claw.

Urza rolled across the volcanic dirt and rose to his feet. He clutched in his hand a dripping drake tooth.

"Now you will take me to your bey." Urza's gaze brooked no discussion.

Rhammidarigaaz dropped the claw from its mouth. Scaly hackles bristled across arched shoulders. Hot plumes of death jetted from its nostrils. Twin flames swept over Urza.

He stood in their midst. Poison and pulverized rock sluiced past him. In moments, he was lost in the dense blaze. The Viashino who had fled once did so again, backing farther from the battle. Rhammidarigaaz vented his fury until lungs were flat and throat was raw. In the aftermath of rolling smoke, there was no sign of the invader.

Lizard men ventured timidly from the rills where they had sheltered. A purring growl that must have been laughter circulated among the creatures.

As if stepping around a corner in space, Urza suddenly appeared. The gory dragon tooth still hung in his grasp.

"Enough bravado. Now take me to the bey."

Rage blossomed blood-red in the drake's eyes. His claws sank deep into the volcanic earth. His haunches gathered to spring. Jaw dropping wide, Rhammidarigaaz lunged through air to swallow Urza whole.

The planeswalker grimaced. With an offhand gesture, he flung an arc of magic across the beast.

He transformed into stone. Rhammidarigaaz, the champion of the Viashino, became a statue frozen in terrific motion. He seemed even more massive and fearsome in that aspect. His jaws gaped wide. His eyes glared blindly. His whole figure was caught in the act of a leap he would never finish.

Urza shrugged. The pulpy tooth waggled in his hand. "Well, now instead of a champion, you have a gargoyle." His voice grew steely. "Take me to the bey."

Though none of the Viashino warriors approached, the largest called out from the lee of a nearby boulder. "No. If this is what you do to our champion, what will you do to our bey?"

It seemed a reasonable observation, and thus, by extension, these could be reasonable lizard men.

Urza approached the drake statue. He took a few visual measurements. Positioning himself carefully out of the line of charge, Urza set the drake's tooth back into the spot it had occupied. It no sooner touched the creature than it fused to his mouth. Urza took a step back. Next moment, the dragon's stony semblance fell away.

Rhammidarigaaz vaulted in his attack. The drake soared past Urza and crashed to the ground before a pile of cooled magma. Its toppling bulk shattered the stone bulwark. Chunks of rock bounded out. Viashino scattered farther. The drake's tail lashed the ground. It rolled twice and fetched up against a rocky knob. There it lay, miserable, a twisted mess of wing and claw and scale.

Urza gazed bemusedly at the creature. He addressed all the lizard men. "I could go to the bey without you to guide me, but there may be more mayhem."

The drake rose. He probed his jawline and gasped out wonderingly. "My tooth. It's back!"

"I can kill, or I can heal," Urza said plainly. "You decide."

Viashino and drake exchanged sullen glances. The leader of the lizard men nodded meaningfully to their champion.

"I r-regret my actions," Rhammidarigaaz stammered resentfully. "Violence is not the way."

"All is forgiven. This is a lesson I took years to learn as well." Urza said. He gestured up the trail toward the mana rig. "Shall we proceed?"

With a wounded bow, not quite courtly but not quite mocking, the drake led Urza up the path. Viashino warriors fell in line behind them.

Jhoira stood in the east forest guard post along the path from the academy to the harbor. It was a small, remote tower, provisioned for three guards with a single cot to allow a sleeping shift. Tonight the battlements and the short length of wall were manned by only two, but Karn did not need to sleep. He stood below, beside the locked iron gate, and watched through an arrow loop in a curved section of wall. Nothing would get past him. Nothing ever did.

One end of the wall verged on a deep fast-time rift where a contingent of eighty runners and scorpions were stationed. Anything living would be slain by the temporal curtain, and anything unliving would be swarmed by the academy's machines. The Glimmer Moon shimmered from their silvery shoulders and watchful optics. On the other end of the wall was a steep cliff at the edge of Angelwood. The puma patrols would slay any monsters moving through the forest and the falcons any moving through the air beyond.

It had been ten years since Jhoira had lounged away the day in one of the warm pools of Angelwood. She looked no older outwardly, but inwardly she felt ancient. The slow-time water that sustained her and all the older scholars and students preserved her body, but her spirit was no longer that of a child. She had been on her vision quest. She had learned how to "break through"—not merely to save Teferi from his isolation, but to save herself as well. She had found not a soul mate but a spiritual twin and had found that she had discovered her destiny. It was not a life of bright seas and distant shores, though. It was a life of Phyrexians, forever bubbling out of K'rrik's dark kingdom.

Tonight would be no exception.

"All clear down there, Karn?" Jhoira asked, pacing the top of the rampart.

"All clear, Jhoira," came the response in a voice like distant thunder.

"We have a full complement of runners tonight?"

"Yes," he replied quietly.

Jhoira sighed. Karn was not much of a conversationalist while he was on watch. Her education complete, the academy built, and her post among the scholars secure, Jhoira had had her fill of lectures and demonstrations, experiments and designs. She could have used a little conversation.

"How many negators do you think we will see tonight?"

"The average number at this location is one for every watch of the day and three for every watch of the night," Karn noted.

"That number might change now that Malzra is gone—gone to Shiv," Jhoira said sadly. "I don't know if would even recognize the place. I was eleven when I left it. That was over forty years ago."

She shook her head, picking up a chip of stone from the top of the battlements and hurling it off into the forest. The stone ricocheted off a pair of trees, sending a deep and mournful echo through Angelwood.

"I'll probably never see the place again."

"Malzra said that he'd be back to collect you, once he had prepared the way," Karn noted.

"By the time he's done that, I certainly won't recognize the place," muttered Jhoira bitterly. "The Viashino and goblins will be massacred, the drakes will be enslaved, and the mountains will be leveled into fields of glass."

Over the years, Karn had developed a nascent sense of humor that relied heavily on irony: "You have great faith in Master Malzra."

"Master *Malzra*? Do you know who Master Malzra is? He's Urza Planeswalker! He's caused every great disaster in the last three thousand years."

"Yes, I know," Karn said quietly. "I overheard Barrin and Urza on numerous occasions when they thought I was deactivated."

Jhoira growled, tossing her hands into the air and staring daggers at the silvery figure below. "You might have mentioned it."

"Urza seemed to want it kept secret."

"Didn't it shock you? Didn't it seem impossible for the man to be a three-thousand-year-old legend?"

Karn's silvery head shook slowly. "I am a man made of silver. My best friend is a Ghitu genius who is fifty years old but looks twenty. I dwell on an island where a day might pass in minutes or years. No, Malzra's real identity didn't shock me,"

"Aren't you outraged? Here's a man solely responsible for every wicked thing that has happened to our world. He makes messes and leaves—"

"He has given Barrin a beacon," Karn said.

Jhoira's rant was caught for a moment short. "He what?"

"Barrin has a beacon, a jewel-handled dagger that is magically linked to a pendant around Urza's neck. Barrin can summon him at a moment's notice should the war turn suddenly. He can appear as quickly as the island's native defenders."

Jhoira shook her head. "You're defending him. Don't you see? Urza should have stayed here until the Phyrexians were no longer a threat. He's the reason the Phyrexians are here at all—"

"We are the reason the Phyrexians are here," corrected Karn. "You and I are the reason K'rrik is here. Urza might have been the reason they came, but we are the reason K'rrik got in. It's up to all of us to get rid of them."

Even as these words sank in, Jhoira glimpsed, in the deep distance, the movement of something vast and multilegged, scuttling like a giant flea. Karn struck the alarm.

A contingent of five runners darted emulike from the fast-time rent beside the wall. They loped forward along the trail. Their legs ratcheted in the darkness.

The distant monster wheeled about, retreating.

In moments the runners closed in. They flashed silver in the light of the Glimmer Moon. The small snap of quarrel rounds rattled though the forest night.

The Phyrexian shrieked but turned. It was small and fiendish between the solemn trees.

The scything sound of the runners' scimitars ended in five pairs of meaty thuds. One by one, their internal charges went off. Hunks of meat and blood and mechanism leaped up into the air. In moments, there was only smoke and the tangle of legs, monster and machine.

"We brought K'rrik here, Jhoira," Karn repeated in the drifting silence.

"Yes," she agreed, "and we need to get rid of him."

"Yes, Majesty," Urza said graciously as he bowed before the lizard lord, "I am a planeswalker. I, and all Dominaria, need your forge."

Urza made a broad gesture, taking in the high hall, its rings of balconies, and its conic vault. He had seen much of the ancient facility on his way in—the coke chambers and blast furnaces, the mold rooms and rollers, the ancient gearwork and chain drives. He had seen enough to know that the forge was capable of producing far more than trinkets—if it was given over into the right hands.

The bey was an elder Viashino. A gray-grizzled wattle hung at his neck, and a bright red crest topped his head. Robed in purple, Bey Fire Eye stood at an ornate rail, the equivalent of a throne for a species with neither the physiology nor the need to sit. The rail was carved from one wall of a giant piston chamber. The circular space had become a pulpit, protected from attack on three sides. Its symbolism was clear—whoever stood within the ancient piston chamber embodied the power of the arcane machinery all around. Fire Eye exuded that power. His eyes were small and implacable as they moved across the gathered throng in his audience chamber. He glowered especially at the young drake who had been sent out to best Urza.

At last, Fire Eye spoke, "What would you build with this forge?"

Urza blinked, taken aback a moment. "Machines. Living machines, like this one." He reached out into empty space, and in his hand appeared a large sheet of paper—the plan of the silver man, Karn—and spread it on the floor before the bey. "Men like this. I will make them from your metal. I will make them to defend our world."

The bey stared for some time at the plans before hissing out his response. "This machine will work?"

"I will show you, yes," Urza said emphatically. "I will bring a prototype made of metal. An old model—too soft. You will see. He works well."

Again, the silence. Urza was not accustomed to waiting for the decisions of others, but he needed these creatures. They knew more about the rig than any other beings on the planet. They knew the secrets of making Thran metal.

At last, the bey spoke again, "You may make your metal men with our forge—on two conditions."

"Yes?" prompted Urza.

"First, there is a certain ancient enemy of ours—"

"The goblins?" Urza guessed.

"No. The goblins are a menace, yes, but our patrols are more than able to dispatch them. The enemy I speak of is the fire drake Gherridarigaaz, mother of our champion. She has plagued us since her son joined us," the bey said. "You must halt her attacks."

"It will be done," Urza replied, "and the other condition?'

"Second, grant us as our property into perpetuity the prototype creature you speak of."

Urza stared a long while at the lizard lord, sitting there enthroned on the massive piston. His gemstone eyes lifted, searching the darksome balconies above, as though an answer would lie there. "It is quite a sacrifice you ask."

The bey nodded placidly. "Among our people, sacrifice for the tribe is the highest honor."

There was wisdom in this saying. Urza thought of all the sacrifices in this war so far. As always, the Phyrexian threat came screaming back to the fore of his mind.

"Yes," said Urza Planeswalker, "you may have him."

Monologue

With Urza gone, things are quiet here at the academy. We have had the usual Phyrexian incursions on the borders. They are only tests, of course, and by killing off each of these beasts, we are only helping K'rrik perfect his invasion force for the day when they will all come across. But, for now, we are safe, and we build more machines.

I can only wonder what Urza is doing on the other side of the world. I can only hope that the lessons he has learned here at Tolaria have made him more human again. Human or inhuman, I pray he succeeds. Otherwise, we are all doomed.

—Barrin, Mage Master of Tolaria

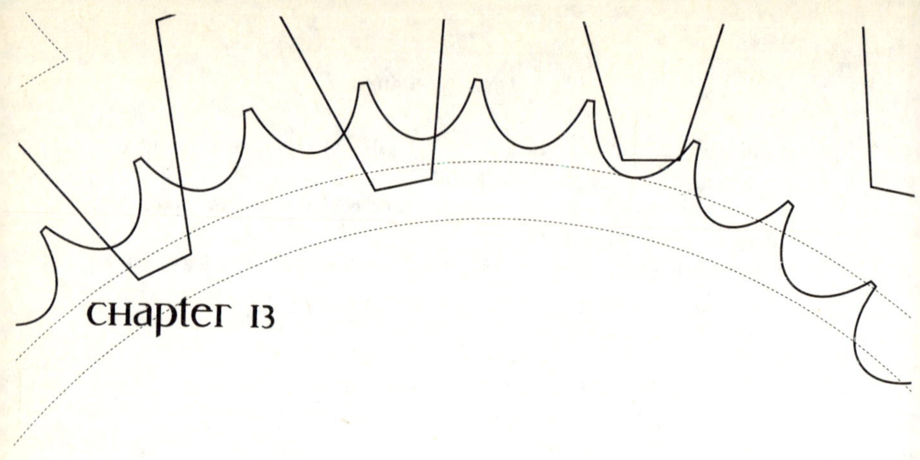

chapter 13

The line of Tolarian runners darted across the grove, their long legs flashing like swords. Sunlight slanted through the forests to either side. The lead machine coursed along a deer path, mounted a gentle slope, and emerged onto the crest of a summit where it paused. The others loped up alongside it. Hydraulics whined as the machines turned, surveying the plains below.

At the far end of the fields, Angelwood bristled with moving figures—Phyrexians. Fangs and claws and barbed tails flashed among the tree boles and undergrowth. Skin as pale as bone gleamed sickly. Leathery folds of hide, knobby shoulders, jagged scales, barbed manes, and eyes like slivers of midnight . . . they were monsters of mutation. Now some of the scavenged bits of metal from fallen falcons and runners and pumas were making their way into the beasts' bodies. Not merely war armor, not merely body weaponry, these hunks of metal were badges of violent valor. They were kill trophies, recovered from fallen machines.

On the fields ahead, metal troops gathered to oppose these monsters. Runners in their hundreds flooded onto the belly of the land. Pumas bounded down from treetop glades and stalked through the tall grasses that verged on the Angelwood. A large phalanx of scorpions filled out the center of the army.

The runners on the summit creaked and moved aside, making room for a new arrival. A large runner, fitted out with saddle and control panel, vaulted into the cleared space. Its rider stood up in the saddle and lifted an olive hand to her brow, peering out across the battle.

"Karn, get up here," the rider called over her shoulder.

A gleaming figure labored up the deer path behind her and stomped to a standstill.

"I am not built for speed, Jhoira," the golem said simply.

Ignoring the comment, Jhoira said, "The main body is coming straight through Angelwood, as the falcon watchers reported. They must have mined their way into the cave complex on the southern edge of the forest. It's just as well. Angelwood is a mild time slough. While most of our forces stop the advance. we'll be able to move through the forest eaves and reach the cave mouth where they are emerging. We'll cut off the advance and then hammer them from the rear."

"How will six runners, a young woman, and a silver golem stop an army of Phyrexians?" Karn asked, his metal frame whining in doubt.

Jhoira flashed a smile over her shoulder and sent her runner bounding down the slope ahead. "You'll see."

The other runners followed. They were fleet-footed, striding like ostriches. Their three-pronged feet scrambled across the shifting stones as they half-slid, half-ran from the hillside into the verges of the forest. They wove their way among great black boles and crashed through damp undergrowth. To one side, the dark dome of the Phyrexian gorge hulked. To the other, Angelwood glowed, infested with hundreds of slow-moving, shambling monsters. Ahead lay a mossy mound of stone. It was a volcanic extrusion, a wound in the earth, riddled with caves. It was through those thousand catacombs that the demonic troops had emerged into the forest.

Jhoira directed her mount up the ancient rill and into the slow time of Angelwood. She charged up the mounded pile of stone, knowing even then that fiend hordes moved through the caverns beneath her. The other five runners bounded up behind her. Karn toiled in silvery languor at the forest's edge. Jhoira's runner leaped up a knob of stone and scrambled across it to the other side. Before them loomed a sheer drop into the mouth of the main cave. Jhoira halted. The five other runners bounded into position beside her, their legs whining in complaint.

From the mossy cave mouth emerged a steady stream of Phyrexians, ambling four abreast into the hot undergrowth. The monstrous column fed the army massing on the plains. The tide could be stemmed right here.

Wishing Karn were faster, Jhoira wrangled her mount up beside a leaning boulder and drove the machine against it. Servos realigned, and the main thrusters of the modified runner flexed. The great stone grated heavily in its cradle. It tilted. Sand sifted from beneath it and rained down over the cave mouth. With one more shove, the runner sent the stone over. Jhoira frantically brought her mount back beneath her. It regained its balance on the verge of the cliff.

The boulder rolled out, tumbled for a moment in massive silence in midair, and smashed down atop a trio of hulking Phyrexians. The stone split like a peeled orange. Golden oil-blood, shattered bone, and pulped muscle mixed with stone shards and sand. The column of monsters behind the site drew reflexively back into the cave. They bunched up at the head of the army. It was now or never.

Jhoira rode her runner over the edge of the cliff. It came to ground on the oily ruin of the boulder and the beasts. Beside it, five other runners dropped. They landed on wheezing legs and pivoted. Crossbow bolts, sixteen from each runner, pelted into the Phyrexians massed in the cave. The ninety-six shafts struck and stuck in meat and bone. The vanguard of the Phyrexian line crumpled, and those behind withdrew a few paces more. It was enough.

Jhoira led the charge into the cave with her runner. It clambered over rock shards and the bodies of Phyrexians. The five others followed. She drew the slim sword that rode at her waist and brought it slicing down through the carapaced head of a negator. It gurgled but flung out its massive arms to drag her down. Leaving the blade in the thing's head, Jhoira vaulted from the saddle. Her mount charged on, out from under her, and swung its scythe blades to engage the fiend. To either side of it, the other runners latched onto their quarry. Ten blades swept out and caught five beasts.

Jhoira, meanwhile, ran toward the cave mouth. It would take only moments before the self-destruct mechanisms activated. . . .

The first, biggest blast came from her own mount. It macerated the beast that it held and sent Jhoira's sword flinging up into the ceiling of the cave. Bits of gore spattered the walls. The blast threw Jhoira free. She crashed among dewy leaves as the other five bombs ignited.

Fire and smoke, bone and stone, waves of belching sulfur . . . with a great, roaring rumble, the top of the cave went to pieces. It collapsed, slowly and magnificently, across the army of fiends, mashing them. Rubble sealed the passageway, mortaring it with glistening oil. The shattered hillside slumped downward in a vast landslide, and like a figure out of a dream, the silver man solemnly rode that slide down to ground.

He clambered from among the tumbled stones and charged to Jhoira's side, drawing her up in concern. "Are you all right?'

The woman smiled tightly, bloody scrapes across her face. "Well, we sealed off the advance."

Karn raised his head and stared warily into the forest.

Many of the lumbering monsters that had emerged ahead of the blast had turned at the sound of it. They converged in a fierce semi-circle on the silver man and his friend.

"Yes, we sealed off the advance. Now we can attack them from behind like you said."

Jhoira staggered weakly to her feet and saw the approaching hordes. She sighed in resignation. "I don't imagine you could pick me up and outrun them—"

"I'm not built for speed," Karn answered sensibly.

A solemn nod was Jhoira's reply. "We didn't get rid of K'rrik, you know."

Karn seemed to consider. "We fought. That is all anyone could expect."

Jhoira looked up sadly at the golem and saw, reflected in his silvery hide, the hundred fiends tightening their circle. Some had teeth as long as swords. Others clawed their way forward on limbs as gnarled, strong, and numerous as mangrove roots. Lupine heads and barbed hackles, coiled stingers and bone-studded jaws, naked haunches and cloven hooves, pulsing poison sacs and pulsing brain sacs. . . .

"It has been a pleasure being your friend, Jhoira of the Ghitu," Karn said with elaborate solemnity.

She smiled brightly. "If I have to die—and all of us have to—I am glad I die beside you."

With an ululating cry, the monsters rushed in upon the pair. A forest of fangs and claws and stingers converged. Karn shielded Jhoira with his silver bulk.

There was only shrieking and blood and limbs flung outward to thrash the trees. Amid talons and teeth came blue flares of magic. Some coalesced into dagger swarms that buzzed like bees through the melee. Others spattered eyes and woke in them cannibal rage. Still others melted tooth and bone into chalky pools. Growls and gurgling. Blood and burning. Death and dismemberment. In moments, the furious carnage spent itself.

The forest grew still again.

Karn turned, confused. Jhoira emerged from the haven of his arms. There was someone else beside them suddenly, a blue-robed man with gray-brown hair. He brushed his hands together as though he had just closed a rather dusty door and then withdrew his fingers into sleeves designed for spell battle.

"Ah, here you are," Barrin said matter-of-factly. "The main battle is going well. When I heard the explosion here, I thought it must have been the work of you two."

Jhoira breathlessly surveyed the killing grounds. The forest reeked like an abattoir. "The fiends. You killed them. You cast a spell."

"A series of sorceries," Barrin replied. "Some of my best summonations and enchantments. They were well spent, though, and I can get them back. That's what libraries are for. I couldn't have gotten you two back."

"Gotten us b-back . . ." Jhoira repeated absently.

"Urza needs you in Shiv," Barrin said.

The master had been gone for a few months, and in the escalating Phyrexian war, Jhoira and Karn hadn't had much time to wonder about the success of the mission for Thran metal.

"I summoned him to aid with the battle—one of the reasons it is going well. Anyway, he says he's struck a deal with the Viashino. He needs you to be a liaison with them. He needs you and Teferi and a number of other students and scholars to help run things with the lizard men. I will stay behind with most of the academy. We will carry on this war until you return."

"And me?" Karn asked. "Does he need me?"

"Yes," Barrin said, his expression darkening. "Yes, Karn, he needs you perhaps most of all."

"No, the gray lever, not the red one," shouted Jhoira down the line of steaming pipe-work. Remembering herself, she repeated the instruction in Viashino.

Her dialect of the language was, of course, Ghitu and therefore somewhat difficult for the lizard men to understand. Even so, after half a year of working daily with lizard men, Jhoira was the only human who could speak Viashino at all. Urza couldn't exactly be called human. Just now, the creatures she spoke to cast quizzical looks up the foggy line of pipes.

"Gray, you know—the color of your blood. Red is the color of mine." Jhoira was almost frustrated enough to bite her own hand to demonstrate what she meant.

One of the younger lizards, a Diago Deerv, gestured emphatically at the appropriate lever. The scaly imbecile to his left grabbed the red lever anyway. Diago dealt a slap of his webbed hand—a bit of correction used by many members of Viashino society—reached over, himself, and drew the right lever.

A blast of steam came from the pipe stack behind Jhoira, venting into the black heights of the cavernous room. The stench of sulfur and superheated rock permeated the place. It boiled across the unseen vault, jiggling loose the condensation clinging there.

Hot drops pelted across her sweating back. Jhoira drew up a cloak of drake feathers, standard issue for workers in the lava pits. The feathers were proof against even the hottest temperatures, and yet they wicked sweat and heat away from the skin. Beneath the cloak, she wore only a loose, light shift of linen and similarly loose pantaloons. Her feet were shod with drake-feather slippers, and she had matching gloves in case she needed to handle any of the red-hot controls.

The vitreous pipes began to glow as lava came pumping up them. The heat of the chamber redoubled. In a few minutes, it would be a veritable oven.

"Let's get up to the blast furnaces," Jhoira instructed.

The scales of the lizard men prickled from faces, arms, and tails, struggling to bleed heat into the air. Wide-eyed and panting, the Viashino nodded their eagerness. It was one gesture they had picked up from their human colleagues.

"Good. Follow me."

Climbing over a jumble of dark tubes, unused and cracked from centuries of neglect, Jhoira led her contingent to the wooden ladder. Its iron rails would be too hot to touch, and even the wood was bearable only with drake-feather gloves. Jhoira ascended. Diago Deerv followed. His comrades came in his wake. Jhoira reached the hatch above, turned the thick metal wheel that disengaged the locking mechanism, and flung back the hasp. Hot air roared up around her as she clambered from the shaft.

Those in the chamber above—a bright, airy, space filled with giant, fat-walled furnaces and great slag buckets—turned to watch the sooty and sweating creatures emerge from their infernal underworld.

Among the workers in the furnace room was Teferi. The young man had traded impish games for a keen forcefulness of will and a relentless search for knowledge. Tall, lean, and wiry, Teferi was handsome and clear-eyed. His dark skin was yet unmarked by the care wrinkles of age, but his brown eyes held an amazingly intense focus. Though chronologically he was one-third Jhoira's age, they seemed physical as well as metaphysical twins now.

"Jhoira," he said, approaching her. The mage and the artificer were equal partners in this endeavor, overseeing the full deployment of the mana rig. "How many conduits do you have working now?"

"Twenty-five, if this one holds," Jhoira responded.

"That should be enough to fire all five furnaces," Teferi noted with approval. He flashed her an appreciative and dazzling smile.

"It's only a tenth of the major pipe ways," Jhoira replied. "I still can't get it out of my head there should be a lot more to this facility than making metal. The power this place could draw from the volcano would be sufficient to run fifty furnaces, but there aren't fifty here. They must have used the power for something else."

Teferi moved in close to her, and a hint of his old capriciousness glinted in his eyes. He was still arrogant enough to use magic to enhance the twinkle in his eyes.

"I tell you, the answer lies in the taboo halls. I've been begging you for months to explore the place with me—"

"And jeopardize the alliance?" Jhoira hissed.

"As long as the drake Gherridarigaaz lives, the alliance will not be broken," Teferi said. "Come on. Say you'll come with me."

Jhoira sighed in resignation. "Once the metal works are fully operational. Until then, we have no time for messing around."

"That could be years," Teferi pressed.

"Well, make years into months, and you won't have to wait so long."

The approach to Gherridarigaaz's aerie was forbidding in the extreme. The lands in a ten-mile radius were goblin territory, and in it the voracious creatures were as thick as maggots on a carcass. In a two-mile radius, the dragon's nest was surrounded by a boiling sea of lava. The aerie itself perched atop a jagged pinnacle of stone that stood like a crooked finger in the center of the caldera. Other tumbled monoliths lay in the bubbling basin. They were spaced just far enough apart that no terrestrial creature in its right mind would try jumping stone to stone to reach the nest.

Neither Urza nor Karn were known for being in their right minds. Neither were they exactly terrestrial. They stood silently on the rocky verge of the magma pit. They had been in Shiv for over a year and still felt they walked the surface of an alien world. The audible shuffling of goblin feet, furtive and feral, in the wastelands behind them only added to the impression.

Urza stared for some time at the distant drake's nest, a huge encrustation of tree boughs woven together with black pitch and fired clay. He stooped, picked up a large stone, and hurled it with incredible force across the surface of the caldera. The stone skipped twelve times before melting away into nothing.

"We are, each of us, capable of leaping stone to stone to get there." Urza said idly.

"Yes," Karn replied.

Urza nodded, his nostrils flaring. Any living creature would have been poisoned by the gasses venting in twisted columns past them.

"I could cast a sorcery allowing us to lava-walk or to fly."

"Yes," Karn said.

Urza stooped to lift another stone, but thought better of it and squatted for some time, watching ghosts of steam promenade across the lava.

"I could conjure my own fire drakes and send them to slay this one."

"Yes," Karn said laconically. "You are Urza Planeswalker. You can do anything. You can wish us into the nest and wish Gherridarigaaz from existence. You can do anything you want. You are Urza Planeswalker."

It was Urza's turn to be laconic. "Yes."

Karn turned toward the scintillating man. "You can do anything, so why did you trade me away for an army of Thran-metal artifacts?"

The planeswalker's eyes hardened. "You answer your own question. Why wouldn't I trade one silver golem for an army of Thran-metal men? There is a great war coming. We must all make sacrifices."

"But you sacrifice me."

He had hardly spoken the words when, with a sudden, vertiginous whirl of movement, the cliff top melted away. The scarlet sea and sooty sky disappeared as well.

Karn stood still. Urza was planeswalking them into the aerie. A human could survive that trip only by being carried in a protective embolism, or turned to stone, or made a flat creature of immutable geometry. Karn merely rode as he was. Urza had sent him on more troubling journeys.

They arrived. The sooty sky remained above. The rest of the world was replaced by a vast, woven bowl of wood and clay, the lair of the fire drake. One corner was filled with a midden of bones, bleached and bare in the brimstone breezes. Beside it lay the half-eaten hulk of a small whale. It had apparently been plucked from the water like a herring caught by a kingfisher. The reek of the rotting sea creature was borne outward on clouds of flies. It mixed with the stench of sulfur and another smell—savage and salty and keen-edged like wood smoke—

Gherridarigaaz. The great drake herself lay in the opposite corner of the nest. She seemed at the moment only a huge pile of red skin, scales, feathers, and fur. Her great muzzle oozed twin streams of smoke. Soot tangled languidly among her spiky brows and rangy mantle. A pair of massive claws lay beside her face. Wings of skin folded over her flanks. The creature's scaly tail coiled on the rock-hard base of the nest.

Urza stepped toward the creature and said, without preamble, "I am Urza Planeswalker. I can kill you with a thought. I will kill you with a thought if you make any move to harm us, and I will kill you unless you cease your attacks upon the Viashino settlement."

The drake slowly lifted her head. Giant lids drew back from slit-pupiled eyes, filled with gold and black striations. The beast spoke. Her voice was vast and purring. "Not much for parley, are you?"

"Our message is understood," Urza said with finality.

"Understood, yes," the drake responded. "Obeyed, no."

"You have no alternative," Urza said.

"I do have an alternative," Gherridarigaaz corrected. "Death is an alternative."

"What creature would choose death over life?"

"A mother would," came the immediate response. "You have clearly not been a father."

Urza cast a long glance at the silver man at his side. "I have been a father."

"Oh, yes," purred the drake in remembrance. "Urza Planeswalker. I'm well enough aware of human mythology. Yes, you had a son. Harbin was his name. You blinded him when you destroyed Argoth. Some say you even sank his boat and killed him."

"I tried to keep him away from the war," Urza replied as if in reflex. "What I did, I did to save all Dominaria."

"You sacrificed your son to save the world," the drake said. "That is the difference between us, Planeswalker. I would sacrifice the world to save my son. I will not give up the fight to free him."

"Rhammidarigaaz chose to leave you. He chose to join the Viashino." Urza pointed out.

"Your son chose to join the war."

Urza's features drew into an angry knot. "I could kill you now."

"Yes, you could, Planeswalker. History says you would, but why, then, am I still alive?"

Urza cast one last, fierce glance at the creature. "You have been warned." With a thought, he and the silver man departed the fiery aerie.

Barrin ran. Fronds slapped him. He thrashed through underbrush.

The thing behind him was huge and sinuous. It slithered in his wake—a giant python, muscular, fleet, silent and cold-blooded. Its homed head was as large as the mage master himself. If it unhinged its jaw, it could swallow him whole. Two man-sized bulges distended its gut already.

"There have to be sorceries to defeat this thing. I know hundreds of them. It's just a matter of thinking . . . something about swamp-walking—?"

The mage master ran. He had been in the heat of combat when the thing had broken through the line. The beast's sudden appearance had interrupted a complex casting. Mana burn had lashed Barrin. He had fallen back. Jangled, he had racked his brain for a defense but found none and ran.

This thing wasn't Phyrexian. It was summoned. The python had been invoked by a Phyrexian capable of casting spells. That was new. Apparently K'rrik had been decanting time-resistant mutants long enough to raise a wizard from their ranks, a wizard or two—or perhaps a small army of them. The giant serpent behind him was not only a terrifying man-eater, it was also a harbinger of greater evils to come.

Breath sawed Barrin's throat. Vines clawed his arms. The creature's cold breath billowed out around him. It almost had him. He redoubled his speed. Think! Think! Treacherous ground stole his feet. With a curse, Barrin tumbled. He crashed through a brake of undergrowth and smashed against a tree.

The serpent coiled into view. It reared up on a broad, shimmering belly of scales. Its mouth glimmered with teeth. Its jaw yawned wide and dislocated.

Barrin clawed behind the tree trunk. He hissed instinctually and glared into the thing's eyes.

"What is that summonation spell Teferi is working on? A creature that can cross time streams . . . Not the imps, but the other one—Teferi's Duck? No, that's wrong."

The monster coiled rapidly around the mage. It looped the tree and lunged.

"Teferi's Drake!"

A yellow-skinned dragon phased into being beside Barrin. It spread its wings in the tight confines of the jungle, and its head darted about angrily. Though the python was gigantic, in the shadow of the drake, it seemed only a worm beside a chicken. The drake's head jabbed downward. Its beaklike mouth snatched up the python.

The serpent writhed in the monster's mouth. One of the man-sized lumps in it convulsed too, whether in defiance or digestion, Barrin couldn't tell. Arching its neck backward, the yellow drake sucked down the python and swallowed it in one gulp.

Barrin slid back down beside the tree, panting in dread. If he had been killed by that python, there would have been no one left to summon Urza, no one to lead the students. And there would be more giant pythons, more minions of evil. More Phyrexian mages . . .

How many wizards does K'rrik have?

Into his musings came the acute realization that the summoned drake stared down at him. Its eyes were at once empty and accusing, like the eyes of Karn. Then, as suddenly as it had arrived, it phased out of being.

That was the flaw in Teferi's spell. To date, the creatures he summoned could cross time rifts but remained in existence for only minutes. Barrin had known of this side effect, but he had been desperate. The drake had been created only to fight, disposable.

How like Karn. . . .

Karn sat on a stone escarpment on the mountain side of the mana rig. The ceramic arteries beneath the structure glowed with pulsing lava, pumped up from the caldera below. Within the plant, massive articulated arms would be cranking huge shafts. Steam shot in vast columns from the top of the rig. The whole thing rumbled and roared in a foul-tempered fury. The rig seemed a great beast, crouching in the red-black sunset, hissing into the sky, slurping from the lava pool.

They had brought it to life. After a year and a half of labor, Jhoira and Teferi and Urza had brought it to life. Jhoira had proven herself yet again the critical connection between Urza and the folk under his command. Teferi had come into his own as an innovative leader and mage. Together they had achieved an uneasy alliance between the human students and the Viashino workers. Urza, meanwhile, strong-armed the drake Gherridarigaaz out of attacking the facility. Even his presence was enough to reduce the constant goblin border battles to only sporadic incidents. The mountaintop was ruled by an iron fist in a velvet glove. All had progressed according to plan, and the first new castings of Thran-metal were only moments from being poured.

They had brought it to life, but Karn felt dead.

Perhaps it was because Teferi had replaced him as Jhoira's closest companion. Their work to vivify the facility had made the close contact necessary. Their species had made the close contact welcomed. Karn felt no jealousy about this growing relationship and even was happy for Jhoira to have a friend made of flesh and bone. But between her work and Teferi, Jhoira no longer had time for long strolls or afternoon conversations with the silver man. He wished again for those bleak days together in the guard towers of Tolaria, but that was not what dragged at Karn.

No, the feeling of dread and death came from the sentence on his life. When all was said and done, he would belong to the lizard men. Urza had offered to move his intellectual-affective cortex to a new shell of Thran-metal, though the man could not promise Karn's mind would move with it.

With a sudden roar, the facility erupted into motion. Though the forbidden sections of the rig remained dark, windows across the rest of it flared with light. The very walls of the great machine rumbled and glowed. The patient roll and plunge of the facility's crankshafts and pistons accelerated to a deep and trembling drone. Jets of steam above the facility coalesced into a great, sooty cloud that blotted out sun and sky both and enwrapped the rig and the silver man in a choking fog.

He sat awhile longer, shrouded in gloom. The forges would be firing, the metals forming, the molds filling. Within the structure, a new army of metal men was being born. Outside of it, an old metal man was being killed.

All around him, small red eyes emerged from nearby crevices and caves. Unseen by the downhearted golem, goblins ventured up to the very verges of the rig, stood atop each others' shoulders to peer into windows, and set hundreds of tattered claws to whatever loose plate or door gap presented itself.

In one place, they found their way inside, hundreds of them.

Monologue

I do miss Urza, Jhoira, Karn, and—yes, I'll admit it—even Teferi. Their labors on the island before they left have given us a solid defense against Phyrexian incursion. I can only hope their labors in Shiv will do the same for the world itself.

K'rrik's machinations advance exponentially. Just because our artifact machines can repulse his current generation of negators does not mean they will repulse the ones that emerge in a few months—let alone any more negator mages who might make it out. We tracked down and slew the one who had summoned the python, but there will be others.

The students, colleagues, and I work hard to improve and adapt our designs, to suggest new machines and to create new spells, but even our fastest fast-time laboratories run at half the speed of K'rrik's.

It will come down to a final conflict—both here on Tolaria and out in Dominaria at large. To win our little war here, we'll need Urza and Jhoira and all the others. To win the coming conflict, we'll need a new machine, one designed by Urza himself, one that can adapt to anything, one with firepower greater than that of the whole island.

Urza started a design before he left. Perhaps he has finished it by now.

—Barrin, Mage Master of Tolaria

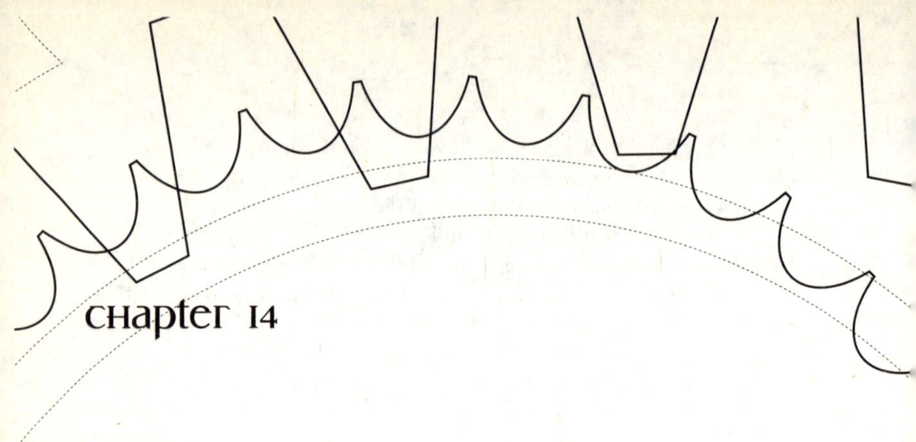

chapter 14

"This is our salvation," Urza said.

He paced before the array of plans. They filled the semicircular wall of his high study in the mana rig. The room was an approximation of his library back on Tolaria, though the books that lined the shelves here were largely Thran, unreadable to anyone but Urza. Tonight, the shelves served to hold tacked plans, the latest wild imaginings of the artificer genius. With a slim pointer cast of the new batch of Thran-metal, Urza indicated the sleek structure of the device.

"It is a flying machine, made entirely of Thran metal. It is driven by a matrix of powerstones, which take up much of the hull. With these stones, it is capable of faster-than-sound travel. Power can be diverted from the drive systems into various gun batteries—"

"What is it for?" Jhoira asked.

Among the group gathered, including Teferi, Karn, and a handful of other top scholars, the Ghitu woman seemed the only one willing to question the master.

Urza pivoted mid-sentence and looked at her, blinking. "Why, it is for war, war with Phyrexia."

Jhoira's brow furrowed. Teferi's hand clamped over her arm, but she spoke all the same.

"The metal and powerstones needed to construct that ship could be used to make armies of warriors, which would be more effective against armies of fiends."

"Armies are slow," replied Urza. The lamplight of the darksome study glimmered from his queer eyes. "This machine will be able to move like lightning for quick strikes against specific targets—targets such as dragon engines and landing craft."

"How many such engines do you suspect the Phyrexians will have?"

"Perhaps hundreds," Urza said grimly, "perhaps thousands."

"Shouldn't we plan to build hundreds or thousands of machines like this?" Jhoira asked sensibly.

Urza looked nettled. "There aren't enough active powerstones on Dominaria to build two of these devices and any mechanical defenders."

Jhoira sighed, crossing her arms. "As fantastical and appealing as this idea might be, it seems to be impractical in the extreme. Unless we find some underground trove of powerstones, we must make the best use of the few we have."

A fiery light glimmered in Urza's eyes, and he seemed on the verge of snorting. He placed the tip of his Thran-metal pointer on the table and pressed upon it. The rod trembled with the master's anger. Instead of breaking, the metal only made a jagged line across the obsidian top. Wheeling, Urza tore the plans down from the wall, crumpled them, and flung them savagely in the corner.

"No more delays. I want the prototype Thran-metal man completed this month."

Teferi finished undoing the final bolt, pulled away the age-crusted grating, and gestured Jhoira into the dark crawlway beyond.

"The plans say that this space leads into the heart of the forbidden zone." His eyes gleamed with mischief. "The secrets of the mana rig await."

Jhoira glanced around again, trying to make sure no Viashino patrols were coming down the passage. "I think this is a mistake. If the lizards find out—"

"Tribal law forbids Viashino from entering the forbidden zone. It says nothing about humans," Teferi said, and his smile glinted in the dark space. "Besides, you promised. The metal works have been running at full capacity for a year now. I'm well overdue."

A laugh of resignation came from Jhoira. She shook her head, staring in amazement at the handsome young man. "Yes, Teferi, you are well overdue." She paused. The cloud of bygone days passed over her eyes. "You followed me down another passage like this, once."

Teferi only smiled.

"Some things never change."

So saying, she drew a dimly glowing powerstone from her pocket and waved it in the cobwebbed crawlspace before her. Taking a deep breath, she entered it.

Teferi followed closely behind. The space was tight, its height slightly shorter than Jhoira's thigh, its width slightly thinner than Teferi's shoulders. The effect was claustrophobic. Instead of an actual crawl, the two explorers had to move forward with an inch-worm motion. Even so, the shaft did not seem an air duct. The floor was too solid, the walls were sided with moldings, and in places along it, constricting the space further, dull-edged hooks jutted from the walls.

Getting caught on one of these for a third time, Jhoira halted. She half-turned, panting, and let the dim glow of her powerstone reach out through the passage ahead. The walls, ceiling, and floor regressed to a gray-black square of emptiness. A cool, dank breeze came from it.

"There's got to be a reason it is forbidden," Jhoira whispered, sending sibilant echoes both ways from them.

"Yes, because whatever is in there is valuable, precious—"

"Perhaps even deadly," Jhoira finished for him. "It occurs to me that since this was your idea, you should have been the one leading."

Teferi didn't respond immediately. The sudden silence made Jhoira nervous. She craned her neck to make out the man. His powerstone flickered, and wedges of light danced wanly about them.

"Jhoira," he said at last, voice awed, "these hooks in the wall. You know what they are?"

"Triggers for deadfalls," she ventured wryly, "or poison darts?"

"Lamps," Teferi said, answering his own question. "These are lamp sconces. Look."

He lifted his powerstone toward the small curl of metal jutting near the top of the wall. The stone pulsed brighter as it rose, showing up a small, shiny parabola, and in front of it, a clip in a sconce. Teferi positioned the glowing rock in the clip, and suddenly it flared.

The explorers fell back, shading their eyes. Bright ribbons of light coursed out around them. Soon their eyes adjusted to what had once seemed a blinding glare, and they saw the hallway clearly. That was what it was, a hallway made for creatures much shorter than the two humans. The floor was composed of venous marble, the walls of riveted metal, and at even intervals along the passage, lantern sconces hung.

"Who was it made for? Viashino?" Jhoira wondered aloud. "They'd have as much trouble as we are getting down this passage."

"Maybe the ancient Thran were little guys," Teferi speculated.

Jhoira shook her head. "Don't you remember the stories of Urza and Mishra finding the first ornithopter? Its seat and controls were human sized. No, this must have been someone else."

"You mean that someone other than the Thran built this place?"

"No," Jhoira responded, "I mean that the Thran built this place for someone else to run."

"A slave race?"

"Perhaps." Jhoira pivoted. "I see something ahead, off to one side. It looks like a doorway."

"Lead on, but be careful. Some of the Thran slaves might still be around." Teferi withdrew his powerstone from the sconce, and immediately the hall was plunged into darkness. It took awhile for their light-acclimated eyes to adjust to the murk.

Taking a deep breath, Jhoira inched forward until she reached the doorway. It was a short opening and narrow. The space beyond breathed hot, dry air past her. Cautiously, she extended her powerstone into the swimming blackness. It showed up a set of ceramic pipes, conduits crawling over each other like the viscera of some great leviathan. As her eyes grew accustomed to the darkness, she could make out, low in the tangle of tubes, a number of the greater pipes glowing faintly with the heat of the lava they carried.

Teferi crowded up beside her and confirmed her thoughts. "This is where those other channels empty. They are meant to power the machinery in the forbidden zone."

"We've accounted for only thirty percent of the lava tubes. If the other seventy percent were used for these other devices—"

"What would take that kind of power? What if it was mutagenic research, the kind of thing K'rrik's been doing?" Teferi volunteered.

Jhoira was dubious. "I can't imagine using such thermic power to create clone creatures. K'rrik certainly doesn't have that kind of power. Mutagenics comes more from tampering with the power of growing things. Remember the stories of Ashnod? Vats and chemicals and muscular fusion—"

Teferi's reply was wondering. "You really listened to all of Urza's lectures?"

Pushing onward down the corridor, Jhoira said, "The cool, dank air comes from ahead. There must be a big room up here."

Crawling, they came to a tight bend in the passage—a kink, as Teferi called it. Beyond, the passage widened and dipped into a debouchment with a pair of open doors. The chill in the air was undeniable here. The rustle of clothes slipped outward into silence before coming echoing back at them.

Jhoira extended her arm, powerstone held on her open palm. The light was too feeble to show up anything. Even with Teferi's glowing crystal alongside it, the space ate up the light.

"Well," Jhoira speculated, "either we venture blindly forward—"

"To fall into some open pit or other—"

"—or we try to find another light sconce or two."

"Here's one," Teferi said, slipping his powerstone into the bracket. As light leaped blindingly outward, Jhoira fitted her powerstone into a niche on the opposite side of the room.

The resulting glare filled the vast chamber, driving shadows back beyond a vault of riveted ribs. Metal struts and trusses lined the walls and ceiling, shot through by more tangles of pipe-work. The countless tubes—bristling here and there with valves and pressure gauges, pumps and release valves—entered the room through walls and floor, snaked in writhing piles of pipe across the chamber, and converged on a great central mass encased in scaffolding many stories high. To compare the network of tubes to vessels surrounding a giant heart would be to vastly underestimate the number of tangled channels. They formed a veritable thicket, through which the central mechanism was hardly distinguishable.

"What is it?" Teferi wondered, staggering to his feet before the massive machine.

Jhoira rose also. "Maybe you were right about the mutagenic experiments."

"Let's go see."

Teferi brushed dirt from his coveralls and started forward. He clambered over a dust-mantled manifold, noting the small ladders and causeways that gave access to them all.

Jhoira followed. Each footfall sent lint rolling up into the air. "It looks like the forbidden zone has truly been empty for some time."

"Unused, but not empty," Teferi ventured, pointing to a small, three-toed footprint on the far side of a cluster of pipes.

An adjacent channel held a three-fingered hand print. More tracks led away from the spot, into the lurking shadows behind the main mechanism.

"It's as though somebody watched us approach and scrambled away when we lit the place."

A wary look crossed Jhoira's face. "We've seen enough to make a meaningful report to Urza."

Teferi ignored the implication. "There's a porthole on the side of the main machine. It's only ten paces farther."

Without waiting for her approval, the young man strode onward. His footfalls obliterated the skittering tracks he had discovered. Jhoira fell in step behind him. Shadows deepened. The glare was reduced to triangular bright spots cast in kaleidoscope across the metal-plated bulk of the mechanism. Teferi and Jhoira reached the porthole. Teferi wiped centuries of dust from the face of the glass.

A dagger of light stabbed through the porthole glass and glinted across something within. The explorers crowded together at the window and gazed in.

"By the stones of Koilos!" Jhoira gasped.

That huge gem—the powerstone that had sundered at the touch of Urza and Mishra, driven the two into their fratricidal war, and opened the door to Phyrexia—could not have been a larger, more perfectly formed crystal than the stone at the center of the dark chamber. Beside it, glimmering in their hundreds, were many more gems, fist sized and double that, all lying in a dark jumble. If charged, any one of them could have powered a dragon engine.

"That's why this place is forbidden," said Teferi with awe. "It is a trove of powerstones."

"Not a trove," Jhoira said. "This is a machine for making them." In the moment of that staggering realization, Jhoira made a second. She hissed, "Teferi, we aren't alone."

The two whirled to face a toothy wall of short spears, thrust their way. Behind the savage shafts, small red eyes squinted in wicked little faces. Light from the wall sconces outlined the creatures' rumpled brows, their pointed ears, their wiry frames, and the obscene proliferation of bristly hair from ears and moles and shoulders.

"Goblins," Jhoira said.

Teferi raised his hands to cast a spell, but a ragged net fell over them both, interrupting the enchantment.

The net cinched tight. The wall sconces went dark. The spears converged.

They came from everywhere. They came from the caves where they had hidden from the Viashino patrols. They came from crevasses that sliced down into their underground warrens. They came even from the forbidden zones of the mana rig itself.

Goblins.

They came from everywhere, and they came in their thousands. Many of the hip-high invaders were the red-scaled Destrou clan that inhabited the hillsides around. They bore polearms surmounted by sharpened ram's horns, which curved close enough to their heads to leave ragged cuts along the creatures' shallow pates. Their long ears were pinned back—a sign of all-out war—and their prominent noses flared with battle howls.

Others were gray-skinned Grabbit goblins, somewhat smaller than the Destrou but nastier in combat due to their tendency to bite with small, serrated, and invariably filthy teeth. They also employed body slams, wearing studded-leather jerkins, breeches, and putties. Hurling themselves screaming into battle, Grabbits swarmed their victims, biting and spinning, shredding with teeth, claws, and hunks of metal, bone, and stone sewn into their clothes. They were savage, relentless, and formidable foes—but they weren't normally allies of the Destrou.

Nor were the third group of invaders, the silver-scaled Tristou goblins. Tall and thin, Tristou occupied the distant ridges of the caldera. Not normally a warlike race, Tristou were bone-rolling oracles and goblin visionaries given to week-long trances that yielded lengthy and largely unintelligible predictions of doom. Since the arrival of Urza, Tristou prophets had foreseen an upcoming war that would unite the goblin tribes. It would be an all-out battle against the Viashino.

The day of that war was at hand.

The Viashino and their human allies had desecrated the holy necropolis. Destrou sentries had captured two humans peering into the gemstone tomb. No goblin had looked upon that sacred place in a century of centuries for fear he would be struck dead by the ancestral spirits that dwelt in the stones within. These two humans not only gazed into the space but shone a light into it and hadn't even the courtesy to drop dead.

The united tribes determined the violators would drop dead—the violators and their Viashino allies. Word of the atrocity spread like wildfire from Destrou patrols in the necropolis, to the Grabbit warrens that riddled the volcanic hillsides around, through the steam tunnels and the guard posts stationed at the head of the sulfur vents, and to the distant oracle caves of the Tristou. The wave of angry whispers crashed upon these far shores and then returned, bearing on it a unified army of thousands of goblins. They bore torches and scourges, claw-headed warhammers, notched cleavers, dart-tubes, acid bladders, nets, daggers, teeth, claws, and the will to use them in all-out war with their neighbors.

They would fight to the death, and the two human hostages they held would assure their victory.

Urza had been working over his prototype Thran-metal man when the alarm went off. He looked up, gemstone eyes glinting in frustration. Whenever Jhoira and Teferi were off-duty, the alarms were almost continuous. Closing his eyes, Urza rubbed his temples. The sites were only mental projections, of course, but thus were all the more susceptible to psychosomatic ailments such as muscular tension and nervous spasms. He opened his eyes again. The half-assembled metal man stared blankly back at him.

It wasn't working. Thran metal grew. He had not recognized that fact before. He had assumed only that Jhoira's trinket necklaces were fashioned in various sizes. Now he knew that the large lizard pendants had grown from small ones.

The pieces of the Thran-metal man were growing too. His chest plates were already grating against each other and binding up the shoulder joints. Worse, the clockwork gears ground together, breaking off cogs, bending shafts, shattering flywheels. Even as Urza sat there, considering the slowly deforming mechanism, a great clang announced the sudden catastrophic failure of a strut in the creature's pelvis, and a groin plate slumped ignominiously.

Urza slouched back in his seat, wondering how long this alarm would be allowed to blare. The mana rig was like a giant bucket, amplifying the clamor until it was unbearable. Around the ringing corners of his mind, Urza chased an elusive thought . . . something about aligning growing parts according to the geometry of life, so that the pieces could expand in concert rather than in opposition. . . . A sphere shape or a three-dimensional oval, with internal mechanisms organized in nested shells, would allow for the growth of each level and that of the whole. Even in the shrieking air, he recognized the irony of designing a machine after the plan of Phyrexia with its nested planes. His gaze strayed to the abandoned plans for the Thran-metal ship—it was ovoid. Perhaps he could use the concentric organizational plan to structure . . . to allow the Thran metal . . . organization with the . . . make a growing—

"Enough—!" shouted Urza at the reeling ceiling.

The alarm was suddenly louder, jarring into the room with a flung-back door. Urza whirled angrily, seeing the silver man crouching in the too-small space.

"What is it?'

"Goblins. Goblins everywhere. Three tribes. The Viashino are losing," Karn said in a rush.

"That's it," Urza growled, standing and growing a war cloak about his shoulders.

The stylus he had been holding grew into a glimmering staff, and he strode ahead of the silver golem, out the door and toward the battle.

The forge room was chaos. Viashino workers in their leather coveralls fought side by side with disheveled, human students. Wrenches and spanners flashed among double-bladed paortings, wrist daggers, and dragon-headed throwing axes. The lizard men fought in ragged clusters, backed up against the vast, glowing furnaces they tended. With desperate jabs and off-balance swings, they held at bay the loud, lapping tide of goblins.

They were everywhere. Gray Grabbits swarmed at the front. They hacked and gnawed at knees. Red-scaled Destrou crowded up behind their short comrades and swung ram-horn polearms above their heads. Here and there hooks caught lizard-man sleeves or wattles and dragged the victims onto the impaling gray horns. Behind that line, a few silver-skinned Tristou held the center of the floor and flung fire and lightning into the defenders' ranks.

Viashino were falling. Already seventeen workers and four warriors lay in pools of gray blood among the advancing goblins. Grabbits fed violently on these dead forms. Two more lizard warriors hung smoldering on the sides of furnaces. They had been backed against the sizzling metal, and their skin adhered. A few flailing minutes followed, and then the cooked reptiles turned to coal. Two human students also had died, one impaled on the end of a stolen paorting, and the other beneath the toothy tide of Grabbits. The remaining defenders, outnumbered, ill-armed, and overheated, languished in the verge between fire and spear.

Diago Deerv brought a gaping wrench down on the head of a Grabbit before him. It staved the beast's skull. He kicked the body among the mass of its comrades, giving them something besides him to eat.

"Where is Jhoira?" he gasped out to the workers around him. "She'd have an idea."

"An idea?" roared a nearby mechanic. A goblin torch rammed against his chest. The lizard man reared back on his tail and kicked the fire-wielding monster back among his fellows. The torch set another pair of Grabbits aflame. "We need an army, not an idea."

Diago blinked at the burning Grabbits. "Sometimes an idea's worth an army." He whirled, pulled a forge pole from its rack beside him, and slipped its hooked end into a large latch on the side of the forge.

"What are you doing? We're fighting goblins, not forges."

"Get back!" Diago shouted forcefully.

His comrades fell back. and in the next moment he flung open a slag gate in the side of the forge. Out poured a river of molten metal, spilling across the goblin hordes. Even the heedless and senseless Grabbits retreated from the blistering flood. Many weren't quick enough, swept under the tide and exploding as every liquid in their bodies turned instantly to gas. These small blasts sent red-hot spatters of metal out to burn other goblins.

Panting behind the flood, Diago gasped out, "Gives us a moment to breathe."

The warrior beside him was prickly, his scales jutting out all across his body. "I'd rather die by spear than by fire."

Diago looked up, toward the wide stairway that led down into the forge room. "Maybe we won't have to die at all."

Another tide rolled down the stairs—Viashino warriors, fully armed and armored, their paortings gleaming in a thicket as they waded into battle. Above the tide of warriors, another figure came, floating above the floor and emblazoned with fiery light. Urza Planeswalker drifted down, a second sun above his army. From his fingertips, bolts of power lanced outward. Where the red crazings struck, goblin bodies flipped up into the air. They tumbled like charred toys before clattering to the ground.

The straggling defenders let out a cheer.

Urza hovered into the center of the forge room. He lifted his hands together overhead. A white light awoke between his fingers. It shone across metal struts and trusses that hadn't been illuminated in millennia and then swept out in stunning waves. Rings of illumination moved over the gathered monsters, stilling them in the midst of battle. Upraised cleavers did not fall, frozen in air. Scourges followed one last course before going limp in the hands of their wielders. The magical staves of the Tristou flared and became rods of fire before fizzling away into sifting ash. In his last labor before the stilling waves of magic lay hold of him, Diago hauled hard on his hooked staff, drawing the slag sluice closed and stopping the flood of metal.

Next moment, even the war cries died away. All eyes turned to the floating figure.

Urza shouted over the throng. His voice was guttural, a collection of growls and harsh barks. The words, nonsensical to humans, made sense to the goblins and their ancient lizard foes.

"Surrender, all goblinkind. Throw down your weapons or face immediate destruction."

He made a sign, and three goblin figures—taller and more elaborately mantled than their fellows—rose into the air. The three chieftains kicked in struggle against the invisible claws that gripped them. They drifted toward the imperious figure.

Below them, among the goblin rank and file, nerveless claws opened, letting cleavers and axes fall to the floor. Grabbits withdrew, bloody mouthed, from corpses. Destrou dropped to one knee in sign of surrender. Tristou stood, spells forgotten on quivering lips. Even as they did, the pacifying waves of white energy gently cycled among them.

"I will speak with your chiefs about terms of surrender," Urza announced to the room.

He made a final gesture, bringing the floating creatures to a stop before him. They hung uncomfortably in the air, their robes of state trailing in bloody tatters.

Urza examined them. His uncanny eyes rested on each in turn. The Tristou chief was a wizened old creature, his eyes large and solemn behind a nose as withered and dark as a date. His robes were once fine—midnight blue with silver piping, though a scorch mark showed where his staff had blazed away. One claw had been burned brutally. Beside him, the chieftain of the Destrou was a warrior female, clad in gray leather armor from which taut red arms and legs protruded. She wore the scowl of bitter undefeat and kept her eyes lifted defiantly in the presence of her foe. The third chieftain was a mad imp, its small body wrapped in bloodied armor studded in teeth and metal shards. It fought angrily against its captivity.

"I am the lord of this rig," Urza said in forceful goblin tongue. "You and your folk will withdraw. None of you will be left within five miles."

"These are our ancestral homelands," objected the silvery Tristou.

"You were permitted to live here until you attacked," Urza pointed out. "You have brought about your own exile."

"Our attack was provoked," the Destrou warrior chief said. "Two of your lieutenants desecrated our sacred necropolis."

"That does not matter," Urza said dismissively. "You have been utterly defeated. Withdraw from this facility and the lands around, or I will slay every last one of you who remains."

"We hold these lieutenants captive," the Destrou continued. "We hold them in a death cage. It is linked to me. At a moment's notice, I can make the cage collapse with them inside, killing them instantly. If I die, they die."

Urza studied the warrior woman. "You are lying."

"Their names are Jhoira and Teferi," the warrior chief replied.

Urza began a response. but the words jumbled on his tongue, and he quieted. He breathed, perhaps for the first time since entering the forge room.

"Take me to them. I must see they are alive."

"No," the Destrou chief replied. A file-toothed smile spread across her face. The tables had turned, and she savored the shift. "But you may speak with them." She nodded to the Tristou oracle, who used his charred claw to draw a black circle in the air.

Noises came from the circle—the jabber of goblins, the crackle of a fire, the shift of midnight winds.

"Teferi, Jhoira," Urza called, "can you hear me?"

A shifting sound came, and the clang of metal. "Who is it?" came a woman's voice.

"It is Urza. Where are you?"

"We don't know. A dark cavern. They have us in a strange cage."

"Is Teferi with you?"

The young man's voice answered, "Yes."

Urza's features darkened. "What is this they tell me about you desecrating their sacred necropolis?"

Teferi sighed. "We went into the forbidden zones. That must be what they mean."

Urza turned to the silvery oracle. "Your sacred necropolis is within the rig?"

"It is sacred to our ancestors. They dwelt in it, long before the lizard men," responded the Tristou with a twitch of his prune nose. "They dwelt in it with the old masters."

Before Urza could respond, Teferi offered, "It looked like it was designed for them. Everything is goblin sized—corridors and ladders and consoles. Viashino couldn't have operated or maintained any of the machines we saw."

The silvery oracle blinked placidly back at Urza.

"Are you saying your ancestors served the Thran?" Urza asked in hushed tones.

"There's more," Jhoira interrupted. "That sector of the rig—the largest sector—is devoted to making powerstones."

The planeswalker, despite himself, turned white.

The oracle spoke into the following silence: "Now, do we surrender to you, or do you surrender to us?"

Monologue

Urza arrived today with strange and marvelous news. He has just brokered a peace accord between five races.

Yes, Urza Planeswalker—defiler of Argoth, scourge of Terisiare, bane of Serra's Realm, destroyer of Tolaria, he whose name has become synonymous with mad and savage war—Urza has brokered peace. Viashino, Tristou, Destrou, Grabbit, and human now work hand in claw within the mana rig. To make matters more incredible, the two human prisoners of war caught desecrating the sacred necropolis of the goblins have been set in charge of returning the goblins to their ancient homelands in the rig and training them once again to run the machinery there. And, most incredible of all, what Jhoira, Teferi, and their goblin hordes will be producing are powerstones—large and perfectly engineered for whatever task Urza wishes.

He seemed mad again, relating all these things to me. He seemed as delighted as if he had just finished designing some vast, improbable, and powerful machine. In a way, that's what he has just done.

I was sad to report less stellar results for my own efforts. K'rrik's negators are growing more powerful by the week. Our laboratories can hardly keep up with the old designs. New versions of our runners are still months away from their initial trials. The spells we have marshaled have succeeded in blocking whatever summoned creatures and artifacts the Phyrexian mages have conjured, but we cannot keep up with their studies. I sense a final conflict coming. Even if K'rrik's forces do not overrun us soon, we will deplete our resources and workforce. Whether they win in a moment or in a million moments, they will win.

It was with this assessment that I pleaded for Urza to return and bring Jhoira and Teferi with him. He shrugged off the request, saying he had complete trust in me. Be reminded me of the beacon, saying I could call on him at a moment's notice, and that was the end of it. He couldn't wait to return to his mana rig and the marvelous machines it would produce.

I cannot help feeling abandoned. Urza has learned much, indeed—he no longer forgets his past obligations, only ignores them.

—Barrin, Mage Master of Tolaria

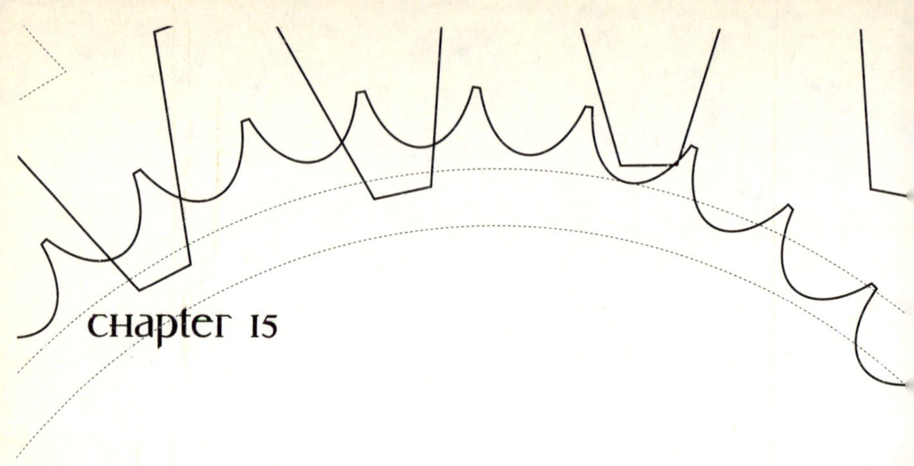

chapter 15

"This is our salvation," Urza said.

He addressed the same group of scholars—Jhoira, Teferi, and Karn at the head of the group—in the same study where he had first presented the design. The plans hanging behind the pacing master, however, were completely rethought. Thran metal was used only in key places. The rest of the structure was wooden.

"It will be capable of faster-than-sound travel, will be able to planeshift, will be fitted out with powerful offensive weapons, and is designed to bear its crew into the most hostile Phyrexian environments. It will be the ultimate strike weapon, arrayed to penetrate the enemy's defenses and destroy the heart of their attack."

Urza paused, as if waiting for Jhoira's objections. She coughed discreetly in her hand but offered no comment.

"One of the key changes to this design, you will notice, is its wooden hull. Given the properties of Thran-metal—specifically its tendency to grow—I have determined that it is best used in conjunction with living materials, in this case wood—a specific kind of wood." Urza set down the pointer he had been using. "Given the excellent progress you have made in the new alliance, I feel the time is right for me to take a brief absence to secure the wooden components."

The once-silent crowd was suddenly on its feet, protests coming from them all.

"What are you talking about—"

"—bring us to this inferno and then leave—"

"—how are we supposed to keep them from killing each other—"

Jhoira's voice rose above the others. "—only reason the accord has worked as well as it has is because you are here, the everpresent and incalculable foe."

"Let them think I am still here then," Urza said. "If you want, I can even arrange a few illusory appearances during my absence. I'm speaking of only a few days away."

That assurance quieted much of the objection. Jhoira was still dubious. "What if it is longer?"

Urza seemed to consider, his eyes twinkling, and then he gave a small shrug. "You will manage. You always have. In the meantime, I have some new specifications for Thran-metal castings—the fittings for the ship. I want you to get started on them. Also, I have these specifications for the size and shape of the powerstone I need for the ship's engines. Jhoira, I want you and Teferi personally to oversee its creation."

Urza descended into the heart of a dense jungle, into the heart of an ancient dream.

It was called Yavimaya. Its ancient trees reached three thousand feet into the sky and three thousand feet into the ground, and three thousand years into the past. Just beneath Urza's feet—shod in gold-gilt sandals, suitable to his role as ambassador for all Dominaria—spread the tumbled landscape of treetops. Multiheaded crowns nodded sagely in the high winds. Among their shifting forms, giant limbs twisted, as large and brown as whole hillsides elsewhere.

In the hollows of some of the massive boughs, clear waters gleamed in wide and twisting lakes, thirty feet deep above smooth-skinned bark. Daily rains filled these raised lakes. Their verges hung with shaggy curtains of moss, and elven settlements crouched at their edges. Waterfalls cascaded from the lakes, down bows or empty air into the darksome forest below.

Urza did not stop among the elven folk. He sought none of the forest's inhabitants individually but all of them collectively. He sought the spirit of the forest itself—Yavimaya.

In places, a magnificent tree had succumbed at last to the colonies of worms and termites that riddled its city-sized trunk, or to the rot of deep roots in lightless slime, or to the implacable time clock within it, and had fallen. Many dead giants leaned against their neighbors, forming vast decaying ramps down into the murk. On such slopes, whole new ecologies of undergrowth and grazing beast and sharp-eyed hunter grew up. Other trees, the titanic ones that could not be held aloft in their creaking plummet toward ground, opened vast pits in the forest canopy, giving view down thousands of feet, past the mounded and rangy bulk of the world trees to the tangle of roots at their base.

Urza entered one of these empty shafts now. He watched in appreciation as the huge sprawl of tree summits rose to close out the sky. Only a large, ragged hole remained overhead. All around him, single-tree forests shivered bright green against the blue sky and its scrolling clouds. The high brakes of branch and bloom gave way to lower ranks of coiling vine and draping lichen. They in time surrendered to dark, cold, plunging depths, reached only by manifold waterfalls and the ever-dimmer sunlight. The air turned cold, wet, and biting.

Urza formed a thick, woolen cloak atop his silken robes of state. The fabrics fanned out on the cool wind, making him seem some great black spider descending an invisible thread.

In time, his gemstone eyes adjusted to the murk. He saw whole new worlds around him. The curved boughs were inhabited. Giant antlike creatures swarmed blackly over a knot in one of the ancient trees. The rotten center of the knot formed a great archway that gave into an enormous interior chamber. As Urza slid downward, he peered past guard ants poised at the brink of their colony and saw into the teeming blackness inside. There hunks of fruit and severed segments of leaf and dead carcasses of tree goats were borne along in caravans to inner storage places. Translucent white larvae lay in careful nests tended by tireless workers. A queen, who was the size of a parade of elephants, laboriously dragged her moving bulk, leaving a trail of wet globs in her wake. Just below the colony, placid herds of long-horned cattle grazed on terraces of bark. These beasts were tended by the ant creatures as though they were mere aphids in a garden.

A sheer drop lay beneath the cattle fields. A few hundred feet farther down, giant cobwebs clung. They held rolled white pouches—some vaguely cow-shaped, others ant-shaped, and still more with human or elven form. Urza was careful to steer clear of the sticky strands of web in his course toward the bottom.

Wherever life could cling, it did. Villages of elves dwelt on shallow swoops of tree bark. Forest sprites lived in spangled beauty among the deep dew fields. Dryads peered out distrustfully at him from folds of bark, and naiads glared from the silvery cascades that dropped from aerial lakes. Tree goats bounded up the sheer faces of the tree boles. Black-and gold-skinned cats stalked among fields of moss. Beneath it all, on the tangled roots at the base of the trees, druids appeared once in a while. They stared up at Urza in fierce resistance before disappearing beneath the ground.

He gazed down at the root cluster. As vast as the boughs above, the roots of the trees climbed over each other in a muscular jumble. In places, the tightly laced structures held dark pools of water or small banks of new tree growth. Where the roots did not connect, though, were triangular wells of darkness. During millennia of growth, the trees had depleted all the earth beneath them, drawing it up their boles. The result was a vast emptiness under the root cluster, broken only by more waterfalls and fat taproots. At the distant base of this murk, waters toiled in perpetual darkness. This was the realm of the forest druids, crisscrossed by thousands of causeways, stairs, and cave passages.

They would put up a fierce resistance to any program Urza might suggest. They would know of Argoth.

As Urza settled his gold-gilded feet on the root bulb of a massive tree, a sudden dread rose through him. This place was uncannily like Argoth. Its elves descended from those who had fled the forest he and Mishra had destroyed. There were ghosts here, the ghosts of Urza's past, but he had not come to commune with ghosts. He had come to discover the future.

Urza lifted his hands in invocation. "I am Urza Planeswalker. I have come for an audience with Yavimaya. We must discuss the coming war. I wish to ally myself with you. We must confer upon the fate of our world."

Multani had known the invader even before he spoke his name. The forest recognized the monster much as a body recognizes a contagion it had once suffered.

Defiler of Argoth, Destroyer of Elves, Terror's Twin, the End Man, Slayer of the People of the World—Urza Planeswalker.

Even as the man descended through the foliage of the upper forest, Multani surged up the bole of a great magnigoth tree. He gathered himself in myriad surges of sap and pulses of green wood. From the roots of that ancient colossus to its spreading crown thousands of feet above, the magnigoth came to exquisite life. The soul of the forest quickened every twig and leaf and tendril. Multani could have flexed the massive roots like the tentacles of a squid and marched the enormous tree through Yavimaya. He could have reached out with any of the magnigoth's hundred thousand boughs and snatched Urza and crushed him. He could have slain the man ten thousand times, in clouds of mold dust or swarms of arboreal spiders or lashing storms of boughs, but he did not, not yet.

This man was no mere man. He had become a power since Argoth. He had drawn the might of the land into him and was perhaps a match for Multani and Yavimaya. He had become a planeswalker and could wink into and out of existence with a thought. It would take a careful trap to capture this one. It would take all the mesmerizing force of the forest's mind to drive from the planeswalker any thought of escape. Only then could he could be contained. Only then would Argoth have its vengeance.

Until then, though, Multani would seduce the planeswalker into a trap. He watched patiently, following Urza down the trunk of the great tree. He would marshal the might of Yavimaya and lead Urza into doom, just as surely as Urza had led Argoth into doom.

A pang jagged through Multani. The man was calling on the land. He was summoning its power as he had back in Argoth. He was daring to compel the forest he said he had come to consult.

Multani sifted all the faster downward, hurrying to reach the spot where the man stood. No matter how many creatures Urza summoned, this was Multani's forest. He would take them back, free them from the bidding of the Defiler.

To treat with Yavimaya, Multani thought bitterly, you must treat with me.

Urza had finished his invocation, but the forest had not answered. He stood for some time, letting the verdant air sift over and around him. He could wait, of course. The forest knew he was here, sensed his power as assuredly as he sensed its, but Urza was never content to wait. He always felt better if he could tinker.

He reached into his vast reserves of sorcery and summoned forth a swarm of sprites.

A flowing cloud of gold and silver cleaved from the treetops high overhead and danced down on the breezes toward him. Urza watched in silent amazement. Though the cloud was still a thousand feet above, his gemstone eyes made out the tiny darting creatures within it. Winged and delicate, the sprites approached, a high song in their tiny throats. The melody ranged hypnotically through many tonal structures, sinuous and ineffable. Soon Urza could make out words in the song.

Return among us, child of ages.
Sing the reconciling song
And burn the pages where long
The sages condemned thee.
Sing, forgetful, sing
Of mild, regretful things
Before the forest's nodding head.
Let dead bury dead and then
Arise to sing again.

The words plucked strangely at Urza's mind. He remembered those voices, small and chimelike against the waterfall roar of wind in the leaves, remembered sprites fighting among druids and elven archers, their voices raised then in fury and condemnation. These creatures sang, instead, of reconciliation. They sang as though they were miniature Barrins.

Delighted, Urza moved to cast a second summoning spell. The sorcery was never completed. Already the forest responded. New ambassadors arose.

To the convolute roll of the gnat song came also a slow, low, gulping sound. It came from among the roots of the oriatorpic trees—shadowy gnomes within their barrows. Their tones made a basso counterpoint to the whistle-high melody.

O nations, rise into the dawning light
Where, bright, our generations' hope has come.
Speak, O dumb, and dance, O lame, the night
Of blame advances round to sun
And morning comes again.

Urza stood in the midst of the swelling chords, daring to hope that this ancient forest had grown up outside of the pall cast by Argoth's death. Perhaps short-lived sprites and gnomes would simply not remember that time. The folk who would not forget, could never forget, would be the elves. Urza needed to know their mind.

As though summoned, they came—elves of the high forest.

They came from behind every tree, from within every fold of root upon root. Their eyes were bright and wide in the gray twilight of the place and glowed, luminous and green. They came, singing too, their voices at last providing the main body of the chantlike round of the other creatures:

Hello, Urza, we know of you
From dark times past that nearly slew
Us, every mother's son, and tore
Our bodies limb from limb. That war
Was hateful, true, but now we live
In peace and health. We wish to give
You all you ask, to save
Our world from such a grave
As once you dug that terrible day.

The three groups of singers converged around Urza. Sprites danced in glowing daisy chains in the air around him. Shadow gnomes scuttled from their burrows to crouch like toads upon the moss beds. Elves treaded with preternaturally light footfalls among the roots. Urza listened to their singing—his mind could hear each strain separately and all of them together. His foot lightly tapped the root ball where he stood.

He heard another voice, a deep rumble more massive and hollow and mournful than even Karn's. The sound came from all around, as though the air itself spoke. The clammy breath of it, though, came from behind Urza. He pivoted, seeing only a vast wound in the base of the tree. The gouge was three times his height. Bark had struggled hard to close over the gash. Great rolled lips of wood still strained to come together. Next moment, those same bark lips drew apart, and smaller rents in the side of the tree opened above. Knots rolled beneath. The wound spoke:

"Welcome, Urza Planeswalker. We are Multani, spirit of Yavimaya." The face in the wood was utterly mournful, the mask of tragedy with only shadows for eyes. "We remember you."

The planeswalker bowed his head and actually dropped to one knee on the root cluster. "Forgive me. What I did three millennia ago, I did to save Dominaria from hideous invaders."

"To Argoth, you and your brother *were* the hideous invaders," replied the voice, haunting as a chorus of the dead.

"I had to sacrifice Argoth or sacrifice the whole world," said Urza, almost pleading. "I did not doubt Titania of Argoth would have made the same choice were she strong enough to."

"Titania had been strong enough before they were despoiled," the tree spirit replied.

"As I said before, forgive me—"

"We are not Titania. We are not Argoth. We are Multani of Yavimaya. We have welcomed you," the voice said, and the lagging chorus of sprites, gnomes, and elves resumed.

The melody coursed, coy and yet somehow cloying, through Urza, like the dank wind moving through his robes. There was a wild geometry to the tones as they twisted in and out of each other. The notes trickled upon Urza. Waves of sound lay beside waves of energy, nudging them into their pattern. He closed his eyes a moment, struggling to assemble a response to Multani. Whenever a pair of words connected in his mind, though, they were soaked apart by the gentle nudge of the song.

"We would speak to you at length of this coming invasion."

Urza nodded, his eyes opening. He was slightly startled to realize he was standing. When had he risen to his feet? The question melted away on the pulsing song. Such matters were unimportant. There were allies here. There was music. For the first time since his ascension, Urza felt true joy. The sharp-edged box of his intellect softened into a warm, hazy buzz, like a swarm of bees—or a swarm of sprites.

"We would first treat you to a festival dinner to celebrate our newfound association."

Yes, thought Urza, I am hungry.

There was something wrong with that thought, something Urza could not quite identify. He couldn't remember the last time he had eaten. Of course he was hungry. If the forest's fare was as sumptuous as its music, he would eat himself sick. Surely there would be wine and other delights to the appetites. Urza would indulge them all.

There was something wrong with that thought too. The nagging objections bubbled up, drowned, through the flood of music:

Return among us, child of ages.
Sing the reconciling song
And burn the pages where long
The sages condemned thee.
Sing, forgetful, sing
Of mild, regretful things
Before the forest's nodding head.
Let dead bury themselves in dead
Sing, forgetful, sing.

When had he begun to sing? When had he ever not sung? Urza's voice, deep and resonant in the edifice of sound, moved among the smiling tones of the sprites and gnomes and elves. The mouth of the tree opened wide. The company of fairy folk guided Urza forward. He paced, solemn and happy, into the yawning space and down the throat of the enormous tree. There would be a feast in these deeps. There would be more music and lights and festival.

Except that all of it was behind him now. Darkness and wood and the irresistible power of Yavimaya pulsed in the very heart of the gigantic tree. Then, these things were all around. The mouth spoke one last time.

"We would speak to you at length, also, of the last invasion."

With that, the tree's mouth closed. Its throat as well. Urza, caught in wood and the thick darkness, wondered dimly where he was, and how he was, and who he was. He would be able to think, were it not for all the pervading mind of the forest, curing him like cedar smoke, changing him, preserving him in place.

But not preserving him. Urza felt his body dissolving away into wood. His fingers were the first to go, each burning with incandescent agony. His every nerve sizzled beneath the skin. His bones turned to chalk and rubbed away in the gnawing of the heartwood around him. His fingers and toes, harvested slowly by the massive tree, turned into mere minerals.

"When Harbin, son of Urza Planeswalker, landed upon Argoth, he sought a green limb to replace a spar on his flying machine. In its mercy, the forest showed him a fallen limb that perfectly suited his needs. In repayment, the man returned to the heart of Argive to bring back armies of ravagers to harvest the forest. Men and machines felled ancient trees, slew druids, hunted creatures into extinction, pillaged, burned, raped, destroyed, all to the glory of Urza and his brother Mishra. Slowly, they ate away at Argoth, killing Titania, her spirit."

The words were needless. Urza had become Titania. His body had become a vast forest. He felt in every tissue of his being the destroying, despoiling work of his own armies. Minute creatures invaded his body and, mote by mote, turned him into mere minerals, mere resources.

Urza would have screamed, but he was no longer Urza. He would have planeswalked from the spot, but that would mean leaving his body, the forest, behind. He could only hang there, encased in wood, and endure.

Monologue

Urza is arriving in Yavimaya even as I write this. I know the forest's position, as unreachable and forbidding as Shiv. He hopes to return in two days' time. Knowing Urza's sense of time—and guessing about the reception Yavimaya will have for him—I'll give him a week before I become unsettled.

This could well be the pivotal point for Urza. He has shown he is capable of building human alliances, and more than that—building coalitions among many races. Perhaps by creating an alliance with Yavimaya, he can make amends for Argoth. Perhaps no amount of penance could ever make amends for such atrocity.

We have our own atrocities under way in Tolaria. Just today I led a charge of scorpions against Phyrexian entrenchments at the border of Slate Waters. Given the physiology of my mechanical forces, a pincer movement naturally suggested itself. We flanked the main body of Phyrexians left and right and trapped them in their trenches. They were caught between us and the temporal curtain. I sent scorpion units flooding into their dens. Meanwhile, I drove a wall of wind down the middle. Flushed from cover, the beasts fell back into the time curtain at the edge of that charred swamp. I ordered a charge. We hurled them into the rift.

That passage would have killed any human. It did little more than further jangle these fiends. Even so, the extreme slow time of Slate Waters halted the Phyrexians in a thick wall. I ordered the scorpions to fire. Quarrels stormed out in a killing gale. The front line of Phyrexians was nearly sawed in half. They were spewing glistening oil in a cloud before them by the time a human contingent arrived to reinforce us.

One young woman tore a hunk of cloth from beneath her armor coat and doused it with oil from a fallen scorpion. She stuck the cloth on a spent quarrel, ignited it, and hurled the thing into the gap. It entered the spray of glistening oil. A dull orange glow spread from the spot. The fiery quarrel hung strangely in the air as slow flame rolled laterally out along the Phyrexian lines.

We stopped firing. We stood, staring in a mixture of exultation and dread. Languid tendrils of flame coiled out around fiendish arms and legs. We watched as our foes ignited. The cheer that came from us when hair and carapace were limned in flame devolved quickly to a groan. Eyeballs ruptured from the heat. Limbs were blasted away. The deep, horrid roar of dying monsters struck us.

"Back!" I yelled.

Even I was cemented in place when the blaze went critical. White hot, the flash was blinding. We fell back then by instinct alone. Clutching our eyes, we clambered over stalled scorpions and mired dead to escape the coming blaze. When the blast at last emerged from Slate Waters, most of us were half a mile into the forest. Even so, it flung us to our faces and, like the warriors on Argoth of old, we could only pray the sun-bright blast would someday end.

It will be another Argoth, this conflict. The Phyrexians press us day and night. Their numbers grow greater with each sally. Their magical might will soon be the equal of mine. The students are weary of fighting, and though I have employed my most awe-inspiring battle spells, I am not a charismatic leader. Jhoira and Teferi were better suited for that. Urza, despite all his inhumanity, perhaps leads best of all.

—Barrin, Mage Master of Tolaria

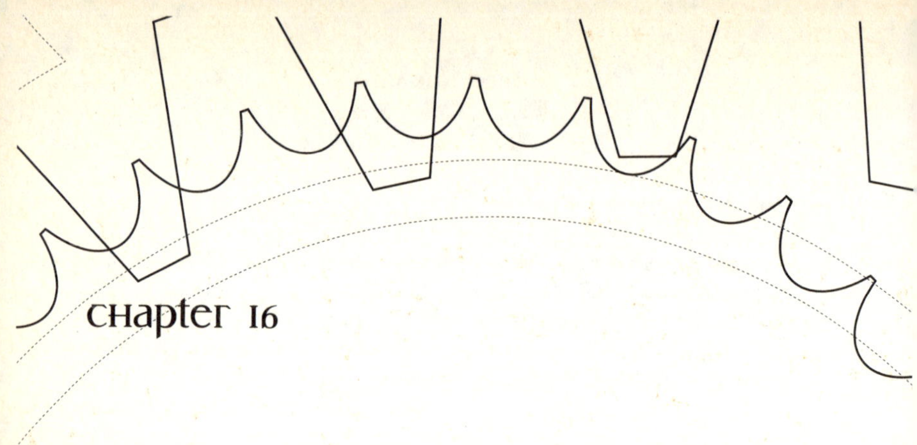

chapter 16

Jhoira stood on the lofted control platform at the nexus of the mana rig. To one side of her stood Teferi and to the other, Karn.

Teferi watched over his workers—the goblin hordes that tended the crystal-manufacturing wing of the factory. It had been nearly two years since the Viashino-goblin war had concluded, and the forbidden zones were now fully functional. Each of the three clans of goblin—the silvery Tristou, the red Destrou, and even the irrepressible gray Grabbits—had aided in the cleaning and repair of the facility. In doing so, they had risen to their individual levels of ability. Chieftain Glosstongue Crackcrest of the Tristou had become the nominal leader of the three clans, but a certain manic Grabbit machinist had won over the masses with his antics, his nonsensical but volatile speeches, and his instinctive and incessant glad-handing. Though all decisions were made by Chief Crackcrest, they had to be approved by Machinist Terd.

The gray creature even now climbed to the observation post.

He scrambled up a ladder engineered for goblins considerably larger than he. His much-spattered coveralls jangled with small shiny tools that no one had ever seen the goblin use—bits of metal Terd wore like talismans or awards. Despite his inability to perform actual work, the creature was in constant motion. His eyebrows—great knotted tufts of hair that were even more prominent than his prominent nose—were raining sweat down on his knobby chin. As he grabbed the rails of the control platform and pulled himself up beside Teferi, Terd gave a bright, sharp-toothed smile. It was one of his proudest features. A goblin with a full set of teeth was a rarity. One with white teeth was a messenger from the gods.

Terd kowtowed obscenely, tipping a little rag of felt that he considered a hat. "The rock thingies all ready." Terd's reports were no more explicit than his speeches. Interpreting them typically took a tedious game of charades.

Teferi gave a long-suffering sigh. "The ore conveyers?"

Terd shook his head with such abruptness that an umbrella of sweat unfolded from him onto all those around.

"The crystal presses?" Teferi guessed.

Terd pursed his scabby lips in thought and then whipped his head as though he were trying to rend the suggestion with his teeth.

"The Thran-metal molds?"

Ecstatic, Terd touched a withered finger to his nose. "Yes, yes. We make rocks today? Yes?"

Teferi shook his head. "Not until the ore conveyers and crystal presses are ready."

"You make Terd a pretty big rock."

"Yes," Teferi assured.

It had been one of the incentives provided the goblin workers that, once a month, when the rig was in operation, each would receive a small crystal—in fact only a cast-off shard from a cut stone. Even if a goblin had happened to get hold of a larger stone, none of the crystals from the rig would be imbued with power until it was charged with mana. Even the smallest of stones would permanently drain the mana from a large tract of land. To power a stone the size of the one Urza had designed for his flying ship would require the mana destruction of a whole world.

"Terd use his stone to be big magic man. Terd become big king of goblins."

"Yes," Teferi humored, "and that will be a bright day for us all."

"Terd go tell goblin scum—'Work faster! Work faster!' Then he be king sooner."

"Go do that."

Even as the irascible little fellow scuttled away down the ladder and shouted commands to his kinsmen, a very different liaison officer climbed the opposite ladder. Diago Deerv had proven himself a capable and level-headed lizard man in regearing the Thran forges. Now with the ancient enemy of the Viashino occupying half of the rig, it was only creatures such as Diago and Bey Fire Eye himself that kept the creatures from all-out revolt—Diago, the bey, and Jhoira's continual reminders that Urza would return any day.

Jhoira was not the official manager of the Thran forges. That job fell to Karn, the very creature who was promised to the lizard men in payment for their labors.

Diago rose to his full height on the platform—he had grown in the last four years—and looked Karn directly in the eye. "We've finished the castings Master Malzra requested. We ask that you come to approve them."

Karn nodded. "I am waiting for a report from the lava batteries. Then I can come with you."

Diago took a deep breath and spoke with a strained voice. "With the completion of these castings, we have fulfilled the terms of our agreement. We ask for payment of the price owed us."

Before Karn could answer, Jhoira interrupted, "Actually, we have still not successfully created a Thran-metal man." She glanced warily between reptile eyes and silver ones. "Those were the terms of our agreement."

"You've abandoned that project," Diago objected.

"Actually, no," Jhoira said quickly. "We have a new design, one that takes into account the metal's growth patterns."

"May I see these plans?" Diago asked.

"Tomorrow," Jhoira said. "I will provide them to you tomorrow. We can begin our castings then."

Diago wore a suspicious expression. "And once these new machines are cast—"

"Yes," Jhoira said, "then you will have your price. You will have the silver man."

Diago bowed low and backed down the ladder.

Jhoira, Karn, and Teferi traded sober looks.

"You don't have any new plans, do you?" Teferi asked.

Jhoira shrugged. "I have old plans—for Tolarian runners. I'll modify them tonight, taking into account Urza's nesting-doll pattern of construction. It'll hold them off awhile more. It may even prove a useful fighter for the Phyrexian wars."

That mention brought all of their thoughts around to Barrin and besieged Tolaria.

Jhoira spoke for them all. "I hope Urza returns soon."

Every axe-blow that struck the trees of Argoth bit into the man's limbs. Every fire that mantled his magnigoth trees flared through his veins. Every killing blast and grating landslide enervated him.

Urza was on the island. Urza and Mishra. Their names were plague and famine, fire and flood. From opposite ends of the land they tore at each other. They converged, and whatever stood between them was destroyed by their fury.

The man in the wood watched as ancient trees leaned and crackled and fell. Their bulk did not even rest on the root cluster before vast machines yanked and hewed and hacked them into beams and joists and planks—but mostly scrap. Bark and thin branches, leaves, and buds became only mounds of debris over which the killing machines rolled. Black snakes of smoke coiled into the troubled sky. There they joined great mountains of darkness, hovering as though in mourning.

What could drive those killing brothers? What passions?

And yet, the question seemed false. It was forced into the man in the wood from the outside. He knew just what drove them—ambition, curiosity, competition, vitality, and all of it enwrapped in a thin, tragic blanket of distrust. What drove them? The highest intentions and hopes. What directed them? The lowest emotion—fear. They were monsters, yes, but only because of their power. Were it not for their machines and their armies, they would not be monsters, but only little boys.

That thought brought a surge of anger from around the man. He railed. As sharp and tenacious as resin, reproof flowed into him. Urza and Mishra were true monsters. They despoiled all they touched. Their very flesh was corruption. Their only motivations were pure hatred.

The man in the wood resisted the welling flood of recrimination, holding his breath. He pushed back against the thoughts. They overtook him anyway and soaked into every pore and poured into his lungs—for every man must breathe.

There was something wrong in that thought, but the distinction drifted away on a fresh wave of agony. In that screaming space, there was no room for any excuse, any forgiveness, but only the undeniable sentence of guilt.

At the man's throat there came another sound of screaming and more visions. Not trees burning now, but people—white-robed students. Not axe machines and levelers, but loping artifact creatures, some like headless emus, some like pouncing pumas, some like giant scorpions. Not armies of Argivians and Fallaji, but armies of fiends and negators, of killing monsters. They swept over another island, far away, not Argoth but . . . but . . . the name would not form in his mind.

In the face of this new, horrific assault, the armies of Urza and Mishra seemed civilized and noble. Felling trees seemed nothing in the face of burning children. An idea lurked there, something about the better war to fight, the war that could prevent the apocalypse.

That thought, too, was squeezed out of being in the furious fist of wood around the man. If only he could think. If only he could hold a thought in his head—thought of his own . . . but then there was only pain.

Barrin watched from the gorge tower. It was the highest spot in the academy. Poised beyond reach of Phyrexian weapons, it curved out over the wall to peer into the dark swath. This spot was manned day and night, and of late, mainly by Barrin. From here he could gauge the movement of

K'rrik's forces to any of the four bridges from the time pit. From here, Barrin stemmed the fiendish tide with long-range sorceries and enchantments. Intelligence gathered here allowed him to deploy his machine and human forces to intercept the attackers. And here, perhaps most importantly of all, lay the triggering mechanism for the beacon pendant Urza wore.

Barrin had just activated the beacon.

It had been nearly three years since Urza had gone to Yavimaya, and no one had heard from him. He could be dead, Barrin knew. Though planeswalkers were extremely long-lived, they could be killed, especially if their life-force became unfocused or dissipated. Still, it was a very difficult thing to kill a planeswalker, but not so to trap one. A planeswalker could be trapped in deception. If Urza did not think he needed to escape, he couldn't. If he forgot he could planeswalk, he could be trapped indefinitely. With Urza's fragile sanity and top-heavy psyche, such tricks could be easily accomplished. If he lived at all, he was trapped.

Perhaps, though, the beacon blaring into Urza's mind would startle him out of whatever malaise had laid hold of him.

Of course, there was a third possibility. Perhaps Urza had moved on. Perhaps he had gotten what he had wanted out of Tolaria and Shiv and Yavimaya and had gone some fourth place to assemble it all.

Whatever the cause of Urza's absence, the beacon summoned him. He must return to Tolaria in the next year, or there would be no Tolaria to return to.

The Phyrexians had just discovered a new bridge out of their pit: a deep spring that fed the academy's wells. One moonless night, they had poured up through every well head and cistern in the academy. The forces of Tolaria rallied and thrust back the monstrous intruders, fighting in their own home as they had fought beyond its walls. The beasts were slain wholesale, grates were affixed over any access to ground water, and new guard posts were created. The Phyrexians had yet to exact their worst death toll. Their dead bodies poisoned the water. Any who drank from the school water supplies in the next days developed a flesh-eating disease that turned their muscles to bloody mush and made bone as brittle as crackers. Twenty-three students and scholars died before the source of the contagion was discovered.

All water for drinking or washing had to be brought from distant wells beyond the school walls. Now, Phyrexians could rise right in the midst of the academy.

The Tolarian fortress had disappeared out from under Barrin. The siege had suddenly turned into a jungle battle—dark, desperate, chaotic, and finally, hopeless.

Barrin's hand squeezed the jeweled dagger that triggered the beacon. The enchanted item would convey to Urza whatever Barrin saw, whatever he thought—scenes of flesh-eaten friends and over-running foes. Barrin said a silent prayer that Urza lived, and that Urza heard.

Jhoira paced uneasily before the line of Thran-metal defenders. Just behind her, Diago Deerv marched. His scaly hide bristled with nervousness as she looked over the machines. They were flawless. The original plan of the Tolarian runner had undergone numerous changes, including a more ovoid body, a deeper bend to the legs, and more capacity for armaments. Jhoira had overcome the difficulties of growing metal in this design, and these twelve fighters, if they ever reached Tolaria, could well prove indispensable in its defense.

If they ever reached Tolaria . . . she had stalled the lizard men for two more years, waiting for Urza to return and broker Karn's freedom. The man had not returned. Jhoira had decided he was dead. Once the Viashino and goblin tribes decided the same, the tenuous peace of the rig would be at an end.

Worse yet, news of Urza's long absence had at last reached the ears of the Shivan Drake Gherridarigaaz. She had resumed her strafing attacks on Viashino patrol posts, had cut off trade routes to the Ghitu tribes of the sea shores, and had dropped numerous boulders into the vent shafts above the city. Her son, who had willingly defected to the Viashino cause, decided he wanted to return to her. Apparently he was a typical child runaway, more intent on making a point than on gaining true independence. The Viashino had adamantly held him to his alliance agreement. The young creature went from being their champion to a caged and chained traitor.

What would they do about Urza's agreement? With the return of the fire drake, half of the bargain Urza offered had fallen through. This morning the other half was in danger.

What would it matter? Jhoira asked herself. If Urza is dead, Tolaria is destroyed, there will be no flying ship, and there will be no hope for Dominaria's delivery from Phyrexia. If Urza is dead, Shiv might well be the nicest place for Karn and the rest of them to live out what remained of their lives.

The words she spoke were somewhat different. "Excellent work, as always, Diago. You and your workers are extraordinary craftsmen."

"Judging from your tone, you have no more reason to delay the payment of our price," Diago said as the two of them reached the end of the line, where Karn stood.

Jhoira's jaw clenched. Muscles in her temples hardened. "No, Diago. I will delay no longer, but I offer you a different bargain. Instead of taking this one silver golem—nearly half a century old and battered and filled with all kinds of emotional entanglements—I offer you these twelve Thran-metal warriors."

A harsh edge entered Diago's eyes. "The agreement was for the silver man."

"Yes," Jhoira agreed, "and now I am offering you a different agreement."

A metallic hiss came from the lizard man's teeth. "No. We know how to build these creatures. They are not intelligent. We wish to have the silver man, to learn how to build an intelligent creature."

"But, he's not just a silver man, Diago," Jhoira said. "He's Karn. He has worked beside you all these years. Don't you care what he wants? Doesn't it bother you to make him your property, your slave?"

"We all are slaves to the tribe. To serve selflessly is the highest honor," Diago said. "Yes, he is Karn, a comrade. When he is given to us, he will be part of our tribe. He will be our greatest defender. He will teach us how to make armies of intelligent machines."

"Karn can't teach you that," Jhoira said. "I know more about his construction than he does. Master Malzra's the only one who really understands his emotional and intellectual abilities. Would you imprison me? Would you imprison Malzra?"

"We do not imprison creatures."

"What about Rhammidarigaaz?"

"He agreed to join us. And, as for Karn, Malzra agreed to grant him to us," Diago said. "And Karn can teach us how to build an intelligent machine. The secrets are inside of him. We will gain them. . . ."

"Enough," Karn said to Jhoira, cutting off her response. "I will go with them. I will teach them what I can. It is the highest honor to serve."

Open-mouthed, Jhoira watched as the lizard man and the silver man turned and walked away into the depths of the humming mana rig.

Monologue

They are everywhere. We cannot stand. We will not last the day. All will be dead. I still clutch the beacon, yet Urza does not come. We all will be dead.

—Barrin, Mage Master of Tolaria

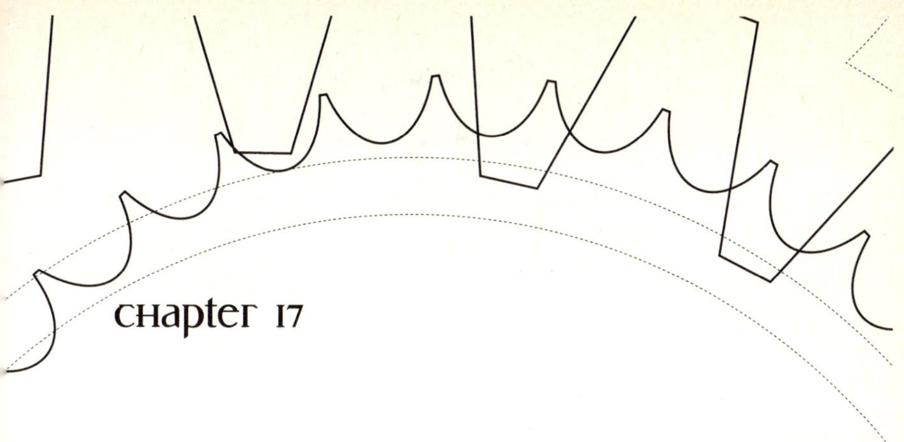

chapter 17

Barrin stood, white-knuckled and wide eyed, in the gorge tower. He clutched the beacon dagger in his hand and gaped as the world disintegrated around him.

A great roaring tide of Phyrexians swept toward the walls. As a whole army, they were terror personified. As individual creatures, they were worse still. Many of the beasts were gigantic, white and meaty, seeming to have taken their forms from the blind shrimp larvae that infested the gorge lake. They scuttled on sharp, darting legs, their scaled hacks hunched in heinous intent over minuscule eye nubs. Barbed antennae tasted the air. The warm brine of human blood drew them on. Others had wolflike figures, all warped and elephantine, with a mane of mange over leathery skin speckled in black and pink. Only their heads diverged from the lupine plan, small, yellow, puffy, and indrawn, like the heads of jaundiced babies. A vast number of the company were human or semi-human, though their bodies had been torqued and tortured into forms unrecognizable—leering death masks of flayed muscle, spidery arms with sinews realigned so that radius and ulna became opposing pincers, rib cages inset with spikes of stone or metal, bellies implanted with poison bladders that splashed foes in acid, hips that were no more than winnowed bone and tarry ligament, and legs that ended in sharpened spikes of bone. Most of the beasts bore weapons stripped from ruined runners or falcons. In a few places, machines of K'rrik's own design shambled among the monstrous hordes.

"We ourselves have armed them," Barrin whispered.

Against this onslaught of horror came the defenders of Tolaria. Barrin activated an array of powerstones, linked to mechanisms across the island. What falcons remained streaked down in furious flight. The white vapor trails behind them traced a converging fan across the sky. Impacting along the surging front, the falcons seemed to be allied lightning strikes. They brought with them a vast, rolling thunder. Fiends were hurled back into the chopping jaws of their fellows. The falcons' incandescent arrival was followed by the ratchet and whine of their shredding mechanisms. Blood—glistening oil and some substance that was bug-black, lime-green, and a shade of lavender that might have been pretty if it weren't steamy and acidic—fountained amid bounding chunks of meat and bone.

Barrin's delight at this grisly assault was short-lived. The hordes behind only splashed through the remains of their comrades and pressed the charge. Barrin squeezed the dagger handle and simultaneously signaled the second wave of defenders.

Hundreds of Tolarian runners lunged up from their trenches at the base of the wall. The machines loped into combat, their scythe wings poised to strike. They darted out, long-legged and fearless. The twang and whoosh of quarrels sounded from the ports that lined their bellies. Shafts soaked in anti-oil—a biologic poison designed to separate Phyrexian blood—thudded home in the pelting lines of monsters.

Phyrexians released a corporate shriek that rattled stones and sheared leaves from their branches. Another line of dead and dying went down, these not in a slick slough but a quaking mound of muscle and bone. The monstrous charge followed on, clambering over the fallen.

Tolarian runners met them, striking with twin blades. Some of the beasts were cut in half. Others were torn open at the belly and ran on a few paces before light fled their eyes and they rolled wetly in the dirt. A few were unstoppable. Though runners hung from scythes buried in their bellies, the beasts advanced, dauntless. They and a healthy horde of fiends surged into the waiting phalanx of scorpion engines.

Urza's scorpions were not designed for speed. With six legs, massive pincers, and darting tails, they were made to stand and fight. They held their position as the beast army fell on them. The first monsters literally fell, legs cut away. Their bleeding bulks dropped atop the stooped shoulders of the scorpions, who merely shrugged them off to snag the next comers. More Phyrexians lost their legs. A third wave leaped onto the backs of the beasts only to be undone by darting tail stingers.

The dead mounded up. In time, the machines' pincers became pinned beneath tons of oozing flesh. All the while, fiends fought onward into a hail of shafts from human guards on the walls.

Then, the first Phyrexian won through. It was a giant creature with a body as bulbous and pitted as an old gourd. It lunged past furiously stinging tails, rolled over the wall of dead, and crashed mightily against the stone rampart around the school. White arrows stood in a thicket across the beast's figure, but they did not stay it. The thing lunged again, smashing into the wall. A jagging crack opened from the battlements to the footings. More monsters clambered past the buried scorpions and reached the wall. They added their bulk to the giant's assaults or scampered up the cut edges of stone or flung tentacular digits to haul themselves over.

In moments, the walls would be breached, Barrin realized. They were already breached. The wells and cisterns poured monsters into the midst of the school. The battlefront had broken into a thousand pieces, and every scholar and every student would fight the legions of hell alone.

Not entirely alone—Barrin's fingers danced across the glittering gemstones. He called all remaining pumas from their forest posts into the school. He awakened every mechanism in the Hall of Artifact Creatures—from Yotian warriors to Tawnos's clay men to *su-chi* loaders and conveyers and logging machines. Every last one would fight today—on this last day of Tolaria.

His summonations done, Barrin turned and descended into the dark spiral that led to the yard below. He would fight, too, with spells and staves and this dagger that had proven no other defense—and even his nails and teeth and bones, if it came to it. When it came to it.

Urza was dead, and soon all of Tolaria would be.

In the midst of all the shrieking wail of forest fires and trapped animals and tortured elves, the man in the wood heard a greater conflict: Phyrexian cries, macerating machines, whistling arrows, men screaming, children dying, and in the throat of them all echoed one name.

Urza! Urza! Urza!

He knew the name of the Defiler. He knew the Bane of Argoth, but this Urza was a different one—a benevolent creature of great power, a mentor, an advocate, a protector. These voices did not cry out in hatred and rage, but in need and hope, in supplication. They cried out to a very different Urza.

They cried out to him.

In the deafening clamor of their voices, Urza remembered who he was.

The mind of the forest pressed in upon him with sudden violence, straining to quell the thought. After five years of torture and penance, Yavimaya's fury was spent. The forest had come to know the man it had so hated. It had subsumed him into its web of life. No, Yavimaya's fury was spent, and its rage was nothing beside the fury of the battle that summoned Urza.

He forced back the mind of the wood. He recomposed his being from the drifting shreds of it within the vast tree. He brought his mind into sudden, keen focus.

Yavimaya made one final grab at him. Multani, the soul of Yavimaya, impelled himself into the form of the awakening planeswalker. He fused with the forming figure, struggling to root him in place, but it was too late.

Urza vanished from the heart of the tree. He was suspended for only a sliver of time in the fold between worlds, but during that moment he could feel a presence imprisoned within him: Multani. In a single instant, his captor had become his captive.

There was no time to think of Multani. Urza stepped from the wheel of eternities into a precise moment, a precise space. Walls of ancient, gray metal took shape around him. Large windows of dark glass, levers and gears, fire belching from glowing forges. It all came into being. None of these things mattered; only the sharp-eyed and dark-skinned Ghitu woman in their midst mattered. She had been crouched over a set of plans, arguing some point with a gesticulating goblin, when Urza arrived.

Jhoira whirled about, slack-jawed.

"Gather your best fighters. Tolaria is overrun. I will return and take you there."

He was already fading from being before his orders were complete. The shocked stare of Jhoira followed Urza into the spinning spaces. He sensed a similar amazement from Multani. That amazement redoubled the next moment as Urza stepped into the chaos of Tolaria.

The walls were breached. The guards along them were merely boneless heaps or red streaks on white stone. Phyrexians poured like roaches through the gaps. They flooded up from shattered grates hurriedly fastened over well heads. They swarmed through burst doorways and down stone corridors. They fought those who could resist and fastened teeth on those who couldn't. Throughout Urza's field of sight, monsters tossed students and scholars like white rags.

Urza rose from the dirt where his feet had alighted for a moment. He floated straight into the air and unleashed red bolts down the ring of wells in the main courtyard. The blasts of energy sailed down the throats of the channels. They flashed past the shadowy forms that scuttled upward. At the waterline, a sudden inferno erupted. Red water and black-charred bodies geysered from the wells. The ground around each well head mounded up in swollen distress. In the next moment, rock and mortar and dirt cascaded down into fire-fused plugs. The wells were closed. The Phyrexians below would drown.

Urza spun about and cast another sorcery. Red beams darted out to each jagged breach in the walls. Limestone grew molten. It folded over the creatures struggling through the gap. It solidified. The wall was once again whole.

Urza kept rising. He hurled more fire outward, rings of the stuff. Force hissed from his hands in arcs of steam and coalesced over the walls to sweep away the raging throng. The vanguard of the attack turned to black statues and then sifting ash. Flames broke out in a great ball. Dancing orange fire shimmered across the black surge and headed toward the verges of the forest.

Still the killer, aren't you? said a mind within Urza. *You would slay ever, bird and beast to kill the creatures that oppose you.*

The wall of fire whirled in one last red roar before dissipating, not singeing so much as a leaf tip. The accuser within fell conspicuously silent. Urza allowed himself a small smile—until the next wave of monsters emerged from the eaves of the woods and stomped forward among twisted bodies and piles of dust.

"This is the horror I sought to stop in Argoth all those years ago," Urza explained to the presence within him. "This is the horror I still fight, but there will not be another Argoth."

Again only silence answered.

Urza's eyes glittered in their gemstone aspect. Extending a hand outward, he made a certain sign. One wing of the Phyrexian host swung in upon the other. Fiends leaped on fiends, bit through brains, sliced off heads. With another sweep of his hand, Urza dragged fallen beasts from the dead pile by the wall, digging free his ranks of scorpions. The machines hauled themselves from the slimy darkness where they had been buried and clambered toward the new line of advance.

"That should hold them for a moment," the planeswalker told himself. He drifted back down within the walls.

Below him, scores of machines, students, and scholars fought against the ubiquitous foe. Among them, one gray-haired man battled with an especial fury. He carried only a dagger but made it work like a sword—slashing, striking, parrying, piercing. Already around him on the dusty ground, monsters lay in piles. The dagger he wielded called to the pendant around Urza's throat. Even more, though, the man drew him. He sank a fatal blow in the dinner-plate eye of the creature he fought, and it spilled sloppily out of his way. Urza alighted where the beast had been and for his efforts got a dagger in the gut.

He smiled tightly, "Barrin, good to see you as well."

Turning white, Barrin drew his blade from the master's belly. It emerged, bloodless, and the man's belly and shirt formed themselves behind the retreating knife.

"Urza, I th-thought you were dead," he yammered stupidly.

"Not quite. I have mended the wall and staved off the main attack," Urza said urgently. "But this must end today. I must go kill K'rrik."

"We cannot last," Barrin gasped, almost pleading, "outnumbered, outmaneuvered . . . out of breath."

"I will bring reinforcements." So saying, Urza winked suddenly from existence. Like a man stepping across a hall from one room to another, Urza strode across the corridor of worlds and stepped into the forge-room of Shiv.

A sizable assembly awaited him. Jhoira was at the front of the group, with a rank of twelve modified Tolarian runners behind her—creatures of Thran metal. The platoon of humans numbered thirty-five, and included Teferi and all the other scholars and students brought to the land nearly a decade before. They were serious now, grown-up, and fire-hardened, like the metal they so expertly made. Beside them was a contingent of forty lizard men, including Diago Deerv and the picked warriors of the bey's personal bodyguard. The young fire drake Rhammidarigaaz accompanied them, along with Karn, the silver man. Next to these clean and orderly troops, a ragtag collection of jumpsuited goblins clustered. Many bore the crude tribal weapons they had brought to the rig five years ago. Others carried only the largest, heaviest, sharpest, or most wicked-looking items from their toolboxes.

Jhoira stepped forward with a military snap, accompanied by Diago Deerv and a scrappy little goblin with eyebrows that reached beyond his nose. This warrior gave what it considered to be a rigid salute. Jhoira addressed Urza.

"Your troops are assembled. Your allies have provided more than token forces."

"I see that," said Urza, his eyes flashing on Rhammidarigaaz and Karn. He indicated them and turned to Diago. "You realize, of course, that these two prizes of yours may be sacrificed in the coming battle."

"Sacrifice for the tribe is our highest honor," Diago responded with stern sincerity.

Urza's eyes passed one more time over the forces. Despite their numbers and their resolve, they would not be enough. He breathed deeply and said simply, "Come with me."

The planeswalking wave that swept out from him encompassed them all in an eye blink. It bore with it Urza's latest enchantment—a mass effect spell that turned the troops two dimensional while in the space between worlds. Thran-metal walls melted away to whirling chaos. Ancient enemies—Viashino, goblin, fire drake, human, and machine, hung flatly together in the emptiness, and then the company resolved out of air into the boiling battle of the Tolarian courtyard.

There was no time for orders. There were no columns marching into battle. There was only space for a breath and pivoting on one heel and striking whatever horrific figure loomed blackly up out of battle. The jangle of Thran-metal paortings joined the clang of goblin axes on carapace. The silver man fought with bare hands and gargantuan strength. The fire drake, the only beast that was a match in size for the gibbering monsters, slew with tail and claws and teeth and breath—all.

Tolaria's defenders gave a ragged cheer as the monsters faltered.

But it would still not be enough.

Urza planeswalked again. He left Tolaria for the lofted aerie of the ancient dragon, Gherridarigaaz. In moments, he appeared in the woven nest as he had before—sudden and stunning, businesslike.

"It is I, Urza Planeswalker," he announced.

The drake was huge and red against the great weave of tree bough and tar. She raised a grizzled head and regarded Urza angrily. "I thought you were dead."

"I can regain you your son, Great Gherridarigaaz."

Her head came erect. "Say on."

"You must fight for me. You must fight for me and the Viashino and the goblins. Your son fights for us, even now. I will take you to the place where Rhammidarigaaz is, and you must fight side by side with him, ally yourself with us, and save us in battle, and your son will be returned to you."

A suspicious glare entered the beast's narrowing eye. "Fight whom?"

Urza's eye was a sharp mirror of the drake's. "You must fight the enemy of us all, the creatures that would kill every last one of us, the monsters at the door."

"Ah, yes," said the drake slyly. "Urza and his Phyrexians."

"I have no time for games," Urza said sternly. "Come with me now and fight to regain your son, or do not come at all."

The drake lifted herself to her full, impressive height. She drew her wings tightly about scaly shoulders and darted her massive head in beside the planeswalker. "I go."

Urza took hold of the beast's shaggy mane and climbed onto her long neck. "Unfurl your wings," he ordered, "and prepare a gout of flame."

The drake complied. Her leathery wings stretched to their full extent.

"We go," Urza said.

With a thought the deed was done. Urza and the dragon folded into immutable geometry. Planar creatures, they careened through the pitching corridor of space. In moments, the veil of that middle place dropped away, replaced with rushing treetops and a bright, cloud-cluttered sky. Urza and his drake regained their third and fourth dimensions. Wings unfolded into rushing air.

Ahead, the Tolarian academy huddled on the hillside. Ropy black pillars of smoke rose from it. Gherridarigaaz gave one magnificent sweep of her wings. Pitching treetops rolled away. The drake broke out over the battleground. Below, monstrous creatures ran in their loping hundreds toward a thinly defended wall.

Drawing a deep breath, she hurled fire down on the Phyrexians. They burned away to greasy black smudges on the littered earth.

A cheer rose up from behind the academy wall. The great dragon soared and banked out over the Phyrexian gorge. Ballistae bolts leaped up from the rent and cracked past her wings. With a single surge, she climbed beyond their reach.

"Yes," Urza shouted to the creature through the wheeling winds. "Fight beside us, and you will have your son."

Then he was gone.

He stepped from the back of the wheeling beast.

The next moment he appeared elsewhere, in a peaceful corner of Tolaria.

His feet came to rest on a dam of rubble and mortar. The mighty barrier diverted water from the Phyrexian gorge. To one side of the broad pile of stone lurked the dark dome of K'rrik's fast-time loop. To the other side lay a vast, blue reservoir, water saved from the dank depths of the gorge. The lake was placid and mirror-still, far from the mad battle. Fishes darted through its depths. Trees around its edges cast their souls in its surface.

"Forgive me," Urza said simply.

Force blasted from his lowered fingertips. It pulverized the dam and hurled Urza into the air. Rocks separated. Water burst forward. The flood turned suddenly white, bearing in its brunt scouring teeth of rock and lime. It roared over the precipice and punched into the gorge. The belly of the lake slumped downward and followed.

Urza plummeted into the blue wall of water. It bore him along.

It would disguise him.

It would protect him.

He would not be torn by crosscurrents of time.

He would not be impaled by ballista after ballista.

He would not even be seen in the jetting flood.

And once within the time rent, he would destroy the spawning grounds where these Phyrexian monstrosities were made, would hunt down K'rrik and kill him, and would cleanse Tolaria forever of the Phyrexian menace.

Jhoira brought her Thran-metal sword crashing down onto the head of a gigantic fiend. She split the creature's sagittal crest and sent it sprawling back against the broken wall of the infirmary. The beast's divided head came to rest against the sill of a second-story window. Within that window, more monsters preyed on the bed-bound patients. Giving a roar, Jhoira climbed the sloping corpse of her foe as though it were a staircase. Her sword crashed against the glazing and sent a spray of glass within. Roars and screams burst outward. Another swipe of her blade bashed flat the toothy shards of glass at the base of the window. She clambered over the sill.

Many of the patients were already dead. The rest had put up the best resistance they could with crutches and canes for weapons. One of the more alchemically minded students had made impressive use of the various anesthetic compounds in the chamber. He had also concocted blast powder in small vials and kept three Phyrexians at bay by casting exploding philters at the feet of the attackers.

Coming up behind them, Jhoira swung her sword at the thick, reptilian neck of one of the monsters. The Thran-metal blade sliced through flesh and bone like a knife through water. The head lolled free and toppled toward Jhoira, its eyes rolling and rows of triangular teeth snapping. By instinct alone, she caught the snarling thing by one pointed ear and thrust it away from her.

One of the beast's comrades—a giant with a wattle of bristly flesh—spun about to engage her. Its jaws roared open for a bite that could cut her in half. Again in reflex, Jhoira rammed the snapping head in the path of the teeth. The head clamped its dead bite on the living beast's tongue. Jhoira hardly had withdrawn her hand before the larger Phyrexian chomped down on the severed head. Bone and tooth crunched and burst outward in a tangle of flesh that lodged itself chokingly in the giant's wattle. It gasped and staggered aside, retching. Jhoira ended its agony with a jab up one nostril and into the creature's frontal lobe. It fell with a sick roar, wrenching Jhoira's blade from her hand and pinning it under its body.

A sharp pain exploded in her side. Jhoira flew limply across the room to crash into the wall. Something stalked toward her, a huge something with gray-scaled skin, small insectile eyes, and ears that flared into venomous spikes. It cast aside cots with the same ease it had cast her aside. Jhoira struggled backward but got caught in a tangle of canvas and broken wood. The beast lunged. Its claws spread wide.

Abruptly, against its gray bulk, there was a small figure in white. In one uplifted hand, the figure held a metal case filled with vials of the yellow-gray powder. Next moment, vials and case both were gone, rammed among the teeth. The monster's head blasted away, pelting the room with its pieces. The vacated corpse slumped heavily atop Jhoira.

"Are you all right?" Jhoira shouted into the sudden calm.

Her rescuer had spoken the exact same words. He rolled the dead bulk of the beast off of her, ducking away, and pried her sword from the other body.

"I'm all right," they assured each other, again in unison.

Jhoira gladly received the blade. She thanked the slight young man who handed it to her.

"Do you think you can make a stand here? Do you think you can hold the door and keep more of these things out?"

"Yes," the young man said bravely. "Yes, if nobody climbs in the way you came."

Jhoira struggled up and staggered to the window. The yard between the infirmary and the academy wall was nearly deserted now, occupied only by hundreds of dead Phyrexians, humans, Viashino, and goblins. Even Rhammidarigaaz had left the courtyard, taking wing with his mother. Together beyond the wall, they roared down from the skies, sending lines of fire and sulfur into the host there.

"There should be no more attacks from that quarter, unless they breach the wall again," Jhoira guessed. She strode toward the infirmary door. "The battle has moved inside. It'll be room to room now. Can you hold this one?"

"Yes," the man repeated.

"Good," Jhoira said and strode out into the hallway.

A great ruckus poured from the Hall of Artifact Creatures ahead. Sighing wearily, Jhoira ran toward the sound.

A room-to-room battle, with her friends in the rooms—Karn in the observatory, Teferi in the great hall, Diago in the master's study, Terd in the cellars, Barrin in the rectory, and Jhoira herself in the Hall of Artifact Creatures. A small smile played about her lips. What Phyrexian host could be a match for a group like that? She would have to remind Urza, as he constructed his flying warship, to make sure to man it with the best of crews.

Her face darkened. She would remind Urza if they both lived through the day.

Urza rose from the vile sludge at the base of the canyon. With an exertion of will, he sloughed the muck of dead fish and tenacious seaweed from his robes. The shallow lake churned with the flood that poured into the gorge behind him. Up in the Phyrexian city, though, all was still. Barrin had been right. K'rrik had thrown every able creature into the assault, wanting at long last to eradicate the school. The only Phyrexians who remained were ballistae crews, sentinels, and those incapable of passing the temporal barrier. Chief of those was, of course, K'rrik.

There would also be another crop of vat-grown monsters. Urza would not leave until they all were dead. From decades of observation, Urza knew where the mutagenic labs lay—deep within the basaltic extrusion on which the city was built. With a thought, he was in a dark, deep cavern.

An aisle of vats extended ahead of and behind him. Stonework stanchions stood between panels of smoky obsidian. Behind these panels were bays of glistening oil—Phyrexian blood and placental fluid. K'rrik had likely filled these cells by draining thousands of his citizens. The emptied husks would then have been diced and jerked to make food for the creatures developing in the tanks. Phyrexians had switched from natural to artificial means of reproduction when placentas began, in utero, to consume their mothers from the inside out.

The grotesque figures within these tanks seemed utterly capable of matricide. Though immature, most were the size of a full-grown human, with nictitating membranes over large and rheumy eyes, knobby shoulders, soft claws, oil-breathing lungs, and rows of legs, some thickening into actual limbs and others withering and dropping away, leaving only hip-nubs. In a number of the dark vats, vestigial leg bones hung from the half-formed teeth of the blind beasts, a snack between scheduled feedings.

Urza was sickened. He rose toward the cavern ceiling, out of the aisle of vats. It dropped away beneath him, revealing row upon row of vats beyond. One hundred, five hundred, twenty-five hundred . . . A network of bone catwalks ran above each row. Across the ivory causeway, machines scuttled, dipping probes into the glistening oil, dumping chips of dried meat onto the heads of hungry creatures, and skimming waste from the top. Urza recognized pieces from his falcon engines in the design of these nursemaid machines.

No wonder K'rrik has sent the whole city on this attack. In months of his own time, mere weeks outside, K'rrik would have a whole new city, a whole new army.

Not any longer—as Urza drifted up into the dark vault of the cavern, he lowered his hands, spread his fingers, and sent great blue flashes of lightning down into the vats. Where the bolts struck glistening oil, massive plumes of fire rose. The figures within the oil writhed. Blue-white sparks traced out their curved fangs and the venom sacks beneath their throats. Arcs leaped finger to finger, knee to toe. The creatures convulsed, churning the oil, feeding the fires. In moments, flames wreathed their exposed heads, and then mantled their shoulders, and then girded their hips. Thick skin burned and cracked and split and curled back, looking like bark. Muscle cooked. Bones burst. One by one, the waiting army of K'rrik stewed where they stood. At the last, as all the glistening oil flared into the air, the sudden intense heat change shattered the obsidian shells. Shards of glass and bits of burnt Phyrexian scattered down the aisles.

More lightning flared; more vats erupted. Half of them were gone. Urza panted, feeling the drain of power on him. He would recover quickly, of course, and needed only one spell to slay K'rrik. Until these all were destroyed, Tolaria would not be safe. Blue

energy leaped from his fingers. Orange columns of fire blazed in the cavern night. Black clouds of soot and smoke belched up to roll at the height of the chamber. Dizzy with exertion, Urza blasted the last of the vats and watched as their inhabitants burned in putrid pyres.

This ought to flush out K'rrik.

Urza stopped breathing. The air in the space could be nothing but sheer poison. He lifted his eyes wearily toward the vault. There black smoke rolled in the deeper blackness of the cave. Something else moved there, too, something silvery and fleet and . . .

The shriek of the stooping falcon engine sliced through smoke and fire and oil. Urza raised his gaze just in time to see the creature's fierce eyes glinting above its knife-edged beak.

Impact.

Urza fell, struck from the sky like a sparrow. He crashed among oil-dripping glass shards. They were the least of his worries. His belly was filled with a mass of rending steel, macerated liver, and bone chips. The cometary creature had sliced into him and flung itself open. The whining whir of its shredding mechanism was unmistakable. The thing tore through muscle and viscera. It snapped ribs and rattled against backbone.

With a supreme effort of will, Urza stanched the flow of blood, reassembled tissues and organs, reconstructed himself out of the remembrance of being whole, but the machine was too quick. It destroyed any tissues that reformed.

Urza was being slain by his own invention, reprogrammed no longer to seek glistening oil but the smell of Urza's own blood.

It was his turn to writhe. He jittered across the shards of glass. Every moment, his mind threatened to blank out. There was not enough left of his physical form to sustain belief, to power the thought that would allow him to planeswalk and escape this horror. Perhaps if he had not spent such power on destroying the Phyrexian army, he could have mustered the strength. Now, though, he was pinned like a fly to a card. His gemstone eyes speckled with his own tossed blood. He struggled to reassemble himself, to draw each of those spots of blood back into the streams and vessels whence they came. The task was nearly impossible. He could not escape the machine, nor could he let himself merely die. He could only feel forever the ravening teeth of the device.

At least he had destroyed the army, if he hadn't destroyed K'rrik.

As though summoned by the thought, the *man* appeared. The term man could little apply to him now, though. K'rrik was little more than an animate skeleton. His time-vulnerable flesh had been mortified from his body over the centuries of his imprisonment. It had been replaced in patient succession by grafts of flesh from each new generation of negators. He had been slowly rebuilding himself, hoping some day to escape the gorge where he was imprisoned. His body now had a sinewy look to it, as though he were not a single man but a series of eels sewn together in the shape of a man. At the extremities of his figure—fingers, toes, knees, elbows, and brow—spikes had sprouted, most of them hollow-tipped and venom-dripping. Only the man's face remained roughly human in shape, and his eyes . . . they were bright and blue and human.

"After your last visit, Urza, I knew your weakness. Keep you near to death, and you cannot escape. Ballistae bolts and sword strokes are too clumsy, though. They leave moments of lucidity, and one moment is all it takes," K'rrik purred as he approached. His clawed and iron-heeled tread cracked chunks of glass as he walked. "This solution is much safer—and a nice piece of poetry. Thank you for the falcon engines. I have forty more, stationed around the gorge, should you succeed in planeswalking."

Urza, unable even to draw breath to respond, could only stare in stunned agony at his nemesis. As he focused his thoughts inward, on perpetual healing, one curl of his mind marveled that this monster spoke so well the tongues of men.

"That was your great mistake, Urza, coming here the first time. It taught us everything we needed to know. That has always been your great mistake, Urza, stumbling into our realm, letting us look you over, and then retreating while we prepared what we needed to kill you. You did it first in Koilos, and we followed you out. You did it again in Phyrexia, and we followed you out. You led us to Serra's Realm, you know. We attacked and invaded. They think they eventually defeated us, but we're still there. We've never left. We never leave a place, once you lead us to it. We've been engineering the transformation of Serra's Realm. The angels think they rule it still, but it is ours. It is one of our staging grounds for the full-scale invasion of your world.

"We've never left this place, either, and now, today, we have taken this island from you."

Urza wished his could spit his defiance. He wished he could remind K'rrik that his mutant army was dead, both inside the gorge and outside. He was left with only a handful of guards, and no matter how many modifications he underwent, K'rrik would never be able to squeeze his brain out of the time-cage where he was trapped. Urza wanted to say all this, but he could do nothing more than hold onto consciousness as he shivered across the rubble-strewn floor.

He didn't need to say any of it. K'rrik seemed to know. "By the way, you haven't destroyed all the vats. This is only the smallest chamber. I have three others. I have eight thousand warriors there. I have two thousand that are ready to emerge."

That was it then. K'rrik would taunt Urza awhile more, then draw his sword and lop off his head. Even if Urza could somehow muster the strength to planeswalk—which as that moment, he could not—he could not escape the time pit, could not even step beyond this death chamber. Three other falcons circled within the rolling black smoke overhead. That was it. Urza would die; K'rrik would live. Two thousand more Phyrexians would emerge to sweep away the final resistance. Six thousand more would emerge to make Tolaria a Phyrexian stronghold on Dominaria. The invasion Urza was only beginning to prepare for would be fully under way. That was it. All was lost.

"I see by the look in your . . . remarkable eyes that you have at last grasped your defeat, Urza Planeswalker. The seed of it was contained in those first moments at Koilos. From the beginning, you had lost everything." K'rrik advanced, drawing a scimitar with slow relish. "I had been hoping to watch your torment a bit longer, but it was only fun before you broke."

Urza shuddered with the unholy motion of the thing shredding his innards. He almost let go in that moment, if only to steal K'rrik's final victory, but an impulse arose in him to remain a moment more.

K'rrik towered over him now and lifted his scimitar high. "Good night, Planeswalker." The blade descended.

In the moment before it struck, a sudden surge of power filled Urza—strength from within him, but strength that was not his. Multani. It was strength enough for a single planeswalk. With the power came a whispered word, the one place to which Urza could planeswalk that would mask him from the falcons and give him the final victory.

K'rrik.

With a thought, Urza stepped out of space. He disappeared from the floor and the rattling creature. For a breath, he was in a nowhere place, but he did not linger there, lest the Phyrexian would understand. With a second thought, Urza stepped back into reality. He emerged at the exact core of K'rrik's body. Urza's form of scintillating energy swelled into being from the spot, bursting the Phyrexian's flesh in a rain of meat and glistening oil. K'rrik exploded, and in his place stood an oil-drenched planeswalker. Bits of eel-skin spattered out across the ruined vats.

Urza held still, not daring to blink or breathe.

The falcon that had moments before been rending him rattled to a stop on the glass-strewn floor. It withdrew its gear-work wings and shredders, folded them against its sides, and turned its head quizzically. The machine seemed to sniff the air. It trotted forward a few paces and pecked experimentally at the glass shards. Then, in a rush of metal wings, the thing leaped into the air and climbed into the smoke clouds above, to join its counterparts.

Move quietly, came the voice of Multani within Urza. We have three more chambers to cleanse.

Urza complied. He rose quietly into the air, sought out a doorway leading from the cavern, and slid through the air toward it. As he drifted smoothly along, Urza sent a thought inward, toward the forest spirit that inhabited him. *Then we are allies?*

Multani's response came without pause. *You have known the agony of Argoth. We have known the agony of Phyrexia. If these are the creatures you fight, we are allies.*

A sigh escaped Urza. He watched nervously to see if any of the falcons would pick up the scent of his breath. When none did, Urza sent, *I am glad of it. I'll need your strength to finish cleansing the gorge.*

Multani replied, *When we are out of this pit, and back into the forested isle, I can conclude this battle for you.*

Jhoira had linked up with her old comrades as they purged the academy of Phyrexians. They had pursued the beasts out of every chamber and corridor in the place, at last cornering a knot of twelve monsters in the far courtyard. Here, though, the tide had turned. The defenders of Tolaria found themselves fighting for their lives.

The situation was the same elsewhere. The Phyrexians had been forced from the battlefields by the drakes, runners, scorpions, and human fighters, but once in the woods, they held their ground, destroying whatever pumas dropped from the trees onto them. They would have slain thousands of Phyrexians, but whatever hundred survived would only return to the fast-time rent to rise again.

The defenders despaired.

The forests themselves rose. Tree branches swiped down to lash Phyrexian faces and tangle them in boughs and strangle them. Vines fastened around limbs and ripped them from their sockets. Mosquitoes and gnats and flies swarmed the monsters and flayed they alive. Leaves, hardened by some strange will, cut like daggers across fleeing legs.

Within the courtyard, the very grass beneath the feet of the twelve Phyrexians shot up in sudden life, piercing feet and slicing through legs and dragging the monsters down to their graves.

The shout that went up in that moment was weary and scattered, but it was the shout of victory.

Monologue

It is finished. The invasion of Tolaria is finished. I have never in my life felt so weary, incapable of even the simplest spell, incapable of even releasing this dagger I clutch so tightly.

But I did not save the island. Urza and his six-part alliance saved it, and if he can rally the folk of Dominaria like this, perhaps he can save the world after all.

—Barrin, Mage Master of Tolaria

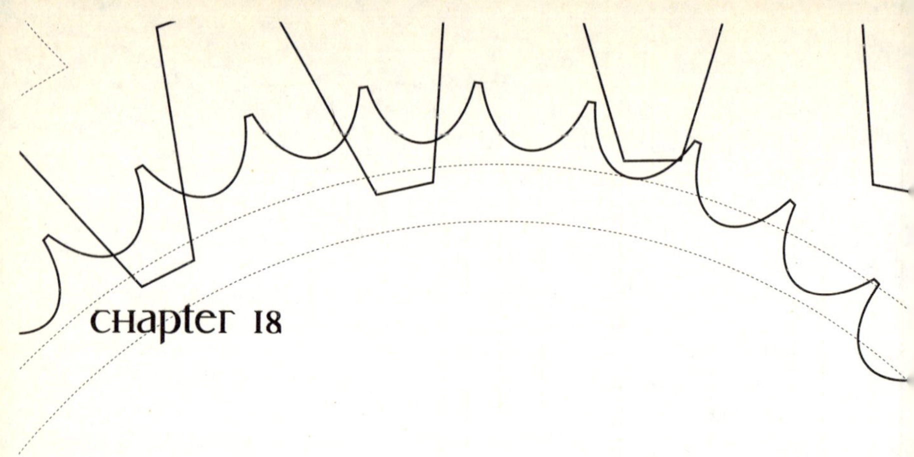

chapter 18

"They are in Serra's Realm, Barrin," Urza said nervously. Barrin was straightening the master's white and gold ceremonial robes, and all the fidgeting attention nettled Urza. "They've been engineering the whole decline of the plane, preparing it as a beachhead for their invasion of Dominaria. You aren't even listening."

Barrin released a long hot breath that only seemed to make the small pavilion tent more uncomfortable. "There will be time for war counsels later. Today is a day of alliances." He punctuated this speech with a snap of Urza's stole.

The master let out his own snort. Sweat seeped at his temples in the warm tent. He was so distracted with thoughts of devils among the Serra angels that he did not think to adjust his personal core temperature to be comfortable.

"They've followed me wherever I have gone. When Xantcha and I traveled the planes, wiping out Phyrexians, we were sowing them like seeds through the worlds. I tell you, the battle we have just fought is only the mildest prelude of the war to come."

"Yes," Barrin agreed placidly, dragging an errant strand of the man's hair back from his burnished brow, "and we just won the prelude. It is time to celebrate our victory with our allies." He backed up, looked the man over from head to foot, and nodded. "You look every inch the conquering hero."

"I feel defeated. There is no time to waste on ceremonies—"

Barrin grew suddenly stern. "To win the Battle of Tolaria, you had to enlist the aid of students and scholars, Viashino, goblins, fire drakes, and even the spirit of an ancient and distant forest. To win the Dominarian War, you'll have to enlist the aid of the whole world. The speech you give in the next few moments will cement the current alliance and lay the foundation stone for your planetary defenses. For once, Urza, don't run off to your clockwork contraptions. For once, Urza, be the statesman, speak to these delegates you have gathered. Reward them for the battle won and prepare them for the war ahead. Afterward, we can go sort things out in Serra's Realm."

The planeswalker's eyes flashed with something halfway between resentment and hurt. In that moment, Barrin remembered why it was that this great man, this near-god, so routinely retreated to his machines: among other humans, he was in fact a shy and fragile man.

"How do I look, Barrin?" Urza asked.

Barrin hitched his head. "You look ready."

Taking a deep and conscious breath, Urza clenched fists within his robe sleeves and strode toward the narrow, bright flap at the front of the pavilion tent. He emerged from the dark, stuffy enclosure onto a field awash in light and air.

The gathered delegates cheered.

Urza smiled. He could not help himself. There, arrayed before him in the bright glade, were the select representatives of his alliance: Jhoira, Teferi, and a contingent of Shivan students; Karn, Bey Fire Eye, Diago Deerv, and the bey's personal bodyguard; Glosstongue Crackcrest, Machinist Terd, and the Destrou chieftain; Gherridarigaaz and Rhammidarigaaz; Multani and a contingent of Tolarian wood faeries; and of course Barrin with two other Tolarian scholars and a group of elite students. Sworn to secrecy about the location of this glade and what they would see here, the assemblage were nonetheless brought to witness for all their people the salvation Urza initiated for Dominaria. They represented the army of survivors. But they were more than survivors, they were victors.

Only a week ago, fires and Phyrexians, the dying and dead had filled the island. Tolaria's defenders had won the battle. They then had turned with equal vigor to scouring stones and rebuilding walls. The honored fallen of Tolaria now lay in decorous shrines about the old Teferi monument. The dead of Phyrexia had made a pyre that burned for three days, high and blue, beside the gorge whence they had come. Not even bones or carapace had survived that oil-fed flame. Thousands of spider artifacts, created by Urza and his associates in fast-time plateaus throughout the island, had been deployed to ensure that Phyrexians would never again plague the island, never again survive the rising of the Glimmer Moon. All that had remained of K'rrik and his negators was the vacant gorge and a reek that cleared away once the last ember of the funeral pyre was out.

There was no scent of death in this glade. Morning air shifted brightly. The forest was verdant, untouched by battle. Centennial trees hung green banners of leaf over the quiet space. Nature wore its finery.

The people did, too. Clothes of labor and mourning were gone, replaced by resplendent finery. The students' and scholars' robes of silk and linen shone in a panoply of ranks and colors. As they cheered, the fabrics flapped like flags in salute. The corps of Shivan humans were garbed in clean jumpsuits of red and wore expressions that were both grave and joyous. Bey Fire Eye's lizard warriors were clad in brightly dyed skins and carried the totems of their houses. Even Terd had submitted to a bath and a session with Tolarian tailors. At the back of the company, the fire drakes wore ornate red barding, surreal against the green jungle. Smoke drifted like dolorous incense up from their muzzles.

As the cheering died away, Urza found himself smiling again. He noticed the sweat was gone from his temples, and he took a deep breath.

"Children of Dominaria, welcome to this new dawn. We dwelt for a time in deep darkness, but now we have light; and I am thankful for the darkness if only in that it made us allies.

"I have hidden this island of mine from the world. I hide it still, that the forces of evil we have battled not find it again. But to you, my friends, it is open. The learning of this land—the clockwork and spell work—is open to you now, open to Viashino and Ghitu, to Grabbit and Destrou and Tristou and to you, Gherridarigaaz and Rhammidarigaaz. The machines we have built will defend you as well as us. The knowledge we have gained will be shared among us all."

Applause answered this pronouncement, accompanied by eager hoots from Terd.

"By coming together—by ceasing our wars and burying our pasts—we arm ourselves for the future. Gherridarigaaz has regained her son not by slaying Viashino but by allying with them."

The ancient fire drake bowed her head in acknowledgment, and something akin to a grin spread across her toothy and fearsome face.

"The silver golem Karn—once owned by me and then by the lizard men—has won his freedom, proving himself in battle and service to us all."

Karn nodded his thanks to the Viashino bey stationed nearby.

Urza flung wide his hands in a grand gesture. "The Viashino, through our decade of alliance and with the guidance of Jhoira and Teferi, have produced this magnificent gift for the defense of our world."

He winked from existence for a moment. A murmur of uncertainty moved among the Viashino and goblins, but Teferi and Jhoira wore knowing smiles.

In the space of a long breath, Urza reappeared, hands still upraised. Before him, hanging in midair, was an ethereal ship. Glowing motes of blue magic outlined its long, sleek gunwales, its deep keel, its sideway-jutting masts and winglike spars and twining lines. Here and there, though, the ship was solid—metal pieces that gleamed like graphite but looked harder than steel. A sleek ram fronted the forecastle, trailing in its wake a series of floating portholes, joist plates, mast mountings, spar collars, cowlings, hinges, strike plates, doorknobs, and rivets. A large anchor and chain rested in the fore, just behind the ram. A pair of lateral sail mounts extended from the starboard and pen walls. At the heart of the ship hovered a massive metal core that could only have been an engine.

There was no applause now, only sighs of wonder and open-mouthed stares.

"The workmanship of these fittings is superb. They will last an eternity. They will forever grow, drawn on by final causes from these fine beginnings into perfection. They will reshape themselves and become what is needed to save us all, to save our world.

"But this great ship, of course, is incomplete. It is not by artifice alone that, our world will be saved. It is by life, too, by green mana. Our newest ally, Multani, spirit of the great and distant forest of Yavimaya, has brought with him a gift for Dominaria." Urza lifted a piece of wood, a large seed. "This is the Weatherseed, from the heart of the oldest magnigoth tree in Yavimaya, a tree that remembers the world before the Brothers' War, before the Phyrexians. It bears in it the essence of the ancient forest. It is the forest's heart."

A strange light had entered Karn's eyes. He stared at the Weatherseed as though it were his own affective cortex. In a way, the heart of Xantcha and the heart of Yavimaya were much the same. They would give life to Urza's machine.

The master held the Weatherseed high and strode to a clear oval of grass. "From this seed, through the aid of Multani, the ship's hull will grow."

So saying, Urza drove the wedge down into the soft earth. His arm disappeared to the elbow. When he drew forth his hand again, black soil clung, crumbling, all around it. He looked at the wound in the grass, seeing even then the forest spirit moving to weave the spot together. Urza stepped back as a bright cloud of shimmering creatures approached. Faeries. They strode from the woods, their very presence setting a hum in the air. They bore with them leaves folded into little cups. Gathered dewdrops glistened in each cup. As the faeries walked past the site, they poured the cool water onto the ground. The creatures bore their empty cups back into the woods as a continuing stream of their comrades followed with more water.

Once the line of cups ceased, other faeries marched out of the woods. Accoutered with slim battle blades and carapaced armor, they were stern-eyed and martial. They surrounded the spot where the Weatherseed had been planted, faced outward, and planted pikes.

Dumbfounded, Terd watched the fey creatures parade into position. The goblin wore a beatific grin on his face. His hoary claws twitched as though he wished to pluck at the faeries, but he resisted.

The Viashino, meanwhile, were watching the ground where the seed had disappeared. Already, silent and slender, a shaft had grown up from the mended hole. It spiraled up into the light, sending yellow leaves out to gather sunshine. In moments, the leaves deepened to green and proliferated. Twigs sprouted. swelling into branches. The small sapling shivered in a breeze that only it sensed and rose upward.

Urza made a gesture. With slow magnificence, the ethereal ship tilted, its prow rising into the air and its stem swinging down to hover over the growing tree. Soon, the great vessel stood on end. The questing boughs of the tree reached up to it, running along the metal plates and lines of force like rose branches up a trellis. They would spread out along the enchanted framework, taking inspiration from its design, melding without conforming.

All the while, quiet lingered in the glade. Urza's footsteps seemed loud as he retreated toward the tent. No one watched him, their eyes and minds and hearts captured by the spectacle of the ship taking form before them—the conjoining of mechanism and blossom, of artifice and nature, of history and destiny.

"Even now, the goblin tribes, once at war with Viashino and Ghitu and drake—"

"And each other!" shouted Terd. The group responded withlaughter.

"And each other—these creatures are working on the matrix of a powerstone that will drive this great, saving machine."

Terd released a whooping cheer, which was taken up by Glosstongue and the Destrou chieftain, then spread to the rest of the crowd. There was accord in that sound. For a moment, they had ceased to be Viashino and goblin, human and machine. For a moment, they had become the voice of Dominaria. The cheer rolled out through the forests and startled birds from their placid perches.

The sound died away, and Urza spoke again. "To complete this great ship, I will need all of you, my allies, my friends. The Phyrexians are gone now from Tolaria and gone forever, but they are not gone from our world. Even now, they are taking over a world connected to ours, one step away from ours. I need your help to build this ship, but I also need your help to save another realm, for if it falls, so shall we."

Monologue

Well, I suppose I should have expected it. I'm the one who set this ball into motion. I am the one who insisted that Urza regain his past.

He began the road back to sanity when Xantcha provided him a facsimile for his brother—Ratepe. It was when this second Mishra died, again in an attempt to rid the world of Phyrexians, that Urza at last accepted the truth of his brother's death. He had begun to regain his sanity.

Then came the explosion of the time-travel machine. That blast did to Tolaria what the Brothers' War had done to Terisiare. In the dark hours after the blast, I had thought Urza was lost for good, but the death of Tolaria at his hands worked on him just as the death of Ratepe had. At last, in present-time microcosm, he had a facsimile of his past-time, macrocosmic mistake. With the destruction of the first academy on Tolaria, Urza began to understand the destruction of Argoth caused by the sylex and by the decades of war that made the sylex necessary. Urza returned to Tolaria to rebuild, to face the children of fury. He was nearer to sanity.

There was more penance to do. In its destruction and resurrection, Tolaria allowed Urza to make amends with the human world for the crimes against Argoth. He yet needed to be reconciled to the natural world.

Then came Yavimaya. Urza had gone there to seek the avatar of the forest, an entity that could grow the hull of his flying ship. What he got instead was a five-year penance for the agony of Argoth. Yavimaya remembered Argoth. Multani remembered Titania. He recognized Urza and made him pay for his past. In purging the guilt of Argoth, Multani returned Urza's sanity. And with his sanity, Urza could at last destroy the Phyrexian children of fury in his midst.

I've tried to tell him he is well, now. I've tried to tell him there is no more need to venture into the past, that now is the time to focus on the future. He only shakes his head and speaks of leading Phyrexians to Serra's Realm.

That will be Urza's next journey, perhaps his last. If K'rrik is to be believed, Phyrexians are there among the angels. I cannot imagine how Urza will survive, trapped between angels and devils.

—Barrin, Mage Master of Tolaria

PART IV

between Angels and devils

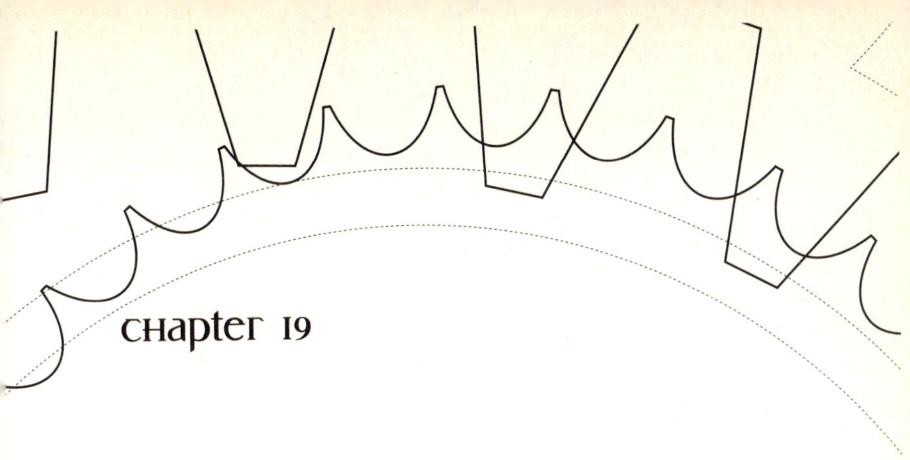

Chapter 19

Once again Urza descended. It was his preferred approach when arriving in unknown and hostile territory, and Serra's Realm, as it had devolved in the last few centuries, was indeed unknown and hostile.

It was still an empyrean skyscape, an arcing firmament stacked with rafts and mountains of cloud. Now, though, the once-blue sky was tinged in yellow and gray. A brimstone stink of Phyrexian glistening oil filled the air, and the realm's illusion of limitlessness had fallen away like a tattered robe. Heaven seemed cramped. The curve at the edge of it was just perceptible. The angel realm had once been a place of white cloud mesas, with large garden berms drifting placidly among them. Now the great berms had disintegrated into small clods, some only the size of shacks, and the sublime mountains had tumbled into pessimistic hills. Their color was muddied too, as though they were losing their quintessence and transforming into dirt. All the lines had been blurred. Every constitution was diluted. Each ideal was debased.

Phyrexians were here. They excelled in such transformations. Urza turned a slow spiral as he descended. Gemstone eyes marked out signs of habitation. At one time, the realm had needed no dwellings, for there was neither cold nor rain, night nor predators, and the very air nourished any who breathed it. Then, the only structures were built for sake of art or philosophical contemplation—pillared gardens, ivy-covered amphitheaters, high halls of state, groves of mana stones, galleries beneath the whirling heavens. Now many of those edifices clung in broken ruin to disintegrating clods of ground. Buildings not firmly rooted had fallen away in the tumbling chaos. Their foundations jutted like shattered teeth from rolling chunks of ground. Among these foundations new structures had been fashioned that seemed more the beige hives of mud-daubers than the homes of angels. They were hard-packed outside, and inside delved into spinning darkness—entrenchments against inclement weather and sudden night and marauding predators.

Phyrexians were here.

The smoke that rose from some of these deep hovels told of fires within to heat and dry the dark, cold spaces. The scent of flesh on that smoke told of creatures being hunted and slaughtered and eaten. No longer was breathing sufficient to sustain life. Now life had to be stolen from others who had it. Angels lived upon mortal flesh. The plane, once a living creature in its own right, had died. Every tissue and corpuscle of its being struggled to survive—preying on neighboring cells, drawing nourishment from the decaying body all around.

Phyrexians were here. They had killed the plane and taught the dying to eat the dead.

Only one fine structure remained, Serra's Palace. Urza glimpsed the palace, floating distant and dark within the gray sea of sky. It looked like an inverted question mark, a fact that had seemed fitting when Serra resided in the crystal aviary at its pinnacle. She had devoted herself and her realm to the constant debate of perfect society, perfect virtue, and perfect beauty. Questioning and discussion were an inescapable part of her realm. Now, though, the inverted question mark of the palace symbolized a place adrift, constant questioning become eternal doubt. It no longer meant debate, but confusion.

Toward that sign of confusion, Urza floated. As he neared the spot, he saw that it glinted more with rusted steel than silver. Its great banks of golden glass were shrouded in an orange grille, spiked and forbidding. Its ivory pilasters were chipped and yellow. The windows of its fanciful turrets had been knocked out to make space for batteries of ballistae and barracks of angel warriors.

These latter flooded out upon the acrid air, approaching the invader.

They were led by three archangels. Gigantic eagles' wings bore these creatures hurtling forward. In their hands glinted magnaswords. Single-edged and curved at the tip, the blades were halfway between scimitars and axes. A carapace of massive silver plate armor covered each of them, and a skirt of metal mesh trailed behind. Silver masks hid their faces. In the wake of these three fierce defenders came a contingent of thirty-some warrior angels. Smaller and more lightly armored than the archangels, these creatures nevertheless bore wicked-tipped lances, round bracers, and expressions of fanatical loyalty.

Urza watched as they came. He readied the supernatural defenses of his planeswalking form. He would not fight these creatures, but they might fight him. Even if he could survive such a conflict, there would be more forces in the palace—archangels, angels, the Sisterhood of Serra, human warriors, and the citizens of the realm. He would have to win past them all and do it without fireballs and killing, to reach the embattled creature at the center of this collapsing plane. He had come not to conquer but to ally.

They swarmed up around him. Wings beat the yellow air. The three archangels formed a triangle that hemmed him in, and angel warriors orbited in a large sphere all around. Droning wings almost drowned out the stentorian command of the lead archangel.

"Approach no farther," the archangel said from behind the mask. Cold, ruthless, and almost metallic, the voice was neither male nor female. "You are uninvited."

"I am Urza Planeswalker," the man responded, his white robes of state stark against the brown clouds and fetid winds.

"We know," the archangel replied. "We remember the smell of you." The comment was spoken matter-of-factly, without humor or malice.

Urza's lips tightened. "Yes, but I do not recognize the smell of this place."

"Much has happened since you came. Much has happened because you came." With or without inflection, the implication of this statement was clear.

"That is why I have returned," Urza replied. "I have come to help restore the realm to its former splendor."

"It is not your concern, Planeswalker," the archangel said. "It is not your war."

"It is if I become your ally."

"Lady Radiant needs no allies."

"Radiant? Yes, I remember her. So, Radiant is in command now?"

"Yes."

"And she needs no allies?"

"Yes."

Urza cast an ironic glance around at the devolving realm. "It would seem to me she could use whatever help she could get."

"That is not for you to decide."

"Nor for you. Take me to her," Urza said in sudden command.

"You are uninvited."

"I could merely 'walk there." Urza lifted his hands threateningly to either side, and the sphere of angels widened just perceptibly. "I am Urza Planeswalker."

The angry buzz of wings deepened. Angels nervously fingered their lance hafts. The lead archangel drifted toward Urza. From behind its mask, air emerged, hot and steely.

"Come with us." The creature backed away from the planeswalker, its unseen eyes remaining ever on him.

Without further word, Urza followed through the droning air. All about him, angels hovered in static threat. Their shadows, pale and diffuse in the sickly glow of the sky, passed languidly over Urza as they went.

Ahead, the dark, overturned question mark grew. With each moment, its transformation was more apparent. Ogee arches above landing platforms bore boxy portcullises like iron false teeth. Fine traceries had been removed to make room for bulky grills. Crystal mana collectors had been replaced here and there by smoking chimneys. Lines of soot traced across buttresses, and blast points showed where the palace had sustained attack.

"Your palace has become a fortress," Urza noted, and he remembered a similar transformation of his academy.

"Only a temporary measure," the lead archangel said, maintaining his backward flight. "but, as you can see, the defenses are warranted."

Urza could see. He imagined Phyrexians swarming the palace, riding on their wicked skyships or flying on wings of steel. He could imagine salvos of bolts arcing from the engines and smashing against the floating city, could imagine angels much like these pouring from the shattered windows and staved walls. There was war in heaven, and he had brought it.

"Yes. Warranted. That's why I want to speak to Lady Radiant. Her foes are my foes. I know of the monsters lurking here, and I have armies of my own to help destroy them."

Behind its quicksilver mask, the archangel did not respond. It merely drifted backward, without apparent effort, toward a large landing platform at the base of the inverted question mark.

The platform jutted like an angry jaw from beneath a dark archway. Its edge was ringed with curved horns, the teeth of a great carnivore. A few flying machines hung in dock around it. Clusters of figures stood in their midst. Three were archangels and another handful of angel warriors. Most of those on the air dock, though, were moiling crowds—angels and humans. They clustered together like fearful sheep. Guards strode around their group and jabbed with the butt of their spears. Some of the humans, packs on their backs, staggered up a wobbly gangplank and onto a waiting air boat. Meanwhile, in sad knots, angels broke from the rest, laboring out into empty air.

"Who are they?" asked Urza on the final approach to the landing.

The archangel before him sank lightly to stand on the crowded platform. Other angels around alighted as well. "Refugees, mostly, fleeing the rebels of the far reaches. They have come to the city for protection, but we have no room for them. Others are dissidents, heading for exile."

Urza nodded, setting feet to ground. The marble floor felt gritty, scored with stone chips broken off in some recent assault. "To what plane will they be exiled?"

"They will remain on this plane. No one leaves the realm, not even dissidents."

"And what of planeswalking visitors?" Urza prodded.

"Radiant awaits above," the archangel declared.

Walking backward in the midst of the landed flock, the angel guided Urza into the once-great city. The divine figure moved with a smooth ease, as though its feet still did not touch ground. It floated beneath yawning embouchement where refugees and dissidents huddled and brimstone breezes blew.

The spaces within were vast, dwarfing even the mob of angels around Urza. Tall, slender columns held aloft vaults of stone. When last Urza walked these halls, those vaults rang with lyric music and the sounds of lively debate. Now they roared with the shouts of sparring soldiers. Along the walls, rank upon rank of stone golems stood in mute insolence, ready to slay any army that might land upon the platform. The windows behind them were covered in black iron, giving the place a cave-gloom.

In the center of the main plaza, a great fountain stood, five stories high and ornately carved with angelic figures. If Urza remembered from his last visit, the statuary depicted the great virtues of Serra's Realm—Art, Discourse, Freedom, and Peace. No water flowed over that fountain anymore, though, and the figures representing these virtues stared out from beneath great rags of dust. At their feet, martial mounts—griffons and pegasi—drank from a half-full, stagnant pool.

Beyond the fountain, a great amphitheater sank into the floor. Urza remembered the glorious wall of golden glass that had stood beyond it. A rubble-and-mortar bulwark now sealed off the rear of the theater, protecting its users from aerial attack. A platoon of human holy warriors used the site. Before them paced an archangel, its sexless voice instructing them in techniques for cleansing and sealing off Phyrexian catacomb complexes.

"—want to be certain none of them survive. Do not assume that any number of spell blasts will cleanse a warren. Enter, but do so with caution and in teams. Once within, there will be burned bodies. Make certain they are dead. Behead them. Do not let a single neck remain intact. Black mana spells can bring them back, even so. They heal with preternatural ease. Do not assume a warren is cleansed simply because all visible foes are dead and quiet. Search every space. They hide like rats. Look for secret chambers. Look especially for their offspring. These will be hidden best of all. Kill them. Behead them. Let not a single one remain, or it will become twenty and return to slay you. Use your soul torches to make certain the job is accomplished . . . ."

Urza reflected grimly on this advice, the same he would have given to anyone going with him into K'rrik's fast-time gorge—if anyone had been able to accompany him.

The archangel leading him glanced upward. The party had just reached a broad shaft that rankled upward past hundreds of floors and balconies and promenades. Even in its decayed state, the space was awe-inspiring, disappearing into blue distance a mile overhead.

"She awaits, above."

The angels, like a startled flock of doves, leaped suddenly into the air.

Urza accompanied them. As they rose, he saw the city in cross-section. The streets were deserted, the public squares taken over by encamped warriors, the windows darkened by plates or locked away in cages of steel. Hollow groans moved through the haunted structure. Smoke seeped from forges. Boot steps echoed from armories. A jewel box no longer, Serra's Palace had become a weapon. It was a city under siege.

Urza thought of his distant Tolaria. It had once seemed as lost as this place. Now it was the nexus of a new alliance that spread across Dominaria. It had been a long battle to save the island. It would be a longer battle to save Serra's Realm, but it was a battle he would willingly fight.

They arrived. Urza drifted from the shaft into an enormous space, a circle of marble thousands of feet across. A vast hole in the center of the space opened onto a deep, verdant forest, a literal hanging garden, in which exotic birds flitted and sang. Above the marble circle rose mile-high windows of stained glass. All along the outer walls of the aviary tower, platforms and perches hung, where Lady Radiant's court conversed or planned or discussed. Banners of state, some with the sun-and-wing heraldry of Serra, and others with Radiant's own lantern-in-darkness design, floated on wires across the center of the tower.

Most impressive of all, the glistening-oil stink that tainted the air everywhere else was gone. Urza sensed the filtering work of great magic in the air.

He exhaled in awe. The aviary was the only pristine place in the realm—quite an exorbitance, given the aerial army it would take to protect the place. An angel nudged him with her staff and gestured toward the pinnacle of the aviary.

The archangel at the head of the party rose into the air. "Up."

As the contingent ascended up the tapered tower, the spaces around them closed in. Heat grew. In moments, palatial promenades gave way to large balconies. Golden windows narrowed. They changed too. As the parry rose, simple triangles of glass gave way to powerful lenses. Light-bending enchantments lay thick on the panes. Some gave fragmentary views of other rooms in the palace. Others showed ruined gardens near the edge of the plane. Still more followed over the shoulder of one angel or another. Every floating continent, every tumbling clod, every shattered wall of the place had its own window. Figures—angelic and mortal—moved kaleidoscopically through the panes of glass.

All about Urza, angel warriors averted their eyes from the jarring mosaic of images. For them, the sight must have been dazzling and absurd. But Urza's multifaceted gaze could make sense of it. In this spot, he could see every corner of the realm. If he stayed here long enough, he could peer into every mind and heart in heaven. This all-seeing chamber had been the single most powerful tool at Serra's disposal. In it, she, or any other planeswalker, would be omniscient.

In the midst of the glaring windows hung her throne. The seat was grand, a pendulum dangling from the apex of the aviary. Its back was fashioned of pearl-inlaid gold. It was draped in red samite that curtained down into the hot space. It could pivot completely around and thus provide easy view of every pane of glass. The throne was politically well positioned too, requiring all supplicants to hover in air and crane their necks toward the one seated there.

The planeswalker Serra no longer occupied the throne. Now the seat held a mere angel—Radiant.

The woman sat the throne as though it were her eternal punishment. Myriad images shone from the windows and swam sickly over her. She endured their ceaseless caress, but her eyes showed no sign of deciphering the images. For her, the throne was no all-seeing seat but a torture chair dangling in the midst of an off-balance carousel. Her eyes were glassy from long exposure, and her hands clutched the throne like a pair of talons. She sat with the aspect of one terrified of heights and did not deign to look upon the company that hovered, up beneath her. Golden hair and white wings draped in regal majesty about her, but her face showed nothing like royal grace—only desperate resolve. She had never been suited to rule the realm, not even at the height of her power. She had fallen far since then. The realm had decayed around her, and war had begun. She seemed grimly determined to see it through to the bitter end.

Though she did not look down, Lady Radiant recognized the prisoner. "Ah, Urza Planeswalker, returned at last to the scene of he crime?"

"Greetings, Lady Radiant," Urza said formally. He bowed in midair. "In a way, I have. I have returned for an alliance. I have returned to save you from your foes."

"Foes you brought to this place," Radiant pointed out. "Foes such as your consort, Xantcha."

"Xantcha was a friend, not a consort," Urza corrected placidly, "and she did not bring the Phyrexians here. I did. They followed me."

"They followed you and ruined us," Radiant said. "We drove them out once, but never has their taint left us."

Urza nodded in understanding. "Yes. The stench of Phyrexia is in the air. I sensed it the moment I arrived, faint but omnipresent. It is in the air, in the wind, off angel pinions, even in the lower palace. Only here, in this aviary, is the stench gone."

Lady Radiant's voice was strained. "It takes great feats of magic to make this air pure."

"But you cannot cleanse the whole realm. For that matter, you can never restore it to its old grandeur. With or without Phyrexians, all artificial planes collapse in time. This one is no exception. But I offer you salvation. I will bear you and all your people from this place and give you a new home on Dominaria. It will be as beautiful and grand as this place. And it will be yours. In return, you need only pledge your alliance to fight at my side against Phyrexia. Do not despair for this realm or for Serra's vision. Once the plane is empty, it can become part of our greatest weapon. It can charge the powerstone at the center of an airship that will defend our world."

"*Our* world," asked Radiant. Her eyes flashed with malice. "No. Dominaria is not *our* world. It is *your* world. *This* plane is our world. It is collapsing because of the fiends you brought here. I am fighting a war against those fiends. How dare you suggest we abandon our world? Would you abandon yours? Your old arrogance remains."

"Forgive me, Lady," Urza said, bowing. "Much of my old arrogance does remain. I did not realize how committed you were to this battle. I should have. I have just concluded my own private war against Phyrexia. They can hide in plain sight. They take human form, perhaps even the form of angels. There is no more insidious foe. In apology for my presumption, I would like to share with you the technologies I devised and the spells my mage master devised, to destroy them. If you will not ally with me on Dominaria, at least let me ally with you here. I offer myself, my machines, and my enchantments to aid in this private war of yours."

"It is exactly that," said a new voice, a man's voice, coming from a platform behind Urza. He pivoted in air to see a tall, thin man with a black goatee and eyes as slim and yellow as wedges of lemon.

"It is a private war."

"Allow me to introduce my minister of war, Gorig." Radiant said regally.

The goateed man gave a shallow bow, though he never lowered his baleful eyes from the planeswalker. He gestured to his own features. "As you can see, I am a wielder of mana magic. I am also an able general. Our war is in hand, and it is private."

Urza demurred with a small smile. "I have, learned no war is truly in hand."

Though she said nothing, Radiant suddenly drew all eyes to herself. Her face wore a strange, beaming intensity. "When first we knew you had returned, Urza, we expected you had come for war. You must excuse us for being so surprised by your offers of peace."

"It is a new man who stands—who floats before you," Urza explained.

"Yes," Radiant agreed, somewhat dismissive. "Before you commit yourself and your armies to this conflict, perhaps you would wish to accompany us on our next raid. We would like to view your combat strategies as well. Our next offensive will be launched in a few weeks. Stay with us and feast until then. Once we have battled shield to shield, as the saying goes, we will know if this alliance will benefit us both."

Urza nodded. "This counsel is well considered." He bowed low. "I gratefully accept your invitation."

At a motion from Radiant, the swarm of archangels and angels melted away beneath them, leaving only the planeswalker, the angel ruler of Serra's Realm, and the dark-bearded man, Gorig.

In one noisy wing of the Shivan mana rig, Jhoira and Karn peered through a glass port in the side of the crystal matrix chamber. Below the floor, magma engines channeled their searing heat into a concentrated beam of ruby light. It rose up a series of tubes, reflecting from panels of silvered glass positioned in exact alignment, and lanced into the matrix chamber. There the beam was split by a large lens, and split again, the four resulting bands of light rebounding through the space to sketch out in air the exact dimensions and cut lines of the airship's powerstone.

"An ethereal stone for an ethereal ship," Jhoira remarked acidly.

Karn glanced briefly toward her, wondering at her mood. "At the rate Multani is growing the hull, the ship is more than ether now. It's been over a month."

"I know," Jhoira snapped. She rose from the riveted superstructure, dusted off her hands, and whistled toward the scampering teams of goblins, signaling the magma pumps to accelerate. "Almost two. Urza is off on another of his endless journeys."

A quizzical gleam entered the silver man's eyes. "He has saved Tolaria. He has made alliances with Yavimaya. He has devised a great ship to save the world. Now he seeks to drive Phyrexians from another place. You can't fault him for that."

"I don't," Jhoira said impatiently. She stooped beside a pair of arguing goblins, entered the disagreement in their own dialect, pointed to a schema one of them held, delivered a pair of thumps to their heads, and sent them on their way. "It's just that Teferi is gone."

"He's what?" Karn asked.

"He'd said when we were leaving that he'd be heading for his homeland, Zhalfir. They were having a war of their own, and they could use a mage of his caliber. He wanted to say goodbyes three weeks ago, but I put him off, said we'd have time when I'd returned from Shiv. I'd thought we would be here only two weeks."

"Perhaps he is still at Tolaria," Karn said. "Perhaps he is waiting for us to come back. What difference will a few weeks make?"

"Much difference, in time of war," Jhoira said. She angrily threw a great lever, sending lava into chutes around the matrix chamber. These channels of rock would solidify around the ionized center of the jewel matrix, providing a compression mold. "No, he's gone. He wouldn't wait for me. He couldn't wait for Urza. Last time Urza stepped out for a week, he was gone five years."

"He's changed, Jhoira," Karn replied. "Before that trip, he traded me away to the Viashino. Afterward, he negotiated to get me back."

Jhoira at last stopped working, letting labor slough from her shoulders. "This isn't about Urza; this is about Teferi."

Stomping up beside her, the silver man stood, awkward. He had long ago learned not to drape one of his massive arms over Jhoira in consolation, lest he crush her.

"We were best friends before Teferi. We can be best friends again."

She turned toward him, a trembling smile on her lips and tears welling in her eyes. "You're right, Karn. We've always been best friends. I was silly to think I needed more." A tremor of uncertainty underlay her words.

Hesitantly, Karn reached out to take her hand. "Urza has taken me back, and now you have as well."

"Yes," Jhoira said. She melted sadly against him.

Karn stood there, even more lonely than before. He was the only thinking, feeling machine among Urza's artifact creatures, and because of it, Urza had no idea what to do with him. Karn was not a colleague; nor was he a mere creation. He had been designed to journey through a time machine that no longer even existed. He was kept busy with a thousand duties, but he had no real purpose. Had he been any other artifact creature, Urza would already have junked him, melted down his parts, and made new machines.

Now, though Jhoira called him "best friend," her voice told of disappointment and resignation.

Standing there, Karn wondered if joining the junk pile would be a mercy.

Monologue

Teferi left just this morning. He took the refitted *New Tolaria*, and a small army of runners, pumas, and scorpions. I kept half the force—some five hundred units—but probably did not need to. The island has been cleansed of Phyrexians. Spider crystals fill the land. Zhalfir needs the machine warriors more than we do, but Teferi's ship would not hold more. As it was, I had to argue quite a while to get the proud young mage to accept the mechanical aid. I do not blame him. Though my association with Urza makes artifice a necessary study, I much prefer spell battles to mechanized ones. Of course, if one wants to win, one employs both.

I am seeing such necessary connections everywhere these days. The hull of the skyship is taking shape, day by day. Wood fuses with metal, and both grow together. I have spent many evenings with Multani. Weary in the suspiring night, he relates to me all he has learned from our fast- and slow-time forests. He speaks of young worlds and old, of the cycle of growth and decay. He tells how the blast that tore through Tolaria brought death in its first moments, and new and diverse life thereafter. He says that had it not been for the destruction of Argoth and the sinking of Terisiare, Yavimaya would never have risen. Life and death oppose each other, yes, but it is only in their opposition that either can exist at all. There is no death without life, and no life without death.

Magic and machine, metal and wood, life and death, Shivan fire drakes and Tolarian sea drakes, somehow, Urza has brought them all into alliance. Somehow, in the words of Multani himself, Urza has come to embody each of them. I have never had such hope for our world as I do now.

Urza has been gone too long in Serra's Realm. He seemed to think he would be able to quickly tell angels from devils. I have to wonder. If fire and water can become allies, perhaps good and evil can, too.

—Barrin, Mage Master of Tolaria

chapter 20

Urza flew among echelons of Radiant's purification army. He wore a battle suit, much like the one he had devised for his assault on Phyrexia. The mechanized assault armor bore special protections against fire—he remembered well the conflagration of glistening oil in the gorge—and airborne poison. It was also proof against ballistae bolts. He bore a great black battle lance tipped with numerous blades, including a narrow axe and curved spearheads. From earlobes to toes, he was covered in black metal, scale mail, and power conduits. He realized with a certain irony that should he slay Phyrexian sleepers this day, he would seem more the monster and they more the humans.

Ahead of Urza to his left flew the commander of this echelon, an archangel as faceless and sexless as the others, its name unknown to Urza but its command unquestioned. It bore a magna sword that could cleave the head from a bull with one swipe. Behind the archangel, in a great cone, flew a contingent of fifty angel warriors, some armed with whips and nets, others with enchanted torches that flared blue-white and were said to turn the skin of Phyrexian newts yellow. The remainder carried swords for summary executions and head bags that would allow the dead to be counted and the skulls to be immolated, preventing grave magics from reviving them. At the rear of the party sailed an airship loaded gunwale to gunwale with white-suited holy warriors. These humans stood statue-still as the ship surged along. Their eyes stared golden and dead from their heads. Righteousness had been part of these warriors' demeanor when they first arrived in Serra's Realm, and ruthlessness had been learned along the way.

The flight of angels and avengers sighted their target ahead—a tumbled cluster of pulverized earth. What once had been an archipelago of aerial islands had been shattered into fragments of rock and grass. The remaining planetoids turned listlessly in midair. Some of them spewed uneven spirals of soot from the hovels dug in their sides.

"The Jumbles contain the single largest infestation of Phyrexians in the realm," Radiant had explained some days ago over a course of tea. The porcelain settings rattled with each stomp of boots drilling in the palace below. "They masquerade as angel folk and human outcasts—and to be sure, there are settlements of each among them—but there are wolves hiding among the dogs. You'll know them by their yellow-green cast in the light of the soul torches."

Urza lofted one such torch now. Others did the same. As yet, the light from the arcane brands was too distant and dim to pick out any creatures on the rolling boulders and hunks of ground. They would see soon enough. Angels swooped down with lightning speed.

The archangel commander made a series of crisp hand signals. The outer wings of the attack column broke away into sweeping lateral dives. Urza stayed with the leader, its core flight of twenty fighters, and the air barge. The other two units—fifteen angels each—soared outward to converge on their target like a pair of hammers. The main flight rose, following the archangel.

The field of rolling rubble dropped away beneath, revealing for the first time in its midst a series of larger aerial islands. The central force would land on the largest of these, purify it, and post a contingent there to secure it while proceeding to the second largest. Already refugee hives of mud and stick were visible below. The colony crouched in a hollow of stone beside a dead forest of gray stumps. The refugees must have been scavenging the ruined forest for firewood.

Another hand signal from the archangel indicated a flat rock bed just below the warren. They would land there. Like screaming falcon engines, the angels stooped from the sky. Their enchanted torches blazed all the brighter in the rushing air. The sight must have been horrifying from below—two-score sun-bright lights blazing down like comets, bringing with them a host of warrior angels and a boatload of angry humans. The sight must have seemed an apocalypse.

The angels came to ground at a run. They dashed up slope toward the gaping entry to the warrens.

Within, faces shone, yellow-green and wide-eyed. They flashed away into shadow.

The angel warriors homed in on those fleeting faces. Their strides lengthened. Their blades rose. There came no shout of fury or terror, as comes from mortal armies on the charge. Only the sizzling torches and the relentless boots announced their coming. Blue-white light bleached the gently rolling landscape. Glaring circles spilled into the shabby warren entrance.

As the charge closed, a mighty crunch and thud sounded behind. The ground leapt. The barge of holy warriors had beached itself. A clank and boom announced the fall of the troop door. Then came the human roar of fury and fear.

Meanwhile, Urza and his archangel commander had reached the warren's entrance. They charged within and rounded a corner. A pair of desperate blades swung weakly out toward them. The first caught on the archangel's massive shoulder plate. The second scraped dully against Urza's armored flank before clattering loose to the floor. The wielders—two young human-looking males—staggered back from the assault and flung up hands to ward off the archangel's torch-cudgel. In the blue-white glare of the torch, the young men glowed a ghastly shade of green.

A spell arced from the angel's gloved hand, pinioning the limbs of both men on spits of lightning. They paused only a moment before bursting outward in a rain of charred flesh. White flashes of life-force flared from the falling bodies and were drawn violently into the torches. Without pause, the archangel strode over the smoldering forms and into the narrow passage beyond. It was a spiraling descent that led into the heart of the aerial island. Urza followed.

Behind them, the main body of angel and human warriors entered. Two warriors took post at the cave mouth.

"They live in cold, squalid darkness down there, afraid of the light, of the truth," Radiant had said as she nibbled on a corner of toast. She had followed the comment with a wistful sigh. "It is as though the air that had once nourished all of us is poison to them."

The archangel led Urza and the rest of the cleansing contingent down the spiraling passage. It let out into a large central chamber. It was deserted. Five small fires leaked smoke into holes in the ceiling. A few middens of bone and trash lay near disheveled sleeping mats. From this central chamber, many dark side passages opened.

The archangel drifted regally into the middle of the cavern. He signaled the troops after him to scour the passageways. Two by two, the warriors pressed into the darkness. Torches flared. Voices cried out in terror, lightning crackled. Teams emerged.

Efficient, rapid, and ruthless.

Except that something was very wrong. As they had descended into the cavern, the Phyrexian stench of the air had lessened until it was gone.

Urza swept quickly ahead of the brute squads, into a dark passage. His gemstone eyes dismantled the darkness, and he saw:

A very human family huddled in that tiny alcove—mother and father and child. Phyrexians did not make sleepers to resemble children. These folk clung to each other, cowering against unyielding stone. They stared through the blackness at the hulking figure of Urza. They muttered prayers to their angels.

Then the killers arrived. They swept past Urza. Their torches sent mirror-shards of blue and white scattering across the wall. Urza saw his own shadow cast, huge and malevolent, over the family.

Then torchlight broke out over them, and their skin glared yellow-green.

An axe rent the father's head, and a spear impaled mother and child both. Red blood came from them all in the moment before the incinerating blast. White fire gave way to black smoke and red welts in the eyes. In the midst of it, spinning ghosts poured from the cloven forms and were sucked away into the beaming torches.

An angel cast another sorcery. Glowing motes of sand followed the inner contours of the wall, seeking secret doors. When none were found, the killing team gave the all-clear whistle, shouldered their weapons, and marched out past the holy warrior posted at the entrance.

Urza followed them out. He soared to the archangel who hovered in the cavern midst. Arriving beside the commander, Urza spoke rapidly.

"Those torches don't work. They show human skin to be yellow-green also."

The archangel's response was unimpassioned. "We have no better way to proceed."

"You are killing your own folk. You are killing humans and angels, not Phyrexians!" Urza insisted.

"This is a private war," the archangel replied flatly.

"I can smell their blood."

"We cannot send you like a scent hound into every burrow—"

"You cannot keep killing innocent people—"

"You have done so—"

"I have done so to battle Phyrexia!"

"Phyrexia is here. You said it yourself!"

"The reek isn't here. It is in the palace—"

And then he knew he had said too much.

Even as the lightning bolt jagged out from the archangel's fingers, Urza stepped into the space between worlds and walked the halls of chaos.

Urza emerged in the height of the aviary. He was alone, for the moment. Radiant's throne stood empty. The nearest angels or guards lingered on platforms hundreds of feet below. He was alone, save for hundreds of spell triggers, silently tripping, one after another. He felt their sorcerous hooks drawing over him and retracting into the walls. He waited—for Radiant, for her personal guard, for whomever would answer the alarms. In the all-seeing panes of glass around, Urza glimpsed images of slaughter and death. The cleansing squads had not ceased their labors.

A globe of light leapt into being around him. Its surface roiled with fire. A score of angels rose in a fierce circle from the floor and, in moments, hemmed him in with spears.

She arrived. Whatever other enchantments lay upon the space, Radiant apparently maintained a summoning alarm. She appeared, seated in her punitive throne, wings and hair drooping over her sides. As her robes of state spread across the high throne, a darker being took form just behind Urza. Minister of War Gorig drew his tall, lean figure together from empty air and strode to the edge of the platform. His lemon-wedge eyes glared balefully at the planeswalker.

"To what do we owe this intrusion?" Lady Radiant asked from her lofted throne.

"Forgive my effrontery," Urza said, sketching an elaborate bow, "but the situation is urgent."

"You were to accompany our cleansing army at the Jumbles," she said. "You were fully provisioned and briefed. That battle is even now in progress. Why are you here?"

"Your cleansing army is killing humans and angels as well as Phyrexians," Urza said urgently. He flung a hand toward the images in the windows. "Look! See for yourself!"

Radiant involuntarily peered toward the scenes, and then reeled, her eyes swimming with violent images.

Gorig blinked in irritation. "There will always be civilian casualties in such operations. There are weeds among the grain. To root out the weeds, a few heads of grain will be lost. But to leave the weeds, they will all be lost."

"I sensed no Phyrexians in the main cavern we entered, and yet every living creature within was being slaughtered. They were humans. They were angels. They were not Phyrexians, and yet they died all the same."

Gorig's response sounded like a growl in his throat. "They were dissidents. They were traitors to the state. They were in league with Phyrexia, were in all respects but physiology Phyrexian. You do not know their crimes against the state and so cannot judge their fates. This war is a private matter."

"If you wish to be rid of these refugees—"

"These dissidents," corrected Radiant serenely.

"—these dissidents, I will prepare a place for them on Dominaria."

Radiant's fair features were tainted with distaste. "You would bear them to your world, even knowing Phyrexian sleepers hid among them?"

"Yes," Urza said without pause. The response seemed to surprise even him. "I would do my best to root out whatever Phyrexians lurked in their midst, but better the multitude of mortals survive to shield a handful of monsters than that they die to eliminate them."

Radiant glanced a question at her war minister.

Anger jagged across Gorig's features. "How can you possibly make this offer? If even one of the beasts survives, your whole world could be destroyed."

"I know that very well," Urza replied sternly, "and yet I make the offer. Lady Radiant, do you give me leave to rid you of your refugee problem?"

The woman's face had regained its placid composure. "I suppose it would save us casualties and weaponry merely to ship out the dissenters—"

"No," interrupted Gorig. "No one leaves. The doors of the realm are closed and will stay closed. No one leaves."

A protest formed itself on Urza's lips but never emerged. In a sudden flash, Urza understood. "No one leaves except me."

Even as he stepped across the dimensional threshold into that shifting space between worlds, the roar of Gorig followed him out, "Return and you will be slain. You are an enemy of the state, Planeswalker. You are Phyrexian!"

"Phyrexian sleepers are indeed in Serra's Realm," Urza said as he paced in his private study, "and they are transforming it, using it to prepare their invasion of Dominaria, but not as we had thought."

Mage Master Barrin sat grimly at the black-wood table. The shadows of the high study gathered about his shoulders. Beyond the window, in a distant glade, the nearly completed hull of the airship creaked in its slow, final expansions.

"The sleepers have fomented rebellion in the realm. They have sparked a civil war. They've done it not by stirring up dissidents among the citizens but by filling the palace with fear. Their leader is War Minister Gorig, who has shut down the discourse and debate that once filled the terraces and gardens of the realm and replaced them with tribunal and terror. Every day he declares more citizens traitors to the state and evicts them from the palace. They cannot leave the realm, though, and flee to refugee camps on broken islands at the edge of the plane. There they are hunted down as though for sport. All the while, the realm shrinks."

Barrin was nettled. He ran a hand through his ragged hair. "How does any of this advance the Phyrexian invasion?"

"White mana," Urza said. "Phyrexia has discovered a way to decant it, draw it off, and convert it into black mana. By slaying the refugees, they are harvesting white mana, drawing it into sorcerous torches that store the power until it can be taken to Phyrexia. Between raids Gorig must empty the torches into a soul battery. All the while, Serra's Realm is shrinking, and Phyrexia's reach is growing. Gorig will allow no one to leave because he is harvesting their souls."

A specter crossed Barrin's eyes. "Harvesting them . . ." He shook his head, dumbfounded. "How much has the realm shrunk?"

Urza rubbed his jaw in consideration. "It has already fallen below its critical mass. Its collapse is inevitable."

"If all of that white mana is harvested by Gorig and reaches Phyrexia—"

"We are doomed," Urza finished.

Barrin could sit no longer. He bolted to his feet, chair toppling behind him. He paced feverishly.

"If we could find Gorig's stores of white mana and divert them into the powerstone for your flying ship . . ."

An astonished look crossed Urza's face. "I can't believe what you are suggesting. It is Argoth all over—using the souls of others to power my own private war."

"No," said Barrin. "No, this is different. This is no longer a private war, Urza. And you would not be harvesting souls. You would be resurrecting them. They are gone already. You would be bringing them back, saving them from Phyrexia, and giving them new life in the heart of your ship. You would be giving them a chance to avenge their own deaths."

"Perhaps," Urza allowed. His eyes glowed with remembered atrocities. "Perhaps."

"This is not Argoth at all, Urza," Barrin assured. "We're too late to save Serra's Realm. The Phyrexians have already destroyed it, but you can still save her people."

Urza's voice was fervid as he picked up the thought. "I'll find where Gorig is storing the souls—they must be in Serra's Realm, perhaps in the palace. But he'll know I've come back. He'll know what I'm looking for. He'll tighten his defenses. I'll have only a few chances. Perhaps I can bring back some refugees each time. I could take a hundred at once if they would gather together—but there are thousands." He looked up. His eyes sparkled intensely. "We need the ship, Barrin. Once I find the battery of souls, we'll need the ship to go get the rest of them. How soon can it be ready?"

"The hull is almost complete. The engine and metal pieces are already in place. The sail crews finished months ago. By now Jhoira and Karn will have completed the powerstone core. We've got to train a crew, of course. Find the soul battery, and I'd say we could fly in a month. Three weeks, if we work day and night."

"I'll find the battery. . . and save those I can . . . and muster the rest."

Barrin smiled broadly, rubbing his hands together in astonishment. "I had thought our victory over the monsters in the gorge had been your crowning moment, my friend. But you have made wars before, and it takes no great man to kill. It takes a great man to save, Urza. It takes a great man."

The cranes were in place around the upended airship, block and tackle threaded through great straddling braces of metal. Terd kicked the base of one of the stanchions, scratched his head in vexation, and shouted instructions to his gray-skinned comrades. They scurried up about him and stared in puzzlement at the bottom of the metal beam. It sat almost but not quite atop the stone it was supposed to rest on. As his workers looked downward at the spot, Terd took the occasion to fling his arm out, winging them all in the back of the head. More shouts followed, and the workers turned to a set of ropes stabilizing the great piece of machinery.

Meanwhile, Diago Deerv and Barrin consulted diagrams spread across the field table. They discussed torque and stress loads. Diago assured the master mage that the metal cross members could support two flying ships. If any aspect of the arrangement were insufficient, he insisted, it was the network of ropes. With a quirked lip, Barrin likewise assured the Viashino engineer that Tolarian hemp was extraordinarily strong in all of its applications.

Nearby stood another table. It was stout and stone. Four runners surrounded it, a watchful scorpion was stationed beneath it, and falcons circled high above it. Atop the table lay a black cloth, beneath which huddled a mass the general size and shape of a man. To one side of the table stood Karn. Though he was utterly still, the focus of his eyes shifted nervously across the crowd of students, lizard men, and goblins clustered beyond the ropes.

Jhoira sensed the tension in her friend. "Relax, Karn. There are no Phyrexians among us today."

"The stone is priceless," Karn said. "It wouldn't take a Phyrexian to try to steal it."

"It would take a mammoth," Jhoira pointed out.

"I'll just feel better when the stone is in the engine," he said.

Jhoira shook her head wonderingly and teased, "You're constantly complaining about having a purpose in the grand scheme of things, and once you have a purpose, all you can do is worry."

"Perhaps my affective matrix is flawed," Karn said in impressive deadpan.

A shout came down the line of goblin laborers. Ropes that had been slack went suddenly taut. The great hull of the ship creaked as lines tugged it in cross-directions. Long and slender, the ship quivered within its drydock framework. Its bowsprit wavered, three hundred feet up in the blue sky, and with a tremendous groan the prow tilted down toward the horizon. More shouts came from the goblins, and lines shuddered with the strain. The curved metal stanchions overhead bowed just slightly beneath the ripping burden.

Mage Master Barrin sent streamers of blue magic out to wrap themselves around points of stress. Scintillating power sank into metal or hemp, adding magical strength.

The tapered stem of the airship, once lying against the ground, tilted upward, showing a row of windows and an insignia shaped like a giant seed.

"The Weatherseed," Jhoira said, pointing to the spot.

"Yes," Karn agreed.

"Multani says the ship is complete but unfinished," Jhoira said. "It's still alive, still growing. It is as much a creature as it is a machine."

Karn was silent.

Jhoira pressed. "You are no longer alone, Karn. Urza has designed and built his second living machine."

"No, Jhoira, you are wrong," Karn said. "I'm a thinking, feeling machine, but I am not alive. This ship is Urza's only living machine. It is always growing, integrating new parts into its structure. I am not growing. I am disintegrating."

Jhoira sighed heavily. "Disintegrating—aren't we all."

Masts and spars that had for long months jutted sideways from the upended ship stepped into the sky. With a final shudder and thud, the vessel settled atop the landing spines. Ropes that had eased it downward grew slack. The teams hauling on those lines leaned forward and let them drop to the ground. There was a sigh from workers and artificers and even the ship herself. Upright for the first time, the sleek-raked craft looked large and muscular against the whispering forests of Tolaria. Crews reverently approached it, staring in awe at its glimmering portholes and its elegant webwork of lines.

Then the commands started again. Workers set ladders to the side of the vessel and climbed aboard. Ramps were hauled into position to ease loading. Weapon crews swarmed the various beam weapons embedded in the prow and along the length of the gunwales. Master Mage Barrin levitated himself into the air and floated along the curving rail of the craft, surveying it on all levels.

"Well, Karn, let's get this stone inside," Jhoira said.

She pulled back the black cloth, revealing a massive and beautifully shaped stone, configured in a long lozenge like the Weatherseed itself. It caught the sunlight, amplified it, and sent it stabbing outward in a blinding corona. Karn leaned down, gathered the heavy gem against his gleaming chest plates, and hoisted it into the air. The combination of silver and crystal was dazzling. Karn was transfigured, a man made of lightning. He walked reverently toward the ramp that led into the ship, and a cadre of four runners surrounded him.

Jhoira fell back, astonished by the bright spectacle. It suddenly occurred to her that Karn and the airship were of a piece. They were not two different generations of invention but one continuum. Perhaps Karn didn't realize it—perhaps Urza did not even realize it—but the silver man and the skyship would go down together through time, parts of a single legacy.

Urza crouched in a dark chamber in Serra's Palace. Gorig's forces had located him and were closing in. Their boot steps rang in the hallway. He still had not found the soul battery. He had not even discovered where Gorig kept charged soul torches. Time grew short. With sudden violence, soldiers' boots pounded against the barred door.

Urza stepped away. He crossed the echoing crawlspace between worlds and emerged in the empyrean reaches of Serra's Realm. Here the palace was only a distant black speck drifting on the horizon. Ahead of him, the Jumbles formed a chaotic sea of tumbling stones.

A golden regatta of troop landers and angel wings glinted above one of the larger masses. They descended toward a refugee hive. Their white-blue soul torches trailed smoky crazings in the air. There, just beneath a green ridge where grasses clung to a ruined temple, was the entrance.

With a mere thought, Urza disappeared from the spot where he hovered. He stepped in a flashing moment into the mouth of the hive.

A handful of young guards started at his appearance and pivoted to hurl their crude spears. One man fell in a tangle of grimy clothes. Four others managed to send their spears Urza's way.

The planeswalker swept his hand in an arc before him, and the spears cracked from a sudden, invisible barrier. They rattled to the cave floor.

"Save them for the cleansing army," Urza advised. "Like it or not, I am your ally against them. I am going within to take with me any who wish to escape to a new place." He retreated quickly down the passage while the sentinels stared, stunned, after him.

One of them, a young angel warrior, rose on her wings and followed. Urza sped away from her. She shouted in his wake.

"Who are you?"

"I am Urza, the planeswalker." The broadening cave walls picked up the announcement, bearing it inward to the people clustered about fires there. Without pause, Urza continued his oration, "The armies of Radiant are coming. They will kill anyone they can find in this place. Any who wish to escape, gather here beside me."

His summons was met with only dull stares.

"There is no time. If you would live, gather here."

Though most of the folk beside the fires—grimy men and women and dispirited angels—stayed where they were, a few young folk rose tentatively and made their way toward Urza. Behind him, several metallic thuds sounded, and then came the distant roar of warriors charging. More of the cavern's inhabitants gathered to the stranger's side, a group of nearly twenty. Flashes and shrieks sounded from the mouth of the cave. Now no one remained by the fires, either fleeing to Urza or fleeing away to the dens carved into the rock off the main hall.

"Those who will not come," Urza shouted out as he focused his mind on the coming planeswalk, "if you survive, get yourself to the colony farthest from the palace—the Arizon colony on the aerial island called Jabboc. I will return there in two weeks' time to save you and anyone else you can bring with you."

Gesturing the fearful, starving mob into a tight cluster, Urza extended his consciousness to surround them. Just as the air began to flare and spark with lightning, Urza folded them into two dimensions and 'walked with them from the world.

Radiant sat on her throne at the height of the aviary. In the last few weeks, it had become a much more soothing place.

When Urza had joined the rebel cause, Gorig at last convinced Radiant to fortify the aviary. She let him surround the glass tower in a web of steel grills. That measure did not satisfy Gorig though. He pointed out that any flying creature with a crossbow could slay her on her throne by sending a bolt through the glass. Radiant relented. She allowed Gorig to fasten thick plates of steel atop the grillwork. Of course the aviary grew dark. The plants died. The birds fell into an unnatural slumber from which they never awakened. The place became cold and dank, but at least it was safe—except for those cursed windows and their violent images. Last of all, Gorig had convinced Radiant to let him dispel the far-seeing enchantments and convert all the panes in the aviary into mirrors.

Now Radiant sat in a dark and safe aviary. The only light came from her glowing presence. The mirrors all around her shimmered with her image. For the first time in centuries, she felt at home on the throne of Serra. Here she sat, searching the eyes of a multitude, the eyes of Radiant.

"Lady Radiant," came a voice from below. It was Gorig. He had emerged on his audience platform. The whine of servos told that he yet wore his battle armor. There was another sound, too, the untidy whisper of a large and heavy bag being drawn along marble. "I have something to show you. Something that will please you very much."

"Not now, Gorig," the angel said distractedly. "I am seeing the future. I am gazing into my own eyes."

His voice was impatient but as sly as a serpent. "Look down for a moment and you will see the future."

"No. The future is here. It is in my eyes. That's where Urza Planeswalker will find his fate. He will look into my eyes. This war will come down to us. I will fight him myself. He will look into my eyes and see the beauty there and remember what this place was when Serra sat this throne, what this place was before he brought death here—"

"We had a successful harvest today—"

"I will look into his eyes and understand at last what madness makes a man bring devils to heaven and then return to aid them."

Gorig's voice was suddenly hesitant. "I would advise you not to look directly into the eyes of Urza Planeswalker, my lady. They are unnatural things—like the eyes of a bug. They will only hypnotize you."

"No, Gorig," Radiant said with a bitter smile. "I will look into his eyes, and he into mine, and we'll know which of us is right and which of us is mad."

"Please, dear lady," begged Gorig. "forget about Urza for a moment. Look down and see what I have brought you." His entreaty was followed by a clattering sound, as though the bag he dragged disgorged hundreds of large wooden balls.

Her curiosity piqued, Radiant at last glanced down. Her eyes lit with delight. "Oh, heads! There must be two hundred heads! Oh, how beautiful, Gorig. How beautiful!"

Monologue

In the last three weeks, Urza has gotten four hundred and twenty-three refugees out of Serra's Realm. He estimates that at least that number has been slaughtered by Radiant's cleansing army.

He also believes each of his intrusions into the embattled plane only accelerates Radiant's genocidal war. All of the large concentrations of refugees have been harvested—aside from the Arizon colony on Jabboc. It holds thousands.

For them, there is only one hope—the airship. Once it is fully operational, it should be able to hold most of the remaining Serran "rebels." The trouble is, the vessel will be fully operational only when we find the soul battery.

Urza still hasn't located it. He has searched Gorig's private chambers. He has penetrated the deepest vaults in the palace. He has fought his way into and out of the best-defended sections of the realm. Still, nothing.

On one of his journeys, Urza was forced into a showdown with an angel contingent. After the smoke had cleared and the bodies had fallen to dust, he recovered twelve mana-charged soul torches. A week's study, night and day, revealed the trick of them. They held enough white mana to provisionally charge the ship's powerstone. We estimate the vessel will be able to fly, planeshift once, fire a few bolts from the deck-mounted energy ports, and maneuver to the refugee encampment.

The twelve emptied torches are now mounted along the lines of the hull, power conduits running from them to the core of the ship. Urza hopes they will draw enough white mana from the air of Serra's Realm to recharge the stone for another planeshift—with the refugees aboard. The power will not last, of course. We need the soul battery to permanently charge the stone. But Urza is less concerned about completing his airship than he is about rescuing refugees.

He acts as though these folk are modern-day ambassadors representing the bygone thousands killed in his wars. Perhaps they are. Perhaps in saving them, he is saving himself.

—Barrin, Mage Master of Tolaria

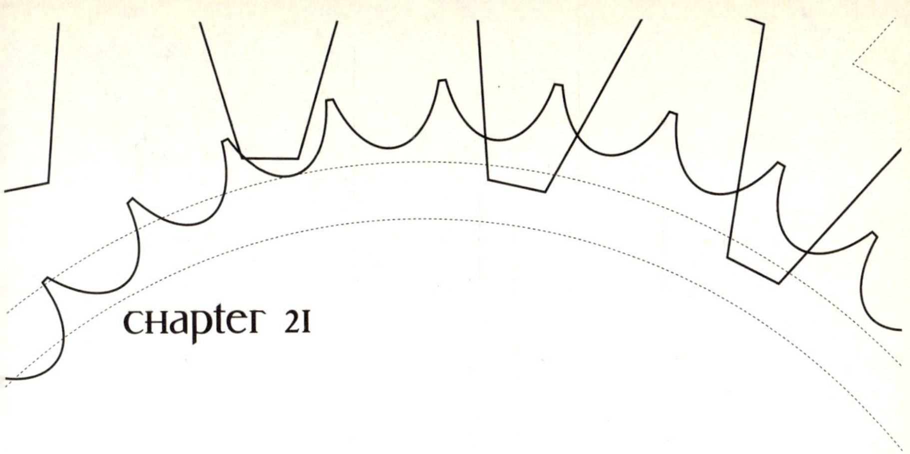

Chapter 21

The day of launch had arrived. A great crowd filled the Tolarian glade—student and scholar, elf and artifact engine, Viashino and goblin, angel and human. Half of them were refugees from Serra's Realm. They pinned all their hopes on the rescue force at the center of the glade. The other half of the crowd had worked for years to assemble that force. Now the work was done. All that remained was to wait and watch. The crowd pressed inward, just out of reach of the war-barded drakes but as close as they could get to the great skyship.

Aboard the vessel, Master of Engines Karn made his rounds in preparation for launch. He peered down into the open hatch.

Artifact creatures clustered in the hold, shoulder to shoulder—two hundred runners, twelve pumas, two hundred scorpions, and a hundred modified Yotian warriors. These creatures formed the planetary defenses meant to guard the refugees as they boarded the ship. The mechanical men shifted in the close quarters, some of them packed so tightly they could not stand. There would be no room for them on the return trip, Karn knew. They would be left behind to be blasted into nothing, or captured and dissected and melted down. Barrin seemed impressed by Urza's willingness to sacrifice the artifact creatures, speaking of Urza's newfound humanity. Karn felt only saddened by it.

Disintegration.

He drew the hatch closed over the main hold and turned away, striding across the narrow deck to the roosts where three hundred falcon engines awaited release. They would perform a new task, providing aerial cover for the fleeing refugees. In addition to this function, they would home in on Phyrexian blood, impaling themselves in any target, and shredding the creature from the inside out. They would also fight any foes that threatened the refugees. Just in case the falcons did not purge the plane, Urza had filled bombards with modified spider capsules, which would resonate in the presence of strong white-mana sources.

He spoke of saving the refugees and cleansing the plane.

Of course, Karn thought darkly, neither the falcons nor the spiders would be returning either.

He moved along the gunwale toward the first bank of fog-cutting lanterns along the bow. They were fitted with focusing lenses and parabolas that rendered their light into powerful beams. In tests, these ray weapons could ignite clothing from two thousand feet away, could make deadfalls burst into flame, and could etch stone. The lantern crews were goblins, selected due to their familiarity with the Thran ray technology used in the crystal forge. Terd and a pair of gray, stumpy Grabbits manned the lantern Karn checked over.

"Everything in order here, Master," Terd declared with a salute snapped so rapidly that his fingertips left welts on his forehead.

Karn only nodded, continuing his inspection of the device. "The sighting mechanism is dirty."

Eyes widened into saucers on Terd's face. In a gibbering tongue, he upbraided his companions. He stomped on one's foot and twisted the other's ear before returning his attention to Karn. A toothy grin crossed his lips.

"It so clean, you see your face in it—" the thought shimmering in his eyes grew a bit cloudy. He blinked uncomfortably "—or not. We not shine ray at your face. You shiny enough, it bounce off anyway! 'Course, it then kill everybody else. We not shine at your face. Malzra say angels got shiny faces, too. We shoot for whites of eyes. Wait, we not see whites of eyes—"

Karn left the creature in midsentence, following the rail to the glasspitter—an invention of Jhoira's. She had been inspired one day by the deadly sprays of molten metal that occurred when water dropped into a blast furnace. The bombards hurled spheres of glass-covered energy among enemies. Where the balls burst, melted shrapnel was flung outward. Her design was finished and presented to Urza before she had fully thought through the lethal consequences. Before she would allow the devices to be built, she made Urza promise they would be used only against dire and deserving foes. She got her wish—and command of the flying ship.

Even now, Jhoira crouched in the prow beside the ship's final ranged weapon—an acid atomizer. The device used an unstable energy field to disperse a caustic spray among foes. Karn approached her.

"Is the atomizer in working order, Captain?" Karn asked.

Jhoira startled. She stared at Karn, blinking stupidly for a moment before shaking the visions from her eyes. "Sorry, I was just mentally preparing for the coming battle. What were you saying?"

"The acid atomizer, Captain," Karn repeated, "is it ready?"

Jhoira nodded, crossing arms over her chest. "Yeah, but don't call me captain. Call me Jhoira. Just because I've been given command of this vessel and crew doesn't make me a captain. As for the atomizer—the fog from this thing will be as destructive as a blast of the fire drakes' breath."

They both reflexively cast glances toward Gherridarigaaz and Rhammidarigaaz, positioned on either side of the long, sleek ship. The fire drakes would provide an aerial defense of the ship and the refugees. The beasts would be planeswalked into Serra's Realm by Urza himself.

Just now, Urza was to starboard tightening saddle straps on the ancient drake dam. To port, Barrin packed wands and tomes into the saddle bags of the young dragon. Though Jhoira was in charge of the ship, Urza and Barrin would direct the entire operation, employing an arsenal of white-mana spells from the backs of the fire drakes.

Urza even then stood in the drake saddle and made a gesture to silence the buzzing crowds. "They will call us invaders," Urza said, his voice amplified by a quick spell from the mage master. "They will call us invaders, just as they have called their own citizens traitors. They have even called us Phyrexians, so powerful is the web of delusion that traps them. We will not listen to what they call us. We will listen to what history calls us. We will save them despite themselves."

A mild ovation answered these words.

"We are not invaders. We are defenders. We are the alliance of Dominaria. We are human and divine, Viashino and goblin. We are builders and enchanters. We are the power of the forest and of the sea, of the mountains and of life itself. We have cleansed our own island of Phyrexian hordes, and we will cleanse Serra's Realm as well. But, most of all, we will return, and bring with us the rest of her refugees, a new army of allies."

A roar of joy began among the humans and angels gathered there. It swept through the ranks of lizard men and goblins, elves and artifact creatures, students and scholars, until the very forests and oceans echoed the shout.

As the sound mounted up, Jhoira nodded to Karn. "Initiate the startup sequence, Master of Engines."

"Aye, Captain," Karn replied.

He crossed the narrow deck to reach the bulkhead where stairs descended into the hull of the ship. In moments, he had reached the engine room. Diago Deerv and three other red-scaled Viashino came to awkward attention as Karn entered.

"Initiate startup sequence," the silver man ordered.

The Viashino snapped salutes and scrambled to their posts. Switches were flipped, levers adjusted, and gyros set into motion. Groans came from the massive engine. A chatter of commands and verifications arose among the lizard men.

Karn meanwhile moved to the center of the curved console bank, beneath an ornate speaking tube that led directly to the bridge. Before him, a pair of deep ports delved into the inner reaches of the engine. Karn inserted his hands into the holes, feeling for the twin bars at their bases. He found them and clasped his hands. When turned, the rods would trigger the engine's start up.

"Open the superfluid manifold," Karn ordered.

He pivoted both handles inward, and felt the mechanisms engage and lock. A great warmth was abruptly born within the engine. In moments, it had drowned out the ovation outside.

Before Karn could withdraw his arms, bracers emerged from deep within the machine and fastened over his wrists. Small wire probes slid smoothly into the joints in his knuckles. Magnificent surges of energy prickled along his hands. Jolts moved up arm and shoulder conduits, converged in the silver man's chest, and fountained into the powerstone at the center of his head.

Suddenly Karn could sense the green superfluids coursing through the great engine block before him. He could feel the warm bath sluice around the glimmering powerstone at the heart of the machine. He could see out the fog-lanterns of the ship, fore and aft, starboard and port. He could kinesthetically sense the weight and alignment of the ship's hull, its sails, its lines, even its young, strong captain as she stood at the ship's wheel. The airship had become a second body for him. Its engines and controls and defenses were suddenly his own.

Integration.

To welling cheers, Karn lifted the great skyship into the air. It rose amid the red-flapping wings of the fire drakes. It ascended into the bright skies over Tolaria, the bright skies of Dominaria.

Jhoira felt small and overawed as she stood on the bridge of the airship. As yet, there was no need to steer. The vessel was merely rising into the blue Tolarian sky. Not until it made headway would the warping of sails and the bending of airfoils make any difference at all to the craft's movement. But clutching the wheel now made a definite difference to Jhoira's position: it allowed her to stay standing.

Beneath her feet, enormous, hot engines labored. They dragged into clear air a payload of five hundred war engines and a crew of thirty. She tried to forget that the fully loaded ship weighed four thousand tons. She tried to forget that this was the vessel's first time aloft—its shakedown cruise. She tried to forget that she would be sailing this vessel into a war with angels.

Something huge and red arced with sudden violence above the ship's rail and then disappeared again. It returned, a leathery mountain, translucent—the bones of a great drake visible through it. The wing dipped a second time. When it reappeared, it brought the red-mantled head of Gherridarigaaz above the rail. A gray snort escaped one craggy nostril as the she-drake pulled herself higher into the sky. Urza, standing in his saddle, lurched into view. He held something in his hand, something that looked like a club but sparkled like a wand. His face was clenched with effort, and he drove the drake toward the prow of the ship.

Something is wrong, Jhoira thought, clinging to the wheel. Something has come loose—or something that was supposed to come loose hasn't.

Gherridarigaaz surged toward the bow of the ship. Urza leaned so far in the saddle he appeared in danger of falling. He swung the shimmering club at something clinging to the prow. A dull thud sounded, and then a wet shattering sound.

"I name thee, *Weatherlight*," Urza declared, holding aloft the fragmented neck of the bottle. His mount soared away over windswept treetops.

Jhoira laughed. There was no monster, nothing amiss. The planeswalker was merely blessing and naming the boat on its maiden voyage. Jhoira felt the weight of dread and impossible futures sag away from her and drop among the rattling leaves below. She laughed.

"Full ahead! Follow that drake," the first captain of *Weatherlight* commanded.

Gherridarigaaz darted out over the forests of Tolaria. Rhammidarigaaz slid into her wake. *Weatherlight* followed them both. Wind coursed over the prow and back to reach Jhoira. She drew the fresh air into her lungs and remembered another place she used to stand—at the edge of her world. She remembered an earlier time, when young courage filled her heart and she dreamed of a soul mate. The man had never arrived, but she had lived a full life without him, and now, young courage poured again into her heart.

Gherridarigaaz was merely a crimson jag on the horizon. Rhammidarigaaz was just behind her. *Weatherlight* gained on them both. The helm had grown active in Jhoira's grip, tugging at her the way an eager horse pulls at the rein. She returned its forceful play, holding the ship against cross winds.

"Trim the sails," Jhoira commanded the human crew. They scampered to cleats and drew on lines. "Reconfigure the port and starboard fans into airfoils." More workers clambered onto the lateral rigs to rework the canvas.

With each tug on slack lines and each shift of sail, the ship gained speed. It coursed above the green sea of trees with greater velocity than any water-bound craft. A turgid wake of tossing tree-tops spread out aft. The wind washing over the deck threatened to blow the lighter crew members overboard. Terd and his diminutive comrades hunkered down beside the rail. Lines throughout the rig hummed in the bluster. The ship's hull creaked as it eased itself into the stresses of its new orientation.

Jhoira smiled. She had almost caught up to Urza and Barrin. At the shoreline of Tolaria, the drake riders nudged their steeds to match the ship's speed. Gherridarigaaz and Rhammidarigaaz flew wing and wing. Churning storms of air spread in twin cones behind them. Jhoira steered the ship past the shore and into the twin gales. Wind lashed brutally across the deck.

"Hang on!" Jhoira shouted to her crew. "We will slow once we enter Serra's Realm."

Until that time, they had to fly in close formation. Urza's planeshift would barely encompass both drakes, and it could be tracked by *Weatherlight's* apparatus only if the field effects overlapped. Whitecaps thundered below, and gray cumulus clouds thundered above. The very air seemed to turn solid, tearing at sail-cloth and hemp, wooden hull and metal fittings. It clawed also at the captain at her wheel, but now she felt only exhilaration.

A bubble of magical might swelled out from Urza. In a heartbeat, it stretched to encompass both drakes. Already they shimmered, punching into the portal.

"Planeshift!" shouted Jhoira.

Another bubble welled up from the heart of the ship itself. The curtain of magic cracked out, whiplike, and dimmed sea and sky. Blue Dominaria glimmered for one tiny moment more, and then it was gone. The roar went with it. Black chaos swept in to displace all. Beyond the ship's rails lay only a churning world of emptiness, and the laboring wings of two great drakes.

And then blue and black both were gone. In their place came a vast skyscape of tinged light, sulfuric cloud, and troubled, tumbled chunks of land.

"Serra's Realm," Jhoira said into the sudden roar of wind, the edge of Serra's Realm. She reached down to a slot in the deck and drew forth a glass-encased map of the Jumbles. The cartography was unmistakably Urza's—detailed, turbulent, overworked. It showed three landmark isles. One was pear-shaped, and it tumbled in rapid succession. Another was long and flat like a great stone knife. The third, lying just beneath the descending brow of sky at the utter edge of Serra's Realm, was the rock called Jabboc.

There, on that distant and broken world, in a colony called Arizon, waited a thousand souls.

"Start a rapid swing round to starboard on heading ninety-five, three twenty-eight, eight. We're heading for Jabboc." Steersmen trimmed in the airfoils and Karn, below, channeled what remained of the ship's power into the banking descent. "Release spider bombards from alternate sides every thirty seconds beginning on my mark." The bombard crews scrambled to load their first salvos.

Meanwhile, Terd clambered up the ladder to the main deck and grabbed at Jhoira's sleeve. "They are here already, Lady. Lightning bugs!"

Jhoira peered out along the line of the goblin's gnarled finger. To port, she glimpsed a beautiful and terrible sight. Glimmering in air like gold dust, were the cleansing armies of Radiant.

"Mark!"

"They've released the first spider bombard," shouted Barrin. He brought Rhammidarigaaz through a sweeping turn to the flank of Urza.

"Good," Urza called back from atop Gherridarigaaz. "We'll know who we're fighting." He looked to his left, where the cleansing army of Radiant swarmed, their wings making a distant drone in the air.

"How many do you think there are?"

"Hundreds," Urza called back, "perhaps thousands. We will need every advantage."

Urza flung out his hands, drawing to himself the white mana of the many places he had traveled in the realm. He fueled a pair of powerful spells. White lightning crackled out from his fingers and spread across the two drakes, feathering around them in a thousand leaping lines. Power surged through them. The enchantment made scales seem gossamer feathers, made red mantles seem rainbowed coronas. There was a sudden glorious aspect laid on the beasts. They were transformed into divine figures, terrifying in their beauty and power. With another gathering of white-mana magic, Urza cast a scintillating aura around each rider, a whirling circle of what appeared to be snow.

"That will protect us from white-mana spells or creatures," Urza explained.

Barrin, unfamiliar with the realm, drew on blue magic instead of white. He summoned a pair of Tolarian drakes. Giant kin of fire drakes, these two dragons had skin as smooth and translucent as reef water. Their wings flashed blue against the yellowing clouds. Their spiky manes, as barbed as tridents, oscillated in the roaring wind. Barrin reached into the core of his memory, tapping memories of the forests of Tolaria. He thought of Jhoira's Angelwood and the Western Reaches and the many fast-time subarctic scrub forests, and cast an enchantment on the two creatures. Green scales sprouted across the backs and bellies of the summoned drakes, providing them additional protection against attacks, magical or mundane.

"Impressive," shouted Urza over the growing buzz of angel wings approaching.

"I have a leviathan up my sleeve, if things get really desperate, though summoning it would tax my every reserve."

There was no time for more discussion. The approaching army's drone had become a roar. They grew from golden motes into arrows of flame.

The angel army of Radiant arrived.

They soared in with the speed of falcons. Two score archangels led the vanguard, each bearing a magna sword, broad as an axe but long as a lance. The archangels came in a vertical circle and held their blades inward like a ring of fangs. Behind them, forming a lethal gullet, were hundreds of angel warriors bearing lances. A great leviathan in its own right, the cleansing army of Radiant opened its toothy maw to swallow the drakes and their riders.

"I'll meet you on the other side!" Urza yelled as he plunged into the hailstorm of white fangs and silver masks and flashing steel.

The other side of what? Barrin wondered.

The angel thicket closed around him.

Magna swords struck the tip of the fire drake's pale muzzle and sparked along its scaly neck. The enchantments held, repelling steel. Even so, the blades converged, tracing their way toward the rider.

Barrin yanked hard on the drake's rein. Rhammidarigaaz curved broadside to the speeding angels. His leeward flank arched away from attack, and his windward flank became an impenetrable wall against which archangels and angels smashed in bloody wreck. Barrin urged Rhammidarigaaz back into his charge. The beast surged his wings, flinging loose a pair of angels who had swarmed up behind him, and vaulted deeper into the throat of the attack. He breathed a great gout of fiery breath into the onslaught, and angels fell from the sky like burning pigeons. Rhammidarigaaz plowed into the vacated space.

The dragon's side was dotted with blood, most of it angelic, though there were a few long wounds where swords had broken through the enchantments. Instantly, Barrin cast a healing spell on the drake, and the gory gashes along his sides, knitted together with threads of white energy.

Another blast of fire emerged from the beast. More angels tumbled in black smoke and melted quill. Silver masks cleaved to screaming faces. Magna swords fused with skeletons.

Distant in the fight, the flames of Gherridarigaaz carved an equally hellish swath through the swarm of angels.

The blue drakes fared less well. Their steam breath killed many, but the press of bodies and the hack of swords ripped the creatures to rags. A bolt of healing radiance leapt from Urza toward the beleaguered Tolarian drakes, but another sorcery, cast by an archangel warrior, deflected the spell en route.

Barrin was beginning his own healing enchantment when an angel choir shrieked down upon him and laid to with swords. A familiar sorcery leapt from his fingertips. The kindled fire arced across the pitching air into the face of an angel warrior, waking flames in her mouth and eyes. He unleashed a second spell of the same kind, drawing additional power from the first. A third conflagration blazed out to strike an archangel, blasting a hole through its armor and out the other side. Three bodies tumbled away, but twenty more clung to the drake's back and attacked with swords and barbed whips.

Massive blades descended. They struck Barrin in head, neck, belly, and back. Magna swords rebounded from his enchanted flesh as though they had struck stone.

Barrin sent Rhammidarigaaz into a sudden dive, flinging free the attackers and bringing the beast's fire breath against new clouds of the foe. Exhilaration moved through the Mage Master of Tolaria—until he saw the bleeding hulks of the Tolarian drakes.

They were below and behind, their carapace enchantments dispelled, and their blue hides marked with gashes as numerous and ominous as hieroglyphics. The killer angels still clung to the beasts, maggots on dead corpses, until their wings at last gave out. In quick succession, the summoned beasts dropped from the sky. Angels peeled themselves from the falling forms.

Chastened, Barrin brought Rhammidarigaaz soaring back into the fray, fiery breath and steel-hard wings slaying angels in their hundreds. The master mage cast sorceries, death blossoming all around him. He would kill as many as he could as quickly as he could, hoping to keep them from the refugees.

Suddenly, black and grotesque in the midst of that angel throng, there came a beast that could win right past Barrin's white mana protections. Bewinged, befanged, and Phyrexian, the monster dropped like night from the sky onto Rhammidarigaaz's neck. It reared up, and Barrin recognized the lemon-wedge eyes Urza had described.

The man otherwise was utterly transformed—his figure hulking and muscular, fitted with countless implants and weapons—halberd arms and dagger-tipped feet and scythes at the elbows. The greatest weapon of all, though, was built right into the beast's torso—a black manifold that blazed in twelve places with the white-blue fires of soul-stealers. He drew white mana into his very being, storing it, harnessing part of it to transform himself. He grew more powerful with every creature he killed.

Gorig *was* the mana battery.

Barrin had time to see no more. Gorig lunged atop him.

Karn felt *Weatherlight's* fading power as a torpor in his own frame. The soul torches weren't gathering enough white mana from the surrounding air to recharge the stone. It only glimmered weakly within its superfluid bath. The ship had enough energy to fly, perhaps enough for a few brief bursts from its ray weapons, but the vessel would not planeshift again.

"We'll need more torches, Jhoira," he called into the speaking tube over his head. The sound of his voice was empty and weary, made doubly so by the metal pipe work. "Just to carry the refugees away, we'll need power from more torches."

"Aye," came the clipped reply from above. "Prepare for landing."

Below the ship—Karn still saw all the world through the ray weapons at bow and stern—the aerial island called Jabboc floated black and forbidding against the descending dome of Serra's Realm. It was a dark place. The eternal light of Serra was failing in these reaches. The life-giving air was thin and tainted. The very edge of the plane hovered only a scant mile beyond the black rock. In everchanging array, its frayed fabric showed the gray chaos that lay between worlds.

"Reduce speed," Jhoira's order came.

Gratefully, Karn scaled back the power flow from the tepid crystal.

"Decrease altitude."

Sails shifted, the prow rose just slightly, and the ship's keel eased downward. The massive aerial island swelled to fill Karn's field of vision. He saw there a twilight roil of hills and rocks. Dead fields lay gray within the perpetual murk. Tangled trees stood in dead woods across the isle. It seemed Hades or Sheol, a place of shadows, sunless land of the dead.

"Lanterns ahoy! Bring the ship to ground beside those lights."

Through the eyes of the ship. Karn saw the flickering glow of lanterns, oil and wick pushing back the darkness. The tepid light traced out arches against the dark—the entry to the Arizon colony. Light reflected in tiny gleams from something clustered within. They seemed almost wasp eggs, piled inside the mud-daubers' nest, but with a certain wonder and dread, Karn realized what they were—

Faces, thousands of faces—waiting and hoping for salvation.

Karn drew upon the strength of his own power matrix to bear the ship across the cold reaches before the cave. A black vale below led past a field of rubble and a forest deadfall. The *Weatherlight* nosed through the tangle of trees and to the flat plain, just below the cave. Landing spines emerged from the lower sweep of the hull. Easing the ship slowly down. Karn felt in his own being the vast shudder of the hull settling.

"Open hatches! Release falcons! Deploy runners and pumas and scorpions! Ready cargo holds! Ready ray weapons!" There was a new urgency in Jhoira's voice.

When Karn peered through the stern lanterns, he saw why.

Angel armies descended on them in a golden cyclone.

Urza stood in Gherridarigaaz's saddle. The Tolarian drakes had plunged out of the battle there, where the swarm was thinnest. They had tumbled away into the gray-blue depths and, some mile below, flashed out of existence entirely.

Only a mile below . . .

The plane had shrunk considerably before their arrival, but it was dissipating even more quickly now. Urza drew hard on the reins, sending Gherridarigaaz into a blistering attack. Angels tumbled from the dragon's blazing onslaught, white and inconsequential like popped maize from a steaming kettle. They, too, dropped away and disappeared in the ever-nearer edge of the world.

With every angel death, the plane was collapsing. The more fiercely the drakes battled the main army, the less time any of them had. Soon the mana depletion would reach a critical threshold, and then the collapse would take only moments. Any living thing left in the plane would be destroyed.

"Hold fire!" Urza commanded the drake. He reined her in a huge circle. "To Rhammidarigaaz, to Barrin!"

The dragon entered a shallow dive that would speed her toward her son and his rider. Angels flung themselves in dense clouds about her, but she held back her killing breath. Magna swords shrieked across her armored hide. Some bit through the enchantments and sliced open long rents. Urza's magic healed them even as they formed, letting not a whisper of air spill from the drake's wings.

Even so, agony won through. Gherridarigaaz roared, smoke trailing from her jowls. She barely contained the fires that ached to spew forth. She focused her fury instead on the battle ahead and on Rhammidarigaaz caught in it. Another three surges of wing brought her to soar just beneath him.

Urza shouted toward Barrin, saddled above, "Break off! To the *Weatherlight*."

In a flash, they were past. The drake sliced through air and angel both as they made their way along. Air made small booms at the trailing edge of the drake's wings. The thickest swarm of warriors fell away. Gherridarigaaz punched through the final wall of them and shot into the gray spaces beyond. Ahead lay the Jumbles. At its distant end hung a large floating isle, and on it glinted the lights of *Weatherlight.* Those lights were dim beneath the gold and white shimmer of angel warriors and soul torches.

Another army.

Urza urged his mount to greater speed. Even as they closed on Jabboc Isle, he could see the advancing curtain of chaos at the edge of the plane.

There was less time than he had thought.

Jhoira helped a staggering old man into the hold of *Weatherlight.* He was garbed in tatters, his face drawn into a scowl of concentration, his eyes turned down from the loud battle that raged only a thousand yards aft. How anyone survived in the Jumbles was a mystery to Jhoira, let alone how an old, infirm man had. How old had he been when he was cast into that world of flotsam? Perhaps he had lived in the isles for years, perhaps all his life.

"Quickly, please, Grandfather," she urged gently, "and move as far aft as possible."

"Is there sunlight where we are going?' the man asked, tottering a moment on the steps.

"Yes, sunlight, water, forests—everything," Jhoira assured as the man moved forward. She stared across the bow at the snaking column of refugees.

There were too many of them. They were too slow, too weak. Beyond their desperate cave-colony, the crackling wall of chaos verged nearer and nearer. Soon it would not matter that there were too many of them. Soon the edge of the plane would begin its disintegrating march across the isle.

Matters aft were just as grim. The falcon engines fought fiercely, dropping angels from air atop the front line of ground combat. The ranks of runners thinned, their crossbow quarrels already spent, their scythe blades snapping out to trap their foes. Orange explosions crackled out along the line. Clutched together, angels and machines both blazed into nothing.

Soul torches fell to ground at the front and crackled and spat, absorbing the hundreds of souls that perished there. The infernal devices blazed, white hot.

The mathematics was against Jhoira. Even if each machine destroyed one warrior with its blast, Radiant could overrun them with hundreds more.

"Karn, can you muster enough power to use the ray weapons?" Jhoira called.

The answer sounded dour and hollow. "I have barely enough power to lift off."

Jhoira stared at the infernal line of battle and considered. She had been told, as commander of the ship, she was not to leave it, but if she didn't, there might well not be a ship to leave. They needed to charge the stone, and only a thousand feet away, power lay sparking and crackling.

"I'm going to get some torches," Jhoira told Karn, her voice hushed. "I'll bring back as many as I can carry."

Karn's response was slow—too slow—but Jhoira did not need to hear it to know what it was. He as much as forbade his captain.

It is mutiny, pure and simple, thought Jhoira ironically as she dropped amid the lines of scorpion engines, marching into oblivion.

A scraggly figure leapt from the rail to land at her side. "You need fighters, I think," Terd said, matching her stride for stride.

"You're right," said Jhoira kindly.

"The more torches, the better," added another familiar voice. Diago Deerv blinked placidly at their looks of surprise. "After all, my folk built half this ship."

Side by side, the woman, the goblin, and the lizard man waded forward through the press of metal, heading toward the burning front.

The Phyrexian smashed atop Barrin, breaking ribs and flinging the man from his drake saddle. The Mage Master of Tolaria tumbled across the dragon's spread wings and fetched up, broken, in the crook of one reptilian elbow. His mind whirled, unable to fasten on anything. Wind roared over him. He clung to the drake's wing, shaking his head to clear it.

Gorig crouched on the saddle, jowls drawn back in a dagger-toothed leer. Long, barbed legs drew up beneath the insectoid creature. The twelve soul-stealing ports along its manifold torso flared in hungry anticipation. Its wings spread outward, and again it lunged.

The first blast of air over Barrin brought with it thought of a spell. He summoned his memories of distant Tolaria and hurled before him a wall of air. The creature smashed heavily against the sudden gale. Gorig roared. It tumbled helplessly backward, away from the mage master and his mount.

Rhammidarigaaz rolled beneath the turbulent barrier. Barrin could only cling raggedly to the drake's wing. Rhammidarigaaz pivoted and soared out from the angel swarm. His fiery breath carved an avenue of soot and burning flesh before them. Barrin could not care. He could only hold on, inching slowly back toward the saddle.

"Urza ordered the retreat," Rhammidarigaaz gasped out between breaths. "*Weatherlight* is under attack."

Barrin nodded dizzily. He clawed his way back to the saddle and clung, gulping ragged breaths.

A ferocious roar came behind them. The bright blaze of the wall of air shattered. Out of the heart of that conflagration came the shrieking Phyrexian. Gorig soared, faster than even the archangels who followed in a shrieking cone behind. Devil and angels alike, every last staff and wing and magna sword was intent on destroying Barrin, Mage Master of Tolaria.

He could not care. He could only hold on and stare at the battle that raged around *Weatherlight*. If he reached Urza, the ship might be saved.

Monologue

Death is not so horrible a thing when one is broken and clinging to the burning back of a fire drake and plunging through a heaven that seems in all ways hell. Death is not so horrible at all.

—Barrin, Mage Master of Tolaria

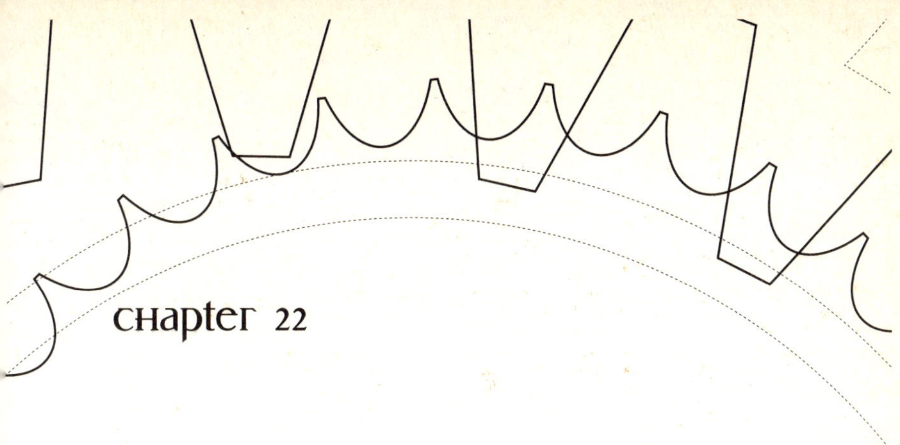

CHAPTER 22

The front lines were thick with angels and scorpion engines, so thick that Jhoira had to battle her own forces to reach it. From behind she grabbed a scorpion's stinger and let the darting tail fling her up onto its back of metal carapace. She caught a foothold and sent her sword swinging into the epaulet of the angel warrior before it.

The creature was fast. His soul torch clattered up and hurled her blade to one side. He followed the stroke with a dagger slash. Jhoira reared back from the strike. She kicked the creature's dagger hand, spinning him to one side, and stabbed with her sword. The angel grasped his side and whirled. The soul torch swung in a blaze toward Jhoira's face. She staggered, trying to bring her sword to bear, but she was too slow. With a white-blue sizzle, the torch impacted. Jhoira instinctively crumpled atop the scorpion's back and cradled her face, expecting to find only charred tatters of flesh. Her skin was whole and healthy.

The torch had impacted the scorpion's intervening stinger. The metal tail thrust back the magic brand. It slid from the angel's grasp and toppled. The sizzling tip of it fell against the wound in the angel's side. In a white-blue flash, the creature's soul was sucked away. Lifeless, the angel collapsed. The torch flared.

Jhoira scrabbled across the scorpion's back and snatched up the torch. She lifted it, just in time. The brand blocked a descending magna sword. The broad blade clattered aside and sliced deep into the scorpion's back plate. Jhoira rose. An archangel towered over her, struggling to wrench its magna sword from the collapsing scorpion. She rammed the white-hot tip of the torch up beneath the archangel's silver mask, catching it in the fold between throat and jaw.

The archangel shuddered, caught between a snagged blade and an incandescent death. Then, in a terrific clamor of wings and armor, the creature convulsed its life away. The torch shuddered and trembled as it drew in the powerful being's life-force. Jhoira gritted her teeth in determination to hold on to the too-hot handle. A roar erupted, fury and agony embodied, and death clutched the archangel. Its own soul torch dropped, and Jhoira let go of her dagger to catch it. Meanwhile the angel toppled back, a great tree falling in a forest. Its wings cleared a broad path beneath it.

As Jhoira caught her breath, she saw Terd scurry out upon that fallen giant and snatch up three more torches lying among the angel dead. They were overflowing with power, having drawn into themselves the souls of hundreds of warriors. Terd used the ragged end of his tunic as a hot pad to grab the torches. He scuttled back just as another angel descended to strike him down. One wave of the three sputtering brands pushed the creature back among its cohorts.

Jhoira grabbed Terd's collar and hauled him away from the front.

In his turn, Diago caught Jhoira's collar and hauled her back. Moments later, a fireball struck the spot where she and Terd had been, driving the destroyed scorpion into a blackened crater.

"I have two torches," Diago gasped out as he drew back his comrades in retreat. The lizard-man's scales stood on end in the heat of battle. "You have two torches, and the goblin has three. That should be enough. We have to get back to the ship."

"Yes," Jhoira agreed, breathless from fighting and from holding onto the cometary torches. "Back to the ship. . . . This will be enough to get us flying . . . shoot some deadly shots. . . . Maybe even to planeshift."

Jhoira looked toward the ship. It was a carnival-lit hulk on the hillside, beside the glowering caverns of Arizon and the black masses of refugees, crowding into the ship. Behind that tableaux, the curtain of chaos gnawed at the edge of Jabboc Isle.

"Maybe even to planeshift. . . ."

"Cease this battle!" Urza cried imperiously. His figure blazed with light aback Gherridarigaaz. Dragon and rider descended in a column of mana energy before the storm of angels and falcons.

"Cease this battle or be destroyed! I am Urza Planeswalker!"

"Tremble before him!" came a voice in mocking answer from among the angel horde.

Radiant emerged. Her figure was lit with an incandescent heat equal to Urza's. A group of archangels accompanied her, four before, four behind, and four more around the ruler of the realm. Her appearance brought a sudden hush to the battle lines. She was strange-eyed, beautiful, and terrifying.

"Tremble before this petulant god-child, this despoiler of worlds, destroyer of planes. Urza has come, my children, and when Urza comes, death always follows."

"I have come to take you out of death. I have come only to carry away those I call refugees, those you call refuse," Urza shouted from the hovering drake. "Let us leave in peace, and we shall kill no more."

"It is too late for bargains. Your war is collapsing our plane around us." She gestured with her war staff toward the advancing curtain of chaos. "You come first bringing Phyrexia, and you come last bringing destruction."

Urza lifted his own battle staff. "Forgive, fair lady. I brought Phyrexia here, true, but you have given it a home in your war minister, Gorig, and throughout your court. The very spells you created to drive the stink of Phyrexia from your palace are the spells that allowed Phyrexia to dwell there and surround you and turn you against your own people. Your plane shrinks not because of me, but because of these soul torches of yours, harvesting the life of your people, your plane, for Phyrexia. That is why chaos threatens. That is why your plane is dying."

In the echoing stillness of the battle, whining servos and pulsing wing beats gave the air a dead drone. Beyond that sound hovered the approaching rumble of matter giving itself over to chaos.

"Come with us, all of you. Come with us to another world. Come where all who are good can live and where Phyrexians, beneath the Glimmer Moon, will die. Come with us, Radiant. Cease this senseless war, and come with us."

She seemed to consider, her face for a moment lovely amid swirling hair and wings of light. Then she spoke, and death followed her words. "Kill them all. To a man, kill every one!"

Radiant herself made good the command. She hurled a wall of force from outstretched fingers. The vast wave of energy ate the very air. It arced toward Urza, too fast to stop, too huge to escape. It would not kill him, but it would stun him long enough that angelic death could fall on him from the sky.

Gherridarigaaz rose. The ancient fire drake spread her wings in a giant shield before Urza. He had to cling to her back not to be thrown from the vertical saddle.

The blast struck Gherridarigaaz full in the belly and chest. Scale and skin and muscle disintegrated. She dissolved away as though in acid. Ribs hung for a moment, vacant of flesh, and then dripped into white smears. Gherridarigaaz released one last, long wail before lungs and throat and head all were gone. Wings, too, vanished. By the time the wave spent itself, all that remained was spine and shoulder blades and half a pelvis.

She had sacrificed herself. It was the highest honor among lizard folk.

Urza escaped the tangled traces of the saddle just before Gherridarigaaz's remains plunged away. He roared too. He roared as though she were his own mother.

The time of negotiation was done.

The time of moderation and sanity was finished.

The time of killing had come.

Gathering magical might. he hurled himself at the tyrant of heaven.

Radiant was ready. She hung in the skies, savoring this moment. Her eyes gleamed madly in the fray. Lithe hands swept out to her sides and forward, as though in a curtsey. Her fingertips trailed long lines of archangels in their wake. They converged on Urza.

Heedless, he shot toward her. With a thought, his flesh turned adamantine. Magna swords fell in a flurry upon him. Their broad blades rang and clattered. His head smashed them back like a soaring cannonball. What archangels managed to hold onto their blades shuddered in nerveless jangle. Others lost their swords. A few even lost their arms. Urza blasted past them all and ran headlong into Radiant.

A lesser being would have been torn in half by the attack, but Radiant had been waiting for this moment. She dodged back in the instant of impact, grabbed hold of the rocketing planeswalker, and with a surge of her wings, hurled herself along with him. She clawed at his face, seeming surprised at its impenetrable warding. Then, hands soft as silk clutched his sides, and lightning arced from her fingertips. It traced out nerve and muscle and bone, a storm within the planeswalker.

He trembled, enervated. Electricity possessed his every tissue. Aside from spasms, he could not move.

Smiling bitterly, Radiant carried him above the boiling cloud of angels and falcons and into the wheeling heights. "You are not welcome here, Urza, not now, not ever."

Those soft hands turned iron hard. She flung the paralyzed man upward, into the descending ceiling of chaos above the realm. As he went, the last jags of lightning danced across his frame. A white tempest cycloned from her upraised hands. The storm bore him fistlike into the shredding curtain. Urza smashed into the verge. He dissolved away. Chaos grated muscle from bone. He was gone as quickly as Gherridarigaaz had been. The wind dissipated, and Urza Planeswalker was not even a stain on the dark chaos.

Radiant shook her head and brushed her hands off.

Something suddenly was between those hands. Urza took form against her. One hand caught her beneath the jaw. The other arm wrapped her waist. No longer adamantine, those limbs were still implacable, inescapable. He flipped her over and dragged her back down into the roaring battle, down toward the struggling refugees and the battle-torn ship. He forced her to gaze at the sight.

"Look, Radiant. Look who you are killing. Look what you've become."

"I know what I am," she gasped out. "I know what you are too."

She cast a quick series of spells, prepared and laid aside for this very moment. All defenses were stripped from Urza's head. Her fingers grew as long and sharp and curved as daggers. She drove them into his skull. They punched through bone and into his frontal lobe.

Urza roared, reconstituting shattered bone and ruptured brain.

She was not done, though. Her fingers curled into claws. She raked through gray matter and shattered sinuses and optic cavities. She scooped up the gemstones that were his eyes. With a brutal yank, she hauled them forth.

Blind and gaping, his head staved, Urza struggled against tumbling walls of pain.

He clutched to her. She was all that kept him aloft.

He had to heal.

He had to rebuild his being.

He could not. Part of that being—the only part that was not a mere projection of his mind—had been ripped away. Those gems defined him. They were at the heart of the Brothers' War: Mightstone and Weakstone. They had been his eyes since the blast at Argoth. They had been his eyes since he had become a planeswalker. They were at the heart of his madness, his power.

Even in his dying agony—for, yes, he was dying: his power was also his weakness—Urza realized how like Karn he was. They were both defined by stones set in their heads. Both lived with them and died without them. Mightstone and Weakstone—they were Urza's affective and cognitive cortex. Without them, he was destroyed.

Radiant knew it. With relish, she hoisted the gory things overhead, beyond Urza's feeble reach, and she actually laughed. "Gorig had told me about these. He had told me you were like Xantcha. She had had a Phyrexian heart, and you have Phyrexian eyes. I told Gorig I needed only look into these eyes to know that you were mad, that I was right. Yes. This is my moment of triumph. I've found the Phyrexian in my realm, Urza. I've found the Phyrexian, and it is you."

She smiled, a faint and wicked thing that Urza could no longer see.

"I've won, madman," Radiant said, staring into the glimmering crystals. In their bloody facets, the battle below played itself out. "My work is done, Gorig will finish off your forces and our rebels. He will cleanse the realm. That is his job. He will even capture your ship—what a curiosity! And with these powerstones—the Eyes of Urza—I will restore my heaven." A thought occurred to her. "Funny that you tried to destroy my world to charge a powerstone, but in the end it is your powerstone that will save it." She glanced down at the convulsing body of Urza, clinging to her in its death throes. "I rather like whispering these things into your dying ears. Perhaps I will take you with me. Yes, no better way to assure you are dead."

So saying, she cast a final spell and disappeared from the decaying heights of her plane. She took with her the Mightstone and Weakstone and the dying body of the planeswalker.

Before *Weatherlight's* bow roared a wall of absolute destruction. Entropy ground rock and grass and tree to nothing, nothing at all. Behind the ship's stem roared another wall—angels turned demonic, rending the machines thrown hopelessly against them. Both walls advanced, closing in on the ship and her overflowing hold.

"There's no more room!" shouted Terd from the hatch. His webbed foot stomped on the shoulder of one refugee as if he could pack them more tightly.

"Then let them stand on deck," Jhoira replied testily.

She lifted the third soul torch over the exposed conduit. They'd had to tear up planks beside the wheel to find where the lines of power descended to the crystal. The ship had shuddered with each stripped board, as though it felt the wound in its very being. Beneath the planking ran a channel of metal sinews, like an exposed nerve bundle. It led down to the powerstone in the core of the engine. Taking a deep breath, Jhoira lowered the sizzling torch so that its butt contacted the conduit. With a lightning jolt, the torch emptied its charge, and the tip of it went black.

"How is that?" Jhoira called down the speaking tube to Karn.

"Better," came the metallic reply. "Almost enough to lift off. We'll be top heavy. We'll need more power to keep the ship upright. How many more?"

"Two more torches," Jhoira said, casting the emptied one aside and lifting another.

"No, how many more refugees?"

As energy surged into the conduit, Jhoira looked at the almost-full deck and the crowd struggling to reach the ship. "Too many. Too many."

"They've broken through!" shouted Terd. He clung to the rails of the ship and pointed at the sky. Angels flooded down in a great storm. "Permission to fire? Permission to fire!"

Jhoira fitted the last torch into the slot. "Fire! Fire!"

Between goblin fingers, fog-lanterns rattled violently. Their parabolic plates slid into position. Twin red beams stabbed out from them and tore into the cascade of angels. Fire erupted among them. The down-rushing wave faltered a moment. Roars of rage turned to howls of despair.

Jhoira glanced over her shoulder. The final hundred passengers were rushing up the gangplank and packing themselves in on deck. In moments, the ship was fully loaded. "Castoff the gangplank. Castoff the grapples. Draw the anchor. Prepare for liftoff!"

Power surged blue-white through the exposed conduits. Jhoira backed away. She caught hold of the ship's wheel and shouted, "Take us up, Karn! Bring us around in a quick turn to port, heading one sixty-five, thirty-one, sixteen. Lantern-rays, clear us a path through the battle. Hold on!"

A tremor of anticipation moved through the crowd and through the great hull itself. The tremor turned into a rumbling groan. The engines below decks growled to life. A grinding noise rose between landing spines and ground. Knees buckled under the first jolting advance of the vessel. Ponderous and clumsy, *Weatherlight* nosed up and away from the rocky niche where it had sat. Energy coursed in dazzling rivulets along the exposed conduits. The prow curved dangerously near the advancing curtain of chaos.

"Hard to port!" Jhoira shouted.

The ship listed away from ravening oblivion. The refugees crouched on the deck clung tightly to the rails and each other. With a magnificent roar, the ship nosed up and away from the planar envelop. A ragged cheer moved wavelike across the deck until the new danger came to the fore. Flights of angels and archangels converged on them, magna swords swung toward the refugees like scythes to heads of wheat.

"Down, everyone!" Jhoira ordered, her voice raw. "Fire at will."

Beams of killing light erupted from shuddering lanterns and cut jagged lines across the vanguard. The acid atomizer dissolved away any creatures that lingered. Angels tumbled from the skies, their spirits whirling ghost-like from their riven forms and into the soul torches along the ship's hull. With each new life, *Weatherlight* gained speed.

Still, the beams did not catch them all, and angels poured over the rails. Refugees shrieked. Magna swords sliced into them. Red fountains erupted.

"Glasspitters fire! Beams fire! Fight, all of you! Fight!"

Swords and belaying pins and chains—the crew led the charge. Viashino and goblin and human, they fought. Great blasts of molten glass belched out from the bombards, catching and slaying angels in their hundreds. Rays of crimson light burned through feather to muscle to bone. Still they came. Out of the throat of heaven came the killer angels. Spirit after spirit poured from sundered bodies into the torches, into *Weatherlight's* power-stone. Out of it flowed red beams that slew all the more. Every death fed the killing machine.

"Faster, Karn!" Jhoira shouted. "Punch through them. Planeshift speed!"

There came no answer from the speaking tube, only the roar of engines and the hot smell of heat-stressed metal.

Radiant reappeared in her throne room, her sanctuary. Ever since Gorig had cast mirror spells on the windows, this room had become her refuge. Now into her refuge, she had brought the dying form of her foe and the gems that were his life.

It was a simple enough thing to decide what to do with Urza. She stripped him from her waist and tossed his crumpled figure to a nearby platform. She wasn't much interested in Urza anymore. He had been merely the package that had carried these stones. Now, broken open, he lay discarded on the floor.

These stones, though . . . Radiant lifted them in a gory hand. She had not spent the energy it would take to transform her fingers from the dagger-claws they had become. She rather enjoyed them in their fierce aspect. They looked so powerful like this—reflecting the gentle glow of the stones and mantled in the planeswalker's blood.

Radiant glanced up. The mirrors were full of her glimmering victory. From every angle, the darkness gave back fragmentary visions of her beauty. A forest of eyes gazed at her—no longer merely her eyes, but the Eyes of Urza too.

"You were like Serra, weren't you?" Radiant said. Her quiet voice echoed ceaselessly off the dark mirrors. "You could see in this room—even when the windows were lenses. You could make sense of the visions of this throne. Of course you could. Your eyes had a facet for every window, and now your eyes are mine."

Urza did not move. His sundered head leaked blood and brain onto the floor.

"Gorig will be sad he was not here to collect your soul," Radiant said wistfully. "Ah, but I have your eyes. Such beautiful eyes."

The crystals rolled languidly apart on her hand. She saw only then the ragged point of fracture between the two stones. She had known the Mightstone and Weakstone were halves of a whole, but seeing how they might be joined intrigued her. Taking one crystal in each hand, she studied them.

"It looks as though they fit together just like—this—"

Breath failing, strength failing, Barrin had crawled to the saddle of Rhammidarigaaz and strapped himself in. The young fire drake struggled toward one army of angels and away from another. Before him, a refugee ship fought through the battle, mantled in spectral lights. Behind him a furious demon labored at the head of a hellish legion.

It was a unique vantage there, suspended in the relative calm between two deaths, between pain and despair. Barrin knew he was done for. He could not fight. He could not escape, but he did have one final spell and the power to bring it into being. The question remaining was one of timing and focus. What would be the best use of the spell? Perhaps he could compel Radiant to kill Gorig, or Gorig to kill Radiant, or an archangel to make a suicide stand to cover the ship's retreat.

Gorig was more than a Phyrexian monster. He was the soul battery.

Suddenly Barrin knew what he would do. He rolled onto his back. Gorig labored down toward him out of the darkening heavens. The beast's torso blazed blue-white in anticipation. There was a simple ratio—something about the velocity of A minus the velocity of B divided by the distance between them over against the velocity of B plus the velocity of C divided by the distance between them—something Urza could have calculated with a mere thought. Barrin was more mage than mathematician, and he had trouble breathing, let alone calculating. Instead, he simply waited until the demon—eyes ablaze and dagger-teeth drooling over the mage master's legs—hovered just out of reach. Summoning the last bit of his strength, Barrin cast a ray of command.

The fury in the beast's eyes shifted from Barrin down to the approaching *Weatherlight*, down to the main deck, where the captain stood. With new, ardent speed, the Phyrexian monster dropped into a dive and screamed his way toward the beleaguered ship.

Mightstone in her right hand and Weakstone in her left, Radiant slowly brought the two together. As the rough facets of the split edges approached each other, the light in the crystals redoubled. They suddenly glowed brightly in her hands. They cast her shadow, giant and menacing, through the aviary. In a million mirrors, Radiant glimpsed herself transfigured by the light.

A glinting smile crossed her teeth. "Such power. Such power."

She brought the stones closer together. Light flared brighter still and brought with it heat. Intense beams leapt out of each facet of the stones. They struck silvered glass and ricocheted through the aviary. The vast structure seemed the interior of a giant gemstone, glimmering brilliantly around Radiant. Light bathed every dark corner. It shone across the ruined gardens below. It danced on bodies of dead birds. It gilded the still form of Urza Planeswalker. Refulgent, nimbic, luciferous, radiant light.

"If they were lenses instead of mirrors," Radiant mused idly, "all this light would spill outward and be lost. But, clever me, it remains here. It is mine."

She turned the Weakstone slowly, matching its fracture marks exactly with those of its brother. With a final slow ecstasy, she eased them together. . . .

The stones never touched. Lightning awoke between them. The glare was blinding. The heat was incinerating. The crystals, glimmering faintly when apart, were holocaustal together. Their effulgence filled every mirror. The light had nowhere to go. Each moment grew exponentially brighter. Each instant grew exponentially hotter.

Radiant tried to pull her hands apart, but the stones called to each other. They burned out her eyes.

"I'm the mad one!" she gasped.

Next moment, it did not matter. Angel flesh seared away. Angel bone exploded. Blood flash boiled. Innards puffed into black smoke that itself was bleached white and then dispersed altogether.

Radiant was gone. The lantern in darkness had burned herself out from within.

Someone else was there in her place. Someone hovered there, the embodiment of the stones, the creature created and sustained by them. It was the conflict between those stones—the world-shattering conflict of irreconcilable opposites that were even, so halves of a whole—that granted Urza life. It immolated his old flesh, and in the same flash, fitted him with a new body, a glorified body. It formed around the locus of his being. It formed around the stones that were his eyes.

And next moment, the core of heat and light could no longer be contained. Every mirror in the mile-high atrium shattered. Hunks of silvered glass flung outward and crashed into the grids and plates Gorig had said would save Radiant. They buckled out and flew away, insubstantial as paper. The blaze followed them. It arced through air. It filled the yellow and shrinking skies.

Urza gazed out through the blinding brilliance. He saw the explosion peel back the skin of Serra's Palace. He saw it pulverize walls within. He watched as blast lines punched holes deep into the floating citadel. Shattered and crushed, the palace listed slowly. Streamers of force tore through its web of levitation spells. The place released an horrific moan and rolled over. The massive hand of gravity tightened its fingers around the thing and dragged it downward. It receded. A coiling sea of smoke trailed behind it. The broken hull soon seemed only the falling, spinning seed of a maple tree.

Then it struck the rising floor of the plane. Chaos swallowed it whole.

All around Urza, the edges of the blast were disappearing against the closing. Before the tide of destruction could sweep him under, Urza stepped from the dying realm.

Only moments after the deafening explosion that destroyed the palace, Jhoira heard an even more ominous sound. Through the groan of overheated engines and the shriek of dying refugees and the howls of rabid angels, she heard a high, keening wail. Something was falling out of the sky, too fast to avoid. She looked up. The meteor hurtled through the angel throng, ripping wings from bodies and rending anything it stuck. It grew larger, its maniac teeth glinting in the moment that it hung above deck. Its eyes were yellow as lemon wedges.

With a sudden, horrific boom, the demon creature struck the white-hot powerstone conduits. Its head was pulverized by the impact. Its wings peeled away, but the thing's massive metal torso remained. The soul-portals on either side of it flared, emptying their charges into the engines.

Weatherlight lunged forward. The beam weapons stabbed out with twice their previous intensity. Whole flights of angels disintegrated. Souls en masse flooded into the flashing torso. The ship gained speed. Angels flung themselves away from the juggernaut and hovered in stunned terror in space for a moment before realizing the curtain of chaos had closed on them.

The plane was disintegrating. The point of critical collapse had been reached. Nothing would stop it now.

The white mana that rained from the folding skies poured into the powerstone of *Weatherlight.* Every creature caught by the advancing curtain turned into a spiral of life-force, which was drawn into the sparking torso of the beast, into the engine.

Jhoira could do nothing but stand and stare in grotesque fascination and awe.

The angel armies fell back as the refugee craft sped into the clear space beyond.

To starboard appeared Rhammidarigaaz, with Barrin lashed to him. There was no sign of Urza. Unless the dragon flew just above the ship at the moment of planeshift, it and Barrin would be left behind.

"Planeshift before final collapse!" Barrin shouted. "Any mortal left in the plane will die!"

"I know! I know!" Jhoira returned. "You hear that, Karn! We need full speed! We need it now."

"Too many passengers," Karn roared from below. His voice was strained, as though he propelled the ship by main strength. "Too much weight!"

Before the bow, another army of angels hung. They were disintegrating before another collapsing edge of the plane. And suddenly they were gone.

Only the *Weatherlight* and Rhammidarigaaz remained in the collapsing plane. Curtains of chaos closed ahead and behind them.

"Now or never, Karn!" Jhoira shouted.

They reached the wall. The prow of the ship sank into chaos and dissolved. In the breath afterward, the ship and all those aboard were gone.

The invasion force had been gone eight hours, and the sun had at last quit the skies over Tolaria. The crowd that had had gathered for *Weatherlight's* launch had remained, but their high spirits had dissolved. The festive morning had given way to a speculative noon, which in turn surrendered to a fearful and prayerful evening. Night now lay full and cold over the academy walls. Someone had fetched candles from the great hall, but a mocking wind put out the hopeful little lights moments after they were coaxed to life. A few lanterns had replaced them, glaring baldly across the mulling multitudes. The quiet prayers were becoming whispers of doubt.

A restless breeze moved among the trees. The crowd turned its attention to the distant deeps of the sky. Something moved there among the lazy clouds of night. Something large. The shape grew rapidly and silently on the wind.

The crowd that had lingered throughout the long, hot day began to draw back in dread. Those lurking in doorways withdrew inside, and, those out in the open pressed back toward doorways. A reddish streamer of flame outlined devilish jowls and a great, rapacious eye.

"It's a demon!"

"Yes, but one of ours."

The dragon's figure was clear now, above the treetops. In moments it soared over the walls and flapped ferociously above the courtyard. Rhammidarigaaz! In his wake, black against the blue-black of night, there came a giant hull. From its sides jutted smiling faces and waving hands.

The *Weatherlight.*

It was some months later when Jhoira stood again at the prow of the ship, feeling the sea winds in her hair. She breathed deeply and remembered a time long ago when she stood in her secret spot, on the prow of Tolaria, and dreamed of far-off places and soul mates. Her girlhood dreams had not come to pass and had in fact brought her much pain over the years. Life had been good nonetheless. She was among the greatest artificers in the world, a trusted companion of Urza Planeswalker and, for the time being, the ad hoc captain of the grand ship *Weatherlight.* She had explored earthly paradises, had run forges in hell, had fought wars in heaven, and had traveled the planes with a silver man and a skyship.

"How are things looking down there, Karn?" she asked through the speaking tube that emerged at the prow.

"The crystal's supply of energy is limitless," Karn replied.

His energy had also increased of late. The orphaned child of Urza had at last found his home, at the heart of the ship he feared would be the end of him. The planeswalker had returned from Serra's Realm chastened by his victory. Unexplainably to anyone, he had begun to show a fatherly affection toward Karn, saying the silver man was formed in his own image. Whether by plan or happenstance, Urza's first thinking, feeling artifact creature had become the heart of his legacy for the world.

Karn had even learned a little bit about humor. "Is there anything you'd like me to shoot?"

"No, thanks, Karn," Jhoira said. "Steady as she goes."

"Aye, aye,"

Yes, it had been quite a life so far. No soul mates, but quite a life—or were there soul mates?

The tip of Zhalfir jutted just ahead, a rocky prominence behind which stretched a broad and bountiful land. The civil wars were concluded, thanks to the wisdom and power of a certain Tolarian wizard, and the country had pledged a tract of land for human refugees from Serra's Realm. That was the purpose of this trip. Jhoira, Karn, and the crew of *Weatherlight* were conducting three hundred and sixty-three human refugees to their new home in Zhalfir. Jhoira's mind, just now, was not on any of those three hundred and sixty-three, but rather on the figure that stood, red-swathed and magnificent on that prominence of stone.

Heart catching in her throat, Jhoira shouted the order that would bring the ship slowly up to hover just above the prominence. Smiling broadly despite herself, Jhoira called out to the man standing there. "Teferi! Excuse me, Lord Mage Teferi of Zhalfir! Good to see you again."

"And you!" came the genuine reply. With a simple flip of his arm, the man levitated up to the ship board. He spread his cloak in wide majesty as unseen arms of magic lowered him to stand before Jhoira. He bowed low, returned her smile, and set hands on his hips. "I hear you have some new citizens for my nation."

"Yes," Jhoira said. "Three hundred and sixty-three."

"Fine. Fine. I do hope you are planning to help them settle in."

Jhoira tipped her head regretfully. "I can stay the day. Urza wants his ship back for other . . . errands."

Teferi nodded, his eyes darkening in disappointment. "Some other time then, perhaps."

"Why don't you come back with me to Tolaria?" she suggested.

"You have lots of friends there. Arty Shovelhead is aboard. He would be happy to see you."

"I'm lucky to be alive, after all I did to him." Teferi wore a chagrined smile. "It's hard to believe a hundred-pound kid would pick on a twelve-hundred pound golem. Still, I'll have to see him again later. Anyone can fight a war. It's maintaining peace that takes all the real work." He looked her up and down. "Well, Jhoira of the Ghitu, let's take these people to their new home."

"Yes, my friend," she replied. "Yes."

Monologue

I'd really hoped Jhoira and Teferi would get together. After all, a master artificer and a master mage would make natural partners. Oh, well, perhaps it will come in time. And on Tolaria, time is one thing we will never run out of.

—Barrin, Mage Master of Tolaria

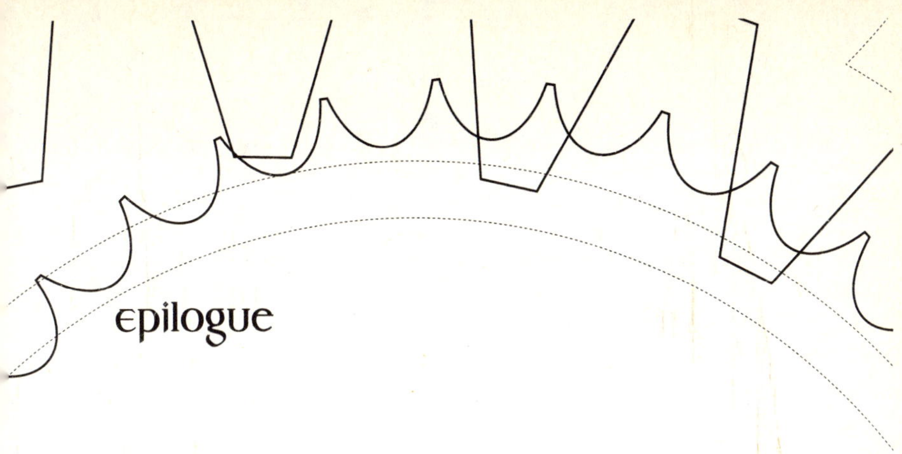

epilogue

At last, Urza is sane.

He remembers battling his brother Mishra, three thousand years ago, and regrets the destruction they caused. He remembers the death of his surrogate brother, Ratepe, and his best friend Xantcha, and is grateful for their lives together. He is capable at last of true regret and gratitude, and that goes a long way. He is at last capable of having true friends.

Urza not only remembers his past, he has taken responsibility for it. He resurrected time-ravaged Tolaria, did penance for Argoth, destroyed a small corner of Phyrexia, and even saved the refugees of Serra's Realm.

As I write this, I sit with Urza in his high study. The evening winds of Tolaria are hot and pregnant with life. The sound of night-birds has begun, haunting and beautiful. The Phyrexian gorge lies quiet, empty now for nearly a decade. The only other sound comes from the great hall. There is a dance tonight, and a whole new generation of Tolarian students are having fun. I tap my foot absently to the distant sound of rebecs and drums.

The master raises his face from the book he is reading. It is his wife's account of the Brothers' War. He has been reading it very gravely during the last month, his thoughtful expression broken at moments into wistful remembrance. The smile that appears on his face now is something different, though.

"How late does the dance run tonight?"

I shrug. "I said they could dance till the Glimmer Moon went down—well after midnight. If the sound is bothering you—"

"No," Urza says with an off-putting hand. "It's just that I've been rereading this wedding sequence. I remember the dances from that day, long ago. I don't imagine modem music would quite accommodate the same steps. . . ."

I rise. "Oh, if not, we can teach the players a few of the old tunes."

Yes, Urza is sane. Now, I suppose I'll see if he can dance.

—Barrin, Mage Master of Tolaria

BLOODLINES
LOREN L. COLEMAN

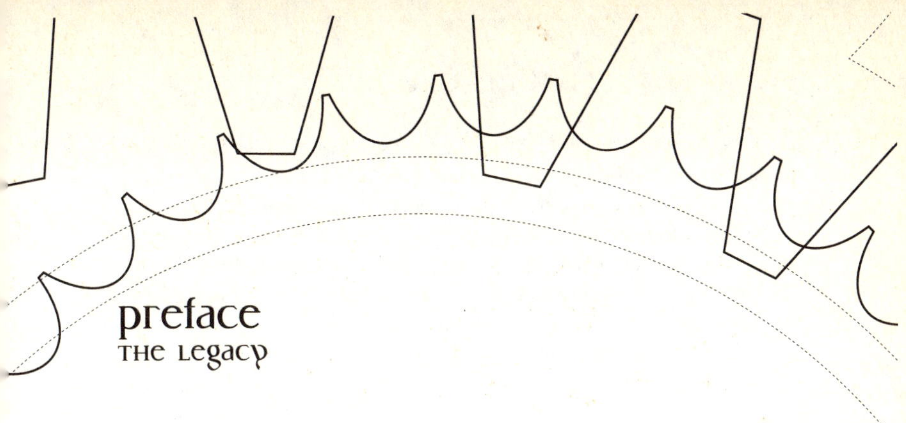

preface
THE LEGACY

Barrin paused in the classroom's open doorway, his charitable mood fading.

Barely an hour returned to the Tolarian Academy, the master mage had decided to walk a quick tour of the main building before retiring, a habit he formed over his many years as the academy's chief administrator. Tonight it possessed the added benefit of giving Rayne a chance to finish her own unpacking. Her private apartment was not far down Scholar's Row from his own, and when she finished, he thought, they might linger over a second exchange of goodnights

Seeing light spilling down the tiled hallway, Barrin decided to offer assistance to what was certainly tutors up late preparing the next day's lessons. Students, of course, obeyed a strict curfew, and the academy's full scholars rarely, if ever, required such late-night preparations. Rayne was likely to be waiting for him—a slight twinge against his conscience—but he knew that in his place she also would be checking in to offer advice. Besides, adding his personal touch helped to keep Barrin in contact with the daily functions of the academy. This had been, after all, his first real leave of absence.

The first thing Barrin noticed was that someone had punched a new door into the classroom. The rough hole in the previously complete wall stood open, not even framed, and at odds with the smooth plaster and elegant woodwork finishes put on academy facilities. A curiosity turned slightly alarming when he recognized the room beyond contained Urza's primary laboratory. That alarm lasted mere seconds, as Urza himself walked from the back room followed by the silver golem Karn. Both of them carried books and scrolls which they added to a growing pile surrounding the lectern. Barrin frowned over the activity. His scowl deepened as he realized that Urza was too distracted to have yet noticed the mage's presence—a fact which should have been instantly registered by the planeswalker's preternatural senses. A distracted Urza could be a most dangerous thing.

The man standing in front of Barrin was known throughout history as the defiler of Argoth and the harbinger of the Ice Age, though Urza himself could not—or would not—admit with one hundred percent certainty that the global catastrophe resulted from his efforts. Barrin was inclined to give the planeswalker the benefit of the doubt, especially since his track record had improved since coming back to Tolaria after the last major disaster, but benefit of the doubt was one thing, careless blind faith was another. The master mage was feeling a bit unnerved by the sight of the deeply focused Urza. As he approached the lectern, Barrin recognized in the 'walker's intense stare and disconnected manner that same fanatical drive that motivated and created the last set of cataclysmic events. He knew that Urza was again obsessing on his personal crusade: Phyrexia.

Those creatures had once been the ancient Dominarian race of the Thran—who at the height of their achievements had mastered a level of artifice unknown to anyone since—save perhaps Urza himself. Then some kind of war tore the Thran from their advanced ways and sent them hurtling down a darker path toward wicked corruption. They were forced to leave Dominaria for an artificially created plane—nine spheres nested inside one another turning blacker and more torturous the closer they get to the center—and after a time they emerged from their exile as the twisted, hideous abominations that have plagued Urza for millennia. For the loss of his brother, for the death of his one-time traveling companion Xantcha, for replacing that which was human with corrupted artifice the realm of Phyrexia had earned its place as Urza's enemy, one planeswalker against nine nested spheres of malignant, venomous force. His vendetta had nearly cost him his life—existence rather—several times over. So far, others had paid that price for him.

Though obsession was doubly dangerous in a being so powerful, Barrin could understand Urza's pain and nearly forgive the planeswalker his costly mistakes. Barrin believed in Urza's war on Phyrexia, believed that they would return to Dominaria (had seen them with his own eyes), and that without Urza and the efforts of the Tolarian Academy there would be little in the way of stopping them. For that reason Barrin had helped create the *Weatherlight*, the skyship that would presumably be the ultimate weapon against the day of invasion. Barrin always doubted the veracity of such an assertion, but Urza had stood adamant—convinced.

If this weapon was capable of defending Dominaria from invasion, why was Urza again demonstrating the distracted intensity which Barrin had learned to recognize and fear?

Karn noticed the mage's approach first, his deep-set eyes widening with recognition. The silver golem certainly would have spoken a greeting if Barrin had not been prepared and spoke first. Seldom it was that Barrin could take Urza by surprise, and usually he learned something from it—never too old to be a student.

"I had not heard of your return, Urza. Welcome back." Urza had disappeared six months ago, after helping to settle the refugees from Serra's Realm across Dominaria and returning only once with a handful of new students and three new scholars, including Rayne.

Urza did not bother to turn around. He simply reformed the patterns of energy which made up his body so that suddenly he faced Barrin. He was obviously too preoccupied for the more subtle nuances which gave the illusion of his still being of normal mortal flesh.

"Barrin," he greeted neutrally, "I expected you back three days ago."

How are you? How was your leave? Such courtesies were left as far behind the planeswalker as normal life.

"My chances for time away from the academy come seldom. We—I decided to take a few extra days at Angelwood. It's not difficult to lose track of time on Tolaria."

The planeswalker did not even bother to feign chagrin at the reference to the island's temporally-shattered areas where time flowed at different speeds, by-products of the catastrophic failure of Urza's earlier experiments with time travel. Angelwood was a moderate slow-time environment where the enhanced sunlight and frequent but gentle rains created a paradise of lakes and shaded glades. It was a favorite among academy staff for sabbaticals, though the time differential worked against those desiring an extended term away from work. Meeting Rayne during his vacation had seemed to shorten it even more, the time passing so quickly in conversation and shared meals.

She was a rarity in many ways, not the least of which being that she was one of perhaps a few dozen adult scholars ever admitted to Tolaria. Phyrexians planted sleeper agents all over Dominaria but always as adults—never children. Security at the academy usually demanded that new students be admitted when they were in their young teens. Senior students were promoted to tutors, and then they could advance to scholars and eventually might serve as chancellor, one of the eight academy administrators. Rayne's natural talent for artifice had won her admission and instant status as a tutor. Four months later Barrin had signed papers promoting her to full scholar, but it wasn't until their chance meeting at Angelwood that the mage had truly learned to appreciate her. She had long black hair that accented her delicate features, and she possessed an impressive mind and commanded a strong yet subtle presence. Barrin couldn't explain such feelings to the planeswalker. Urza, Barrin doubted, would not understand. Caught up in his obsession, the 'walker barely recognized the civilities of friendship.

Not so Karn.

"It is good to see you again, Master Barrin," the silver golem rumbled out of his cavernous chest, putting an end to the awkward pause that followed Urza's lack of response.

To Barrin, Karn still sounded a bit despondent. Ever since Jhoira's decision to leave Tolaria, the golem had been unable to hide his melancholy. Jhoira had been the golem's best friend for several decades, and even though the silver man claimed to understand why she left, time did not heal his wounds.

"Did you enjoy Angelwood?" he asked.

Barrin smiled, as much for Karn's courtesy as for the fond memories of the last few weeks. "Very much, Karn. Thank you."

"Good," Urza said brusquely, "because we have some hard work ahead of us, important work." He waved Karn off. "I will need several new desks, Karn, and a large worktable."

The silver golem nodded perfunctorily to Urza, offered Barrin a grim smile, and then trudged off to fulfill Urza's request.

"So important that it could not wait for tomorrow?" asked Barrin, now resigning himself to a long evening.

"We have delayed too long already." Urza glanced toward the classroom's main sketchboard, covered with a script Barrin recognized as a meld of ancient Thran and the modern Argivian used as the Academy standard. "I've proceeded as far as I am able alone. Completing the Legacy will require the facilities of the entire academy if we are to have our defenses readied against the Phyrexian invasion."

Urza paused, nodded as if agreeing with himself, and then turned away from Barrin and the conversation. He picked up a large roll of plans and moved to the wall, unrolling and pinning them up against a fresh spongewood board. They described an apparatus of titanic size and complexity.

"I will annex this room until the new labs are built." He studied the plans with a critical eye. "I wish I could find Serra and ask her some more questions."

Thrown off by the abrupt changes of topic, Barrin stared at the planeswalker for a moment, then just shook his head. "New labs?" he asked. "Urza, why should we—?"

The planeswalker interrupted without turning. "The existing ones are fine and will certainly be utilized, but cannot accommodate the needs of the Lens and Matrix."

So much for clarification.

"Urza?" Barrin began but was again cut off.

"I know that the auxiliary lenses will capture ambient mana." Urza traced a long finger over one area of the plans he studied. "Filters, perhaps? To separate the mana before focusing?"

"Urza."

"Filters, yes certainly. She must have used them. Even Serra's Realm was not purely white mana. She mentioned that total purity was not possible. The question is can the Matrix focus one source of mana in alteration of the more basic—"

"Urza!"

In the large open classroom, designed with an ear toward acoustics, Barrin's shout rang out like a thunderclap. Urza turned slowly from the board and his new plans, whatever they were for, to face the mage. The planeswalker's eyes sparked with fire, and Barrin recognized them as the twin powerstones over which Urza had fought his brother over three millennia ago. They surfaced in times of weakness or intensity (when the planeswalker was too distracted to maintain the illusion of normal eyes). Barrin possessed no doubts that this was one of the latter.

"The *Weatherlight*," Barrin said simply, naming the sky-borne vessel the academy had worked so hard to create, a warship capable of traveling between the planes of the multiverse. "The *Weatherlight* was supposed to be your ultimate weapon. It is the core of our defense, the one thing that the Phyrexians will be hard-pressed to match."

Urza smiled, a bit sadly. "I was overconfident," he said. "The *Weatherlight* can inspire hope with the wondrous feats already at its command, and it will hurt Phyrexia badly in limited engagements, but it will not win the war on its own." He paused, his eyes regaining their illusion of being still human. "Barrin, you were there—in Serra's Realm. That was one battle, and we nearly lost it. Alone, the *Weatherlight* would have fallen. We still have work to do."

"It was under powered," the mage said, playing at contrariness and defending the *Weatherlight* to keep Urza talking.

"It was inadequate," Urza said with great weight, putting an end to the argument. "The *Weatherlight* is the core of the Legacy, not its entirety. Indeed, it may buy us the time we need to complete our defense. As you once pointed out, we cannot assume I will always be present to direct the battle against Phyrexia. The Phyrexians still hunt me with their negators. Other planeswalkers present a threat as well, and there are always unforeseen . . . occurrences." Urza possibly alluded to the years he spent as a prisoner of Yavimaya. "Fate might yet intervene, and though I tend to believe that even fate will not dare gainsay my claim to oppose this evil, I will not rely on that fact. Plans must be set down against the future to finish the *Weatherlight*."

Barrin considered the *Weatherlight* as she already sailed. The airship had fantastic speed, powerful armaments, and the ability to travel between planes. What more was there? True, Barrin concentrated on magic over artifice, but in the decades he had spent with Urza he'd picked up a feeling for the craft. The *Weatherlight* was, in his opinion, already the ultimate artifact, with design mated to purpose. Perhaps they could add a few trappings—install some minor features. Wouldn't it be better to begin looking elsewhere for answers?

When he put those thoughts into words, Urza readily disillusioned him. "The *Weatherlight* is more than any regular artifact, defined by its purpose and static in its function. It lives." As if realizing the implication of his words, he quickly amended the concept. "Not as you live, of course, nor even Karn, but it shares one thing in common with you both—the ability to *evolve*, to grow beyond its current form and ability. The Legacy will be a series of artifacts, crafted over the years, that can be introduced to the *Weatherlight* at a later date. Before you ask why we did not incorporate such features into the vessel from the beginning," he said, forestalling Barrin's question, "it is because of time constraints and secrecy. There are features I have not even conceptualized yet that will eventually be crafted, I am sure. Even were we able to add all possible features to the ship now, its power signature would stand out like a blinding beacon, drawing Phyrexia after it. As it is, the *Weatherlight* will be hard to track until nearer the moment of its final purpose."

The scope of the project left Barrin nearly dumbfounded. "What is that purpose?" he asked, caught up in the vision and expecting now the grand revelation.

Instead, Urza admitted, "I don't know."

Barrin blinked back his surprise.

"The *Weatherlight* is the grandest artifact ever conceived." Urza flapped his arms, once, in a very human gesture of frustration. "As I envision it, the vessel will be able to evolve and do almost anything imaginable. What is that to be? Who will imagine it? When will the invasion come? Where? What will be the key to its ultimate defeat?" His voice rose, its edge of frustration and frenzy cutting apart Barrin's earlier confidence. "Questions! Only questions. I have no answers, not yet." He took a few seconds to regain control of himself. "This is why the bloodlines will be so important."

Again, Urza had jumped three steps ahead in his thinking, apparently assuming Barrin to be gifted with sight that allowed him to peer into another's mind.

" 'Bloodlines'?" the master mage asked, doubt touching his voice as if unsure he had heard correctly. It was not the kind of term to encourage confidence and peace of mind.

"Of course, bloodlines," Urza said, exasperated. "The second half of the Legacy. A *human component*. Haven't you been listening? We can't say for sure that I will be present for the invasion. There must be someone for the masses to follow who will understand how to beat Phyrexia, someone who will know how to use the *Weatherlight* in order to save Dominaria." He gestured back to the sketchboard where flowing Thran script mingled with Argivian. "Within the bloodlines we will discover the inheritor of my Legacy, and in the meantime the project will provide us with warriors with which to stand against Phyrexia and its agents." He stepped closer to the board, his voice softening and taking on messianic tones. "They will be Dominaria's soldiers. One among them will be its salvation."

"You expect to train a successor then?"

The administrator within Barrin took over, considering the years, decades perhaps, that it would take for Urza to even locate enough suitable candidates, especially if he wanted to form an army from such a program's detritus. The sheer logistics for such a limited return did not seem prudent.

"Not train," Urza said, dismissing the idea with the easiest shake of his head. "Not as such. What I have in mind will require of a candidate too many specific traits that could never be learned, even in the time given some mortals here on Tolaria." He turned from the board, fixing his hard gaze on Barrin. "Our new army and the heir to the Legacy must be bred."

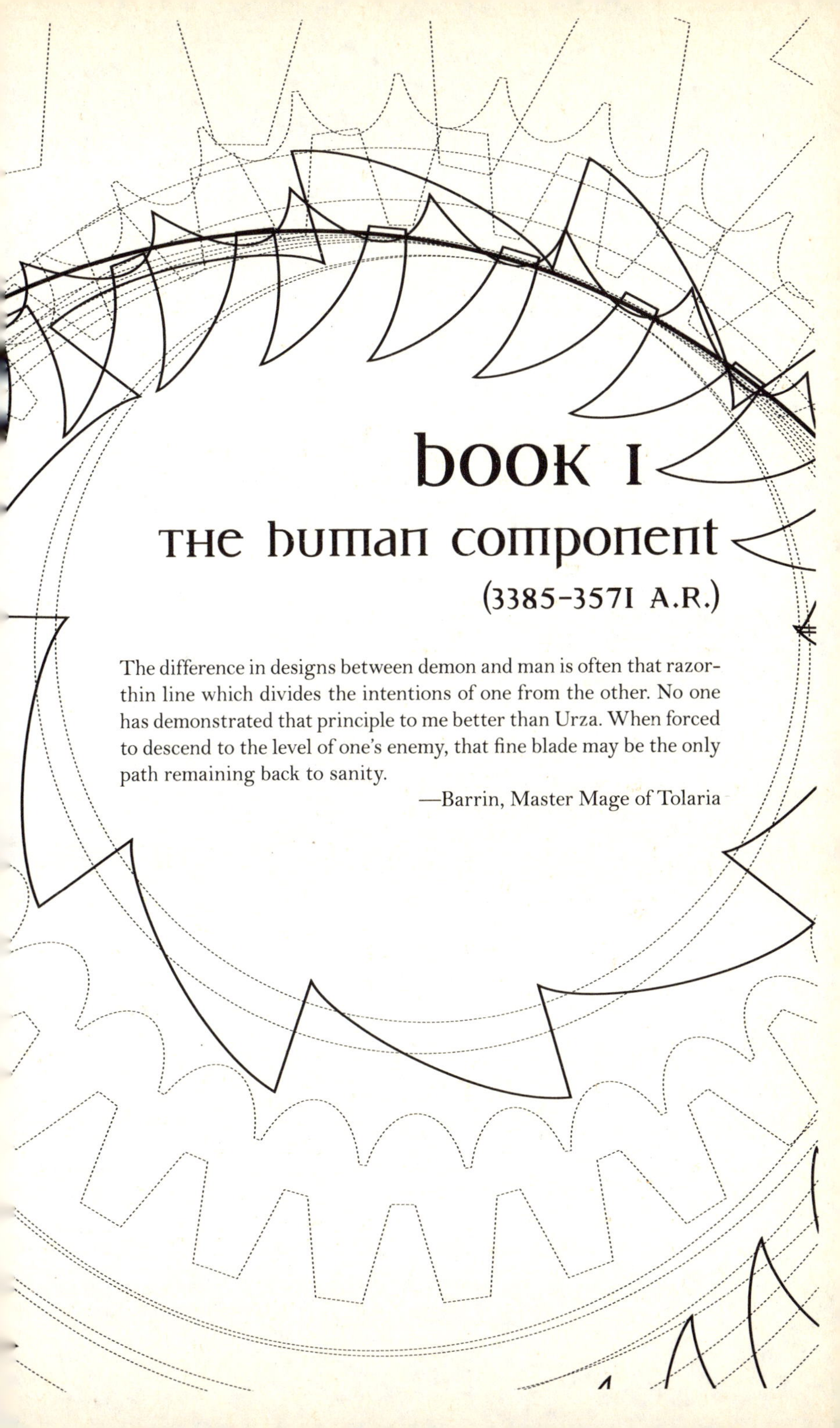

Book I
The Human Component
(3385–3571 A.R.)

The difference in designs between demon and man is often that razor-thin line which divides the intentions of one from the other. No one has demonstrated that principle to me better than Urza. When forced to descend to the level of one's enemy, that fine blade may be the only path remaining back to sanity.

—Barrin, Master Mage of Tolaria

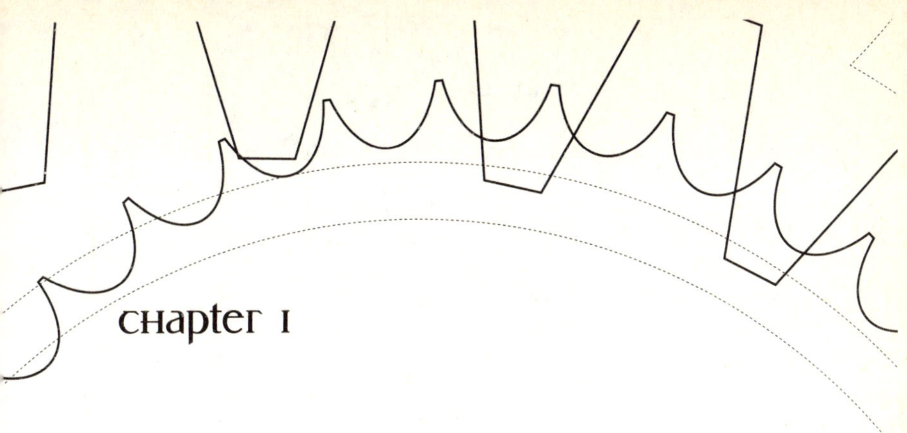

Chapter 1

Gatha gazed out one of the nearby teardrop windows, his arms crossed defiantly over his chest as Barrin answered questions for a batch of new students. Smoke-tinted glass stained the outside world a dull gray, physically expressive of Gatha's own darkening mood as Barrin continued to make him wait. Rain spattered off the window's upper curve, at times hard and insistent and then fading to a light drizzle. The latest buildings for Urza's new laboratories had been completed just in time. Tolaria's stormy season had begun.

"We've been over this before," Master Barrin explained in answer to a question Gatha had ignored. The mage's voice remained patient, though at a glance the senior student noticed a tightening around Barrin's hard green eyes which forewarned of a darkening mood. "The magic presents no direct influence on the developing child. It is a procedure used prior to conception, to accent the traits which the child already stands to inherit from its natural parents."

He was still discussing the Bloodlines project: Urza's controversial plan to develop some kind of master warrior. It was now six years into its first generation of subjects. Gatha shrugged aside concern for Barrin's argument and began tapping his foot to illustrate his impatience.

Like sheep with their shepherd—in Gatha's judgment—the new students flocked around Barrin at the front of the workshop. The space had been cleared and cleaned by the senior student in preparation for this orientation class. Except for the half-built gestate cradle pushed into one forward corner, it was the same as every lecture hall in the main academy buildings. Gatha might have found better uses for his time, though a request from Barrin was never to be ignored, and there was something to be said for any recognition by the academy's chief administrator. The senior student held his silence and his place, occupying himself by studying the latest arrivals to Tolaria. The group was one short of a full dozen. Their eyes burned brightly with interest over the tour of the new labs and the information imparted by the master mage. Many of them aspired to be the next prodigy, of course—the next Teferi or Jhoira—or like Gatha himself. At the island academy such visions of personal grandeur were expected, even encouraged, if one owned the talent. A few students fell outside such a generality, though. They glanced about, troubled and nervous. Gatha labeled these ones right away as the next set of 'able hands.' They might work on the major projects, even on the Legacy itself, but always under the exacting direction of others, tools in the hands of masters like Barrin, Rayne, and one day soon, himself.

One such student raised a nervous hand. He was whipcord thin with hair the color of rhubarb and a nose which battled and defeated the rest of his face for attention.

"The plans for these 'Metathran' we've heard discussed in the hallways and amphitheaters." His reedy voice grew in strength and confidence as he progressed. "Simulacra given true life through focused mana? Forced development, probably through overlaid patterns cloned off desired predecessors?" He glanced around for support, found it wanting. "A slave race?" he asked, confidence finally waning and telling in his restless stance.

Gutsy, Gatha decided at once, awarding the junior student credit for calling Barrin on the morality of Urza's newest plans. Strong opening, near-brilliant supposition but ultimately dumb.

The senior student looked back to the window, catching a light reflection of his own face in the tinted glass and of course unable to ignore the triangular tattoos decorating his forehead. It was a debatable honor to be given an artificial set of the Keldon triple widow's peaks. The marks were placed on his entire family after his father served as military liaison to a Keldon warhost hired to fight for Argive.

He turned his attention back to the group of new students. Gatha looked at the gutsy inquisitor who had engaged Barrin. The younger student dwelled too heavily on the methods, not enough on the potential. He would amount to little. Urza Planeswalker supported the plan, and therefore it would happen. It became now, to Gatha's way of thinking, a question of who would lead and so be recognized by the chancellors for promotion to tutor status. Anything else was a waste of a student's time.

Barrin, however, seemed able to dip forever into a well of patience when it came to the newer students. "Timein, isn't it?" he asked, favoring the student by remembering his name.

Gatha shrugged off any concern for competition. The other's scarecrow build guaranteed some measure of easy recall.

"We were speaking of the Bloodlines project, dealing with human generations. These 'Metathran' you ask about are, as you said, *simulacra*," Barrin continued. "Still, I won't disagree with the idea that we are raising new *philosophical* issues at the academy," he said, switching his address to the entire class. "You've all had your first classes in Phyrexian physiology and psychology by now, so you have some idea of what we are up against. We'll need the Metathran to fight them, and no," he returned to Timein on a more personal note, "they will not be slaves. Gatha," he called out, "what is the second criteria of Metathran psychology?"

Caught in the midst of his personal reflection, Gatha started. A hot flush raced from the back of his neck up over his scalp—a discomfiture which lasted all of three seconds. He swallowed away the dryness in his mouth his brief embarrassment had brought. Eyes were upon him now, and he managed to look both contemplative and studious as he turned back to the assemblage. Gatha did not mind an audience.

"To restrict their mental functions to areas of personal survival and martial ability," he recited verbatim from Urza's text, adding his own dramatic touch to the quotation, "with a *limited* concept of self and society." He traced one finger along his jaw, then smoothed a pleat along the front of his white robes. "In effect, they are a type of golem."

Nodding his approval of Gatha's conclusion, Barrin's steady gaze still conveyed a measure of warning to the senior student that he should pay more attention. "Like any artifact, the Metathran will obey its programmed instructions. As with the *Weatherlight*, they are instruments of our defense."

No one raised another question, though the shuffling gestures of several students—Timein among them—suggested that the issue was not completely answered to their satisfaction.

Barrin seized upon the opportunity to end the session. With one hand he tugged at the golden mantle to his robes, straightening it, and with the other he waved toward the workshop's door.

"That will be all for today. Return to your regular classes." They moved toward the door. "Gatha, you will remain, please."

As the students filed out, Gatha caught mixed looks of curiosity, admiration and jealousy from the new students. He drew strength from those stares and glares. Such expressions meant that his name was known, as he wanted it. Only Timein offered nothing for him at all, glancing over with a simple expression of frank appraisal, as if he were weighing Gatha's worth by observation alone. Gatha smiled back, tight-lipped and challenging.

"What do you think?" Barrin asked when the room cleared and Gatha had shut the door.

It was a purposefully vague question, meant to elicit more than basic information but also something as to how Gatha himself thought. The student did not mind, confident in his own ability.

"A verbose way of saying that the ends justify the means," he said, immediately seizing upon the earlier drama in which he'd had a part. "Most of them are still trying to untangle the argument."

The hints of a smile tugged at the corners of Barrin's mouth, though not necessarily one of encouragement or humor. "You think you see more clearly than they do?" No hints of approval or disapproval in his tone.

In place of answering, Gatha walked over to the half-completed gestate cradle. One of the new modular designs that Urza had requested, its sledge-shaped body would be capable of full growth support for the Metathran soldier created within, if the artificers worked out the majority of the design problems, that is.

"I've read the academy histories," he finally answered, circumspect. He reached out to place a hand upon the slick metal casing, noticing a touch of oil to its surface. Being able to touch a thing always made it seem more real. "I have yet to find even one project that has advanced this far along that was not carried through to completion." A polite way of saying that arguments were pointless at this late stage.

Barrin nodded and then headed over toward the door. He paused, hand on the knob. "Coming?" he asked.

Gatha quickly fell into step behind the mage master.

"Your achievements have not gone unnoticed," he said as they walked down a long hall, past doors leading off to other workshops. The labs still smelled of new construction, raw wood and finishing paint. "You have made certain of that. Still, self-promotion aside, you excel in your studies of the magics and your natural grasp of artifice is impressive as well." He pulled a key from within the folds of his robes and used it to unlock a door at the end of the hall.

This new workshop had been modified and outfitted for immediate use. Blue metal file drawers had been mounted into one wall. Metal tables sat in the center of the room with trays of instruments, some obviously magic in nature but most of pure artifice, arranged on top of it. The room was well lit and spotless, but it was very cold. Their breath clouded in front of them. Gatha shivered involuntarily, one hand clutching at the front of his blue tunic trying to draw it tighter against his skin.

Barrin closed the door behind them and locked it. He gave Gatha another frank look of appraisal, eerily reminiscent of Timein's earlier expression. The student bore up under the scrutiny, for the first time feeling a bit awkward. Finally, Barrin awarded him with a reluctant nod.

"I'm adding to your duties," he said, moving to the file drawers. The master mage threw a catch on one of them, then leaned his weight outward as if pulling it open against great weight.

Gatha sucked in a cold breath and held it. Resting in the drawer, on a long plate of metal, was a blue-skinned humanoid of impressive height and elongated skull. Dark blue glyphs—magical sigils perhaps?—decorated the naked body, reminding Gatha of his own tattoos. There was an elegance to the sexless, lean-muscled creature. The master mage did not need to tell Gatha that he looked upon his first Metathran. Part of Urza's newest labs were obviously functional.

He looked to Barrin, found the elder man staring at him levelly.

"What do you think?" the mage asked again.

What did he think? Gatha recognized immediately that he had achieved the next step in his education here on Tolaria. He was being trusted with a new responsibility and his next break would come from his own ingenuity and his ability to make things happen.

Gatha let out his breath and smiled. "Where do I begin?"

Rayne bent farther forward, leaning far out over the lens to inspect for flaws. Tall and lithe, she reached nearly to the middle of the four foot radius device. The muscles along the backs of her legs tightened and quivered, holding her from smashing through the delicate item. Silk bands tied back the wide sleeves of her flowing robes to prevent even their light brush on the lens's surface. Hardly daring to breathe, wary of fogging the area over which she worked, she continued her search.

The sapphire tint to the material partly reflected her own image, making detection of a flaw harder than if it had been clear crystal backed by a deliberate pattern. She studied her own raven-black hair, her thin nose, and her long slender eyebrows in the reflection. There, near the single curl of hair that tucked down in front of her ear was a mar in the lens's otherwise perfect reflection.

She rotated the special magnifying glass that a student had created for her over into her field of vision. The glass clipped comfortably to her forearm and moved about on a pliant, telescoping arm. It was light enough to almost be ignored and left both of her hands free in case they were needed. She couldn't be sure if Gatha had put a touch of magic into the glass or not, but it cut the glare and allowed her to focus on the most minute object. Now it showed her the lens's flaw in great detail, a large irregularity in the lattice structure.

"Ruined." She straightened up cautiously, still treating the lens with extreme care. It represented too much work to rate anything less.

Karn moved forward, the silver golem's massive frame dwarfing Rayne. He had waited quietly against the wall for three hours. "The crystal lattice again?" he asked, his voice soft and deep.

Rayne smiled at him, recognizing his regular attempt at courtesy now that she had disengaged from her study.

"Yes, Karn. Over five hundred student-hours, all told, ruined by a microscopic defect." A flawed artifact, she turned her back on it. There was no wishing it to perfection. "Place it on the rack, please. Urza will want to inspect it himself, though I know the flaw is too large."

A scholar of artifice at the academy, Rayne normally commanded enough authority on such projects to make her own decisions—but never when it came to Urza. The planeswalker always double-checked her work when it involved his own projects.

With a delicate care belying his great strength, Karn used a large, grooved fork to grasp the lens securely by its edge rather than the plane. He hefted it, pivoted and slid it carefully into a storage rack next to two others that had also failed to meet standards.

Rayne had already moved on to a new activity. Her private shop always held at least three different ongoing projects, not counting students' work that she had to check over in order to gauge and track their progression. The room smelled of oiled leather and metal. Tables appeared cluttered with tools and parts; though in truth, the *clutter* was actually a complicated but well-ordered system of easy access sorted by probability of use. Most residents of the academy failed to grasp the concept. A few of her better students had picked up on the system. It was also the one time she believed that she'd impressed Urza Planeswalker. On his one visit after her assignment to a Legacy artifact, he had walked in and actually said, "Very nice," in reference to the layout. He never touched one tool, but four of his assistants were sent over that day to study the shop design.

At a table, Rayne puzzled over a new clockwork engine built from Thran metal. The living metal kept growing, binding up joints and gears if not perfectly balanced for the expansion. She flipped the magnifying glass back into her line of sight, staring through it while working on the smooth, intricate pieces. Behind her, Karn finished moving the lens and then resumed his patient vigil

"Barrin will be late again, will he not?" She paused to correct her own Argivian. "Won't he?"

"I do not know, Mistress Rayne." Rayne stopped working and glanced back at the silver man. With a slight hitch to his shoulders, surely a learned trait, Karn elaborated. "He did not communicate such to me, but he did seem very involved in studying Gatha's recent accomplishments."

Gatha was one of Barrin's best pupils. "But as much a curse, that one," she said aloud, a touch of dry humor to her voice. First there was Teferi and Jhoira, and now Gatha. "Why do the brightest ones always bring with them so much trouble?" She glanced back to Karn. "What did he do this time?"

The golem cast his gaze away. "There was an incident at the labs, something to do with enhancing certain traits among the Metathran. Gatha experimented with the Eugenics Matrix without the permission of Urza or Barrin. The facts bore him out, but the result was," the golem paused, "messy."

Rayne shook her head, as much over the trouble surrounding Gatha's lack of caution as the problem the engine presented her. Everything rests on the details, she thought in relation to both problems. It would help if she knew what the engine's ultimate purpose was, but Urza had left her in the dark. Part of the Legacy, perhaps, or another refinement to the Metathran labs. Rayne felt frustrated working like this. It would be more frustrating, she imagined, to be saddled with Barrin's problems.

"Bring me a stool please, Karn. It will be another late night."

Conversation waned as she worked further into the delicate engine. What more was there to say? They both knew Urza to be a hard taskmaster at times. Barrin followed because he believed in Urza, in the 'walker's vision for defending Dominaria. Rayne's vision was more limited to her own work, the creation and maintenance of artifice. In matters of greater scale, she trusted Barrin's judgment. If the master mage thought his presence elsewhere important enough to remain away, then she could do no less than keep working as well.

The vault sat at the heart of Urza's labs, a domed room of titanic proportions devoted to the creation and full gestation of Metathran warriors. The grand arches that buttressed the lower walls allowed better than thirty feet of head clearance. Enchanted globes set into the walls filled the cavernous room with soft light. Conspicuously missing were the gestate cradles. Barrin had ordered Gatha and others to remove the devices before Rayne's students were brought in to fit a new lens into one of the mechanisms. The mage doubted that such a precaution was really necessary. Most students knew the labs were already functioning to some degree, but Urza's orders stood.

The students worked high above the floor on scaffolding set next to one large pillar, junior students steadying the platforms or passing up tools as they were called for by their seniors. Voices and the sounds of work echoed around the vault. Rayne stood out in the open floor, her hands tucked into the opposing sleeves of her robes, supervising her students with a critical eye that missed nothing. Barrin did not approach her yet. An earlier nod and brief smile told him that she knew of his presence. Now he awaited some signal that her attention was no longer required on the work in progress. As he would with any scholar of the academy, Barrin allowed her full authority over the area in which she worked. Besides, the master mage needed a few extra minutes to muster his courage.

Soon the students had finished their task, and they sealed the pillar where the lens had been placed. Rayne waited while the students disassembled the scaffolding and were beginning to remove tools and equipment from the vault, then turned toward Barrin and awarded him with a full, warm smile for his patience. Barrin's legs felt weak, but they managed to carry him forward. As always, he was struck by her delicate beauty, porcelain skin and slender frame—not the usual image of an artificer.

"Hello, my dear," she said, reaching out with one hand to accept his embrace.

He folded her into a quick hug, for a second oblivious to the nearby students. "Greetings," he paused, now a touch self-conscious about the nearby onlookers.

Rayne sensed more in the undercurrents of his voice, no matter that he had tried to hide both his distress and nervousness. She frowned lightly, curious.

"There is news?" she asked, deliberately trailing off the question to allow him an easy time of response.

Nodding, the mage met her searching, dark brown eyes. "Gatha completed the latest tests, and Urza is less than happy with the results." He took a deep breath, tasting the chill air of the large chamber. "All indications point toward forty generations, he says, in order to develop the heir to the Legacy. We are unsure, so far, how many subjects we can hope to raise in fast-time environments, but the island's shattered time streams might work for us. How Urza is calculating this is anyone's guess."

Rayne gave the lightest of shrugs. "Numbers do not lie," she said simply.

Barrin caught the implication: Numbers do not lie, but Urza might. The master mage pushed that disturbing thought from his mind. There was a time and a place to have that discussion, but the planeswalker who founded the Tolarian Academy was not the subject Barrin had come to talk about.

"My new quarters in the slow-time area are complete," he said without further preamble. "Close enough to complete anyway, for me to take up residence."

The possibility had been considered years ago, and preparations were made in case a large facility in extreme slow time was necessary. The Legacy, especially the Bloodlines project, required an overseer other than Urza—one whose presence was considered more dependable. Drinking of the island's slow-time waters, the proverbial fountain of youth, arrested aging, but forty generations demanded more extreme measures. The island's temporal anomalies offered the solution. Some of the best and brightest would move into slow-time areas, those who would coordinate the various projects and keep the Legacy focused over the centuries. Barrin would be first among them. They would be in slow time for twelve hundred years relative to the rest of Dominaria but only thirty or so subjective to the person.

"I've already ordered my assistants to begin moving my offices and labs," he finished weakly.

Rayne stepped back, arms folding protectively across her body. "So soon," she said, hugging herself tightly. She looked up, apparently ready to say something but then shook her head. "This is goodbye then?" she asked calmly.

"That depends on you." It bothered him, the idea of living out such an extended and isolated life in slow time. It bothered him more when he considered that this move could take him away from Rayne forever. It was that thought, more than anything, that had driven him forward on this course. "You could come with me."

Was that a flash of joy in her eyes? Barrin couldn't be sure.

"I could?" she said, part question, part statement.

"Yes," he said, verbally stumbling forward. "I would like you—I am asking you to join me. I am asking you to marry me."

Now Barrin felt the cold sweat standing out on his forehead. Rayne stared back as if not comprehending what he had just asked of her. He felt several long heartbeats marking the seconds.

"There is nothing else for it then," Rayne said, smiling beautifully. "Of course I will."

"Yes?" Barrin asked, marveling at Rayne's acceptance.

He flushed suddenly warm in pleasant shock then smiled and gathered Rayne in for another hug. They embraced each other heavily, and Barrin counted himself fortunate to have found such a person to share his life. It was a good omen, perhaps—certainly good fortune—which Barrin was not about to dismiss for all his other concerns.

He felt immortal in a way that a slow-time life could never provide.

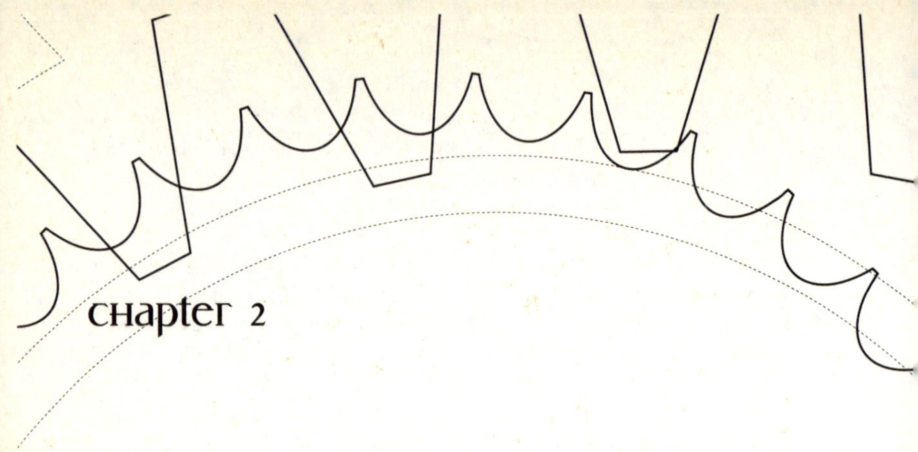

Chapter 2

Croag began to awaken from a long slumber of rest and preservation, the member of Phyrexia's Inner Circle beginning to stir within his bath of soothing, glistening oil. The insinuating fluid seeped through microscopic ducts into his semblance of skin—gray-sheened and stretched tight over ropy wire-braided muscles and a cleft skull. Small on an otherwise large frame, the skull looked out with eye sockets currently capped by protective shields. Teeth bared in frozen maniacal grin, Croag consumed more of the life-sustaining oil through gaps in his sharpened teeth. One skeletal hand of razor-sharp fingers and corded with muscles of metallic fiber rose from the glistening oil. It screeched against the bath's metal rim and finally locked around a scarred lip. Oil ran down along the Phyrexian's arm, dripping back into the pool from the sharp spiked point protruding from what must have been the monster's elbow.

In his state of semi-consciousness, Croag heard several thunderous whispers which reverberated through his skull and brought with them pleasant memories: the scents of smelted iron and fresh oil. A dark shape loomed out of his dreams, black against a night that lacked both moon and stars. The landscape was lit by sparks from the venting of countless forges, and far above, burning cinders rained down from a metallic sky. The shape grew in size, striding across the plane until all grew insignificant by comparison. The dark leviathan stopped, recognizing Croag among the infinite reaches of his mind.

This night Yawgmoth had come to speak with him.

It was the dark god of Phyrexia, creator of their plane and architect of their improved bodies. In all the multiverse, there was none so perfect in form as he. From his slumber over the millennia, the Ineffable spoke to the Inner Circle and made his will known. Croag easily recalled the one time the dark one actually woke, and the grand terror that physically shook the nine spheres of Phyrexia until all recognized his power and were bent to the task of remolding the Dominarian Nexus with Phyrexia at its center.

A querulous rumble shook Croag, still locked in a dream. The council member trembled before the display of power. *Urza Planeswalker lives*, the dark god confirmed.

Eyes of molten red flashed out of the darkness in anger and disapproval. Their searing heat threatened to cripple Croag's body. Compleat though they might be, even a member of the Inner Council could not stand before their enraged god. *Report*, thundered the Phyrexian lord.

Croag understood his master's anger. Urza Planeswalker had been born in the shadow of Phyrexia, mastering the powers of a very unique powerstone left behind in the mountain portal of Koilos. He had also managed to somehow lock away the Dominarian Nexus, preventing any Phyrexian reprisal and thwarting the full inception of the Dark One's plans for over three millennia.

Insult to this injury came when Urza launched his own attack on Phyrexia. Many members of the Inner Circle were lost in that attack, and many more were later returned to the vats—rendered, decanted, and compleated again according to a better plan. Four Spheres Urza fought his way through, showing the Phyrexians where they were weak and nearly waking the Ineffable himself. Urza was eventually driven back and pursued by negators. They were to destroy the planeswalker and be rid of him forever.

Somehow Urza managed to escape, time and again, always leaving behind the ruined corpses and burned out shells of the negators for the Phyrexians to reclaim and study for faults. He led the Phyrexians into Serra's Realm, an artificial plane constructed by another planeswalker and devoted to pure white mana which threatened the existence of any Phyrexian. Distracted by so tempting a target, here the negators lost Urza's trail. Serra's Realm fell prey instead. Assaults against the abominable plane finally drove Serra away, and then the Phyrexians' corrupting influence worked to turn the realm into a dark mockery of what it once had been, until Urza reappeared, challenging the corruption that had finally made the artificial plane habitable by Phyrexians sensitive to white mana.

Not a single detail was forgotten or omitted in Croag's report to his dark lord. Indeed, the Phyrexian was powerless to withhold anything from his master. His mind was simply drained of all information—relevant or not. When finally finished, the member of Phyrexia's Inner Circle waited for judgment, knowing it could come either swift and terrible or prolonged and cruel—all at the whim of their god.

The raging thunder that was the Ineffable's ire for Urza Planeswalker spent itself inside Croag's dreams. Tendrils of furious, molten energy slashed at his frame, and darkness squeezed upon his mind. The death scent of scorched oil permeated his body, but this was not punishment or condemnation, and Yawgmoth spared his subject his full fury. Then, under control once more, the Phyrexians' self-made god left Croag with other images from his own mind.

The Inner Council member was shown plans for Rath. The ceaseless spread of manufactured tan flowstone as it swept over the limitless horizon and would one day sweep over Dominaria itself. It was to be the staging ground for the coming invasion. He was told of the evincar, the one who must one day rule Rath and work the will of Phyrexia. This one would come of its own time, and until then Croag would be responsible for administrating the duties of evincar or finding someone who could.

Lastly, the half-conscious completed Phyrexian was shown the penalty he would suffer if plans did not proceed according to schedule. Interference from Urza Planeswalker would not be tolerated. If he failed, his flesh and metal components would be disassembled by the hunched-over, skittering creatures known as birth priests. The raw material of his artificially perfected body would be stripped down and reused. Nothing would remain of Croag, his name burnt from the minds of all Phyrexians.

Croag chattered his understanding.

The dark god retreated from Croag's mind. Smoke left in his wake dispersed on the hot winds of forge bellows, but the stench of burning metal never completely vanishing.

Beneath the surface of the bath, Croag came fully awake. His eyeshields dilated open, revealing large sockets that immediately filled with oil. His vision glowed amber from the cold-burning lights above the surface of the pool. It swallowed large amounts of the fluid. Tightening his grip on the bath's outside edge, Croag hauled himself upright, breaking through the surface and immediately calling to his servants.

The dark god had given him a task.

The pain distracted Davvol. As best he could, the Coracin native compartmentalized the agony of the mechanically-taloned hand locked with vice-like strength around the back of his neck. He ignored the tremors of his own traitorous muscles, and with a focus of will, he cast his mind forward from his body. For a brief second he stood there, looking back into his own eyes—black orbs with just a touch of steel-gray in the center. He cringed away from their lack of compassion and the obvious signs of illness in his pasty, corpse-like flesh.

The creature standing next to him, holding him in its grip, was hardly better to look at. Its body was a meld of machine and flesh, with one real arm and one of metal framework and corded muscle grafted back into place. Grillwork replaced its mouth and covered the bony ridges of what must have once been ears. Davvol extended his consciousness to touch the thoughts of the creature before him. Interspersed between the hate and contempt which ruled most of the Phyrexian's thoughts, it only knew of its own purpose. It was a speaker, one of the few who could speak Coracin's language.

Free from his body's entrapment, Davvol's mind now drifted through the antechamber of his world's most sacred temple. Usually lit by torch alone, it now stood illuminated by strange smokeless lights brought by the Phyrexians. The temple was an ancient ruin of rough stonework with one set of metal doors that took up the entire northern wall of the antechamber. To Davvol's knowledge, and that was saying something, no one had been past those doors to view the *Gift of the Gods* in over three thousand years. Even the antechamber was forbidden to all except the most powerful of Coracin's leaders. Twelve years as his nation's historian had once allowed Davvol the right to visit this supposedly hallowed place. Here he had taken his mental powers to new strengths. Then his forced retirement stole that privilege from him, until today.

Now he visited the temple again. Two score Coracin leaders were held in attendance by half as many black-armored soldiers. The speaker, the soldiers and another larger Phyrexian who appeared to be in charge stood across from the captive Coracin heads of state. This large Phyrexian was the one who could save Davvol's life—the one who could protect him from his own diseased body. The Phyrexians traveled across worlds. They could exchange the weaker flesh for metal and machine. They would do so because they needed him, could use him elsewhere, just like they relied on him today. Among the Coracin, even those rare ones with mental abilities similar to his own, Davvol was unique. Because his body had begun failing him so early on, he had spent the entirety of his thirty-four years of mature life developing his mind until none could match his strength. His mind was all he'd ever had.

Flares of black and red energy sparked at the edge of his consciousness. He saw the wards that guarded the doors react to his disembodied presence. His mental intrusion however was not quite enough to trip any alarms or traps. He entered another chamber, and there it was, the so-called *Gift of the Gods* that had sat at the heart of the temple for millennia: a machine, spiderlike in that its slab body would move forward on six articulated legs was obviously made of metal.

It gleamed as if age could not touch it in this vault. Davvol marveled at its physical timelessness. He studied the head, thrust forward from the slab body, savage in its likeness of natural physiology. The speaker had shown him a picture of it, calling it an engine of some kind—a Thran war machine brought here long ago. Yes, that is what it was, a war machine sitting at the center of Coracin's lip-service religion. This was what his leaders fought now to protect for themselves.

"It's there," he said, returning to his body with the speed of a single thought. He winced from the painful pressure applied by the speaker's mechanical hand. "Two sets of doors. The engine sits in the second chamber approximately thirty paces inward from this point."

The larger Phyrexian, the one showing less flesh and so obviously in charge of the situation, screeched something to the speaker—the sound of tortured metal and popping rivets. The hand released Davvol, and he slumped to his knees in weakness.

"Which one can defeat the wards?" the speaker asked. Its Coracin language translation came out harsh and rudimentary but understandable.

Davvol coughed wetly then rose shakily to his feet. The answer was already within his mind. Many people knew who among them was the keeper of that secret, and he felt no shame in giving that up. He had been a welcome member of the ruling elite once, before his physical appearance and health began to deteriorate. His perfect memory had been an asset, giving him a handle over administrative tasks few could match. He had given his mind over to his countrymen in hopes that they, in turn, could find a cure for his diseased body, but these people had been unable to heal him. They had stopped trying once he was expelled. Now they shunned him on the street as if his body's state was a fault he could control.

The fault was theirs.

"That one," he said, pointing out the correct man. The man shivered in fright, and the eyes of thirty nine other Coracin leaders cast venomous daggers at Davvol.

The speaker chattered and hissed back to the other. After a moment, "That one we have interviewed before. He was most resistant. Remove the knowledge from his mind."

A chill shook Davvol as the Phyrexian asked for the first thing he would be unable to deliver. "That may prove difficult," he began, and hastened when the speaker reached out for him. "What I mean is that my talent cannot root around in another's mind. I can read only surface thoughts, generalities." He swallowed hard, tasting a metallic sting at the back of his throat. "He would try to sabotage my efforts. He should open the wards himself."

"He refused earlier even when tortured," the speaker said.

Davvol pulled himself erect. "Yes, I'm sure he cherishes the solemnity of his position." He walked over to the other man. "It's only an artifact he guards—a machine." Something so easy to give up in return for life, thought Davvol. "I'm sure there is something he cherishes more, perhaps something he is more afraid for than his own life."

The elder man stared back. His expression twisted between loathing and hatred, and then he spit into Davvol's face.

Davvol did not flinch or move to wipe away the spittle. He felt it trail slowly down his left cheek. It didn't matter, he promised himself. The image was there in his mind—the other man's weakness. This insult only proved to him how little he still owed these people. He turned back to his Phyrexian masters.

"He has a daughter."

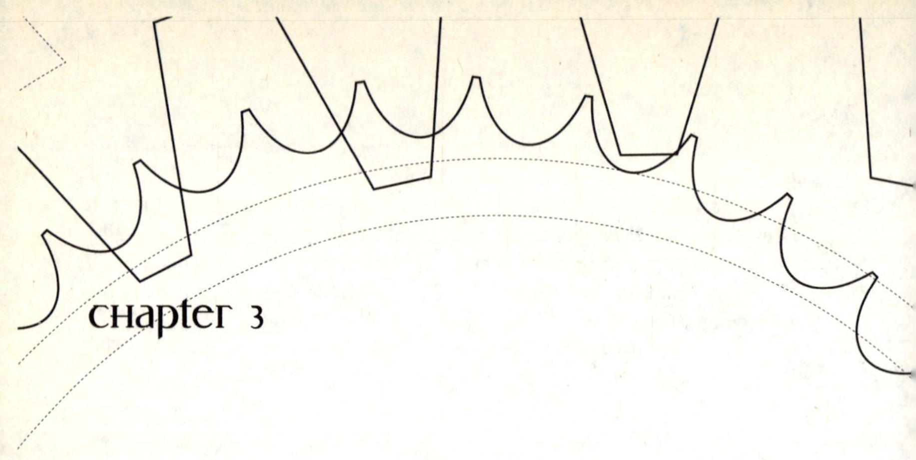

chapter 3

Gatha stood in the Grand Vault, as it had now been formally named, the focal point for the creation of Metathran warriors. It was also the central hub to the various labs and workshops in which the bulk of the work for the Bloodlines project—and to a lesser extent the ongoing Legacy project—was accomplished. He still could not help admitting to being impressed by its sheer magnitude—the arches, the central pillars that housed most of Rayne's mana-focusing lenses, the *space*—Urza certainly did not think small. Neither did the young tutor.

Gatha paced a short path alongside one of the gestating cradles, its curved nose sticking out of the large socket into which it had been plugged until full gestation of the Metathran warrior was achieved. This one was *his* warrior, one of those which would owe its existence—not exactly a life—to Gatha. His hard-soled boots beat a slow rhythm against the polished stone floor. One hand trailed along the side of the cradle, over rough gear teeth and the alternating smoothness of polished metal and glass viewports that looked into a dark interior. He did not attend the "birth" of them all, but this one might be special. He would know soon.

Timein found him there. "Master Gatha," the younger man said by way of address, voice devoid of any emotion. The senior student waited for acknowledgement before continuing.

Gatha glanced over and nodded curtly. Six subjective years had done little for Timein except to sharpen the student's mind. Still a tall and gangly body that looked ready to fall apart in a strong breeze and an adam's apple that almost split through the skin on his neck, at least his voice had lost the reedy tenor of youth. Timein began to bring him up to date on some of the minor experiments being conducted in real time, leafing through a stack of reports he carried in his knobby hands. As he listened Gatha compared and admired his own features in the reflection of a cradle viewport.

Eight years, again subjective, had brought Gatha into the comfortable stages of manhood nearing thirty. He now wore a trimmed goatee that he reached up to stroke while listening to Timein's report. He had filled out physically, and his mind had never been so brilliant. A tutor, one of the youngest ever, though he fell shy of Teferi's mark by a solid two years. Master of time, he considered himself. He felt himself second only to the Master Mage Barrin and Chancellor Rayne, who lived in the more extreme slow time and rarely ventured forth. Eight subjective years, passing in between moderate slow-time environments and real time, while for Dominaria forty-two years had passed. In the moderate fast-time envelopes, where much of his actual work was accomplished by students, over seventy years of research and production had accrued. Preoccupied with their own relative immortality and the fate of Dominaria as real time progressed, most other tutors and scholars underused the fast-time outposts. Gatha prided himself on never wasting opportunity.

"Results of recessive gene enhancements, post-birth, *negative*." Timein's voice barked out the word, bordering on disrespect and definitely capturing Gatha's full attention. "*Surviving* subjects show high rate of mutation, considered inadequate for further bloodline development."

Wheeling, Gatha strode over to Timein and snatched the report. It still smelled of fresh ink, and his thumb smeared one of the red circles that highlighted various figures. Gatha's strong hands wrinkled the parchment, clutching it tightly. Teeth clenched hard enough for his jaw to ache, he read down the list of three years' relative work—wasted. The red circles were no doubt Timein's notations, calling attention to numbers that supported the student's own predictions of four months ago. Gatha spared the student a quick glance, but Timein had settled a careful mask into place. The preparedness of the student allowed Gatha to place an easier handle on his own rage.

"What do you make of this, Timein?"

Gatha had learned years ago that Timein did not volunteer information, not to him at least. Though a promising sorcerer, Timein made no secret of the fact that he disapproved of the Bloodlines project. The trouble he occasionally stirred made it easy for Gatha to sidetrack the younger man's own studies, keeping him junior through extended assignment in slow time. It helped, more often than not, having an assistant nearly as brilliant as himself. Also, Gatha was not about to let Timein remain in real time where the sorcerer could conceivably age and learn faster and be promoted over him. That wouldn't do at all.

Timein merely shrugged. "I made my opinion known months ago, Master Gatha." A not-so-subtle method of reminding the academy tutor that Timein's *opinion* had also been right. "I imagine Masters Urza and Barrin will not care to hear that this tampering *post-birth* exceeded their guidelines."

Ah, a threat—Gatha smiled at the challenge. As he had noticed years ago, Timein simply did not know when to stop while ahead.

Waving over a junior artificer who worked on a nearby cradle, Gatha ignored his young charge. "This cradle," he said, kicking at the device that held his latest Metathran experimentation, "is to be unplugged at once and the subject delivered to my workshop."

If the other experiments had failed as badly as the report suggested, a similar procedure used during this Metathran warrior's gestation would prove similar. Autopsy would provide that answer and perhaps a suggestion for new paths.

The artificer turned back toward her workspace.

"Do it now," Gatha ordered, though he knew standard practice for artificers as ordered by Chancellor Rayne was to always keep an orderly space. Likely, the girl was going to set about putting tools away or some such bother. "The subject is within hours, perhaps minutes, of full gestation. I do not want it brought to full term." Damn the standard procedures.

Timein had evidently caught the nuances of Gatha's early termination of the Metathran gestation, connecting the tutor's displeasure with the report he now held. Gatha noticed the gaze of frustration and sorrow which his apprentice directed toward the failed experiment. He almost laughed, wondering what Timein's reaction would be if privy to Gatha's more recent alterations, most of those with the tacit permission of Urza Planeswalker. To recapture his attention, Gatha held up the report Timein had furnished and slowly ripped it down its length.

"This report," he said with a quiet hardness, words underscored by the tearing sound, "has obviously been exaggerated to the point of error. I will visit these labs myself." The report was in two pieces now. Gatha folded them together and proceeded to tear again, this time across the shorter axis. "Timein, you will take the rest of the reports to my office and compile all data." He quartered, refolded, and tore the report again. "Let me know what Barrin's people are working on as well."

The fragments of the report went into an outer pocket. Gatha frowned at the smudge of red ink staining his thumb. He reached over and rubbed it out against the dark blue border of Timein's sleeve.

The student mage could only stare in dumbfounded silence. When Gatha nodded a dismissal, Timein blinked away most of his shock and then turned to do as he had been bid. In Timein's years on Tolaria, Gatha doubted the apprentice sorcerer had ever seen data purposefully destroyed. The shock value, seeing it wash over that gaunt face, had been exquisite.

"It doesn't matter," Gatha whispered after the departing figure.

The report concentrated on the past. Only the present, the *now*, mattered. Behind him, the echoing clangs of a cradle being unplugged from the central machinery ran out, echoing in the cavernous theater. *Now*, Gatha had other projects to begin.

Karn discovered himself actually stalling. The silver golem had been asked to summon Gatha into the presence of Barrin and Urza and had already managed to be sidetracked by two other errands.

In the timelock, passing into the slow-time area where Gatha had settled his own quarters and a modest workspace, Karn had paused to study the device. Without a cushioning effect a human body could not withstand the transition of extreme temporal changes. The instant alteration in blood flow that occurred on the cusp, one part of the body extremely slower than the other, made for radical embolisms and instant hemorrhaging. Here, in the timelock, slow-time waters were pumped out of the same well that served Gatha's facilities. They were then misted into a series of chambers, which stood just outside the radical change in temporal flux. The density of mist in each chamber stepped up the farther one penetrated, preparing the body for slow time. The water was then reclaimed and returned to the water table via another shaft. It was very efficient, a variation on the first device built by Jhoira, who had noticed water's tendency to retain the temporal qualities of its original environment and so could be used to alter time in small areas.

Jhoira. She was rarely far from Karn's thoughts, his first true friend after the golem gained sentience. He had thought her dead once, only to regain her companionship and then lose it again as she moved on to a life that did not include Tolaria. He saw her occasionally, perhaps once every decade, but for Jhoira time had already mended the wounds of separation. Karn could expect no such relief. Ironic, that with Tolaria's ongoing mastery over temporal mechanics, he had yet to find a way to distance himself from a pain better than fifty years old.

After his emergence into the slow-time environment, Karn stopped by the side of a small, fragrant flower garden to pick a chrysanthemum. Its deep purple reminding him of Jhoira's darker hair, and its sweet scent the light perfumed oil she had worn on occasion. Finally the golem admitted to himself that his delays were moving further from the realm of plausibility and toward the denial of his task. He abruptly handed the flower to a passing female student and set off for Gatha's tower without an answer to her look of surprise. Stopping to smell the flowers simply was not a cure for his pain or a fair delay in his mission.

Still, memories of Jhoira were not so easily set aside. Drawn to make human contact, the golem could not help establishing relationships with those around him even though he recognized each one as another potential loss—more pain to deal with.

Gatha had set up a stasis field in his small workshop where failed Metathran warriors could be brought and kept in isolation while he ran his own tests. Four subjects currently crowded that field, two of them so deformed as to look more animal than humanoid. A third was hunched over, misshapen but recognizable. The fourth looked perfect in every regard, right down to the blue skin and Thran script that appeared as tattoos but were actually natural marks—never two identical. These creations would remain in stasis indefinitely. The alternative was to destroy a failed subject since the regular stasis fields were used to store *viable* warriors for use during the time of a Phyrexian invasion. Karn couldn't say for sure that destruction wouldn't be preferable, and therein lay another problem. Gatha didn't care. The tutor was brilliant but reckless. Karn had compared him to Teferi at first, but Teferi had been a spoiled boy who grew out of his troubles and into a responsible wizard. This Karn did not say to Gatha but hoped it would be implied.

"Don't look so glum, Karn," Gatha said as he noticed the golem's arrival. "You're too bright to be gloomy." Gatha chuckled at his own joke, then glanced back to the warriors. "I've been expecting you. Barrin's unhappy again, I take it."

"He wants to see you right away."

Gatha returned to his observation of the Metathran, shaking his head either at Barrin's summons or something to do with the fourth warrior subject. There it was again. A lack of any real concern for anything but what he focused on at the moment, and here every moment cost severe delays in real time where Barrin and Urza waited.

"Look at him," Gatha said. "Perfectly formed. Beautiful." He ran one hand back over his head to smooth back his own hair. Karn had noticed in the recent years that Gatha preferred to display his own tattoos, as if this somehow related him to the Metathran warriors and their own markings. "And completely psychotic. It can attack when angry or pleased, or it might simply curl up and become catatonic for days."

"And those others?" the golem asked, nodding toward the malformed warriors. He watched the young tutor's face for any sign of misgivings but found none.

"Older subjects." Gatha dismissed them with a wave of his hand, then reached up to stroke his goatee. "No, this one is the closest I've come yet to my goal. My fast-time laboratories will be concentrating on data from its gestation for several subjective years."

"No," Karn told him. "They won't." He hated to be the one to bring such news to Gatha, but Master Barrin had been direct: If Gatha did not respond immediately to a summons, Karn should deliver the news himself. "Your fast-time labs are being diverted to other projects.

Bloodlines work, but under another tutor and this time overseen by an academy scholar."

This grabbed the tutor's attention as nothing else could. "Barrin's orders?" Gatha did not bother to hide his anger, even when Karn confirmed it with a slow nod. "We'll see about that."

He grabbed up his cloak and strode immediately for the door, leaving the golem to follow or not as he pleased. Karn trailed behind, feeling miserable. He received only slight justification in the obvious foresight of Barrin's orders. Apparently the only way to motivate Gatha was to deliver such blows.

Barrin and Urza had commandeered a classroom which could seat one hundred students comfortably. It was the closest empty room at hand when Urza had reappeared. The planeswalker spent so little time on Tolaria these days, hounded by Phyrexian negators and not wanting to lead them back. The *Weatherlight* visited less often for the same reason.

Occasionally, some cases at the academy still required Urza's presence, and Gatha was certainly one of them. The rogue tutor stood alone in the dead space that separated where Urza and Barrin sat from the first level of seating where Karn now waited. A thin, placating smile on his face, Gatha affected an air of someone wronged at great trouble and personal expense—a child, convinced in his own superiority and put upon only for his smaller size and fewer years.

On the surface, the young tutor bore up under the rebuke admirably. Standing in silence, a slight flush to his skin and the hard cast to his eyes were the only signs of his inner feelings. Hands clasped behind his back, he simply nodded to every point made by Barrin and bowed to Urza's final demand.

"You must adhere religiously to the guidelines as set down for the Bloodlines project and exercise more discretion when it comes to the presentation of your work." Urza waited, then prompted for a reply. "Is that understood?" he asked.

"Yes, Master Urza. Of course." He was unable to hide the spark of anger that still smoldered behind his narrowly focused eyes. "My fast-time laboratories. Without them—"

"Without them," Barrin interrupted, voice hard, "you will be forced to slow down and adhere to the guidelines we've set. Your third generation subjects tend toward anger and brutality, even in their early years, and your rate of mutations are far above the average."

Urza rubbed at his chin with his right hand. "Anger and brutality are fine, each in its place, but these are unfocused." He shook his head. "Most third generation subjects show an increased lack of emotional focus. That's a step backward, and you're leading in that direction. We need to discover what is setting us back. We'll commit more generations to the fast-time pockets, try to generate data at better rates. If we solve this problem, you *may* get those labs back." He waited, and this time Gatha volunteered a curt nod. "That is all."

Gatha bowed his leave from the two of them. He did not look at Karn at all on his way out, a fact the golem did not miss.

The silver man made as if to leave, unsure of whether or not to follow. In the end he waited, and Barrin set Karn's obvious problems aside for now.

"He will ignore us, Urza." said Barrin. "He'll be more circumspect, for a while, but nothing will slow Gatha down except to further strip him of resources."

Urza, as was typically the 'walker's way, concentrated more on his own concerns. He shuffled a paper from out of a nearby stack, glancing over the report. "Why the step backward?" he asked again to the room in general. He glanced up. "You have more to say about Gatha?"

"He's incorrigible," Barrin snapped, "drunk on power and his own genius and now bitter that we've interfered with his fast pace plans. We'll regret every day that we do not curtail him."

"You once thought the same about Teferi." Urza actually allowed a touch of humor to his voice. He continued to scan the report.

Barrin shook his head forcefully. "Teferi deserved a good switching, but he did not destroy lives. Urza, this man is out of our control, and it is affecting the work of other students and tutors, raising again the same moral issues I've wanted to avoid—*we've* wanted to avoid—in the past. Gatha takes too many chances."

Urza evidenced no reaction, unimpressed by the dramatics. The mage sighed, feeling his years. He tried a new tack.

"Do you know how many of his failures are stacking up in the stasis chambers? Some of our newest students, those born on Tolaria, are now trying to discover magical ways to cure deformities we've left for them as a Legacy."

"Gatha is responsible for several of what few breakthroughs we've had augmenting the bloodlines," Urza argued calmly. He lifted his gaze to find Barrin's. "You know what he did to help bring the Metathran labs on schedule."

Yes, Barrin knew. He had assigned Gatha the work, hoping that getting his hands dirty might knock the indifferent edge off of the boy. Instead, Gatha had acquired a taste for it. He dressed in dark clothing these days, not the precise Argivian uniform he had when he arrived at the academy, the better to hide bloodstains Barrin felt sure.

"The Metathran are our own sin, but you've convinced me of their necessity. The bloodlines, though, involve and affect real lives." Barrin swallowed, trying to coax life back to his cotton-dry mouth. "Don't remind me that they are all volunteers, because this goes beyond that." He glanced toward Karn and then continued. "He's introducing Phyrexian material into the main Eugenics Matrix," he said matter-of-factly.

Now Urza paid attention. "How did you find that out?" he asked sharply.

Barrin stammered at the 'walker's reaction, his scalp prickling. The Eugenics Matrix was a Thran artifact that Urza recovered and modified and was the key to genetic manipulation. The Matrix and the simpler devices based on it offered the only real chance for success on the Bloodlines project. They also represented the opportunity for terrible abuse. All new procedures were supposed to be cleared by Urza or Barrin. The mage had heard unconfirmed rumors only but had hoped to shock a reaction out of the planeswalker never thinking that, if true, Gatha could be operating with permission.

"You knew?" he asked in a hoarse whisper.

"How else would Gatha get hold of *Thran* genetic material?" Urza stressed the different name, though of course they were one and the same. Noticing Barrin's frown of confusion, he said, "Acquired from more recent incarnations, of course, but as descendents of the Thran we can hope to reacquire their better traits." He brushed the semantics aside with a quick wave. "Where did you hear this?"

"Karn," Barrin answered, nodding to the silver golem. "He brought some rumors to my attention which led back to Gatha." He noticed the golem's start. Karn began to speak, and then with a confused expression, obviously decided against it. "I'm still investigating," the mage finished.

"Then you may stop investigating," Urza said simply. Noticing Barrin's look of dawning horror, he continued. "Nothing is more important than the Legacy. We agreed to that years ago, yes?" He waited for Barrin's reluctant nod. "It *does* matter that they are volunteers. I would not burden you with such troubles here on Tolaria if they were not. I must have the heir to the Legacy." Urza's eyes burned away, and in his illusionary mask of a young face the twin powerstones shown out in their stead. "Someone who can empathize with the Phyrexians enough to outguess them—to understand how to employ the Legacy to defeat them, possibly inside Phyrexia itself. Once Karn has joined with—"

"Speaking of whom," Barrin interrupted as soon as Karn's name was mentioned, talking over Urza's next few words. "Karn, would you mind finding Rayne? She's visiting some of the real-time labs. Let her know I'll be late and help out if she needs anything."

"Of course, Master Barrin."

Karn bowed stiffly from the waste, the relief in his voice telling how happy he was to finally have an order. The golem exited through the same door Gatha had used.

Urza had turned back to the report he held as soon as Barrin mentioned Rayne, his intensity of the moment before forgotten just as easily as it had come. This was not the first time Barrin had noticed that Urza seemed uncomfortable around the idea of the mage being married. It nettled him slightly and led him to wonder at the 'walker's odd manners.

"She *does* worry, sometimes," the mage said by way of explaining Karn's mission.

Looking up from the report, Urza nodded. "I'm sure."

To the swamps of Urborg with Urza's indifference! This chance upon him, Barrin said, "I am married, you know. Her name is Rayne."

"I know that." Urza's expression did not change.

"Do you disapprove?" Barrin asked directly.

"What makes you think I do?" Again no expression, but there was a hint of curiosity in his tone.

Barrin leaned forward onto the table they shared. "You avoid her, even the mention of her. I've noticed before that you take special pains to prevent encounters." He paused. "I'm sure she notices too, though she will never say so."

The 'walker nodded. "So you think I disapprove. Barrin . . ." His voice trailed off as if he were trying to organize his thoughts or was deciding what not to say. "Barrin, my own experience in relationships does not . . . I do not claim to have a clear understanding of mortal events. I try to leave well enough alone where my concerns are not needed and my presence is possibly disruptive."

It was a plausible answer—slightly evasive—but plausible. "You do approve?" Barrin asked, fishing for a straight answer for once. He held Urza's gaze, as if he could will the truth from the 'walker.

"Life must endure, Barrin," Urza finally said. "That more than anything defines our purpose on Tolaria." He paused, then, "I think you have done well. I certainly would not have chosen any other mate for you."

Barrin should have known better, hoping for an easy answer.

Urza stood, gathering up the reports he had been reading. The perfunctory way he went about collecting his papers might have signaled an end to their conversation, and Barrin was willing to let it go. Ending a conversation on a positive note for once would be nice.

Urza was of another mind. "Why did you want Karn to leave the room?" he asked, pausing half way to the door.

The 'walker was not *always* obtuse to the mortal events around him. Barrin nodded. "You were about to say that Karn would be joined with the *Weatherlight*, weren't you? And right in front of him."

The planeswalker stared back, waiting.

Barrin shook his head. "Urza, he isn't a cog or a gear. Karn is a sentient being, capable of making decisions which affect his life. I doubt you've even noticed, but . . ." The mage trailed off, drawing a strange parallel between Karn's obvious personal troubles and the previously discussed problems with the bloodlines. Could one be *too* empathic? Or have too perfect of a memory?

Urza shrugged indifference to Barrin, either missing or more likely not caring that the mage had interrupted himself. He hovered in the doorway. "The *Weatherlight* will require a governing mind when it comes time for its grand purpose, as directed by the heir. Karn is perfect for that task. He will complete the *Weatherlight*." With that, he walked from the room.

The planeswalker's use of the term *complete* ran a chill through the mage. That was how the Phyrexians described the replacement of flesh with artifice, as the *compleation* of the body. Barrin slid into a nearby chair, his strength deserting him. In all the years he had known Urza, Barrin could not remember hearing the planeswalker use the term in a similar context.

Ever.

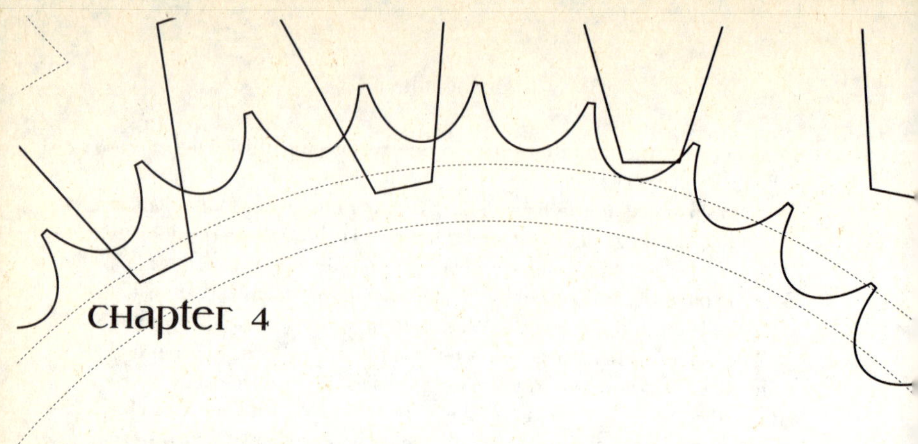

chapter 4

Leaving the kingdom of Zhalfir in its wake, hardly a dark smudge set against the graying coastline, the *Weatherlight's* crew checked all horizons and called them clear. Karn glanced back toward the ship's stern. A colorful sunset framed the aft end of the ship. Ilsa Braven, the vessel's current captain, commanded from the quarterdeck, and she bellowed commands which would not be heard again on the *Weatherlight* for some time.

"Rig the ship for sky. Take her up."

Crewmen shifted the sail rigging, and engineers brought the ship's magical engines up to power. Slowly, the sleek vessel rose from the embrace of blue-gray waters and into a sky washed pale red by the dying sun. The skyship's sharp bowsprit whistled as it cleaved the air. The sails remained full—billowed by magical energies which wrapped themselves about the sky-borne vessel. Most of the sailors and students aboard would agree that this was one of the best moments—when the freedom the *Weatherlight* offered was palpable especially to those who rode the open deck.

Karn did not revel in that moment, though this would be the final flight of the *Weatherlight* before security issues forced it to remain in the role of a simple ocean-bound vessel. He remembered other times well enough when he had enjoyed his time on the ship—pleasant moments on deck or down in the heart of the vessel where the silver golem could physically link with the *Weatherlight's* powerstone engine and command the ship's flight with a level of precision no human crew could hope to match. Those were heady times in the golem's life, good times indeed, now lost.

Over the last ten years Tolaria had begun to feel like a prison to Karn. His constant movement between the different temporal zones made him uneasy, unable to really know any of the students anymore. They were lost in a mayfly life while the silver man stepped into slow time to assist Rayne, Barrin, or Gatha.

Against his better judgment, Karn remained Gatha's friend—the tutor's only friend, it seemed. Other academy staff avoided him. Many of the students who worked under the tutor were afraid of him. Gatha did not seem to mind the lack of human contact, content in his work and a periodic acquaintance with Karn. That Karn needed something more came to a head when, during one of those visits to slow time, the golem missed one of Jhoira's rare appearances on Tolaria. The silver golem did not hold resentment for Gatha's summons, but it did cast him into a personal depression which only Barrin and Rayne had noticed and finally worked him through with a few kind words and gestures.

It was Gatha's continued use of Phyrexian material in the bloodlines that finally convinced Karn to seek a leave of absence from Tolaria. So many of his subjects were born malformed, and nearly all of them, so far, turned malevolent to some degree as they matured relatively quickly in fast-time environments. The golem had found himself unable to reconcile his friendship with Gatha and the revulsion he felt toward the man's practices. Karn remembered the years of fighting against the small Phyrexian community that had once infested Tolaria. He remembered the terrible creatures that repeatedly rose in newer, more hideous forms and the many good lives lost because of them. He easily recalled their grotesque features—artifice and flesh intermingled—and the caustic scent of the slime and oil that they called blood. He could still hear the screeching cacophony of noise that was their speech and screams. Worst of all, he remembered his own empathy for the black nightmares—that tiny spark within him which recognized Phyrexians as kindred.

Karn knew of the black powerstone which gave him true life—Xantcha's Heart. It had been first tied to the life of Urza's former companion, a Phyrexian newt who turned against her old masters and old world. It had retained its powers after she gave her life to defeat the Phyrexian Gix, and so Urza had bound it to the golem and brought about his first sentient artifact. The powerstone responded to Phyrexians still. The principle of similarity, Barrin had called it, trying to relieve Karn's anxiety with an explanation. Like must recognize like, but Karn had felt that same spark of empathy for Gatha's creations, and it frightened him. He did not want such feelings confusing his true friendships with good people like Jhoira, Barrin and Rayne. Upon hearing that Rayne and the forest spirit Multani would lead an embassy to Yavimaya on the *Weatherlight's* next tour, its final flight, Karn volunteered to help crew the vessel in hopes of reliving a few of those better days and so reclaim some hold on the present, except that hadn't worked.

Karn heard the *Weatherlight's* call to him even now. That deep hum of power that bled up through the polished wooden deck—a sound so bass it was felt more than heard. It was different this time; missing were the other people who had made those times alive for the silver golem, mostly Teferi and Jhoira. Always back to Jhoira, for whom, Karn admitted now, he had made this entire trip. He wanted to talk to his first and best friend, but neither she nor Teferi had been in Zhalfir—the ship's first port of call—and no one had been able to say where they might have gone off to and whether alone or together.

There would be no absolution on this journey, only the hard, cruel truth the golem now faced standing alone on the ship's deck. He had tried to run away, but his past would never allow that. It followed him, tormenting and tireless. Right then Karn wished it all away.

Never once did he consider what such a wish might cost him.

Multani moved to the edge of the quarterdeck, away from the tight knot of academy observers whom Captain Braven had invited up into her domain for landing. The nature spirit gripped the rail. He could feel the life in the ship, a life which was still as much a part of Yavimaya as a being of its own essence, much like himself.

Even from a distance, Multani would fail to pass for a human or one of the more humanoid races. His trunk exactly that, a medium-sized bole too thick and cylindrical to remind one of a body. His arms and legs were thick branches, very knobby at the joints and his fingers and toes rootlike extremities. Barklike skin covered the backs of his hands, forearms, and the tops of his feet, and his face seemed to *sprout* from the top of his trunk. Hair the color and texture of spring moss fell back from his scalp and upper shoulders, the mane tumbling halfway down his back. He had chlorophyll eyes, green irises staining veins into the white, and a leaf-shaped pattern tattooing the left side of his woodgrain face. He was created from the essence of Yavimaya, the sentient forest packaged in humanoid form.

Now, after better than a century away, he was leading a Tolarian embassy and Llanowar ambassador back to his homeland.

Blue-green waters rolled up to a thin outer arc of beaches which alternated between light yellow to reddish browns and the intermittent green of coastal growth. The beach territory quickly faded toward pale washes of rainbow color as the *Weatherlight* moved inland. That was new. The forest green had once stretched from one side of the island to another, before Yavimaya had begun some . . . changes. The interior remained a dense canopy of greens, interrupted only by a few dark mountain peaks. The canopy rippled in places, as if by an intense wind that no one else could feel.

He felt the forest's anticipation and just a trace of concern for allowing so many outsiders access to its lands. The nature spirit sent back a soothing call.

"It's wondrous," Rofellos said, the Llanowar elf bounding up to the rail beside him.

The young warrior's dark, unruly hair fell in a tangled cascade down his back. He leapt up onto the narrow rail, leaning far over with one arm looped casually through nearby rigging. The bottom hem of his leather tunic waved in the moderate breeze created by the ship's passing. His sword dangled from a rough leather belt—an item he never set aside no matter the company or situation.

Multani had moved aside to avoid the others, especially Rayne with whom he had already spent so much of this voyage in conference, but Rofellos, for all his energy and rough ways, was welcome. He was one of Gaea's forest-born, though more violent than most, but then the same could be said of most Llanowar elves. That was the reason Yavimaya had asked the Llanowar warrior clans send an ambassador. Perhaps the Llanowar might learn from Yavimaya something more of harmonious living.

Respectful as always to Multani's slightest comment or movement, Rofellos jumped back down to the deck. "I'm sorry, Multani. I didn't mean to disturb you."

So close to home, Multani doubted that much could truly disturb him. Soon, he promised himself, he would know the forest's soothing touch again.

"Do not worry, Rofellos, Yavimaya welcomes you.

Rofellos drew himself up proudly at the recognition, whether from Yavimaya or Multani himself the nature spirit couldn't be sure. In reality, it didn't matter. Perhaps Rofellos could not fully appreciate the unique creation which was Yavimaya yet, but certainly he stood in slight awe of the nature spirit. Multani watched the elf carefully as, still racing the wind at a good clip, the *Weatherlight* flew over the island perimeter.

The elf started only slightly. "No beaches?" He grinned, obviously enthralled by the prospect. "No sand or rocks," he said in wonder, "only Yavimaya."

"You will find no sand," Multani promised. "None safe."

Below them the beaches had been consumed by a tangle of thick, thorny rootwork. The roots extended out from the small copses of coastal growth, then curled and bunched as they ran across the open space and finally dived into the ocean shallows. A few last tips stuck out like huge spikes, as if to impale landing ships. When Rofellos mentioned this, the nature spirit nodded.

"They are meant to do just that. You see years of patient growth at work here. Though Yavimaya's defenses will tend to spread from the heart outward, an initial perimeter guard was deemed of great importance."

The elf forced on himself a moment to consider this, a sign of extreme patience in a Llanowar. Finally he asked, "Does Yavimaya tell you this?"

"I simply know it to be true. Yavimaya speaks through me. It has no need of speaking *to* me."

As the coastal root network and isolated copses fell away, the *Weatherlight* crossed over what had appeared at first to be painted desert. The air chilled and quickly turned to an intense cold. The nearby humans chattered excitedly, and Rofellos continued to stare over the side, oblivious to the temperature. Multani shivered in his physical shell, turning his face upward to stretch toward the sun's warming rays.

"More roots, thinner ones, blanketing the ground." The elf fell silent for a few seconds. "Writhing over . . . are those dunes?"

"Trees," Multani whispered without looking. "The boles of ancient trees, centuries old, which Yavimaya shaped and then recently fell here in perfect order so that no gap remains. The ground here reflects no heat. The warmth is pulled into the decomposing trees so that the root desert may grow faster." The spirit looked ahead, at the high cliff of wood that barred their path. "Captain Braven, you may rise above those trees, but slow your speed. Your landing area is near."

The captain barked out the appropriate orders.

"We are not traveling into the Heart of Yavimaya?" Rofellos asked.

Multani tensed at Rofellos's choice of words. He obviously knew nothing of what he asked, merely reflecting some of Multani's earlier statement. The true Heart of Yavimaya would never be known to the Llanowar. Likely, it would never be known by Multani, so protected it was by the sentient forest. Though it was forbidden even to him, Multani knew a slightly jealous protection of his homelands.

"For our purposes," he said simply, "the borderlands will be close enough."

The vessel settled down in a clearing of dark grasses dotted with small, lavender-cupped flowers. The field rippled under the same unfelt breeze that had earlier shaken treetops in the distance. Trees which reached hundreds of feet into the air surrounded them, visibly impressing many of the students. Multani recognized it as new growth raised in the last few years. Several of the larger hills around would be partially decomposed trees from the ancient growth, brought down by Yavimaya for the raw material.

The Tolarians went about their routine of making the vessel fast. Sails were reefed, and the telescoping circular gangplank hauled out and dropped down over the side.

Multani winced at the harsh clanging sounds as the staircase unfolded. He move toward it once secured, but Rofellos ignored it completely. With a wild shout for his own bravery, the elf vaulted over the lower gunwale and slid down the outer curve of the hull. At the last moment he kicked outward, breaking his fall with an easy tumble across the grass. He rose only to one knee, though, suddenly transfixed by the rippling motion of the sward. Multani could only guess at the other's sense of wonder as he descended to the ground.

The air was vibrant with life, singing Gaea's song as wind shook the tops of trees and whistled past sharp grasses. Pollen, which Multani had never scented before, distracted him, every taste calling an instant explanation from Yavimaya. The earth felt spongy beneath his bare, rootlike feet, and he found it hard to control the urge to dig his toes down into the rich soil and taste his homeland again. Yavimaya withheld him, waiting on the others.

The elves appeared as if by magic. One instant they were absent and only the forest sounds surrounded the clearing. In the next, all forest sound but the distant fall of a tree disappeared, and a dozen lithe bodies appeared at the clearing's edge. They moved into the clearing with cautious grace, as if unwilling to leave the protection of the forest. All were of fair hair and skin, with features so delicate they appeared fragile. Rayne moved up to Multani's side, and the nature spirit stepped away to distance himself from her.

"Yavimaya welcomes you," a female elf said in traditional greeting to Rayne and the other humans. Her voice was light and musically cast.

Rayne smiled warmly. "We are here on behalf of the Tolarian Academy—"

"To request some rare hardwoods for the crafting of your artifacts," the elf completed for her. "For Urza Planeswalker." She smiled with shy amusement at Rayne's apparent confusion. "Yavimaya was present for all your discussions with Multani, of course."

Multani nodded his own greeting. "Long life, Shahira," he answered: A typical elven salutation. Yavimaya stirring at the edge of his mind, Multani turned back to Rayne. "The forest will provide you with your request for materials. Some of the hardwoods will take a few days' effort to grow."

As if to underscore his statement, the rolling creak of twisted wood resounded about them followed by the staccato snapping of limbs being stripped away. Within the forest, only much closer this time, one of the trees toppled, then another, this one at the edge of the clearing. Multani did not bother looking, having expected the pruning. Three more trees fell in quick succession, the canopy rippling with movement.

Frowning in thought, Rayne studied the surrounding forest. "Decay?" she asked.

Multani looked sharply to Rayne, insulted but tempering any outward show. Surprisingly enough, though, it was Rofellos who answered first.

"The cycle of life," the young warrior elf said, brushing the back of his hand across the rippling grasses. "Accelerated, but natural."

Rayne's dark eyes widened with amazement. Bending low, she examined the strange movement of the field. "The grass and flowers, they are dying off and regrowing so fast they sprout from the withering shell of their former incarnation. It creates the illusion of wind."

Multani had never doubted Rayne's intelligence. "*Decay* implies failure," he said formally. "Nothing happens here that Yavimaya does not approve and control." He nodded in the direction of the latest felling. "The forest is in a state of accelerated growth cycles," he explained. "Building up the forest's store of raw matter from which we may draw new strengths. Phyrexia is not the enemy of Urza Planeswalker alone."

The Tolarian artificer nodded her agreement. "It is good to know we have allies," Rayne said, "and tell Yavimaya we appreciate the offerings."

Smiling tightly, Multani reminded himself that Rayne could not be expected to learn of the forest's ways as fast as she might learn about artifice. He allowed himself a light laugh at her expense.

"You should have listened more closely to Shahira, Mistress Rayne," he said. "You just told the forest yourself."

Rofellos glanced about quickly, still feeling eyes upon him. The thrill had worn off hours ago—the persistent gaze that followed his every move, crawling over his skin with a gossamer touch. His hand stayed near his sword hilt, fingers twitching as he scanned trees and ground and sniffed the air. Danger surrounded him, stretching his nerves taught.

The young elf had taken to the treeline with Multani's permission, eager to explore the land that would be his home for years, maybe decades, to come. He'd rolled in leaves far different from those he'd ever seen, raced miles of near invisible trails never before run by a Llanowar, and used some crushed berries to paint a simple hunting mask across his eyes. It was the way Llanowars claimed land, making it theirs through intimate knowledge. A warrior race, Llanowars often lived or died on the honing of their instincts. Rofellos was not about to allow his stay in Yavimaya blunt those senses. Ambassador he might be, but first and foremost he was a warrior. Yavimaya, he felt certain, recognized that in him and approved.

Right now his instincts warned him of a threat—a watcher—someone dogging his tracks and a better tracker than he. Multani? Possibly. If so the humor of the situation was now lost on the wild elf. His grin was feral as his eyes darted among possible hiding places. Always the feeling that he merely had to turn a bit faster, look slightly harder, and the presence would resolve into the figure of his tormentor.

Now came a brush at the back of his neck. Rofellos spun about, sword drawn and flashing in a high-lined attack. He checked himself a split second before slicing into the tree that stood behind him.

"Who's there?" he called loudly, instantly regretting it. You never gave yourself away so easily, except this was supposed to be friendly land. Silence greeted him.

Rofellos backed up a step and then another. He glanced frantically into the canopy above him and deeper into the undergrowth—nothing. Spinning about again, he set off at the strong pace he could keep up for a day and night and half a day again if need be. He would run this presence into the ground.

With every step the disembodied gaze followed, nagging at the back of his mind.

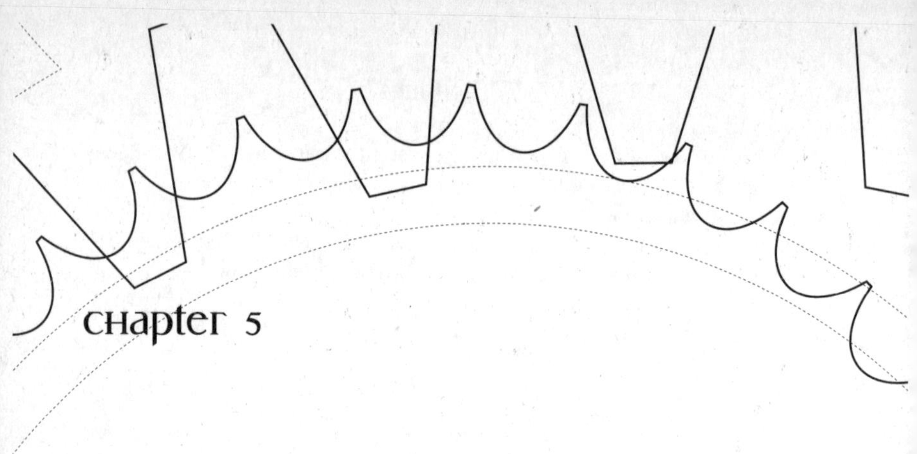

chapter 5

Davvol stepped through the doorway of dark energy, followed closely by the speaker sent to summon him from his work. He quickly fell to his knees as the heat rolled over him, and scorched air burned down into his lungs a caustic and oily brand. Flaring eruptions from the mile-high furnaces lit up the eternal night sky of Phyrexia's Fourth Sphere a hellish red-orange, spewing tons of ash into the air. High above, a tangle of pipes and mechanisms which formed the underside of the third plane rained down a light mist of oil. The metal rooftop on which Davvol rested radiated a near-blistering heat of its own, working its way through Davvol's armor and forcing him to stand or roast against the oven-temperature plating.

Another Phyrexian moved nearby in the shadows cast by a large gout of flame and oily smoke. It looked the part of a monster of Coracin fable—skeletal arms and skull, and that terrible grin of sharpened metallic teeth. Its clothes fell over it as a funeral shroud, seemingly tattered and ruined. When it moved closer, Davvol noticed the cloth's writhing movement as the tattered ribbons constantly shifted to cover a new portion of the Phyrexian's body. Instantly he knew that cloth to be alive and integral to the Phyrexian. No doubt this was the most powerful creature he had ever stood witness to. What a magnificent creation! Davvol trembled, his strength giving out, and he fell to his hands and knees before its power.

The new Phyrexian hissed and screeched something in its own tongue to the speaker. "I am Croag of the Inner Circle," the speaker translated into Davvol's language, though with a tortured squelch behind every word. "You do not approve of our world, Davvol?"

Davvol forced himself to his knees alone, hands already blistered with burns imparted by the searing metal floor. Pain can be controlled, he thought, cursing his weaker flesh. Fear can be controlled.

"I look upon your world as perfection," he answered, "but my body is weak." He remembered the Phyrexian term that would describe flawed meat, not yet augmented by artifice. "Incompleat."

At least his body was no longer dying. The Phyrexians had done that for him, though little more in his forty years of service. They gave him only enough to keep him alive, allowing him to live out a Coracin native's full years while he helped seeker teams find and uncover treasure troves of lost artifice.

More hissing and screeches. "I have chosen you to serve the Ineffable's plans. You will come with me."

Croag lifted his thin arm, braced with metal straps and cords, and summoned another Phyrexian from the shadows behind him. The new beast carried another portal, its fingers already setting stones into place to direct the channel that could step between worlds. It placed a rod upon the ground, and a doorway rose from it.

Davvol swallowed against the dryness cutting into his throat. The Ineffable had summoned him? The Phyrexian dark god himself? Never before had Davvol been allowed past the Second Sphere of Phyrexia, and here the Fourth almost killed him. Was Croag leading him to the next sphere? If his death was sought, why not rend him down into the vats? How had he earned such torture? Davvol rose on shaky footing to stumble after Croag, the last vestiges of his courage prompting him onward. There was nowhere to run, not here and never from the Phyrexians. They owned him and had made that clear from the start, though they had yet to honor any part of their promises to compleat him. They kept him alive but only that. Croag disappeared into the new doorway, and Davvol followed, nearly passing out with the final step he took in between portals . . . and planes.

By comparison, Davvol stepped from the Fourth Sphere of Phyrexia into paradise. He, Croag, and the speaker stood on what appeared to be the rim of an extinct volcano. A sharp wind billowed out Davvol's smoldering cape and rustled Croag's living garments with a rasping sound. Its chill touch brought back to mind the blistering pain in his hands, but Davvol set his teeth against the agony while surveying the alien landscape. No sun stood in these overcast skies and likely never did. Blanketed from one horizon to the other, the gray cloud cover glowed evenly with a muted light. Red and orange lightning crackled and leapt in the skies, cavorting to the accompaniment of booming thunder.

The ground around them was a dull, tan sandstone, fused and smooth as if from intense heat. It flowed out for as far as he could see, interrupted only by the mountain chain that trailed back from the volcano. In a few places nearby, Davvol saw the facsimile of boulders, noticing they were little more than sculpted bubbles in the seamless flow of ground. Down inside the caldera, as if raised up from an old eruption, stood a magnificent tower fortress.

"What is this place?" he finally asked.

"This is Rath." The speaker waited for more of Croag's grinding screeches. "It is the instrument of the Dark Lord, a new plane, set in the Dominarian Nexus, from which we will complete his task."

Davvol stood on a new artificial plane, still in its infancy by the look of it. He brought his hands together in contemplation, fingertips almost touching but mindful of his burns. Turning about, Davvol contemplated the entirety of Rath. His eyes, steel within black, searched the horizon for further signs of life but found none.

"I am required here?" he asked.

"You will oversee and accelerate the schedule of Rath's expansion," the speaker said for Croag. "You will hold it in stewardship until the Ineffable names an evincar to rule." Croag must have seen something in Davvol's face, for another series of noises spat from the speaker. "This does not please you?"

Davvol studiously blanked his face. No matter his personal feelings, he knew better than to try the Phyrexian's humor. "It pleases me greatly," he said, lying only slightly, wounded that they had not simply named him evincar. With greater authority might have come stronger steps toward his own compleation. Still, what they offered impressed him, and hadn't his memory for details proven its worth long ago in an administrative position? "By expansion, you mean—"

Croag's chattering interrupted him, and the speaker quickly translated. "Rath is still growing." It pointed down to the caldera fortress. "The Stronghold taps into Rath's lava furnaces. Flowstone is created which continues to expand the borders of this plane, pushing back the energy envelope. Flowstone production must increase, and you must control any dissident troubles."

Davvol glanced around. "Dissidents?"

"A city of slave labor beneath the Stronghold." The speaker pointed to the smudge of forestland Davvol had noticed before. "They were brought over from Dominaria long ago."

The Coracin native thought to ask more about this but then realized that it no longer mattered. The situation would be as he observed it, time enough for questions later. What truly mattered would be the resources at his disposal. Already his mind worked at several plans for optimizing production.

With a strong gust of wind snapping his cape out behind him, he folded his hands carefully together and asked, "What may I draw upon to complete this job?"

"The flowstone," was Croag's first, not entirely helpful, answer. "Also Phyrexian troops, for keeping order, and the negators."

He would have negators at his command? Davvol had seen the terrible powers wielded by Phyrexia's elite hunters only once, and that had been enough. Terrible, sinister designs, compleated for the hunt and destruction of Phyrexia's enemies. Negators, troops, and slave labor, the power swam in his head. He glanced down into the caldera. The Stronghold was his to occupy. The Phyrexians withheld the merger of flesh and artifice he craved, but here they had given him a world to rule. Certainly that could only bring opportunities later. He nodded to himself, eager to get to work. The Phyrexians would know his worth; nothing would be left to chance.

"Negators," he said. "I wouldn't have thought the locals strong enough to warrant them, but they are most welcome."

There was a pause for translation, and then Croag shook his cleft skull in a human gesture of the negative. He chattered a new flurry of squeals and hisses. A clammy hand clutched at Davvol's heart, forewarning him that whatever the negators were for, the problem would not be so simple as he'd wished.

"The negators are not for you to control the Vec," the speaker said. "They are for the protection of Rath itself, for the destruction of the only one who might upset the Dark One's plans.

"You, Davvol, are to assist me. You will hunt down and destroy Urza Planeswalker."

In the Stronghold, Croag walked unattended through the wide hall that led to the throne room. The lower steel bands of his robes brushed the flowstone floor on occasion, smearing a glistening band of light oil wherever they touched. A set of pipes followed the corridor at shoulder level, radiating heat. His hidden footfalls, eerily silent, left behind only scratches and pits in the floor. The doors to the throne room were of thick metal, set on tracks that led back into the tan walls. They rolled away to the accompaniment of a dry metal grinding. A sound which angered Croag, telling of the neglect by Rath's current steward.

Davvol, he had left behind, the member of Phyrexia's Inner Council preferring to come alone. The Coracin native would be singularly useful in the administration of Rath, but he was weak—meat—and would only be a liability in this encounter. Nothing could be allowed to threaten Croag's newest plans, not even Koralld.

"I have been expecting you, Croag, yesss," Koralld hissed when Croag stepped into the dimly lit throne room.

A Phyrexian overseer, Koralld had been brought to Rath to steward the expansion of the artificial plane—he had failed. The overseer sat on the room's large metal throne, hunching back into the seat of authority as if physical contact would improve his ability to hold the position. His legs remained tensed, the fibrous muscle that showed between the gaps of his armored skin coiled and bunched. His articulated hands grasped the arms of the throne, each finger ending in a razor-sharp talon. He had mandibles instead of teeth, and each one dripped a viscous substance that would burn meat and pollute blood. A single eye stared out from the middle of a large, armored skull.

Croag worked his way farther into the room but kept an appreciable distance from Koralld. The overseer was not about to go easily.

"Rath is still behind schedule. You failed."

Failure carried only one sentence with Phyrexians. Failure implied imperfection. Imperfection had to be corrected.

Koralld tilted his head to one side. A serpentine tongue flicked out to clean the metal tipped mandibles.

"You bring a full meat body to replace me, no. I do not think that is ssso."

From the floor to both sides of Croag the flowstone softened and bulged up in two large cylinders. These quickly hardened into spears and drove unerringly toward Croag's body. They were too slow. Koralld's mastery over the flowstone, while impressive for its control, lacked any real power. Croag's skeletal arms flashed out in blurring speed, smashing aside the lances that shattered into stone fragments and chips.

This was only the prelude to an attack, however. The chamber lights flickered out, plunging the throne room into darkness as Koralld sprang for Croag. The Inner Circle member slashed out blindly, his razor-tipped fingers slicing easily into Koralld's carapace even as the overseer smashed into him.

Croag's robe of steel bands absorbed a great deal of the impact, allowing him to keep to his feet and slip away from the enraged Koralld. Croag's eyes burned brightly now, filling the normally empty eye sockets of his skull with an unfocused, reddish light. The darkness retreated before his compleated eyesight. There was the actual throne of Rath and the doors, he picked out the broken cylinders of flowstone and the broken pieces scattered about but no Koralld.

Where would he go? Croag turned a slow circle, his steel bands rubbing together. He had to be here. Koralld's only opportunity was to kill Croag here and now and so prove his superiority—earn his ascendance.

Ascendance!

Koralld fell from his overhead holds even as Croag snapped his attention to the ceiling. The member of Phyrexia's Inner Council saw the handholds crafted into the stone above, prepared no doubt for this occasion. In the same blinding motion he had shown himself capable of before, Croag shot his arms up to bear the brunt of Koralld's attack. The other

Phyrexian's claws ripped past the steel bands this time, digging down into the wire-cord muscles. The overseer bit in with mandibles to pierce his victim's shoulder. Croag's right arm fell useless, the shoulder flaring in a deep pain as Koralld's venom disrupted the mixture of glistening oil and serum that all members of the Inner Council relied upon for blood. The overseer's attack then turned against him, as his own weight tore the mandibles from Croag's shoulder. He scrambled to get his feet beneath him, landing awkwardly.

Here Croag struck back, snapping forward to sink his own polished steel teeth into Koralld's. No poisonous discharge, but it held Koralld fast and left him unable to use his best weapon. Croag's left hand flashed outward and then in, talons piercing the overseer's right arm and driving farther into his body to pin it in place. Steel bands snapped at Croag's mental command, some whipping out to wrap around legs and the overseer's one free arm. Others snapped back and forth, flailing at the trapped Phyrexian, their razor edges methodically scoring and slicing past Koralld's armored skin.

The lesser Phyrexian screamed his rage and pain, thrashing about desperately for release. Croag's eyes burned more sharply now, their unfocused fire coalescing into twin coals that began to sear into the side of Koralld's head. There was a second pulse and a third. Each time the searing rays burned deeper. On the fourth, Koralld quit struggling and simply hung in Croag's deadly embrace, feeble tremors shaking his body. On the sixth pulse, the overseer's scream gave out, and the tremors stopped.

Croag was not finished. The Phyrexian kept up his efforts, fiery pulses boring into Koralld's head while the razor bands sliced deeper. He waited until his artifice-bonded cells repaired themselves and he regained use of his right arm. Croag brought up both hands to crush Koralld's carapace skull. Flesh brains pulped out.

"You did not think, Koralld," the Phyrexian finally said, responding to the overseer's comment before the attack.

He threw aside the ruined skull and walked toward the throne while the steel bands of his robe reknitted themselves. No, Rath needed something else besides an overseer's hard-handed rule. Davvol? Was he the key to the upkeep of Rath and the destruction of Urza Planeswalker? Perhaps. Davvol's mental powers suited him for administration, and perhaps a fresh outlook might solve the puzzle of how to kill the planeswalker. Croag certainly needed to find some answers. He had not forgotten his master's commands or the punishment that awaited him if he failed. At least Davvol would be much easier to control.

Croag knew complacency to be a common downfall of even the most powerful Phyrexians. Could Davvol be dangerous? The Phyrexian Inner Council member could not see how. Davvol had yet to show any ambition except in the matter of his compleation. *That* could never be allowed to happen—not fully. Davvol would be kept alive so long as he proved useful, so long as he was kept motivated, and what mortal did not fear death?

In the darkness of the Stronghold, Croag seated himself upon Rath's throne.

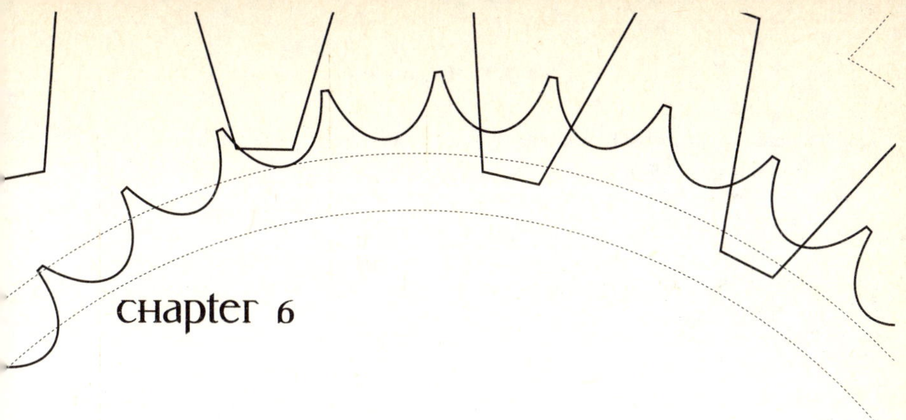

chapter 6

Barrin stepped into the workshop, noticing first the disarray of tools left out on the workbenches. Timein stood nearby, staring out one of the gray-blue tinted windows. A slight chill crawled over the nape of the mage's neck. Timein's posture and position reminded Barrin of a time eight subjective years ago—sixty-five in actual Dominarian years—when he had first offered Gatha a position in the Metathran experiments. Barrin doubted it to be coincidental that Timein had requested their meeting here in the very same workshop Barrin had then held his orientations on the bloodlines. Timein had specifically wanted this room—wanted Barrin to remember.

"I'm here, Timein."

The student sorcerer turned around slowly, awarded Barrin a bow of respect. "Thank you for your time, sir. You will find the papers on the edge of that first table."

The mage did not look immediately. He instead met Timein's placid gaze and tried to discern what could be so important that the senior student had deliberately bypassed the usual administrative chain to come directly to the academy's chief administrator.

"If you wish to register a complaint, you should do so through proper channels. Working under Gatha can't be easy for any—"

"I will register no complaint concerning Tutor Gatha," Timein interrupted, though his voice remained respectful, "but I do have a discovery I believe should be placed directly into your hands."

Barrin thought he knew Timein better than to expect grandstanding, so he shrugged him the benefit of his doubt and picked up the stack of papers set nearby. The top page looked to be pasted back together from several pieces that had been deliberately ripped. Barrin did not recognize the report and glanced back to the young sorcerer.

"Who did this?" he demanded.

Timein stood mute. That told Barrin enough. So much for the idea of accurate records. He began reading.

The first page was not the only one that looked as if it had been pasted back together or fished from the trash. By the time he had read a fourth of the way through the pile, Barrin was seated and arranging certain papers over the cluttered desk for ease of referral. All told, the stack covered about forty years of real-time research into the problem currently facing the bloodlines—the growing lack of empathy for Dominaria and an embrasure of their darker . . . elements.

"You can prove this?" were Barrin's first words.

Timein nodded. "In the next room."

A few junior students waited there, escorts for a sullen, elderly man who frowned at Timein's entrance and glared hostility at Barrin. The man's head had an elongated curve going back over his shoulders.

"This is Rha'ud. He's a bloodlines subject raised in fast time."

That explained the skull's elongation to Barrin. Several subjects had evidenced a few unusual physical characteristics after some of Gatha's experiments. They were also known for a natural hostile approach to anyone associated with the academy.

"Why are you here, Rha'ud?" Barrin asked softly, feeling for the other man. "You were not compelled?" Barrin ignored Timein's wounded glance.

Rha'ud shook his head once. "This one," a nod to Timein, "said he might be able to help my little girl. She don't get along so well with others." He swallowed. "With anyone."

The mage let it go, not wanting to parade over the man's pride. "Let's hope he can," he said.

Timein brought out a small box and removed from it a stone streaked with cobalt and milky white. Some areas sparkled green or red from less obvious mineral deposits.

"A Fellwar Stone," Timein explained. It was a naturally occurring stone capable of channeling the five types of mana.

He placed it on the table, close to the elder man, and cast an incantation over it. The stone rolled toward Rha'ud, once, twice, then fell still. The young sorcerer picked it up and placed it closer to one of the escorts. The stone began rolling at once and was prevented from falling off the table only by Timein's quick grab. He nodded to the students.

"Thank you." They got up and left the room, Rha'ud between them.

"That doesn't prove much, Timein." Barrin waited, sure the student would explain himself.

"Just a quick demonstration," the younger man said. "The stone will roll slower and turn less often depending on the generation. It barely trembled for Rha'ud's daughter." He placed the Fellwar Stone back in its box. "I'm using a variation on the laws of contagion. If a person has memories for the lands of Dominaria they are drawn to anything of a similar type. Using wood, the spell will work only for those with an affinity for nature—green mana. A hot coal or piece of obsidian likewise for the mountains or red mana. I promise you, Master Barrin, that the bloodlines are developing without an affinity for any part of Dominaria. The fast-time labs we are using to accelerate the turn of human generations do not allow them to gain memories of the land."

"These are not mages," Barrin said, troubled and looking for an argument, "and if they were it is a matter of bringing them outside—"

"A person's connection to the lands of Dominaria means more than his ability to draw upon the mana he possesses," Timein interrupted again. "I can prove to you that that connection directly affects the person's natural empathy for the world around him. How far back a lack of such ties causes irreversible harm is uncertain, but theory suggests that it could be at birth or even conception or *over generations.*"

Barrin stood speechless. He paused, his gaze meeting Timein's, while considering the implications. "The entire project could be in danger of permanent contamination. Is that what you are saying?"

Timein simply nodded.

The mage sighed. "All right, Timein, I'm convinced, but we'll have to turn this over to a larger workforce at once for independent verification and study of possible treatments, and I'll have to tell Urza." He was certain the 'walker would not be pleased about these findings or the destroyed reports. Barrin would *not* tolerate such blatant disregard for protocol, especially when lives were affected.

The sorcerer braced himself up at the mention of Urza Planeswalker. "He will be back to Tolaria soon? I heard he had just visited."

"Yes, but we have another problem that requires immediate action. In fact, it's ironic that the bloodlines problem is so similar to Karn's."

This appeared to catch Timein off guard. The younger man frowned. "Karn? How can he suffer from a lack of memories of the land?"

"His problem is just the opposite. He suffers from an *infinite memory.* It is paralyzing him, though slowly, over the course of decades." Barrin shook his head in implied pity. "Rayne and I have noticed it affecting his performance in any task requiring human interaction, and he will continue to grow increasingly inflexible as time passes."

"Did Urza have any ideas?" There was no questioning Timein's concern.

Barrin shrugged. "I don't think so, not yet. He simply said that the situation would have to be dealt with 'decisively.' " The mage braced Timein with his gaze. "I'm telling you because I'll want you to work with Rayne and myself on this. Perhaps your empathy research can help."

Timein nodded gravely, accepting the charge. "If it can't?"

"The solution will be entirely in the hands of Urza Planeswalker."

The workshop was one of the larger ones, with an overhead gallery for students to observe the progress below. Several tables stood upon the floor. Racks of tools and equipment lined the walls. The room smelled of aged wood, leather, and oil. Rayne thought the room much bigger than required for so simple an alteration, and the gallery remained clear, which surprised her; the academy was still a place of instruction, for all its preoccupation these days with the Legacy. Only Barrin stood solitary in attendance above, and she suspected her husband of turning away the idle curious for the sake of the patient. Rayne approved and nodded her support to Barrin.

She stood at Karn's left shoulder; the large silver golem lay down upon the centermost and largest table in the shop. Turning her gaze back from the gallery, Rayne placed a gentle hand on Karn's thick arm.

"It will be all right," he said, his voice a soft rumble, stealing her thought for him.

No one else in the room cared for nor actually needed Karn's comforting assurances. Urza stood at the table's other side, discussing some finer points of Thran metal with Gatha who managed to at least look curious whether or not he actually was. Rayne doubted it. Gatha was here on the order of her husband. He had helped design "the cage" and consulted with Urza on the magics that would be employed.

"Learn some compassion for the lives he touches," was Barrin's private comment to Rayne, though both doubted it would happen. Even after two years, Gatha still chafed at the new restrictions to his own work. He complained about the "insignificant duties" placed upon him such as teaching classes and filling out extra paperwork to ensure that no more research was "misrouted." His single appeal to Urza had met with stony silence, and there was no higher court.

Urza moved to Karn's head and without preamble reached beneath the neck to unfasten the clasp. Even for the planeswalker this took some doing, trying to manipulate the intricate lock hidden inside a small cavity. It was designed to be difficult, and the combination was known only to six people, including Karn himself. The lock released with an audible snap. Urza lifted, and the golem's entire head swung forward to rest with his face touching his chest. Rayne noticed that the assembly was not hinged, but the silver metal itself seemed to bend and fold to allow the movement. Karn shuddered once and then went completely stiff as Rayne reached in and removed the black powerstone that gave the golem life.

The Heart of Xantcha. Rayne never before had the chance to examine it. It was the size of a grapefruit and perfectly black, where most powerstones were constructed of a clearer crystal. Rayne thought that she could feel the power that resided within the stone, imagined it as Karn's spectral voice asking for help. A single tear welled up in the corner of her eye, but there was nothing she could do for her friend. Urza Planeswalker had decreed it would be so—Karn's recallable memory would be capped at twenty years, to prevent the golem's slow failure toward compelled dormancy.

Rayne glanced back up to the gallery, wondering how her husband must be feeling over the results of his insight. She saw that a single person had joined Barrin. It was Timein, the sorcerer whose latest work had suggested that a subject's empathy for Dominaria was better than ninety percent based on the ties developed over the first eighteen years of life. His evaluation of Urza's plan—before discovering the use it would be put toward—could find no reason why a "floating memory" of twenty years would not adequately duplicate the formative years repeatedly over the lifetime of a subject. She wondered if foreknowledge of Urza's plans might have changed his answer—if only in presentation.

They all shared responsibility, everyone now present. Rayne possibly the more so as it had been her initial theory that the increasing pressure of growing Thran metal against the powerstone might somehow be used to restrict memory recall. That theory had held up despite numerous student attempts to break it, despite her own best attempts as well, once she realized the single flaw that Urza had decided Karn could live with and probably be the better for. Despite the research, no one could say how this procedure might affect the golem's mind.

In the meantime, design of the cage had gone forward. The planeswalker now lifted it from a nearby box. A two-part shell, it looked delicate but was stronger than any other known metal. The basket had been fashioned from a pattern of whorls and segmented braces which perfectly enclosed the heart of Xantcha. Rayne set the powerstone inside one half, and when Urza closed the basket it magically fused into a solid piece. A full-year's growth of the metal would squeeze the stone and begin to suppress Karn's older memories. Over two centuries of accumulated experience and knowledge would be lost to time's press in as little as a single decade, after which Karn's memories would fade as any regular person's might, locked away but with a full recall capacity of only twenty years. It was hardly a young man's lifetime, but according to Urza, "More than adequate."

Rayne winced as Urza replaced the powerstone—no more concern showing in the 'walker's eyes than for any other artifact. Rayne glanced away. There were worse things than death, certainly, and so far Urza Planeswalker seemed capable of them all.

Rain pounded Tolaria, the first heavy fall of the year's stormy season. Special covers went up over the academy's tended grounds, protecting flower beds and in some cases the food gardens on which the students and staff relied upon for fresh produce. The deluge pounded against paving rock, clay shingles, and wooden slat roofing. Over fast-time areas the water was wicked away so quickly that the downpour simply appeared to lighten or even stop. The slow-time envelopes, as seen from without, appeared as strange bubbles, the water building on the surface until it began sheeting off the sides. It might be hours or even weeks before the first drop hit the ground as seen from real time.

Inside the island's protected harbor, rocking in the hard wind, the anchored *Weatherlight* sat with gangplank extended to the nearest dock. A few final supplies were carried onboard—the ship's schedule not to be interrupted by mere acts of nature. The crew loaded on provisions for the voyage, slow-time waters to be delivered to those few academy alumni allowed a return to the real world, and Legacy artifacts to be hidden away in other cities until needed again one day.

Gatha stomped his way up the gangway, working his fury out on the iron grillwork. He ignored the purser who was responsible for all stores loaded and passengers brought aboard. The man was currently debating the additional equipment being brought up the ramp by two of Gatha's assistants. Bypassing formalities, Gatha instead presented himself to the captain, who stood in a small sheltered overhang while supervising the last of the cargo being secured aboard his vessel.

"Help you, master?" she asked, using the title clearly out of habit than any awe for the academy insignia on Gatha's cloak.

She certainly did not move out into the rain so that Gatha could stand protected from the elements. Twenty years commanding a vessel might inure anyone to the regular formalities, Gatha supposed. Still, the tutor loathed her for his dry position, the buttons on her foul-weather coat done only halfway up while Gatha squirmed from the cold water leaking in at the neck of his cloak.

"I've been added to your passenger list," the tutor lied, presenting the forged papers stamped with Barrin's own seal—"borrowed" during one of the master mage's few classes he still taught.

Gatha could have more easily laid his hands on the seal of a chancellor but had decided against it for various reasons. Though Gatha despised Barrin for the other's weak stomach and lack of vision, there was no doubting the master mage's formidable powers. Since Gatha considered the other man a peer—even if he was a rival—only Barrin's seal would be used. Shut down Gatha's primary labs would he?

"So I see," Captain Braven said after a cursory glance at the seal. "And that?" she asked, nodding toward the commotion at the head of the ramp.

"My equipment and some supplies. All papers are in order." Gatha tucked the documents back into the relative dryness of his dark cloak. "You are to transport me and my equipment. I will leave the ship at your first port of call." His tone left little room for arguing, and the captain seemed ill inclined to do so anyway.

"Erek, check the seals on that equipment and get it secured below," Captain Braven bellowed, ignoring Gatha's flinch at the volume of her order. "It's too wet to be arguing their timing."

Nodding an insincere thanks, Gatha backed away from the captain and returned to his assistants. The purser scrawled a brief description of each piece to his master inventory, estimating weight when necessary.

"Ether Mixer, what's that?" he asked, stopping a female student at the head of the gangway.

Gatha spoke up before the student could answer. "Lab equipment," he said. "For mixing ether, of course. Light, very durable. Store it wherever." It was his own private joke. How did one mix ether? By stirring around empty air. It was a reference to speaking without knowing of that which you spoke.

Naturally, the purser did not understand the reference. He nodded, grunted, and jotted a few notes. "Forward hold," he said.

Gatha fell in beside her for a few steps."Remember, I count on you." The female student glanced over, rain plastered hair laying between her eyes and down over her face. Gatha nodded his support.

"You are my eyes and ears back here on Tolaria, in case I ever need to come home."

Not very likely, unless Barrin ever stepped down. Still, Gatha might eventually need access to slow-time waters if he were to run out of the supply he'd stolen and information on the latest academy breakthroughs when they happened. She nodded reluctantly.

"Master Gatha," the captain called out before he could bolster his student's confidence more. The rogue tutor stopped by the captain's alcove, bracing himself for discovery and the quick, violent action that would necessitate, but Isa Braven posed no true concerns of that nature. "You may take the first passenger cabin" she said simply. "You are our only guest."

The tutor nodded. "Where is you first port of call?" he asked.

"Argive."

Gatha smiled. "Argive," he said, repeating the name. "Well, well." After seventy-five years, Gatha would apparently be returning home.

The academy slept. Only a night watch roamed the real-time areas of the island. A few assistants monitored critical projects which required twenty-four hour surveillance, but for the most part, silence gripped Tolaria.

Karn never slept. His body did not require it. Though in times of decreased activity he could suspend his higher brain functions and enter a kind of hibernation—just to pass time until he was with purpose again. In years gone by he had done just that, but not tonight or any night in the past year since his alteration. He vowed he would never sleep again, though of course in time even that vow would be lost.

No bed ate up space in the golem's room. It simply was not required. There was a table and several reinforced chairs, but the most functional pieces were the shelves where Karn placed the memorabilia he had collected over the decades—the centuries—books and pictures, keepsakes and souvenirs. The aggregation of a lifetime. Nothing in this room was without meaning, without a memory attached, but there soon would be. All of it would become meaningless to Karn as his memory faded, except one thing.

A picture of Jhoira, sketched for him by a student of artifice also gifted in art.

It was all he had left of her, his best friend. Karn couldn't bear the thought of Jhoira returning to the island and him not remembering her. Karn stared at the picture and quietly spoke to himself. "Jhoira is my friend—my best friend. We met in the original academy, before the accident drove us from Tolaria. She named me. Karn, from an old Thran name. She said it meant strength." His voice sounded heavy in the confines of his small room of memories.

A wave of intense anguish rolled over the golem. All this for a person he had not seen in better than a century. There were events from as little as four days prior which he could no longer recall with exacting detail, fading for their lack of emotional significance as they would in a human mind. How did they stand it? Karn could not remember ever feeling frightened, and these days his lack of a memory no longer meant that it was true, but he felt frightened now.

Standing there, his memories arranged around him like trophies of the past, Karn started again. "Jhoira is my friend. My best friend . . ."

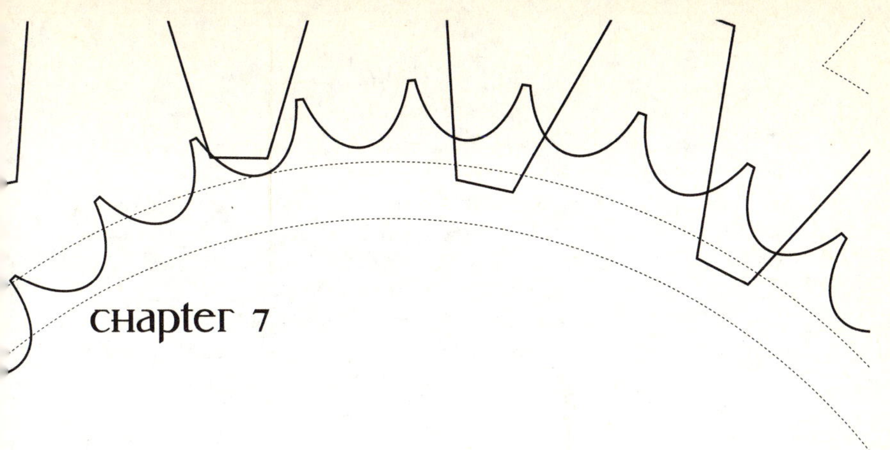

Chapter 7

Gatha leaned heavily on a staff of dark ebony, its headpiece a pair of ironwood crescent blades stained a deep crimson. Picking his way over the slide of rubble that obstructed the mountain trail, one of the larger rocks rolled underfoot and the mage earned a new cut against his lower shin. His quality calfskin boots—bought in the lowlands and assured of rugged wear—were nearly at an end to any useful life, scarred and scuffed against the sharp rock they'd clambered over these last several days. The thick wool coat, however, held up admirably, and it was a good thing. The sharp wind that whistled down from the snow-drifted peaks cut through anything lighter. As it was, the wind found its way past cuffs and collar to keep him always on the verge of freezing. The sweat from the climb stood out cold on his face. Gatha considered magicking himself warm again, but that was a draining use of power, and it never lasted long enough.

His guides, a Keldon trader and his son on their return from the lower port city of Agderisk, plodded on steadily and without complaint of the rugged terrain or cold climate. The shaggy colos hides they wore kept them warm. They did not bother to check on the young mage's progress. They showed the same disregard for the slaves who were leading a caravan of large colos—something between a war elephant and a shaggy mountain sheep, to Gatha's eye—loaded down with their wares and the mage's equipment. The slaves would follow because to disobey apparently meant a lingering death. Gatha would keep up or he would be left behind, likely to die.

The Keldons were apparently not big on alternatives.

They were, however, the largest men Gatha had ever seen. Drahl, nearly fourteen and still two years away from entering military service, stood nearly six feet with a build to match his fathers, heavily muscled, the two of them, with forearms and lower legs longer than upper arms and thighs. They had grayish skin, networked with scars, and thick, dark hair with the triple widow's peak that Gatha's tattoos simulated. They also tattooed themselves, filling in the skin around their eyes with a dark ink that lent a fearsome appearance. The elder trader sported a pike in the place of his lower right arm, the limb lost in battle at the age of eighteen he'd said.

Gatha understood so little about these people, even though his father had once served as the Argivian liaison to a Keldon warhost. He knew the basics of course, that the Keldons based their society almost completely on the waging of warfare. They existed as mercenaries, their mountainous lands effectively one large armed camp. Other nations paid for their services and paid well, since Keldon negotiation techniques were fairly straightforward and violent when opposed. Try to bargain down the price and the warhost was just as likely to claim the balance by force on their way home. Worse, they would simply claim the full price from your nation and then head home anyway. They carried back to Keld their blood price as well as pillage and slaves taken from the land invaded. Glancing back, Gatha counted at least three different nations among the human slaves. Benalish were easily placed by their cast markings and the Surrans by their ritual scarring of the face. He returned his gaze to the trail. Slaves were of little use to his efforts here except as potential subjects for experimentation if all went well.

Farther on, Gatha saw his first example of Keldon architecture, high enough into the mountains these hard people began to feel at home. The buildings sat on a small cliffside plateau half-buried into the mountain slope. Constructed of stone, several of the structures were three stories high, tiered as they rose to a steeply pitched roof of tan-colored wooden planks. They looked incredibly solid, as if called up from the ground on which they sat. The windows were dark.

"Stopping here?" Gatha asked in simple Argivian.

He had heard the trader speaking Keldon with a few others in the lowlands. A rough language that would be hard to learn. The Keldon people knew the basics of many languages, though, from their constant campaigning.

"Nah. At war," the trader said. He pointed toward the red banner spiked into an upper wall of one of the buildings then looked back. He made a gesture of butting his one fist into the sharp end of his pike. "Battle. Fighting." He bared his teeth enthusiastically.

Gatha nodded his understanding, wiping sweat from his forehead and pulling his greatcoat closed tighter at the neck. Soon, he hoped, they would rest.

The rogue tutor had discovered it more difficult than he'd thought, trying to set up a lab outside of Tolaria. His work was not looked upon favorably by most nations. Argive, in fact, had been merely the first of several nations to refuse him. His experimentation did not allow for a secret laboratory. The room required and indelicacies of the operations themselves were certain to attract attention sooner rather than later, twelve years of wandering, twelve *real* Dominarian years of work, lost, before his arrival in Agderisk and a talk with the local traders.

Everyone the world over knew something of Keld and its aggressive ways. Learning more of them now, in the shadow of their mountains, Gatha had been intrigued to hear of the rituals surrounding the creation of the Keldon warlords. The largest and most violent of the young, still several years out from entering military service, were sent on a pilgrimage through the deep mountains' frozen wastes. Those who survived were then enchanted to further their growth into larger, superior warriors. They became capable of extraordinary battlefield prowess that also worked to excite the troops being led into a frenzied state. To Gatha, this sounded very much like a eugenics program, if a bit crude in its methodology.

His trader guide, when Gatha first found him, had not been inclined to talk with the mage. Noticing Gatha's tattoos had changed his mind. Apparently they won him the courtesy of an interview, if that's what one might call Gatha's simple speech and the trader's even simpler grunts. In the end, Gatha simply paid the man as a guide to the Keldon Necropolis, their capital where the *doyens* of the Warlord Council met.

The Keldons were a people very interested in anything that could improve the way they waged war and had already worked with the early stages of enhanced genetics. It had sounded too good to be true, Gatha remembered, then stubbed his foot against a sharp rock and nearly fell—too good to be true, until he had started this treacherous climb.

The Keldon Necropolis crowned a mountain peak, the fortress capital rising up out of the hard land. Frost and snow lightly dusted some surfaces but drifted deep in the several large crevices where sun never struck ground. Homes rose up from the dark gray stone—single dwellings lower on the slopes, and higher up, loose clusters were tied together by trails worn into the hard earth over centuries. Nearer the summit the buildings suddenly sprang up in thick numbers with little room for trails, most paths winding through caves carved into the mountainside. Above this mountainside city towered the great tombs themselves.

Here the Keldon warlords were finally laid to rest. This majestic vault defied gravity and earth as it challenged the sky. It was almost two hundred feet high with steeply sloped sides, and one entire mammoth wall was open to the thin mountain air. When he had seen it from a distance, it had reminded Gatha of the great Surran burial pyramids. Only these were steeper pitched and the top carried away to make room for the living witch kings' council chambers—the Necropolis, where Gatha now waited to address the Keldon ruling body.

The cold, thin air sat heavy in Gatha's lungs, as if reluctant to give up any oxygen. The mage had to work at breathing after his long climb. Waiting for his audience, Gatha's muscles burned in silent protest. He felt a poor excuse for an ambassador, especially one representing himself. He gave his wool greatcoat to the trader who had guided him up the mountain in exchange for a pair of tough coloshide boots and thick furs. He felt in need of a hot bath and smelled of the large animal that had given up this particular set of hides. At least he would appear more presentable, or so he thought. A footsoldier escorted him through a set of large bronze-plated doors and into the main council hall.

The same magical architecture that held up the great tombs below must certainly have been used for the hall. Like a giant cylinder it rose five stories straight up, with galleries set about each level for observers. Flags and banners from other nations had been crudely spiked into the walls. There were hundreds, thousands perhaps. Likely these were brought back from every war ever fought by Keld. The meeting area itself was actually an inverted amphitheater, a tiered pedestal carved out of the gray bedrock. The uppermost platform stood empty, possibly awaiting a speaker. On every ring after that sat the chairs of the council, each one different and again with some designs clearly belonging to nations represented on the walls. On those chairs sat the *doyens*—the warlord elders of Keld, half a hundred at least. The trader and his son, who had seemed so humongous to Gatha, could not begin to touch the smallest of these men, a great number of them easily topping seven feet. They wore thick leather clothing, ceremoniously studded and colored. No one wore furs or hides that might provide warmth. Many tunics bared chests and arms to the frigid air, scars standing out whitish on gray skin. The cold was a long-vanquished enemy of these people. Some carried weapons at their sides, those lower down the platforms. Those higher up carried short staves or rods of carved bone. A mist from warm breath haloed the great room, and from out of that mist fiercely tattooed eyes stared at the mage who suddenly felt very small and alone.

It was a state Gatha was not too familiar with and, secure in his own power, he quickly rallied from. He knew what he needed, and he would have it, somehow.

"Warlords of Keld," he began slowly, speaking Argivian. He had already been informed that Argivian was a language most knew, and that they would not speak with him unless he presented a subject suitable for their notice—or offered a direct challenge. He had decided to offer a little of both. "Into your lands I bring a gift, knowledge, which can help you and your nation grow mighty. Magics, which will make your sons stronger on the battlefield, your warlords more fierce and your victories more complete."

A few stirred at that, possibly taking Gatha's words as a slur against their own prowess. The mage waited for a challenge, but none rose immediately. He stepped farther into the council hall. Briefly he considered making his way up the platforms to the empty spot where all could easily see him, and then he decided against it. He possessed no way of knowing yet what the local rituals might demand. There was an obvious pecking order implied in the seating, and Gatha did not want to challenge anyone's pride, not yet. So he instead circled the tier slowly, explaining the basics of his studies and experimentation. No details, he doubted anyone here would understand. He couched the more unpleasant facts in vague references or dismissed them completely, concentrating instead on how his own work mirrored that which the Keldons already employed in the creation of a warlord.

"I only need a lab, support, and time," he finished. Always time, the devourer of his accomplishments that had stalked him for twelve years now.

A warlord on the lower tier near Gatha rubbed at his coarse beard. He growled a reply in broken Argivian, "Why *puny one* think we need his strength? Who is he?" There followed something more, this in the Keldon tongue that could only be derision from the laughter barked out by a few others.

Debate the mage would tolerate, but not even Barrin had ever insulted the tutor's genius. Gatha speared the large man with an angry gaze, eye contact being a challenging gesture in any culture.

"One who is strong enough to be able to think, *before* I speak," he answered with scathing disdain. Only in afterthought did Gatha wonder at his rash action.

The warlord sat forward abruptly. Muscles bunched and twitched, and one hand strayed toward the short stabbing sword he wore.

"You speak to me? Varagh? You, lowlander?" His dark eyes flashed dangerously.

There was nothing for it now but to establish himself in some form of ritual duel, a test of strength. Gatha walked slowly toward the warlord, carefully drawing mana from the lands he had touched in his recent travels. He remembered the river delta of Agderisk, its chaotic channels of muddied waters. Power swelled within his mind, begging for release. Eyes never flinching from the hostile warlord, the mage stepped up onto the first tier with calm and deliberate motion.

Varagh stood abruptly, one hand darting for his sword as the other clamped down hard on Gatha's shoulder, pinning the mage in place. Such deliberation in killing saved Gatha's life. The mage brought up one hand in a twisting motion. Energy danced from his fingertips and into the warlord's eyes. The giant man stumbled, sword falling from nerveless fingers, blinking away the sudden confusion. Gatha gathered himself up and physically forced the larger man from the platform so that he now stood at the same height, eye to eye, as if physically dwarfed.

The warlord rounded on Gatha, spinning in a fluid, catlike motion. Gatha thrust his left hand forward, sparks of blue energy dancing around his outstretched palm. Snarling, Varagh clawed his own face with his thick fingernails and then charged forward. It caught the mage, who had expected the Keldon to take more time to recover, off guard. He dodged to one side, releasing another blast of mind-numbing energy. This time the sparks danced outward . . .

. . . and glanced off the warlord's bared chest.

Gatha was picked up by his shoulder and hip then slammed down onto the tier. Darkness swam before his eyes. He felt detached, as if this could not possibly be happening. Battle magic! This is not how I die, he thought. Even so, he saw through the haze as Varagh reached one hand back and clench it into a hammerlike fist.

A dark blur landed heavily behind the Keldon, grabbed the raised fist and pulled it back. The pressure eased from Gatha's shoulder. He sat up and scrambled backward until he found the next tier. Another warlord had pulled Gatha's attacker away. Now the two circled each other, crouched low and barring teeth. Varagh shouted, attacked, and was dealt a cruel clawing across the face. The answering punch was weak, and the new warlord caught it up, snapping the arm at the elbow as easily as matchwood. Varagh never uttered a sound for the pain. He simply stood there with a snarl of anger on his face while the other warlord held onto the wrist of his broken arm. He glanced down then bowed his head at the neck.

The victor released the wounded arm, turned his back on Varagh, and stepped back onto the first tier, looking down on the mage. Gatha came to his feet slowly.

"I Kreyohl," the new warlord said in Argivian. He reached out slowly, placed a hand on Gatha's chest, and shoved him from the tier.

The mage stumbled and nearly fell to his knees. Anger welled inside Gatha, but he held it in check. This one might know battle magic as well, and there was no fighting them all at any rate. He broke eye contact and bowed his head as he'd seen the other warlord do. Both *doyen* retook their seats, Varagh below and Kreyohl on the next tier higher up.

Kreyohl studied Gatha in silence for a moment. "You alive because I hear you more. Not want you dead."

Yet, Gatha finished for him. Still, he recognized now the procedure he had witnessed, the stronger male disciplining the inferior. They respected strength and little else.

"I *can* make you stronger," he said cautiously, not wanting to offend but not ready to give up. " I have special magics, and I need only time and a little help."

No one answered right away. Gatha saw Kreyohl glance from the side of his eyes, obviously reading the body language of his neighboring warlords.

"You make many promises," he said slowly. "Maybe keep, maybe don't." He paused. "What can you show us now?"

Now *there* was a sentiment Gatha could understand. Unfortunately, it was also one he had not decided a ready answer for. Few were those who thought of the present first and future later. It was that thought, of *the present*, that prompted a solution.

"I can scry the world of Dominaria." How to say that more simply? "Magic sight. See troubles and wars. Today and any day, where the Keld might find the best employment." No, not correct. "Take the best plunder."

That appealed to the assembly. Subtle nods were passed. A warlord on Kreyohl's tier spoke the group consensus. "Prove it, and your work supported."

Gatha smiled, breathing out between white teeth a cloud of frozen vapor. Proving himself was not a difficulty. It was, in fact, one of his favorite pastimes.

Two years and Gatha still could not stand the smell. The small room stank of the peat used for walls, corrupting the crisp scent of new snow which had fallen in the night. The tan wooden planking laid directly over earth shifted slightly beneath Gatha's feet as he crossed the temporary laboratory. He slapped his hands together for warmth and held them over a barrel of slowly burning animal fat. The sharp, final tock of a clockwork timer drew his attention to another table, but the sound of rock being quarried distracted him from checking results. He paused at a window cut into the southern exposure, looking downhill on the site of his permanent labs. *His* labs.

A winding trail cut down the snowy mountainside toward an area roughly leveled by natural erosion. The site was large, befitting the importance of the work Gatha intended to do there and the efforts he had already put forth on behalf of the Keldon people. A *doyenne,* one of the Keldon matriarchs, strutted imperiously around the site overseeing the project. The females oversaw everything which was not associated directly with warfare.

Slaves worked to burst away some remaining outcroppings. The dark gray rock was collected and then moved by colos to the building pile used by the Keldon builders. Among that small percentage of Keldons ill-suited to war—dishonored and sent to live as general laborers, traders or farmers—these outcasts would rate master builders in many nations Gatha could name. They worked slowly and methodically, building to Gatha's specifications but following their own designs when practical. In his fourteenth year of self-imposed exile from Tolaria, Gatha could finally hope to begin soon a serious continuation of his earlier work.

The Keldon armies were constantly on the move these days, preying on Dominaria wherever Gatha's scrying and a nation's coin brought them. The mage's commitments called for a great deal of his time and efforts, especially when the council preferred his presence at the Necropolis higher up the mountain. Those efforts were now being scaled back in favor of his experimentation. Permission had been granted to begin his work on slaves and second-class Keldon citizens.

He had already begun setting up his Matrix and the rest of his equipment in this shack the *doyenne* had built for his temporary use. The first trials on native Keldons showed incredible response. Slaves were not quite as easily altered, but they served as good subjects for initial experiments. The colos were even more so, their tough nature adapting to his changes and giving Gatha more ideas. He used the colos as testing boards for his more radical ideas, moved up from there to slaves, and then to the Keldons to observe an end result. No one complained of his few setbacks. Many of his Keldon subjects actually expressed appreciation that the mage had found a way they could serve their nation one final time. Gatha drank in the heady results as each day brought him closer to resuming a full work load. His work had certainly found a home here in the bloodlines of Keld.

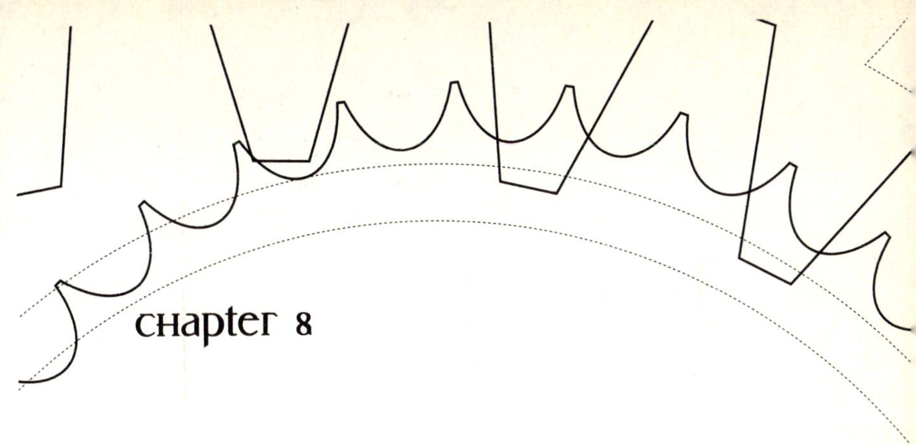

chapter 8

Urza was unprepared for the Phyrexian attack. One moment the planeswalker had been studying a cliff face for traces of Thran artifice, and in the next, a stream of hellish energy had slammed into him from behind and pinned him to the rock wall. It had required of the 'walker every ounce of his willpower to hold together his form in the face of the surprise attack. The second negator hit him from the side, a flurry of rending claws and razor-sharp fangs. Only by throwing the second Phyrexian into the energy attack of the first did Urza manage to break away and recapture a portion of his strength.

Now the three danced about wildly. Urza moved with preternatural speed. His attention divided between two negators, they came close to matching him. Lightning crackled at Urza's fingertips, striking out like some kind of whip, keeping the negators at bay. Where the energy touched the creatures it split the armor, exposing black, corrupted flesh beneath. He couldn't seem to reach anything vital in these robust creatures, and the energy cannon that replaced the arm of one Phyrexian continued to strike at him with dangerous effect.

Wherever the reddish stream touched him, the equivalence of mortal pain ate into his concentration. The more he devoted to keeping his form intact the less he had to deal with the his own offense. Urza settled into a defensive pattern, gambling that the Phyrexians could not come up with another surprise while he built up his own power.

The negator predisposed to physical assault uttered a long and piercing shriek that threw a disrupting ripple throughout the 'walker's entire form.

A wisp of fiery energy from the cannon caught Urza in the arm, and for the briefest second he recalled the mortal pain of a burn as well as the disruption to his immortal form, a sensation he would have been happy to live without remembering.

Drawing power from his memory of the Hurloon Mountains, calling forth the powerful mana they offered, Urza cast lightning from both hands which began piling up in front of him. The collection pulsed and grew, spitting out arcs of snapping energy. No more time left to him, Urza cast the large ball of lightning forward. It sped toward the negator brandishing the cannon. It dodged the first pass but was caught up trying to shake the inexorable advance.

It gave Urza all the time he needed. Bringing his staff to bear, the planeswalker triggered one of its many functions: a sonic attack, one that he had devised decades before to deal with the Phyrexian infestation of Tolaria. The sound interfered with the composition of glistening oil—the lifeblood of Phyrexian living artifice. The high-pitched harmonics slammed into the second negator with incredible force, throwing it back and pinning it to the earth. Sprays of gray-black liquid gushed from the negator's open wounds, and it trembled and shook. Urza moved forward, the head of his staff pointed directly at the creature. With a final spasm the negator fell still, its fluids leaking into the ground and staining the soil black.

Only then did Urza notice that the second negator had ignored the attack of harmonic sound. It still dodged about nimbly, evading the pulsing collection of energies that trailed after it relentlessly. There would be no escaping the strike, only delay, but the 'walker couldn't be sure of it being enough to kill the negator. Tapping the mana as he had a moment before, Urza quickly built up another such electrical storm and flung it toward the cornered Phyrexian. Weak from the attacks against him and concerned that the remaining negator might have sent a summons to others, Urza cast his form into the chaos that existed between worlds and 'walked away.

While the pain of the burn had long faded, its memory continued to worry the back of his mind.

Flanked by four of the armored Phyrexian soldiers, their black armor gleaming dull orange in the fiery glow of the lava tubes, Davvol toured the main facility concerned with the production of flowstone. The massive, bladed dials spinning in their housing above generated most of the mechanical power required. Giant corkscrews pulled up the lava in black-crusted tubes from the geological furnaces of Rath far underground. They would be cooled by waters siphoned off a nearby lake and then fed farther up into the processing machinery. Yellow steam escaped the joints of nearby pistons, scalding and sulfurous. The machinery this far down had turned rust-red over time, standing exposed to the sulfurous steam.

Davvol filed away a mental note that the machinery should be overhauled as soon as the secondary additions were built and in full production. The megalithic proportions of two new attractors demanded an incredible investment of labor and time—another fifty years of work before the new facilities would be ready, this as the Vec and the Phyrexians measured time, both referring back to the old Dominarian calendar of their ancestors. The Coracin native measured years a bit longer. It didn't matter either way. Davvol never forgot a detail he had committed to memory. It was now one hundred thirty-three years since the Phyrexians brought him away from Coracin, and he could review notes made to himself over a century back that had still not come due.

So far beyond his normal lifespan, the Phyrexian collaborator still resented being trapped in the weak and diseased body for which Coracin physicians had once predicted an early demise. Now he had certainly outlived those physicians and any other Coracin living then. The Phyrexians kept him alive and offered a few improvements—when it suited their needs—but little else. They guaranteed him virtual immortality so long as he kept the machines running here on Rath, so long as he completed whatever task was set before him—so long as Croag decided that he was useful.

The Vec workers, a humanoid race with blunt features and knobby joints, stood nearby during the inspection. Their pale skin—from so long trapped away from any sun—flushed in the room's heat. They despised him. He knew that, but they would never do anything so long as the Phyrexian troops stood guard. Any one of the spindly limbed warriors could kill them all, easily, before Davvol was put in any mortal danger that the Phyrexians could not repair. That was the trick, to beat the Phyrexians' ability to remake and *improve.* Davvol was learning something of this in his attempts to kill the hated Urza Planeswalker.

"I want production increased," he said to the Vec supervisor in charge.

Nothing indicated a difference between her position and a common laborer, but Davvol still knew. It paid to single out those who should know that their lives would answer last if any trouble should arise. His policy was simple. If a supervisor failed to accomplish the tasks given to him, he would watch those who reported to him die. The policy was quite effective, and the Vec policed themselves to keep supervisors who would not throw away their lives needlessly.

"The borders must be pushed back faster with enough excess for my special use. See that it happens."

The Vec nodded, sullen but compliant. Sweat ran down her face. Her face a mask, only her brilliant blue eyes spoke her hatred.

Davvol departed, leaving behind two guards. The others came with him back down a long corridor lined with corroded metal pipes that ended in a large balcony open to the outside. He stepped up onto his flying disc. Traveling around the Stronghold was no easy feat. From the caldera rim he had been unable to accurately judge its size. It was better than three kilometers in height as measured from the lower machinery to the top of Stronghold's cyclone funnel tower and twice that in width, its entirety filled with Phyrexian artifice or denizens over which he had authority.

His guards joined him, and Davvol mentally commanded the disc to rise and move through the open wall. The immense cavern, almost a second caldera beneath the first, knew a perpetual twilight. Some lights issued from the bottom side of the Stronghold, while the Vec city below offered slightly brighter areas where its thinly arrayed neighborhoods clustered together into shared warrens. The air was warm and very humid, with condensing steam eventually falling down onto the city as a caustic rain. The disc rose rapidly toward the sculpted ceiling and then through one of the holes that dilated open and allowed a vent to the upper caldera. Davvol noted that he must—in the next year or so—look into the sulfuric rain, not that he cared for the Vec's troubles. The escape of so much mineral content in the steam spoke of inefficiency in the machinery, which must translate into slower production of flowstone.

Flowstone, a wondrous substance. He had discovered its merits almost immediately upon assuming responsibility for Rath. Reaching into the wide sleeve that covered his right arm, he removed from a hidden pocket the sample of flowstone he carried with him always. Warmed by the trip into the bowels of the Stronghold's machinery, the fist-sized hunk of tan stone still seemed unremarkable, as plain as it had been when the steward had torn it from the barren landscape that stretched between horizons. It was so much more. Without much effort, Davvol mentally shaped it into a series of rough figures—a cylinder then a cube. The tan substance would soften under his command then melt like a candle in an oven, except, the stone would not run out of his hand but toward whatever new shape he desired—a ship, an egg, a short staff. It was much harder than any regular stone and apparently had no limits on what it might accomplish. He concentrated a bit more, and the short staff melded into a knife with a fine bone handle and a very sharp edge. A touch more thought and the handle softened as if wrapped in leather. Davvol had made such weapons with blades so fine as to be able to score the hardest Phyrexian metal.

Flowstone apparently obeyed those with power over the plane of Rath, both in small portions like he held or in massive plains of the material. An evincar, named by Phyrexia, would possesses full mastery. Now Davvol and Croag shared that power, the member of Phyrexia's Inner Circle a permanent *guest* of the Stronghold and constantly looking over Davvol's shoulder. Davvol did not doubt with whom Rath's final authority currently rested, but Croag showed little interest in manipulating the flowstone, and it was control of the flowstone that might end up being the deciding factor of who truly ruled Rath. The knife softened and changed shape in his hand.

The disc exited the upper vent and flew over the Stronghold's lower surfaces. Black metal gleamed as lightning cascaded in the sky high above and bathed the caldera in an unnatural and beautiful red wash. Davvol sent the disc on a long glide around the main tower to the throne room. In his hand he held an exquisite flowstone crown. Yes, flowstone was one of the two paths into full power here on Rath, power Davvol meant to have.

Urza Planeswalker guarded Rath's second path into power. The Phyrexians despised Urza as no single other entity in the known multiverse, and an unimaginable reward awaited the one clever enough to rid the dark race of him. Despite Davvol's best efforts through the six decades so far—planning traps and instructing negators on new tactics—the planeswalker kept right on existing.

Something had to be done—not just planned, but physically accomplished—not exactly one of Davvol's strengths.

He paced the floor where a seeker had brought the latest negator corpses after their discovery on another plane. Two this time, smaller than most but very deadly and extremely fast. Rath's steward had hoped that their augmented reflexes would offset Urza's defenses. Not so, obviously. Their armored carapaces had been melted open in a dozen places. The blackened flesh of the first corpse appeared thoroughly disrupted, and Davvol found it desiccated of glistening oil. The second negator arrived in three pieces, having been caught in a maelstrom of energies that Davvol could only begin to guess at. This one leaked oil in a spreading pool, the room's light flashing over it in a filmy rainbow. The area stunk of charred meat, scorched oil, and hot steel. He stood, watching the oil spread over the polished metal floor, and thought.

He heard the rasping of metal fibers sliding over each other—Croag.

"Urza Planeswalker lives," Croag said, not a question. The Phyrexian stopped beside Davvol, his cleft skull staring down at the ruined negators.

Davvol nodded. "Obviously."

The council member's voice still sounded to him like a series of chattering squeals and hisses, but the Phyrexian had found it convenient to compleat Davvol's inner ear, so those sounds actually made sense to him now. Removing the language barrier had also mellowed Davvol's fear of the Phyrexian, who was no longer *quite* so alien. Besides which, living in the shadow of death for better than a century would harden anyone to its presence.

Croag turned in Davvol's direction. "What do you do now?" it asked.

"I am thinking."

Davvol prodded at a severed arm with the toe of one armored boot. The arm was actually a cannon of sorts, capable of delivering a stream of hellish energy that could disrupt a planeswalker's energy patterns. It rolled over, leaving behind a trail of soot and oily sludge. They were fortunate to have the corpses to examine. Quite often they were never recovered.

"They did not perform as I'd hoped," Davvol admitted, not that predictions could be made easily.

Negators did not conform to any particular design. These Phyrexians ranged from short, bulky creations to large dragon engine war machines. Bigger did not always mean better, except at times a better target. For Davvol, who relied upon an ability to organize and categorize, such maverick functions made for difficult evaluations.

"Urza Planeswalker must be killed," Croag hissed. "He must not interfere again." A skeletal arm reached out toward Davvol, razor-sharp fingers raking slowly through the air before the steward's face. "You are failing."

Davvol's wide-set eyes stared at the talons hovering inches from his face. Swallowing against the knot in his throat, he kept any waver from his voice. "I am doing the best possible. Urza has lived for over three millennia. He will not go quietly into the void." That gave Croag a moment of pause, possibly reminded of the failure of so many others. The arm lowered a fraction.

Davvol sidestepped away, crouching down to closer inspect the desiccated negator. Croag expected some kind of action. The steward would find something. The easiest excuse would be to blame the negator's design. Obviously they were flawed, though perhaps Croag would not care to hear him maligning more perfect Phyrexians. Against any regular form of life the negators were fearsome assassins, but a planeswalker called for a new outlook—and innovation. There Davvol met an impasse. True innovation, the ability to make radical leaps forward, would be beyond him. He had a feeling that Croag understood that—that his immersion in the details and inability for radical thinking was an important reason he'd been selected for this position in Rath. It made him the perfect steward, able to be trusted so much as the Phyrexians trusted anyone not of their own race.

He did see areas in the Phyrexian negators that *might* be improved upon. The difficulty lay in his lack of understanding for the planeswalker's strengths and weaknesses.

"It will take time," he said after some thought. He reached out and traced a scar melted into the negator's armor. His pale fingers came away with just a smudge of black. "More time than I first thought," he said, stalling with careful words, "but I believe it is possible." He stood. "Urza Planeswalker can be killed."

Croag was not one for easy conversation. "How?" he screeched, and Davvol caught the hint of intensity behind that one word.

For the first time, Davvol wondered if Croag somehow had a personal interest in the death of Urza Planeswalker. Did the Inner Council member, too, live under the shadow of death? Punishment by the Ineffable—the Phyrexian Dark Lord? A chill trembled his pasty skin. It made sense, looking back on the last six decades of Croag's presence and constant interference. The data had been incomplete until now. Davvol had been unable to place a mental touch upon this Phyrexian, his mind too alien, and relying on speakers for so many of those years.

He answered Croag with his own question. "Can negators be compleated to my own specifications?"

Metal cloth writhed, wrapping itself up and about Croag's face for a second, leaving a glistening sheen over the Phyrexian's taught gray skin. "This can be done," he promised.

With such infrequent contact between negators and the planeswalker, it might take decades merely to enhance the negator's sensory abilities so that recovered corpses could provide better data on their observations of Urza as well as a negator's own ability to fight him. It could be centuries more before Davvol could hope to improve on their design. It was how he worked best, though, able to organize and manipulate an infinite array of details to find the most efficient path. His plan would show constant progress, purchasing an existence for him that would stretch out several times over the natural lifetime of a Coracin native. Also, this evolutionary process would allow him to create an army of negators the lethal ability of which Phyrexia had never known. With this presentation alone, Davvol might be brought to compleation himself and named evincar of Rath. Wasn't that the Phyrexian way, after all, to improve in the current generation that which failed in the previous?

Davvol felt the planeswalker's death was assured. The power of numbers was on his side. Eventually, Urza would be overwhelmed, but under a slow program of constant refinement to the creatures that hunted him that could stretch out perhaps another five centuries. Davvol would have his monsters and eventually the life of the 'walker as well.

With any luck, Urza would take a long time to die.

chapter 9

Multani dug his toes down into Yavimaya's soil, enjoying its warm, moist touch. He felt young and energetic, revitalized. From halfway around the world he had felt Yavimaya's strength build, his body reflecting the sentient forest's state. As older trees fell to make room for newer growth, his own limbs grew more supple and strong. His size increased, and the mosslike growth from his head and shoulders that served for hair grew in thicker and more luxurious. Here, actually standing in the shadow of Yavimaya's coastal trees, his feet buried beneath the soil, Multani could almost forget Rofellos's greeting.

"Yavimaya welcomes you," he'd said as the *Weatherlight* had come aground.

To hear the words spoken even as Yavmaya's greeting was made known to his own mind felt strange to the nature spirit. It was unsurprising that Yavimaya had initiated contact with Rofellos. In the absence of Multani, what other way could the forest and the Llanowar elf directly communicate? Through the dual greeting the nature spirit felt the forest's casual use of the elf—its hold over him—and the elf's uncertain knowledge of his own place. Multani also sensed that Yavimaya had relied on Rofellos for some time now to also act as its voice, an ability the sentient forest had apparently grown to miss in the seventy-three years since Multani had last been called home.

In that time Yavimaya had also stepped up its accelerated mulch cycles. Even within the less dense coastal forests the creaking sway and final, limb-tearing crash of falling trees never quite ended these days. It would fade, as a distant tree toppled, and then rebound as a nearer growth bent to Yavimaya's will. One could actually see the trees growing, their limbs stretching upward and out as boles thickened and root systems swelled the ground around them. The grass continued to mulch itself too, new shoots growing up within the decaying green blades. Farther back in the forest's shadows the underbrush writhed, thinning itself and then growing back with slight changes to flowers and leaves in a never-ending process of forced evolution.

One student had exclaimed sharply, noticing that even the insects along the ground were growing and dying at an accelerated rate.

"Of course," Multani had answered. Rofellos took the opportunity of the distraction to slip away, back into the forest. "They are as much part of life's cycle as any plant. In so many cases, one can not exist without the other. Many of Gaea's creatures will follow the same pattern, though in some the changes will be brought about without actual rebirth." This had excited several of the student mages for some reason.

As natural as the process might be, however, Multani couldn't help now but wonder about his absence during the accelerated growth cycles, whether or not it could be another reason for Yavimaya's greater empathy with Rofellos. In the last seven decades how many generations had he missed in the forest? Sharing his thoughts with Yavimaya, Multani still had no good answer. The forest, for all its intelligence, had never undergone such a treatment either. It knew mistakes, trying to direct the evolution of its plants and creatures. It feared mistakes, worried at losing any life forever. That was the nature of the forest, to live in a ceaseless cycle where the living died but new life could always hope to be born from such loss. Multani wanted to stay this time, to remain with his parent forest, but he knew that Yavimaya had decided his work to be elsewhere. He was an ambassador and teacher, the forest's voice among other nations and peoples.

"Enjoying the day?" a voice behind him asked. Rofellos stepped from behind a large bush. His arrival had been silent. The Llanowar had truly made this his home.

There was no denying the undertone of challenge to his question. Multani opened his mind with that of Yavimaya, sharing the sentient forest's consciousness with Rofellos. As on the beach, he could feel the turmoil roiling within the elf—the relationship between he and Multani, between he and Yavimaya. Rofellos now saw the nature spirit as something of a rival. It cast Multani into an uncertain position with Rofellos, and the adversarial nature of the Llanowar was winning over memories of the awe he had once felt for the nature spirit. Multani recalled those times, and with the memory he realized something else about the elf—Rofellos was not aging!

Not as he should be—Yavimaya had obviously taken hold of the elf's life-force, binding Rofellos to itself. While the sentient forest built its strength,

Rofellos tapped into it in a way similar to Multani. The Llanowar looked to be only in the early stages of an elf's middle years, the long period that accounted for so much of their extended lifespan.

"You're happy to be back," the elf said.

It was not quite a question, that last. Multani could sense the elf merely reflecting many of the feelings Yavimaya already shared with him. The Llanowar simply put them into words, at times apparently unable to fully distinguish his own thoughts from the ambient feelings of the forest.

"I enjoy returning to Yavimaya," Multani answered in voice, sparing the elf any trouble in understanding "Yes."

The nature spirit moved closer toward Rofellos, stopping on his way to feel at the bud on the new grenade flower. He sensed the violent energies stored up within, energies that would eventually burst the pod open, raining seeds farther out so that the plant could spread. In later evolutions those seeds would grow larger and might be thrown so far as to cross rivers or rocky surfaces. The burst of strength now might also hope to discourage any of the larger herbivores from making a meal of the plant. That defense, too, would grow.

"A fascinating new growth," Multani said, testing the Llanowar.

"I have not had the chance to inspect it," Rofellos admitted.

An echo of his words, truer perhaps to his original thought, filtered through Yavimaya's consciousness to the nature spirit. Multani knew that Rofellos had plenty of opportunities these many years but failed to take full advantage of them. If the plant did not provide food, clothing, or any other practical use, the Llanowar could not be made to pay attention. How sad, Multani thought, to keep so limited a view of nature.

"You should try," he said to the elf, encouraging on his own behalf as well as Yavimaya's.

Rofellos stepped forward hesitatingly, his features so obviously clouded with doubts. Multani tried to feel for the Llanowar's spirit, but it eluded him. Rofellos was not a true part of Yavimaya, not yet, at least. The elf reached out, gripped the stem roughly. The pod burst with a light snapping sound, as if sensing an attack, and dozens of tiny, sharp-tipped seeds exploded outward. A few stuck into Rofellos's arm, enough to catch but not enough to even draw blood. Still the Llanowar jumped back as if attacked, hand darting to the sword at his side. More of Multani's gentle words of encouragement died unspoken as the nature spirit noticed Rofellos's wild-eyed expression of shock and confusion. The Llanowar was under more pressure here than the nature spirit had ever thought.

Then, swiftly, silently, Rofellos faded back into forest shadows and disappeared as easily as Multani himself could have done.

His feet hardly seemed to touch the forest floor, its soft bed of earth unblanketed by grass this far under the canopy. Thin branches whipped at his face as Rofellos allowed instinct to lead him, the roll of a hill pushing him toward easier paths, the warning creak of a nearby trunk as Yavimaya took hold and wrestled it toward the ground detoured him back toward the clearing but did not slow him. He clenched at the empty air.

Landing in a natural ditch formed between two gentle hills, Rofellos pulled up sharply and tested the air. He scented only the perfume of nearby flowers, grenades and poison mothers, their fragrance belying what would eventually be a dangerous effect. He heard no sound of pursuit, nothing but the distant echo of a felled tree and some birdsong overhead. He crouched to place one hand against the earth, feeling for vibrations of silent movement, and searched the nearby shadows for Yavimayan elves. Nothing. Even Yavimaya had retreated from his mind, for now, the forest's language forgotten in his mad dash. It would be back, slow and insidious, taking root again within his mind.

Rofellos had hoped that somehow Multani would help him—explain how the nature spirit coped with such a pervasive presence. The Llanowar should have known better than to place trust in anyone not of his home. If the forest spirit had tried, if there had been some hidden meaning in their discussion of the grenade, the elf did not understand it, so he had fled. It was the second rule of a potentially hostile situation, the first being immediate violence. Yavimaya had not allowed him that, so he ran and escaped Yavimaya. For a moment he was simply Rofellos, though already he felt the insinuating return of Yavimaya, felt it reaching into his mind, calling him. Soon it would simply *be* there, but for now the choice remained.

The Llanowar ran.

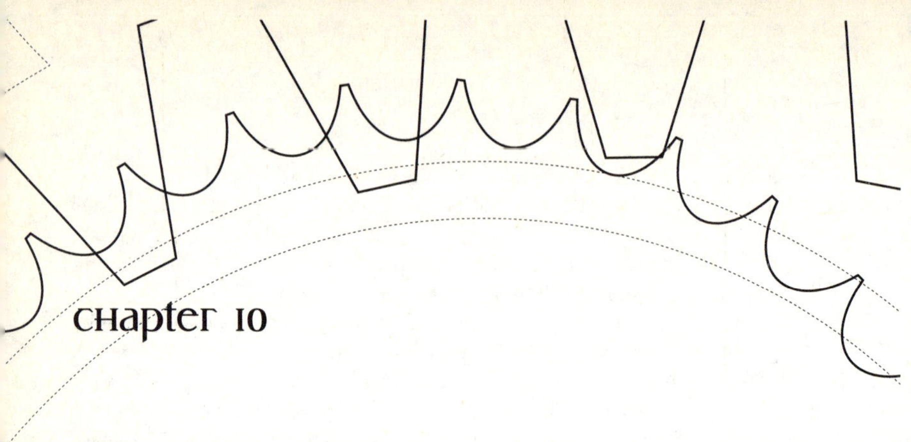

chapter 10

A large fire blazed over the hearth in Gatha's main laboratory, holding at bay the freezing air outside. Snow drifted against the northern window, protected by stone and shadow far longer than the drifts that had begun to melt last week with the thaw. The labs smelled of smoke but were otherwise kept spotless by the slaves assigned to Gatha. The slaves were courtesy of the more influential warlords who were in the mage's debt. Keldons always paid a debt, whether for good or ill.

So far, in better than forty years of experimentation, Gatha had balanced out the good over the ill. It was not that he hadn't made mistakes, just none lethal to date. It was a simple matter of counterbalances. If he made an enemy of a warlord, he simply had to befriend a more powerful one. As he'd noticed early on, the pecking order was well established in Keld. Body language could tell you at a glance who was dominant between any two warlords or any two *doyenne*, except that those positions could change at any time through design or simple misfortune. Gatha knew that one of these days he might choose wrong, but that was something to worry about later, when it happened, not now. *Now* was for his work.

The voices of his slaves rose in the hall, interrupting him as he placed a tray of colos muscle on the table and reached for his sampling tweezers. There was a heavy thud, no doubt the body of one of them hitting the wall, and then the door was thrust open. Trohg stomped into Gatha's lab kicking snow and mud from his thick leather boots. Seven feet plus, the Keldon dwarfed the mage by a good sixteen inches and over one hundred pounds. Immune to such size differences anymore, Gatha did not flinch from the hard stare. He scowled at the interruption to his work but nodded for a slave to remove the tray he had been about to sample from. There would be no work while Trohg remained inside.

The Keldon grabbed one of the chairs near the fire and pulled it farther back into the room, away from the warmth. He sat then nodded toward the hearth.

"You put it in a good place," he said, speaking in the *low Keld* tongue for Gatha's benefit.

It was a language relying more heavily on words, fit for ordering around slaves and non-warrior Keldons. He pointed to the ripped standard that hung down from the large iron spike driven in between the mortared stones. The other half hung in Trohg's manor near the Necropolis, and a second banner of the same kind also decorated the council hall. Trohg had shared the standard he'd brought back for himself from a victorious campaign. Such was a sign of rare admission that a warlord or witch king owed someone a debt for that victory.

Grandson of Kreyohl, the Keldon warlord who had saved Gatha's life, Trohg had been brought to the mage at the age of ten for augmentation. A runt birth—as the smaller Keldons were often called—Trohg had no chance of selection for the warlord trials. His father preferred to see his son dead in the frozen northland wastes or by the mage's unpredictable magic—and said as much to Gatha—than be bypassed for selection. For most Keldons this would not be so disastrous, but as the first son of a mating between a strong warlord and an influential *doyenne*, Trohg's failure would directly affect the position of both his progenitors. His son would not be passed over and indeed hadn't been. Trohg not only responded to the genetic alterations, but he was also one of the rare warlords now referred to as a witch king. In battle he excited his troops to a furious, fanatical pitch and could then draw off their combined strength to legendary effect. Young as he was, Trohg sat on the highest tier in council, a warlord with few peers.

Moving over toward the fire, Gatha took the more comfortable and therefore weaker position. Familiarity only went so far in Keld, and he never forgot the delicate niche in which he lived here. His mastery of their language and the Keldon cut of his clothes would never make up completely for his lack of a warrior's background. A warlord could take his life at any time, provided Gatha could not first maneuver a stronger one into his path.

"I am honored to share in your victory," he finally said, staring at the torn standard rather than be tempted to make eye contact with Trohg. Argivian—his birth nation.

The witch king grunted in agreement. "I take strength from the warhost," he said, voice strong and deep. "Nothing hurts me. I stomp out the lives of my enemy as if they were snowbound, slow and weak." His dark eyes sought out Gatha. "You did this for me, and I remember." He paused. "You will do same for my son."

Gatha glanced back to the warlord, courtesy forgotten in the shock. What he had thought would be a social visit, such as they passed for in Keld, had turned suddenly to business. The magical ability of the witch kings created incredible demand for Gatha's work, no matter that fewer than one in ten survived the process in any shape to fight. He had even begun cutting Phyrexian genetic material back into the Matrix, using it as he used colos genes—the adaptable material working to fill in the "gaps" his own work left behind. Still, a stable process had yet to emerge. Gatha did not want to make an enemy of this man.

He averted his eyes, swallowing against the dryness that had suddenly parched his mouth. "I did not know you had a son," he said, stroking the rough goatee he maintained in nervous habit. "Congratulations on your new warrior." Even as he answered with the standard salute for a son, Gatha was estimating the boy's chances: not good.

Trohg shook his massive head. "I have no son, yet. You will help me make him a witch king too."

Preconception? Gatha had done very little of that in his four decades in Keld except with captured slaves. Keldons wanted things done now. They worked for the day, never next year or into their children's lifetime. The future took care of itself. Trohg must have a strong dose of his grandfather's genes to look so far ahead for himself. Gatha had given up trying to convince a warlord or witch king to allow preconception adjustments years ago. Why should they suffer his unpredictable magic before they see the result of their labor?

"You will do this," Trohg repeated, hard voice on edge now.

The mage nodded. "It is possible," he said, the Keldon language thick in his mouth, "but not easy, and there is no way to predict if magical ability will be passed on to your son." Basing the new life off Trohg's genetic make-up, a successful subject, would dramatically increase the chances. It would take additional resources in equipment, the development of some new procedures, and time of course. He cursed silently. There was always a cost in time. "You have *doyenne* who will agree with this?" No small concern there. Trohg had two mates that Gatha was aware of, and he couldn't see either of them trusting the mage enough to allow preconception magics.

Trohg nodded. "I have a new manor and a new *doyenne.* She is eager."

Meaning *ambitious.* "It may take a few tries," Gatha warned him, "but I believe I can do this."

Standing abruptly, Trohg saluted with a clenched fist held in up in front of his face, the hand blocking part of his vision. Gatha was sure to return the salute but not hold it nearly so long. The inferior could never afford to impair his vision for as long as a superior. It implied insult to the stronger warrior.

"You will make my son a witch king," Trohg said, "and his son. For as long as you do this, Gatha, you will need nothing. If you ask, you will receive. If you need, we will supply it." He paused, then in *high Keld* continued. "You will sit on the Warlords' Council. This I pledge to you."

This was the highest praise, both the switch of tongues as well as the message. Gatha took a chance and replied in similar fashion, with a grunt of thanks and slight bow at the neck to signify his unworthiness before a superior warrior. Trohg grinned, baring his teeth, and the mage bowed again as the witch king took leave of the labs. The strength fled his legs and Gatha stumbled for a chair. An impressive pledge Trogh had made him, though Gatha knew it to be a false promise. No one sat in the presence of the Warlords' Council atop the Necropolis.

However, with a witch king and Keldon warhost at his back, Gatha would never fear for his life again and would never want for anything again. That was power the mage knew how to spend. Labs to rival Tolaria? Done. The Tolarian academy itself? Done. Barrin's head on a Keldon pike? Done. The future was opening up before him. Gatha only had to seize upon the course he favored, and if it did not quite suit his liking, then the mage would remake it to his desire.

"I don't like it, Urza." Barrin threw the pages of material down onto his desk. They spread across the marble slab top, a few sheets drifting to the floor with a whispered flutter. "We—I—curtailed Gatha's work because it represented a danger to morality as well as the lives of his subjects. His defection proved that he was never to be trusted, though you later defended his right to leave. Now he has set up his own labs? With one of our minor Eugenics Matrices?" Barrin rocked back in his chair, shaking his head, voice plaintive. "Urza, I wanted him stopped, not set loose on Dominaria."

The planeswalker stood on the other side of Barrin's large desk. He appeared the Urza of his youth again, years numbered in the teens instead of the thousands. His seamless face was too serious and intense for his apparent age.

"It's not as if the Keldons are suffering him involuntarily," the 'walker said. "They gave him a home and labs because they *want* what he is offering. They've practiced selective breeding and magically enhanced evolvement for far longer than you or I, Barrin. Why debate their choice, especially when it gives us the chance to observe such useful events?"

Barrin rubbed at eyes red and scratchy from late nights at work. He stood, fingers sifting among the loose pages that had spread over the desk until finding one of the rough sketches Urza had provided.

"There," Barrin said, drawing the page out from the others. "Have their breeding cycles ever turned out something like that before?"

Roughly man sized, the creature was a misshapen excuse for a Keldon—monstrous in size with an exaggerated bone structure that hunched it over and built an almost domelike carapace across its broad back. Sexless. It had malformed hands and feet with webbing between what few fingers and toes had formed. Bony barbs protruded from its heels and elbows.

Urza shook his head, his appearance aging a few years as Barrin cut into his excitement. "We've had similar catastrophic failures here on Tolaria," he said. "I think that one was from Gatha's cutting colos genes into the Eugenics Matrix."

"That thing was not borne from a faulty experiment," Barrin said, exasperated that Urza would compare the two programs. "That was created out of a living being in retroactive manipulation, something we have never done except when Gatha broke the guidelines."

Urza slammed an open palm down against Barrin's desktop. "It *is* possible. He has created from under-strength subjects viable warriors worthy of the high criteria Keldons hold for warlord selection." He sat back into a chair, calming himself obviously by force of will.

"Barrin, I'm not saying we should adopt Gatha's methods, but they might be used to temper our own. What if they would allow us a higher success rate? No radical mutations but simply to nudge and guide a subject into the pattern we tried to establish prior to conception. Preventative therapy, Barrin."

As much as he wanted to resist the idea, Barrin could not help considering it. Though deformities were rare after a century and a half of relative real-time work, they still occurred. Many of those born normal still exhibited signs of personal maladjustment later. Those were nightmares the mage could do without. He gripped the edge of his desk.

"In that light, I am forced to agree that there might be *some* benefit to review of this matter, but why should we allow Gatha to continue his work?"

"You've seen the latest reports. Most bloodlines have entered cascading failure because of earlier fast-time growth. We can treat them, but they will never be viable generations leading to the heir. Of the Tolarian generations, only the ones raised strictly outside of fast-time environments are looking strong enough, and Tolaria's ambient blue mana is beginning to influence their heritage too strongly. We are facing a serious setback. I'll need the kind of data Gatha is generating to start again and make up for lost time."

Barrin slowly stood, an eerie chill shaking the mage. *Tolarian* generations? Urza was not one to qualify a statement unless necessary. He swallowed dryly through a blocked throat. When he spoke, his voice was little better than a hoarse whisper.

"How many?" he asked. "How many bloodlines exist off this island?"

"A few," Urza admitted as if the subject bore little consequence. "Nothing different from what we have done here on Tolaria. Dominarian, raised in heavy white mana-rich areas, most influenced by Thran genetics." The planeswalker frowned. "My first generations were much more stable as well, though later generations did not degrade nearly so badly as the ones here on Tolaria because they stayed in contact with the white mana lands most likely."

A second program carried out by Urza alone. Barrin sat back into his chair, numb. "Why didn't you tell me?"

Urza shrugged. "They were not part of Tolaria's program, and you already had so much to worry about. If you recall, I worried from the start about using Tolaria's mana to make adjustments to plains-dwelling subjects, and then with Timein's work—"

"Stop, Urza." Barrin held up his hand in a gesture of submission. "Just stop."

He massaged the bridge of his nose, feeling a throbbing headache building. He remembered once, so many decades ago relative time, when all he had hoped for was a simple life. He did not want virtual immortality or to be in control of so many lives other than his own. He did not want to be caught up so intricately in the insanity that was Urza's program against the Phyrexians.

Even threatening to walk away now, though, would accomplish little. Urza Planeswalker could not be argued with and certainly couldn't be controlled. All Barrin could do was attempt to mitigate the collateral damage. Like it or not, Barrin was responsible for those lives, not the least of which were his wife's and—eventually he hoped—his children.

"Do you have data on your outside experiments?" he asked, hating himself for the question.

Urza visibly paused then nodded slowly. "Of course, with arrangements that all data would be delivered to you in case anything ever happened to me."

"I want it now," Barrin said. "I'll put Timein on it. Tutor or no, he is still one of the best—most *reasonable*—minds we have." Even to his own ears, the mage's voice sounded tired—defeated. "I'll put the academy on it, Urza. We'll see what might be done to correlate all the data—yours, mine and," he couldn't keep the disgust from his voice, "Gatha's. I'll do what I can."

"I never doubted that for a moment, Barrin." Urza stood. "You are the best I could have ever hoped to find for this work." He started to say more, hedged, then continued on anyway. "Go home and rest," he suggested. "Visit with your wife." He was gone, with a step between worlds.

Barrin sat alone, his work prior to Urza's arrival forgotten and absolutely no enthusiasm for the new work laid before him, but he would do it, he knew. Not today, not until he had completely assimilated it into his brain, but he would do it because it needed to be done, and because there was no one else who could.

Timein met Barrin on the hill overlooking the Colony—the small hamlet of bloodlines subjects who had moved to this far corner of the island to distance themselves from the academy and the project into which they had unwillingly been born. A few people were in evidence, a couple still bearing evidence of the bloodlines legacy. A man with a withered left arm worked a sparse field of vegetables. One large woman, her upper body swollen out of proportion to her lower, lifted a large rock out of the way of a plow.

"Don't they know that we can fix most of the gross deformities?" Barrin asked, the light wind pushing the front hem of his cloak back against his legs.

Timein nodded. "They know." He reached up and tucked back a stray lock of hair. "I'm not sure why they don't come in." He spread his hands expansively. "Look what magic has done for them so far."

Barrin glanced over sharply at the sarcasm. The student met his gaze easily, secure in his own ability though he still refused anything resembling promotion.

"You brought me out here for a reason, Timein. What is it?" He looked down on the Colony again. "I know you don't pick your meeting places casually."

"I'm leaving the academy."

Barrin's face hardened into a mask at the declaration. "I don't have to allow that you know. Only scholars are allowed access back into the world, and you are not yet a tutor."

The sorcerer smiled thinly, sensing Barrin's bluff. They both knew how much was owed to Timein.

"I didn't say I was leaving the island."

The master mage caught on immediately. He glanced downhill. "Here? Will they let you in?"

"I'm hoping so. I'll need help to build any kind of home before the storms arrive."

Barrin shook his head, in frustration more than denial. "Timein, you could be reassigned. Other projects . . ." he trailed off.

"Not so long as the academy supports Urza's Bloodlines project," the sorcerer promised, folding thin and spindly arms over his chest. "I've gone as far as I can. Now I need some distance. The Colony is about as far as I can get and remain on Tolaria." He paused, uncertain. "Maybe I can do something here to help these people. Master Barrin, I'm tired of fighting an enemy I've never even seen and with questionable tactics at that. It's over."

The look of despair that flashed briefly on Barrin's strong face nearly bent Timein from his purpose. He knew that in a way he was running out on the academy, on Barrin and Rayne and especially Urza, but the truth was in his words. He had gone as far as he was able, and by Barrin's slow nod, Timein knew the other man understood that. He watched as Tolaria's master mage braced himself up, shouldering that much more of the burden himself.

"When you are ready to come back, Timein, the academy will be there."

Timein watched as Barrin turned away from the Colony and headed back along the path. With the decision made and accepted, there was no longer any hesitation to the mage's step. He would go forward because there was no one else, and Timein respected him for it. As the sorcerer marched downhill in the opposite direction, he only hoped the feeling was returned. Entering the Colony, he put such debate from his mind.

There was work to be done.

Urza's lab holding the Thran Eugenics Matrix was one of the most secure sites on Tolaria. Two chancellors were required in attendance for any work. No one adjusted the complex machinery except Urza or Barrin. Rayne stood near the device cradling a massive leather-bound volume in her arms, her husband next to her. Marking her place in the Thran Tome, she studied the intricate artifact. A complex design built from delicate-looking components of Thran metal, it had lasted underground over many millennia awaiting Urza's discovery. The Matrix also had a touch of magic to it, very rare to find in Thran artifice, and in Urza's belief, an inadvertent addition.

"In all probability," the 'walker had once said to an assemblage of the scholars, "the Thran never realized the significance of magic, and so even they did not know exactly how their Eugenics Matrix worked."

If that was supposed to make them feel better for their tampering in a science they only half understood, it failed to do so. Rayne was one for the more straightforward work of artifice—clear established relationships and predictable results, yet the order of accomplishments of the Thran empire suggested greater understanding than Urza suggested. Rayne couldn't be sure that the planeswalker was correct in his theory.

"Can it be done?" Barrin asked, impatient and unable to help the question.

Rayne glanced up, sighed a frustrated breath. She gathered up her long, dark hair with a quick twist around her hand and tossed it over her shoulder then bent back to her task.

"Thirty generations," the mage whispered, shaking his head and pacing off to one side.

Rayne sensed her husband's weariness and wanted to console him, but she also needed to concentrate on the work at hand. She hadn't seen Barrin so despondent since the day Karn's memory had been capped.

She certainly understood his concerns. Newly promoted to chancellor herself, one of the administrative leaders of the academy now as well as a head scholar of artifice, she had reviewed the final results from Timein's research. It would take approximately thirty generations to approach the empathic mixture Urza required of the heir to his Legacy. Better than six hundred years and it all had to be in real time. No more shortcuts could be taken, not in the actual rearing of bloodlines subjects, and all needed to be raised off of Tolaria in virtually uncontrolled experiments. In the end, who could be sure that the empathic mixture would produce an heir with the exact qualities Urza desired? The person he wanted was strong and willful with as much empathy for the enemy as for the world of Dominaria itself—the ability to understand and so defeat the Phyrexians, without turning to their dark purposes.

Rayne set the large tome on a nearby table and allowed it to fall closed with a quick, dry ruffle of pages and a heavy slap from the binding. She breathed a heavy sigh, rubbing at her temples as if trying to massage into place within her mind all the information she'd just absorbed.

Barrin was back at her side in three quick strides. "Can it be done?" he asked.

She smiled wearily at his impatience. "Never bet against Thran artifice," she said. "There wasn't much they apparently couldn't accomplish." She placed one hand on the tome. "I even found some references to the idea of binding artifice with flesh on the most basic cellular level. I wonder if that remained theory?"

Her husband shook at that thought. "Having seen the monstrosities of artifice bonded to flesh, I can only imagine the horror of artifice *blended* with flesh."

Frightening shadows stirred at the back of Rayne's mind. Still, the thought would not let go. There was potential there.

"We only want to be able to make subtle alterations to a living being," Barrin said, as if reminding his wife of their current goal, "but they will have to be applied throughout the entire biological system to prevent genetic rejection from causing rapid breakdown."

This was a vague way of saying that a change must seem to be naturally present from birth to prevent what could be a terrible death. Rayne nodded, her eyes dark with the strain of reading into the late hours. She glanced around, suddenly uncomfortable to be in one of Urza's workshops.

"I think we can do this," she said, "and with greater effect than Gatha's crude experiments since we'll rely more on the precision of artifice over his unpredictable magics." She looked to Barrin with a frank openness. "The question is, should we?"

"A question I ask myself every day, my love," Barrin answered after a moment's pause, "but after learning from Multani and others about Yavimaya's forced evolution, Urza believes more firmly than ever that we are on the right track, as if our work here reflects nature's own course. Urza will proceed with or without the academy's assistance."

Rayne glanced over at the Thran Matrix, the ancient artifact so compact and precise and utterly devoid of malice or empathy. *That* would come from its user. "I believe it would be better *with*," she said.

To that Barrin simply nodded.

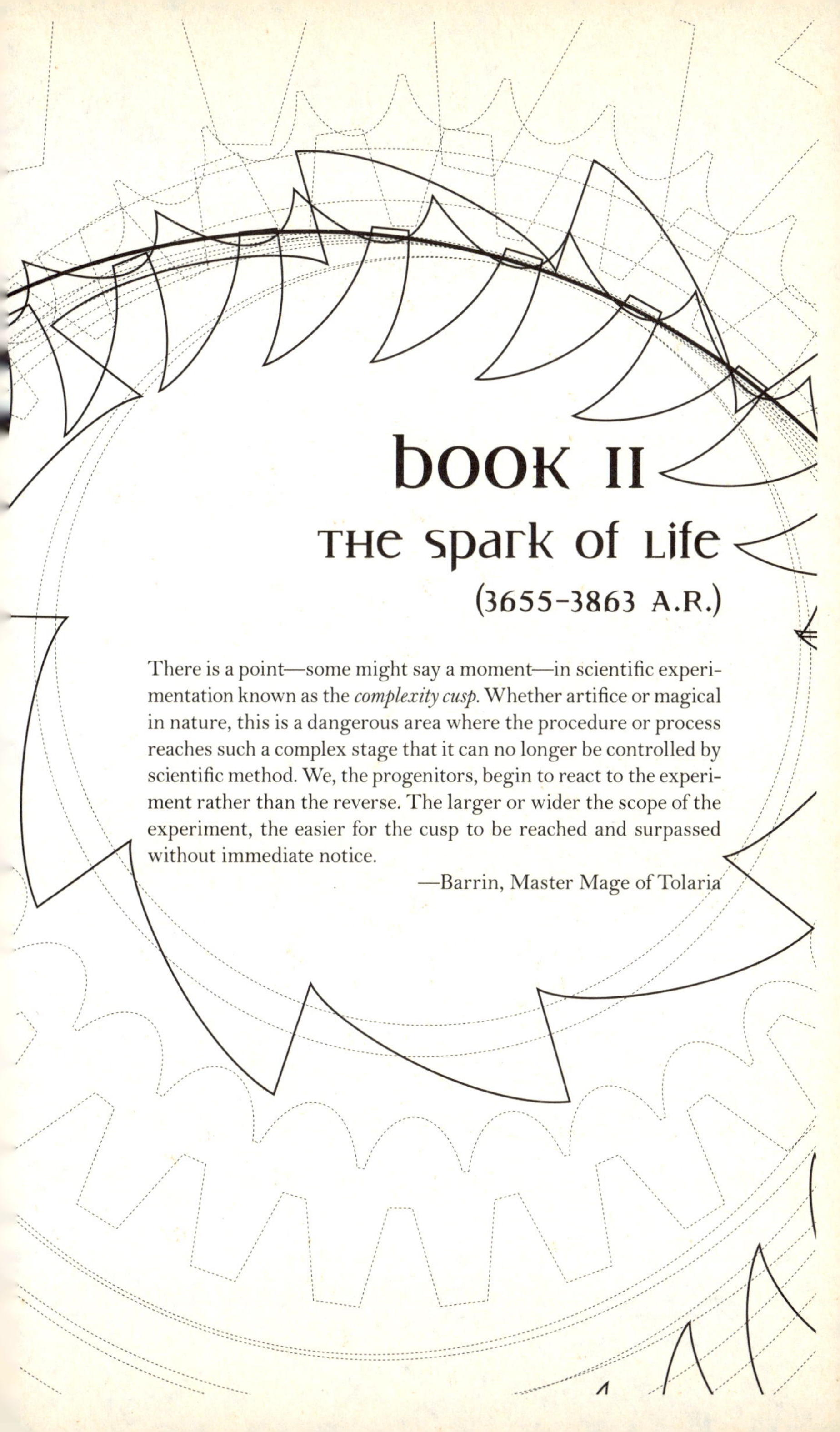

Book II

The Spark of Life

(3655–3863 A.R.)

There is a point—some might say a moment—in scientific experimentation known as the *complexity cusp.* Whether artifice or magical in nature, this is a dangerous area where the procedure or process reaches such a complex stage that it can no longer be controlled by scientific method. We, the progenitors, begin to react to the experiment rather than the reverse. The larger or wider the scope of the experiment, the easier for the cusp to be reached and surpassed without immediate notice.

—Barrin, Master Mage of Tolaria

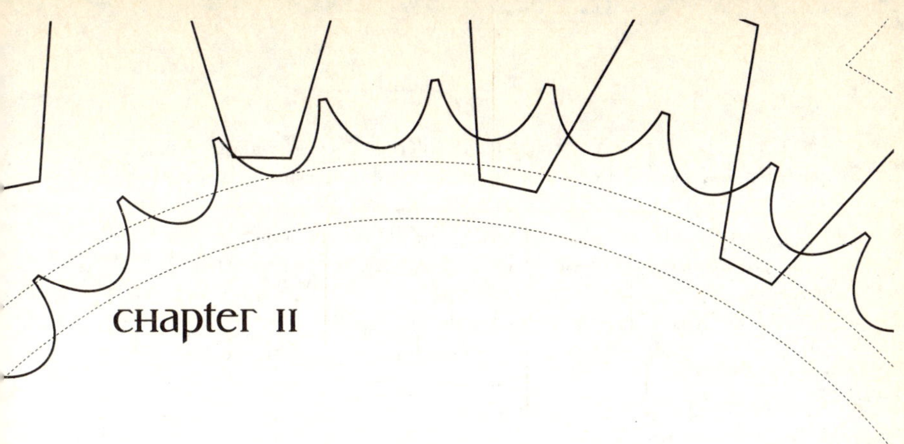

Chapter 11

The sun rode low in the west. Lyanii doffed her helm as she approached the caravan's merchant leader, holding the visored headgear in her right hand in a display of neutrality—not quite peace. A few long strands of her chestnut-brown hair drifted next to the high cheekbones of her face, the majority of her long tresses caught up in the tie she used to keep it out of the way while in armor. Merchant swordsmen took ready positions at the sides of the caravan wagons. She carried no weapons herself, but the phalanx of archers backing her by one hundred paces argued her strength. The merchants would only be able to guess at what forces remained behind the gates of the newly-built village of Devas. It left her in the superior position, where she would remain. As a former marshal of Serra's Realm, the artificial plane fallen in the war between Phyrexians and Urza Planeswalker, it was what she knew best.

Still several paces out, she began to gauge the merchant's measure. He looked to be sharp of mind but soft of body, commanding through his purse. The merchant displayed the tan of a traveler. His clothes were fine silks threaded with spun silver. He had an earring in each ear, large rubies both, and a gold tooth, which flashed in the sun when he smiled. He returned her interest, finding no help in her unsmiling face but obviously impressed with the quality of her armor. The opalescent finish to the light steel promised well-guarded wealth. The Serrans' ability to blend in was one of the reasons Lyanii had chosen Benalia for her people, second only to its affinity for the ambient white mana of sun and plains and open sky.

Lyanii spared barely a second for the merchant's personal guard of four pikemen, unconcerned with their presence. "I am Marshal of this village," she said in greeting, neither challenging nor welcoming.

The merchant would have to make the first effort. The Serran people were too new to make assumptions. Assumptions had hurt them before as well.

"Trader Russo," he said, smiling wide. His Benalish accent rode his voice in softened vowels, though the heavy-scented oil he wore spoke of trade with foreign lands. "I travel through here once a year, usually stopping at the river bend where your village is being built. It is beautiful work and erected with impressive speed."

White stone was favored in Benalia. Their village used it in abundance, polishing each wall until it shone like alabaster. Fluted columns rose to impressive heights to either side of the gates, ending in platforms far above like those which might carry statues but currently remained empty—the lookouts having winged back down into cover. Inside the gates, rising over the few finished clay-tiled roofs, were the beginning walls of what would be their cathedral fortress.

"This is our land now," Lyanii said, speaking for her followers as well as herself, "but Devas welcomes trade. You may camp nearby."

The trader allowed the touch of a frown. "Capashen or Ortovi?" He spread his hands in a gesture of ignorance. "You sit between their ancestral lands, but I can't place you by the architecture."

Lyanii had hoped to brush over the heritage of her people and the method of their arrival, but clearly some explanation would be warranted. "We are refugees," she said, and that was true. "We hold no allegiance to the Benalish clans." His frown deepened. "Surely they would not object to the presence of a new village?"

"One that raises solid walls and employs its own guard in the same custom and fashion as a proper clan manor?" The merchant ran fingers back through his curly black locks. "They just might." He glanced back to the line of archers, and again at her crest, as if trying to place them. "Refugees from where?"

"A land devoted to Serra," Lyanii said, measuring out truth with a careful hand. This trader was obviously well-traveled, so he might have heard of those Dominarian sects that knew of Serra and worshiped her as a goddess. "On the continent of Jamuraa," she said, pretending to relent. "We were attacked. The invaders drove us away, despoiling our lands . . . " Her explanation didn't even begin to touch upon the whole story. The destruction of their homeland and how the Phyrexians had found the Serrans was left out. Now the surviving refugees from Serra's Realm were scattered in small groups, hiding. "Armies of the dark lord with no name."

Russo tried a tight grin. "Ah. Another Lord of the Wastes," he said with false solemnly, trying to recapture a lighter mood. When Lyanii did not respond he flushed in embarrassment and explained. "I hear a lot of old tales in my travels. There is one about a dark figure and his armies of evil minions who will one day sweep whole nations from Dominaria. I've heard everything from the Ice Age to the small wars in Efuan Pincar blamed on him." He laughed, hollowly. "Of course, who actually believes that?"

Lyanii found no humor in the idea. "Who indeed," she said simply, voice tight with her loss and upset with herself for the momentary loss of control.

The merchant stumbled through an apology for his bad humor.

"No matter," she said finally. "I will have to contact the local clans then to make them aware of our presence and our preference for solitude."

"Yes," Russo agreed, "but do you know which to approach? Such procedures can make all the difference in Benalia."

She didn't see why, but then ignorance was not to be ashamed of—only corrected if possible. Russo might have suggestions, but then he could not appreciate the Serran refugees' position. As marshal she must choose. "Where are you bound for next?" she asked.

"I've just come from Ortovi and am on my way to Capashen Manor and the Capashen villages west of there. That doesn't matter. You need Clan Blaylock. They're the ones overseeing foreign diplomacy, until the next moon of course."

Lyanii nodded her agreement, but frowned at that last. "Next moon?"

"You did fall from the sky," he said, trying to recapture some of the mood lost earlier. "How did you travel so deep into Benalia and not hear of the Clans' lunar rotation?" Lyanii only shrugged. "On the glimmer moon's lunar year, two months from now, the ruling clans all rotate their duties. After that it'll be Clan Capashen's turn at diplomacy for a year, while Blaylock moves to the ruling clan." He grew thoughtful. "You could, I suppose, hold on until the moon's change. Then you are dealing with a local Clan. The Blaylocks would want to enforce the caste system on you sure enough. The Capashens are more tolerant of outside ways." A glance to the ranks of archers. "Your warriors will be a sticky point, regardless. It might be better if you formally adopted their system to begin with."

"That will not happen," Lyanii said, head swimming with all the new information.

She was marshal because Serra had decided it so, just as others were archers or guards. They were suited for their positions because they had been created as such. Why should they let an outside force determine their roles? Still, the trader had been more helpful than she'd at first thought.

"Thank you for the advice, Trader Russo."

Russo shrugged, neatly separating himself from the matter. "Advice is free. Here's hoping you do well, Marshal Lyanii. In the meantime, shall we see what my caravan can offer you and yours?"

Lyanii nodded for him to lead then turned and signaled for administrators from Devas. They would better know what was needed and what could be traded away. She would accompany the administrators and later perhaps invite Russo into the village for a discussion on Benalish customs. This land was their home now, and Lyanii would need to know everything possible if they were to survive.

The formal reception took place in Capashen Manor's ballroom. Gold flake had been mixed into a sealant and brushed over the white stone walls, leaving a smooth golden-glitter finish. Stained glass windows along two walls offered multi-colored views onto the impressive grounds in the back of the estate. A cathedral ceiling arced majestically overhead, rising up to the stained glass dome heavily trimmed in gold. The open space muted the soft music that rained down from an overhead musician's balcony, the perfect volume to enjoy while also engaged in discussion.

Karn walked into the room at the side of Nathan Capashen, leader of his Benalish Clan. Around them the Capashen nobles mingled cautiously with those of Clan Ortovi—their guests. Karn noticed that a strained cordiality had settled over the assembly as everyone carefully skirted the purpose of the state visit. By custom, it wasn't until the second day of a visit that business could be discussed. Of course, everyone already knew from the guests in residence what that business would be. Now they merely awaited the final member of the convocation—the third party that tradition demanded put the question forward, though certainly it would be rejected—again.

"This race of lizardmen, the Viashino, they actually live over a live volcano? Amazing, Karn." Nathan Capashen looked sideways at the silver man. "*Almost* incredulous."

He shook his head, obviously trying to compare such a life with the open plains of Benalia. Nathan was an avid audience for news of the larger world.

It was Karn's turn for a question about Benalia, trading his knowledge of Dominaria for more intimate information on this land. He found it interesting, as his journals were mostly filled with memories of Tolaria until only thirty years back. He began to accompany Urza in frequent travels about Dominaria. The golem knew some pain for those he saw so little of these days—Barrin, Rayne, and Timein. Delving into the details of new lands helped to ease that sense of loss. His question was interrupted by the sudden heightened pitch of conversation in the room as people passed along a single name and then fell into an expectant hush. Malzra.

Urza Planeswalker strolled with intent across the large floor, bearing down on Karn and Leader Nathan Capashen. He wore a closed-collared garment of royal purple and a blue leather vest. Urza stopped, glanced about as if just now noticing the silence and smiled at the surrounding people. Conversations picked back up but at a much more subdued level, and many crowds edged in closer to Nathan and Karn's location. Three others broke from their own groups and moved in for the official matter, one taking up position behind Nathan and two joining Urza.

Nathan nodded a friendly greeting. "Master Malzra, you honor us with your presence here. Am I to understand you wish to put forth a formal proposal?"

"I do," Urza said. The 'walker's blue eyes were sharp and bright, and Karn followed his gaze past Nathan to the clan leader's young cousin Jaffry.

The young clansman was nervous, acutely aware of the attention focused on him. He was also just as obviously smitten with the woman who trailed Leader Trevar Ortovi, his eyes always coming back to her.

Urza nodded to the young noble lady, Myrr Ortovi. "I am honored to invite both clan leaders present today to consider accepting Myrr Ortovi as wife to Jaffry Capashen."

Benalish law stipulated that leaders of each clan had to consent publicly and in the same forum before a marriage could take place between clans. In this match, Clan Ortovi gained most of the advantages. Though she would live among the Capashen, Myrr would forever be Ortovi—clan affiliation was determined by birthdate and nothing else. Her loyalty to Clan Capashen would always be secondary. So on those years when the Capashen ranked higher than the Ortovi in Benalish government, she might hope to use her influence in favor of her clan.

Nathan Capashen didn't even look to his cousin. The feelings of the couple came second. "This match was denied last year, Master Malzra. Why should I reconsider now? Your sterling recommendation notwithstanding, of course."

"Leader Trevar offers as dowry control of the lands and both villages bordering the river Larus. Also, in his position as head of taxation this year, a reduction to only one part in ten of all crops." Urza turned to look at the young girl.

Myrr nodded, showing that she was a willing participant in this ritual and stepped forward, offering Urza her hand.

Nathan shook his head sadly. "I cannot agree." Several gasps of disbelief erupted across the room. "In two months the Capashens take over foreign policy while the Ortovis handle trade. After that, the Capashens shall rule Benalia, and the Ortovis will be in place for diplomacy. I would be a fool to ignore the serious advantage given Clan Ortovi by placing Myrr within our manor." He paused. "I might consider such a marriage in the year after, of course."

Of course, then the Capashens would be back at the lowest position while Ortovi ruled. Karn looked to Urza, as did all others, knowing that the matchmaker would not have brought forth the invitation without something new to offer. Urza did not disappoint.

The 'walker had not released Myrr's hand, pulling her forward gently to stand next to him. "It saddens me to see two people kept apart over a trivial matter of dowry. I'm certain Trevar Ortovi would offer more to see Myrr's happiness if it would not be a detriment to his own clan. So in his place, I would like to add to Myrr's dowry."

An allowable custom, though Karn doubted anyone could remember the last time a *neutral* third party had done such.

Urza nodded to his golem. "I offer Karn as part of Myrr's dowry, his services devoted to their family in specific and Clan Capashen in general for no less than fifty years."

All eyes speared the silver golem. Karn dwarfed all present, but at the moment he felt very small under those piercing gazes. Fifty years! Better than twice his memory span. Forgotten would be Tolaria and his friends there. He was shocked that Urza would simply make such a decision without first warning the golem, but then something also spoke up inside of him that warned that this was not the first time.

Urza's offer had struck the right target in Nathan. The clan leader couldn't help the smile that followed his initial surprise, but then he sobered, looking at the silver man carefully.

"Karn, is this what you want as well?" he asked his friend.

Did it matter what the golem might want or decide? If Urza was to be believed, nothing else mattered but the threat of Phyrexian invasion. The golem had seen one battle already, a negator catching the 'walker and golem as the two traveled to inspect the mana rig under the Viashino's care. He could only imagine the horror of an army of such creatures. If Urza believed Karn's service to the Capashen was warranted, could he gainsay the planeswalker?

"I will stay," Karn said slowly, feeling out the words.

Nathan nodded once, abruptly, then turned back to Urza and Trevar. "It is a good match," he said. Nathan motioned Jaffry forward, and Urza joined his hand with Myrr's, then said loudly, "We welcome Myrr Ortovi into our manor."

It was a signal for the others in attendance to flock in and congratulate the newly engaged as well as each other for a fine bargain struck.

Urza found the golem quickly. "I will be off, Karn. I will bring the balance of your personal effects on my next visit." He paused a long moment, giving the golem an evaluating stare. "I had hoped your travels about Dominaria would give you an appreciation for its lands and people. It's good to see that I was right."

Karn read into that a reluctant admission that Urza might actually consider the golem a being of his own, not that it mattered in the larger picture of course. Still, it helped to reinforce Karn's resolve that his choice had been the right one. So long as he—and Urza—believed that the golem could make a difference in the preparations against Phyrexia, Karn felt compelled to answer that higher calling. What else was there in any life—human or artifact, mortal or immortal—beside a useful existence?

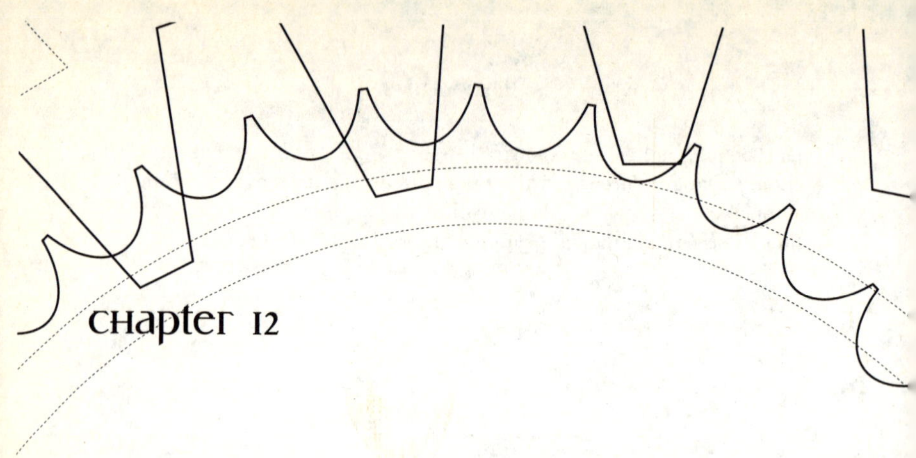

Chapter 12

Gatha's colos pens were heavily reinforced. Extra thick walls were tipped with spears of valuable iron pointing inward and down to keep the beasts from getting too aggressive. Now a head reared up, the colos butting aside one spear. It had learned to use its protective scale already.

From his viewing platform, Gatha studied the single incredible beast for the results of his latest experiments. The massive colos—larger than most by five hands at least—clawed at the ground with razor-sharp split hooves. Its rank breath frosted in the crisp morning air. Gatha found no physical deformities except the one he had given it—the same hard bone armoring its horns now grew in plate-sized scale over half of its hide. It was patchwork still, spaced in between large areas still shaggy with the usual coat, but no longer suffering degradation problems. His attempts at developing a superior war beast were hitting closer to the mark. Another three trials and he might try cutting the armored scale into the Matrix and use it on some Keldons crippled by earlier testing and now good only for experimentation, perhaps after one more trial.

Though occupied with studying the beast, Gatha still kept a wary eye on the party being led carefully down the trail toward his labs. In Keld, it never paid to be unobservant. Gatha knew his visitor would be no descendant of the long-dead Trohg. All warriors with a pedigree from the witch king had been given the safe routes and passes to his lab. Even now, a pair of Trohg's descendents, six times removed, stood guard at the laboratory's main door with wickedly barbed halberds. Twelve years old, the both of them were already standing above six feet and taking early warlord trials the following year. Gatha considered them mild successes.

The approaching party passed beneath the crude arch erected over the path. He recognized Varden, a minor witch king and—lately—a troublemaker in council. His escort was none other than Kreig, another of Trohg's descendents and Gatha's best subject ever. This would demand his personal attention, and he scaled back down the short ladder to the frost-bitten ground below.

He doffed his fur-lined cap and gloves and tucked them beneath his armored breastplate. The armor of Keldon design was made of thinly beaten, overlapping steel plates trimmed in red leather and gold. It was one of many rich gifts presented him by Kreig's two *doyenne.* He ran a hand over his oiled hair, slicking it back so that his tri-widow's peak tattoos stood out prominently. On the back of his right hand the personal sigil of Trohg had been tattooed. It bound Gatha to Trohg and the witch king's lineage and signified his acceptance in Keld with all rights and privileges. More, it shielded him from any immediate danger—by tradition any dispute with a protected person must be taken to the senior warrior of that line. Kreig, with Gatha's latest help, that would forever and *always* be Kreig.

"My friend," Kreig greeted, a *high Keld* salutation rarely offered inside the Keldon nation and never to an outsider. Gatha steeled himself to prevent a wince as Kreig squeezed down on his shoulders. "Varden demands an audience with you," he said dropping back into the lower tongue. He shot a glare back toward Varden who averted his eyes from the more powerful witch king. "I took his manor and mate hostage to insure his good behavior."

This meant that Varden came with an argument and possible challenge. Kreig may have overstepped himself slightly—certainly Varden thought so, his nostrils flaring with pent rage—usurping what was traditionally the censuring power of the council. Gatha doubted many would argue with *his* witch king.

"I will hear him."

Varden wasted no time. Though several inches shy of Kreig, the smaller warrior showed no fear of the other's presence. "You," he thrust a thick finger toward Gatha, a fighting offense between any regular Keldon males, "you refused my request for The Gift." *The Gift* was how Keldons referred to the preconception process Gatha had started with Trohg and applied judiciously depending on his own needs and whims. Usually, the effort was not worth potential returns—not with the strong line already backing him. "I desire another son, one who deserves warlord trials."

Varden's first son had been born lame, guaranteeing him a position in Keldon society barely more than slave labor. At least with a battlefield injury, one might expect to live out life as a craftsman.

Gatha had expected something like this. "No," he said.

Hands balling into sledgelike fists, Varden barely controlled his fury. "No? What do you mean, no?" he yelled.

"No," Gatha replied with quiet strength, his *low Keld* tongue perfect these days. "I refuse your request. I thought it was clear from the message I sent. If you need to hear it from my lips, then so be it." He shrugged. "No."

"Lowland fodder," Varden stormed, spittle flying from his lips. "You will change your mind," he said, more a command than a threat.

Carving his place within Keld had taken Gatha better than four decades. He still remembered those early years, always self-effacing and at times cowering because it was expected. Trohg had changed that, first ever to name the mage a friend after the successful advancement of his own son to warlord and then witch king status. Gatha had over a century since to grow into his new power, and he knew how to wield it. Varden neither frightened nor even worried him, and the warlord's lack of understanding of that only proved the legitimacy of Gatha's refusal. He was genetically damaged in body and mind—in the mage's opinion.

"I will not change my mind." Gatha folded his arms across his chest, resolute. "Your son is not fit for enhancement." He dug the barb in deeper. "Though perhaps I will request him for," and he had to drop back into Argivian for the word, "experiments. I will never use *your* blood in my work again. I expect your diseased line to die out." Gatha turned to Kreig. "This interview is over," he said. The message was apparent—Varden no longer mattered.

Varden shook with rage. One hand fastened onto the hilt of his broadsword. His darkly tattooed eyes glared fiercely down on the smaller man. "You do this to us," he yelled, "To me. Your work over the years, deciding who travels on and who falls. It will stop soon, little one. I vow it."

Varden stomped away, his terrifying exit made comical when he realized that he would require Kreig or another escort to pass him safely through the snares that warded Gatha's labs. Gatha waited for him to bluff it through alone, but in the end Varden waited just past the arch, fuming.

"You have made an enemy for us," Kreig said, careful to keep their conversation from Varden's ears. "Varden will summon his warhost. Other warlords might stand against me now. I had hoped this wouldn't happen for another year."

Left unspoken but implied with his last statement was the fact that Kreig *had* anticipated such a day. Gatha had merely accelerated the timetable. It left the mage feeling confident in his greatest subject, who would grow greater yet with the slow-time waters being given him the last several years. His initial supply kept preserved in a stasis field, the both of them could easily live another century, then, if necessary, Kreig's warhost could visit Tolaria and *request* more.

Gatha was not about to see his work ruined now by something so easily overcome as chance. "Give me the names of those who might stand against us. I will entice them to stay away from Varden." The easy offer of withholding of his magics could influence most warlords. Kreig cocked his head to one side, considering, then grunted a simple acknowledgment. The mage smiled. "You then only have to crush Varden."

Even as breath came in frosted clouds, the battle cries of the Keldons warmed the air and stirred bloodlust. There were screams of challenge, personal conquest, and the bellowing of orders as commands of the opposing warlords were routed. Only a few shouts of pain were heard, except perhaps in the most tragic of cases where limbs were lost or backbones cleaved, allowing those final seconds of painful clarity before oblivion. No fearful shouts were called—not so much as a whimper—not from these men. They would bleed their flesh white, staining the frostbitten earth and stone dark with the red of their life before admitting to cowardice in any fashion or guise. It was a clashing of titans, marauders who would fight and die to the last man if so ordered here on this lonely plateau, no ordinary contest. Mist wreathed the land farther down, piling into a dense fog that cascaded down the mountainside to fill the lower valleys. It was as if the gods themselves had elevated the battleground above the ken of mortal man.

A broken ridgeline split the plateau unevenly, the scarp of sharp rocks pushed up during a recent movement of the earth. The battle raged only on the larger side—a thousand warriors joined in ferocious combat. A few had claimed the higher ground for their fighting, loosing hand-pitched rocks and the occasional axe down on those below. Boulders large and small littered the battlefield, minor obstacles Keldon warriors dodged to get at their enemy.

Leather-armored footsoldiers carried hooked longswords or wickedly spiked maces. Nearly all tied smokesticks of colos horn into their hair. The smoke drove many Keldons into a battle frenzy and was known for the nervous anxiety it bred in other races. They fought in single combat only where a blood feud was acknowledged between two warriors. Mostly they clumped together and dashed madly into enemy groups, bristling juggernauts of steel and sinew. Against any other foe, a Keldon warrior would have trusted the tough coloshide leather and his own strength to stand up to a blow, setting up a killing stroke of his own. Those who relied on such tactics lay among the fallen here. This was not a battle to be won on ferocious strength alone. Here strength and skill carried the battle only so far. It would be won by the warhost commanders, the Keldon warlords, the witch kings.

Kreig held the inside flank of his warhost, turning his broad back to the sharp ridge as he slashed his way through the thickest fighting, well armored with metal gauntlets and greaves, interlocking plates covering chest, shoulders and hips. His helm allowed a narrow slit for vision, the opening guarded from a lucky sword thrust by twin crescent-shaped blades. A ridge of curving spikes stood out from his shoulders, each one vented to a cavity built into the neckline where smoldering embers had been placed to wreath his headgear and shoulders in fearsome smoke. The leather joints in his armor were made with the shaggy colos hair still in place to bring about the illusion that the armor concealed beast rather than man.

Gatha's greatest witch king wielded his Keldon greatsword with both hands, the silvery finish of the blade now marred with gore and running droplets of blood. The bloodlust of several hundred warriors coursed through his veins, exploded in his heart, pounded at his temples. He drew upon the warhost's strength, their courage. His eighth opponent lay in two at his feet, cleaved from right shoulder to left hip. The warrior's stabbing sword had pierced the witch king's right thigh. The Keldon simply drew it out as if it was a mere annoyance and tossed it aside with a howl of derision for Varden's warriors.

"Varden!" he called out, challenging the other witch king to stand against him.

His own warriors, those close enough to hear the challenge, called out his own name in a chant. "Kreig! Kreig! Kreig!" It left little question from where the great witch king commanded. Sporadic calls of "Varden" were little more than half-hearted answers to the general chant, not a reply to his challenge. None could stand against this witch king. No being of Dominaria could hope to match him.

Another warrior came at him, this one slashing with a halberd. With a spinning cut, Kreig took the head of the polearm off just behind the blade. He continued his spin, coming back around in a straight-armed attack that took the warrior's head easily from his shoulders. Kreig picked up the head and tossed it into a knot of Varden's men who were trying to protect the lower slopes of the scarp. A sickle-axe sunk into the ground near his foot. Kreig picked that up as well. His return throw found an enemy warrior halfway up the slope of sharp rocks. Even throwing upward, his strength punched the point of the weapon through armor and chest to stick out the other's back. No one would be protected from him.

Where Kreig walked the battle turned in his favor. His closest warriors fought and died to keep abreast of him, which pushed the witch king forward all the harder. They were lucky to simply trail back from his lead in a deep arrow, leaving behind a field littered with dead or dying men and a few scattered fights. Kreig could see Varden now, leading his men from behind—ordering them forward while he and his private guards advanced much slower. A thick line of Varden's supporters separated Kreig from his enemy—but not for long.

His greatsword flicking like a dragon's tongue, Kreig forced his way into a knot of mace-wielding soldiers. He left amputated limbs, shattered bone and cleft armor in his wake. Two heavy-spiked clubs stuck into him, abdomen and elbow. A downward slice took the arms off one man. The other he dispatched with an easy thrust through the chest. The weapons still sticking in him, he felt no pain and never slowed from wounds which would have killed a mortal man. He was more than mortal at this moment, the energy at the core of his being multiplied several hundred-fold. He was Kreig. He was *Keld.*

Kreig looked over the field at two Keldon warhosts joined in battle. Each one, by himself was a superior warrior. Together they were a proud and fierce nation. Where each warrior fell to a brother the nation diminished. *His* nation diminished.

He chopped the head off a war sickle aimed for his neck, his sword edge slicing through the wooden shaft with ease. Instead of a return stroke, taking another life, Kreig fastened one gauntleted hand onto the other's long hair and pulled the warrior to arm's length to stare into the witch king's dark gaze.

"Keld!" he bellowed a new war cry, taking the nation's name for his own.

He shouted it into the warrior's face, turned him with an easy roll of the wrist, and set him facing against his former comrades. He could feel the man's loyalties swaying on the field, caught between the powers of two witch kings. Kreig took up a stabbing sword from a fallen warrior of his own host and thrust its hilt into the warrior's hands.

"Keld!" he yelled again, a cry the warrior took up for his own.

Kreig swept forward—invincible in his power. Any warrior brave enough to meet him was converted with the call of home and nation and set back on the side of Kreig. With each convert Varden's power waned. More rallied to Kreig, in singles, then pairs and then trios. Finally the remaining enemy forces fell back, regrouping around a solid center. Varden pushed his way to the fore, broadsword in one hand and his personal crest in the other. Kreig summoned his own colors, taking the greatsword one-handed despite the awkward grip.

"Varden," the smaller force called out, summoning the last of their strength in a mad rush at the opposing center.

"Keld," the warhost of Kreig answered.

Led by their mightiest, the army swarmed forward and over Varden's group. The witch kings came against each other. Kreig's greatsword punched through metal plating to slice into Varden's left leg. Varden's own stroke slipped into an unprotected space and stabbed deeply into Kreig's side. Powered by their greater strength, each witch king felt the pain of near-mortal wounds. Kreig rebounded faster. He swept his blade down and then around in a grand overhead sweep while Varden barely had time to bring his own sword up in an attempt to parry. Varden's broadsword shattered under the vicious stroke, and Kreig followed through to split open the witch king's head. His blade turned slightly by Varden's spine, Kreig's stroke finally died when it stuck into the other man's left hip.

Kreig stood over the fallen witch king, the battle over. He wrenched his weapon free, held it aloft with blood dripping down in a christening shower. No more challenges were called forth, only the victory bellows of his followers. Keld was his now. He would lead its greatest armies into the field, and here in the mountains he would rule. He saw a tiered throne in his vision, decorated with bodies of his fallen enemies. He looked his nation in the eye, challenging it, and it glanced away, subdued.

Gatha remembered a time when he had stood in Council, ready to address the assembled *doyen*, and had deliberated taken the uppermost tier in order for all to look on him as he spoke. He had demurred then, unsure of protocol. This day, standing with Kreig as the witch king set forth to claim that empty spot, the mage could only think back on that moment and count himself fortunate to be alive for even considering the idea.

Kreig carried the tattered and blood-stained colors of Varden. The other witch king's warhost no longer existed, all survivors having pledged their loyalty unto death to Kreig. He had come to the council as the greatest warrior—the greatest witch king—ever known. Dressed simply in ceremonial leathers, his chest and arms bared to the cold, he walked over to the wall, withdrew a spike from his belt, and used it to stab through the heavy cloth and into the wall. Never before had a warlord's crest been displayed here among the spiked standards of every nation the Keldons had ever fought against. It was both proof of victory and threat to those who would stand against him. Kreig nodded to Gatha, and the two walked straight over to the lowermost tier. Kreig mounted it first, staring down those nearby, and then turned to offer Gatha a hand in aide.

Where the mage may have come into his own power here in Keld—able six months ago to stand up before a furious Varden and believe himself sacrosanct—here his nerves sang tightly for the role Kreig expected him to play. The witch king did not need to include him but did so for an old promise made by Trohg himself. Shrugging aside the offer of assistance, Gatha mounted the tier and stared directly at the warlord to his immediate side. The Keldon stood, his massive frame towering over Gatha, but after a quick glance to Kreig he averted his gaze and stepped back, leaving room for Gatha to stand as an equal—as *doyen*, one of the leaders of Keld.

Gatha swallowed a tight knot in his throat, his mouth dry and scratchy for lack of spit. For the first time ever the council hall did not seem cold, a full-body flush warming him.

Kreig, however, was not finished. He stepped upon the next tier, then the next, again meeting no challenge.

On this third tier a crippled warlord rose, his age impressive and showing in the weathered face and slightly stooped shoulders. One arm had been replaced by a stabbing sword, his left leg a sharpened stump of metal.

"I do not speak against you, Kreig," He thrust the bladed hand toward Gatha, "but he does not belong there."

Gatha knew that those warlords crippled in battle still retained their place. The council of the aged was given weight in all deliberations, but in the end the strong ruled. Kreig locked gazes with his elder.

"He is here because my great sire, Trohg, promised that one day Gatha would sit on the council. I am keeping that promise. Gatha has proven himself as the greatest ally of the Keldon nation. My victories are his victories."

Kreig's death would likely be Gatha's own as well. The mage was again thankful for his hoard of slow-time water. Now he was merely gambling on Kreig's martial prowess. His entire life in Keld had been a gamble. At least here he had loaded the dice.

The elder glanced away first. For his challenge, he decided to step down a tier rather than be thrown down later. The warlord next to his abandoned seat, though, rose and drew a dagger. No words passed nor needed to. Kreig leapt for him at once, taking a savage slash to his side but fastening his hands about the other man's neck. Muscles bunched on his shoulders. A sideways twist and the other man's neck snapped with a bone-crunching sound. It echoed in the chamber. Kreig threw him from the tier.

A warlord *doyen*—no witch king this one—rose beyond him. Kreig moved forward, and the other dropped back into a defensive stance. The witch king paused, then walked forward slowly and with great deliberation to each step. He stopped barely a foot from the other warrior, hands at his sides and eyes boring into the other man's face as if daring him to strike first. Brutal seconds passed, and then the warlord broke away his gaze and bowed his head in surrender unable to bring himself to follow through on the challenge. He also demoted himself to the second tier. Kreig continued to stare down at him. Still there were no words spoken but some subtle body posturing that Gatha could not quite follow. The warlord stepped back down to the first tier, and Kreig turned his attention back to the final level.

Behind Kreig, the *doyen* shook themselves into a new structure of power. With three vacancies now on the third tier, a witch king from the second tier stood and moved up next to Kreig. Toward the dominant witch king he kept eyes averted and head slightly bowed. To his right he stared his neighbor in the eye and then sat. No one challenged. Another rose from the first tier and took a seat in the second. A few of the younger but stronger witch kings replaced older warlords higher up as well. To Gatha's eye, it became apparent who supported Kreig and who was simply bowing to his greater strength.

Kreig ignored it all. With deliberation he stepped up to the fourth tier, holding only six chairs—one of them his usual seat on the council. One witch king stood in challenge. At this level none carried weapons, considering it beneath their martial prowess. The fighting was brutal and silent. Kreig held up under a stiff-hand blow to the throat and a rib cracked by a knee body blow, giving as good as he received. Finally he managed to catch his opponent on the jaw with his elbow. Kreig picked the stunned man up by shoulder and crotch and threw him from the tier, his skull caving in when it dashed against the hard floor below. The witch king then picked up his own chair and threw it down after the body, leaving him no actual seat. He stepped up into the open space where no chair had ever been placed and where, by his action, none ever would. This place of power was his by right if no one challenged.

No one did. The four remaining *doyen* who sat on the high tier averted their gaze, and Kreig's power was assured. Again the *doyen* maneuvered around to fill vacancies. No fights marred the quiet. The others did not presume to compare their ability with Kreig's glorious rise. They recognized and honored Kreig's strength—and Gatha's, the mage realized, remembering how Kreig had shared all victories past and future.

It was a feat never before managed, an event out of legend. Kreig had taken the uppermost level. From before recorded time the promise had come down: When the Necropolis below the council hall filled with the warlord dead, they would all rise in an invincible army and sweep Dominaria. The warlord who sat the final tier would lead that army. Gatha had never understood if that warlord would be one of the dead, the greatest of them all through history, or whichever warlord had seized the position for the great event. Here, with the mage's help, it seemed that Kreig might be able to await that rapturous time.

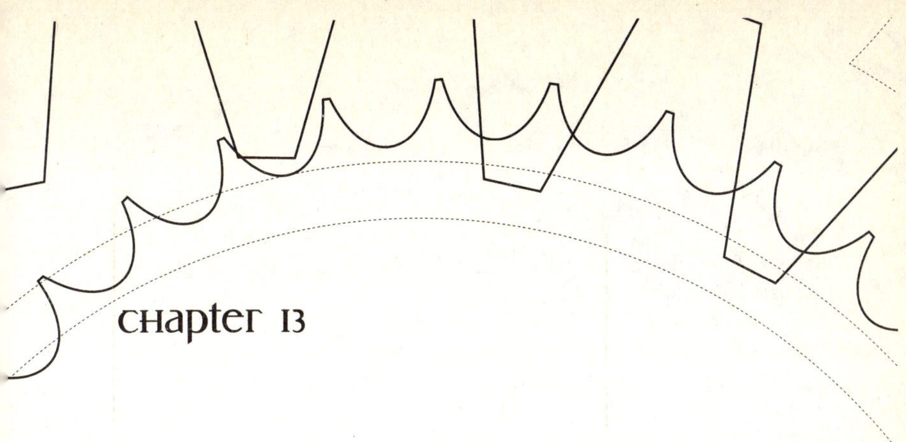

chapter 13

Davvol stood on a small rise that he'd shaped up from the mountainside's easy slope of dull tan flowstone. His flying disc rested upon the ground behind him—a black altar guarded by two Phyrexian soldiers standing a silent guard. On the horizon the great volcano that held the Stronghold thrust its imperial presence into that chaotic sky. It dwarfed the mountain on which he currently stood and reminded Davvol of that which he ruled.

A cutting wind sliced through the gaps in his armor, breathing chills against his grayish flesh and billowing his cloak out behind him like the leathery wings of a giant bat out of nightmare. The cold also gripped at his head, squeezing it in an invisible vise, except where the black Phyrexian skullcap armored and protected it even from the elements. A Coracin physical characteristic—in his mind, a defect—was that the bone plates in their wide skulls never quite closed and so left a vulnerable spot over the brain, a vulnerability that Croag had agreed to remedy, as Davvol's mind was of importance to both Davvol and the Phyrexians. Only one feature to the skullcap bothered him: The small circular indentation high over his forehead. Phyrexians did not adorn their work with art or meaningless design. That indentation had a purpose, which Croag had not seen fit to pass on and Davvol preferred not to draw attention to by asking.

"You intend to attempt a transfer." Croag's voice squealed and cracked behind him. This was not a question. Croag obviously knew.

Davvol looked over his shoulder, his black eyes guarded against his surprise at being interrupted here. The member of Phyrexia's Inner Circle stood next to the steward's disc, a portal still opened behind him and flashing as Davvol's soldiers passed through and away—back to the Stronghold, no doubt. Now Davvol frowned. The soldiers were a precaution since the Vec had been known to roam far from their underground city searching the landscape. Of course, Croag could easily handle anything a common soldier could, but those guards were *his*, to be dismissed only by Davvol himself.

"I am considering it," he finally admitted.

"It would be better if your troops did not see a failure." Croag glided forward slowly, the metal bands that formed his semblance of clothing rasping against each other. Croag carried his staff today, a twisted metal creation with no apparent purpose. Davvol knew better than to assume such was true. "Failure is too often the genesis of recycling. You might weaken their loyalty to you."

Croag had done him a favor? Perhaps. Davvol did not blind himself to the possibility that Croag might be concerned that the guard witness his *success*. The centuries were stacking up behind the steward of Rath, and with each passing year he accumulated more data through which he better understood his position and that of those around him. Davvol smiled, thinking that none of his race could ever have hoped for such a long life holding the power he did. He would gain more so long as he maintained appearances and worked carefully.

"My appreciation, Croag. I hadn't considered that." Because he truthfully hadn't considered failure as an option, "What would happen to the subjects if a failure occurred in mid-transference?" Would the Phyrexian even know?

"They would be gone," Croag said simply. "Lost between worlds. It has happened before, yes. During the first steward's reign."

That told Davvol quite a lot that he hadn't known before, the most important, of course, being that Rath's rulers had changed in the past, and by extension could easily be changed again in the future. The thought bred hope and concern both. He turned to the task at hand, staring down the slope at the smooth wash of flowstone.

Davvol mentally reached back to the Stronghold. There the great control machinery for transference currently lay dormant, though it, like the flowstone, was attuned to the mental commands of both Davvol and Croag. The machinery sparked to life with his mental touch. When Rath was complete, ready to provide access to Dominaria for the armies of Phyrexia, this great machinery would overlay one to the other, the mutable quality of flowstone bridging the gap between planes in one final expenditure. Until then, the ease of a transference was limited by many factors, the closer to Rath's final form, the better. The size of the attempted transference and physical distance from the Stronghold's control machinery made a difference as well. The only variable was apparently the strength of mind of the steward or evincar. As always, Davvol trusted his mental abilities.

First in the valley, he sensed the machinery powering to life, softening the flowstone over an area measuring in square miles. Pressure built within his mind, an avalanche of malleable stone poised overhead, threatening to engulf him. Just beyond the promontory the land sank as if undermined by some great cavern beneath. Edges to the valley appeared as flowstone sloughed downhill.

As the flowstone continued to evacuate, the machinery built up the lower sides and generally shaped the valley into the picture Davvol held for it—slightly crescent shaped with weathered southern slopes and a steep cliff face to the north. His consciousness plunged into the land, following the forces at work. The pressure eased, the incredible raw weight of the flowstone falling away as the valley took its basic form. The machinery then began to pull details from Davvol's thoughts—from the memory of his trip to Dominaria. The seeker opening the portal for him had promised the perfect site, enclosed and isolated, and such had been delivered. Davvol spent days memorizing the finer detail, from the spicy pine scent to the cool touch of dew-laden fern. Now he transferred that detail to the Stronghold's control machinery, and again his mind strained under the weight of his undertaking. Flowstone leapt up in columns and spikes, filling out to become trees and bushes and grass. They stood in frozen relief, a true-to-life forest valley apparently sculpted from simple sandstone.

Only it was not so simple. It was an incredible display of power, both from Davvol and from the flowstone itself.

The process continued, memory becoming reality in this artificial valley. Now buildings rose up, adding to a renewed mental weight. Never before had Davvol felt his mind so completely at work, the machinery simply taking all he allowed. He saw animals in the forest and people on the streets and walks between buildings. They moved—were alive—and many stared up into a sky turned suddenly dark. Voices cried, shouted, and screamed. Davvol stood on the threshold of worlds and planes, looking between the chaos of the multiverse as the great machinery folded one into the other. The people were aware of Rath, of *him*, and many fell to the ground out of abject fear for what they could not understand.

Several hundred lives, the town residents, were but tiny sparks within his consciousness. The true life carried across the hole he had opened in the void, their sobs and screams of terror piercing the background roll of Rath's eternal thunderstorm. Their tormented cries distracted Davvol, forcing the machinery to pull stronger at his mind. Slowly Rath's steward sank to the ground, his hands splayed down against the flowstone promontory as he came to his knees under the stress. Still he did not take his eyes off the valley, then the pressure receded, and the forces raised by the machinery brought Davvol back from the threshold. The tortured wailing faded. He felt a few small sparks of life evade his final grasp. Some were lost in the chaos between Rath and Dominaria.

It was done.

A deer sprang nearby, jumping from verdant valley to the lip of Rath's unnatural flowstone landscape. It froze in fright then scrambled back to the safety of trees and undergrowth. Far in the distance, carried to Davvol by the final vestiges of his connection with the Stronghold's control machinery, came the terrified cries of people now gazing into an unfamiliar and hostile sky of dark clouds and vivid lightning. These were the newest residents of Rath.

Davvol smiled fully. These people would be taken as slaves. Davvol planned to accelerate the schedule and bring Rath closer to the point of final convergence, then Rath itself would cross the threshold and merge with Dominaria, bringing with it the armies of Phyrexia. Davvol would rule Rath and open the way for Phyrexia. He saw no other future. Even Croag would admit this now.

When he turned back Croag and the portal were gone. Davvol stood alone over his valley, left with his creation. The steward laughed, his harsh voice carried away on the sharp wind. That was fine by him. He felt no desire to share the moment, preferring the solitude of his success—his first success, but certainly not his last.

Storm clouds over Benalia hid stars and the blurry reflection of the Glimmer Moon. The Null Moon, a hard point of light often mistaken for a bright star, had recently cleared the overcast horizon. Only one being in the Capashen village of DeLatt knew the Null Moon's exact position, no need of direct sight to sense the satellite. Its lips curled back revealing a feral smile of sharp, gnashing teeth. Thunder crashed, shaking clay tiles and rattling window panes.

The blackness that formed inside the small courtyard had little to do with the dark Dominarian night. Pale gray flagstones reflected a cascade of lightning into the most remote corners. The bright wash bathed everything in a preternatural glow for one split second, except the round portal of pitch dark that sat tucked behind a wall of hanging plants. The home of the village magistrate framed three sides of the courtyard, the fourth opening up onto a wrought-iron fence with a gate offset on the right-hand side. An engraved metal shield over the gate offered a welcome to those who passed within. Though the gate remained locked, three figures moved among the shadows of the courtyard. Lightning flashed again, the scar standing out in the dark sky for a long second as violent thunder assailed the earth.

Croag already felt at home here. The electrically charged air felt invigorating, reminding the Inner Circle member of Rath and certain portions of Phyrexia—and something more, a sense pulling at Croag's mind in a way that more closely spoke of home and *kindred*. He could detect the barest scent of glistening oil—the scent exuded by meat once bathed in the vats. Croag chattered a brief acknowledgement to the seeker who had found this place. The minor Phyrexian stepped back with a groveling bow, taking a subordinate position to Croag and Davvol.

Davvol studied the surroundings, no doubt committing every last detail to his extraordinary memory. Croag did not mind—encouraged it, in fact. Davvol proved ever more useful as the centuries played out. Though he had yet to kill Urza Planeswalker, his improvements to negators could not be gainsaid, and his management of Rath was adequate, if uninspired. He had surprised Croag those months ago, able to guide a transference between Rath and Dominaria. That was not to say that the Inner Circle member considered the other dangerous. Davvol displayed no real aggression or ambition, not in any way the Phyrexian could gauge at least. Perhaps in another century or two he could be trouble, but who could plan so far ahead when today there was so much to accomplish?

A twinge, more direct this time, centered Croag's attention toward a pair of glass-paned doors. "There," he said, a simple screech of sound. It pointed one skeletal finger.

Rath's steward squinted in the direction, unable to pierce the gloom so deeply as Croag with his uncompleated eyes. "Where?" he asked as more lightning streaked across the sky. "The doors?" He moved off, his armored boots scraping against flagstone.

Croag moved quietly, making only his usual metallic rasp and the occasional scrape of metal bands against stone. With the booming thunder and a damp wind rattling the metal gate, the sounds of their passage should go unnoticed. If not, there would be one less Dominarian. Davvol tried the door latches, and they opened easily on well-oiled hinges. Croag was the first through, shredding the diaphanous white curtains as he passed. He moved directly to the side of a bed on which an old man slept. Weak and frail looking, as were most Dominarians, Croag found it difficult to reconcile the dark call that pulled him toward the human. He was not a sleeper but something very similar.

Reports from Dominarian agents—the sleepers, negators and seekers who came into contact with many of the weaker races—had spoken of such humans. Meat creatures with a dark affinity and a special strength building within that drew the Phyrexians toward them. Croag had considered such reports in error, confusing the nature of humans born in black mana environments with true Phyrexian purity. The Vec and others now living in Rath knew such empathy.

Croag had changed his opinion when he had walked Davvol's new settlement. Most of the people there had fled in terror, but one did not. Donning chain mail and mounted on a similarly armored horse, he came at the Phyrexian, intent on destroying Croag—no fear or hesitation showing in his steel-blue eyes. Croag had felt that connection then, as if both beings recognized in the other that which was black—that which was *Phyrexian.* It brought the human strength enough to resist and to fight. Spurring his mount, he thundered in at the alien creature with furious hatred. The Inner Circle member destroyed the human with very little conscious effort. He plunged his talons deep into the lesser creature's brain to draw out what final information he could. Delicious in its intensity, Croag reveled in the sensations that only meat could know.

In light of this attack Croag had come here, to the home of a Benalish nobleman serving as village magistrate. Here a seeker had recently sensed that spark of dark matter in the soul of a human. Again Croag knew the pull toward one not of his kind—but similar.

With a gesture from the Phyrexian, Davvol placed the artifact Croag had ordered him to carry near the human's head. A braided metal cable uncoiled and slithered across the pillow to set itself into the old man's ear, whispering a series of tones and noises. At normal volume, issuing forth from one of the larger Phyrexian war engines, the sound would frighten and confuse. At sufficiently high levels it might even be enough to interfere with the nerve processes. Here, at such a muted volume, it would merely induce a deep slumber. The human would not awaken, though he might remain aware of the nightmares that Croag would subject him to. The Phyrexian rested his left hand over the man's face, first and fifth talons rotating inward to burrow through flesh and bone above the temples and into the soft brain matter beneath. It was not enough for permanent damage, not yet, but meant to draw upon memories of the sleeping man. Croag was searching for answers.

The old man's eyes opened. Alarm and then terror flashing through them, quickly replaced by a furious hatred. This was not supposed to happen. His hands came out from the covers to fasten around Croag's wrist. Blood ran down his arms and splashed against his face as the skin on his hands split against the razor-sharpness of Croag's construction. Still he did not let go and actually budged Croag's hand, forcing the talons to cut laterally through sensitive brain tissue. His hands locked as the seizures took him, and he thrashed in the bed. Croag dug deeper, pulling out what information he could.

His name was Jaffry Capashen, son of Steffan and distant cousin of his current clan leader Thomas. The concepts and context of family and clan and caste all flooded the Phyrexian's mind. There was no time to enjoy the sensations, the knowledge pulled deeper to be reexamined later as the frail body faded into death.

Croag drove inward, cracking bone and squeezing the gray meat for more. He sensed the other's affinity for Phyrexian methods and manners, the reason no doubt he had resisted the artifact. Dim images of years spent in a large clan manor swam at the Phyrexian. He saw brief memories of a battle fought in service to Benalia, an arranged marriage and the birth of two children, the death of his wife Myrr, and the taking of this assignment to the local village where he dispensed justice and collected taxes for his clan.

Croag withdrew his razored talons, leaving behind a pulped mess of bone fragments, brain and blood. He turned to find Davvol waiting patiently, but the seeker was no longer in the room.

Davvol did not wait for the question. "I sent the seeker away," he said calmly. "The old man was certainly never supposed to wake up and defy you. I thought it better for the seeker to not see a failure here. It might cause," he paused, "problems."

Immune to the embarrassment of feelings, Croag still knew of the respect due his status and that in Davvol's eyes he was now being subject to very careful ridicule. The Phyrexian hunched down, not to diminish himself but in preparation of attack, though Croag restrained himself. Davvol remained too useful a tool to dispose of at this time.

"Yes," he said in a metallic screech. "At this time." It was not an answer to Davvol's comment but a reinforcing of his own thoughts.

Davvol apparently sensed some of the danger he stood in, turning back toward the ruined mess of a man who slowly soaked the white linen dark red. "Anything useful?"

Use would be determined later, but certainly Croag had been given a measure to pause and consider. "There are two offspring," he said slowly.

A plan formed, reflecting Davvol's efforts with the Phyrexian negators. Perhaps Croag could guide the development of a few Dominarian natives who showed affinity for the Phyrexians similar to Jaffry. Such an empathy was rare enough to justify further investigation at the least. If such affinity could be manipulated . . . this he would not speak of to Davvol. It was not truly the steward's concern. This was a matter which demanded Phyrexian attention, and hope as the steward might, Davvol would never be of Phyrexia, never compleat.

"Urza," Croag said, remembering one other image. "Urza Planeswalker was known to this human. He has been here." Croag could not afford to take chances wherever Urza might be involved. "I want an account of everywhere Urza Planeswalker has been tracked on Dominaria, everywhere humans with a dark affinity have been noticed. Seekers must be sent to investigate those areas." If there was a relationship between the two he would find it. A taloned hand slashed at the air between them. "You will kill Urza Planeswalker, soon."

Davvol nodded slowly, obviously unable to help a look of resignation. "This can be done," he said, echoing Croag's words of so many years before.

The Phyrexian did not wait for further conversation. With one final glare, eyes burning like hot coals within his cavernous sockets, he stalked from the room and back toward his portal. He had had enough of Dominaria, but he would return soon.

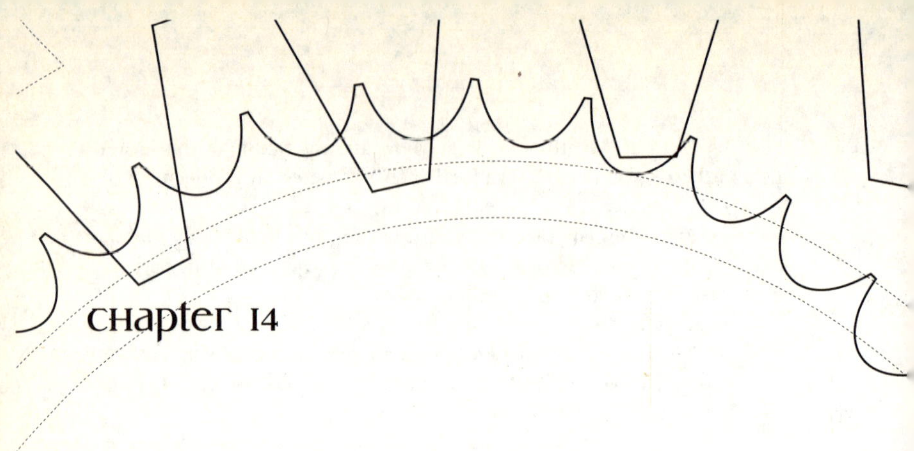

CHAPTER 14

Fire rained down in a burning cascade, washing over Urza's arm and scorching the golden finish on his staff as the planeswalker failed to move in time. A flaming, gelatinous substance which stuck even to his form of energy seared into him at a dozen places now. Each wound drew off that much more of his strength, leaving him more vulnerable to the negator's next attack. Urza's options were rapidly decreasing in direct proportion with the waning power left at his command.

The planeswalker had come back to Efuan Pincar to see after the bloodlines in this small nation. He hoped to mix the best results from here into a weak Femeref line, rejuvenating it. Though marriage and preconception treatment of the parents with the Eugenics Matrix was preferred, the 'walker was prepared for more drastic methods as necessary. With a few genetic samples from the local subjects, he could *cut in* appropriate traits and qualities—*post*conception. As a rule, he tried to avoid such procedures, but with the strange loss of the bloodlines in Femeref, Urza lost one of his best. The people simply vanished, by all accounts just over ten years ago, and only a few insane tales of a night of storms were left to offer any explanation. This was a matter of needs versus means. Dominaria's safety required it.

Urza still couldn't be sure what had drawn him back to his old home in Efuan Pincar—the remote cottage he once shared with Xantcha now falling into ruin. In this place the two of them worked on ways to defeat Phyrexian incursions into Dominaria and later, with the help of a local boy Ratepe, had finally won the battle against Gix. Nostalgia? Not likely. Maybe he came to remember Xantcha whom he'd traveled with for so long. She would've understood the necessity of the bloodlines, he felt certain. The Phyrexian couldn't have simply been waiting for him. Either this location was checked often, and Urza had simply chosen the wrong time, or the negators were getting better at tracking him without giving away their own presence. The planeswalker preferred to believe the former, so he did.

Now the cabin burned, having caught a spray from the negator's fire-throwing weapon. Small trees sprouting up in the clearing were also afire. A sooty smoke trailed the area, the gritty clouds having trouble escaping into the sky and beginning to wear on Urza's visibility. The large creature-construct appeared to have little trouble tracking the planeswalker. A long arm snaked past a blazing pine tree, the crackling flames of little bother to it, swiping at Urza's side and scoring bloody furrows from ribs to hip. Such an attack would rarely have shown blood, the manifestation of energy bleeding away from Urza's consciousness, but on top of the burning wounds the 'walker was simply unable to regenerate the illusion after clawing.

A large dark shape loomed through a hazy black cloud, standing twice as tall as Urza. Its incredibly bloated body expanded and contracted with an over-exaggerated breathing motion. One arm nearly dragging the ground ended with razored claws. The other looked stunted, but in actuality it had been replaced by a type of slender cannon that spewed the dangerous substance. Urza swept back, avoiding a new stream of fiery gel and focusing mana into a lightning strike. A blue-white arc leapt from his fingers and smashed into the negator's carapace of hard, glossy black skin. The energy danced over the outer form, all of it drawn over to the Phyrexian's left hip where it entered. The glossy carapace split down the outside of the left leg. Corrupted flesh sizzled and burned as the lightning was somehow channeled down into the ground and away from anything vital.

This negator was immune to natural fire and resistant to lightning. The two creatures Urza had found time to summon early on had met with fiery deaths, and now the 'walker was losing too much mental strength to tap more mana. It was a hard realization for Urza Planeswalker to admit. He was losing this fight.

When one understands the nature of a thing, one knows what it is capable of—a saying once passed to him and his brother both from Tocasia, the old Argivian archaeologist who first taught the brothers about the recovery and restoration of artifacts. His attention was divided between an attempt to build his powers up and searching for the Phyrexian he had lost again among the thick gritty smoke. It took Urza a moment to understand why he had dredged up that old memory, then transposed it. Once a person understands the capabilities of a thing he might also know its nature! The creature was disgorging an incredible amount of burning fluid, but even the Phyrexians could not violate the laws of conservation. That substance had to be stored or somehow produced by the negator. The bloated body and its bellowlike breathing suggested a combination of both.

As a planeswalker, Urza was capable of casting all colors of magic, but his first love, his initial rise to power, had been with artifice. He thumbed a stud on his staff's contoured grip. One of the crescent-shaped tines on the staff's head reversed itself on a clockwork gear, bringing a special edge to bear. Another switch triggered the harmonics that attacked glistening oil. The 'walker had made adjustments to the sonic device after its failure with the one negator decades before, hoping for an improvement. This he received, but not much.

The Phyrexian screeched in pain and anger, wading forward through fire and smoke to reach the hated device. The fire cannon tracked in, but a slight tremor in its musculature gave Urza all the edge he needed. The planeswalker swung his staff around, slicing the blades into the creature's shoulder joint—the one that held the slender cannon to the negator. The blade, magically sharpened, cut through reinforced skin and metal supports. The cannon fell to one side, a gush of glistening oil and burning gel vomiting forth before the negator's body clamped down on the wound. Still, the escaped gel burned into the Phyrexian's outer flesh, distracting it even more.

Urza was already moving, circling about the negator and trying nothing fancier than slicing at its bloated body. Now the Phyrexian suffered the same problem as Urza, deciding between the strength and attention necessary to deal with its physical wounds and how much to spend on the 'walker. It became a race to see who could strike a fatal blow first—a race the Phyrexian lost. Urza sliced long and deep across its wide back and then quickly swept back to avoid the unstoppable gush of gelatinous fluid.

There was no stanching this wound, and once the substance was exposed to air the negator apparently lost the immunity it possessed that allowed it to store the material. It screeched in agony, high pitched and actually painful to Urza's hearing as the gel continued to eat away at it. The planeswalker picked up the severed arm carefully and moved back from the conflagration. The scent of scorched oil and burnt meat followed him.

He stood back and watched his old cottage burn.

Rayne slipped out of her usual work habit, donning instead the special garment she had designed for increased protection. A long jacket of blue cotton, thin pads had been sewn into its entirety and specially woven steel threads reinforced the chest and abdomen area. It was a bit heavier than she preferred, but when dealing with Phyrexian artifice it seemed better to be safe than comfortable.

Ehlanni assisted, an academy tutor who had proven herself very adept in disassembly and evaluation. An added benefit, Ehlanni was of a human tribe that shared the Hurloon Mountains with the minotaurs. Powerfully built, she could be counted on to help move the large objects and test equipment. Also, in terms Rayne had once heard Gatha employ, Ehlanni knew how to take a hit. A Phyrexian device had blown up in her face a year ago, and she had walked away from it, though Barrin's best healer-mages spent a good week restoring her to full health. Again, this was just another precaution for dealing with Phyrexian machinery.

"Only not quite machinery, this," Rayne said softly, bending down to examine the cannonlike device, a weapon which, according to Urza, had once sprayed a fiery, gelatinous substance that clung even to Urza's pure-energy form and burned ceaselessly.

What the 'walker had not mentioned was its origin. Rayne first assumed that it had either been taken from an artifact creature like the dragon engines or was more of a handheld device. She swung her wrist-mounted lens over to peer at the destroyed mounting hardware. What could only be artificial fibers exuded from a steel coil and burrowed into a small blackened lump. She had wondered at this earlier, until cutting into it and discovering it to be a slice of tissue similar to human muscle. This close, she also smelled the charred scent of the flesh. The fibers were bonded to the meat by a process she had never seen before. It was at once hideous and wondrous.

Ehlanni did not share Rayne's latter sentiment. "What is it, then?" she asked.

Rayne squinted and readjusted her looking piece. "I would guess that it was once part of a Phyrexian negator." She felt at one of the fibers with a bared finger, cool and smooth to the touch. Flexible. "Some kind of special metal alloy, maybe a metal enhanced form of cloth." Who could tell? "Urza must have removed it after a recent fight. These fibers are actually fixed to the muscle as if they were large nerve endings. I've found three other cables with similar function, including the thick metal-braid tube that had residue of the fire-gel." She looked up at her assistant. "Do you think this creature could be biologically producing the burning gel?"

"I think I'd rather not find out," Ehlanni said with a look of disgust for the artifact. "You're saying this was actually part of a living being? An artifice graft?"

The chancellor nodded. "Far beyond anything we are capable of here at the academy." Rayne had serious doubts saying so about Urza. Master artificer that he was, Urza almost certainly knew how it was done, but would he ever attempt to duplicate it? Would she herself if she understood how it was accomplished? Her initial reaction said no, but then immediately her mind seized upon circumstances where such grafting might be desirable. It could be useful for replacement of an arm lost to misfortune or war or as a treatment for a birth defect. It was such a small step from there to improving on the natural order. Improved eyesight? Stronger heart? Faster reflexes?

"Where would it end?" she asked no one in particular, bending back to work.

The magnifying glass brought her a level of detail she could only have guessed at without it, and even so, the intricacy hinted that buried even deeper than she could see might be found a third level of complexity.

"It violates the law of simplicity. At some point the construction of this device should begin to get simpler as we deconstruct it, not more complex, unless the Phyrexians are able to work on a scale we can't even observe much less touch." In the back of her mind she recalled the Thran Tome and its suggestion of artifice and flesh blended on the cellular level. Excitement touched her voice, warmed her skin as she considered artifice on such a level of mastery. "Urza never mentioned anything about this. I wonder if the Phyrexians are improving or just sending their better designs after him these days?" Or both?

"Are you feeling well?" Ehlanni frowned her confusion and not a little shock. "The closer I study these creatures and their work the more I see that Urza was right in his pursuit of *anything* which might destroy them. What I can't believe is that others haven't noticed this as well." She shook her head. "I swear you seem to be admiring them."

Lost in her observations, Rayne barely acknowledged the comment. "There is something to be said for the *theory* behind such accomplishments."

Ehlanni reached out and tapped the device, her finger thick and blurry under Rayne's glass. "Would you like to see one of these grafted to your husband?"

Rayne recoiled at the question, the horror of such an idea hitting her like a slap. She realized then that earlier she had considered exactly that. Shivering for a deathly cold touch caressing her back and scalp, Rayne pressed such thoughts from her mind. Ehlanni was right, this was nothing to be admired. No matter the *potential* for good, such artifice was only in the hands of those who used it in the birth of abominations and the support of evil desires. Improved eyesight and reflexes were nothing. Where would it end, she had wondered?

The scent of the charred meat now suddenly stung at her sinuses and burned acrid in her throat. She swallowed dryly and removed the wrist-mounted magnifying glass as if it represented the same principle of augmentation. This type of procedure would create a never-ending process of replacement and refinement until . . . what? The word came to her at once, both appropriate and obscene in the same instant: until compleat.

Timein had scheduled no meetings. He had, in fact, dismissed for the day those few students who had left the academy to join him at the Colony. He felt exhausted in that pleasant way which reminded someone of a full day's valuable effort. From the new well he helped dig to the students he—hopefully—enlightened on a few of the finer points in thaumaturgic studies. He needed a warm bath and perhaps some time for private reflection. He was looking forward to an early retirement for the day.

Why, then, was there a light on in his home?

The sorcerer did not think to be worried. Nothing dangerous happened on Tolaria—not counting Urza's catastrophes of course. He paused a moment upon discovering the door to his home still locked. His mind still puzzled on this as he turned the key in the lock and swung the door open. Someone waited within. The man's back was to the door and he studied a shelf of books all written by Timein. Timein saw only blond hair trimmed at shoulder length and a coat of finely tailored leather.

"Can I help you?" Timein asked, noticing the golden staff leaning nearby—its headpiece of joints, wires and gears—just as the figure turned. It was Tolaria's one recurring catastrophe—Urza Planeswalker.

"Timein, it is good to see you again." The 'walker looked about the single-room home. He nodded approvingly. "You've done well here."

Timein steeled himself against the false flattery, doubting Urza ever lived in such fashion. "It's simple," he said of his surroundings and the Colony both, "but it suits." He crossed his arms over a narrow chest. "It pales next to the academy, of course, but then we've had far less to work with in the way of material and resources."

If Urza caught the reference to the island's slowly deteriorating state, the 'walker either did not care or was more concerned with other subjects. The two stared at each other for a silent moment before Timein reminded himself that Urza was not of true flesh and so would win any staring contest.

"What is it you need, Urza?"

The 'walker looked nonplussed. "You act as if I've done something against you, Timein. I can read it in your posture as well as your voice. Have I given you cause for anger or grief?"

Timein unfolded his thin arms, relenting only a little. Pulling off his hat, the sorcerer tossed it over to his bed. "If you haven't you are likely about to," he said, loosening the drawstrings on his cuffs for comfort.

This apparently amused the planeswalker. "Sorcerer *and* soothsayer?" He smiled, his face lined and careworn as a middle-aged man. "Do you think you know why I am here?"

Nodding, Timein moved over to his desk and leaned back against its edge. Urza, he noticed, had a way of wearing people down very quickly. He wondered how Barrin stood up to it for all those centuries.

"You're here to bring me and the others back into your program," he predicted. "Come to bring the strays home?"

"I want your help, yes," Urza said, shaking his head. He picked up his staff and laid it in the crook of one arm. "But I've never forced anyone to do work he hasn't wanted or at least agreed to do, ever, Timein. Remember, you never complained about serving under Gatha's instruction. And so long as you didn't I needed you there."

In Timein's view, Gatha had kept control of the younger man's life those early years. The sorcerer had never had the chance to complain. "You're saying I have the choice to refuse you or not?"

Urza shrugged. "Of course."

Timein almost said it then—refused without hearing the proposal to be rid of Urza Planeswalker. The Colony was Timein's home now. It was a place where occasionally Tolarian students sought refuge when they could no longer reconcile conscience with the work being done at the academy. Some returned to the school, eventually, but others were often ready to take their place here. So long as Timein hosted this refuge, he wanted it kept clean of Urza's influence.

"What do you want of me?" the sorcerer asked.

Urza accepted the invitation to speak with a simple nod. "I need more detailed processes for judging empathies—a person's connection to the lands of Dominaria and any predisposition toward . . . *other* . . . lands as well."

Toward Phyrexia, Timein translated. He had no doubt that Urza could talk straight out about it but was hedging for the sorcerer's benefit. "Why not do it yourself?"

Urza spread his hands. "No one is as adept at these magics as you are, Timein. You are a mage of the natural body, the near-physical spirit. By inclination and more than three millennia of work, I am still primarily an artificer. Not even walking the planes changes you so much that you deny your basic nature." He lowered his arms. "Nothing you develop will be—can be—used to change someone's nature, if that helps, but the Bloodlines project will continue, and the better my tools the fewer my mistakes."

Now *that* admission rattled Timein's belief, if slightly. Urza Planeswalker admitting to mistakes had to be a rare sight indeed. His cynical side argued that the 'walker could afford to save such momentary admissions for just such occasions. Dealing with Urza reinforced Timein's admiration for Barrin.

"Directly or indirectly, I would still rather not," Timein said, surprised that he did not say no at once. It felt more as if he was slowly talking himself out of it. Obviously, Urza's appeal on behalf of the bloodlines subjects had hit him hard. "I've worked hard to help this colony survive on its own and to make a small refuge here away from the madness of the academy."

"I have no wish to disrupt the colony," Urza said. "I wouldn't think to spoil your exemplary work here. I'm simply asking *you*. Indirectly you help all the time, Timein. This refuge you've created gives students something we never thought to include—a place to escape for a time and so come back with minds fresh and unburdened by too many years of pressured work. Also, there's your silence. Barrin and I would trust you to leave Tolaria, but once away you could ruin the Bloodlines project by making it public.

What local nations did not find out and interfere in, the Phyrexian sleepers would." He looked at Timein with frank interest. "If you are so opposed, why haven't you done this?"

Timein couldn't help but wince at Urza's detailed evaluation of the sorcerer's work and life. He felt as if Urza had laid bare his mind and knew better the sorcerer's reasons and motivations than Timein did himself. Truth be told, Timein knew that so long as he remained on Tolaria he wasn't truly free of the academy and its work. He was still a part of the pattern and likely forever would be. Had he been waiting all these years for someone to arrive and offer him a reason to come back?

"I'll do it," he said softly. "On my own time and without anyone else's involvement, but I'll do it." He shuddered, knowing the nightmares he would open himself to because of this. "I've often wondered, Urza, what my research would show me of your nature. Have you ever wanted to look into it?"

"All the time, Timein." Urza nodded, slow and slightly sorrowful. "All the time." Then, with a final tight smile, the 'walker was gone.

Timein cursed both Urza and himself for the necessity that had drawn him back into the 'walker's plans. If his work could prevent the suffering of people in Dominaria, didn't he owe it to them to try? He sat behind his desk, leaning his lanky frame back in the padded chair as he stared up at the ceiling. Urza just might be right. That was the problem Timein faced anytime the 'walker came for assistance.

If Urza was right, would Timein's years of inaction necessarily be proven wrong?

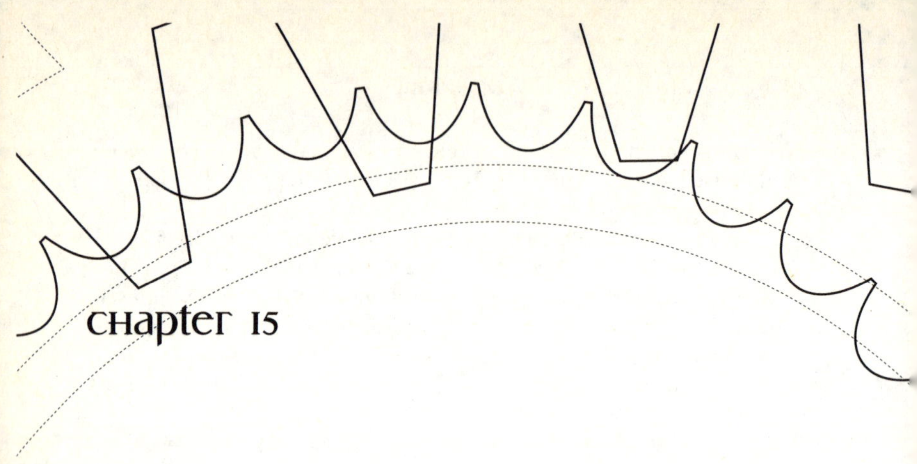

chapter 15

Summoned to the Stronghold's throne room, Davvol smothered his anger over Croag's blatant ploy to show the steward as subservient. His armored boots struck heavily against the floor, grinding his rage against the flowstone surface. Before entering the room he settled a neutral mask over his face.

"You requested my presence, Croag?" The words were drained of any emotion, spoken between thin, humorless lips.

The member of Phyrexia's Inner Circle seemed melded into the huge metal monstrosity that was the Stronghold's throne. Sharp edges gleamed dully in the cold lights of the room, and the ridged back shone with a light sheen of oil. Even as uncomfortable as it looked, Davvol craved it for his own—to be shared with no one.

"You were inspecting the machinery?" Croag asked, voice full of rasps and squeals. "Down in the secondary attractors?"

Not that Davvol needed the reminder because the summons had come while he was doing an inspection only added fuel to his ire. Flowstone production was up to levels never before known to Rath, pushing back the energy curtain that surrounded the artificial plane.

"Yes," he finally answered. "Some structural supports gave way last week from poor calibration of the bladed dials."

The screws turned easier now with Vec blood to grease the equipment, the responsible workers having been made a proper example of. Davvol wondered briefly how well the Inner Circle member would act as a lubricant. Very well, he thought—glistening oil being so much a part of his body.

"You have a *request?*" he asked, stressing the word. The summoning message from Croag had used "demand."

Some bands wrapped up over Croag's face, trailing oil over the taught gray skin that surrounded his mouth. His voice did not sound muffled when he spoke, as if the sounds were not made by his throat or mouth but simply reverberated from his entire being.

"I would like you to conduct a new transfer," the Phyrexian said.

Davvol waited, but nothing more followed. He crossed his arms defiantly, deciding to risk a touch of Croag's displeasure by pressing for more information. "Why?" he asked. When Croag volunteered less, it usually meant the Phyrexian trod uncertain ground—like the night they both visited Benalia.

The Inner Circle member waited a moment, as if deciding what or how much to say. "Our sleepers in Askaranton reported a skirmish with a large number of warriors. Some possessed heavy affinities for Phyrexia. These warriors were not acting on their own interests but for Askaranton's rival. Dominarians call such warriors mercenaries. Phyrexia might call them negators. I wish to assess their level of threat."

Croag was admitting that the Coracin was needed for more than the simple stewardship of Rath—even needed for something other than killing Urza Planeswalker. That concession alone was worth quite a bit. It was a simple enough request, Davvol decided.

"Where and when?" he asked.

"The armies are traveling back to their own lands now. We will meet them once they arrive."

"You want me to bring them here, to Rath," Davvol said, predicting the request.

"No," Croag replied, the red embers burning dully in the dark recesses of his eye sockets. "I wish you to send an army there. To Dominaria. To Keld."

War cries echoed off the steep passes that lead deeper into the Keldons' mountain nation. The grinding internal noises of immense mechanical engines roared, and massive treads chewed at these softer, lowland grounds. Fire spewed out of heads forged into the shape of dragons and demons, raining a burning substance over rock and earth and Keldon warriors. For a very few, it was all they could do to stay on their feet while the fire ate down to bone. Others, too caught up in their own bloodlust, ignored the pain and fought on until they finally dropped lifeless. Blades and armor were splashed with dark ooze and glistening oil which sprayed from engines. One massive engine rocked and then toppled, its treads ripped from heavy iron wheels and internal mechanisms so ruined that balance could no longer be maintained. It fell onto a knot of heavy fighting, crushing the black-armored warriors and Keldon footsoldiers alike.

At the head of three warhosts, the battle fury gripping Kreig elevated the witch king to new heights. Filled with the strength of his followers, he stood a titan over the battlefield. The sun's corona licked at his temples, its fiery arms wrapped over his eyes coloring the field red as blood. He stood shoulders brushing mountaintops, raking down avalanches of white snow and gray rock. The cold touch of Keld anchored his feet firmly, and no creatures of Dominaria could shake them loose. He was the witch king, undisputed heir to the supreme army of the Necropolis. He was *Kreig the Immortal*—and in the histories of the Keldon people, nothing more need ever be written.

Laden with plunder taken from the former kingdom of Askaranton, the army had shipped back to their own continent to begin the trek up into the mountains. An enemy encampment had held the main pass. Massive engines of warfare backed a legion of spindly limbed, black-armored troops. At their center stood such beings of grotesque shape and nature that Kreig had been reminded of Gatha's failed subjects. They had leathery black skin, some parts scaled with a natural armor. Some were carrying or melded with strange devices. One immediately leveled an arm at the combined warhost, a stream of hellish energies whipping into several Keldon warriors and burning them alive. Kreig did not know of this enemy or how they might have brought a small army into his lands, but such an act he understood perfectly. Yelling the war cry handed down his line from Trohg and Kreyohl before him, Kreig charged forward leading his host to battle.

Three witch kings fought at his side, each in nominal command of a separate warhost. They held the center of the field. Their courage and savage nature excited the warriors around them to greater acts of ferocity, even as those same warriors lent back a portion of their strength to encourage their leaders beyond bounds. No witch king inspired Kreig. He drew from each directly, just as he tapped every warrior brought to the field, filling his mortal shell with their strength and lifeforce. In return he offered them the pinnacle of Keldon achievement to which they might aspire but never reach.

Now even *he* was brought to a standstill against the black abominations that fought with a savagery most Keldons would be hard pressed to match. They shrugged aside lethal blows. Hooked claws, bladed fingers, and artifice weapons struck back with incredible force, enough to rend a regular warrior in one swipe. The enemy warriors in regular black armor were more easily dispatched, arms and legs cut or ripped from the body with ease. He learned after splitting one open that those limbs were merely mechanical extensions, and the true warrior was a stunted growth of a creature hidden away in the main armored shell. It took several sword thrusts through the armored body to finally kill one of the strange knights.

In the fifty years since his ascension, none had stood against the witch king Kreig, not his own people and certainly no outside force. Unlike some *doyen*, Kreig took to the field nearly every year, constantly challenging the world to match him. That these creatures even dared step into his domain offered an insult that demanded punishment, and here they presented a challenge that so far matched the best fight three warhosts offered. In a lesser race this would certainly have raised fear—in a lesser witch king, perhaps doubts or concerns.

In Kreig it engendered a near-blinding rage, lending new strength and stamina to his already terrifying nature.

The caustic scent of his own charred flesh overpowering the smoldering colos horn, Kreig shouldered his way past a stream of burning energy and closed with the largest of the demon-spawn. Nine feet high where its curved back finally hunched forward, head and shoulders actually at a lower level, the creature might once have been humanoid. Its evacuated abdomen was ringed with bands of blackened metal. Several steel tubes sprouted from its upper back, wrapping down to connect where the base of the spine might be on a normal being. Its feral grin of steel teeth was stained with the green-glowing slime. Large crystals set into its upper body threw out searing waves of focused heat which shimmered in the air and burned through armor and flesh. Kreig leapt into an embrace with it, his greatsword held high and angled back down in front of him like a rock scorpion's striking tail.

It moved impossibly fast. Serrated talons fastened onto the witch king's armor, points piercing through to flesh beneath. Its teeth clamped onto the hollow beneath his left arm, and the chest-mounted crystals flared with renewed assaults of scalding heat which seemed to strain at the very bones of his body. The viscous slime on its teeth burned through the wounds and into his blood, lighting his entire body afire. Kreig brought the point of his greatsword down into the muscled joint that held the creature's shoulder and thick, scaled neck. Reveling in his own pain, a sense he had not known for decades, Kreig drew hard upon the battle frenzy of his warriors and continued to place his full strength behind his sword. It drove through, spearing the creature along the length of its body. It shuddered, claws now removed from the witch king's body and flailing the air, but its teeth set in harder, crunching bone and rending flesh.

It was as if a giant hand had reached down to swat at the Keldon who had thought to place himself on par with the gods. An eruption of flame picked him up and lifted him into the air. The roaring thunderclap deafened his ears to the shouts of his followers and the metal grinding of the war engines they fought. Acrid smoke clogged his nose, ran acidic down his throat and into his lungs, and then he was falling back to earth and into the charred ruin that had once been his opponent. The ground rushed up with bone-jarring speed, embracing him with crushing force.

The witch king rose shakily to his feet. His armor gone, bare skin braced with blisters and angry burns, he barely felt the chill touch of the air. Blood trickled and then clotted as his wounds responded to the powers the combined warhost still engendered within him. Where the green spittle clung to him, those wounds did not close immediately and continued to pain him with agony like molten iron dripped into his veins.

He could not remember coming so close to the threshold of death, ever, yet here he stood, in defiance of the Keldon Necropolis for eighty-six years of life and enough mortal wounds to slay a full warhost. Kreig pulled his greatsword from the foul remains of the creature, its length deformed from the explosion but still deadly in its weight and edge. Laughing his rage at the sky, the witch king stood bare-skinned against the battle continuing around him.

Whatever these things were, they could be killed, and he was still Kreig. He could not know defeat by mortal hands.

Snow-chilled lands fell away to blankets of hoarfrost. An overcast sky of gray cotton, touched darker with pockets of rain, promised a storm. A light rumble voiced the heavens' discontent—answered only by the dull echoing of footfalls and shouted commands from within the mountain pass that led to the lower lands surrounding Keld.

Warriors in full armor led the way from the pass, their red leathers and bright metal weapons standing out against the dark ground. They moved with military precision, anxious for battle but still wary of ambush. The lead elements finally trumpeted back an all clear with small instruments made from hollowed-out colos horn. Another band moved from the mountain pass. This was Gatha's personal guard, their armor bearing his adopted crest—the ancient Keldon sigil for life, from the times before Keld developed a true script for writing. The military procession was followed by a baggage train of three colos pack animals, slaves tending them or laden under packs of their own.

Gatha walked at the center of his guard, nods of respect following his every movement. At times when he passed close to a warrior he received an awkward bow as the Keldon stepped aside. Despite his smaller size, Gatha felt the tallest among them, resplendent in finely designed armor of the best Keldon craftsmanship. He wore metal greaves, chestplate and shoulder mantle, trimmed in red leather and a black, heavy cloth cape with everything tooled in gold. He carried a riding crop—a leather-wrapped handle on a sharp, hooked piece of steel that might have been called a footman's pick back in Argive. The crop served more as a badge of rank. Gatha never attempted to ride the large colos beasts.

The traipse down from his mountain labs caused a regrettable delay in many experiments, but it was necessary after reading the reports and then spending long hours with Kreig in honest conversation. The witch king's detailed description of the invaders sent chills through Gatha's spine, and then had come Kreig's reluctant admission of what had followed the battle—the enemy's method of retreat. Such an event Gatha would prefer to consider a bloodlust-spawned illusion.

Bodies of the Keldon fallen, those that had not been *taken*, Kreig had ordered carried deeper into the mountains for burial beneath rocky cairns. One minor witch king had been interred in the Necropolis. One never returned. The Keldons were most distressed about *that*, one of their chosen denied the Necropolis and so eventual resurrection. In the Keldons' long history, not one warlord had ever failed to be brought home to rest.

Signs of the battle were still obvious in the scorched rock and the scraps of blood-stained leather. All metal had been scavenged, including that of a fallen war engine—pieced down so Gatha never did get a fair look at its original design. The warming air, moist with spring's coming, held a touch of carrion in it. Gatha paused and knelt over one large patch of ground stained black. He pinched up some dirt between his fingers, rubbing it and then bringing it closer to his nose. It felt gritty but not as true soil should. It was a fine dirt ruined with the saturation of some foul substance. The scent gave it away. Oil. Glistening oil.

"Phyrexia," Gatha whispered, naming the foe.

He placed a sample of the soil in a metal container and moved on, his dark eyes sharply deconstructing the battlefield and missing no scrap, trail of blood, or splash of gore. He found some globs of dark flesh that no scavenging bird had touched set about an area of scorched, pockmarked rock. It was the remnants of the thing Kreig had destroyed. A negator? He gathered every last piece of the ruined meat. Genetic comparisons back inside his labs would confirm it as Phyrexian, and the rogue tutor actually considered this procurement of fresh genetic material a small boon to his work. Who could tell what advantages the Phyrexians had bred into their minions since the samples he had stolen from Tolaria, advantages Gatha would attempt to duplicate for the Keldon people, breeding them into the bloodlines he controlled?

It was thought among most Keldons that there was little Gatha could not accomplish, but one must prove himself worthy of any requests and then more so if the magic was to take hold. Of course there would never be any recriminations, no resentment or rancor held, if the request was denied or the process failed. Not since Varden *the foolish* had anyone challenged Gatha's decisions. Never since Kreig's rise to power and the preternaturally long life that followed had another thought to criticize Gatha's presence in Keld. Such were the conveniences of deification, except that now the game had changed with the arrival of Phyrexians.

Gatha did not actually require tests to tell him that his theory was correct. He knew, just as he felt sure that the force Kreig had fought was little more than a scouting party sent to investigate. How had they learned of his work? What more did they know now? He stood from gathering another sample and looked up into the blanket of gray clouds, expecting to see the "face of the sky" staring back down on him. Gatha would like to believe that Kreig's explanation had been more of the religious trappings that layered their lives these days, except that the witch king had always seemed to know the truth behind it all even if he did enjoy the benefits as Gatha did.

That left the method of enemy withdrawal as a fact. That the sky had suddenly roiled with steel clouds broken only by cascades of lightning—red, green, and glaring white. Eyes of gray metal within black orbs stared down out of the chaotic sky like twin cold suns. A face of pale skin, sagging and without animation like the flesh of a corpse, appeared over the battlefield. It was cut only by a thin, cruel mouth that issued orders to the invading army in booming thunder. Kreig and others all reported feeling a pull tugging at them as enemy troops stepped away and simply faded from plain sight. Several Keldons surrendered to the arcane forces, vanishing under the gaze of those cold eyes and the call of its thunderous voice. Gatha did not want to believe it, but he did. Kreig had said something to him had made him believe.

Kreig the warrior, the mightiest the nation of Keld had ever seen, had felt afraid.

Dwarfed in power, the witch king had known his first moment of fear, but rather than be cowed, he railed against the forces tugging at him—challenged them. His warriors borrowed from his great strength, rallying. Fewer Keldons slipped away, as with a final scowl of displeasure the creature faded, and the sky cleared. Kreig's combined warhost had stood alone on the battlefield.

With the Phyrexians defeated at the hands of the Keldons—*his* Keldons—Gatha hoped for a reprieve. Perhaps they would not return, seeking easier prey elsewhere. Defeat couldn't sit well with them. Defeat never sat well with anyone.

Croag threw the lifeless body to the ground, skull shattered, gray matter mingling with yellowish fluids, white splinters of bone, and red blood. Two weeks he had spent in interrogation of the prisoners Davvol returned with. One every day, no matter how tempting it was to rush through them. He savored the moments—the memories—but also took the time after each to consider the information imparted. Davvol had taught him something of patience, with the other's slow process of improving negators in the steady and relentless hunt of Urza Planeswalker.

He chattered an order to a nearby guard who removed the corpse. The guard would add it to the others, Keldon and Phyrexian alike, for a seeker to later take the entire store of meat to Phyrexia for the vats. Resources were never to be wasted. Perhaps the Keldon matter would serve to make newts stronger and improve the compleated Phyrexians they would eventually become. In that way, the defeat today would only lead to a greater victory in the next generation.

In a few of the Keldons there had been large deposits of the same essence that the member of the Inner Circle detected in the old man on Dominaria, recognizing in them that which was familiar to his own nature—that dark perfection of the Ineffable from which all else should and would be derived. Only in the old man—a white-mana creature—that dark core repelled Phyrexian influence. In the Keldons, it made them stronger and therefore a threat.

So this was Urza Planeswalker's plan! An army of Dominarians with the physical resistance to meet the invasion on an equal footing. How broad the vision and yet so juvenile in the attempt. Of course Phyrexian substance made Dominarians stronger, bringing them closer to perfection. If the planeswalker had a thousand generations he might hope to spread such resistance over enough of Dominaria to make a difference. Here and now, with the scope Croag sensed, that influence would barely be felt, except, of course, in the Dark One's displeasure.

Organized resistance to Phyrexia's plans for conquest could never be tolerated. The Dark God would see it as Croag's failure. *His* anger would consume the Inner Circle member and deny him continued existence. Croag must destroy such efforts—subvert them. Davvol would be encouraged to continue testing forces against Keld, so that Croag might receive a better idea of the effectiveness of Urza's current plans. Croag would then destroy the system perpetuating the danger, including the capture and consumption of this Gatha—surely a scion of Urza and possibly with knowledge of the 'walker's private retreats. Other large programs of such a nature must also be located and destroyed.

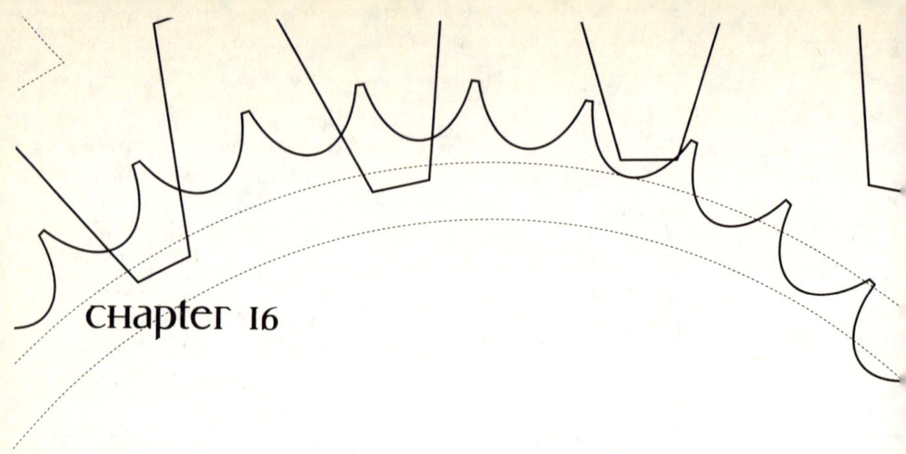

CHAPTER 16

Passing through the gatehouse, its gleaming white spires thrusting upward into a blue sky, Ellyn entered the flagstone-paved courtyard of Capashen Manor. She carried a collection of scrolls bundled loosely under one arm, occasionally dropping one and having to stoop for it. They were taxation estimates for local villages. No matter how important they might be, especially this year, she couldn't bring herself to invest much enthusiasm. Why should she care how well the crops came in, so long as the farmer caste supplied the manor with plenty? Instead of the scrolls, her hand itched for the comfortable feel of a sword hilt, for the chance to prove herself.

Strange creatures stalked Capashen lands these days. Monsters, some called them, of black flesh and metal with a taste for devastation. Farms had been left in ruins, and the people were frightened. Some of the clan's best warriors had already taken to the field, leading bands of Benalish soldiers as they tried to protect harvests and clear Capashen territory of these things. Only "some" of the best, though, because *she* hadn't been considered. Even in the noble Benalish clans, one's position was so often determined beforehand.

Since the marriage of Jaffry Capashen and Myrr Ortovi, her great-grandparents, Ellyn's family line had been relegated to minor status in an attempt to contain any attempts by Clan Ortovi to abuse the relationship. Ellyn's parents followed a similar course, as taxation officials and village magistrates and minor diplomats depending on the year and needs of the clan. Ellyn had been born . . . *different.* She challenged the rules whenever possible, stubbornly pushing forward. Whenever a person of higher stature made a mistake, they turned around to find her ready to assume the greater position. She learned the ways of the sword, drawn to weapons like a piece of metal to lodestone. Sometimes she felt that the metal called to her, a feeling she could not shake, as if a piece of her were missing.

Ellyn heard a whisper at the back of her mind, felt a dark presence seconds before her sharp ears picked up the sound of booted feet hammering against the bleached flagstone courtyard. Shouts of alarm echoed through the manor followed by a screeching snarl. Ellyn turned away from the manor front, walking swiftly at first and then running for the corner, a trail of scrolls bouncing on the flagstones behind her. She slid around to the east side of the great building, where the manor's shadow fell, just as three guards raced up from the other direction to catch the creature between them and her.

The semblance of a young dragon, it was like nothing Ellyn had ever heard described. Five feet at the shoulder, the creature's leathery wings stretched up another three feet over its mutilated back. Its head and neck were devoid of flesh or muscle, cleaned down to bone. Thin metal cables connected the eye socket to the base of the skull, and long, coarse hair sprouted from the thick scale armoring its shoulders. Its four legs and a long barbed tail were spot-covered with muscle and some skin, but in several areas ran uncovered down to bone or steel replacement. It screamed again, the chilling screech of metal knives scored against slate.

Two nobles lay on the bleached flagstone, throats and chests clawed open, staining the ground with Capashen blood. A third figure was pinned up against the manor wall by the creature's bulk, robes tattered and bloody but obviously still alive as he tried to crawl past. The soldiers attempted to drive the monstrous form back. It struck out with its metal-tipped claws, shredding the arm of one soldier who dropped his sword and staggered away, screaming shrilly for the pain. Ellyn's gaze flickered to the abandoned weapon, part of her eager to seize it and join the battle while another part stood immobile, unwilling. This creature was from one of her recurring nightmares from as far back as she could recall—turned from imagined image to deadly reality in front of her.

Ellyn might not have broken from her trance, torn between loyalty and a strange, unholy sense of fear and familiarity for the creature, but then the beast reared back, one massive back leg coming down on the fallen noble and pinning his leg against the ground. He cried out in pain, hands grasping at his leg to pull it free. Ellyn recognized him, even past the smears of blood masking his face.

So did one of the guards. "Leader Purceon!" he yelled. It was the leader of their clan. The warrior didn't hesitate. "Capashen!" he yelled out in battle cry, rushing forward. The dragon beast's tail whipped around and impaled him, the tail's bladed tip driving through his midsection and thrusting out of his back.

The danger to her clan leader and the sacrifice of the guard broke Ellyn's catatonic state. She dove forward, snatched up the fallen sword and rolled to her feet as the creature cast away the broken body. The leather grip felt strange, too soft, but the balance was familiar. She moved shoulder to shoulder with the remaining guard, adding her swordplay to his. Checking one slash, Ellyn almost lost her sword as it vibrated madly in her hand. It felt as if she had slashed her sword into a steel post.

As one they advanced, forcing the beast back from their fallen clansman. So close to the creature, Ellyn could smell the reek of oil—at once foul and enticing.

With a last swipe at the two sword-bearing humans, the dragon beast turned and held them at bay with violent slashes of its bladed tail. Its scream resounded with pure fury and hatred as it reared over Purceon. It slashed down once, twice. The creature's head bobbed in time to its clawing, always keeping its attention divided between the fallen noble and the two wielding swords.

Th guard standing next to Ellyn moved toward the beast, and she followed. The creature turned with incredible agility. Its claws struck out, rending long mortal furrows down the guard's face and chest even as its tail sliced deeply across both legs. Its attention diverted for a crucial second, Ellyn slipped past and ran her sword through the dangling loops of metal cable running from the creature's eye sockets to the base of its skull. She thrust downward with all her strength, pressing her full weight behind the stroke. The cables parted, and the metallic screech of the dragon beast's pain half-deafened her. She stumbled forward, fell and rolled out of the way.

A slashing breeze brushed at her hair. The creature's long tail, barbed with a dagger-sized blades, whipsawed the air over her. Ellyn tried to bury herself down into the flagstones, thankful the beast could no longer see her. The furious beat of wings buffeted her, digging grit out from between the flagstones and dusting it into the air. With a screech of rage the blinded beast took to the air as new guards ran around the corner, weapons drawn.

Ellyn rolled over to Purceon's side, her breath coming in short, gasping fits. She felt as if she had passed a test of sorts, though to pick at the thought any more brought only confusion. Instead she checked her clan leader for life and found him staring at her with guarded eyes. One side of his face bore a parallel set of deep scars ripped through his cheek. He nodded a cautious greeting to her.

"My thanks, Ellyn Capashen."

She nodded back, not trusting her voice just yet. Ellyn stood up and walked over to a fallen guard. She stripped him of his swordbelt and buckled it on over her tunic. Ramming the sword home, the weight of its steel comfortable on her hip, she moved back to where soldiers were applying pressure to Purceon's open wounds.

"More of those creatures are out there," she said simply, knowing it to be true. "I will take charge of a band and hunt them." Ellyn knew that further tests awaited her.

Purceon paused, winced as a new bandage was applied over his leg, and then looked skyward for the retreating creature that had taken the lives of five other Capashen. He nodded to himself.

"Yes," he finally said. "You will."

The village of Devas spread along the river, the normally white stone bathed pink in the late afternoon sunlight. Stubbled fields lead away from the settlement as far as the eye could see. The harvesting season in Benalia had just ended. A few missed stalks of grain wafted in the warm breeze that drifted in off the western plains. The high fluted columns flanking Devas's gates cast long shadows east over the parade grounds established just outside the walls. Those shadows ended in winged silhouettes, the platforms up high occupied by a pair of sentries who watched the surrounding lands with a hawk's gaze.

The bulk of Devas's martial force gathered outside the white oak gates for a training session. Archers tacked paper targets over bales of straw. They practiced long flights in which arrows fell from the sky in a thick, steel-tipped rain. The House Guard worked with sword and halberd, their dance as graceful as it would be deadly. By counterpoint, lancemen thundered by on the plains-bred *eponaes.* It was an impressive sight, and one the Serran refugees allowed few to witness.

Lyanii gauged the sky, judging another thirty minutes of good light left. Raising fingers to her lips she blew a shrill whistle then circled one arm overhead and pointed toward the archers who would need more time to gather their equipment together. They set about picking arrows out of the bales and the ground. Lyanii looked back to her soldier *under instruction* and frowned lightly at the sword he rested, point first, into the ground.

"That was not meant for you, Isarrk. Again. Another pass."

The young Isarrk did not bother coming back to attention, but he rubbed the blunt point against his leggings to clean it. "Apologies, Marshal. It won't happen again."

He grimaced his false contrition toward Karn. Lyanii hid a deeper frown at the youth's somber spirit. As he came back *en guard*e she focused her attention on his every movement, watching for a mistake. His body suddenly taught with lean but well-toned muscle, the youth nodded a reluctant readiness to his two sparring partners.

As the two young Home Guard attacked with fluid sword strokes, Isarrk turned one blade into the other, fouling both. He checked his own answer cut short, leaping back to avoid the swift response of one assailant.

All three paced an uneven circle, the two guards never allowing the young man a respite and Isarrk always wary of allowing them to split apart and trap him.

"How is he doing?" Karn asked, the golem's deep voice reminding Lyanii of the rumble of distant thunder drifting across the plains. "Well, it would appear."

Lyanii pulled a cloth from the belt of her training leathers and dabbed away sweat built up from her own exertions in practice. Her lips were salty with the residue.

"Adequate," she said.

Rarely did she take on a Dominarian. Isarrk's training came at Karn's behest, the marshal remembering the time when Urza Planeswalker had rescued so many of her people—herself included—from the decaying plane that had been Serra's Realm. Karn had been there, and Lyanii understood the debt owed all who risked their lives to bring them away from the Phyrexian infestation.

Once she had tried explaining this to the silver golem, only to find that he knew nothing of the episode except from brief historical notes Urza left for him at ten year intervals. In fact, Karn's return to Devas every few decades always came in the same manner, as if he had never been to the settlement before. He would simply arrive with a new student, asking the Serrans to please instruct him or her in combat—until now always a young noble. Lyanii remembered her sorrow, learning that Karn's memory had been capped. In a land of mortal humans, the Serrans were incredibly alone in that they outlived all around them. The first generation aged, but slowly—a human life but a splash of time to them.

Here was Karn, as near immortal as the Serrans except that he simply relived a life of twenty years—endlessly. For a while he would become a bridge between Clan Capashen and the village of Devas. Karn could be counted on during these times to help allay suspicions, at least in regard to the Capashens, then the golem's other duties called him away, and when next Lyanii saw him they began again. It didn't matter that he couldn't remember the debt the Serrans owed him. She did.

"No," she yelled when Isarrk overextended to score against one guard but left himself open to the striking sword of the second. "No, Isarrk, not a parry. A riposte. *Riposte*! You turn the one blade back against itself, and that leaves you still ready to defend against the second. Again. Do it again." She glared at the young man, daring him to make a remark. Isarrk blew out a long sigh of frustration and set himself back on his guard.

"Is there a way to accelerate his training?" the golem asked after a moment's silent observation. "To make him," here the golem paused, trying to capture the words for what he meant, "better?"

Lyanii had noticed that this time Karn's preoccupation with a student had taken an edge to it. "This boy is different, somehow, isn't he?" she asked.

"More than just being a commoner's son?" She wondered if it had something to do with Urza Planeswalker's last visit to Benalia, or the unsettling tales of dark creatures preying upon the Benalish people.

The silver man nodded. "He is different, yes, but not *quite* a commoner. One parent was a Capashen noble, though he died before it could be proven. That leaves Isarrk a farmer for the rest of his life, trapped by the caste system. Purceon Capashen asked me to look after his training this year."

"He has the ability," she admitted, "but he must have the drive as well. You can't force a person's basic nature."

"Don't be sure," Karn said softly.

Lyanii glanced over, Karn studied Isarrk with a gesture of fondness. "Is it the Capashen Clan or is it Urza?" She felt certain now that the planeswalker might have more to say on this than Purceon Capashen.

Karn stiffened, wary, but then whispered for her ears alone, "Urza."

That was enough for Lyanii. Any debt she owed Karn was far outweighed by that owed to Urza. "He can be pushed to excel, Karn, but I'm not sure if it will help. A just cause isn't enough. He has to have the heart to defend it. If he cannot rise to my challenge, I may do more harm than good."

On the field Isarrk skipped back, arm clutched to his side against the pain of a solid hit. He tossed his sword down in disgust, not for his opponent but at himself.

"I can't do it, Marshal. It's not that either one is stronger than I am, but they aren't committing to probing attacks I can turn easily. When a sword comes in driven behind their full weight, how am I supposed to match that with the strength of my arms alone?"

Lyanii looked over at the silver golem. She knew Karn liked the young man, and that he must be weighing that fondness against his orders from the Capashen noble and Urza. It surprised her how long he stood there, immobile, the sky's riot of sunset colors washing his silver sheen with a touch of red.

Karn nodded. "Push him."

Lyanii drew her longsword and stepped into the practice circle. She threw it to Isarrk, who caught it properly by the hilt. An easy flick of her foot and his abandoned weapon flipped into the air. She struck an *en guarde* position with it, anchoring her feet flat against the ground.

"Come at me."

Isarrk studied her with wide-eyed amazement. "This sword will break that one in two, Marshal."

"If I let you do that, I deserve to bleed," she said, voice steel. "You'll come at me," and she quoted him, "driving with your full weight." She gestured with her weapon, and when he hesitated she slashed at the air and screamed in her best commanding voice, "Do it now!"

Isarrk leapt forward, almost as if not by his own volition, the gleaming sword whistling a quick feint and then driving in with a slashing attack that would hope to overpower any defense the marshal could offer. Lyanii brought the smaller weapon up at an angle to the flat of Isarrk's blade, catching it in a spinning parry that she held into a full arc, until turning the blade back toward Isarrk's right shoulder. She kept her feet planted. Not wanting to drive the sharp instrument back into the young man. She released it and extended her arms to rap the side of Isarrk's head with the back of her closed hand. The youth crumpled to the ground, dazed.

Lyanii stood on her guard, ready for another attack. Tossing the small sword down onto his chest, she stalked back to her place of instruction. Isarrk came reluctantly to his feet, one hand pressed to his new bruise.

"Do it again," she ordered him. "Do it right."

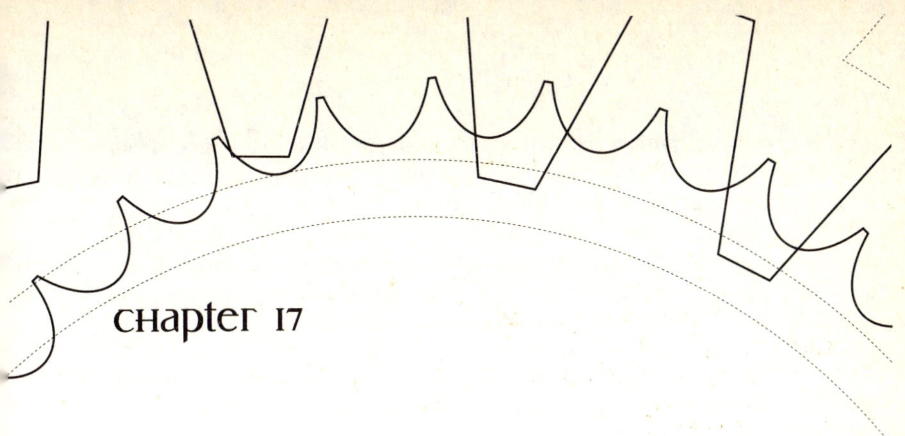

CHAPTER 17

Rayne stood in the shadow of the captain's raised quarterdeck near enough to the gunwale that she could stare out past the peaked bow and watch Yavimaya's appearance. The tall forest grew slowly out of the horizon, like an immense wave suddenly frozen in permanent relief. As it spread across the horizon, color tipped the lower edge, a long pale strip promising fair beaches. It was a false promise, Rayne knew.

Captain Pheylad brought the vessel in under topsails only. This was Pheylad's first and likely only visit to the sentient forest, and this without Multani to forewarn Yavimaya or direct their course. Multani was in the elven lands of Shannodin inspecting some forest sites where entire villages had supposedly gone missing. Rayne was here—needing a break from Tolaria and her study of Phyrexian methods in creating negators.

Why she had thought a visit to the sentient forest might allow her the chance to reclaim some peace of mind, she could not now say. Yavimaya bothered her with its unnatural cycles and strange growths. There was a process at work here she could not understand. There were no set laws and relationships like she dealt with in artifice. Allowing for the forest's sentience, Rayne sometimes wondered if the feelings of unease were mutual. Yavimaya might be as uncomfortable with their presence—with her presence—as Rayne was with it.

Rayne grasped the polished railing and stared down, watching as the first slender root tentacles reach out to brush against the *Weatherlight's* hull of living wood. The impaling points pulled back, and on the shore the root network writhed and split open, allowing a path of firm ground from beachhead to the magnificent coastal forest. Rayne breathed a short sigh of relief. At least Yavimaya still recognized the *Weatherlight.*

It was a comfort which lasted only long enough to bring the longboat ashore. No elf met them. No sound of birds or even insects cascaded through the trees. Silence reigned except for a light breeze wandering the trees and rustling brush. Leaving the strange root network behind had helped to ease nerves, the students and crew present spreading out in the relaxed setting of calf-high grasses and flowering underbrush. Now they each shifted uneasily, suddenly nervous in their unannounced arrival with no welcoming party.

"Too quiet," Rayne said, uncertain of what else she expected. Suddenly she put a name to it. "No falling trees."

Rayne's previous visits had been during the advanced mulching cycle of the forest as it built up stores of raw matter. Now the sound of falling trees was absent, replaced with a simple whisper of the wind through treetops and interlocked branches rubbing lightly together. The tall sparse grasses rippled only with natural movement, their own fast-growth cycle apparently complete. It was as if Yavimaya slept.

"The forest must know we are here," she said. She nodded to Pheylad but wondered who she was trying to convince. "The elves will be along soon enough."

The captain glanced uneasily at the dark shadows beneath the trees, his shipboard confidence lost on dry land. "They might already be here," he said. "Can't see 'em unless they want to be seen."

One of Rayne's senior students pointed farther into the forest. "There, isn't that new?"

Rayne didn't bother to point out that after fifty years, everything was likely to be new. The normal rules didn't apply to Yavimaya. "Yes, looks like a tropical flower of some kind."

The new plant was extremely large, its finlike growth reaching ten meters high. Colorful winged bugs flew around it, some of them occasionally flitting out to fall into the grass. A caustic stench welled up over the meadow as several bugs were stepped on by advancing students and ship's crew. The offending crushers exclaimed sharply, trying to wipe the residue off against the ground.

Rayne stood off to one side, indecisive as she waited for some form of contact. Rofellos, would he still be alive? The academy chancellor did not like the silence that continued to greet them even after these long first minutes. Rayne noticed beside another of the strange tropical plants some thorny vines and another plant with spikes standing out three inches like small daggers. Something off to her left rustled as with hidden movement, though she did not believe it to be the elves. Their passage tended to be silent and hidden.

She had just decided that they would all return to the ship—to await the arrival of Yavimaya's emissaries—when she noticed the color shift in the nearby trees. It was subtle yet fast enough to be tracked by the eye as light green darkened and shifted to various blue hues. The trees closer to them were in advanced stages of the color change, while deeper into the forest the change was just beginning. From her previous journeys in the *Weatherlight*, Rayne immediately grasped what it would look like from an aerial view and how Yavimaya would no doubt sense it—an expanding circle of disturbance at the center of which was the *Weatherlight* and her people.

"Back to the ship," she said, voice low with carefully concealed concern. Only a few turned to look. "Back to the ship!"

Everything seemed to happen at once. A trio of wolves, so heavily muscled their shoulders blended in with their neck, sprang from concealment to suddenly encircle one of those crewmen who had protested the stench of a squashed bug earlier. Another offender found herself encircled by a cloud of stinging creatures. With a shrill scream she tried to plunge into a thick wall of brush, hoping to lose the winged insects in the heavier growth, and was caught in a tangle of vines covered in sharp thorns. Blood welled in cuts and streamed down her face from the crown of vines wrapped about her brow. Another creature, a sledge-headed beast, shouldered its way past the thorny brush to snarl a challenge.

The chancellor took a step in the direction of the trapped crewman, whose thrashing drove thorns deeper into her skin, and the forest suddenly closed up in front of her. She saw a pair of vines leap up to opposing trees for support, animated like a pair of striking snakes and forming an immediate barrier. They suddenly sprouted enough thorny vegetation to create an impassable wall. The wall then sprouted jade-green blooms which Rayne recoiled from as if struck. The innocent looking blooms touched at her core and drew strength away.

Acting from instinct, Rayne reached into a pocket for globe-bombs, an invention of Barrin's for those traveling away from Tolaria in case they should meet with Phyrexians. She tossed one into the wall. The globe shattered, its force automatically channeled away from the thrower, shredding the thinner plant life and scoring deep scars into nearby trees. A Tolarian student was not far behind Rayne's action, tossing one of his own globes at the wolves and careful not to throw too near the beset crewman. The wolf yelped as splinters of glass impaled its hind quarter. The wounded beast and one other companion streaked back for the safety of the forest. Rayne tossed another of her globe-bombs at a suddenly active bush covered in globular blossoms. The plant disintegrated under the force. Behind it, previously screened from view, an elf riding a great moa raced toward her, cradling a war bow in one hand and reaching back for an arrow. Rayne drew back for another throw.

"Stop!"

The voice sounded off trees and quivered in the branches and leaves surrounding them. It seemed to shake the very ground and was reflected back from the upper boughs of the great trees. The reflections echoed among the plantlife, which shook under the order. It was as if the forest itself spoke, except Rayne remembered that voice. Rofellos.

The Llanowar elf stood nearby, just inside the forest and at the top of a grassy knoll. He carried what appeared to be a halberd, a long smooth pole of silver wood topped with a wide, green leaf that seemed to possess the rigid sharpness of a blade. He had changed little in the relative centuries since Rayne's last visit, except now he boasted a trimmed mustache.

Rayne suddenly realized that her intended target was an elf—not the animate vegetation or even one of the creatures that had assailed them—but a sentient resident of Yavimaya. The elf's own wild-eyed glare of anger faded, his face going slack with a sudden lack of animation. He lowered his bow as Rayne brought down her own hand, returning her globe-bomb to a pocket. She noticed that the creatures had all retreated, and the vines released their grip on her student.

"Everyone calm down," she said as easily as she could, heart pounding in her chest with the adrenaline rush. "Just stand where you are until Rofellos tells you otherwise. Don't worry. We are among—" friends? Not exactly— "*allies* here."

Watching Rofellos's slow approach, his weapon still held tightly at the ready, Rayne could only wonder if that were still true.

"The forest is," a pause, "distracted," Rofellos said. Standing on the beach as evening fell over the island, his polearm resting in the crook of one arm. The Llanowar focused on Rayne alone as he spoke. The coastal roots had closed up, allowing only a narrow path from the water's edge back into the forest. "Yavimaya is working to tailor its defenses before the Phyrexian threat finds its way here."

Rayne had watched Rofellos treat the wounded with herbs and a jelly-like salve taken directly from the folds of a large violet-colored plant. He moved with purpose, efficient in his every act but lacking the energy and enthusiasm with which he had once assailed life. Certainly this was not the same elf Rayne remembered from before. Now, listening to him explain the initial lack of contact, she couldn't be sure that his reference to Yavimaya came from an individual's view of the situation. It reminded her too much of the imperial *we.*

"Are *you* saying Yavimaya is dormant?"

Rofellos shook his head lightly. "Not dormant. The accelerated mulch cycle is complete, and Yavimaya is spending intense resources in the evolution of the forest and its servants."

"And you, Rofellos, how have you been?"

Obviously the elf had not aged much, but without slow-time waters even a long-lived elf should be showing signs of time's passage by now. She performed a quick review of the years, checking her dates. Rofellos should actually be dead, though here he was, looking still to be in the middle part of an elf's long twilight of middle age.

Frowning, the Llanowar concentrated on the question. "Ro—," he began, then corrected himself, "*I* have been well." He blinked hard, his brown eyes momentarily clearing of their indifferent gaze. By the mage-lit stones some students had set out on poles, burning with their own cool fire, those eyes seemed to broadcast a private pain. He blinked again and it was gone. "Yavimaya takes care of my needs."

He then walked over to a net bag of glowing stones set up on a pole, inspecting it at close quarters while Rayne continued to observe him. Technically their business was complete, having gained a new supply of special woods for use in developing artifacts. Rofellos, though, appeared to be in no hurry. Rayne couldn't decide if the delay was on Yavimaya's part or his. She waited, uneasy with the heavy forest scents pressing in from the dimming lands. Captain Pheylad waited near the longboat with a few crewmen. He shook his head in confusion.

As before, during their approach, Rayne sensed her own unease with the sentient forest. There were no set relationships she could take apart and understand—no gears or cogs. The mechanisms that drove most people were so complex as to be unfathomable.

"Excuse me?" she asked as Rofellos muttered a question. Something to do with Multani?

The elf started, then turned back. "Yavimaya would like to have one of these glowing stones. The light is a good match for one of the forest's needs."

To Rayne the light was too soft for proper illumination, a subtle white-blue inappropriate for working under, but then, she didn't have the superior eyesight of an elf either. "Take it," she said, certain that the request was not his original question. Rayne walked over and unhooked the net bag from the pole then handed the small bundle of glowing stones to Rofellos.

Again there was a flash of pain in Rofellos's brown eyes. He glanced about carefully, searching the shadows as if for dangers. "Have you seen Multani?" he asked, voice quiet and trembling.

Rayne could only shake her head. "No, not for many years."

"I should like to see Multani?" The words came out as part question, part uncertain statement. His face tightened, a hard look of determination dominating his features. "You should not come back, Rayne. Yavimaya has become dangerous."

"Tolaria may need further supplies," she said. "Without the *Weatherlight*—"

"Not the *Weatherlight*," Rofellos interrupted. "You, Rayne. *You* should not come back. The troubles in Keld make Yavimaya too uneasy."

To wonder what possible connection she had with Keld was Rayne's first reaction. Other than her previous acquaintance with Gatha there was nothing else. Rayne dismissed the thought as the outright affront of the recommendation hit her. True that she'd wondered about the forest's own unease, but to have that confirmed struck her with a cold slap of reality. She would've asked after such a dismissal, except that Rofellos now hurried to the path left for him and disappeared into the rootwork. Only the glow of the magicked stones marked his trail, and those too finally vanished as the coastal roots closed after him.

Rayne stood on the beach, hugging her arms to keep back the sudden chill that had swept her, lost in her confused thoughts of Tolaria and Yavimaya, and not of Keld.

The *Weatherlight's* departure was marked with a more rapid speed than its arrival. It danced over the rough swells, gaining headway until it hit the gentle roll of deeper water. Soon it was a pale smudge beneath the gray light reflected down from the Glimmer Moon.

Where dark promontory jutted out into the ocean, the weathered rock able to grow no heavy plantlife despite Yavimaya's relentless attempts, a black oval spread open. It grew in size. When viewed side-on it disappeared, the portal so impossibly thin because it did not actually exist but was more a hole in the chaotic energies that separated the planes. A leg thrust through, black armor gleaming as it reflected the Glimmer Moon. Arms and a body followed, the thin form stepping through and rising to its not-so-impressive height. Its compleation did not demand size but a compact, tough form that could visit countless planes and bring back detailed news to its masters. It required neither breath nor food, not anymore. The rush of glistening oil through its artificial veins was sustenance enough.

It turned non-augmented eyes toward the ocean, but the Weatherlight was gone. The seeker's gaze fell back to the forest-island. No dangers here, it seemed, but orders were to be followed. It would explore and observe. Others would evaluate. First it needed to return and provide a report on this location for Davvol and the Master, Croag. After a last scan of seemingly defenseless coastline, the Phyrexian left Yavimaya.

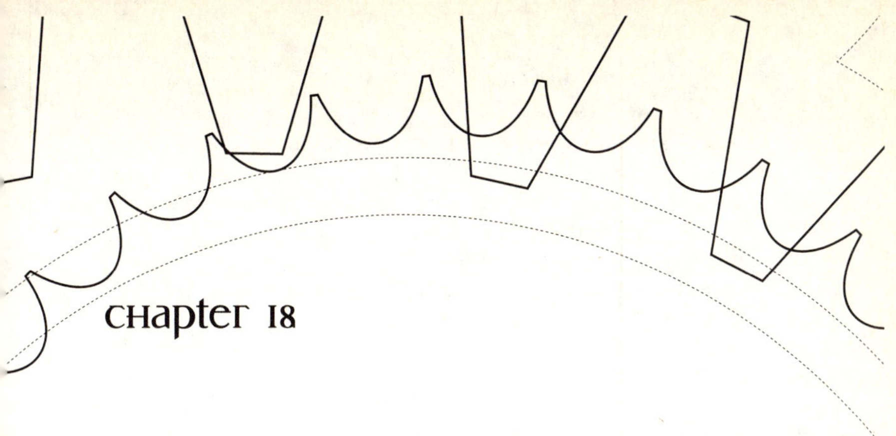

Chapter 18

Smoke from the burning granaries trailed up dark against Benalia's clear-blue sky. To one side of the flaming structures, the hamlet's soldiers had driven back nearly twice their number during the furious first moments of their counterattack. Other men worked beneath them, dumping grain into barrows and wheeling it quickly away, never concerned for their own safety. The flames, fueled by the incendiary mixture the strange enemy was using, could not be extinguished. Any moment the fire might lick through to one of the grain-dust filled voids which would then go up in a great explosion. Every barrow of grain removed fed a family for that much longer.

Sweating from exertion, Isarrk pushed his barrow under an overfull load of grain. It had been twenty-three years, he figured, since he had last held a weapon in his hand—since Karn and Marshal Lyanii gave up forcing on him a life he didn't desire. The memories hounded him as the now elderly man strained to lift the full barrow, choking on grain dust. He didn't want to remember. He was afraid to.

His arthritis bit into the joints of his hands, but it wasn't enough to distract him from the shift in the fighting. By sheer numbers alone the spindly-armed warriors in their black armor were regaining the edge. More than from their impossibly-thin arms and legs, Isarrk knew these things were not human. A gut sense told him they were fighting drones—better trained than the local soldiery though perhaps not so good at working together as a unit. However, the Benalish soldiers weren't taking advantage of that, allowing themselves to be drawn away from each other—broken into several small fights where the enemy's two-to-one advantage would spell immediate ruin. Isarrk knew the soldiers should be sticking to a tight line of battle, even a three-sided box, where the attackers would foul themselves if they pressed in with greater numbers. He also knew he should be keeping his mind on his own responsibilities.

What good would saving the grain do if the battle was lost? The black enemy would only set upon it again.

If they did, *when* they did, then he would defend it. They *all* would, but what would happen if all the farmers, now busy moving grain, placed aside their duty and ran to battle now? The enemy would be defeated and the grain lost to fire. That was the advantage of caste. Everyone knew his place and responsibilities. Almost everyone.

One person broke away from the granaries. Grabbing a wide-bladed, curved hoe used to push the grain around, he set one foot against the head and another on the shaft and bent the blade out straight. With his improvised polearm, he ran to the side of the Benalish warriors yelling, "Capashen!"

Isarrk stumbled, spilling his barrow over onto the ground, as he recognized the other by build and voice—Patrick. His son.

"No!"

Isarrk made it five paces before slowing to a confused halt, glancing between the fight and the workers who continued to rescue the grain. His instincts pulled him onward while his basic beliefs warned him to go back. Both sides needed him. He remembered Lyanii's comment about having the heart to defend a just cause. He stepped in the direction of battle then quickly worked back up into a run. Right now, the warriors needed him more.

Patrick was already in trouble, never having been trained for such action. He had also split the Benalish line with his presence, forming a weak link that two enemy warriors were pressing against. The young man, barely out of his teens, slashed about wildly with his device while yelling his defiance. One wild swing smashed the strange longsword from the grip of a black-clad soldier. It cost him, though, as the force spun him halfway around. The second enemy dealt Patrick a vicious slash across his ribs, parting the thin sleeveless shirt he wore and flaying back skin and muscle. The youth screamed in a mixture of his pain and the anguish for failing. He fell back as another swing aimed for his head missed by mere inches. Stumbling, he dropped against the ground as the enemy shoved aside its disarmed companion and came at him.

Isarrk had one chance. Ignoring the fallen sword that lay next to Patrick, no time to snatch it up, Isarrk lashed out with his foot, aiming for the other's wrist. He connected solidly, knocking the other's stroke awry and falling to the ground next to his son as he lost his own footing. Pain flared in his hip for the rough landing. Still, not the worst move to make, he decided, grabbing up the sword that now lay between the two farmers.

Its long, metal handle felt strange in his hands, and his arthritis protested the angular grip, but the lethal weight seemed to suddenly add strength to Isarrk's arms. He brought up the slightly curved, black-metal blade, parrying a quick backhand slash which would have opened up his own chest. The sword had an impressive reach, so he brought it around and bit deeply into the standing creature's ankle. It screeched as it stumbled back, giving Isarrk the time he needed to climb back to his feet.

"Pull in!" he ordered. "Don't split apart. Form a solid line!"

For the Benalish warrior to his immediate left, the advice came too late. A sword thrust snaked past his defense, skewering him through the heart. The withdrawn blade dripped crimson, and the man crumpled without a scream. Isarrk immediately bought a measure of revenge for his comrade. He lunged forward against the warrior Patrick had disarmed. He expected the blade to turn against the armored head, but he was surprised when it pierced metal and sliced through the faceplate. There was a stuttering screech, and the creature toppled. A jet of warm, black blood gushed out as Isarrk removed the sword, staining his lower arm and the front of his own sleeveless cotton shirt. The fluid was tepid, reinforcing his assumption that he fought something not quite human.

The remaining guards were pulling back into line, but now Isarrk faced a pair of the dark-armored soldiers—his own remaining and the opponent of the luckless fellow who had dropped on his left. They hammered at him with their own weapons, pressing forward in staggered attacks trying to drive him back, except on the ground just behind him lay his son, hands pressed over his wounds in an attempt to preserve his life.

Isarrk refused to give up one inch, turning back each stroke. He planted his feet solidly against the ground, waiting for the next disconcerted rush. It came, one of the enemy warriors leading the other by a long second. Isarrk parried with the circling maneuver Lyanii had demonstrated to him so long ago, using the attacker's strength against itself as he twisted the blade's tip around and led the cutting edge of his opponent's sword right back into the creature's own shoulder. It severed its own arm, the mechanical limb dropping off with a spray of foul-smelling oil. Isarrk spun around quickly, catching the second attacker's stroke and again turning it, this time into its companion. The edge bit into the lame creature's side, wedging the black metal blade. A quick backslash by Isarrk took the armored head off the second warrior. Dark slime and oil spewed out, drenching his sword arm and staining a dark swath across his body.

At the far right, the last Benalish warrior in line traded a deadly embrace with one of the enemy. Both swords buried themselves in the other's body, and they fell together in death. Still, the odds didn't look quite so uneven now as five men faced off against seven attackers. There was no apparent communication, but the enemy warriors began to withdraw. The one Isarrk had crippled pulled the sword from its side and limped away on its own strength. They were heading out into the low hills surrounding the hamlet, wary but moving with purpose now.

"What should we do?" one Benalish guard asked, nodding toward the retreating figures.

He glanced around to his companions and obviously included Isarrk. The respect they showed the farmer as each looked to him for guidance spoke volumes.

Isarrk avoided their gaze. His muscles screamed protest for the abuse he had put them to, and his joints felt as if on fire themselves. Panting heavily, he buried the sword he carried point first into the earth and then knelt at his son's side. Patrick didn't look well, but he might pull through yet. The first explosion sounded as a granary burst, raining splintered wood over the area. Men ran, those who could, knowing their time was up. The other two went in close order; brief gouts of fire swam through the sealed chambers, and then a ground-shaking explosion rang everyone's ears as more wood fell from the sky. One burning chunk of wood landed near Isarrk, and he ignored it. It looked as if most of the grain had been saved, but he noticed at least three bodies lying near the granaries. Fire caught on the clothes of one. Isarrk looked down at his own hands, blackened by oil and foul blood.

Silent tears fell against his hand and arms but did not wash away the stains.

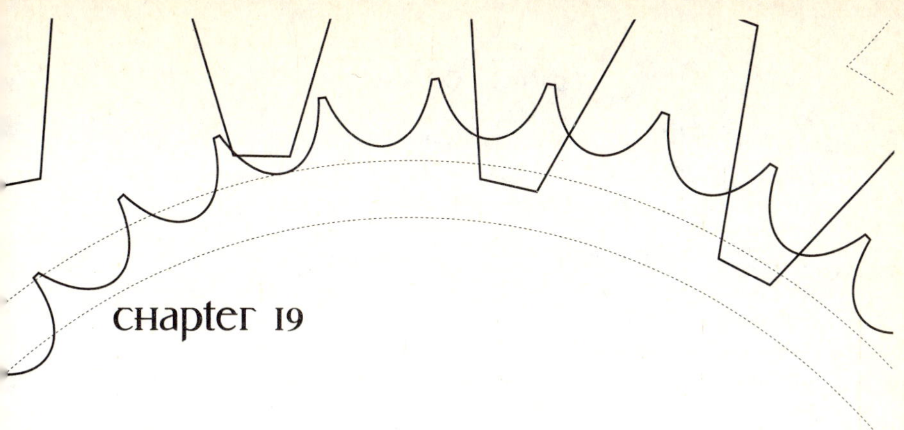

chapter 19

Kreig roared a defiant laugh, his deep voice echoing within the wide-open vaults of the Necropolis—his Necropolis. The bellows challenged the sleeping corpses of better than one thousand years of Keldon rulers. None answered. He growled a sharp oath, enjoying this moment among his ancestors.

Three exterior walls banked inward as they rose majestically overhead to a ceiling of polished, dark-gray stone. The entire fourth side was open to the thin mountain air—as no mortal walls could hope to contain the warlords and witch kings of Keld. The scent of new snow carried in on cutting winds, the frigid grip tugging at Kreig's long, dark braids and brushing an icy touch against his bare chest and arms. Thousands of tombs lined the walls, each no larger than the slab of marble on which a warlord would some day rest. Many of these were already bricked up, sealing fallen warlords into place until the final battle.

A faded mural painted over the ceiling's wide expanse depicted that promised legend. The Call to Return—the moment that marks the end of the world—that would sound of a thousand battle cries after the Necropolis filled. The warlords would rise again to be led by the greatest of their number. An army unto themselves, they would lead the rest of the Keldon nation to war. The mural depicted the great army sweeping down from the Necropolis to conquer all of Dominaria, a bright sunrise over the Necropolis bathing the land red as with blood.

Kreig walked among the several hundred sarcophagi that rested upon the vault's floor, each trimmed in a varied measure of silver or gold depending on the fame and prowess of the warrior within. The greatest of the Keldon leaders were these, placed lower down in the Necropolis and so ready to lead the way out once the dead rose. Only here did Kreig walk among peers. Even the greatest war lords eventually came to rest here, all warlords. Except Kreig?

It was not a question he felt able to answer with any degree of certainty. Not anymore.

In a century and a half of life and warfare, Kreig had never felt the mortal coils settle about him as in the last decade. Since the dark invaders began pushing at the edges of his nation he felt it. Gatha knew something of them as the mage knew about nearly everything. They were beings of another world. *Phyrexians*, he had called them—born of nature and made over again with machine. Such ideas confused Kreig's sense of the natural order where the strongest led and others followed. These Phyrexians bled and died the same as other races. They were innumerable, perhaps, but not invincible.

In twenty-three battles against them, Kreig had yet to personally know defeat. Four other witch kings with their warhosts had, though. The Keldon warhosts no longer traveled out into Dominaria except on the very rare and highly paid expedition. It was only enough to support the nation, if barely, as the majority remained home and continued to fight the dark ones. Kreig tracked the battles over fifty years, at first beginning only with minor raids and probing maneuvers. Those attacks gradually stepped up in strength until no other nation on Dominaria could have matched such an enemy. The Keldons remained battle-ready, even in their own homes, their lands having always served as a large armed camp. The mountains were known to them, comfortable to them. No one could hope to fight as well in this territory.

And they were losing.

The Keldons were not in danger of being completely overrun, though Kreig believed that the invader could do so if they wished. He understood warfare like nothing else, and he recognized a purpose in the enemy attacks. They had spent decades learning the Keldon strengths and weaknesses, as if a thousand dead—even ten thousand—meant nothing while probing at those depths. They turned heavier strength against the foundations of Keld, destroying the best of the witch kings—those on which Kreig relied and whom Gatha had named as his superior bloodlines. This was a purposeful campaign to isolate the two, slowly dismantling the work of a century and a half. One by one the witch kings finally succumbed until only he was left to hold the nation together: Kreig the witch king. Kreig the Immortal, Kreig, who had come to the Necropolis to visit his own crypt.

Made of obsidian, it was glassy and mirrorlike in its thousands of facets. The small building was trimmed in heavy gold with weapons adorning outside and inside walls both. A gate of wrought iron barred entry but allowed for viewing within. A hanging rack for his armor occupied one corner, and the sarcophagus waited with lid half-drawn as it had for one hundred years. No similar structure decorated the vaults, just as there had never been a warlord such as he. It had been built a century before, on his order, right at the very lip of the vaults, built where Kreig knew he could hurl a spear out over the edge and have it not smash into ground for a good half mile drop or more, depending on the winds. The warlord had never thought to occupy that crypt, knowing within himself that no Dominarian could ever hope to kill him. He had been right—the Phyrexians weren't Dominarian.

Fingers wrapped into the iron bars of the crypt door, the cold metal sticking to his warm skin, Kreig ground his teeth in fury. One hundred fifty years of experience promised him that the enemy would come for him soon—for Gatha and he both. His warrior instinct drove him to fight, and he would, at the head of the largest combined warhost the Keldon nation had ever known. An event which would survive centuries of retelling, it would be known in the oral histories until the day when The Call to Return finally sounded.

His muscles bunched and strained, his mortal limits set against metal and stone. Coarse-threaded screws set into a mortared jamb wrenched free. He yelled his anger and defiance in a guttural shout. The iron gate twisted and came away in his hands. He held it overhead and with another savage cry pitched it from the lip of the Necropolis out into the thin, frozen air. He heard it whistle away, fade, and be lost. It fell down far enough that he never heard it hit, and that sat well with Kreig. Let it be lost.

If he was ever to be laid to rest here, it would not be within confines which could be built by man—not even Keldon man.

Rough blankets draped most of the equipment in Gatha's labs, gray shrouds rank with colos sweat having been used as saddle blankets in the past. Gatha hated that scent, even after three centuries in Keld where the musk of that mountain animal seemed to permeate every facet of life. He wondered if the Keldons hated the large beasts as much.

He shrugged and shook his head, dispelling his speculation along with any lingering aversion to the scent. It did not matter anymore. Kreig had been to see him at the first of the week, carefully talking around the very point the witch king had come to make. It was something that couldn't be put into words. What Gatha had feared for fifty years—the Phyrexians were coming, and this time there would be no stopping them.

Standing still and silent, Gatha strained his hearing to catch the sounds of the battle being fought on the plateau below his laboratory. No fire crackled in competition. No slaves moved about doing his bidding, where their footsteps might have drowned out that distant ringing of metal against metal. There were only he and two guards who waited like motionless statues outside his main workspace while he prepared it. The fighting sounded as if it had moved closer. Gatha could hear the shrill cry of a wounded colos warbeast echoing up the mountainside, but it was drowned out immediately by the grating roar of a massive Phyrexian dragon engine.

It was the sound of death knocking upon the gates, an Argivian saying which Gatha remembered from long before Keld or Tolaria. Strange, that deep down he had actually believed death would come politely, requesting admission rather than kicking down the barriers and falling upon its victim in a fury of fire and grinding metal.

Well, Gatha did not intend to quit without a fight. Where he had been forced to flee Tolaria, betrayed by those he had called colleagues even when they did not deserve such praise, here he knew strong allies and the strength of his own powers. Kreig had never failed him, never failed the Keldon nation, and Gatha knew that any chance for victory would revolve around them both: warlord and tutor. Witch king and wizard. Gatha remembered much of the Tolarian histories, of the battles waged with the dark forces. He knew many of their weaknesses. He could help turn the tide of battle, perhaps. In case he could not, the lab required preparation.

Moving around the room, Gatha continued to cover each piece of equipment with the rough, strong-smelling blankets as he wrapped them with magical energies drawn from the mountains of Keld. He pulled the mana from the land, feeling its raw power and knowing the destructive force such energies could bring about. Warmth flushed his skin pink, warding him against the room's severe chill, as he layered the magic into every device, every table, into each wall surrounding him. It pulsed at his temples, straining for release, but he held each strand tied into a simple knot at the center of his mind. He buried it down deep, and there he held it with an afterthought. So long as he lived his labs were safe, but at any moment he could bring them down. He would not allow his work to fall into the hands of such an enemy. Better that it go to Urza, who had appreciated Gatha's efforts for many years. He wondered at what Urza might be able to accomplish with the culmination of Gatha's three centuries of research—great things, certainly.

His previous casting completed, the mage stepped over to a large iron-bound trunk. The dark ebony paneling had been carved with scenes out of classic literature, each one depicting the gift or acquiring of knowledge from the gods or through man's own effort. Gatha had been known for both in his years in Keld. Inside the trunk was every scrap of information he had collected: early theories and experiments, two hundred years of refinements, his book of questions, as he called it, new paths of exploration suggested by his work, and many problems he had run up against or simply considered but had never possessed the time to pursue. Always time, his hated enemy, working against him. What he might have accomplished, eventually. Gatha smiled in the face of that consideration. What he *had* accomplished, *today.*

Thinking back on his time in Tolaria, Gatha felt for the magic inherent to the island and drew it for his use. It came in a cool, salt-laden breeze. He attached tendrils of the power to the trunk, and with a simple twist of his mind he transported the entire collection into a fissure deep within the ground. There it would await Urza, the only person Gatha knew who could possibly retrieve it and figure out how to unlock its contents without engaging the protective wards that would incinerate the research.

The lab dead and warded, the trunk hidden away with only a tether held in his mental grasp, Gatha picked up his staff from its resting place by the main door. Made of dark ebony, as the trunk had been, its headpiece a pair of crescent-shaped iron blades stained a deep crimson, it was no longer the simple walking staff he had used to enter Keld. A magical device he had imbued with powers over his long stay, it would aid him today in defending his home.

Passing through the door, he gathered his guards by glance alone and then added that final magical tendril, connecting his boon of knowledge to the knot of magical threads already tied within his mind. It was readied to search out and whisper a message to Urza Planeswalker. It would bring Urza here, eventually. What happened after, in the future, was not Gatha's concern.

It never was.

Kreig commanded his warhost from the left flank, near the edge of the plateau where the fighting was the most concentrated. Here there could be no quarter, no fallback—the opposing forces always aware of the precipice they could so easily be swept over. Already a number of Keldon warriors had plummeted to their deaths, dashed to crimson stains on the sharp rocks below. Kreig had led an assault which toppled a dragon engine to join them. His greatsword sliced apart treads while a white scar of lightning cast out from Gatha's fingertips slammed into the engine's enraged head.

The stench of oil and blood, scorched ground and burnt flesh, assailed the normally chill mountain air now warm with Phyrexian fires. Kreig registered the pain of his healing right leg. The witch king's armor had been burned away from a gout of a burning jellylike substance belched from one of the larger black creatures, that creature now destroyed and left in his wake. Armor-clad warriors, those stunted growths with their mechanical arms and legs, he left shattered by the dozens. They annoyed him, so small and insignificant compared to his expanded boundaries.

His was the personal strength of a thousand men, borrowed piecemeal from the legion of warriors under his direct control. When he swung his gore-streaked greatsword, it struck with force enough to rip through armor plating and shatter metal supports. Flesh and bone where he found it among the dark soldiers, he cleft with ease.

How much more might he have become if he had brought the entire Keldon warhost under his banner? This was not the only battle being fought today. It was one of several, in fact, and the witch king never forgot his responsibilities. He was more than Kreig—immortal or not, the greatest of the witch kings or not—he was *Keld.* Even in the frenzy of battle the witch king never forgot his priorities. His nation would survive. The Phyrexians were here for him, testing themselves against the greatest warrior Dominaria had ever known. He and Gatha, they were the objectives. So long as Kreig did not put the whole of Keld in between the enemy and themselves, some—many—would survive.

The warlord was able to easily recognize the Phyrexians battle philosophy. They had apparently little use for subterfuge with what seemed to be inexhaustible resources to draw upon, and they had their god of pale flesh and black eyes that could place them for battle or withdraw them as necessary. They wanted to rip out the strength—what *they* perceived to be the strength—of his nation. They would learn that the Keldon strength was inexhaustible as well. It didn't matter whether the Phyrexians won today or next year. They could take all of Dominaria, in fact. One day the Necropolis would be full, and then nothing would stand before his nation and *him.*

A skeletal figure walked the battlefield toward him. Kreig knew of it immediately, sensing the approaching danger in the waning lifeforce of his warriors. It appeared only slightly more impressive than the spindle-limbed warriors in black armor—the only visible differences being its cleft skull and burning red eyes that sat back within hollow sockets. It carried a staff which looked to be a thin, twisted piece of wood, and it wore no more protection than a robe of tattered cloth bands, or so it seemed.

One Keldon warrior charged the thing, and it moved with blinding speed to eviscerate the man with one swipe of its thin, taloned hands. Another met an end with searing bolts from the creature's eyes. The one blow Kreig saw the creature take was shrugged aside as easily as the witch king himself might have done, hardly scratching through the tattered robes that writhed with their own life.

Rage gripped Kreig, watching his warriors so easily cast aside as if they barely merited a warrior's death. He kicked an impaled creature off his sword. The warlord shouldered his way past or through several skirmishes, trailing the smoke from smoldering colos horn back from his shoulder vents. A Phyrexian's clawed hand took off the bladed antler that guarded part of his helm's eye slit. He shrugged it aside, raking his armor's elbow spikes into the creature's midsection and tearing through several hoses acting as veins for thin, glistening oil.

The other creature finally noticed his advance and paused to meet him. It screeched out an attack of tormenting sound. Waves of preternatural sound assailed Kreig with stunning force, as if he had hit an invisible wall which then toppled back over him. His armor shook, and small stabs of pain worked through his gut. He shouted his war cry, cursing his own muscles for their treasonous behavior, and then he was past the wall and set upon the Phyrexian.

His greatsword rose and fell three times in rapid strikes. The first two glanced off the bands of metal that rustled and rasped over the creature like living snakes, but the last connected solidly to the side of the Phyrexian's head. A few metal bands fell to the ground, writhing a moment before falling still. The vicious slash to the creature's face caused it to stumble and opened up a large cut in the taught, glistening-gray skin. Kreig moved to make a disabling blow but found his sword deflected by a flick of the creature's hand. A stiff-armed stabbing motion followed from the Phyrexian, allowing a pair of talons to pierce his armor and dig into his ribs.

Kreig backed off immediately, knowing to not press an attack after being taken unaware, and he watched the cut on the Phyrexian's face heal. Strands of fiber spun out from one side of the wound to the other, pulling the flesh tight again. Small spinning devices, fused right into the skull it seemed, spun and stitched the skin back together flawlessly. His own wounds burned painfully. He noticed a sludgelike black fluid dripping from the creature's two talons that had found his skin. Growling defiance, Kreig swung again. Another lightning flash of motion and the Phyrexian's poisoned claws scored again along his right shoulder.

Burning, the substance continued to eat away at him regardless of how much strength his warriors lent him. Kreig stumbled, going down on one knee, his swordpoint stabbed into the earth for balance. He hated the Phyrexian for humbling him in such a manner. He couldn't draw a breath, the burning now in his lungs. Kreig wrenched his helm away, drawing in deeply the steaming, smoky air.

Chattering a cacophony of squeals and hisses, the creature moved in to deal a death blow. A crackling, snapping arc of energy scored the air over Kreig. Gatha's lightning caught the Phyrexian in the shoulder, driving it back a step as two more warriors fell on it. One arm apparently fused into place, the beast clawed the throat out of one footsoldier and then threw him into his partner, driving them both over the cliff edge. It then worked at its shoulder, twisting it back into a full range of motion within seconds.

With a struggle to control his pain, Kreig levered himself back to his feet and brought his greatsword back up in challenge. He could feel his own blood trickling down his side, the wounds failing to close as that burning sludge worked deeper into his body. The Phyrexian advanced, striking out with long, skeletal arms that moved with blazing speed. Kreig countered, giving back a step under each blow but holding off the deadly embrace. More of his warriors leapt in to the fray—only to be thrown back dead or dying—and then the creature advanced again. Kreig knew that the space behind him was limited. There would be Gatha and then open air as the plateau fell away to the lower valleys. He would have to act soon.

The Phyrexian never gave him that chance. As if tired of the game, it simply grabbed his sword on a parrying stroke and wrested it from his grip. A razored claw shot out, piercing his armor and digging claws into his midsection. It lifted Kreig from the ground, its hollow sockets only inches from the witch king's tortured gaze, as it pumped more liquid fire into him, then it tossed both Keldon warlord and sword aside as if broken toys. Kreig slammed into the ground, and there he lay in wordless agony. So easily discarded, the greatest witch king ever known rolled over enough to see the face of his destroyer. He stared into the skull's lifeless expression.

The Phyrexian turned, no longer concerned with the broken Keldon, and its ember eyes found Gatha.

Hellfire scents of burning flesh and scorched ground rose to choke Gatha. Metal clattered against other metal. The grinding of gears at times threatened to drown out the orders passed among minor warlords and their witch king masters. A haze hung over the plateau, smoky and wraithlike, and from that haze the Phyrexians kept advancing. Warriors went down beneath physical weapons and blazes of energies, and some simply fell sick as if by sudden disease.

Kreig fell to the Phyrexian champion, and the shock value itself drove the Keldon army back several precious yards.

Gatha could not wonder if he hadn't somehow been responsible. The more magic he expended, it seemed, the greater the opposition brought forward by the Phyrexians. His cast of lightning helping to topple a dragon engine, and then two more of the juggernauts rolled forward. He'd summoned a giant at one point, which had been quickly overwhelmed under a surge of black-armored warriors. Then came the particularly draining cast, drawing upon his entire store of mana to summon a rock hydra to block the lower pass, trying to limit the influx of more enemy soldiers.

The Phyrexians countered with their god.

The mage had glimpsed him in between castings while trying to marshal the energies at his control for another lightning strike. The image fit Kreig's description too well—pasty corpselike flesh and wide-set eyes of steel gray within black. The thin, hard line of his mouth grimaced under strain. Gatha did not believe the figure to actually be a god, no more so than he himself was, though the Keldons had for decades considered him and Kreig both as near-divine. He sensed the bridge form between worlds, saw briefly the dull tan landscape overlaid onto Dominaria. Planeswalker! The word shouted out in his mind from his earlier association with Urza. It was the closest he could come to naming the powers he saw demonstrated. From across the bridge stepped a new group of Phyrexian nightmares, the skeletal figure among them, bypassing the hydra.

Urza help us, was Gatha's first thought at witnessing the crossover. If he could have hoped to shout for the planeswalker's attention, right then he would have done so, but he had spent too much of his stamina already, manipulating heavy magics as well as maintaining his hold on the wards that protected his labs. Now he could only try and recover, witnessing the horrible passage of the new Phyrexian as it slaughtered its way quickly and effortlessly across the battlefield to put down Kreig. Even a solid strike of lightning failed to do more than slow it—and draw its attention. Right then as it looked to him, before its final confrontation with Kreig, Gatha sensed the hatred it felt. It froze the mage in his place for a moment—long enough for Kreig to fall—and then the dark creature was past the dethroned witch king and facing Gatha himself.

Backed against the plateau's precipice, his magical strength waning, Gatha began a sacrificial casting that would expend his own life in one final attack against the Phyrexian. One of the most powerful and dangerous spells he'd brought away from Tolaria, he held it in reserve for just such an occasion. With Kreig vanquished and the army poised at its breaking point, there was little else he could accomplish with his life. He could only hope to accomplish something more by his death.

Time betrayed him. The creature's red eyes darkened, becoming twin orbs of dark power within cavernous sockets. The black mana swept from it in a mind-rending wave—a banshee wail that drove the mage quickly to his knees. The spell he had held in readiness was lost to the chaos, torn from him in a painful struggle. It left him weak and defenseless. He rose back to his feet on shaky legs, his mind numb. He stared into the orbs, and they froze him to his spot. The Phyrexian reached its hands out toward Gatha's head—razor-sharp fingers on hands of metal framework and cable. One finger on each hand opened up to allow a short length of braided wire to escape. The ends probing the air in front of his eyes, searching. Gatha realized then that all his preparations to keep his research from Phyrexian hands were for naught, and worse, he was about to give up Urza's best-kept secrets—Tolaria, the *Weatherlight*, the Legacy and the bloodlines. He understood now. The Phyrexian was here for his mind.

In his entire life, Gatha had always lived by what could be done now, not tomorrow or the day next. Leaving his knowledge for Urza's recovery was in many ways an act of today, though it also prepared for the morrow when that knowledge might surface again. Seconds away from betrayal of Dominaria to Phyrexia, Gatha made the final commitment. Gauging his distance from the plateau's drop to a deep valley, Gatha released that buried knot of magical energy within his mind, collapsing the wards that protected his labs and held the call for Urza in place. Far up the slope from the plateau, fire blossomed as the destructive force of the mountain's stored mana welled up in a cataclysm of energy and raw power meant to destroy his labs completely. The roar of the explosion was matched with a magical shock wave which rode the recoil of such a heavy mana draw. The creature glanced away for a second.

That was all the time Gatha required.

Kreig had watched the Phyrexian advance on Gatha, his jaw clenched against the pain and refusing to give it justice through voice. His friend and advisor stood transfixed like a bird caught in the mesmerizing stare of a rock cobra. Kreig rolled to his stomach, ignoring the fire that burned within as he got his hands under him. His helm laying off to the side, Kreig's face pressed into the ground. It smelled of fresh dirt—no oil or blood to taint the ground of Keld here, no scorched earth, not yet.

The sweat of exertion runneling from his brow, Kreig levered himself back to hands and knees. He still maintained his hold on the warhost, still felt their combined strength and rage coursing through his veins as it warred with the foreign substance invading his body. He focused on the back of the creature that had laid him low. He saw the sky over the invader's shoulder deepening into purple as his bloodlust mixed with the normal blue. He rocked back to his feet as Gatha shrank to his knees—the two trading places. He stumbled for his greatsword, drawing it back from the dust where the Phyrexian had cast it. The Keldon nation was not finished. Neither was he.

The powers of a witch king were never without their limitations, even in him. He drew from his warrior nation that which he needed to make himself stronger and gifted back to them, in his exploits and energy, a lust for life and battle which would carry them through and home again with the spoils of war. Only here the spoils were Keld itself. He could feel the dark matter killing him. It certainly would have killed any mortal man already. Kreig had never known defeat before, but if it must happen, it would happen on his own terms.

The explosion of Gatha's labs did not distract the witch king's focus. He saw Gatha pitch himself backward, rolling for the cliff edge. The Phyrexian recovered quickly but not soon enough. Gatha was lost in the vast space that fell away from the plateau. Cheering his friend, defying death at the hands of Phyrexia, the witch king leapt forward sword reversed and poised overhead like a scorpion's stinger, the battle cry on his lips his own.

"Kreig!"

The skeletal creature spun quickly, arms flashing in on the attack. Kreig drove forward into the deadly embrace. Talons ripped through armor like a sword through old leather, digging deeply into each side. Pain blossomed—an agony unlike any he had ever known or imagined. Kreig retained hold of his weapon with a determination honed over one hundred fifty years of battle, and he felt his steel bite at the joint where the creature's thin neck met with armored bands covering its shoulder. Screaming his war cry, Kreig drove the blade down with his every ounce of strength and kicked forward.

The blade worked in and plunged deep, driven by the strength of every warrior who still survived and the raging will of one mortal who would never surrender easily to death. The Phyrexian screeched in pain and fury and then caught him fast, trying to hold Kreig in a final embrace. No physical barriers held a Keldon warlord, not even after death. Kreig drove forward, bloody spittle flying from his lips as he screamed his own name. His vision swam, and he stood at the entrance to his crypt facing out into the world, the drop before him leading down from the Necropolis. With his final call to battle, rousing those who woke behind him, Kreig leapt out into the space.

As he fell, he knew that somewhere, down below, Gatha waited for him again.

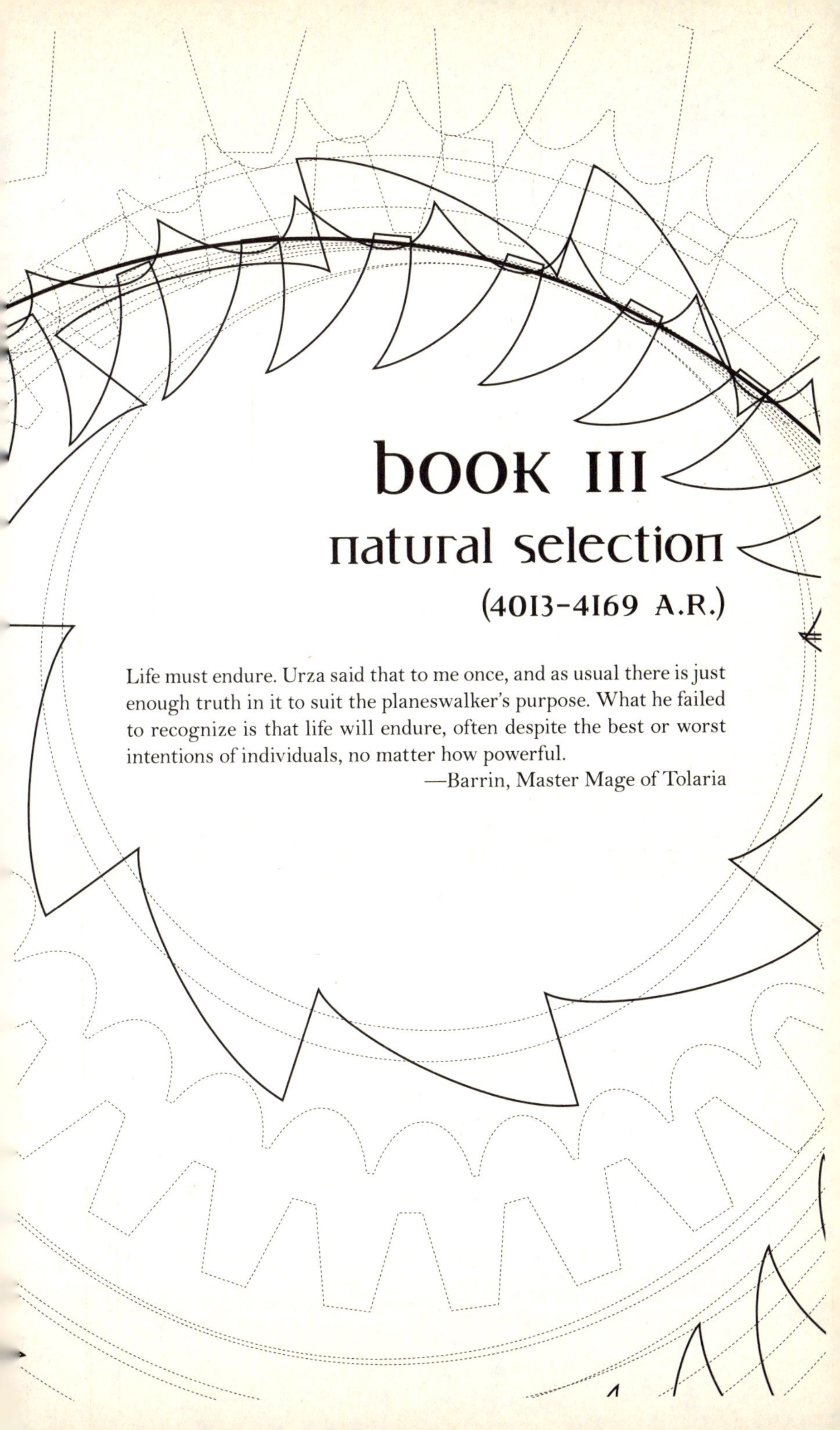

book III
natural selection
(4013–4169 A.R.)

Life must endure. Urza said that to me once, and as usual there is just enough truth in it to suit the planeswalker's purpose. What he failed to recognize is that life will endure, often despite the best or worst intentions of individuals, no matter how powerful.

—Barrin, Master Mage of Tolaria

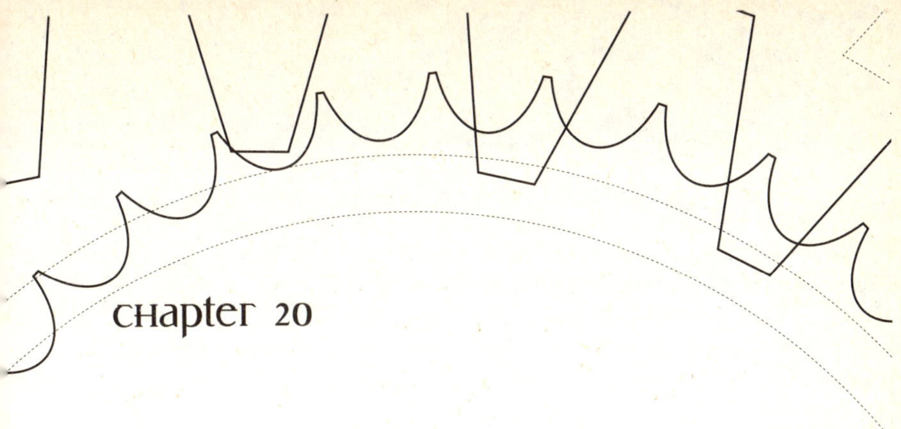

chapter 20

Silence reigned in the Chancellor's Hall, the administrative work of the academy brought to a halt for the night and most offices locked up and darkened. Light spilled through the open door of the last occupied workspace. Timein approached it slowly.

Though he only held the official academy rank of senior student, Timein had passed through security with little trouble. The sorcerer had free access to Barrin or any chancellor on the master mage's own order. The island's night watch had not challenged him. The final doorway, however, was daunting enough to stop him cold. It stood open, inviting, and Timein could see Barrin working at his desk within. That last step across the threshold was one of Timein's most difficult accomplishments in all his time on Tolaria, precisely because it would signify the end of that time.

He stepped through into Barrin's office. The mage glanced up from his work, from reviewing the material he and Urza would be discussing no doubt. The mage had put out the word that he would be meeting with Urza for all those who might have business that needed to be brought to the planeswalker's attention.

"Timein," Barrin said in surprised greeting. His expression hovered somewhere between curiosity and suspicion. "It's been a long time since you've visited the academy."

In Barrin's presence, Timein removed his cap and shoved it into a pocket. "The academy is on my way to the docks," he said, mouth dry. He knew Barrin didn't need to be told that one of the academy's security-cleared trader vessels had docked there this week—and was leaving on the tide tomorrow morning.

The mage settled back in his chair, hands flat in front of him on the marble-topped desk. He studied Timein with guarded green eyes. "I see," he said. "You want papers for leaving Tolaria," he said. It wasn't a question. "What about your students? Your fellow exiles?"

"The colony refuge will sustain itself without me. But my own studies . . . " he trailed off. How much did Barrin know about the work he had done for Urza?

Most of it, apparently.

Barrin rose and offered the sorcerer his hand. "Your work these last years has been of extreme importance and help, Timein. Your refinements to the empathy magics couldn't have been accomplished by anyone else." Tolaria's master mage nodded slowly. "Are you certain you cannot be persuaded to stay?" he asked, a note of resignation present.

"Yes, I'm certain," Timein said.

The sorcerer had too much to work through on his own. While he'd begun to admit to a certain validation behind Tolaria's purpose—behind Urza's purpose—it was hard to balance that out against his lack of understanding for the lands and lives his work affected. Barrin might be able to make those hard decisions, balancing lives against the sometimes harsh necessities of the future. Timein did not yet possess such an outlook.

"I do hope to return, Master Barrin, someday, but I've gone as far as I can with the Legacy and Tolaria." He smiled a sad smile. "As far as I can, for now."

"It's been better than a century since the deaths of Gatha and Kreig, Urza. Still the Keldons haven't fully recovered." The mage shook his head. "I don't care for the idea that we may see that same kind of devastation in Benalia."

Barrin paced the *Weatherlight's* deck, trying to work off some of his nervous energy but feeling that in fact the reverse was true. Though the ship remained sea-bound, sailing emerald waters beneath a brilliant summer-blue sky, the mage sensed the large powerstone that was the vessel's heart pulsing from its protected vault. The magic charged him, a reminder of his part in the ship's design and construction, and of course, in its maiden voyage to Serra's Realm. That felt so long ago, the battle now just one more footnote in his never-ending life. Barrin's world seemed to shrink with each new year added to that span, lost among the incredible history.

Standing near the forward mast, pennants snapping in the rigging above him, Urza glanced upward for a long moment, possibly remembering the time he'd spent on ship climbing into the sails and mastering the ocean's temperament.

"I trust that Keld will survive," the 'walker said with regard to Barrin's first statement. "It has always been a strong nation. I doubt they will ever see another of Kreig's status, though certainly the witch kings wish for it."

The master mage conceded that point. Urza was right in that the Keldons had asked for Gatha and the rogue tutor's experiments, had *embraced* them. Their current difficulties, now that Phyrexia had moved on, stemmed from the witch kings trying to hold onto the power Kreig had once brought them all. Yes, that struggle would work itself out, eventually, but this was not the issue at hand.

"The Phyrexians stumbling over Gatha's work was unfortunate but not devastating," continued Urza.

Barrin disagreed. "It pointed the Phyrexians in our general direction. We have reports of infestations in Femeref, Sardnia, and especially in Benalia. They know of the bloodlines, Urza."

"*Something* of the bloodlines," Urza corrected. "But they seem to be focusing on them as warriors only and not on their future potential."

Barrin shook his head, then drew in a deep breath of the tangy sea air. "It doesn't matter. They *know*, and that's dangerous. It means they will keep looking, finding more of your bloodlines and placing the project in jeopardy."

Urza shook his head. His voice turned hard. "I will keep ahead of them. *We* will keep ahead of them. Even should the Phyrexians try, they couldn't find all of the bloodlines. Not near enough to make a difference, in fact." His voice softened, even as his expression followed suit. "We're getting so close, Barrin. There are so many promising lines, scattered all over Dominaria." He nodded a brief concession. "Yes, I'm concerned that the Phyrexians are stepping up to such an obvious level of interference. The invasion may not be far off, but I still need at least six generations. The Legacy is complete but for an heir to wield it." His eyes glinted hard against the overhead sun. "Barrin, I need that time. The infestations are being controlled. I expect that the Benalish can hold out a bit longer."

"We both know that if the Phyrexians want to take down Benalia or any other nation they will. Right now they are toying with the bloodlines, trying to gauge their effectiveness. You owe whatever time you have to Phyrexia, Urza, and betting on them is not a pleasant gamble to make." Barrin sighed in frustration. He knew he wasn't getting through. "We're lucky they have not discovered Tolaria," he said with a sharp glance to the planeswalker. "What's left of it," he added. The island was no longer holding up well to the centuries of mining and farming and general use by so many people.

"Gatha kept that from them," Urza said softly, ignoring the latter remark. "To the end, he was a loyal student."

Barrin could not allow *that* to go by unchallenged. "Loyal? If he were loyal he never would have left Tolaria. His work was a beacon to Phyrexia. We never should have allowed it to continue."

Urza slashed the air before him with a knife-edge hand, a human gesture of frustration, certainly chosen from the memory of his physical life and used now only to influence Barrin. "It *had* to continue. I needed the insight of his generation to accomplish sooner what might have taken me centuries of trial and error. I don't always have the answers, Barrin, and we don't have the time it would take me to find them myself."

His ears warm with the rebuke, the world swam in Barrin's vision as one particular turn of phrase stuck within his mind and set his hackles rising. The insight of Gatha's "generation." An eerie, prickling sensation crawled up Barrin's spine and spread over his scalp, squeezing in at his brain, which throbbed in painful response against his temples.

"Not possible," he finally said, voice hoarse with doubt. "You gave me the information on the bloodlines. Gatha was nowhere among them, and he's too old."

The mask frozen over Urza's face admitted to Barrin that the planeswalker had indeed given something away he hadn't meant to. His entire form an illusion of energy patterns, Urza could look as he wished. Gestures and expressions were entirely affectations he assumed for dealing with mortals. He simulated emotional responses as it suited him, most often preplanned to generate the effect he wanted. Caught unaware or in the grip of intense concentration, those were the first signs to slip away.

"I gave you the information on all *continuing* bloodlines, not every single bloodlines subject, and Gatha is not too old." The human mannerisms returned, and Urza allowed himself a small sigh of concession. "I began my first experimentation outside Tolaria not long after we discovered the mana rig in Shiv, when I knew the *Weatherlight* would fly, several decades *before* bringing the Legacy and bloodlines to your attention." There was an uneasy pause, and then Urza continued. "I told you then that I had taken matters as far as I could *alone*."

The mage performed some quick math—thirty years! Just enough to raise one generation and breed the next, subjects that, if left unchecked, might have bred thousands, even millions, of descendents by now. Of course, theory never matched reality, but it was still staggering to contemplate.

"So you haven't kept track?" he asked.

The 'walker shook his head. "No need. These were prior to our official Bloodlines program, and the procedures were imperfect. I also relied on a heavier mix of Thran blood in the Matrix. Most of those early lines sickened, and I allowed them to simply breed my work back out. Only a few lines prospered, but they showed remarkable talents. Those I brought to Tolaria for their genius. I turned them over to you better than three hundred years ago."

For their genius. Barrin wondered at all those students over the years. Not Jhoira and Teferi, they fell outside the proper time frame. Gatha for certain, and how many others? How many remained in his classrooms and labs? In his life?

Barrin looked at the planeswalker. He remembered Urza's words spoken so long ago. "I certainly would not have chosen any other mate for you." He locked gazes with the true immortal, but Urza simply looked on, curiously now, which meant either he had no idea as to the question so close to Barrin's lips or was not about to volunteer the information. Barrin blinked, glanced away, and focused his gaze on the far horizon ahead. The wind cut sharply over the bow and welled tears in the corners of his eyes.

"Take me home, Urza."

It was a waking dream—a nightmare, actually. It was a clockwork world—a series of them—one shell world nestled around the next one. The ticking and grinding of gears sounded always at the edge of one's hearing, deep and pervasive as it threw the barest tremor into the ground. The air filled with the scent of hot metal and fresh oil, scents which Rayne knew well from her life as an artificer.

Rayne fought the vivid images, trying to clear her mind and concentrate on her work. A gyroscope belonging to a mechanical dervish rested in the clamps before her, held to a comfortable height such that she could inspect it while sitting on a workshop chair. She leaned in again, checking the wear and searching for tolerance deviations. Her gauge trembled in her slender fingers, and her wrist shook just enough to continuously spoil the focusing power of her wrist-mounted glass. Biting her lower lip in frustration, she tore the glass off her wrist and hurled it across the room. Hearing the glass shatter against the wall brought an instant of immediate gratification, followed quickly by a sense of loss and guilt for having taken her turmoil out on an inanimate tool.

"Rayne? Is everything all right?" Hurried footsteps came down the corridor and then the door of her workshop swung open.

Startled, Rayne stood quickly in the surprise of hearing Barrin's voice. She expected her husband to be gone for several hours yet. Catching her stool before it overturned, she set it carefully against a table as he entered.

"You're back early." Watching him scan the shop with his quick, green eyes, she noticed their haunted look. Frowning, she clasped her hands together. A gesture of concern and meant also to hold them steady. "The meeting went as you suspected, I see." Rayne knew her husband too well. There was no missing his look of fear, quickly smothered under doubting eyes.

"I had Urza 'walk me back to Tolaria," he said in answer to her first statement. Taking passage back to the island should have cost him several days time, though only hours subjective to Rayne.

She noted the despondency in his voice, the too-casual shrug. Barrin was her entire world, always more important than her artifice. After so many years she could read him as she could no other, and she remembered better than he. She could compare her husband's moods and attitudes with previous years, and she noted the failing pattern. Something was wrong or going wrong. So far, though, Barrin had been unable or unwilling to share it.

Now he tried to change the subject. "What happened to your glass?" he asked, nodding toward the twisted frame and pile of glittering shards.

"A mistake," she said. That was truthful enough. "I will have to fix the frame later and order a new lens."

"I'll take care of the lens," he promised quickly.

Too quickly. He was definitely avoiding some problem. "Is something the matter?" she asked, knowing full well there was and wanting to draw him out—wanting also to avoid her own personal nightmares.

She noticed a glistening bead on her husband's forehead and reached out slowly to dab at it with delicate fingertips. Moisture. She almost expected the scent of glistening oil but shoved such thoughts back into the darker recesses of her mind.

"Something *is* the matter."

His eyes met her gaze, softened under the warm concern. Almost, she thought, he was ready to blurt it out. Slowly, almost sadly, he reached over and took her hand in his. "Rayne," he began, voice trembling only slightly. "Rayne, are you happy on Tolaria?"

An odd question, deserving perhaps an inconclusive answer. "I think I have been getting too close to my work," she said openly, her voice tight with the tension but feeling some of the strain draining away by speaking of it. "It does not hold the allure it once did. Not since . . . " she trailed off, uncertain.

"The negator?" Barrin asked, finishing the sentence. He asked it as a question, but something more rode his voice.

She nodded, feeling better for the admission. "Silly, I know, but we have been at this for so long." Her words caught as Barrin winced. "What is it, Barrin?"

Her question was insistent this time—worried. She couldn't remember seeing her husband so concerned. So *vulnerable*, that was the word. His fire was missing. Was the rock-solid strength that had guided the academy for over six centuries of relative time finally eroding under natural stress and the very unnatural pressures of dealing with Urza Planeswalker?

Barrin raised her hand to his lips. Kissed it hard, once. "It's not important." He called up a smile, tight and humorless but there nonetheless.

"You're right, we've been at this for too long. But I don't think it will go on much longer, Rayne. Tolaria can't hold up forever. Urza's plans are near fruition, and the enemy grows bolder. Something is going to give and soon, then we can take a hard look at where the academy is and what *we* want to do." He nodded. "Then." The smile sparked briefly in the corners of his bright green eyes. "It's not important," he said again.

Wanting to trust her husband and believe in a brighter future that could arrive of its own accord, Rayne almost believed the lie.

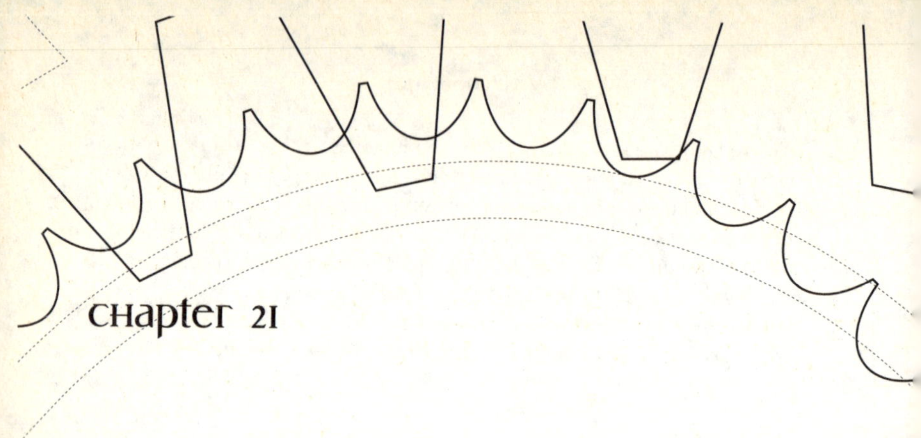

chapter 21

The seemingly endless plains of Rath were, in fact, not. There was a limit to the amount of flowstone the Stronghold had been able to produce in its millennium of operation. Here, at the edge of Rath, the sky boiled as if alive with fire—a riot of red and orange distorted ever so slightly like flames reflected from polished metal. It was a sight to twist the most sane mind into a terrifying shadow of its former self. The physical boundary of a plane was not meant for contemplation by mortal man.

Davvol, however, could hardly count as such anymore. He had been compleated to the point where he lived indefinitely, if at the sufferance of his Phyrexian masters. Six centuries of life, one in waiting and five more here on Rath as steward—evincar really, for in the last hundred and twenty years of his stewardship it could be said that he had truly ruled this plane. Since Croag had fallen beneath the sword of Kreig the witch king, the Phyrexian had been forced to slowly heal over the past twelve decades. He was in no shape to challenge Davvol, whose mastery of flowstone and the machinery of the Stronghold made him powerful. Davvol was finally powerful, out from under the shadow of the Phyrexian Inner Circle member. Croag rested in a place of darkness few knew of and where none could wonder at how the Phyrexian had almost been destroyed at the hands of a mortal Dominarian. Such was their new relationship. Croag was able to delay and heal rather than return to Phyrexia and face possible rending, and Davvol ruled Rath as evincar, with an unspoken but present guarantee that Croag's reports back to Phyrexia would never endanger either of them.

Davvol had come to this point today, the farthest reaches of his realm.

Here would be the most difficult spot to attempt a transference, the forces controlled by Rath's great machinery at their weakest and so relying more on his own ability. Armored troops waited in formal ranks behind him, silently menacing.

Flowstone rippled as he made mental contact with the control machinery under the Stronghold, focusing it against the nearby ground. Tan-colored waves rose in the landscape, shallow troughs running between them, as the machinery first worked the larger features into the surrounding plains. It was a slow process and the pressure within his mind built to a steady ache. Simple vegetation followed in the transference, and then the homes and utility buildings so common to every Benalish village.

This was a Capashen settlement, the clan that had long occupied Croag's attentions until his accident. Davvol had decided to usurp those duties as well, the constant testing and probing, now that Keld was a forgotten experiment.

The village formed as he recalled it, the control machinery pulling it from his memories. The two worlds overlapped as the chaos that existed between planes was feathered aside and the final barriers weakened. He felt that final moment of transference. His mind lay open to the people of the Benalish village who now beheld the chaos storming about them as Rath intruded into their lives. Hundreds of humans—each a tiny flare within his mind as the great machinery seized his consciousness—heard the terrible wailing that encroached upon Rath from the chaos between worlds. He felt that moment, and held it.

On his gesture, the armor-clad troops raised their weapons high and moved into the village, fighting—slaughtering—at once on Rath and also Dominaria. Davvol felt each one's life added to the pattern the machinery forced upon his mind, a tangible weight pressing down on him. The tiny flare extinguished as another Dominarian fell before his troops. The warriors traveled dim streets, now only half-lit by sunlight. Davvol directed his soldiers toward specific people, wanting to bring over those who would represent a good cross-section of the village. Dominaria was his hunting ground. No one could hide from him.

Only, he was not about to get all that he wanted. The attack faltered in places. He found himself distracted by the rising wail of disembodied voices. He was distracted by the press of new wills acting against his own. The intruders interfered with his control over the Stronghold's machinery. This presence took on a luminescent, humanoid form within his mind as it wrestled into the pattern of transference in his mind. Davvol's mind swam, his train of thought barely able to hold control over the great machinery.

He tried to bring warriors against these apparitions plaguing his mind, but they possessed no physical form to attack. As he searched for ways to win the battle in his mind, he found the assault in front of his eyes going not as well as he'd hoped. Some Benalish held their own against the Phyrexian troops. Usually it was a single, leather-clad soldier, caught in the village during the attack or perhaps on permanent assignment, but others joined in as well. Here a blacksmith wielded his hammer and crushed through Phyrexian armor and skull alike. Over there a farmer employed his scythe to great effect, knocking legs out from under Davvol's troops and leaving them helpless upon the ground.

There was no meeting such challenges to his troops, not while the haunting cries continued to threaten his control. As his warriors began to drag back victims, stepping from Dominaria to Rath and leaving those Benalish no hope of return, Davvol slowly released the barriers and allowed them to drift back into place. He had his subjects, though not as many as he would have liked. They would be sent to live among the Vec, the Dal, or the Kor. His final live warrior returned. Straining, an acute pain shot through his mind with each strange haunting voice. Davvol reached out to the places where he had felt Phyrexian lives harmed or destroyed and latched onto their physical forms. He pulled them back to Rath even as the last barrier came crashing into place.

The intrusive forms slipped away as well, melting back into the chaos that existed between planes. The strongest of them faded away last, and Davvol reached out after that final alien presence trying to wrestle his mental touch over its mind. There *was* an intelligence there. He could feel it—a whisper just outside of his range of hearing. He pushed harder, rage over his partial failure today lending him strength.

Soltari.

Then it was gone.

A name? A place? Davvol had no way of knowing and no more strength left to pursue it. He stumbled to one knee, his weakness betraying him. Darkness swam over him, almost laying claim to his consciousness. He fought it off, refusing such a pitiful display in front of his warriors. Then he rose on shaky legs, dark eyes glowering at any Phyrexian watching him. Without a command given, he turned and walked with determined stride to the portal waiting several paces behind him. The gateway back to the Stronghold. He'd been given a lot to think about, and now he simply needed some time to put it all together.

If Davvol had any two resources on his side, they were his ability to think and the time to do so.

Shuffling out from the shadows with an odd hunching motion, Croag made himself known to Davvol with a screeching whisper. "You have news of Urza Planeswalker?"

Croag preferred to announce himself in such a way. It was better than allowing the steward to guess Croag's presence by the dragging foot he kept hidden beneath his banded metal robes or the rasping wheeze of his artificial lung breathing. Davvol appeared to take pleasure in the Phyrexian's damaged state, but like it or hate it—and Croag certainly hated it—the Inner Circle member was in need of Rath's first evincar. Croag required time for self-repair. Certainly he could not return to Phyrexia in such a state.

No, that would not do. Rath certainly was ahead of schedule now, but Urza Planeswalker still lived, and more, he was preparing Dominaria against the day of invasion. He was doubtful that the planeswalker could affect any meaningful widespread change before that glorious event, but admission of the attempt would be enough cause for an end to Croag's existence. Gix's failure had been nowhere near so severe, and he had still been cast into the furnaces of Phyrexia. Croag was of the Inner Circle. He was superior. At such a high pinnacle, second only to the Dark One, the fall would be all the more long and merciless.

He suffered the time spent away from his plans and power. Croag's body contained meat at such a minute level that every cell could repair itself or rebuild its neighbor, given time. However, without the use of Phyrexian devices and assistant operations the cells first returned to their simpler meat form. As interesting and at times as sublime as the return of pure meat might have been, Croag did not appreciate the feelings of helplessness and danger which had accompanied every moment. Davvol might have killed Croag, easily so, and claimed a right to further compleation through such an impressive act as to slay a member of the Inner Circle, except Davvol was apparently not so ambitious or was too infatuated with his self-proclaimed title of evincar.

Croag still could not be sure if Davvol was too simple, too stupid, or just more patient and crafty than the Phyrexian had ever credited. He had spent decades in consideration of such ideas while his body mended, unable to carry out previous designs with the strange subjects in Benalia or even attend to routine on Rath. Even Croag's temporary return to the state of being meat did not bring with it an understanding of Davvol's mind. Later, though, he would have such an answer. He would know Davvol's mind, all in its place.

He asked again. "You have news of Urza Planes—"

"No, Croag," Davvol interrupted, looking up from the newest batch of ruined corpses that lay at his feet. "No news of the negators currently hunting Urza. The 'walker has been very cautious these last several years." He glanced back, his lips pulled into a tight, wide-mouthed grimace. "I can't decide if Urza is worried for his own life for a change or if he has gone to ground in protection of his plans." He paused. "These," pointing at the mess in front of him, "were not sent after the planeswalker."

"If this is not Urza's work, who else has destroyed negators? Not the Vec." Rebellious they might be, but the Vec even in large numbers should not be able to kill a negator.

"Trees and flowers were mostly responsible for this," Davvol said, a frown pulling down the edges of his wide mouth. He brought his hands together, fingertips touching. "Animals. A few elves. The place is called Yavimaya, and it's dangerous, Croag, perhaps more so than Urza Planeswalker."

Nothing could be worse than Urza Planeswalker. Croag looked carefully at Davvol, searching his pale-skin face for signs of duplicity. The black skullcap Davvol wore still offered its inviting eye, the depression Croag had seen fit to design into that protective cap. That would be the only way to be sure, but Croag was not ready to dismiss Davvol yet. He shuffled closer, the few metal bands left on his covering robe rasping dryly for lack of glistening oil. Closer, Croag saw that the corpses had mostly been crushed or blown apart by explosion. Very little suggested magic, though perhaps artifice.

"Trees and plants do not stand in the way of Phyrexia," he screeched and hissed.

Davvol folded arms over his chest. "They do now. Yavimaya is completely hostile. The land itself attacks."

"Urza." The name escaped Croag before he bothered to consider. "This must be the 'walker's doing."

A shudder trembled through Croag's under-developed joints. How many ways could the planeswalker find to interfere with Phyrexia's return? Too many. Even once was too many.

"I don't believe so, Croag. A seeker found this place, and there is no evidence that Urza is involved. Plants that explode? Trees which turn suddenly supple and smash warriors between them?" Davvol kicked at the mangled leg of a negator, its hardened flesh shredded to the metal by some kind of shrapnel. A few wood splinters still protruded from the negator's areas of pure meat. "Too alien for the 'walker," he shook his head. "No, this is something different."

"Different is bad," Croag hissed, Davvol's soft speech beginning to wear on his patience. Croag should order Davvol's voice compleated, able to speak in proper Phyrexian. "Different must be Urza. Destroy this place, Yavimaya."

Even the name caught in Croag's throat. A moment of silence stretched out, marked only by the irregular timing of Davvol's blinking eyes and Croag's rasping breaths.

"No," Davvol finally said, without preamble or qualification, a straight denial of Croag's order.

The Phyrexian drew himself up to his full height, cleft skull at a higher level than Davvol's head. His eyes glowed with the passion of molten steel as he leaned close to Rath's evincar.

"You will do as ordered." There was no room for denial here, or so Croag thought.

Croag didn't account for the negator that suddenly appeared at Davvol's side as if summoned by magic. Small and compact, it moved with fluid grace. It was one of the faster creations Davvol had developed over the centuries. Faster, perhaps, than Croag, even at the Phyrexian's strongest, which this time was not. It carried a saw-toothed shield. The other arm ended in a hand of oversized fingers all metal-tipped and backed by corrosive-fluid plungers. It had no armor to bind joints or slow its incredible response time. Croag noticed suddenly with a tremble of something akin to fear—it had no compleated ears. Would this creation even understand the Phyrexian language? Croag was certain it would not. This negator took orders in Davvol's meat-tongue language. This negator was present to kill Croag, and at this point it could do so. The Phyrexian never doubted that.

Davvol, to his credit, never bothered to threaten or even imply that the Phyrexian should feel threatened. Secure in his power, he simply repeated, "No." Then, only after a slow step away from Croag, he continued. "If you want to attribute every threat to Urza Planeswalker, Croag, you may, if you are that afraid of him. But we do not know enough of this Yavimaya to risk incredible resources. Yet. I refuse to underestimate an opponent. I will continue to press at this Yavimaya and find its weaknesses much as we did in Keld. And when I have its measure, then *I* will destroy it. As a present for the Dark Lord."

Croag shook, every fiber and component screaming for Davvol's death, but buried in the steward's refusal was a truth the Inner Council member recognized. Davvol was correct in that the Phyrexians had a habit of blaming Urza for any and all failures, because in three millennia of time, only Urza had orchestrated the defeat of Phyrexian plans. It could be possible that Croag now overlooked a new threat, and the Phyrexian could ill afford another mistake. That did not make his defeat here any easier to accept. He would know satisfaction, but not yet, not until he had healed.

Eyes blazing fiercely, casting red flickers before them, Croag turned away and moved from the room with his odd shuffling motion. His teeth clicked in exasperation. He still needed Davvol, and Davvol obviously believed that he still needed Croag, or the Phyrexian would have been killed. Croag would rely upon that for just a bit longer, then they would discover who was the true master of Rath.

Perhaps a visit to the newer attractors had not been the best of Davvol's ideas, not after the meeting with Croag, but his schedule called for monthly visits to inspire greater production of flowstone and that meant today. Rath's steward toured the complexes with brutal efficiency, executing workers if standards appeared lacking at all. By the time he reached the lower levels where the massive spinning blades drew glowing red lava up from Rath's molten underworld, the Vec had been alerted to their master's fury and were found climbing over machinery and coaxing every last ounce of effort from the devices—as it should be. Davvol took limited pleasure noting the steady rumble shaking the floor, his equipment holding up to stresses which would have caused the supports of the main attractors to buckle and give way.

A large room surrounded the spot where the encased blades penetrated Rath's flowstone crust to bore down into the lava beds far below. One hundred Vec worked furiously over controls, their blunt features bathed in sweat and soot. The heat pulsed at near-insufferable temperatures, the air hot, sulfurous and hardly breathable. Still, the machinery appeared to be well maintained, the joints greased with black sludge and most metal surfaces oiled for protection. He checked what few gauges he himself knew how to read and found the bladed dials rotating at full capacity, perfect, too perfect, in fact.

"Vec," he called out to the supervisor, ordering his presence. The humanoid ran over. "This facility is pulling up lava at the same rate as the main attractor," Davvol said, tapping the gauge. The supervisor nodded, eyes a pale but furious green and saying nothing. "But these facilities are better cared for!" Davvol shouted his fury into the smaller man's face. "Why are you not outperforming the main attractor by now?"

He flicked one hand toward a random worker, and immediately his negator leapt from the nearby shadows to seize the hapless Vec. With a violent motion it broke the Vec's back in three places. The worker was left laying on the blisteringly hot metal floor, crying in pain.

No Vec moved or spoke. Only the clanging and grinding of machinery spoiled a perfect moment of fear and loathing, then the supervisor barked out quick orders, and everyone fell to work with renewed energy. The noises intensified—a cacophony of metallic protests. The throb that shook the floor quickened perceptibly. Walls shook, and in places a few gauges cracked for the additional stresses. A sudden leak of sulfurous, yellow steam shot out from a ruined piping joint. Under such pressure, the thin stream sliced deep into one worker's leg like a fine blade and nearly amputated it. Everything else held, as Davvol had known it would.

"Better," he said aloud but not with anything resembling satisfaction. The increase in output would barely be felt in flowstone production. Rath's borders stretched out so far that to achieve a constant rate of growth was now impossible. The violence he had just committed had been simply a show of power, but it didn't help him shake the feeling of uncertainty he carried around with him. Casting a deformed shadow over Davvol's work here was Croag. The self-proclaimed evincar strode imperiously from the room, grinding his anger beneath metal-shod heels.

Davvol knew that he should have waited, not tipped his hand so soon to the Phyrexian, but the meeting had not been planned. That Croag had returned to the more active sections of the Stronghold did not bode well for the steward, who had hoped for another half-century or better. Five more decades of progress and Davvol might have accomplished just a little bit more. Perhaps he might have killed Urza Planeswalker by then, and Croag could have been safely disposed of so that Davvol alone reaped the rewards of such a victory.

Croag *had* returned now, and upon learning of Yavimaya he had ordered—to Davvol's mind—a poorly considered plan. Croag had pushed for obedience, so Davvol pushed back. He knew he could kill the injured Phyrexian, but he kept him around. If Croag were gone there would be another. It was better to have the devil you know—especially the one you know that you can defeat.

Even now Davvol sensed his personal guardian keeping pace behind him, the negator stalking shadows with deadly fluidity, ready to leap to Davvol's defense in a fraction of a second. It was of simple construction, very durable, and able to tangentially threaten Croag. Was it too soon? Would Croag now worry enough to move against Davvol or consider the idea that Davvol instead made a better ally than enemy?

It was a question with no easy answer. His echoing footsteps and those of his negator drove home the reality of exactly how alone he was here on Rath. Davvol stalked the Stronghold's lower levels and considered the possibility that today he had chosen wrong. Today, the first time in better than six hundred years, he had made his first major mistake.

Mistakes were not tolerated, not by Phyrexians.

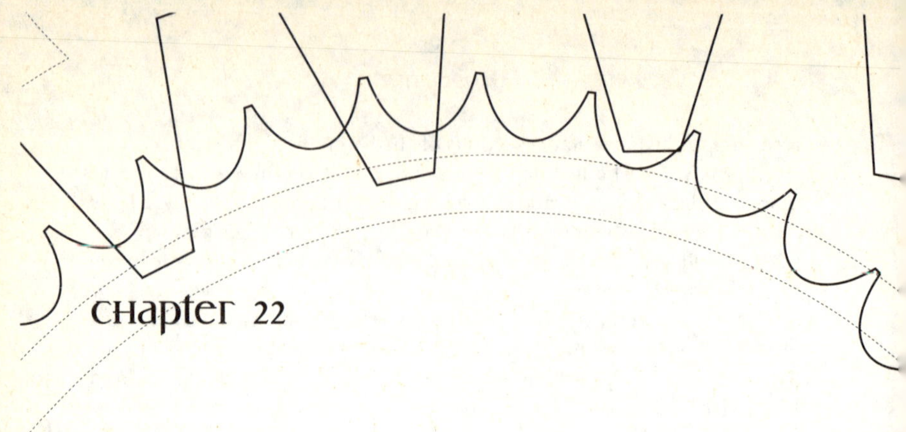

chapter 22

Lyanii hosted the meeting in Devas's cathedral, not a place of stringent religion—the Benalish definition of cathedral—but certainly a place of reflection and spirituality. An incredibly high vaulted ceiling rose overhead, alabaster arches opening up to covered balconies on the third and fourth stories. The Marshal wondered how many of her guests noticed that there was no access from the ground to those balconies.

A long, whitewashed oak table had been set for feasting. The delegation from Clan Capashen occupied one side. Representatives of Devas, most with the characteristic porcelain features that had been common to Serra's Realm sat on the other. The Marshal had placed herself in the middle, her best lieutenants to either side. Administrative diems and valued clerks also sat in attendance. Two former Benalish also sat among the Serrans, emigrants who had earned trust enough to share the secrets of Devas and also the table here tonight.

A table knife tapped on the side of a crystal goblet chimed a musical note repeatedly over the level of conversations. The low buzz faded, giving the man standing everyone's attention. Clan Leader Rorry Capashen placed the knife back on the table, nodded his thanks to all, and then looked to Lyanii. His brown eyes spoke of a calm intelligence. His strong face promised leadership. A descendent of Ellyn Capashen, Rorry had proven himself on the battlefield and at the bargaining table both.

Now he set his warm, steady gaze on Lyanii. "I was hoping we might discuss our business, now that we've finished your excellent repast."

Lyanii had wondered how long the Capashens' patience would last. The

Serran Marshal glanced once to Karn—seated on a large stone block two positions down from Rorry Capashen—and then nodded her acquiescence. "By all means," she said calmly. But before he could begin, she shrugged and guessed, "You want our help in fighting the dark warriors."

Not one to be caught off guard for long, Rorry Capashen simply blinked his surprise while retaking his seat and then admitted it. "Yes. We've suffered their raids over years leading into centuries now, and they steadily get worse. This year it is particularly bad, and who knows what the next will bring? The Benalish court has refused our petition for organized involvement because most do not see a danger. Only Clan Blaylock is in agreement with us, having also met the raiders. But," and his eyes tightened, "I understand that your forces once took arms against them."

She couldn't help another glance toward Karn. He matched her gaze with a curious frown of his own, obviously not understanding the attention. He was certainly welcome in Devas and knew of the winged ones, though he retained no direct memory of the refugees' original ancestry. Karn simply knew that Urza vouched for Lyanii and her people—every ten to twenty years—and the golem would not gainsay the 'walker. More likely one of the students Lyanii accepted from time to time had let something slip. There were at least a dozen besides the silver man who had shared Devas's secrets. Karn would never betray Devas's trust.

The golem's presence, however, did speak for some pressure being brought to bear against them. A long-time associate of the Serrans, he often managed to win concessions that others might not have. Even if Karn didn't remember—couldn't remember—someone in Clan Capashen had noticed and likely wished to play off that connection here and now.

"You support this request, Karn?" It was a simple way of asking if Urza supported the request.

After a slight hesitation, the silver golem nodded. "I think you may want to consider it, Marshal Lyanii. People are being hurt." His pause answered Lyanii's real question.

"The people are frightened," Rorry Capashen spoke up again. "The legend that the Lord of the Wastes is returning has gained frightening acceptance among Clan Capashen." He tried to scoff at the old legends, but he was unable to purge his serious concern for his people.

"You don't believe in the Lord of the Wastes?" Lyanii remembered the first time she had heard of it herself. The merchant who had come upon the refugees their first year settling into Benalia had told her the story.

Rorry Capashen looked nonplussed at the question. "I do not," he said easily. "Are you saying that you do?"

Lyanii glanced to a few of her followers, noting their haunted eyes even now. "I think there is evil out there which we don't necessarily understand or even know about," she said cautiously. "Yes." Karn was leaning forward attentively, no doubt recognizing Urza's warnings in her vague statement.

"There might be several so-called lords, and if I should someday find one, I would fight." She shook her head, strands of hair brushing the side of her face. "But I see no evidence of there being one here, Rorry Capashen. I'm sorry."

The Capashen leader took the refusal with proud bearing, though he could not hide all trace of disappointment from his voice. "As am I. My grandfather spoke of the training he received at Devas. He held you in high regard, Marshal. It would have been an honor to fight at your side." His brown eyes implored what he would not ask again in words. "I'm sorry you do not feel our cause is a just one."

Damn, Karn. Lyanii knew that last sparring attack was the golem's doing. Karn knew them well enough to realize that such a charge would not sit well. She gripped her hands into tight fists, stemming an outburst. Her eyes found the golem, and Karn had the good manners to shift uncomfortably under her non-blinking gaze. This meant something to the golem personally. That carried weight as well, but in this case not enough. This was not a training session. It would risk her people's lives. It might bring Phyrexia down on top of them again.

"Try to understand," she said, careful of how much she could safely say. "Our nation was once prosperous and content. Someone—" She paused, shook off that tack and started again. "We involved ourselves in a war that was not ours, and it cost us everything. That is not mine to risk again, not without better reason. We can't afford to be wrong." She slowly released her fists, wrapping her right hand instead around the stem of a crystal glass. "I'm sorry, Rorry Capashen. The heart to fight and a just cause are not enough."

The clan leader nodded, accepting her final answer.

Karn frowned, his silver face clouded with a dark expression. "That is not what you told Isarrk."

The glass's fragile stem snapped in her hand, cutting her palm and spilling dark wine onto the table. She fumbled with her linen towel but finally got it wrapped about her hand to stanch the trickle of blood. How had Karn remembered that? She had once told Isarrk that all a true hero needed was a just cause and the heart to defend it. Isarrk had eventually done so. Carefully she glanced to one of the Benalish humans sitting at the table on her side—a relative of Isarrk. The boy would not meet her gaze.

"Excuse me, Karn?" Rorry Capashen looked over at the silver golem, confusion apparent on his handsome face. The question was also in Lyanii's mind, and she silently thanked the Capashen leader for asking in her stead.

The golem appeared confused. He glanced from the clan leader to the Marshal of Devas and then stared at his own silver hand as he concentrated. Then he shook his head. "I'm sorry. Something I thought I remembered." His voice told of his own doubts. "A mistake."

The Capashen leader nodded, turned his attention back to their host. "My apologies, Marshal Lyanii, if Karn upset you."

Lyanii shook her head in response. "No, quite the opposite. He reminded . . . " she couldn't very well admit the entire truth, ". . . reminded me of another event. Let's say I will give your request further consideration, Rorry Capashen." She held up a hand at the clan leader's look of pleasant surprise. "Let's leave it at that for now, please." Not one to argue against a second chance, Rorry nodded at his fortune.

The Marshal lapsed back into silence as normal conversation resumed. She had more than an aversion to making the wrong choice again. Here was also the very real fact that after so many centuries Lyanii was finally beginning to understand something more than fighting and leading others in battle. She might want to avoid such things for both herself and her people. Was that wrong?

"Jhoira is my friend, my best friend. We met in the original academy, before the accident drove us from Tolaria. She named me Karn, for the old name of Thran metal. She said it meant strength."

That evening, alone in his apartments, the golem repeated his nightly mantra while pacing the floors of heavy timber. In times where nothing made sense, the repetitive statements allowed him some measure of focus.

Stopping at a bureau, the silver man placed one massive hand on the thick tomes he had filled with his own words over so many changing lifetimes. Why was he so preoccupied with the past when he knew that he could never hold on to it? Karn looked at the one portrait sketch he still carried with him in all his travels. Human she was, with dark hair and intense eyes. It was his oldest artifact from previous times, magically protected at some point in the past to preserve it. All he really knew was that her name was Jhoira, and that she had been a friend. He knew it from the nightly mantra he spoke. It was a promise to himself to never let the old memories completely fade, but they did, and they colored his current relationships, promising that they too would fade in time.

Slowly, Karn turned the picture down on its face. Not tonight. Tonight was for his current relationships, to consider them individually and together, because even as Karn admitted how important these relationships were to him, how they touched and influenced his life, he knew that he also touched upon theirs. How he remained in their memories, even after they passed from his, was suddenly more important to the golem than anything else.

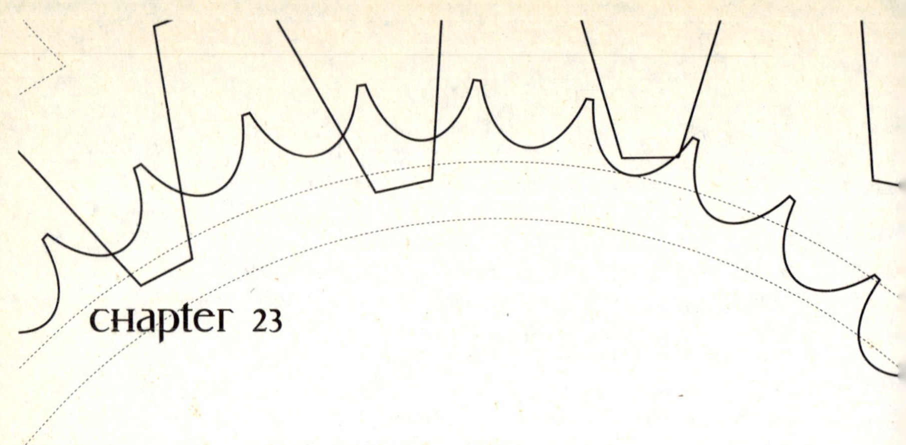

Chapter 23

The sound was of splintering wood, like a hundred tiny explosions strung into long creaking strains, mixed with the shouts of battle and the snarls and growls of woodland creatures. The beleaguered enemy responded with roaring gouts of fire, the screech of wounded metal, and a cacophony of chittering and hisses.

For miles in every direction the canopy had shifted blue, a warning of intruders that continued to spread from treetop to treetop. The colors darkened the closer one arrived to the battle, the area of fighting shaded by trees—their foliage turned darkest black. Here Yavimaya's defenders met the small but lethal Phyrexian probe.

Leaves and thin branches whipped against Rofellos's face. The Llanowar moved too quickly astride his war moa for Yavimaya to shrug the limbs aside. Eyes clenched shut, he tracked his prey by sound and the growing scent of crushed marker beetles. Where most outside creatures found the scent offensive to the point of distraction, the elves knew it only as another piece of Yavimaya. They trusted its guidance just as they would movement reflected in their own eyes. Everything in Yavimaya worked together for the betterment of the whole, from plant to insect to animal to elf.

Now the elves were dashing in on their mounts to slash at the enemy flank, harrying the Phyrexians. They always withdrew before concentrated effort could be brought against them—only to show up in a new place on the offensive once again. Trees bent or shifted, twisting themselves atop their root system, to cover the elves' escapes. Brush would shrug aside, allowing access where before had only been a dense thicket of thorny vines and hardwood brush. Phyrexians who attempted to use such openings were destroyed by sharp brush and dart-throwing plants.

Yavimaya coaxed and guided so that not one of its woods-dwelling subjects was hurt by the forest's own hand. It rooted deep in Rofellos's thoughts, recognizing that here as nowhere else were the Llanowar elves supreme. The forest even allowed Rofellos to overrule a desire to recall Multani, the expenditure in resources and concentration unnecessary for so simple a battle. Their shared mind became the center from which Yavimaya structured its defense. His hand—*their* hand—clenched around the middle grip of his double-bladed sword. Rofellos sliced again at a footsoldier entangled in vines, splitting open its chest. The moa lashed out with its jet-black beak, taking an arm off at the shoulder. Then he—*they*—twisted about and leapt back into the gloom covering the forest. The stinging slaps of slender branches against Rofellos's face were easily ignored in favor of the freedom that came with fighting.

The Llanowar were warriors, but where Rofellos's natural urge to bolt and run free pressed too sharply, Yavimaya soothed him back into dormancy—a wild flower cultivated into a tamed garden. Rofellos found it hard to reconcile the different personalities that were now his: Rofellos the Llanowar, Rofellos the ambassador to—and *of*—Yavimaya.

No matter, Yavimaya promised. This eve he was at least acting Rofellos the Llanowar, and the night was golden in battle.

Rofellos yelled a Llanowar oath, taunting his enemies. The war moa he rode squawked a shrill call of its own, the warbling noise hard to track in the forests and hopefully leading to the enemy's confusion. Brush swayed before him, and he tucked his head down behind the moa's powerful shoulder as it leapt through a newly formed passage. He had circled to the Phyrexian rear, where their single, large war engine rolled forward oblivious to the trees shouldering into its armored sides. Its own demon head chewed at the roots of one tree, tearing through with mechanical efficiency. Rofellos rode along the flank of the juggernaut, taking the warrior picket by surprise. They barely knew he fought among them before his blade of living plantlife sliced deeply into armored carapace.

He whispered to his weapon, and the blades circled inward to reform as his staff, enabling him to hold his mount with that hand without worry about hurting the moa. His free hand dug into the leather satchel that swung at his side. He drew out a handful of acorns, tossing the collection of sharp points and rough caps into the jaws of the war engine as he rode past.

The mechanical leviathan shuddered, its internal gears grinding as they bent and bound. Armored plates, so impervious to outside attacks, split open as pressure from within surpassed its design tolerances. Roots worked their way out, digging for the ground and anchoring it in place. Limbs forced their way up through rents in the upper armor tree widening into thick boles. Rofellos paused in the safety of a thick steelthorn brush, his—*their*—eyes wild with delight at the run through the enemy force. They watched as—within less than a minute—a twisting stand of oak trees had burst from the innards of the giant machine. No mechanical animation left to it, its pieces littered the ground or were held in thick limbs high overhead.

Faster, Rofellos decided, a spark of his own mind flaring in their shared consciousness. The quick-growth acorns needed to sprout and develop faster. It would be even better if nearby trees could throw the little missiles themselves. He felt the twinge in the back of his brain as Yavimaya heard him and agreed.

The Llanowar leapt forward from the brush to race the moa around to a new side, his staff unfurling leaves which sharpened again into massive blades. He had other ideas. The elven mounts handled well enough, but Rofellos would prefer greater jumping ability so as to leap over an enemy line or onto the backs of their war machines. How about increasing the size of a dart-throwing plant for less range but more stopping power? Rofellos's thoughts separated again from the shared mind, briefly. He was surprised Yavimaya had not thought of such tricks on its own, but then the forest, while sentient, was not omniscient, and certainly not experienced at war, though it was learning.

In the shadow of the Stronghold's volcano a small section of Rath and Yavimaya overlapped, but the raging sea of chaotic energy between planes worked to separate them. Davvol fought the Stronghold's machinery to retain control. Never before, not even at the edge of Rath's boundary curtain of swirling energies, had he known such a trial. Here, so close to the seat of power and control, the transference should have been easy. Not even the Soltari wailing could distract him here. Yet the weight forced on his mind slowly squeezed at his sanity, threatening to crush him for his temerity in challenging the laws of reality.

After so many years of receiving information from remote probes, Davvol required a first-hand account of how his warriors fared in the dangerous forest. Certainly he was not about to risk himself in that hostile setting.

He felt the lands, the very nature of Yavimaya, shifting. Nothing seemed to remain static. Trees swayed, conforming to no natural patterns of growth or behavior. They even uprooted themselves, just to spite his efforts at holding the bridge. Now a new stand of oak, thick with intertwining boughs, erupted up from the bowels of his one war engine, decimating it and causing yet a new ripple of pain as a piece of the pattern slipped away and had to be rebuilt again. He felt as if he were in a contest against another mind for control of the machinery. Yet Croag was nowhere near strong enough to upset Davvol's designs, and the strange Soltari could hardly raise a distraction so close to the Stronghold.

Whatever the problem, it kept him distracted to the point of being unable to properly evaluate the assault. He had time to note only a few points. Fire was, of course, a deadly weapon against plant and animal both, though the sap that boiled out of the bark of the trees squelched the flames rather than feeding them. While the compound released by his war engine would dissolve the wood eventually, these growths were proving resistant to immediate effect. At least the animals and elves still fell to blade, claw and tooth. If only the land itself were not so treacherous. How the elves had found mages of such caliber was beyond Davvol—for now.

As with anything, though, he had the time to observe and evaluate. His forces would improve for this battle, while nature was limited to such a slow progression that it could not hope to compete. It was a good thing, since the Phyrexians were not faring as well as he'd hoped. Davvol imagined the rage Croag might feel if he were to witness such a defeat in the making.

There was the elf warrior again, riding atop the large bird that he controlled with a skill that bordered on the two being somehow of one mind. This elf was different from the others Davvol glimpsed in those rare moments he devoted toward the battle. Apparently he was the only one of such size and marking. The elf rode deeper into the Phyrexian formation—a nimble dance frightening in its lethal grace. Davvol winced in pain as the Stronghold's control machinery fed back its effort in adjusting for a large stand of brush that finally succumbed to fire. That brush had separated Rath's evincar from the deadly elf commander. The dark-haired warrior glanced sharply in Davvol's direction.

Then with a blood-chilling cry, the elf spurred his mount forward and stepped out onto the flowstone of Rath itself!

Davvol recoiled in shock, never before suspecting that as his own troops moved back and forth across the threshold so could others make the transference of their own volition, though it made sense. Stronghold's machinery held the bridge, reacting to the presence of any life in the area but not ultimately controlling who might pass through. This was not knowledge Davvol would want an enemy to return with.

The elf appeared just as confused for a moment, surveying his surroundings with a blank expression, then the warrior's fierce gaze locked onto him, dark eyes burning with hatred and rage. Davvol placed his mental touch upon the elf's mind, sensing for any connection to a leader or the mage who opposed the bridge into Yavimaya.

The elf, Rofellos *and* Yavimaya. The names came to Davvol, bleeding out of the elf's mind.

His concentration divided, Davvol was unable to hold the bridge between planes. Rofellos was torn between following the retreating presence and killing the stranger before him.

Like an artifice puzzle of gears and axles, the last piece was snapped into place, and Davvol understood. Yavimaya was part of the elf because Yavimaya was alive and aware. The forest manifested itself through its creatures and plantlife, and it controlled the very land over which it grew. Yavimaya opposed the evincar in holding the bridge. Even as Davvol challenged Yavimaya with the troops and machines under his control, so the forest was sensing at the boundaries of Davvol's control over the machinery holding the threshold. Davvol mentally recalled his warriors, reached out and pulled back what lifeless bodies he could quickly locate and grab. A quick hand motion summoned his negator guard from behind him and set it toward slaying the elf.

The elf was just fast enough to save his own life. Kicking off from the mount, placing the large bird between himself and the advancing blur, the elf pitched backward and rolled into the flowstone jungle that overlapped onto Yavimaya's forested land. Cursing, Davvol snapped after the elf, determined to sink mental teeth into him and drag him back over, but he was gone, cloaked no doubt by the blanketing intelligence of the forest.

His troops faded back across the threshold. Bodies of the fallen formed back up from the flowstone. As he severed the channel between worlds, Davvol cursed his pause, which had gifted that elf his life.

It wasn't until later, remembering the blood and oil dripping down from the elf's green blades, that Davvol wondered what else might have been—if the elf had not been given pause as well.

One half of the way around Dominaria, Multani had felt the changes take root. At the time, he was in the Burning Isles, where the renowned Shipbuilders' Guild was systematically destroying forests through logging. He worked among the villages and city-states who sold their timber off to the guild without thought to the future, teaching them care of the lands and trying to prevent their coming troubles. Already the rains fell less, drying up streams and smaller rivers on which many hamlets depended. Wind erosion cut scars into the land and dropped dust storms over some cities.

Multani's own work consumed him, distracting attention away from the happenings back in his parent forest. He had known of the Phyrexian incursion of years back, of course, feeling the forest's pain reflected as aches within his own body and mind. Alterations were to be expected, and as they progressed his appearance changed with the forest's. The nature spirit's bark skin already possessed the strength of ironwood armor. Multani recognized his improvements and approved as Yavimaya approved. Except the nature spirit did not take into consideration the involvement of Rofellos.

One day, Multani noticed the odd looks given him by his latest congregation. He followed their gaze back to his own shoulders. Growths extended from them in spiky fashion—ridged armor. The same growths sprouted near every major joint. He had gained length in his limbs, his toes thickening into sturdy stands and fingers extending now into the beginning of hardwood claws. Never before particular about his appearance, the nature spirit now looked and did not care for all he saw.

It was then he had heard the first whisper of Rofellos's voice entwined with the thoughts that were Yavimaya's. Multani mentally pushed his mind more in parallel with the forest's sentience to better understand the changes. It was a simple endeavor, usually, to bury his thoughts and intellect back into the stream of consciousness from which it had sprung, only this time he felt a resistance, so he pushed harder.

Rofellos pushed back.

Even as Multani felt at the boundaries now set within Yavimaya's consciousness, the nature spirit heard the forest's call to return. The nature spirit walked into a nearby stretch of forest—and disintegrated.

The nature spirit's physical body was actually but a shell—pieces of wood and bark and moss, shaped into a humanoid form—that allowed him to more easily interact with the various races of Dominaria. Now it fell away, raining to the ground as sticks and twigs and scale flakes of ironwood bark. His mind, all of who Multani actually was, faded back into Yavimaya's consciousness, but it was held distinctly apart from that which the forest now shared with Rofellos. Instantly the nature spirit was back within his homeland, the familiar feel of its high canopy and lush undergrowth. He sensed the incredible resources still buried in the land from the accelerated mulch cycle—so much strength yet untapped.

Multani stepped from one of the massive trees of a coastal forest, a watchtower tree, standing as high again as the surrounding woods. He peeled away from the bole like some new fast-growth, whole again in his bark-skin form and mossy hair. What the tree itself could not provide grew rapidly from his large frame. Yavimaya's incredible reserves fed him from the land through his contact with it.

The Llanowar elf waited in the shadows of a grenade plant, its bulbous growths much larger than the one they had inspected together so many years before. "Yavimaya wishes our physical presence," he said.

Unnecessarily, as Multani received the same knowledge even as the elf spoke it aloud. The ground to one side split and opened, the immense root system buried beneath Yavimaya welling up to allow a cavern into the forest's depths. The two moved toward it together.

Dwarfed next to Multani's larger frame, Rofellos never once showed any discomfort. His gaze had braced Multani immediately, as if sizing up a possible challenge and then turned elsewhere. He looked more the wild elf than before, as if in its latest cycle Yavimaya encouraged the reversion.

Thin, thorny vines had been woven into a few of his braids. While not fully painted, the elf wore blue smudges under his left eye and a small circular design of red and blue decorated the right side of his neck.

"It has been a long time, Rofellos." Multani drew abreast of the Llanowar as the two moved along the dimly lit cavern. He noticed the bow, slung across the elf's back. A quiver of ash arrows rode against his left shoulder. "You fought well against the Phyrexians."

"I live to serve."

Multani did not disagree vocally, though inwardly he knew better. The nature spirit lived to serve—working Yavimaya's will in the world outside. Rofellos lived to war—the forest's weapon against its enemies, subsumed by Yavimaya for his knowledge and expertise. Multani tried to push such thoughts over to Rofellos, make the Llanowar aware again of his identity, but the fracture persisted that separated their minds from each other.

Seed torches lit the interior. Plants which sat high on a stalk and produced a phosphorescent pollen that burned cool to the touch. They sprouted along the wall as needed. Many were the color of Tolarian mage-lit stones, ranging from blue-white to lavender shades. Deeper, one burned a rare golden color that washed the wooden walls with an aureate shine. Rofellos and Multani paused here, knowing that the golden torch marked an end to their walk. A new chamber opened in the wall next to them, and they stepped into it as one.

In the center of the chamber, growing up from the floor, a branch of white-ash wood stood alone. Seven feet high, it was topped with a tapered frond that Multani knew was as rigid and sharp as any human-crafted blade. In his presence, Yavimaya gave the weapon its final living force. A green membrane grew up from the floor to wrap the staff in leathery chitin. That membrane connected the weapon to part of Yavimaya's force, making it able to bend itself into several different weapons such as the bow Rofellos wore or the double-bladed sword he had used to battle the Phyrexians. Multani knew this, though he still did not understand the barrier that now existed in Yavimaya's mind. That knowledge remained outside of his grasp.

"It is yours," Rofellos said, his voice soft yet filled with a mixture of awe and pride as if the weapon was a great honor. To the Llanowar, perhaps it was.

Multani, centuries spent working in harmony with the lands and people of Dominaria, did not look upon it with such reverence. "What if I do not wish it?" he asked, startled at his own words.

His voice rang out stark in the chamber, alone. Rofellos glared coldly. Yavimaya did not answer, did not encourage him one way or another. When Multani thought to push for the forest's mind he found it withheld, completely.

He was alone.

Yavimaya's nature spirit suddenly understood then what it meant to be his own creature. He would not be compelled, where once the choice would have been made by Yavimaya and simply accepted by him without question. Yavimaya was of two minds now. Rofellos and Multani would be allowed to choose their own paths, and if necessary, Yavimaya would then share a separate path with each. The nature spirit almost declined the weapon and left Rofellos to share such experiences with Yavimaya while he concentrated on healing and teaching, which had been his life for so long.

He almost declined, except he recognized that Rofellos required his help and healing more than any. Somewhere deep within the Llanowar elf's mind a tiny spark that was wholly Rofellos still burned. That part of the elf, Multani knew, likely struggled against the oppressive presence of Yavimaya's mind. It was the same spark that had pushed back, resisting Multani's efforts to share Yavimaya's consciousness. If the nature spirit was ever to reach in to help the elf, the two would need a common link through Yavimaya's consciousness.

Multani moved forward, slowly. He grasped the staff, accepting it into the crook of one arm as the base separated cleanly from the floor.

For an instant the barrier fell away. Multani felt it slip, brought down by Rofellos's own feeling of companionship as Multani accepted the weapon. That tiny spark still burned within Rofellos's mind. Multani breathed air to that spark in encouragement for the individual of Rofellos. He sent encouragement for the young Llanowar who had relieved the nature spirit of a portion of his burden and was now lost because of it. Personal identity was just as important as a sense of greater belonging. The nature spirit was just beginning to recognize his own balance between the two. He could only hope to do the same for Rofellos.

Chapter 24

The artificial thunder of hooves pounding the ground stormed across the battlefield as Devas's cavalry tore through a thin advance line of black-clad warriors. Sword and mace and lance rang against each other and glanced off metal armor. The screams of dying men and women, the shrieks of a wounded horse, all added to the cacophony of chaos that enshrouded the field. The air stank of sweat and blood and the gore spilled upon the ground. Beneath it all was the hated scent Lyanii remembered all too well from centuries before. It was the scent of glistening oil—the stench of Phyrexia.

Lyanii parried a slashing attack directed at her by one of the tall, spindle-limbed warriors. She turned its sword with ease, spinning into a riposting arc that severed the head and part of a shoulder from its body. Slime splattered onto her own armor, spotting its opalescent finish with inky foulness. She kicked over the creature and paused to catch her breath. A century ago she would not have even registered the fatigue—One more sign that age was finally claiming her.

"Therri!" The Marshal called out for her aide, a wary eye on the large engines moving in the Phyrexian backfield. Therri Capashen swam up through a thick knot of fighting, moving with a grace that belied her relative newness to the field of battle. "Message to Gavvan," Lyanii ordered, naming Therri's brother whose Capashen forces held the center of the field. "We're holding the flank, but the enemy has moved both war engines opposite our position. If we are going to break the line, it will have to be done from his position. Go!"

Therri was off, but rather than race for the rear lines where she might hope to grab a mount, the young warrior peeled away at a tangent and fought past a number of Phyrexian guard before breaking into open field where her legs carried her toward her clansmen. Lyanii could not help being torn between pride and frustration for the reckless maneuver.

"Remind you of anyone?" Karn asked, his voice easily carrying over the sounds of battle.

The golem carried a large shield in one hand and a huge mace in the other, his normally bright silver finish streaked with black foulness. Two armored Phyrexian warriors clawed and cut their way past one of the Serran Guard, bringing their long swords in at the silver man. The golem took one slash against his shield, stepped back from the other and then brained one warrior with the mace. The polished helm caved under Karn's great strength, and the warrior dropped lifeless.

The Serran officer ran the second Phyrexian through, her blade flat to the ground in proper fashion as it burst through the neck joint. The creature inside died with a gurgling screech. She stepped up next to Karn to take advantage of the natural shield the large golem presented.

"Of any *one*?" she asked, changing the question. "Of every one. All of them. From Rorry all the way back to Jaffrey's first son. They're all in her and more." She felt a moment of pity that Karn could not remember Therri's progenitors, but then a spike of curiosity wondered at how he had come by asking such a question regardless. How many could he remember and compare her to?

There was no time to ask as Karn stepped forward into a new hole broken in the Serran line. A small, stoop-shouldered creature, more artifice than flesh, sprang for the opening and was slammed back hard by the golem's shield. It scampered back, hiding behind the legs of a guard elite. The golem thrust his mace forward like a spear, the large spike on its top piercing the slender ribcage area and winning only a thin trickle of oil.

The creature's slender arm shot out, raking scratches across the golem's near-invulnerable silver form. Its other arm, covered with a variety of blades, tubes and strange artifice, slashed inward as well but was fouled by a spear thrust from one of the Serrans. The Phyrexian turned against this new opponent, tearing past spear and shield and through the Serran's chain mail. It ignored Karn's attacks, determined to put an end to one of its enemies.

Lyanii leapt forward, shouldering aside her own man and taking his place before the onslaught of fast, lethal metal. Karn continued to rain sledgehammer blows against the Phyrexian's back and side. Lyanii's sword kept time with the creature, turning aside its hard-hitting blows with inches to spare. Then the Marshal missed.

The beast's slender arm sneaked past her guard, piercing the armor that shielded her right hip and digging slender talons in bone-deep. Lyanii fell back, rolling away from the creature's grasp. It bought her time, seconds only. She knew she wouldn't rise back up on the wounded limb. The Phyrexian followed, ready to finish her off. It would have, except for Karn.

The golem cast away his shield, wrapping his large hands about the reinforced shaft of the spiked mace. He came at the Phyrexian with an overhead rounding blow that caught the armored creature at the upper curve of one shoulder. The guard stumbled to its knees. Karn spun around, placing his weight and incredible strength behind another blow that buried several points into the Phyrexian's small face mask. It toppled back, screeching in a sound that reminded Lyanii of sharp claws drawn over a board of slate.

Karn helped the Marshal back to her feet, lifting her one-handed. Lyanii winced putting pressure on her leg. "Can you stand?" he asked.

Can *we* stand? That was the question haunting Lyanii's mind through the shroud of pain. For the second time in her long life—the first being on Serra's plane when her people had been subverted by Phyrexians and led against their own—the Marshal felt doubt in battle. This was what she had been created for by Serra. It was all she knew, and it wasn't enough.

Lyanii shrugged off the golem's help, anger at her own weakness making her abrupt. "I'll be all right." She exhaled a short exclamation of frustration. "We'll make it," she answered her own question, regaining control of her emotions.

Shouts of confusion and fear now erupted from the center of the Capashen lines. Lyanii grabbed up her main standard, planted nearby, ready to signal her next order. Her battlefield experience whispered the reason behind the upset even before word finally reached the Serrans. Gavvan Capashen had fallen! Slain by a monster, the word said. The Capashen middle sagged, Phyrexians pressing forward. Lyanii paled, recognizing the beginnings of a rout and knowing the slaughter that would follow.

She remembered that she had sent Therri straight into its middle.

Therri Capashen had been close enough to see her brother fall, his personal guard holding the center of the Benalish line, the Capashen standard driven into the earth while Gavvan lent his own sword to the fight. Never one to sit back, he shared the danger and inspired those around him with his heroics. With sweeping arcs he took the spindly, mechanical arms off a Phyrexian warrior, the edge of his sword striking sparks against the black armor. Spraying oil, the creature fell back and one of the ornate-armored guard moved up into its place.

Gavvan wasted no time with this one, pulling the short rod from his belt and thrusting it forward. An ancient gift from Master Malzra, artificer and matchmaker, the rod was a Capashen heirloom. Malzra had promised it a defense against violent artifice, though it should be used sparingly. One of the Phyrexian guards, so much metal crafted toward lethal intent, seemed close enough to the old artificer's description. The creature's slender arm, slashing in toward Gavvan's throat, froze immediately as if the metal joints suddenly fused. The abomination shuddered to a stop. It became a frozen statue on the battlefield, and her brother simply shoved it aside. As it crashed to the ground, its animation stilled forever, the clan leader's personal guard shouted out a cry of, "Gavvan!"

Except her brother had not noticed the malformed, black-flesh creature stalking the lines and moving against his position. If he had, he ruled it a minor warrior due to its lack of metal armor. Its bloated chest rippled and pulsed as it moved forward on thin legs. Large, hook-shaped claws trailed near the ground at the ends of long arms. Glistening crystal eyes glowed a dull orange as it riveted its gaze on Gavvan. Therri simply knew that this creature *needed* no armor and that it hunted her brother.

"Gavvan!" she yelled in warning, pushing frantically past other Capashen warriors and laying about with her sword when the enemy pressed in too close. One long Phyrexian blade snaked through to slice away part of her leather armor, scoring a shallow cut along one arm. Therri ignored it. "Gavvan, no!"

In the other shouts of the Clan Leader's name, Gavvan missed the warning. The creature leapt forward over the last twenty feet, legs driving out as if it was some kind of titanic insect. Before landing it already began to spew a dark, sludgelike substance that stuck to Gavvan's arm and chest. The chain mail protecting his body held up, but the leather strips on his arm began to smoke at once. Gavvan had time for a single backhand slash at the monster. His blade hardly cutting the tough, wrinkled flesh over one shoulder, and then it stuck fast. Twisting violently to one side, Gavvan's sword was torn from his grasp.

The Phyrexian craned its head forward. Its chest heaved, and its throat expanded. A torrent of black sludge belched over Gavvan's face and shoulders. The young clan leader screamed, hands clawing at his own face as exposed skin began to blister and smoke. Blinded, thrashing about in pain, he made an easy target. The great, hook-shaped claws seized Gavvan, lifting him from the ground, and with a violent scissorslike motion left him in two large pieces, dead.

Therri stood in shock, the battle forgotten as she stared at the ruin of her brother's body. So close—she'd been so close to helping. If she'd taken a horse from Lyanii's flank . . . if she hadn't wasted valuable seconds in any of four different fights along the way.

The Phyrexian army pushed forward, now spearheaded by the monstrous beast that killed Gavvan. Suddenly, Therri realized how close they were to a full rout as news of her brother's death swept the lines and demoralized the Capashen. These black creatures, never skilled in working as a coherent unit, were pushing forward singly to exploit the sudden shift. Beneath Therri's doubts and recriminations she found a spark of rage, which she fanned until it warmed her entire body. She knew these things for the evil they represented, preying on a moment of weakness engineered by some kind of special monster.

Springing forward into the monster's path just as it set upon one of Gavvan's personal elite, Therri parried an attempt to fasten those hooked claws into the soldier and watched for her opportunity. She had recognized the nature of the creature's movements necessary to call up its terrifying weapon. There again was the bellowlike force of its bloated chest and expansion of the throat as it craned its head forward. Gavvan's sword was still stuck in its shoulder, a warning against any slashing attack. Instead she ducked into the creature, risking its claws as she drove her sword forward with all her strength into its throat. She left it there. Sludge leaked out down the blade. She danced back, avoiding the claws that suddenly flailed about as if possessed of their own mad intelligence. No weapon, Therri wrenched the nearby Capashen standard free of the ground. Reversing it, she bore it back at the Phyrexian like a spear, its ornate tip aimed unerringly for one of its crystalline eyes. The dull orange gem shattered, and she drove through into the head. Leaping up behind the attack, she rode the creature backward and into the middle of the Phyrexian line.

Therri counted herself dead. Perched atop the creature's bloated chest, disarmed and surrounded by the enemy, she expected a finishing stroke any time. She didn't care, having avenged Gavvan, having blunted the Phyrexian advance. Then a black-armored warrior to her right stumbled and fell—one arm missing and its chest pierced by a sword. The sword was still held by the Capashen warrior she'd saved seconds before. Only a fraction behind were two more of Gavvan's personal guard, driving in on her left and pushing the enemy away from her. She took quick stock of the battle. The four of them were a tight knot in the midst of the Phyrexian line.

Wrenching Gavvan's sword free, her own covered by too much of the burning sludge, Therri also took hold of the Capashen standard and pulled it from the creature's head. She waved it crisply back and forth, the white and gold ensign fluttering and snapping. Three men to her force and clan still in danger of rout, Therri accepted the only option left to her.

She led them forward, on the attack.

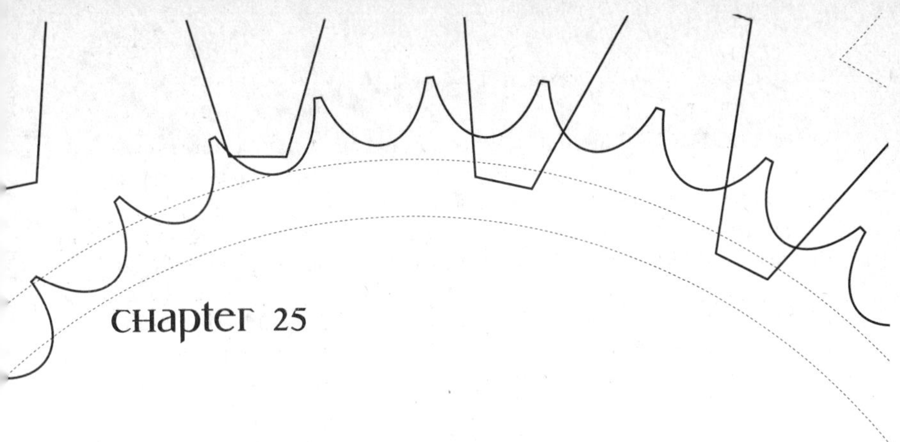

chapter 25

A sea of raging energies broke over Urza in a kaleidoscopic wash. It permeated his mind and nearly drowned his consciousness. As certain as Urza was that there must be a fundamental pattern to this chaos, underlying everything, it remained of such a magnitude that even the planeswalkers could not comprehend it. Propelling his mind through the chaos on will alone, the 'walker was trailing a Phyrexian. He followed a dark beacon—the characteristic pattern left by a Phyrexian portal device. He pursued a trail left by the creature he now pursued—and would destroy.

The negator had ambushed him. Its teeth were blunt, unusual for a Phyrexian, and set at wide irregular intervals. With every breath those teeth rang out with energy-disrupting force. The hisses and screeching that made up Phyrexian speech formed partially translated in Urza's mind, drawing a shadowy lethargy over the 'walker's thoughts. Urza still remembered how he had stood there, only vaguely aware of the mounting problem.

With a voice able to whisper a numbing darkness into his mind, the thing had been on him with little chance to prepare. Except for that strange new power, the negator had relied on physical assaults and an old system of burning fluid. The storage tanks were not even protected by the desiccated flesh covering the rest of its deformed body. The skin was simply split open in three places, and tanks were buried partway into its frame. Metal-braided tubing connected the tanks to a shoulder-mounted weapon. It was an older negator, set after him long ago. Hardly a match, especially once Urza had used his staff to knock away half of the creature's lower jaw. Without its siren's sound, the negator had chosen flight—to report its partial success back to its masters, no doubt.

Urza was not about to allow that to happen. His mind piercing the veil, Urza drew his body into form and set foot down upon a strange plane. For a moment he thought he remained partway into the chaos between worlds, the steel-gray skies cascading with the same energy as did the void. The clouds were real enough, roiling in strange winds, and the ground firm beneath his feet—though he sensed its potential for treacherous footing. The dull tan stone stretched in seamless perfection over a rough plateau and then fell down an impressively long and steep mountainside into the deep valley below. The mountain ended only a few hundred yards above him at a sharp ridge. Halfway up that slope the negator had paused, dark eyes staring back at the enemy who had trailed it.

Urza drew in the winds, striking them by will to fit his own pattern. The wall hammered into the Phyrexian, driving it back downslope. Its progress thwarted, the creature spun and leapt for the 'walker—and died mid-flight, a summoned phantom snatching it up in a large mouth of teeth and shredding desiccated flesh away from a metal-reinforced skeleton. Black, decaying meat clinging to few metal cauldrons and a few dull gray bones rained to the ground.

Yes, it was an older creation of Phyrexia, not too dissimilar from what he might have seen in the days he traveled with Xantcha. So many worlds traveled then, he explored the planes of the Dominarian Nexus and out to the fringe of the multiverse itself. Now this world—a world he had never 'walked before. The chaotic sky lacked a sun, and the ground, this strange stone, was not true soil but manufactured.

Welcome to Rath, planeswalker.

Distracted at the importance of his discovery, Urza did not immediately question the appearance of a new voice. This was a created plane, like Serra's Realm—like Phyrexia.

"Rath is an artificial plane," he said, answering aloud.

That is correct.

Urza now realized that the voice sounded within his mind, not his ears. He guarded his thoughts, wary once again. His expanded consciousness identified the intrusive thoughts as a simple voice, unable to read his mind but "heard" through the same function that allowed him to speak in anyone's language. "Where are you?" he asked, finding no places a body could hide.

Lost. And not even you can redeem our bodies, Urza, if Urza Planeswalker you are. Look above you. Look beyond.

Above him Urza saw only the sharp ridge and heard the cut of wind slicing over it. "Look *beyond*," the voice had said. The powerstones burned within his eyes, replacing the illusion of mortal blue as he concentrated his preternatural senses. He saw their outlines, spectral dances of energy, sometimes twisting into a simple globular pattern but more often holding a humanoid shape with arms and legs and head. There were three of them, then ten, then fifty. Similar to his own form of pure energy, but they were so much more basic in nature. They swam along the ridge, unthreatening.

"I am Urza," he admitted cautiously, continuing to tap the mana of traveled lands should he require the power. "How do you know me? And who are you?"

Who else would bring war to Rath rather than await Rath to bring war to him? We are the Soltari. One of the patterns of energy pulsed. *I am Lyna.*

The Soltari. From the depths of his memory Urza recalled the name, a small city-state of Dominaria, which mysteriously disappeared back in the days when he and Xantcha had worked to free Efuan Pincar from the Phyrexians, over two hundred years before his founding the first Tolarian academy. Lost, Lyna had said. Lost between worlds!

Urza had no need of bending to the ground. His contact with it allowed his consciousness to work against the strange stone—to test its properties and sense its purpose within the plane of Rath. He could feel the movement far below, spreading outward to the distant horizon. It was a flow of malleable stone, able to hold back the energy curtains and force a new plane into existence—able to penetrate the veil and rip pieces of Dominaria away. What had Lyna said? Rather than await Rath to bring war to him? The planeswalker leapt into the air, flying above the ground as he rushed for the summit—the direction from which the strange stone flowed.

He found himself on the volcano's rim, staring down into an incredible caldera. The base of which was spanned by an incredible fortress tower. Dark metals gleamed beneath eerie lightning. This place was obviously Phyrexian in architecture, and it had to be the nerve center of Rath in that the stone radiated outward from it as it continued to push in all directions. Urza reached down through the fortress, testing the production of the strange stone. He felt the tremors shaking beneath.

It can overlap Dominaria. Lyna again. *Such has been done many times. We were the first, and the only failure that cost so many lives, though with any transfer some are lost. They wander Rath or their own lands, always apart. You will destroy this place?*

Though he had contemplated just that, now the 'walker shook his head in a silent negative. "No," he finally said. "It doesn't feel as if I can." He looked hard at the fortress below. "Different from Serra's Realm," he said, thinking aloud. "It will not collapse so easily. The stone holds the curtain back—it would take massive destruction of the land itself, of the world." Then the purpose of Rath hit him—a hard cruel blow to his mind. "This is their staging area for the invasion. No portals. From here they hope to set entire armies across the world."

You must destroy this place—the Stronghold. We have worked to distract the overseers here. We have pushed at the equipment over great amounts of time, but our work is too slow. They will finish soon.

"No," Urza said, offering a grim smile. "Not soon. I felt your work beneath the fortress. The equipment is weakened and being run too hard. Artifice requires more care—a lesson the Phyrexians will learn without my help. It would be better if they never knew I was here."

You will simply leave then? This was no judgment, just a clarification from Lyna.

"I will, but you are welcome to return with me." Urza felt again at their energy forms, certain his strength could pull them across a short 'walk between planes. "I cannot give you back form, but I can return you to Dominaria. And when the time is right, I might be able to give you revenge." How many years had these people waited? A millennium?

We would like that. Phyrexia has much to answer for.

Urza couldn't have agreed more.

The lingering scent of dinner, grilled swordfish from the leftovers that Barrin had walked past in the kitchen, told the mage he hadn't missed the meal by more than thirty minutes. That was subjective, of course. Having just come through the timelock, Rayne would have actually finished hours before Barrin ever left real time for their shared home. The wonders we have done here on Tolaria, he thought, not a little bitterly. For the sacrifice of one meal, Barrin had been able to spend a full day with Urza.

A poor substitute, he decided. If only there wasn't so much to do and now so much more, after Urza's revelation.

The house was silent except for a crackling fire, which warmed the main room, occasionally tossing out a small spark, which glowed dull red on the hearth before fading to a cinder. Rayne waited on the couch, legs tucked beneath her and lost under the folds of her silken robes as she stared into the dancing flames. His wife did not greet him.

"You are still not working?" he asked, lacing concern heavy into his voice.

Barrin couldn't remember the last time Rayne had gone into her workshop. He was concerned, of course, but he also did not want Rayne to hear the doubts crowding his thoughts—doubts for her, for them. Every day he hoped she would solve her problems, uncertain how he might help.

"I didn't want to get involved in a new project just now." Rayne put little feeling behind the excuse. She studied her husband with haunted eyes. "I had hoped you would be home early, that we could talk . . . " She trailed off, waiting.

Barrin paced over to the couch and sat wearily on the opposite end. Usually Rayne would have asked after Urza's reasons for an emergency meeting, especially since the 'walker had simply shown up this morning and pulled the mage away. She was obviously beyond caring about academy business this night. The short stretch of fabric and cushion that separated Rayne from him seemed at once a great chasm with sharp rocks waiting below. He ventured a foot toward the edge, dreading where it might lead.

"We can always talk, Rayne." His spirits lifted slightly as he discovered he actually meant it. The shock of Urza's news, about the artificial plane of Rath, left the mage with a new perspective. Suddenly he saw the avoidance of their problems over the last few years, and he felt the worse for it. "We should've talked some time ago." He heard the regret in his own voice, hoped Rayne read into it as well. "If ever I wished that Urza's time travel machine was still functional to be able to relive a period of my life, this is it."

The time machine. How many problems could be traced so far back? The shattered temporal zones, the constant threat of Phyrexians discovering Tolaria, then Urza's second academy, and the projects developed—when was the last time Barrin had truly considered any of those projects?

Rayne shifted uneasily. "The world has passed us by, Barrin. And we're," she paused and then put it in terms more familiar, more comfortable, "we're winding down. This is a problem we've avoided for too long. Yes or no. Stay or go."

"Easily asked," Barrin said with a heavy sigh, feeling every day of his eight relative centuries of life. Rayne had started with the one problem on which he knew he would have to fight her. "I walked around Tolaria," he said by way of edging into the discussion. "All around it, which is why I'm so late. The island is not in good health." It was a euphemism for the ruined lands now blowing dusty tendrils out over the ocean, the failing crops, and now worries over the water table. "The island is suffering but still the academy goes on, teaching and learning and building. How much more might we have accomplished, Rayne, without the Legacy, the bloodlines and Metathran wasting so many valuable resources?"

"Were they wasted?

"I don't know. And maybe that's the trouble." Barrin smoothed his cloak flat, ran fingers back through his graying hair. "It cost us Gatha, Timein, and dozens of others over the years. The Phyrexians claim their price, even when they aren't attacking, and the Legacy . . . " He paused. "It finally seems we've put all our hopes into one plan, into Urza. If he's wrong, again, or if he simply makes too many mistakes along the way, then it's all over."

Rayne wiped at her eyes with the heel of one hand. "I have to leave," she said simply.

"I know, and I have to stay."

There, it was said. Her admitting her decision freed him to admit his. Living in slow time for so long with only brief vacations back into the real world had left them both drained, but where everything else paled, still Barrin could hang onto his duties. Those duties would be impossible to run from anywhere but here—for now—for as long as it took to complete the Legacy and discover its heir. Urza's revelation had convinced him that he must see this through to the end. He was always the outsider, never at peace with the world, his family or himself. He breathed a heavy sigh and proceeded to slowly tell Rayne about the meeting with Urza—about Rath and why he was needed in slow time now more than ever before.

Rayne had her own private demons to dispel—he knew—from listening in on her nightmares some nights. He knew from the truth Urza all but admitted at their meeting the subjective year before. Trapped inside a slow-time cage with the darkness, her every moment suffused with Phyrexia or the preparations against them, she could never come to terms with that black side of her nature. She could never come to terms with being a child of Phyrexia—whether she recognized it as such or not it was true. She was one of the bloodlines—Urza's child—one of the thousands touched unknowingly by the 'walker.

To his surprise, Rayne shook her head. "Then I stay as well." Not the same emphatic statement she might have made at the project's beginning, but a weary acceptance of the circumstances.

Barrin hadn't expected that, though inwardly his hopes sparked that the two of them could see this through to the end together. "Are you sure?"

"No." She stretched a tentative smile over her face, apparently found that it didn't cause her any new pain. "I can't leave you behind. I refuse to let Tolaria, Phyrexia or even Urza separate us." She stood, one hand catching Barrin's and pulling him up after her. Standing there, both his hands around both of hers, they stared into each other's eyes. "I do not want you lost to me, Barrin, my husband. Do what you must, what needs doing." She released his grip, stepping away in a whisper of silk and the light whisk of leather sandals against the wooden flooring. "I'll be waiting. Always." She backed her way from the room, eyes tearing only slightly but her confidence in her husband never wavering. In that, Rayne obviously possessed no doubts. She turned at the entryway and walked toward their private chambers.

How long he stood there, lost in his own thoughts, Barrin wasn't sure. The fire hissed and popped, the flames offering a small measure of company and solace though never so warm as the touch of Rayne's hands against his. His conscience and sense of duty both nagged at him, finally prodding him from the room and moving him along as far as the long hall. There he paused, staring in the direction of his private offices, knowing there was work to be done, but putting off Rayne who had sacrificed again for their common good. He turned away from the offices, heading instead toward their chambers. Perhaps he couldn't solve Rayne's problems, but he could be there for her as she so often had been for him.

His work could wait one more evening.

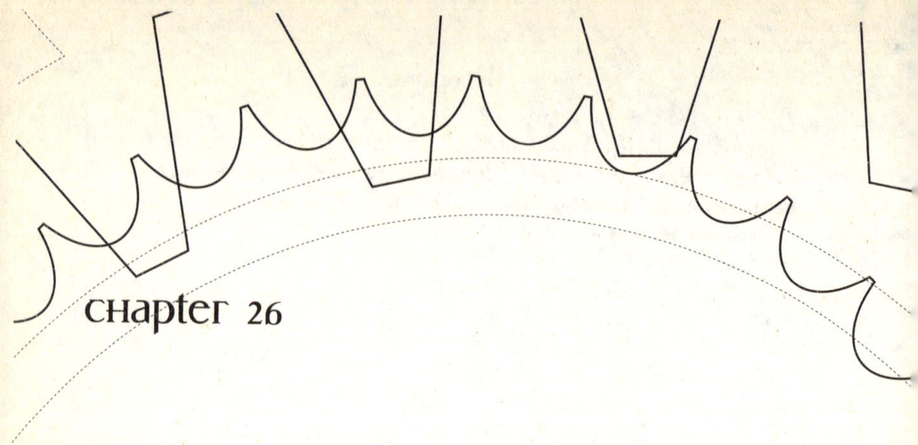

chapter 26

Croag had waited for this day.

A tremor rumbled through the floors of the Stronghold, and in places metal bracing squealed under new stress. Such quakes were commonplace these last several years, the result of running the machinery so hard for so long. With each day the purpose of Rath came so much closer to being fulfilled, then only the task of the Dark Lord would remain, and Dominaria would belong to the Ineffable. Pushing for that day, Davvol had decided on another inspection. He would try to find a way to silence the tremors, but at the same time he pushed the Vec and the machinery all the harder. Guards in tow, he started his routine. He left his negator behind.

For better than two centuries now, Croag had worked to heal himself, a slow and even painful process, though at times the pain had been rather exquisite to feel: the culture and growth of new meat, the slow infusing with artifice, mixing his blood with fresh glistening oil. His strength had taken decades to rebuild, bringing back his powers even as he learned to alter and improve on his old design. Now came the time of testing himself—of reversing the shift in Rath's power that occurred the day he had been struck down by the witch king Kreig. Today he would destroy the first of Davvol's supports.

The negator waited in its alcove near the throne, a saw-toothed shield in one hand and its other tipped in both claws and corrosive-fluid plungers. It shifted when the Inner Circle member entered the room, setting itself into a state of preparedness. Croag would not allow it to turn more on guard. The Phyrexian's eyes blazed a hard red, and searing beams of energy lashed out to split the hardened, wrinkled flesh that covered the negator's face. This would be Croag's second battle for Rath's throne room, and he had every intention of victory.

The negator's movement was a dark blur. Springing from its resting place, shield blocking Croag's attack as it swept in with its claws. Croag could never be so fast, though he came close. The Phyrexian master relied on his armored bands to make up the difference, the metal strips fully repaired as well and equal to the task. They turned the claws of the beast, though a few were spattered by the corrosive sludge. Croag struck back, but already the negator was past and pulling up short on the other side of the room. It stalked back carefully, watching for its opening.

Sampling the corrosive material the negator used had been part of Croag's plans. Knowing his body capable of withstanding any of the older chemical attacks, he had doubted Davvol's latest was too different. Radical leaps were not part of the Coracin's way. He preferred slow, methodical improvement. Such was the case here. The sludge burned into Croag's bands but failed to cause much more than a mild distraction. A rasping slide of metal and new coat of glistening oil, and the annoyance was gone.

Now it was Croag's turn. He leapt for the negator, offering it a deadly embrace. The saw blade shield slammed into his side, cutting past several metal bands and damaging the compleated flesh beneath. More of the claws scored deep wounds, but now Croag had the measure of the corrosive and his body was already working to negate its effect. One of the Inner Circle member's skeletal hands shot out to dig razored fingers into the negator's chest. They cut deeply then began to vibrate with a new life.

Where Croag's artifice-blended flesh pierced the negator a new process began. The negator's flesh reacted with Croag's, merging. The Phyrexian master's entire hand slid into the negator, then his arm up to the elbow. The negator began to twist violently now, feeling the invasion but unable to react as its own flesh and artifice turned against it. Croag reveled in his triumph, knowing instantly that he could consume the negator's entire being in this way. Such an expenditure of power for so simple a creature was not necessary. The negator was fast, deadly in its own right, but could never stand against a fully operational member of the Inner Circle. It would add so little to him, and Croag could wait for a better opportunity.

With a wrenching pull, Croag ripped his arm free and so brought with it the negator's flesh and machinery already consumed. He left behind a hole that bled oil and thick black blood.

The negator was well built, keeping to its feet though all the fight had gone out of it. Croag lashed out with both taloned hands, raking off large swaths of flesh and gouging into bone and metal support. The shield came up, and Croag ripped it from the other's grasp, hurling it with all of the Phyrexian's force so that it actually stuck into the armored walls of the throne room. The clawed hand rose sluggishly, and the member of the Inner

Circle caught it and used searing whips of energy from his eyes to sever it at the wrist. Still the negator remained standing.

Just how long could it stand up under such damage, Croag wondered. With something very much akin to physical pleasure, the Phyrexian set to work.

A violent quake shook the Stronghold, as if the plane's flowstone foundation had shifted under the weight of the towering fortress and its processing equipment.

Davvol slowly paced the short aisle that ran between both lines of negators. Four of the Phyrexians to a side, each was a deadly instrument. They were the result of his centuries of effort, tailoring the best of the negator abilities into ever more-efficient creations. If not for the unknown strengths of planeswalkers, Davvol might have thought any one perfectly suited for the task of killing Urza. As is, they were his best—and last—gamble.

A particularly sobering thought, Davvol was now forced to gamble his hard-won power in this bid against the 'walker's life. Still fresh in his perfect memory was the day of several months prior when he came into the Stronghold's throne room. The oil mixed with blood was pooled in the middle of the room and splattered in streaks and splotches against the walls. He remembered the scent of flesh—meat—spoiling in the fortress's warmth. He found his own guardian negator shredded, fouling the throne room. It was not defeated, not dead, but shredded—rent down into pieces so small that it could only be done with a deliberate and determined effort. It could only be credited to Croag. It was a message, no subtlety at all, that Davvol's immunity from the Phyrexian Inner Circle member had expired.

For the first time in many centuries Davvol remembered a trace of the fear he had once felt for the Phyrexian—the cold touch along his back and the metallic taste of a mouth suddenly dry in nervousness.

Fear, as would forever be the case, was a wonderful motivator. Davvol brought the production of flowstone up yet again, pushing his workers and the machinery well past their limits. The secondary attractors shook with constant tremors, at times twisting against the Stronghold itself, but the counterbalancing torque built into their design allowed for such abuse. Today's earlier visit, in fact, set a new threshold for the equipment. He also stepped up other projects, readying a private army capable of killing the land of Yavimaya once and for all.

Of course, he bent himself strongly to the task of killing Urza. Destroying the 'walker was the one act Davvol knew could assure his continued position as evincar of Rath. It could bring him closer to the compleation he desired. His body was already strengthened to the point where aging and routine damage could not hurt him, yet Davvol still knew many of the physical limitations of flesh: Heat and cold, pain and discomfort. The evincar looked only toward protecting his mind, allowing it an immortal existence free of such encumbrances. For now, however, he could only imagine the benefits of such a form while the threat of Croag hung over his present life. That threat colored everything darker in an already black land. It interfered with Davvol's ability to think straight and to plan.

One final nod completed the inspection. Nothing seemed amiss, and the evincar could think of no other refinements that might make the difference—none he had time for at any rate.

"Find Urza Planeswalker," he ordered. The floor shook again, causing him to stumble to a wall rather than be cast to the ground. Cracks showed in one flowstone wall, then reformed to a smooth surface under his mental direction. "Find and kill him. Go."

Each negator turned away, stepping for their own portals, which already stood open at the back wall, then they were gone, tracking. Davvol stood alone in the throne room, trying to sort through so many mental notes and decide on his next action. Another quake worked its way up through the floor and along the walls, a grinding tremor that seeped up past the armored soles of his boots to churn inside his stomach. This time it did not fade immediately, setting off a sympathetic shaking that reflected back from other directions.

Something was wrong. Davvol sensed it. The Stronghold was by no means a sentient entity, but he had known it for so long that he sometimes felt a connection to it that had nothing to do with the flowstone properties or the great machinery at his command. That connection spoke of danger.

Now the walls shook but not the floor—decidedly unsettling. Davvol called for guards, led them toward one of the bridges he had ordered built in his first century as steward, a construction which held one of the secondary attractors. Even through half a kilometer of flowstone and metal, Davvol felt the grinding of metal tearing into metal, of gears stripped or screeching as the joints threatened to bind. Before he had crossed the bridge's expanse Davvol was running. Why this day of all others, he wondered briefly, allowing his emotions to color his thoughts. Why not tomorrow or the following year? More precise logic returned. Why not last week or the last decade? Whatever the problem, it happened now. To solve the problem was paramount, not to make matters the more difficult by dwelling on his own frustrations.

The upper chambers were frantic with workers running about trying to bring machinery back under control. The sealed shaft that housed the large driving screws twisted against its mountings. Machinery rattled, and a pipe ruptured to pour cold lake waters over the floor. The water flashed to steam where it washed up against hot steel, raising an instant steam bath. Davvol ordered the local supervisors captured by his guards, stopping them to put questions forward. Frantic work degraded into chaos with the workers suddenly bereft of leadership. Davvol grabbed one by the shoulders, lifting it off the floor and shaking it like he might a rag doll.

"What is happening?" he yelled at it, not thinking to place the touch upon its mind. In this hectic environment, he likely would have failed regardless. The entire bridge shook, throwing half the workers and even a few Phyrexians to the ground. "What is it?"

One worker leapt for Davvol's face, its gaze wild and panicked, swinging a sharply-tapered tool. A Phyrexian soldier skewered him on its sword, held the Vec dangling in the air while blood seeped out around the edges of the blade, and then cast it down to the floor. The Vec supervisor waved down other workers who looked about to snap under the stress and sudden violence. The superviser then pointed down, jabbering at Davvol in its own speech. Whatever the problem, it came from below, in the complex mechanisms of the bladed dials that pulled lava up from the furnaces far underground.

Davvol wasted no more time with questions. He kicked at the lifeless worker, venting rage and frustration. "Kill them," he ordered two guards. "All but that one."

As per his standing orders, the supervisors were punished in watching their people die. Then he was running again, his steam-sodden cloak trailing behind him, and his armored boots ringing against steel decking. The bulk of his Phyrexian escort followed. They found stairs and spiraled down into the depths of the machinery—into the main gears room.

The room curved about the central shaft, immense in the open space contained within the walls but made confining by an array of steam pipes, clockwork gears and various machinery. A hideous screeching filled the space, machinery worked too hard and tearing itself apart under the stresses applied. The room was out of a nightmare—awash in an orange glow, the light cast through large portals in the shaft's shielding by lava as it spilled upward, driven by the spinning blades. Yellow steam spilled from cracked valves and warped piping. The scent of sulfur was heavy in the room's jungle dampness.

Dozens, possibly scores, of Vec leapt from overhead concealment or from under deckplates suddenly loose and sliding over hiding holes built into the flooring. They had been driven to the limits of their endurance, and now with the Stronghold apparently collapsing about them, they did all they had left in them to do. They struck out at their tormentor. As other doors opened to admit more into the large theater filled with steam pipes and an incredible array of clockwork gears, they numbered better than a hundred.

Against a dozen Phyrexian troops, such ill-trained warriors were at the disadvantage. The black-armored soldiers hewed their way through the wave of bodies. Blood spattered the floor and machinery, drying quickly into rustlike streaks against the dark metal. The floor trembled and continued to shake longer than it had previously with the earlier tremors. Machinery tore loose of mountings, tumbling about the floor and indiscriminately crushing Vec and Phyrexian alike. A gear arm shattered and came crashing down in a ringing clatter. The screeching wail grew louder until it seemed tangible. This was likely the cause of the violent vibrations. The great complex machinery—Davvol's design—was tearing itself apart under high speeds and stresses.

The evincar screamed his frustration, attempting to find some way to bring it back under control. He didn't know the machinery like the Vec, had relied on them to maintain it, and this group was beyond even acknowledging his demands. They would need dispatching, and new workers brought in to shut down the system. Except there was no time for such a change out of personnel. He spared one thought for the workers in chambers above, before remembering he had ordered them slain. Events had conspired against him in a way even Croag could not have. Davvol made up his mind then to flee—able to recoup his losses another day.

Barely was the decision reached, however, when the floor suddenly pitched up sharply as if struck from below with a mountainous fist. Walls bowed and crumpled, and the ceiling caved downward raining shafts and toothy gear wheels. While still airborne, Davvol felt a metal pinion impale him. He came down hard, spitting blood from between thin, pale lips. Another gear fell across the backs of his legs, crushing them and pinning him into place. Pain flared in his mind, cloaking any thought of saving himself with a panicked desperation. A hideous rumble of stressed and avalanching metal overrode the noise of the overhead gears, still spinning wildly and trying to complete their function. The floor dropped out from beneath them all, as the entire bridge and shaft collapsed down into the lower caldera.

Davvol, evincar of Rath, fell with it.

Scorched metal and molten rock, the scents of hell.,Davvol knew only those scents and pain, never-ending pain, as the mountain of collapsed metal struts and supports, machinery and gearwork, continued to shift and grind. The molten glow of the lava had faded some time before. He could not say when. He didn't think it had touched him, the scent of charred flesh being that of others and long since cleared from the scalding air. Now darkness reigned, broken only by the occasional spark as metal shifted and struck against metal and flowstone. It was light enough to show him that his head and one arm remained free in a small space. The rest of him had been caught under an avalanche of gearwork—toothy wheels, pinions and shafts.

He faded into and out of consciousness, praying for rescue, rescue or death—either one after so long. This was the curse of near compleation. His body was simply unable to die, keeping his mind alive but not strong enough to allow him to free himself. With no voice for calling out, his restricted air intake was not enough for speech. It was barely enough to feed his brain and perhaps not even that. The veil clouding his thoughts threatened a slow torturous death of his mind. It was the only thing Davvol had ever possessed of true value, so he fought, trying to stay alive. He focused on the brimstone scents of his prison and the sound of grinding metal as the avalanche continued a slow fall toward entropy. He listened to the drip of water pinging against steel plates and the rasping whisper of steel bands rubbing together.

Croag.

Twin sparks of flame, hovering in the black, artificial night, flared up to offer a dim light to see by. Davvol noticed the dark doorway of an open portal behind the Phyrexian. There were no Vec laborers, no guards, just Croag, making his way carefully to Davvol's position. No humping walk or raspy breath, the nightmare had been reborn. Davvol remembered the way in which Croag had dismantled the negator set to protect the steward. The Phyrexian could likely free Davvol from this misfortune. Davvol would do anything for release. If he'd been able to speak, he would have promised whatever was asked of him—would have pledged the rest of his life to Croag's service.

Except, the rest of his life was exactly what Croag intended to take.

Extending one clawed hand, Croag set a single finger against Davvol's black armored skullcap, right where the circular depression would be, the evincar knew with a sudden wave of fear. He felt the sharp stab of fresh pain as Croag physically dug into his mind and began to drain the steward's memories, sifting knowledge from experience and taking both for himself. The Phyrexian was heedless of the damage this procedure caused, never planning to release Davvol and always having planned to drain the other in this way. Davvol felt his mind slipping away, leaving only the knowledge that he remained trapped, alone, and in pain. He had been given a long existence of suffering, robbed of the one thing he had ever treasured.

Croag was gone, having taken what he had come for—finished with Davvol, once and for all.

Croag paced the small plateau, feeling with every step how the surface might bend and reshape itself to his will, *his* will, but bent by the skill of Davvol.

Never before had the Phyrexian drained so much from a single subject. Several lifetimes worth of experience and accumulated knowledge were all at Croag's disposal now: the ability of flowstone, the evolution of negators, the trials Davvol had fought in Yavimaya, and the hatred, undeniable and uncompromising, for Croag. Everything was there, including how Davvol had planned to dispose of the Phyrexian, and when Croag circumvented those plans by destroying the negator, how Davvol would have used the death of Urza Planeswalker to elevate his position in the Dark God's gaze.

Urza Planeswalker had found Rath. There was no denying the evidence. The ruined shell of a negator lay upon the flowstone, tortured metal and some desiccated and petrified flesh was all that remained. Croag could see the creature fighting Urza and then escaping back to Rath, leading the 'walker right back to Phyrexia's most secret plan. Why not? Davvol had never thought to instruct them against such a feat. Urza had tracked the negator back, finished it off, and then escaped with knowledge of Rath's existence. Urza would have recognized the nature of this plane—and its ultimate purpose—at once. It was the staging ground for the coming invasion. The planeswalker would sense it, and in the voices of the Vec or one of the other races brought across he could find confirmation if necessary. There were no doubts. In the back of his mind, where Croag had stored the mental essence of Davvol, the Phyrexian heard the evincar's dark laugh.

Could Urza Planeswalker be killed? Davvol had thought so, but Croag no longer felt sure. Perhaps only the Dark One would be able to destroy the 'walker, but no doubts remained now that Croag would have to try. He would have to do it himself personally, and that required drawing the planeswalker into the open, a feat not accomplished in the assaults on Keld or in any fighting since—but Benalia—that seemed so much more likely. Benalia or Yavimaya, either should do. Both of those would have to be dealt with before Croag could ever face the Dark Lord again, even in his dreams.

The negators and troops would be called into battle then—a preliminary strike to herald the coming invasion. The planeswalker would show, and he would fight. Croag would be ready to meet him—to kill him. He would do the job himself rather than continue to trust failing subordinates. He would test his own mettle and metal, as he had once already, proving that he remained Croag, favored of the Ineffable among the Inner Circle of Phyrexia.

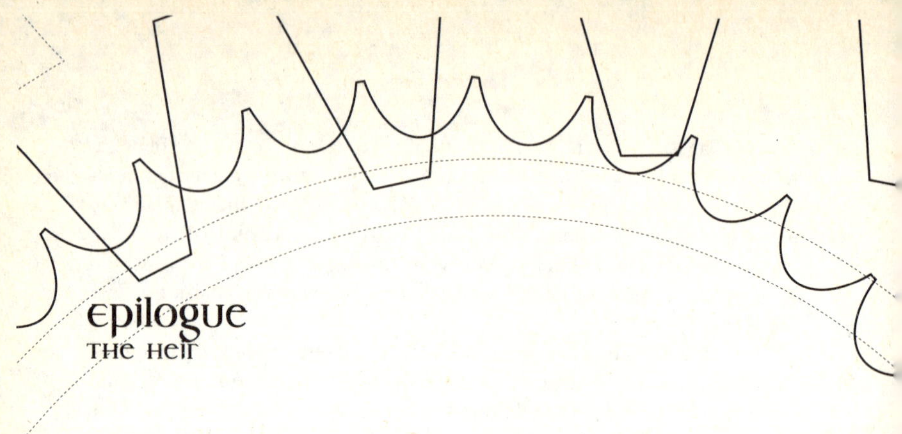

epilogue
THE HEIR

Barrin watched as the last student filed from the slow-time end of the timelock. They would be carting out records and other files today, cleaning out the last of his personal effects on the morrow. The final evacuation of the buildings might take weeks, cataloging every scrap of paper, but nothing would be lost in this move. Eventually the buildings would be torn down for their raw materials. Even the paving stones would be pried out of the ground, and the fresh soil possibly excavated for healthy landfill.

The necessity of such scavenging only underscored his resolve that Tolaria had been left unmanaged for too long. The master mage paused at the timelock entrance for one last look about his home, at the slow-time envelope that had been his world for so long. It was just another lie or a half-truth, once believed for the sake of convenience but no more. Dominaria was his home, his world, and he would not remain isolated in his self-inflicted exile any longer. Recent events had finally driven through the need for his return, the need for Tolaria's return.

The misted slow-time waters were damp on his skin as he passed into the first chamber, the fog seemingly alive in the blue glow of mage-lit stones. It swirled about him reminding of monumental events in his life, and Barrin's mind formed patterns out of the chaos. He could see—constructed of tiny beads of water—the fortress compound of the First Academy, torn apart by magical upheavals brought on by their temporal experiments, the same catastrophe that had shattered Tolaria's temporal fabric and created the pockets of slow and fast time. There in the corner, formed out of mist, was the *New Tolaria*, the ship that had hosted the academy in those years following the destruction of the first school and crashed through the waves until making landfall once again on the island shores. Above his head, near the ceiling in a swirling spire of fog, was the rise of the second academy and the mist wraiths which were of course the Phyrexians come to tear down all they had built. One larger swirl of misted waters sparkled against a mage stone—the *Weatherlight*—smashing through the rest just as it had helped to carry the day on Serra's Realm. Yes, he remembered those years well enough—the dark and the light of them.

The breeze of his passage shredded the mist images. He remembered back on times and events that stood out visibly in his memory. He recalled the early days, acting at times as surrogate father along with Urza and Gatha in creation of the Metathran warrior simulacra, even as he started his own family and locked both he and Rayne away behind temporal doors. He thought about the bloodlines, in their many incarnations, tearing at the unity of the academy and then moving in force out into Dominaria. He saw Keld cast into ruins, its people only now recovering from their several centuries of Phyrexian *testing.* He felt for the Capashen Clan of Benalia—desperately wounded, along with a half dozen other strong centers of the bloodlines. And now, Karn was missing. The master mage shook his head, so many lives disrupted, so far yet to go.

A warm tropical sun shook the chill from Barrin's skin as he passed from the final chamber and back into real time. The deep-blue sky might have been a reflection of the ocean waters except for a few snowy clouds that drifted lazily overhead. He blinked against the bright day and took a deep draw of the salt-tang ocean breeze. No more mistakes, he promised himself.

"Care for a stroll about the island?"

No mistaking that soft, beautiful voice, though Barrin still noted its hesitant approach. He turned to one of the stone benches that sat to either side of the timelock. Rayne sat there, her silk robes gathered about her, each hand tucked into the opposing sleeve. Long, raven hair cascaded down over both shoulders. Brown eyes studied him in a mixture of concern and hope.

"Been waiting long?" he asked.

"Not long," she admitted. "A few hours. I heard that you were closing down all the slow-time offices and labs. I saw the students go in earlier and hoped that you might be coming out with them." She stood, as graceful as ever, though she kept her arms crossed protectively in front of her.

Barrin nodded. "However long we have left," he said slowly, "I'd rather spend it on Tolaria, the *real* Tolaria." He paused, at a loss of where Rayne intended to take the conversation. "The *Weatherlight* has not left, has it?"

"No, though Multani and Rofellos hope to continue on their way soon. Did you want to talk with them? I already arranged for a group of scholars to interview them on what happened in Yavimaya."

"I wouldn't mind speaking with Multani. I also want to send the *Weatherlight* toward Argive. I hope to arrange a new trade of scholars with the Argivian University. They might have knowledge of ways to repair some of the damage we have done to Tolaria. It might give us a chance," he said, the various meanings warming the mage.

Rayne smiled then, bright and wonderful. Her eyes gleamed with a hint of mischief. She took his hand in hers, guided it to the slight swell of her abdomen. "Give us *all* a chance, then. I'm pregnant."

The revelation shook Barrin to his core. A smile in answer to Rayne's own spread across his face, a reflection of the warmth he felt inside. "What better omen to begin with than the start of a new life?"

"Shall we head for the new offices then?" Rayne asked. "There is so much to get done."

Barrin shook his head, enjoying the brief spark of confusion that flashed on his wife's face. "I'll take you up on your first suggestion, a stroll about the island." No more mistakes, he had promised himself. No matter the demands placed on him, Barrin would not—could not—allow himself to ignore the very reasons for which he fought. No one could, not if they were to believe in a better life after the battle.

"The Legacy and the heir—if there ever will be one—can wait until tomorrow." Someone else would simply have to watch over Dominaria today.

Jamuraa's mountain peaks were barely a smudge over the line of the horizon—a promise of the distance still to be traveled. Behind Karn, the sun fell low over the Voda sea. Sunset crimson splashed against the heavens. A sailor's good omen, Karn had learned in taking ship across the Voda, but it reminded the golem of nothing more than the blood spilled behind him in Benalia. The lives lost in protecting Urza's plans were not lost for nothing. Karn made sure of that.

A wind touched already with evening's chill raked the grass. The full Glimmer Moon rose low on the eastern horizon, promising some gray light by which to travel this night. One heavy step followed another—the same tireless pace that had carried the golem away from DeLatt and finally out of Benalia. He had stopped at villages only when necessary, once to engage a silversmith for repairs to his body, four more times to complete at least part of his mission as tasked by Urza Planeswalker. In the water crossing he kept to his cabin and away from prying eyes. He had been brought ashore by longboat, away from any port city, and of a necessity, far from his final destination.

Therri's face still haunted the golem, pale and drawn after the narrow battlefield victory that cost her her brother and landed the responsibilities of Clan Capashen upon her shoulders. Karn had not forgotten her, but again his conflicting loyalties called for compromise. Stay with her or follow Urza's order. Life versus Legacy.

The planeswalker still worried more for his collection of clockwork, sculpting, and magical devices than he ever would the people whose lives he touched. His only words to Karn, after the death of the Phyrexian incursion in Benalia, had been to direct a recovery of Legacy items.

"The Legacy," he'd said to Karn. "Collect what you can and take it away from Benalia. You will find protection in Jamuraa. I will locate you there," and he grimaced, "when I can."

He had smiled with a grim sort of self-satisfaction, and winked from existence—stepping in between worlds. Perhaps it was better that Urza kept his words so simple. The 'walker would never be convinced of anything other than his own genius—his own plans for the future of Dominaria.

Life versus Legacy. For Karn, the choice came easily. Therri Capashen would remain in his memory—for as long as Karn could keep her there. Karn might not even remember this day when the invasion came—if the full invasion ever came—but he would live the next two decades at least secure in the knowledge that the Capashen heroes lived on through at least one child. One more life, then, might someday make a difference. Carry the Legacy from Benalia, Urza had charged him. Protect it until found again by the planeswalker. Karn did carry several artifact pieces of the Legacy, and in his arms, swathed in new, thick blankets, he carried another part of the Legacy—what might well be the last surviving Capashen hero—the infant, Gerrard, Therri's orphaned grandson and her final request of Karn that the silver golem take him somewhere safe.

Urza Planeswalker focused on his *human components* as his path to an end product rather than for their own special talents and abilities. Living among them, caring for them as children and often befriending them as adults, the golem instead recognized in each the spirit that defied Phyrexia and promised any form of salvation. Urza had been wrong in that. Perhaps they would not wield the Legacy in its final form and discover how to defeat Phyrexia once and for all time, but one of them survived. How many more might be critical to the future? This was a simple truth, which Karn in his limited memory had recognized where Urza Planeswalker and his millennia of experience had not. Every one of them, bloodline subject or not, was a separate hope for Dominaria—could make a final difference that might stand between life and loss.

This one Karn would keep safe, so that in his own life, Gerrard Capashen might hope to make a difference, the mark of a true hero.

Confrontation leads to conflagration in this hot new planeswalker adventure.

THE PURIFYING FIRE

By award-winning author

LAURA RESNICK

On Alaroon, among an encalve of like-minded pyromancers, Chandra draws the attention of an ancient faith that sees her as a herald of an apocalypse. Will she control her own destiny, or suffer the will of others?